Praise for L. E. Modesitt, Jr., and the Spellsong Cycle

"The fifth and final no[...]g Cycle' features a resil[...]e songs contain powerfu[...]o flinch from difficult dec[...]-strates a unique ability [...] the intimate minutiae of everyday life." —*Library Journal*

"The book shows no falling off from its predecessors in any way, but particularly in its intelligent system of magic and in addressing the questions of the responsibilities of power, which Modesitt handles as magisterially well as Lois Mc-Master Bujold. Like its predecessors, it merits the highest recommendation, which will surprise Spellsong devotees not at all." —*Booklist* (starred review)

The Shadow Sorceress

Selected as one of the best fantasy novels by VOYA

"The saga continues on course toward becoming Modesitt's outstanding work of fantasy." —*Booklist*

Darksong Rising

"The consistent excellence of L. E. Modesitt makes him by far the most entertaining of today's fantasy writers." —*Romantic Times*

The Spellsong War

"Modesitt tells a damned good tale . . . delightful." —Anne McCaffrey

The Soprano Sorceress

"Highly recommended, as is anything by Modesitt." —*San Diego Union-Tribune*

SHADOWSINGER

A SPELLSONG CYCLE NOVEL

L. E. MODESITT, JR.

TOR®
fantasy

A TOM DOHERTY ASSOCIATES BOOK
NEW YORK

SHADOWSINGER: A SPELLSONG CYCLE NOVEL

Copyright © 2002 by L. E. Modesitt, Jr.

Edited by David G. Hartwell

A Tor Book
Published by Tom Doherty Associates, LLC
175 Fifth Avenue
New York, NY 10010

www.tor.com

Tor® is a registered trademark of Tom Doherty Associates, LLC.

ISBN 0-765-34258-8

First edition: February 2002
First mass market edition: March 2003

Printed in the United States of America

0 9 8 7 6 5 4 3 2 1

For Elizabeth and Drew

••

CONTINENT OF LIEDWAHR

The Winter Coast

Lundholm

Nordwei

Vereisen
Bay

Oskwye

Sandaye

Vyel   WEI

Morgen

ESARIA
Saris River   River Nord   River Ost   Dolov

Itzel   High   VULT
River Syas   Grasslands   Ostfels

Nesalia   Nordbergs   Elhi   Elahwe
Spisen   Blach   • Helmsa   Fal River
                 • Dubuta   Chean River   Synek
Neserea   • Dengiz   FALCOR   Sand Pass
            Defalk   Menares   Ebra
Great   Synope
Western   West Pass   Cheor   Spear River
Forest   Sand Hills

Mittfels   Ranuak
                                        Sand Pass

Great Chasm   Aroodel
                        Sadwei   Stromwer   South Pass
Second Great Cataract   ENCORA

Envaryl   Sudbergs
            Fist Cataract   Shoals of Discord

DUMARIA   Narial   Sylwa

Duvar   Ancient Cliffs

CHARACTERS

Secca *Sorceress Protector of the East; Lady of Loiseau (Mencha); Lady of Flossbend (Synope)*

Robero *Lord of Defalk, and Lord of Elheld, Falcor, and Synfal (Cheor)*

Alyssa *Consort of Robero*

Dythya *Counselor of Finance*

Jirsit *Arms Commander of Defalk*

LORDS OF DEFALK: THE THIRTY-THREE

Alseta *Lady of Mossbach; consort is Barat; son is Lyendar*

Birke *Lord of Abenfel; consort is Reylana; mother is Fylena*

Cataryzna *Lady of Sudwei; consort is Skent; heir is Skansor*

Chelshay *Lady of Wendel; consort is Nerylt, son of Clethner*

Clethner *Lord of Nordland; heir is Lythner*

Dinfin *Lady of Suhl; consort is Wasle, brother of Birke*

Dostal *Lord of Aroch; consort is Ruetha*

Ebraak *Lord of Nordfels; heir is Cassily*

Falar *Warder of Uslyn, heir to Fussen; also consort to Herene, Lady of Pamr.*

Fustar *Lord of Issl; sole heir is Kylar*

Gylaron *Lord of Lerona; consort is Reylan; heir is Gylan; father of Reylana*

Herene *Lady of Pamr; consort is Falar; heir is Kysar*

Kinor *Lord of Westfort (Denguic) and Lord of the Western Marches; consort is Asaro*

Mietchel *Lord of Morra, brother of Lady Wendella of Stromwer*

Selber *Lord of Silberfels; heir is Helbar; sister is Belvera*

Tiersen *Lord of Dubaria; consort is Lysara; eldest son and heir is Lystar*
Uslyn *Lord heir of Fussen; father was Ustal, mother Yelean*
Vyasal *Rider of Heinene*
Ytrude *Lady of Entfels, sister of Tiersen; consort is Cens*
Wendella *Lady of Stromwer; heir is Condell*
Zybar *Lord of Arien*

SORCERERS AND SORCERESSES

Anandra *Sorceress assistant to Clayre*
Clayre *Sorceress of Defalk*
Jolyn *Assistant Sorceress of Defalk*

FOSTERLINGS, APPRENTICES, AND PAGES

Jeagyn *Fosterling/sorceress apprentice at Loiseau*
Kerisel *Fosterling/sorceress apprentice at Loiseau*
Richina *Apprentice sorceress to Secca; daughter of Dinfan*

DEFALKAN ARMSMEN

Elfens *Chief Archer, Loiseau*
Drysel *Captain, Loiseau*
Quebar *Captain, Loiseau*
Rickel *Lord's Guard-Captain, Falcor*
Wilten *Overcaptain, Loiseau*

DEFALKAN PLAYERS

Bretnay *Violino, Loiseau*
Delvor *Chief of Second Players, Loiseau*
Duralt *Falk-horn, Loiseau*

Diltyr *Chief Player for Clayre, Falcor*
Dossin *Lutar, Loiseau*
Elset *Woodwind, Loiseau*
Kylar *Violino, Loiseau*
Nuel *Violino, Loiseau*
Palian *Chief Player, Loiseau*
Rowal *Woodwind, Loiseau*
Yuarl *Chief Player for Jolyn, Falcor*

OTHERS OUTSIDE DEFALK

Alya *Matriarch of Ranuak; consort is Aetlen*
Alcaren *Sorceror; cousin to the Matriarch*
Ashtaar Ashtarr *Leader, Council of Wei, Nordwei*
Ayselin *Holder of Netzla, Neserea*
Belmar *Holder of Worlan, Neserea*
Fehern *Acting Lord High Counselor of Dumar; without consort*
Hadrenn *Lord High Counselor of Ebra; Lord of Synek, Ebra; consort is Belvera; heir is Haddev; younger son is Verad.*
Hanford *Lord High Counselor of Neserea; consort is Aerlya; eldest daughter and heiress is Annayal*
Kestrin *Liedfuhr of Mansuur; brother of Aerlya*
Maitre of Sturinn *Leader of Sturinn; master of the Sea-Priests*
Motolla *Holder of Itzel, Neserea; heir is Chyalar*
Svenmar *Holder of Nesalia, Neserea*
Veria *Counselor, Freewomen of Elahwa*

1

MANSUUS, MANSUUR

Heavy wet flakes drift past the windows of the Lied-fuhr's study, each window hung with maroon velvet drawn back to reveal an early-spring snow that has already dropped more than half a yard of whiteness on the city, and on the ice that still covers the River Toksul.

The man who stands before the windows, looking out, wears a sky-blue tunic with a silver chain bearing the amulet-seal of the Liedfuhr of Mansuur around his neck and a mourning band of black and maroon upon his left arm. For a moment, his hard green eyes flick to the ice-and-snow-covered river that cuts through the city, if well below and beyond the hill on which the palace rests. Then, he turns, standing beside the polished wooden desk that has graced the study for three generations, and asks, "You think Nes-erea will fall before harvest?"

"As matters now proceed, it is most likely," replies the trim overcaptain in the maroon uniform of the Mansuuran Lancers. There are but a few streaks of raven black amid the silver-gray of the lancer's short hair. His thin eyebrows are silvered as well, but the dark eyes are deep and intent. "Despite the efforts of the Sorceress of Defalk, Aerlya and Annayal hold but an area little more than a hundred deks around Esaria."

"If we dispatch the fifty companies of lancers from Un-duval? Then what, Bassil?" Kestrin runs his right hand through short-cropped brown hair that is already half-gray, although he will not reach his full second score of years until the turn of the following spring.

"Are you willing to risk all fifty companies? And to

slaughter all those who do not support your sister and her daughter?"

Kestrin tilts his head slightly as he studies Bassil. "If I must."

"You must. You must also avoid facing the sorcerer Lord Belmar. He is strong enough to dispatch all your lancers with his spells."

"Unless we can catch him in a snowstorm or the rain." Kestrin laughs.

"You risk much if you send your lancers into Neserea," cautions the older man.

"I risk more if I do not."

"Your seers report that the Sea-Priests are readying a fleet to sail from the Ostisles," reports Bassil.

"They are doubtless sailing eastward, but not to Mansuur."

Bassil raises his eyebrows, but does not speak.

Outside the private study of the Liedfuhr, the wind moans. The snowflakes are smaller, and falling faster, and the light dims as the clouds overhead darken, as if winter is returning to Mansuus.

"This Secca—Lord Robero's new Sorceress Protector of the East—she has destroyed all the Sturinnese vessels that had threatened Liedwahr. Do you think that the Maitre of Sturinn will decide to invade us while he has forces in Dumar that are threatened by the sorceress?"

"She remains in Encora for the moment." Bassil pauses. "Yet it is most likely that she will travel to Dumar and use her sorcery against the Sea-Priests there before the Maitre can reinforce them. That will not be easy for her. The Maitre can use the sea to land more sorcerers and lancers, but it will be weeks, if not longer, before the snows melt enough for Lord Robero to send reinforcements to Lady Secca."

"He will not send them even then," predicts Kestrin. "He fears Belmar as much as the Sturinnese. Lady Secca has been successful without further aid. Lady Clayre is slowly losing in Neserea, as you have pointed out, and Aerlya and Annayal may have to flee before long."

"Where?"

Kestrin sighs. "Perhaps to Nordwei."

"It is yet winter there."

"And you question that I should send lancers into Neserea?"

"I cannot see how you could do otherwise—when you can. They cannot cross the snows of the Mittpass yet." Bassil shakes his head. "If you do not dispatch them, once the snows melt, Belmar will take all of Neserea by midsummer. But . . . if he is as bright as he seems, he will turn to face your lancers, in order to destroy them."

"They must not face him. Their task is to destroy those who rebelled against Aerlya." Kestrin's voice is hard. "If he turns, then the Sorceress of Defalk may be able to strengthen Aerlya's hold on the north and east."

"That is possible," Bassil concedes, his voice neutral.

"Not likely, but possible," Kestrin replies with a grim laugh. "Better that than we do nothing. The lady Secca may yet retake Dumar from the Sturinnese, but this Belmar is their tool, and even she will be hard-pressed if Neserea falls and the Sturinnese reinforcements land in Narial."

"Because she will be caught between him and the Sturinnese?"

The Liedfuhr nods slowly. "Because we will then face the Sea-Priests alone."

Outside the study, in the growing darkness, the moaning of the returning winter wind rises with the night.

2

The late-morning sunlight poured over the two-story structure that held the Matriarch's guest quarters, but the wide second-story windows that faced west were still in shadow. The air in the main chamber was hot and still, foreshadowing summer in Encora, although by the turn of the seasons, spring had even yet to arrive.

Rather than using the small working desk that faced away from the leftmost of the three windows, Secca had seated herself at the circular golden oak conference table, her back to the windows. Alcaren sat on the opposite side of the table, leaving four chairs vacant. The tiled hearth on the south wall held several logs set on a pair of heavy iron andirons, but it had been weeks since Secca had needed a fire.

The petite and redheaded sorceress looked at the rose that lay on top of the papers before her on the conference table— a perfect white rose, appearing so delicate that the slightest breeze would rip off the petals. But like so much in Liedwahr, the rose was not what it seemed, for the petals were of white bronze and the stem of a greenish iron—and it had been Alcaren's love gift to her, one she had never expected.

Her amber eyes went from the rose to Alcaren—narrow-waisted and broad-shouldered, almost too short for his breadth to be handsome, yet not stocky, with short-cut brown hair and gray-blue eyes. He wore the pale blue Ranuan uniform and the collar insignia of an overcaptain. As he felt Secca's eyes upon him, he looked up from the map he had been studying and smiled warmly.

In spite of herself, Secca flushed.

"I do the same thing," he said with a slight laugh, adding, "when you look at me."

She shook her head. "It is hard to get used to."

"I know. No one ever looked at me that way."

Secca wondered about that, and yet, she didn't. Alcaren was barely a head taller than she was, and he was striking, but not necessarily handsome. He was a largely untrained sorcerer in a land that feared sorcery, and a strong man in a land ruled by women. "We still need a consorting ceremony," she said slowly.

"You sound dubious, my lady. Am I that much of a burden to bear?"

At the mock-woeful tone of his voice and the twinkle in his eyes, Secca laughed. "You are no burden. Far from that! Still, it is strange."

Alcaren waited, his smile encouraging her to speak.

"It is strange, and it is not. After these years, I had not thought to find love."

"Though I have not traveled as you have, my lady," he replied gently, "neither had I."

"I had thought, were I ever to be consorted, it would be in Falcor, or Flossbend, or even Loiseau . . . not in a strange land."

"We could wait," he suggested. "I would not wish to rush you into such."

Secca shook her head. "Lady Anna waited even to acknowledge her love for Lord Jecks, and I fear she lost years of happiness because she delayed." A sad smile crossed Secca's lips as she thought of the woman who had been more than a mentor, more than a teacher—a mother as well, in fact, if not in name. Secca doubted that she would ever recall Anna without love, emptiness, and a sense of regret that she had not told Anna how much the older woman had meant to her.

After a silence, Secca added, "I need you, both for myself and for what we do. I would not have it said that our alliance was disharmonious or merely of bodily needs."

Alcaren raised his eyebrows.

Secca found herself flushing again, wondering how she had been able to ignore the sheer magnetism of her consort-to-be for as long as she had. "I did not say . . ." She laughed once more, shaking her head as she did.

Alcaren laughed as well.

As the moment of shared joy passed, Secca cleared her throat gently, repeating, "We must have a consorting ceremony before we leave Encora."

"Because you're a Lady of Defalk."

"And so that the Ladies of the Shadows know that I'm going to carry you off away from Ranuak." Secca smiled mischievously for a moment. "Does the Matriarch perform such ceremonies?"

"Seldom . . . but she can."

"Surely, she would do that for a beloved cousin."

"She would more likely do so to make sure her beloved cousin was leaving Encora forever," replied Alcaren dryly as he rose from the chair and stepped back, stretching, before looking past Secca toward the windows and the harbor beyond.

"I think she would like to see you happy," Secca said.

"Oh . . . that she would. Happy with a lovely woman and a beautiful sorceress . . . and happily gone from Encora and on our way to save Liedwahr from the scourge of the Sea-Priests. With song-sorceries used to great effect elsewhere."

Secca nodded agreement, even as she sensed the underlying bitterness. "But she would perform the consorting ceremony."

"I am most certain she would."

"I will send her a request by messenger," replied the petite redhead, "after we meet with the others."

"Will you also send a message to Lord Robero?"

"Yes, but not by sorcery, and not soon. Perhaps I will wait to tell him personally." Secca grinned. "He did say that I needed to consider the matter of heirs."

Alcaren's mouth opened.

Secca laughed once more. "Not now, but with you able to do sorcery, I could have children without fearing all would be after me while I was weakened."

"I am not . . ." he replied slowly.

"You can certainly sing a scrying spell already," Secca pointed out. "That is not forbidden, even by the Ladies of the Shadows."

"The idea of greater sorcery—it feels strange," Alcaren replied.

"Best you get used to it if we are to contend with the Sea-Priests." Secca eased to the working desk, bent over, and lifted the lutar from the case beside the left end of the desk. She began to check the tuning.

"You want me to try a scrying spell now?" he asked.

"Why not? We need to check on the Sturinnese ships before we meet with the others. I'll do the first one, and then I'll write the words for the second."

"You have high visions of my ability."

Secca shook her head. "I know what you can do." She pulled on the copper-tipped leather gloves, then stepped to the conference table and looked down at the scrying glass in the middle before clearing her throat. She'd already run through a series of vocalises before Alcaren had arrived, and they should have been enough for scrying spells.

Chording the lutar, she sang.

"Mirror, mirror, show me clear and as before,
any ships of Sturinn near Liedwahr's shore . . ."

Even after Secca had finished the spell and lowered the lutar, the mirror remained blank silver, showing only the white plaster of the ceiling.

Secca frowned, then handed the lutar to Alcaren. As he strummed it and hummed the spell-melody, Secca dipped the quill in the inkwell and then jotted down the words she held in her mind. Careful not to tilt the paper or brush the wet ink, she set the sheet on the table between Alcaren and the scrying glass.

He studied the words and ran his own chords, not quite

like hers, mouthing the words silently. Finally, he sang the spell in his true and light baritone voice.

"Show me now, most clear and as must be,
ships of Sturinn near our southern sea . . ."

The glass remained blank.

Secca jotted a third spell—one asking to see Sturinnese ships in the Western Sea near Mansuur. Even after Alcaren sang it in his true baritone, the glass came up equally blank.

"My singing?" he asked.

"I think not. Try this one." She slipped a fourth spell before him.

"If this doesn't work, you get to try it again," he said.

"It will work."

He raised his eyebrows for a moment, then concentrated on the spell.

"Show us clear and show us bright
ships of Sturinn that share Ostisles' light . . ."

The glass displayed a bird's eye view of a wide harbor filled with vessels.

Secca swallowed. Never had she seen so many ships in one place—even through a scrying glass. "You see. You can do it as well as I."

"I can do it, but not so well," he countered.

After trying to count the vessels in the glass, she lifted her eyes. "Can you do a release spell?"

"It will fade without it," he pointed out.

"But it takes energy from you. The release spell ends the drain immediately."

He frowned, then sang, chording the lutar.

"Release this vision of what we see,
and let the glass a plain mirror be."

Secca laughed. "I haven't heard that one."

"I couldn't remember yours," Alcaren confessed. "So I made that one up."

"That just shows you are a sorcerer, no matter what you say."

"Don't tell the Ladies of the Shadows, thank you."

"I won't." Secca frowned. "I lost count at threescore ships."

"The spells showed that all those ships are still being readied in the Ostisles," Alcaren pointed out.

"Right now."

A solid *thrap* on the door interrupted their conversation.

"The lady Richina is here, Lady Secca," called Easlon, the lancer stationed outside her door.

"Have her enter."

The tall blonde sorceress—the youngest of all of the full sorceresses of Defalk and not even a year beyond being more than an apprentice—stepped into the main room of the guest chamber, inclining her head to Secca, and then to Alcaren. Her green eyes smiled with her mouth. "Wilten and the chief players will be here shortly."

"Has your glass . . . ?" Secca shook her head. "You can tell us all at once when they arrive."

Richina, more than fifteen years younger than Secca and nearly a head taller, moved toward the conference table with the kind of tall grace that the all-too-petite Secca had often envied in others. "It's most pleasant outside, if with a chill breeze."

"It looks to be," Secca admitted.

"You should get out more often, lady," suggested the younger sorceress.

"The chief players," announced Easlon.

Spared the need for a response, Secca replied, "Have them enter."

The gray-haired Palian stepped through the door, her light gray eyes offering a smile as they passed over Secca and Alcaren. Delvor followed, his lank brown hair flopping over his forehead. Both inclined their heads to Secca, and to Alcaren and Richina, if slightly less deferentially. Two steps behind came Wilten, the overcaptain of Secca's undermanned four companies of lancers. The overcaptain nodded reverently, if stiffly, to Secca.

Secca waited for Richina and the other three to seat themselves before she began, slowly. "The Matriarch has gathered crews for some of the Sturinnese ships." As she spoke, she found herself thinking again how dearly the spell that had destroyed the Sturinnese sailors and armsmen had cost her. Yet, had Alcaren not offered his own life with Darksong to save hers, she never would have known the depth of his love. Still . . . remembering how she had felt sprawled on the ship's deck dying, she almost shivered, and she had to swallow before continuing. "And there are also another half-score of Ranuan ships that will accompany us when we leave for Dumar."

"Are there other Sturinnese warships near?" asked Wilten.

Secca nodded to Alcaren.

"There are none near Liedwahr," explained the Ranuan overcaptain. "The glass shows that the Maitre gathers ships in the main harbor of the Ostisles. That is a voyage of two weeks with the most favorable of winds."

"The seas are clear," pointed out Wilten, "but the Sea-Priests hold Narial and the coast all the way east to the Ancient Cliffs, do they not?"

Secca nodded. "We will have to use the glass to find a landing where we will not have to fight our way ashore. There are few Sturinnese lancers on the lowland coasts west of Narial. It's a longer voyage, but there are roads north to Envaryl."

"They could take Envaryl any day, could they not?" pressed the overcaptain.

"Not with the lancers they have within fifty deks of that city," replied Alcaren. "They have sent companies of lancers throughout Dumar to root out those who oppose them. Even if they tried to regroup the very day we set sail for Dumar, they could not gather more than twenty companies and send them to the coast by the time we land."

"This you are sure of?"

"It might be fifteen; it might be twenty-five," Alcaren conceded.

"That is why we need to sail as soon as we can," Secca said. "We cannot count on the Sturinnese to keep their forces spread, and we do not wish to wait until another fleet is gathered and filled with armsmen and lancers." *And drummers and sorcerers,* she added to herself.

"How long will that be?" asked Palian.

"I hope not long," Secca replied. "I meet with the Matriarch tomorrow, and we will see." She turned her eyes back to Wilten. "Can all be ready within the week?"

"We can be ready," the Defalkan overcaptain responded.

Secca looked to Alcaren. "And the SouthWomen?"

"They have been ready for several days. A few more days will help in training the new recruits."

"Recruits?" asked Wilten.

"Among the younger SouthWomen there has been no dearth of volunteers to go fight the Sturinnese. Captain Delcetta and Captain Peraghn have been able to be most selective in those they accepted."

Wilten nodded slowly, almost stolidly. To his left, Palian offered a knowing smile, while Delvor bobbed his head, and then pushed back the lock of brown hair that always fell across his forehead, and always had in the score of years Secca had known him.

Secca stood. "We'll meet after I've talked to the Matriarch. Then we should be able to finish planning how we can retake Dumar."

As the chief players, Wilten, and Richina stood, and then slipped out, Secca kept a smile on her face, despite the near absurdity of what she had so blithely proposed. With perhaps a half-score of ships, six companies of lancers, two groups of players, and three sorcerers, she was talking about reconquering a land held by more than a hundred companies of Sturinnese lancers, supported by dozens of Darksong drum sorcerers. While she might expect two companies of SouthWomen, her own four companies of lancers were already well understrength, and she could expect few if any reinforcements, while her enemy gathered a fleet of between two- and fourscore warships and transports and scores more companies of armsmen and lancers. To the north of Dumar in Neserea, a rebellion raged, and if that turned out badly, she might find another sorcerer arrayed against her—one who had powers similar to her own, and interests far closer to those of the Maitre of Sturinn.

The smile remained, and she said nothing until the door closed. Then she sighed as she turned to the window and looked toward the harbor, although she could see only the masts of the ships tied at the piers.

"Everyone thinks we can do this," she said slowly.

"If we cannot, the Liedwahr we know is doomed," Alcaren said, stepping up behind her and slipping his arms around her waist, if loosely.

"If we can, it is also doomed," she replied softly.

"I know."

For a long moment, they stood together, enjoying the moment, before Secca turned in Alcaren's arms, hugged him, and kissed his cheek. Then she slipped from his loose grasp and stepped back toward the conference table, looking down at the papers and scrolls. "With the new recruits, the SouthWomen will be nearly as strong as my lancers."

Alcaren shook his head. "You still have nearly three companies' worth."

"And a very cautious overcaptain."

"Wilten does not care that much for me," Alcaren observed.

"We have talked about that before. He does not dislike you. He dislikes anything that is unknown or offers a risk. You are both." Secca tilted her head, thinking, realizing that, even after all the years of seeing Wilten, she would be hard-pressed to describe the overcaptain, except in a general way. He affected neither beard nor mustache, and he was neither tall nor short, neither ample nor excessively slender. His eyes seemed to take on whatever color surrounded him, and his face was not oval or square or round or thin.

"He is like too many in Encora these days, then." Alcaren snorted. "They would have someone else bear the risk, essay the song-sorcery, and then complain that the way in which their liberty was preserved was not to their liking."

"That is true in all lands, perhaps in all worlds." Secca pulled out a sheet of parchment, then shook her head and took one of the crude sheets of brown paper. "We still need to send a request to the Matriarch."

"We?"

"It takes a man and a woman to be consorted. We both should sign the request."

Alcaren laughed. "That way, neither those in Defalk nor those in Ranuak will be pleased."

"Are they ever?" Secca raised her eyebrows.

They both laughed.

3

WEI, NORDWEI

Outside the window of the study, the light from the late-winter sun reflects in all directions from the glaze ice coating the two-yard-deep snow that covers the city and the ice on both the River Nord and Vereisen Bay. Because of the glare, the dark window shutters are almost entirely closed, except for a slit where they meet.

The woman who sits at the desk of polished ebon wood, her back to the window and the thin line of bright light, has fine silver hair and dark black eyes. Once her hair was as dark as her eyes, but those eyes, set as they are in a finely wrinkled skin, still are clear and miss little.

"Leader Ashtaar, the Lady of the Shadows." The voice comes from outside the closed study door.

Before answering the announcement, Ashtaar covers her mouth with a dark green cloth and coughs—once, twice— then sets the cloth aside.

"Enter." Her voice is firm and clear.

The woman who enters is cloaked in black, with a black hood and a gauzelike black veil.

The Council Leader of Wei nods to the polished wooden armchairs across the ebony desk from her and waits for the woman in the dark hood to seat herself. The Lady of the Shadows takes the seat farthest to Ashtaar's left, well away from the thin line of glaring light.

"You wished to see me?"

"Leader Ashtaar, you know well our concerns about sorcery."

As Ashtaar nods, her fingers find the polished black agate oval on the desk.

"Defalk's Sorceress Protector of the East has stretched the harmonies until all Erde vibrated, and then the illegitimate sorcerer of Ranuak used Darksong to save her from her folly."

"That is what the seers reported," Ashtaar replies mildly.

"Is that all you have to say?"

"She destroyed all the Sturinnese warships in the ocean along the south coast of Liedwahr. That was in our interest. Do you wish me to condemn that?" asks the Council Leader.

"This time . . . *this time* it benefited us. Do you not think that the Mynyan lords thought the same when they first unleashed song-sorcery?"

"That may be, but there is little I can do about this. What do you wish of me?"

"At the very least, you could send a messenger to Lord Robero."

A crooked smile crosses Ashtaar's lips. "What will I tell

him? That he must forbid his sorceresses from the sorcery that is all that keeps his realm from falling to the Sea-Priests? Or that we will send the lancers we do not have to attack him?"

"You made sure we had few lancers. That was your doing," points out the hooded woman.

"Indeed it was, and I would do the same again. With the sorcery of Defalk, and the strength of our fleet, we may yet survive and prosper. You would strip Liedwahr of all that would keep it from the chains of the Sturinnese for fear that sorcery you cannot describe might prostrate us in a fashion you cannot define."

"Words, honored Ashtaar. Elegant and well-spoken, but only words. The *facts* are thus. We do not have enough lancers to stop Defalk from using sorcery. We do not have enough ships to stop the Sea-Priests from bringing their sorcery to Liedwahr."

"You sit on the Council, lady. You know as well as do I that we have spent all the coins we could on our fleet, and that fleet has protected our traders well enough that we yet prosper. Would we have prospered had we spent the golds on lancers? Had we any more golds to spend on ships?"

"Yet you risk two of our fleets by sending them westward?"

"As you know," replied Ashtaar, letting a trace of tiredness and exasperation show in her voice, "the Council agreed that it was far better to do that than to leave the fleets either caught in the ice or laid up at their piers and moorings. The presence of our vessels in the Western Sea will at least make the Sea-Priests more cautious." She pauses for the briefest of moments before continuing. "Besides complaining about matters neither of us can change, what do you wish?"

"What we always wish. Your word that you will not support the sorcery of Defalk in the war between the Defalkans and the Sturinnese, and your word that you will not allow your seers to turn to sorcery."

Ashtaar's eyes seemed to darken further. "That I cannot do. It would be most unwise."

"You will regret not renouncing the sorcery of Defalk."

"I am most certain that I will," replied the Council Leader. "I am also certain that I would regret acting as you wish far more. Neither of us would wish to survive under the rule of Sturinn, and if we did, even you would regret most bitterly condemning song-sorcery."

"You presume too much, Ashtaar."

"No. I do not presume at all. Sturinn has been planning to take Liedwahr for years. The Maitres built their fleets and trained their sorcerers and lancers and waited until the Great Sorceress and the old Liedfuhr died. In this time of change, they have acted. We are at a time when the whole future of all Erde will be fixed for generations, if not forever. I will not place Nordwei in the van of opposition to the Sea-Priests. That would be foolish for many reasons. But I will not do anything to harm the efforts of those who oppose them, and where we can help, we shall."

"You are old and mad. You will have sorcery destroy us all, worse than in the Spell-Fire Wars."

"I think not. The harmonies will prevent that," Ashtaar asserted quietly.

"Words. Vain words, especially from one who does not believe in the harmonies."

"I admit that I do not believe in your harmonies. Harmony is a force. So is dissonance. They will balance. We may not like the resulting balance, but it is better to strive for the harmony we wish than to abdicate to those who would use dissonance because we fear the changes that struggle may bring." Ashtaar's fingers rest on the polished agate oval, unmoving.

"We will see." The Lady of the Shadows rises.

"We *will* see, and I will also regret having to use a seer to ensure that your assassins are less than successful."

"We will see about that as well."

Ashtaar nods. "You may go."

After taking a step toward the door, the hooded woman turns back toward Ashtaar. "If I might ask, why did you not attempt to use your fine words to persuade me? Why did you oppose me so strongly?"

"Would fine words have changed what you believe?" asks the older woman. "Would you have believed me if I had promised to look into the matter most carefully?"

The hooded lady laughs, harshly. "We will see."

Ashtaar's eyes follow the dark figure until the door closes.

4

From her seat at the conference table, Secca glanced toward the harbor and the masts she could see from the second-story windows of the guest quarters. The faint smell of spring-damp earth eased through the windows on the light breeze that still held a hint of chill.

Secca's amber eyes dropped to the papers and scrolls before her, the topmost one a rough map of Dumar she had sketched out in her efforts to plan where she and her forces might best land. Envaryl still held out, although Secca had the disturbing feeling that it should have fallen weeks before. The Ranuans were hurrying, according to Alcaren and the Matriarch, but it had been almost a week from the day she had asked the Matriarch to consort her to Alcaren and to hasten their departure for Dumar.

On one day she had set a consorting and an invasion— although few would have considered her meager forces as adequate for such, even with two sorceresses and an untried sorcerer. Then, Alcaren was not untried in battle, just in battle sorcery.

"Chief Player Palian, lady," announced Gorkon.

"Please come in," Secca called as she looked toward the door.

"You asked for me, Lady Secca?" The gray-haired chief player inclined her head to Secca as she stepped into the guest chamber.

"I did." Secca gestured toward the chair beside hers at the conference table and waited for Palian to seat herself.

"You were the one who taught me my instruments all those years ago. You knew me when I was a little girl."

Palian nodded.

"You were younger than I am now, closer to Richina's age."

Palian smiled faintly.

"If I might ask . . . if you would not mind," Secca ventured. "Why did you never choose a consort?"

Palian chuckled, ruefully. "I was never asked . . . and never did I see someone I wished to ask. Before I knew it . . . well, there was little point in doing so." She paused. "After playing for Lady Anna, and under Liende . . ."

"You did not wish to consort for the sake of consorting?"

"Did you, lady?" asked Palian softly.

Secca shook her head. "But now . . . I have decided to consort." Secca looked at the older woman. "I never thought it would be like this."

"You knew that Lord Jecks threw himself before an enchanted javelin to save Lady Anna, did you not? That was when she took Dumar. A Sea-Priest was hidden and cast two at her."

Secca smiled, almost wistfully. "No. She never told me, but I was barely eight when Lord Ehara sent lancers into Defalk. It does not surprise me. It would have taken an effort such as that . . ." Abruptly, Secca laughed. "I'm more like her than I'd known—is that what you're suggesting?"

Palian smiled. "Alcaren could not have shown he loved you any more than he already has. Or than Lord Jecks did for Lady Anna."

"That is true . . . but . . . being consorted by the Matriarch of Ranuak . . . in Encora?" Secca raised her hands. "In less than two days . . ."

"You do not have to. Not even Lord Robero could force you to consort," Palian pointed out.

"I had always thought—Flossbend, or Loiseau. Even Falcor. Never had I thought I would be consorted in Encora."

"Were it not Encora," asked Palian quietly, "would you be consorted at all?"

Secca didn't even have to think about that. She'd already met most of the men anywhere near her own age and position in Defalk. A rueful smile crossed her face, but before she could speak, there was a knock on the chamber door.

"Lady Secca, there is a messenger here," Gorkon announced.

Secca frowned. "A messenger?"

"There are two, with a guard. They're from the Matriarch." There was a hint of laughter in Gorkon's voice. "They very much need to see you, and I would say you should see them."

Neither Gorkon—nor any of her lancers acting as guards—had *ever* presumed to suggest whom she should see. Secca glanced at Palian. The chief player shrugged, her face also expressing puzzlement.

"They . . . can enter—without the guard."

The "messengers" were two girls—and they carried something thin and almost as long as the older girl was tall—something obviously very light and wrapped loosely in dun cotton. "I'm Ulya, Lady Secca," offered the dark-haired girl, bowing. She was not quite as tall as Secca.

"I'm Verlya." The younger and smaller blonde also bowed.

"Mother said that we could bring these. They're consorting gifts from Mother, Father, and us," explained Ulya.

"Mother?" Secca asked, although she suspected who the two must be.

"She's the Matriarch, but we call her Mother still," said the younger blonde—Verlya. She added quickly, "You have to open these now."

"Thank you." Secca smiled as she glanced at Palian. "You're all very kind."

The girls had mentioned gifts, but she saw only the one, carried by both. Ulya lifted it toward the sorceress.

Secca took the light bundle and laid it across the conference table, then slowly peeled back the dun cotton until she had revealed a gown—shimmering blue fabric, but the blue of Loiseau, not the pale blue of Ranuak—with three-quarter-length sleeves and a high-collared neck. Looking at it, as she lifted the garment and held the shimmer-silk before her, she realized it had been somehow tailored for her. She studied the gown closely, then smiled. It was a gown in appearance only, with a full skirt over three-quarter-length trousers, clearly designed to let her ride.

She glanced at Palian, inquiringly.

Palian shook her head.

"Lady Richina let us borrow one of your gowns while you were riding one day," explained Ulya.

"And some trousers. Mother said you would need to ride to the ceremony. Lady Richina promised she wouldn't tell," Verlya said, asking quickly, "Can we come to your consorting? Mother said we had to ask you."

Secca smiled softly. "If your mother agrees, you may come."

"Good!" exclaimed the small blonde. "She said we could come if you said we could." She paused. "Oh . . . I forgot the second gift." She fumbled in her leather jacket and brought out a rectangular box of polished white oak and extended it. "The real gift is inside, but the box is for you, too."

Secca slipped the bronze catch and opened the box gingerly. Her mouth opened. Inside was a necklace—a choker—of white gold. She studied the design of interlocking sections, noting almost belatedly that on one side—set inside a framed gold diamond shape—were a miniature sabre crossed with the symbol for a half note. Where the two crossed was inset with a small diamond. On the other side was a thunderbolt crossed with a note, and the jewel was a small emerald.

"This is gorgeous," Secca said slowly. "I do not think—"

"You have to," insisted Verlya. "It was made for you and Alcaren. He was the best of Mother's guards."

"I gather I have no choice." Secca smiled at the two sisters. "I thank you both . . . and your mother and father for being so thoughtful and generous."

"Mother says a consorting like yours happens but once in the life of a land," offered the older and dark-haired girl.

While she could have disagreed had Palian or Richina—or even Alcaren—said those words, somehow she could not contradict Ulya. "I do not know about that. I do know that you have made it more special, and I cannot thank you enough."

Ulya bowed. After a moment, so did Verlya.

"We must go," the older girl said as she straightened. "Mother said we were not to tarry."

"Or dally," added the blonde.

"By your leave, Lady Secca?" The two bowed again.

"By my leave, and do convey my deepest thanks to your mother."

"Yes, lady."

The two turned and walked solemnly to the door—except Secca caught the glimmer of a smile from the younger sister.

After the door closed behind the departing girls, Palian looked to Secca. "They were most polite and restrained for the heirs of a land."

"They're not automatically the heirs," Secca said absently, her eyes still on the white-gold choker she almost wished she had not been given. "This Matriarch is the younger daughter. Alcaren said that her mother was actually a cousin of an earlier Matriarch."

"That might be better for other lands, as well." Palian's voice was dry. She stepped forward and stood beside Secca, looking down at the open box beside the gown and studying the white-gold choker. After a moment, the chief player turned to Secca. "It carries a message, lady, though none is written thereon."

"I know." Secca nodded slowly. "I know."

"The lady Richina," announced Gorkon.

"Do have her come in," Secca said coldly, winking at Palian.

Richina inclined her head almost before she was inside the chamber. "Lady Secca."

"I understand that you have been lending out my gowns," Secca said sternly. "My only gown."

Richina bowed her head.

Secca laughed. "Best you see the fruits of your deviousness." She held up the gown.

"It is beautiful, lady."After a moment, Richina added, "It is my fault. I wanted you to have a consorting gown, but I cannot sew well enough for such. So I asked the Matriarch for her assistance. You do not mind, do you?"

"You have more boldness than I do in such," Secca confessed.

"In that, you also resemble the lady Anna," Palian said. "Never would she ask anything for herself if ever she could avoid it."

Secca flushed, then looked down at the polished wooden floor before raising her eyes again.

"If you can," blurted Richina, "you might keep the gown a surprise from Alcaren."

"I will say nothing," Secca promised. "That does not mean he will not know. This is his land."

"I do not think any will tell him," observed Palian dryly. "Not about a consorting gift from the Matriarch."

All three women smiled.

Secca held up the gown again, stepping toward the mirror on the inside wall. "It *is* beautiful."

5

EAST OF ITZEL, NESEREA

The two men sit across an inlaid wooden table in a study paneled in time-aged golden oak. Because the day is gray, and near sunset, only the dimmest of light seeps through the ancient mullioned windows, and most of that is blocked by the heavy gold velvet hangings drawn across each casement to block the late winter cold. Even so, the chamber is filled with the golden light that radiates from the almost half a score of six-branched candelabra that surround the table where the two eat.

"This table is almost as exquisite as the one in Jysmar's hold," remarks the younger man, after taking a sip of golden amber wine from a crystal goblet. The darkness of his blue tunic, trimmed in gold, accentuates his piercing blue eyes, fair skin, and jet-black hair.

"Much was lost when you brought his hold down around him, Lord Belmar," replies the man in gray, who at times appears barely older than Belmar, and at other times more than a score of years older than the young Lord of Worlan.

"That was his loss, not mine." Belmar smiles before taking another sip of wine. "Besides, the show of force was necessary. The older lords were beginning to doubt my power." He gestures around the chamber, his hand sweeping past the polished dark oak shelves that hold the scores of leather-bound books, past the Pelaran tapestries hung on the walls between the shelves. "Would we have had such easy entry here otherwise?" He chuckles. "And Lord Girsnah is more than happy to have us served his very best. I could even request his daughter, master jerGlien, and he would offer her willingly." Belmar glances toward jerGlien, as if seeking a reaction. "She is young, tender, and rather attractive."

The man in gray offers a faint smile of amusement. "I imagine he would, under the circumstances."

"I won't go that far. That sort of foolishness was what undid Rabyn."

"Along with his other failings."

Belmar ignores jerGlien's sardonic tone. "The entire south of Neserea acknowledges me. So does the northeast and the far northwest. Only the river valleys of the Saris and Esaria itself stand opposed."

"That is true."

"Now is the time to strike." The black-haired and blue-eyed lord glances at the older man in nondescript gray. "Do you not think so, master jerGlien?"

"Always . . . somewhere . . . it is time to strike, Lord Belmar. The skill is knowing where and how hard."

"Meaning that you think I am too impatient?" asks Belmar.

"If you can stop the Sorceress of Defalk, then you should do what you feel necessary."

"I defer to your experience, master jerGlien, yet I might ask why you think I am too hasty. For your words suggest other than what they say."

A shrug comes from the man in gray. "We have made certain entreaties to Lord Robero, very quietly. He is not totally unreceptive, but he is far from convinced, it would seem to me. We must convince him . . . appropriately."

"And how would that be, and why would I care?"

"I do not pretend to know Neserea, and Defalk even less, but . . ." JerGlien pauses dramatically. ". . . were I about to rule a land, I would prefer not to have an unnecessary enemy on my borders. Lord Robero is constrained by the presence of the very sorceresses who support him." The Sturinnese smiles. "What man enjoys being constrained by women?"

"You think . . . ?"

"One must strike before it is expected . . . or where such

an attack is not expected, and it cannot hurt if one strikes where a loss may not be regretted totally by the ruler of a neighboring land."

"Striking at the sorceresses of Defalk?"

"You face the least dangerous, for all her experience," offers jerGlien. "The younger one is more dangerous."

"She destroyed an entire fleet, did she not? The younger one? That could not have pleased your Maitre," replies Belmar.

The man in gray laughs. "What she has done has gained her little. She remains in Ranuak, and the snows on the Mittfels and Sudbergs still deepen. She has no allies to speak of and will have to face far more sorcerers than she knows if she would wrest Dumar from us."

"She may have gained little," points out Belmar, "but it has cost your Maitre dearly."

"Not so dearly as one might think, and if it positions her to fail . . . why then, it is well worth the cost."

"You presume to judge such for your Maitre, my friend."

"Were the Maitre here, I daresay he would find little to object to in my words."

"He is more trusting than I would be."

The Sturinnese smiles. "He is far less trusting. He cannot afford trust. He ensures obedience. That is safer and wiser. Far wiser."

Belmar pauses, not quite imperceptibly, before lifting the goblet. "I will study the glass and the maps tomorrow. Then, we will see. Perhaps we can persuade the lady Aerlya that her daughter—young Annayal—should indeed consider a consort most quickly in these troubled times."

"If she remains in Neserea."

"In a winter like this, with the snow waist deep except on the roads we have cleared with sorcery . . . where could she go?" Belmar smiles once more.

"Where indeed?" replies the Sturinnese, lifting his own goblet. Although the rim touches his lips, he does not actually drink the wine, excellent as it may be.

6

Outside the guest quarters, a cold misting rain drifted from the low gray clouds, collecting on the window-panes and running down the glass in irregular rivulets. Inside, before the low fire in the hearth, two figures embraced as though they had not seen each other for seasons, rather than just since the evening before.

After a long time, Secca gently disengaged herself from Alcaren's hug, good as it felt, and stepped back.

"Is something the matter?" asked her consort-to-be.

"You have to tell me more about your parents," Secca said. "We're going to meet them in less than a glass, and I know almost nothing."

"You know about my mother—or have you forgotten?" Alcaren offered a mischievous grin, his broad hand reaching out, his fingers caressing her cheek momentarily.

"I remember everything you told me, but it was all about you and your mother, and how you'd never make a trader like she is—or like your sister. You didn't tell me anything really about her. I don't know what she looks like or what . . ." She shook her head. "Please . . . just tell me."

"Well . . ." Alcaren drew out the word. "She's tall, taller than I am, and her hair was sandy blonde, but it's mostly gray these days. She laughs a great deal, sometimes when she doesn't mean it. I suppose that comes from being a trader. She's never liked matters that deal with household-ing, and we always had a cook, because she doesn't care what she eats, and the rest of us would have starved."

"Your sister—I'm sorry I'm interrupting, but this is all so unexpected—will she be there?" Secca paused, then added, "I'm sorry."

"You don't have to be sorry. Nedya will like you."

"She's your sister? You've never mentioned her name."

"I haven't?"

"Not once." Then, in all fairness, Secca had to remind herself, she hadn't known Alcaren that long—less than two seasons.

Alcaren shook his head. "She's small and dark, wiry, like Father, but she's strong. She can hoist cargo with the strongest of the crews. Her voice is like Mother's, though. Even when we were small, everyone in the neighborhood could hear her."

"Does anyone else have a talent with the mandolin or with voice?"

"Father has a pleasant voice. He was the one who first taught me to play, but he dislikes sorcery, perhaps even more so than Mother, and I've never heard him sing."

Secca winced. "What do they think about your consorting to a sorceress?"

"Nedya thinks that it's for the best . . ." Alcaren grinned. "She said that it would be good for me to have someone who can understand me and keep me riding in the right direction."

"How about your father?" Secca wasn't sure she wanted to ask about what Alcaren's mother thought.

"He hasn't said much. He never does. He didn't even shake his head or curse when I broke chisels and ruined stone blocks and broke clay molds. He knew I was trying, and that I just didn't have the talent." Alcaren's lips curled ruefully.

"What did he say when you told him about us?"

"He just smiled, and said it was about time I found someone who could take care of me."

"Take care of you?" blurted Secca.

"Remember? I've never proved particularly adept at what they think is important. My hands can finger a lumand or a mandolin, but not work clay or stone. I get sick on ships in rough water, and I never enjoyed counting up golds."

The sorceress almost shook her head, thinking about how

well Alcaren rode, how accomplished he was with a blade, how effectively he seemed to organize and lead people, and how much he knew. "And your mother?"

"She said that I was consorting well above my station, and that it was for the best, but that I should thank the harmonies and not get airs about it." He was the one to shake his head. "She said that being your consort would be the most difficult task I'd ever tried." The warm smile followed. "She might be right in that."

"Now I'm difficult?" Secca raised her eyebrows.

"What you will attempt in attacking the Sturinnese has never been successful," he pointed out. "Then, what you've already done has never been done, either."

Secca frowned. Anna had done far greater sorceries and become the first woman regent truly to rule a northern land in Defalk.

"No one else has ever destroyed a Sea-Priest fleet at sea. Even your lady Anna only destroyed them at anchor in the harbor."

"No one else was ever foolish enough to try." Secca glanced toward the windows. "I suppose we should go. You said we would be there by midmorning?"

"Before midday."

Secca turned toward her bedchamber to gather her riding jacket and her sabre, but Alcaren intercepted her and drew her into his arms.

"We do have to go," she whispered.

"In a moment."

It was a very long moment before he released her—or she released him.

By the time they had gotten their mounts from the stables, which were a good hundred yards behind the guest quarters and past the barracks that housed her lancers and the two companies of SouthWomen commanded by Alcaren, the cold rain had turned into an even finer mist. The formless gray clouds had lightened, and a cooler breeze swirled through the long, stone-paved courtyard. Infrequent light gusts of cool air alternated with warmer damper air.

"It will be colder tonight," Alcaren said, as Secca mounted her gray.

"I like that better than rain," she replied.

A discreet cough interrupted their conversation. "Lady, Overcaptain . . ."

Secca turned in the saddle.

Wilten stood by the stable door.

Beside him was the SouthWoman captain Delcetta. The strawberry blonde woman had an apologetic smile on her face. "We have taken the liberty of having a squad of lancers from Loiseau and one from the SouthWomen to escort you. They are drawn up and awaiting you. Also, your chief archer Elfens has requested to accompany you with several of his best archers."

"The Ladies of the Shadows have not been released from the White Tower, have they?" asked Alcaren.

"No, ser. But we do not know all who may follow them," replied Delcetta.

Wilten nodded, and added, "It is best that none think you unguarded."

Would she seem more formidable guarded or unguarded? Secca wondered.

As she and Alcaren rode out of the courtyard, the lancers eased their mounts into position, leaving the two of them between the crimson-trimmed, dark blue riding jackets of the SouthWomen and the green of Loiseau. The measured clopping of hoofs echoed through the damp morning as the column headed between the neatly trimmed boxwood hedges that flanked the lane leading to the main avenue.

Secca glanced forward at the SouthWomen lancers leading the way, then at Elfens, riding behind the vanguard.

The tall archer seemed to feel Secca's glance and twisted in the saddle, grinning as he offered an angled half bow.

Secca grinned and shook her head. After a moment, she turned in the saddle to take in the column behind them. "I feel almost like a prisoner."

"You are," Alcaren said with a laugh. "You're a prisoner of your own power. None of us can afford to lose you."

"Even you?"

"Me . . . most of all."

Once out of the lane, they turned their mounts northward, in the direction of the Matriarch's small palace. The misting rain stopped completely, but wisps of fog rose from the gray stones of the avenue, twisting into vague shapes in the seemingly more frequent bursts of cold air that had begun to chill the warmer damp air.

"What is your . . . your parents' dwelling like?" Secca asked after a silence.

Astride the brown gelding that was almost the size of a raider beast, and far larger than Secca's gray mare, Alcaren shrugged. "It is a dwelling with two small wings and a stable that will hold four mounts, perhaps five if we double stall in the front corner. We have no carriage. There is a small formal flower garden off the portico and a much larger vegetable garden. Father has his studio in a small outbuilding. It is all very modest."

"Do you still have a chamber there?"

"I suppose so. I have left nothing there, but Father calls it my room."

They continued riding past the Matriarch's palace and then turned onto another avenue that led uphill and to the northeast. Secca noted that some of the dwellings flanking the avenue were nearly as large as the Matriarch's. None was small. "Is their dwelling on this side of the hill?"

Alcaren laughed. "I fear not. It is smaller and more to the south on the lesser hill."

Secca nodded, but as they rode to the top of the hill and then followed a narrower way to the right and down onto a lower hill, the houses and grounds did not get much smaller. When they rode up into a stone-paved circular drive, Secca was scarcely surprised that the dwelling was more than the simple house Alcaren had suggested.

"Here we are," announced her consort-to-be, gesturing toward the small villa with two wings branching from the circular and columned rotunda that dominated the stone-paved lane leading to the covered entry and the mounting blocks.

Alcaren reined up in front of the mounting blocks, leaving them to Secca. While she appreciated his courtesy as she dismounted, once more she felt almost patronized because of her small stature.

"Alcaren!" The young woman who hurried out through the columned archway was indeed small and wiry, perhaps even shorter than Secca herself, and more boyish in appearance. She glanced up at Secca and flashed the same warm smile that Secca had seen from Alcaren. "Lady Secca . . ." Then she laughed, warmly and openly. "Welcome . . . welcome."

Secca tried to halt the inadvertently quizzical look that she could feel appearing on her face.

"Alcaren never said how beautiful you are," Nedya rushed on. "Or that you were a redhead."

Secca wondered what Alcaren *had* said, since, from what she'd seen and overheard from the younger women in her hold of Flossbend or at Loiseau, they seldom mentioned the physical beauty of women who might be rivals—or consorts to their brothers. Secca didn't have an easy response, but managed to reply, "He's probably had other things on his mind. He's been helping me plan what we have to do next." Realizing belatedly the ambiguity of her words, she added quickly, "Against the Sturinnese."

"He talked about that," Nedya admitted. After a moment, she said, "I'd keep you both out here in the cold chattering, but Mother and Father are waiting inside."

"As patiently as ever, I am most sure," Alcaren said dryly as he stepped up beside Secca. He glanced sideways at the sorceress. "Mother has never been known for her patience. She has other virtues, but not that."

"And my older brother can be painfully honest," replied

Nedya. "His grace is that he is as unsparing of himself as of anyone else."

"I've always found him the soul of care and tact," Secca admitted.

Nedya raised her eyebrows. "For that alone, we should be thankful." She spoiled the arch effect by smiling.

Secca handed the gray's reins to Gorkon, who had ridden up behind them, but not dismounted. Then she walked side by side with Alcaren up the steps and through the door that Nedya had left open. The entry foyer was not large, a circular space four yards across with white-plastered walls and a floor tiled in a pattern of repeating hexagons of alternating white and dark blue. A single tapestry filled the blank wall directly opposite the doors, and the scene upon it was that of a full-masted ship under sail, rendered entirely in shades of blue, save for the golden-braided border.

The broad-shouldered older woman who stood just before the tapestry in the small foyer was a good head and a half taller than Alcaren. She had a weathered face somehow both squarish and angular. Her eyes were grayish blue like her son's—except even more piercing. Beside her stood a smaller, slighter man with dark brown hair streaked with silver.

The woman spoke first. "I am Carenya, Lady Sorceress, and I welcome you to our dwelling."

Secca inclined her head. "I am happy to meet you. Alcaren has spoken much of you and of your success as a trader."

"Were it not for your efforts, I fear, none of us would be traders for much longer." A wry smile, but one with warmth beneath, appeared with Carenya's words.

"I am Todyl." The man who stood in the archway to the left offered a broad smile. "Alcaren has said how talented you are, but he had not told us that you are also beautiful."

Secca found herself blushing, as if she were fifteen years old, instead of more than twice that. "You are most kind, and so is Alcaren."

"Do come in," Carenya offered, turning and gesturing in the direction of the archway in which her consort stood. "We should not be standing in the foyer." She paused. "It is damp outside. Would you like some warm cider? Or a hot brandy?"

"Cider, if it would not be too much trouble."

"For me, also," Alcaren added, almost apologetically.

The trader glanced at Nedya. "If you would . . ."

"I'll be quick," promised the young woman.

The sitting room beyond the archway was both as Secca had imagined it, and not at all the same. Given Alcaren's description of his mother, she found the spareness unsurprising, but not the vivid reds and yellows infusing the few hangings on the plaster walls and the three brilliant green cushions on the all-wooden settee where she seated herself.

Alcaren sat down beside her, protectively, as Todyl and Carenya settled into unupholstered wooden armchairs across a bare low table from the settee.

"Alcaren has said that you are one of the Thirty-three of Defalk, both by ability and by birth." Carenya offered the words as an opening, but without a tone of questioning.

"I am Lady of Flossbend. My father held the domain, but he died when I was a child, and both my mother and my brothers were poisoned by my uncle. The lady Anna defeated my uncle and restored the lands to me. I became a sorceress, and when Lady Anna died last fall, Loiseau came to me as her sorceress-heir."

"If I might ask," ventured Todyl, "what is your hold like?"

Secca smiled. "Neither Flossbend nor Loiseau is terribly large, just enough to support a small household and the lancers."

"Lancers?" asked Carenya.

"The four companies of lancers in green are hers, not Lord Robero's. She supports them and pays them," Alcaren said quickly. "My lady is sometimes too modest."

"Your lands cannot be that small, then," suggested the trader.

"We do as we must in these troubled times," Secca replied, not really knowing how she could answer the implied questions without being deceptive in some way or another, or revealing more than she had any desire to divulge.

Nedya hurried into the sitting room, bearing a tray on which were five mugs. Steam drifted from all five. She deftly set a mug before Secca, then before Alcaren. "Only because this is special," she told her brother with the hint of a smile.

"I'll do the same for you," he whispered back.

"You'll wait a long time, but I'll hold you to it." Nedya handed mugs to her parents, then sat on the stool at the end of the low table, cradling the mug between both hands.

There was a long silence.

"Besides fight battles," asked Nedya abruptly, "what does a sorceress of Defalk do?"

Secca smiled. "Until the last two seasons, I had never fought a battle. In Defalk, sorcery is used to make life better for people. We build roads and bridges, sometimes buildings. Last fall I repaired an old dam and part of the aqueduct that provided water to the people of Issl. I have used sorcery to discover where a well might be dug."

"That does not sound too taxing," observed Carenya.

Secca tilted her head, wondering how she could explain. Finally, she began. "In one day, a sorceress and her players may be able to use sorcery to build one dek, perhaps two deks, of stone-paved road. That much sorcery will exhaust them. Defalk had no paved roads outside of Falcor when the lady Anna became regent. Today, there are more than a thousand deks of roads in Defalk. There is even one that travels most of the west of Defalk, from Nordfels to Denguic." She paused. "It would take scores of men to build and pave a dek of road in a day. While sorcery can do such faster, it takes much effort and skill."

"The roads improve travel and trade," mused the trader.

"We also have had to build bridges and fords," Secca added.

"Defalk had been the poorest of lands since the Spell-Fire Wars," reflected Carenya, "but now . . ."

"Matters are better now," Secca pointed out, "but Defalk is still far from wealthy. It has been more than a score of years since the terrible drought, and the land has still not fully recovered. Even my orchards do not produce what they did in the first years of Lord Brill."

"You could have been a trader, lady," replied Carenya with a slight laugh. "Nothing is as good as it could or should be."

"How will you get to the ceremony?" asked Nedya quickly, as if to preempt another question by her parents. "It's a long walk from the guest quarters to the Matriarch's."

Secca glanced at Alcaren, who met her inquiry with raised eyebrows. Then, he finally shrugged.

"I would guess that we'll ride," Secca replied. "I haven't seen any carriages or coaches in Encora."

"There aren't any," Nedya said. "Unless you count the wagons with benches."

"It's an old custom," explained Todyl. "The Mynyan lords used carriages shielded with sorcery. No one has ever used a coach since."

Secca nodded slowly. Just as she thought she understood Ranuak better, something like the matter of carriages popped up. Then, she should have guessed from the tailoring of the gown sent by the Matriarch.

Wondering how many other surprises she would discover in the course of the afternoon, Secca smiled and asked Carenya, "How did you become a trader?"

"That was easy enough. Once I could stand, my mother put me on the deck beside her . . ."

Secca nodded and continued to listen.

....

While the sun shone through a high and thin haze, the chill breeze out of the northeast reminded Secca that, even in Encora, the season was not yet spring. She and Alcaren rode at the head of the column, preceded only by four of the Matriarch's guards, and followed immediately by Wilten and Richina, with a company of lancers in the green of Loiseau bringing up the rear.

Wearing her green leather riding jacket over the blue gown was practical, if not terribly elegant, but Secca had no alternatives, besides freezing. She shifted her weight in the saddle of the gray mare, then glanced sideways at Alcaren, riding beside her in the darker blue dress uniform of an overcaptain of Ranuak—a much warmer outfit than the blue consorting gown Secca wore under the riding jacket.

"I've never seen that uniform," she said.

"Neither had I, until yesterday. It was a gift from the Matriarch. She said she owed more than a uniform to me, but that the uniform would have to do for now."

"She wants you consorted and out of Ranuak," Secca suggested, "and she might gift her favorite cousin more—once you're safely away."

"Her problem cousin is more accurate," Alcaren replied. "But I'm about to become more your problem than hers. Are you ready for that?"

"More than ready. You've already been the problem. We're past that." Secca smiled, broadly, trying to conceal some of the nervousness she felt.

"You're worried still." His voice carried the understated concern that it had taken her seasons to recognize.

"A little. In a way, I'd given up hope of finding a consort I could love. Getting that feeling back . . ."

"I know." Alcaren laughed gently, warmly. "I do know. I didn't expect to find myself drawn to you. Then . . . I couldn't lose you, and I didn't realize it until I had to act."

"I know. I'm glad." Secca appreciated both his words and the warmth behind them.

The last half-dek of the avenue leading to the Matriarch's palace was lined with lancers—women lancers in the red and blue of the SouthWomen. As Secca and Alcaren rode past, each SouthWoman lifted her sabre in salute, holding it unwaveringly long after the couple had passed.

"They don't have to . . ." Secca murmured.

"They do," replied Alcaren in a low voice, leaning toward her. "The Council of SouthWomen will ask the Matriarch to allow all five companies of the SouthWomen to accompany you to Dumar."

"They told you this?"

Alcaren shook his head. "They were talking about it from the day after the battle with the Sea-Priests. All of the SouthWomen lancers are packing, and all have made arrangements for others to handle their crafts or work."

Secca swallowed.

"You have become their champion, and they will follow you where they would follow no other."

"Me? I'm not even from Ranuak."

"All have seen your work with a blade, and all know that you have slain Sea-Priests with both sorcery and blade."

Secca smiled, ruefully. "You told them?"

Alcaren shook his head. "Delcetta did. Since the time of the Great Sorceress, they have felt they failed, and they would follow you to redeem themselves."

Secca still felt strange hearing Anna referred to as the Great Sorceress. "Redeem themselves for what? What they did created the Free City, and that began to change everything in Ebra."

"Only because Anna defeated Bertmynn and forced the Ebrans to recognize the city as a place of refuge. They feel they owe both of you."

Even after Alcaren's brief explanation, Secca couldn't say she understood, but she wasn't going to pursue it on her consorting day.

Following the Matriarch's guards, they turned their mounts toward the gateless opening in the bluish white granite walls that encircled the Matriarch's palace and grounds. Over the ungated entry rose a high stone arch. Above the keystone of the arch was set a single white-bronze fire lily. Inside the walls, the stone drive curved toward the three-story dwelling set in the middle of a park with wide expanses of grass and irregularly spaced low trees. Under the portico waited another set of four guards in the pale blue uniforms of the Matriarch, standing on the steps above the long carriage-mounting block.

"You will let me assist you in dismounting, my lady, will you not?" asked Alcaren. There was a smile in his tone of voice, as well as upon his lips.

"This time." Secca was smiling as well.

After dismounting, Secca took Alcaren's arm, and they walked past the small honor guard and up the three wide stone steps to the archway into the small palace. Richina followed silently.

Once in the square foyer inside, Secca removed her riding jacket and handed it to Richina. The younger sorceress took off her own jacket, revealing her simple traveling gown of rich green, then passed both jackets to Gorkon, who had followed them inside, with Wilten. Richina led the way up the single staircase, not overly wide, perhaps three yards, but broad enough for Secca and Alcaren side by side, even with Secca's blue overskirt.

"I hope your family is here," murmured Secca.

"Father wouldn't miss it, and neither would Mother and Nedya. They've probably been here for a good glass."

When Richina reached the landing at the top of the steps, the younger sorceress stepped forward toward the open doorway into the Matriarch's formal receiving hall, where the consorting would take place. The Matriarch's two daughters, both in white trousers and tunics, flanked the doorway, each carrying a sprig of fir about two spans long, each sprig wrapped in white ribbon. The two girls bowed gravely to Richina, and then more deeply to Secca and Alcaren.

"Have them enter," called the Matriarch.

As Secca stepped into the formal receiving hall, past the two girls, walking slowly beside Alcaren, her eyes went first to Alya, standing on the dais before the blue crystalline chair-throne, a throne sparkling with an inner light that created an aura around the Matriarch. The diffuse light from the floor-to-ceiling windows on each side of the chamber somehow emphasized the warm bluish aura.

Alcaren's parents stood on the left side of the receiving room, their backs to the long windows, while a slender man with blond-and-silver hair, presumably the Matriarch's consort, stood by himself on the right. He was attired entirely in white, except for a dark blue belt and matching dark blue boots.

Both Carenya and Nedya wore white tunics with lace collars over dark blue trousers, while Todyl wore a blue tunic over white trousers. All three wore crimson leather belts.

Richina stepped forward, and then moved to the right, beside the Matriarch's consort, before turning to face Carenya.

Secca and Alcaren stopped two paces short of the dais and the Matriarch.

Alya smiled warmly. "I would like to say that I never would have guessed that this consorting would come to be. I cannot tell you, and all those here, how happy I am that you two have found each other, and happiness in each other." She paused. "The ceremony is simple."

There was a moment of silence. Then, the Matriarch glanced out across the modest formal hall. "Do any here have any objection to this consorting?"

After a pause, she looked at Secca. "Do you, Secca, Lady of Loiseau and Flossbend, enter this consorting of your own free will, without coercing another, and without coercion by any other being, and in joy, hope, and honesty?"

"I do." Secca felt a lump in her throat, and, somehow, she wished Anna could have been there to see the ceremony, and . . . somehow . . . she felt sad that her mentor had never felt able to consort to Lord Jecks.

"Do you, Alcaren of Encora, enter this consorting of your own free will, without coercing another, and without coercion by any other being, and in joy, hope, and honesty?"

"I do."

Alya looked to Secca once more. "If you would repeat after me . . ."

Secca nodded.

"I, Secca, in the sight and song of the harmonies, offer myself as your consort, forsaking all others. I accept you and no other as my consort for so long as shall the harmonies declare, through all times of trouble, all times of joy, and the times that are neither."

"Alcaren, if you would repeat after me . . ."

Alcaren smiled and squared his shoulders ever so slightly before repeating the words. "I, Alcaren, in the sight and song of the harmonies, offer myself as your consort, forsaking all others. I accept you and no other as my consort for so long as shall the harmonies declare, through all times of trouble, all times of joy, and the times that are neither."

After just a moment of silence, Alya raised her left hand, drawing a circle in the air.

Secca could see the faintest shimmer of a blue orb hanging before the Matriarch for a long instant before Alya again spoke.

"As Matriarch of Ranuak, I declare you are consorts in body, in spirit, and in harmony."

Secca turned toward Alcaren, lifting her head slightly as his arms went around her ever so gently. Their lips met.

Someone sighed.

As she and Alcaren embraced and kissed before the Matriarch, Secca could feel a sense of warmth—and peace— flow over them, and she didn't want the moment to end.

8

ENVARYL, DUMAR

The sharp-faced man in the crimson tunic of the Lord High Counselor of Dumar stands with his back to the low coals in the hearth of the villa's study. "A cold winter this has been. Few have seen one this chill."

The man in gray nods. The two other men, one wearing the uniform of an overcaptain, the other the gold collar insignia that proclaim him an arms commander, do not.

"We watch, and yet your glass, Elyzar, it shows nothing," continues the Lord High Counselor.

"The glass shows what is, Lord Fehern. It does not show what we wish," replies the sorcerer.

"I do not see why the Sturinnese do not move against us," offers the arms commander. "The roads are firm. The mud is gone, and yet they advance not. Or so slowly that they might be a giant tortoise."

"That may be, Halyt," says Fehern. "That indeed may be, but they hold all of our lands save this miserable western province. They rode quickly enough in the fall. Now, they do not. Can your glass tell us why, Elyzar?"

"It can show what happens. It does not show what is in men's hearts." The broad-shouldered sorcerer fingers his neatly trimmed and square-cut black beard.

"It is clear that they wait for something," states Arms Commander Halyt. "Could it be that they fear the Liedfuhr will strike them from the north?"

"Kestrin won't do that." Fehern snorts. "He worries far more about his sister and her daughter. My dear younger brother Eryhal should have consorted with the elder. Then, there would be less support for this Belmar."

"One cannot undo what is done, lord," offers Elyzar unctuously. "One can but take the opportunities offered to change the future."

"We can't do anything about Neserea," points out Halyt. "We needs must prepare for the onslaught here."

"How . . . with more quick skirmishes that kill Sturinnese, but scarcely stop them? Or do you have a score of sorcerers or thirtyscore companies of lancers coming to our aid from somewhere?" Fehern laughs hollowly. "Not a word, and not a single lancer from that old woman of Defalk. All these years we have sent tribute and fealty, and what do we receive in our time of trouble? Not a thing. A sad thing it is when the best ruler of Defalk was a woman and but a regent. She was more a man than the men of Defalk."

"All the mountains are too deep with snow . . ." murmurs the overcaptain.

"Now . . . but were they that deep when the Sturinnese landed in Narial? When aid would have truly helped?"

Neither officer speaks for a time.

Fehern looks hard at the sorcerer. "Your glass has no answers as to why the Sturinnese tarry. Do you, Elyzar?"

"They wait for something, lord. It could be that they think that waiting will gain them more than attacking."

"We have supplies, more than enough. What we do not have is sorcerers who can do battle work and lancers adequate to stop the white tide. You know that." Fehern glares at Elyzar. "So must they."

"They must know something." Halyt laughs heartily. "Otherwise, we would see them on the river road."

"They must. But what?" Fehern turns from the sorcerer, cocking his head slightly. "What could it possibly be?"

Elyzar offers an enigmatic smile, but does not reply.

9

The cold and clear skies that had graced Secca's consorting had departed, and for the two days afterward gray clouds and misty rain had blanketed Encora, not that Secca or Alcaren had paid much attention to the weather for the first day or so.

A stolen pair of days of bliss were all Secca dared take, and Alcaren had but nodded knowingly that morning as she made ready to visit the Matriarch once more. Now, she rode through the light and cold rain, with Alcaren beside her, back northward along the avenue to the Matriarch's compact palace. Behind them rode a company of Defalkan lancers, and before them a squad of SouthWomen in their crimson-trimmed blue jackets.

"I will not accompany you inside her receiving room," Alcaren said. "Neither your people, nor Lord Robero, nor the Ladies of the Shadows would wish to see me as exerting greater influence."

"That would be best," Secca admitted, relieved that she had not been the one to have to make that statement, and pleased that Alcaren had both seen the problem and made the offer not to accompany her. "The Matriarch will still know I listen to you."

"She listens to her consort, and all know that. In Ranuak, consorts are meant to be heard in private."

"That is also true in Defalk, save that the consorts heard in private, until the Lady Anna changed matters, were all women."

"Some lords would not be loath to see that custom return?"

"There are doubtless some, but more in Neserea than in Defalk, and that is why so many rally behind Belmar."

"You worry about what will happen there almost more than what awaits us in Dumar."

"I do." Secca couldn't have explained the dread she felt when considering Neserea, almost as if that land posed a greater danger than Dumar, yet nothing she knew would support that. "I cannot say why, but I do."

"I cannot see that, my lady, but I would not go against your senses for that." Alcaren paused. "I would ask that you consider why you may feel that way. In that fashion, we will not be so surprised as might otherwise be the case."

"I don't think it's Belmar . . ." Secca shook her head. "I'll have to think." She could still recall Anna's words about trusting her feelings. If only she could put words and ideas to *why* she felt as she did.

Alcaren did not press her, and shortly they rode under the archway into the Matriarch's grounds and reined up under the covered portico, where a pair of guards in pale blue stood by the archway.

"You are expected, Lady Secca," offered the taller, even before Secca had finished reining up beside the mounting block.

"Thank you," she replied, dismounting easily, then handing the gray's reins to Gorkon, who also took the reins to Alcaren's gelding.

Secca and her consort entered the foyer, then climbed the stairs to the upper level, where Alcaren stopped at the upper landing, well short of the Matriarch's guard.

Secca stepped forward, and the guard turned to the door, opening it just a trace.

"The lady Secca to see you, Matriarch." Almost before completing the announcement, and before the Matriarch's words to admit Secca were completed, the guard opened the door.

Secca walked toward the dais, stopped, and bowed before Alya, who was again seated on the blue crystalline throne-chair.

"You had asked to see me, Lady Secca?" asked the Matriarch.

Secca bowed. "I would like to inquire as to how might our transportation to Dumar be coming?"

"As quickly as we can finish fitting out the vessels. After all, after freeing our ports and providing us with six more vessels," replied the Matriarch with a smile, "how could I refuse?"

"Especially since it would remove two sorceresses and a sorcerer from Encora," countered Secca.

"But I would be losing my favorite cousin." Alya laughed warmly, before a more serious expression reappeared. "I cannot tell you how happy I am for both of you. I have not seen Alcaren so joyous in all his life. He does not tell others, but I can sense and see that."

"I fear I am carrying him into great danger," Secca said.

"That may be, but it is a danger that you may be able to overcome together. The dangers he faced here could never have been conquered."

Secca nodded. From what she had seen of the Ladies of the Shadows, she understood.

"Do you know where our ships would carry you? When we spoke before, you had not decided, and Narial remains in Sturinnese hands . . ." ventured the Matriarch.

"I had thought the small port of Stygia, south of Envaryl. We are still using the glasses to study Dumar, but, before we went farther, I wished to ask if that destination would be one where you could assist us."

Alya laughed gently. "I think everyone in Ranuak would like to help you on your way, wherever it be in Dumar, if not for the same reasons. The SouthWomen want to follow you into battle. The Exchange wants you to defeat the Sturinnese as soon as possible. The Ladies of the Shadows would like you and Alcaren out of Encora before you corrupt the land to a greater extent, and I will feel great relief, if sadness, once you are safely departed." Alya's expression returned to a somber cast. "You know the SouthWomen have requested to accompany you? All five companies?"

"I had heard rumors of such."

"Would you have them?"

"Gladly," Secca replied. "Five companies would help greatly."

"I had thought as much. They have asked if you would accept Delcetta as their overcaptain. She would take orders still from Alcaren, or from you, as you see fit."

"I have no problem with her being an overcaptain. With the demands of sorcery, I would leave direct command to Alcaren."

The Matriarch nodded. "I will convey both my approval and yours to the Council of SouthWomen . . . not that they need mine, nor have they always heeded the Matriarch, but it is better when we do agree." Alya's last words were delivered with a dryly sardonic tone.

"How soon can we leave?" pressed Secca.

"Before your consorting I had asked the Exchange to make ready the ships. Three days from now, I am told, if there are no storms, and if you are ready."

"We will be ready."

"I will send word." Alya stood. "I wish that times were otherwise."

"So do we all." Secca bowed. "Thank you."

"We owe you the far greater thanks, Lady Secca. Perhaps in time, all in Ranuak will understand that."

"You are kind." Secca doubted that the Ladies of the Shadows would ever be thankful, and with what she might have to do in the weeks and seasons ahead, they would be even less pleased. "We will do our best." With a faint smile, she bowed again and turned.

Outside, Alcaren was still standing by the top of the stairs. He glanced at her.

Secca nodded slightly, and they started down the steps.

"Three days," she murmured, as she and Alcaren crossed the foyer toward the archway leading out to the portico.

"Wilten will not be pleased."

They both laughed softly as they stepped out of the building and under the portico.

Gorkon led their mounts to them, and Secca mounted quickly, and as gracefully as possible, she thought, for a woman as small as she was.

She said nothing as they rode out from under the portico and into the rain that had let up and become more like an icy mist.

"That is not all, is it?" Alcaren finally said as Secca and he followed the squad of SouthWomen back southward toward the guest quarters and barracks.

Secca eased her mount closer to Alcaren's, so close that their legs almost brushed, and she replied in a low voice, "They've asked me to accept five companies of SouthWomen, with Delcetta as overcaptain reporting to you. I accepted. I hope you don't mind."

"Reporting to me?"

"In a battle, I can't worry about lancers. You think I should have them report to Wilten?" Secca lifted her eyebrows as she continued to look at Alcaren.

He shook his head. "Best you let Wilten know that it was the Matriarch's request."

"I will, once we have gathered everyone." Secca used the back of her glove to blot away the melted water oozing down her forehead toward her eyes. Her thoughts went from the sea voyage ahead and the Sturinnese forces in Dumar to Clayre and the difficulties the older sorceress faced in Neserea . . . and back to her speculations about what might await her forces in Dumar.

Alcaren respected her pensiveness, and the ride back to the guest quarters was without more conversation. As they made their way back up the stairs to the second floor of the structure, Secca blotted away more of the water that had seemed to seep into her hair, despite the green felt hat.

Achar and Easlon were the guards at the double doors to her chambers. Secca glanced to the older guard. "Easlon . . .

if you would find Lady Richina, the chief players, Over-captain Wilten, and Captain Delcetta."

"Yes, lady."

"Oh . . . and would you see if you can find another chair somewhere?"

Easlon nodded before turning away.

Alcaren opened the door for Secca, then followed her inside and closed it. He crossed the room to the hearth and lifted another log from the wood box onto the gracefully curved bronze andirons—above the coals that were all that remained of the morning's fire.

"Thank you," Secca said. "That icy rain is almost as bad as the snow."

"I'm not sure it's not worse," replied her consort, taking Secca's jacket and hanging both his and hers on the wall pegs.

Secca glanced toward the bedchamber. "Is your lumand here?"

"It's behind the door," replied Alcaren. "Why?"

"You'll need it." Secca smiled.

"My lady . . ."

"You're going to do some of the scrying spells."

"I can see you are determined." Alcaren laughed, almost ruefully.

"You knew that before we consorted," she pointed out.

He shook his head as he crossed the room.

"Lady Richina," announced Achar.

"Have her come in."

Richina entered, carrying her cased lutar, and offered a slight bow to Secca. "Lady."

"How are you feeling?" asked Secca.

"I am fine." Richina tilted her head quizzically.

"Good. If you would sit at the table while the others are arriving and prepare a scrying spell to call up Lord Fehern of Dumar?" Secca asked.

The younger blonde looked at Secca. "Are you feeling well, lady?"

Secca laughed. "I'm fine. We're going to face the Sea-Priests. Both you and Alcaren are going to get a great deal of practice in sorcery before we land in Dumar."

"She is very determined on this," Alcaren said, stepping back into the main chamber and running his fingers over the strings of his lumand—a unique instrument somewhere between a mandolin and lutar.

Richina offered a smile, and set her lutar against the wall, well away from the heat of the hearth.

"Lady?"

At Easlon's voice, all three turned.

"Here is a chair. The chief players will be here shortly. So will Overcaptain Wilten and Captain Delcetta."

"Thank you." Secca walked toward the door, picked up the chair, and carried it back to the table. She had barely set it beside the table when Easlon announced the chief players. "Come in."

Palian and Delvor stepped inside the quarters. Both bowed, although Delvor slipped from his bow into quick sliding steps to a position in front of the hearth.

"The fire feels good, lady," he explained.

"You can enjoy it until Wilten and Delcetta get here," Secca said.

"That won't be long," commented Palian. "They were but a few moments behind us."

As if to confirm her words, Easlon announced, "Overcaptain Wilten and Captain Delcetta."

Secca took a seat and waited until the others were seated around the conference table, before she began. "I met with the Matriarch earlier this morning. She has agreed to provide us with vessels to take us to Dumar. They will be ready in three days, if there are no storms."

"Three days?" asked Wilten deliberately.

"The Sea-Priests are readying a fleet in the Ostisles. I would prefer that we have some time in Dumar before we face even greater numbers of Sturinnese and their thunder drummers."

"Lady . . . we have four companies that number closer to three. Even with two companies of SouthWomen . . ." Wilten shook his head.

Secca glanced toward the red-haired Delcetta. "Has the Matriarch talked to you?"

The SouthWoman officer nodded. "Would you like me to explain . . . ?"

"Please," Secca said.

Worry and puzzlement warred briefly on Wilten's face as he turned to look at the blonde SouthWoman.

"Both the Matriarch and the Council have agreed," began Delcetta. "We will send all five companies of SouthWomen lancers with your forces. We are prepared to leave immediately."

Palian nodded, the hint of a smile crossing her face.

"Delcetta has also been advanced to overcaptain, but the Matriarch has requested that she still report to Overcaptain Alcaren," Secca added.

"The SouthWomen have agreed to continuing that line of command," Delcetta replied. "It has worked well."

Secca looked to Wilten. "We will have a few more companies, and also another sorcerer in Alcaren."

Wilten nodded slowly. "Still . . . it is a perilous undertaking."

"Very perilous," Secca agreed. "But delaying will only make it more so."

"Where might we land?" asked Delvor. "Will not Narial be defended by the Sturinnese?"

"I had thought we would avoid Narial." Secca stood and gestured to the maps laid across the table. "We don't have the forces to attack Narial, except with sorcery, and I don't see any point in destroying what's left of the port city. Most of the Sturinnese forces are gathering in Dumaria, probably for a march upon those Dumaran forces remaining in Envaryl. That is where Lord Fehern appears to be gathering his forces. If we land at the harbor of Stygia—it's a small fishing port to the south of Envaryl—we can follow the trading road across the low hills east of the southern West-fels and reach Envaryl that way. Also, there is a narrow trading pass northeast of Envaryl that, when the snows melt, could gain us entrance to Neserea to help Lady Clayre."

"What about the Sturinnese, Lady Secca?" asked Wilten. "Could they not follow us from Narial?"

Secca nodded to Alcaren.

"That would be most difficult for them," Alcaren said smoothly. "Much of the coast is rugged and rocky, and they have no vessels to carry them to Stygia. The only other route is by the midland farm roads, and that would take them far, far longer. We would be well in position on the highland bluffs before they could reach us."

"What do we know about Lord High Counselor Fehern? Will he hold until we reach Envaryl?"

Rather than answer the question directly, Secca turned to Richina. "If you would call up Lord Fehern in the glass?"

"Yes, lady." Richina stood and reclaimed her lutar, taking it from the case and checking the tuning. Shortly, she began the chords for the scrying spell, and then the spell itself.

"Bring us clearly and as you will
Fehern's image to this glass fill . . ."

The glass displayed a man standing by a window, a figure seemingly tall, with graying black hair, deep-set eyes, and an angular face.

Both Wilten and Delcetta frowned.

Secca was more interested in the broad-shouldered figure in traveler's gray who stood back from Fehern's shoulder. She studied the man. "He looks like a Sea-Priest, even if he's in gray and not white."

No one else around the table spoke.

Secca smiled at Alcaren. "Can you come up with a spell to see if he is?"

Richina's eyes went from Secca to the glass, then back

to the Ranuan. Then the younger sorceress sang the release couplet for her own spell.

> *"Let this image leave in flight*
> *and clear the glass for another sight . . ."*

After frowning and mouthing some words, Alcaren eased from his chair. He picked up his lumand, an instrument smaller than Secca's lutar and, facing the glass, began to sing.

> *"Show me now and as you can,*
> *Any Sea-Priest close to Fehern the man . . . "*

The glass showed almost the same scene, except that it focused on the dark-haired man with the trimmed and square black beard.

"You can release it," Secca said to Alcaren. "If you and Richina would sit down . . ." She waited until all were seated around the conference table.

"Did you know this before?" asked Palian.

"Not for certain. Jolyn had sent a scroll some weeks ago that suggested Fehern's rise to Lord High Counselor had been sudden and unexpected." Secca laughed once, harshly. "We had Sea-Priests in Ebra. Why not in Dumar?"

"How could he place himself in the hands of the Sea-Priests?" asked Delcetta. "Does he not understand that he will be their slave?"

"Perhaps Fehern doesn't know the man is a Sea-Priest," suggested Richina.

"He may not wish to know," said Alcaren dryly.

"With this . . . can we afford to enter Dumar?" asked Wilten.

"Can we afford not to?" countered Palian. "Fehern cannot know or allow himself to believe that the man is Sturinnese. Otherwise, he would not have fought the Sea-Priests. He would have sought terms or some advantage. Better we act before the Sturinnese learn we know such."

"So long as we never rely on Lord High Counselor Fehern," added Alcaren.

Secca stood. "We still embark in three days. While we make ready, I would like you to think upon this, and how we might turn it to our advantage."

Wilten looked at Delcetta, then at Delvor, and finally at Alcaren. Each met his gaze without blinking. A long moment passed before he murmured, "As you will, Lady Secca."

Those around the table rose and bowed to Secca, except for Alcaren, who merely stepped back toward the windows while the others filed out of the chamber.

After the door closed behind Richina, Secca and Alcaren exchanged glances.

"It's a trap, you know," Alcaren said.

"A snare within a trap, I think." Secca looked at Alcaren. "Yet waiting will tighten the noose more."

"The Maitre has been planning this for years."

"He has been planning longer. We'll have to plan better," she replied. After a moment, she added, "Once preparations are complete, and just before we embark, we should send a message by sorcery to Lord Robero telling him that we are beginning the effort to reclaim Dumar."

"Do you have some thoughts as to how we are to accomplish that, my lady?"

"Not yet." She smiled, half-sadly, not quite truthfully, as she recalled the notes hidden away in her pack, the ones taken from Anna's notebooks with the spells she had shuddered to read, and shuddered more in reading Anna's explanations. "Do you?"

"Not yet, but I have great confidence in you."

Secca shook her head.

"I do . . . It is just that you fear doing what you must do." Alcaren grinned. "Remember, you don't have to do anything this moment." He glanced toward the bedchamber, with a half-leering smile, "except enjoy your consort."

"I never thought . . ." Secca began.

"Neither did I," he replied.

They both laughed, and the sound was a mixture of rue and joy.

10

ENCORA, RANUAK

The Matriarch walks slowly toward the throne-chair of blue crystal that waits upon the low dais at the end of the formal receiving room. Her eyes barely take in the familiar room, or her distorted reflection in the shadowed long windows on the west side of the room, a reflection that does not show clearly the blonde hair that is silvering all too rapidly, nor the drawn face that has become more and more angular with each season.

Silently, she steps up onto the dais, turning and seating herself on the blue cushion that is the sole softness within the chamber. She straightens herself upon the throne-chair of blue crystal, then clears her throat, before declaring firmly, "You may show her in."

"Yes, Matriarch." The voice of the guard is firm and clear, although he stands in the corridor outside the receiving room.

The door opens. A gray-haired woman steps slowly into the formal receiving room, and beams of golden morning light slanting through the long windows bathe her boots. The short cut of her hair accentuates the roundness of her face, but the deep-set eyes are hard and cold. She offers a bow that is less than perfunctory. "Matriarch."

"You expressed a desire to see me. What do you wish?" asks Alya.

"I would like to know how long you intend to keep us prisoned in the White Tower. Or our daughters in the Blue."

"Not much longer, Santhya. It would not have been necessary had you not been so foolish as to try to kill the Sorceress Protector."

"I did nothing of the sort, Matriarch." After a pause, she adds, "As you well know." After a second pause, she continues, "Nor did I consort a sorcerer and a sorceress under the aegis of the Matriarchy."

"You would rather I deny them that small happiness?" Alya snorts. "As for attempting murder, as one of your council, you approved that attempt, even if you did not personally lift the blade." Alya offers a wry smile. "Even so, I keep my word. It may be a week or two, but then you can return to your home."

"But not to the Exchange, I wager."

"No." Alya shakes her head. "You have proven that you place the Ladies of the Shadows above your duty to Ranuak. That is not acceptable for the Assistant Exchange Mistress."

"Dyleroy accepts this?"

"It was her decision, not mine. She is Exchange Mistress."

"For mere golds you will destroy all we hold dear."

Alya's eyes glitter, and a palpable chill issues from the dais.

Santhya shivers, but says nothing, and her own deep-set eyes continue to view the Matriarch.

Finally, Alya speaks, slowly, deliberately. "What we hold dear is the right to determine how we live. What we hold dear is for each woman to be mistress of her own body. Golds are one tool, but no Matriarch and no Exchange Mistress has ever subverted those principles to golds. You, and all the Ladies of the Shadows, fear the use of sorcery so greatly that you would return us to being slaves rather than see sorcery employed to keep us free. Through fear, you would enslave us."

"Through sorcery," counters Santhya, "you will destroy us."

"I doubt that."

"Matriarch . . . small as she is, well-mannered as she is, that sorceress will destroy all that is Liedwahr before the year is out. The Spell-Fire Wars will seem like nothing compared to what she will unleash in the name of protecting Defalk—and us—from the Sea-Priests. The oceans will turn to steam; the land will flow like water; and the handful of folk who survive will die barren."

Alya laughs. "In the time of the Mynyans, during the Spell-Fire Wars you mention so often and so well, there were scores of sorcerers and sorceresses. Today, Defalk has four, perhaps five. The Sea-Priests may have a score, possibly twoscore, after the score or so that the Sorceress-Protector Secca destroyed."

"The Sorceress-Protector has the knowledge from the Mist Worlds, and none had that in the time of the Spell-Fire Wars."

"Enough." Alya does not raise her voice, but the receiving room chills yet more, despite the morning sunlight angling through the eastern windows. "We do not agree. We will likely never agree. I have answered your inquiry, and you may go."

Santhya offers the slightest of bows, then turns without speaking and walks toward the door that opens as she nears it and closes after she passes through it.

Alone in the receiving room, Alya does not rise from the crystal chair. Her eyes are dark, and her face remains drawn.

11

<hr/>

With the sun barely rising over the port quarter of Encora, Secca and Alcaren dismounted on the pier where the ocean trader was tied. Secca still felt tired from having to do sorcery early in the morning to send the message tube to Lord Robero, but she hadn't wanted to send it much before they left, and did not wish to send it later, when she might need all her strength to deal with the Sturinnese. As she turned, Secca glanced again at the wooden plaque below and aft of the bowsprit, where the spare script letters proclaimed *Silberwelle*.

"You don't mind that it's the *Silberwelle*, do you?" asked Alcaren.

"Not so long as you don't have any Darksong in mind," Secca replied. Still, it had been disconcerting to find that the "flagship" of her small expedition was the same vessel from whose deck she had destroyed the Sturinnese fleet blockading Encora—and where she had nearly died.

After unstrapping her saddlebags and lutar, Secca turned and looked once more at the *Silberwelle*. "I hadn't thought . . ."

"You hadn't thought what, Lady Sorceress?" came the question from the ship's railing beside the upper end of the gangway.

Secca glanced up and smiled at the woman who addressed her. Captain Denyst was less than a span taller than Secca and little broader. The captain's broad and welcoming smile, set in a face tanned and weathered, showed even white teeth.

"You'd not be depriving me of the chance to help you strike at the Sea-Pigs now, would you?" asked the *Silberwelle*'s captain in her unique voice, a voice that carried the slightest of rasping edges and seemed to cut through everything around.

Secca shook her head. "I'm afraid I didn't end the last battle particularly well."

"Any battle you win and survive is a good one." Denyst gestured abruptly. "Don't stand there. Come on board. Need to load all those players and mounts coming down the pier, and need to cast off no later than midmorning."

Secca walked up the gangway, trying to reconcile the feelings she harbored with the knowledge that the *Silberwelle* and her captain were the best suited for the voyage ahead, yet also recalling the chill feeling of those moments but a few weeks before when she had gone to the edge of death—and perhaps farther. As her boots touched the wood, and she moved away from the pier, two crew members waited to descend to begin loading Secca's and Alcaren's mounts.

"It's good to see you looking so well," offered Denyst, once Secca and Alcaren stood on the main deck. "Consorting looks to agree with you two." The wiry captain grinned directly at Secca. "Take someone like you to set this rascal's heart afire." Denyst then glanced toward Alcaren. "Good thing, too."

"You'd have me ablaze all the time?" joked Alcaren.

"Better that than an unhappy trader or a guard to the Matriarch, don't you think? Love'd be the only ruler you'd abide." Denyst turned slightly and called to the crewmen leading the gray up the gangway. "Those two in the forward stalls!"

"Aye, Captain."

Denyst turned to the two. "The first, and I'll be sharing her cabin. You can have mine."

"You don't have to . . ." Secca began to protest.

"Aye, and I don't, but consorting happens but once, and there's little enough time before you face the Sea-Pigs." Denyst's eyes twinkled. "Next voyage you take with me, you two can have a smaller space."

"Thank you." Secca hoped there would be the opportunity for another voyage.

"Thank you," echoed Alcaren.

"No thanks till we port at Stygia." Denyst frowned. "There are no Sturinnese vessels in Narial? That is what you said?"

"That is what the glass shows," Secca admitted.

"They don't have anything here to challenge us," Alcaren replied. "But there is a fleet gathering in the Ostisles."

"We best hasten home," Denyst said. "Leastwise, quick enough to discourage them from coming after us. Best you get yourself settled while I tend to the load-on. Figuring the balance with all those mounts will take some doing." With a quick smile, Denyst stepped past them toward the gangway.

Alcaren gestured toward the hatch leading aft.

Secca glanced back up at the poop deck railing, where she had fallen at the end of the battle, and where Alcaren had used Darksong to save her. Then she swallowed and followed Alcaren through the hatch toward the captain's cabin.

12

EAST OF ESARIA, NESEREA

A fire burns in the narrow hearth of the small sitting room. Despite the heat thrown out by the dark iron reflector plates set against the bricks at the back of the hearth, white rime covers the panes of the windows, largely masked by heavy and worn hangings, once crimson, but now closer to maroon. The sorceress pulls back the left hanging and scrapes one of the paired windows clear of the ice for a moment. Through the waning and weak late-afternoon sun, she looks down at the gate of the small keep.

Then, at the knock on the door, she pulls the hangings back over the windows and walks to the door, opening it and looking past the single guard, who has barely begun to speak.

"Lady Clayre . . . your chief player."

"Please come in, Diltyr," Clayre says to the brown-haired chief player, who stands in the chill, stone-walled corridor.

As Diltyr enters and closes the door, he smiles. "You are looking well in such cold weather, my lady."

"If I must choose, I will take the cold over the heat of summer." She laughs gently. "Especially when one must wear what ladies must." Her smile fades. "I know the cold is hard on the armsmen and players. I would not subject them to it, were it not necessary."

"They understand, lady."

Clayre steps toward the table, picking up the lutar she had tuned before looking out the window to study the gate to the small hold. "We must see where Belmar is at the moment, and if we can determine what he essays."

The two figures stand before the glass laid upon the ancient hexagonal table. Clayre's fingers touch the lutar's strings, and she begins a vocalise to warm up her voice.

When the sorceress finishes the vocalise, the chief player clears his throat, then offers, "Lord Nysl frets that we remain here, Lady Clayre."

"I worry that we remain here. Yet we must see what small opening Belmar may offer us. With but two companies of lancers and a quarter-score of players remaining with us, we must take any advantage we can. That is why we will study the glass." Clayre picks up the lutar and clears her throat, before offering the spell.

> *"Show us Belmar and those who play his spells,*
> *bring in view all that spellsong tells . . ."*

The glass obediently displays the dark-haired Belmar standing before a group of more than a half-score of players, with three drummers, each before a set of three drums.

"Drums . . . always where there is trouble are there drums," murmurs the sorceress as she surveys the image in the glass.

After a time, the dark-haired sorceress sings the release spell and steps back from the glass upon the table. She lowers the lutar slowly, then looks at the chief player. "What do you think, Diltyr?"

"Belmar has more players than do we," answers the man with the short-and-square-cut brown hair. "Scarce a half-score of years ago, no one could find enough players anywhere in Liedwahr, and there were neither drums nor drummers. From where do they come?"

"From Sturinn, I would wager, although I doubt Belmar has looked closely into the mouth of that gift horse." Clayre frowns, pursing her lips. "We must strike in some fashion he will not see, and quickly."

"In the snows of winter, Lady Clayre?"

"Better now than in the mud of spring, or the heat of summer, when he can bring all the lancers he has bought and borrowed against us with even greater numbers of players." Clayre lifts the lutar. "We need to find what else we can." She lifts the lutar once more.

13

Secca slipped along the railing, up toward the bow of the *Silberwelle*, where Alcaren stood just aft of the bow-sprit, taking in the cool morning wind and the winter sun that offered but slight warmth. To Secca's right was a long low line of darkness on the horizon—the south coast of Dumar.

"Are you feeling better?" she asked.

He turned, showing a countenance merely ashen, as op-

posed to the greenish cast his face had held earlier in the
voyage. "It's always better up here."

She shook her head sympathetically. "You didn't want to
be a trader, and here I am, dragging you back onto ships."

"But not all the time." A ragged grin appeared on his
face. "I hope." After a moment, he added, "The harmonies
must have a sense of humor. There's definitely an irony
here."

"What?" asked Secca. "That, try as you may, you can't
escape ending up aboard ships?"

"I'm consorted to a sorceress who can't swim and whose
lands are hundreds of deks from any water except small
lakes and rivers . . . and I've taken more sea voyages in the
past season than in the past half-score of years."

"It won't be long," Secca said. "Denyst says that we'll
be turning northward and heading into Stygia shortly."

"I know." Alcaren smiled. "I asked her just a while ago."
His smile faded. "I worry about her return voyage."

"You think the Sturinnese fleet—or some of it—can get
there that quickly? The glass doesn't show—"

Alcaren glanced back at the sails of the vessels following
them. "I would say not, but with the Sea-Priests, one never
knows." He offered a laugh, only slightly forced. "But that
is even more true with you."

"Me?" Secca protested. "I fear not. All know I must attack."

"But not where."

Secca doubted that. The Maitre or his sorcerers certainly
had already marked her progress and would be ready for her
comparatively small force long before she reached Envaryl.

The two stood, side by side, for a time, until several crew
members began to scurry aloft, and the *Silberwelle* began to
swing more directly northward, settling onto a new heading,
her stem pointed toward a slightly higher headland.

"Stygia must be near those bluffs," Secca suggested.

"Directly under them, as I recall." Alcaren stretched. "It
will be good to stand on ground that doesn't move."

"I'd better get my lutar and glass ready," Secca said.

Alcaren nodded, taking a last look at the headland before following Secca aft across the gently pitching deck and through the hatch into the captain's cabin.

There, Secca laid the glass upon the table and took out the lutar, tuning it carefully. Then, clearing her throat, she sang.

"Show us now and in the light of day
Any who would bar our landing on Stygia's quay
or ships that lie in wait to fight . . ."

The glass remained blank, showing only the reflection of the overhead.

Secca nodded, then gathered both the grand lutar and the leather-wrapped traveling glass. Alcaren picked up his cased lumand and took the glass from Secca. Both had already repacked their saddlebags in anticipation of porting in Stygia, but left them on the doublewide bunk when they left the cabin.

The two climbed the ladder to the poop deck, where Denyst stood forward of the woman at the helm. The captain's eyes studied the lighter blue waters inshore of the *Silberwelle*.

"Shallower than I'd like, but there's a channel. Narrow, but not so narrow as the East Bay in Encora." Denyst laughed, once, her laughter cutting through the morning.

"The glass shows no one is there to stop us," Secca observed.

"Wouldn't think so. Not so as this is a place where most would land lancers or the like."

"Except us," Secca said.

The three watched as the *Silberwelle* led the way toward the small harbor that was supposed to lie below and between the gaps in bluffs to the west of the headland.

Secca could just make out the outlines of dwellings on

the grassy bluffs above the harbor when Palian, Delvor, Wilten, Delcetta, and Richina joined them.

Then, from nowhere seemingly, appeared the long-faced chief archer, who bowed. "Should you need us, we stand ready, Lady Secca."

"Thank you, Elfens. The glass shows no enemies, but we will let you know."

After a sweeping bow, Elfens descended to the main deck.

"The players stand ready on the main deck, should you need them, Lady Secca," Palian said.

"Thank you. I don't think we will, but if we do, we'll have little notice."

"Indeed," murmured Wilten.

Stygia was indeed a small harbor, if it could even be called that. Less than a score of dwellings rested on low bluffs overlooking the ocean. Between the two bluffs was a rocky depression or narrow valley where a small stream entered a semicircular bay, barely big enough for two oceangoing traders. From the rocky base of the western bluff a semicircular breakwater extended. The top of the breakwater was paved in cobblestones, and a narrow stone way led from the foot of the dark stones along the base of the bluff toward a narrow flat stretch of land on the west side of the valley where the stream entered the bay. What looked to be a single warehouse was the only structure below the bluffs.

A trail-like road wound up the west hillside—through several switchbacks.

"It's even smaller than it looked in the glass." Secca glanced at Denyst.

"Only a bit of chop. We can unload there. Be a while. We can bring but one vessel in at a time."

Secca looked to Alcaren. "Would you use the glass to see if there are any lancers or armsmen around?"

Without a word, the broad-shouldered Ranuan unwrapped the traveling glass and set it on the deck. Then he took out the lumand. After tuning the instrument, he sang.

"Show us now and in clear light
any of Sturinn close enough to fight..."

The glass remained silvered, displaying only sky and
sails.

Wilten nodded, then glanced toward the small harbor, as
did the others.

"Thank you," mouthed Secca to Alcaren. She should have
realized earlier that the overcaptains needed to see that there
were no Sturinnese nearby, even if she and Alcaren had
already seen that there were none.

Alcaren nodded.

Behind them, Denyst began issuing commands that
sounded absolutely meaningless to Secca, but with each
command, another set of sails was furled, and the *Silberwelle* slowed, almost crawling inshore.

"Look!" called Richina. "Someone's leaving."

As Secca and the others watched, two figures tumbled
from the warehouse, opened a sliding side door, and led out
two mounts. Without closing the stable doors, they rode
quickly up the narrow road, leaving dust hanging in the air.

"Didn't like our look, did they?" Denyst laughed.

Secca and Alcaren continued to watch, but could see no
other signs of people, even when Denyst brought the *Silberwelle* in under short sail, the ship barely creeping up to
the two closely spaced bollards near the end of the quay.

"First squad!" ordered Delcetta. "Stand by to disembark!"

"Green company! Second squad! Stand ready!" ordered
Wilten.

Secca studied the harbor and the single warehouselike
structure again, but it appeared empty, as if the two riders
who had fled had left it deserted.

From the higher poop deck, Secca and Alcaren watched,
with Delvor and Palian—and the players to the seaward side
of the ship—all ready for any spellsong that might be necessary. Not only was the long quay empty, but so was the
entire area below the bluffs—that Secca could see even be-

fore the first squads of lancers from Loiseau and the SouthWomen hurried toward the single warehouse.

In less than half a glass, after the crew and lancers had begun to walk mounts down the gangway and onto the narrow cobbled surface of the quay, Delcetta and Wilten returned.

"No one's here, lady," reported Delcetta.

Behind her, Wilten nodded. "They may be re-forming at the end of the road, at the top of the hill."

"It looks like the houses have been abandoned," suggested Delcetta. "They wouldn't want to face the armsmen carried on eight vessels."

"With the Sea-Priests," Wilten replied, "it is better to be certain."

"We'll check the glass to see if there's anyone there," Secca said.

"Would you like me to do that?" murmured Alcaren.

"If you would," Secca replied.

Alcaren again took up the lumand.

*"Show close and clear the houses on the hill,
and armsmen or lancers near them still . . ."*

All the glass showed was vacant-looking dwellings, not a single lancer or armsman, and not even a single person of any sort.

Secca looked to Wilten, then Delcetta. "Let us be thankful that there are no armsmen here. There will be enough battles to come."

14

The late-afternoon wind moaned out of the north, and the sun hung just above the lower Westfels. Trying not to shiver in a green leather riding jacket that felt all too thin against the wind, Secca looked to the west, beyond the hills with bare-limbed trees to the Westfels behind them, still covered with snow, except where patches of trees rose above the snow or where the rock was too steep to hold snow or trees.

Then she turned her eyes back to the frozen dirt road her forces traveled. The high plains stretched for deks before them, filled with winter-browned grass that had faded into a pale tan and had yet to be supplanted by the green shoots of spring.

"It should not be this cold," said Alcaren, riding beside her.

"You think the Sturinnese have used sorcery on the weather?" asked Richina from where she rode directly behind them, beside Wilten.

"This ground has not seen snow," replied Alcaren. "Otherwise, the grass would be more matted and flattened. Yet the wind blows chill enough to have frozen the road." He looked sideways at Secca. "Could you do such sorcery?"

"Not without much effort and study, and perhaps not then, but the Evult did, with the massed voices of his Dark Monks. That was how he created the years of drought that almost conquered Defalk. It could be that the Sturinnese could do such with voice and drums." She paused before continuing. "I would think they would have to be much closer to the Westfels to create that kind of sorcery. It may be that we face merely unseasonable cold."

"Most unseasonable," confirmed Alcaren, his eyes going to the road ahead.

A pair of riders—one a SouthWoman in crimson and blue and one a lancer of Loiseau in green—rode back toward the vanguard of the column. Wilten eased his mount onto the shoulder of the road, and after inclining his head to Secca, rode ahead to join Delcetta in meeting the scouts.

"What do you think?" asked Alcaren.

"The scouts have seen little, else they would be hurrying," replied Secca.

"According to the glass, the Sturinnese have just left Dumaria on the river road to Envaryl. They may not even reach Fehern's forces, such as they are, before we do." Alcaren frowned. "I like that not."

"Nor I." Secca shook her head. "Yet the glass shows nothing untoward in Envaryl, save that the disguised Sea-Priest still advises Fehern."

"Would that we knew exactly how he advises Fehern." Alcaren snorted.

"He will offer what appears in Fehern's advantage, but is not. We just do not know how he couches such advice." Secca broke off as Delcetta and Wilten rode back and swung their mounts onto the shoulder of the road to ride alongside Secca and Alcaren.

"The scouts report that there is a hamlet less than five deks ahead," Wilten reminded Secca. "It is empty."

That didn't surprise Secca. Every town or hamlet they had entered in the three days since they had left Stygia had been hastily abandoned. "Will it provide enough shelter against the cold and wind?"

"There are several large barns and a half-score of dwellings," Delcetta added. "It will be cramped, but all will be out of the weather. The scouts say there are some animals that are stragglers from those the peasants drove away with them."

"If you can round them up, go ahead," Secca said.

As Delcetta and Wilten nodded and rode back to the vanguard, Secca shook her head. While she disliked foraging off those who had little, circumstances were leaving her little choice. But then, it seemed that very little in dealing with the Sturinnese left her much choice.

"Lady?" asked Richina, easing her mount forward. "Why do the Dumarans flee us? We have done them no ill."

"Not in more than a score of years," Secca replied. "But Lady Anna did invade Dumar, if not this part of the land."

"Peasants fear any lancers. Almost always, they will lose stock and provisions. They might well flee before Fehern's forces as well," Alcaren added.

"Even in Ranuak?" asked Secca with a laugh.

"We have far fewer lancers," he countered. "And . . . there is so little fertile land that the Matriarch cannot countenance such. We must trade or fish for our sustenance, and that is why all appreciate what you did to break the blockade."

"Even the Ladies of the Shadows?" pressed Secca.

"They are governed by fear, and little more."

"Fear is a dangerous mistress," mused Secca, wondering, as she often had since the attempt of the Ladies to assassinate her, how the fruits of sorcery could possibly be as bad as the enslavement of every woman in Liedwahr in chains that a Sturinnese victory would bring. How could any sorcery she might use create something that bad?

15

The dwelling was that of a more prosperous peasant farmer, constructed mostly of fired mud bricks, with a large common room that formed an "L" with the kitchen, and a separate bedroom that held two beds, a large one, and a small cotlike one set against the wall. Despite the chilly air, the cottage held the odor of dirt, rancid grease, and mold.

In the common room, seven figures gathered around the long and battered wooden table, with its two wooden benches. On one side were Secca, Alcaren, and Richina. Holding her lutar, Secca stood between and behind Alcaren and Richina, who sat on one bench. On the other bench sat the two chief players and the two remaining overcaptains.

The fire in the wall hearth took the chill off the room, but little more, as the wind howled around the cottage. A single candle sat in a battered holder in the middle of the table, beside the traveling scrying glass set there. The room was dim in the late afternoon, where, outside the cottage, high gray clouds brought twilight even before the sun had set behind the Westfels. Inside, the puddles of light cast by the fire and the sole flickering candle barely lifted the gloom.

All seven studied the image in the glass, which showed a force of perhaps two companies of Sturinnese. The riders wore heavy white leather jackets with fur-lined caps. Despite the cold, and with no visible orders, they rode in formation, exactly two by two. Another group of riders followed the main body, with packhorses behind them.

In the dimness Secca squinted at the glass. The objects carried by the packhorses appeared to be cylindrical. She moistened her lips.

"Those are quivers lashed behind their saddles," Alcaren said, gesturing toward one of the riders, "and those are bows covered in oilskins."

"The riders are archers, and they're followed by a small group of drummers and players." After a moment, Secca added, "They're headed toward us, but they came out of Narial, it seems."

When the others had studied the image for what seemed long enough, Secca sang the release couplet, then turned from the glass on the rough wooden table and walked toward the window, halting as she realized that the inner shutters were solid wood, and closed. Even with both inner and outer shutters closed, cold air seeped into the small cottage. She turned, still holding the lutar in her left hand, and nodded slowly. "We'll need spells, new ones."

"Even with your current spells, lady, they cannot stand against you and nine companies of lancers," Richina replied.

"That is not their intent," Alcaren said. "They do not intend to get closer than a dek, if that."

Richina glanced from Alcaren to Secca, then back to the broad-shouldered overcaptain and sorcerer. "But how can they . . ."

"The arrows," Secca said. "They will use drums and Darksong to guide the arrows against us."

"They must know you can stop that," protested the younger sorceress.

"Do they?" asked Alcaren. "Lady Secca has not shown any sorcery that carries that far, not on land, and not against an enemy she has not seen on a battlefield. Besides, it will cost them little to try, and could cost us dearly."

"It will also reveal what we can do and cannot do," Secca said slowly, "before they must face us in a full battle."

"Not if none of them escapes," said Palian, her voice flat.

The sorceresses and Alcaren looked to the chief player. Palian remained silent, her eyes meeting Secca's.

"It is hard to project the firesong that far away," Richina said.

"There must be other spells," Palian said, her eyes remaining on Secca.

Secca said nothing, but Palian continued to hold her eyes.

Richina glanced from Secca to Palian and back again. Delvor looked down at the table. Wilten appeared to be looking at no one and nothing, while a faint smile played across Delcetta's face. The faintest furrow appeared on Alcaren's brow.

"There may be," Secca finally temporized, thinking of the notes she had taken from the sealed strongroom two seasons before, notes she had not wished to study again. "There may be."

Palian nodded. "One seldom regrets trying; one always regrets not having tried."

"Unless one dies because of either trying or not trying," Alcaren said, his tone conveying an archness that Secca could tell was meant to provoke a bit of levity. "The problem is that you often don't know which is better."

Secca laughed, softly, but without humor. "I know which is better, but it's not much better."

"Anything is better than allowing the Sea-Priests to take Liedwahr," Palian said mildly.

Wilten cleared his throat.

Everyone looked at the Defalkan overcaptain.

"Ah . . . you talk of spells. I have simpler questions. How far away are these archers, and do you plan that we should ride to meet them or wait here where we have shelter?"

Alcaren laughed, a sound open and without bitterness. "You're right, Wilten." He looked to Secca. "A day and a half, I would say. What do you think?"

"About the same." Secca looked to Delcetta and Wilten. "You suggest we let them come to us, and let our lancers and mounts rest?"

"If you can perform sorcery near here," replied Delcetta. "The hills to the east . . . would they suffice?"

At her words, Wilten nodded in affirmation.

"They would." Secca glanced to the shuttered windows. "It would be better to have both players and lancers rested." And, perhaps . . . perhaps she could find a spell that would stop the archers without dipping too deeply into the spell-songs Anna had prepared.

16

Kestrin stands on the balcony outside the private study of the Liedfuhr. He does not wear a cloak, despite the fat flakes of late-winter or early-spring snow that drift past him. His eyes follow the river, still ice-covered, that flows westward to the port of Wharsus, and there, into Defuhr Bay.

To his left, also wearing neither jacket nor cloak, stands Bassil, in the maroon of a lancer officer. For a moment, as each flake strikes his tunic, it stands out before melting and leaving a small spot of darkness on the fabric.

"What now?" asks Kestrin.

"Your seers report that the Sturinnese fleet has sailed from the Ostisles."

"It will not arrive in time to stop the shadowsinger from destroying the Sturinnese forces in Dumar."

"If she can indeed do that," replies Bassil. "There are more than a half-score of Sea-Priest sorcerers with the Sturinnese forces, and all have players and drummers."

"She has already destroyed more than that, has she not?" Kestrin's eyebrows lift. "Or have I been misled in the reports that have come to me?"

"She has, but it may take her much time to retake Dumar. She landed at a small fishing harbor to the southwest, and now rides across the high plains to aid Fehern. It will be at least a week before she can reach Envaryl. That is if she does not have to fight any skirmishes along the way, and if the weather holds."

"How does that change anything? Once the snows melt, hopefully in the next three weeks, we can still send our lancers into Neserea to support Aerlya and Annayal. The Sturinnese will be in the south, contesting with the shadowsinger."

"You may not wish to send them through the Mittpass, sire." Bassil's tone is apologetic. "Even when the snows melt."

Kestrin turns and faces the lancer overcaptain. "And why might that be?"

"Your seers fear that the Sturinnese have set their course for Mansuur, not Nordwei, or Neserea, and certainly not for Dumar."

"They fear? Do they not know?" snaps the Liedfuhr.

"The course is northerly, and that would be the same at the beginning for a destination of Mansuur or Neserea . . . or Nordwei. But the seers have glimpsed maps of Defuhr Bay."

"Do you believe them?"

"I was doubtful, sire. I asked them to scry for me, and I also saw such maps on the chart tables."

"That can only be a bluff," Kestrin says. "Why would they leave such out, except for us to see? It must be a bluff."

"Bluff or not, can you afford to leave Wharsus undefended—or lightly defended?" Bassil uses the back of his hand to blot away the water that has come from the snow melting in his short hair and that has begun to ooze down his face toward his eyes.

"What other companies can we summon to Wharsus?" Kestrin's voice bears both an edge and a hint of resignation.

"You can bring those from Hafen and Cealur, and detail most of those here in Mansuus to Wharsus."

"That won't be enough," Kestrin says.

"If we took two thousand from the five thousand you have garrisoned in Unduval, we could still leave seventy-five companies there to enter Neserea—when the snows melt. That would be enough to keep Belmar from taking Esaria—if they are careful to strike only those forces that are not supported by sorcery and take care to avoid the sorcerer," suggests Bassil.

"That will not be so easy as it sounds." Kestrin gives a dramatic shrug. "Yet what else can I do?"

"Hope that the shadowsinging Sorceress Protector of the East and the Sorceress of Defalk will be more effective than they have been . . . and trust in the harmonies."

"Send a message to the Council of Wei," Kestrin suggests, "telling them what you have discovered—except that you might tell them that the Sturinnese fleet could easily be headed to their shores."

"It will be difficult to get a messenger there, sire. The Bitter Sea remains frozen, and no passes are open in the Westfels. We can send a ship to Elahwa and hope that the Sand Pass will be open—but that will take weeks, and will not arrive until long after the Sea-Priest fleet does."

"Forget the messenger. We must trust that their seers will see what ours have seen." The Liedfuhr shakes his head. "Everywhere, I must trust others. Is there nothing else I can do?"

Bassil remains silent, even as he blots more water from his forehead.

"Is there nothing?"

"I would not suggest anything, sire, merely to provide an appearance. You can but protect your land, and aid your sister as you can. The snows in the Mittpass melt earlier than all others, and far earlier than the sea ice breaks in the Bitter Sea. You might consider having provisions to send to the Sorceress Protector of the East, should she defeat the Sturinnese in Dumar and start to ride northward into Neserea."

"I should support her, riding into . . ." Kestrin laughs. "What you are telling me is that she is my sole hope of preserving Annayal's succession."

"Yes, sire. Only she has the knowledge of the Great Sorceress. Whether she has the strength and the will to use such . . . that we can but see."

"We will see." Kestrin looks to the river for a long moment before turning back. "We have more than a few orders to draft to redeploy forces, do we not?"

"Yes, sire."

"Best we get on with it." Kestrin motions for the overcaptain to reenter the study, then follows him, closing the door firmly behind himself and stamping his boots on the maroon mat inside the door.

17

In the midmorning, Secca sat in the middle of the battered wooden bench, with scraps of rough brown paper stacked around her on the table. She massaged her forehead with her left hand, blinking eyes that were reddened with the effort on concentrating in the dim light, then tried to hold a sneeze. "Kkkk . . . chew!"

She rubbed her nose.

"You're not getting a chill, are you?" Alcaren sat at the corner of the table farthest from Secca, facing away from her, lumand in hand. On his corner of the table were two sheets of the brown paper with notes, and a grease marker beside them.

"No. It's something in here. When I go outside, I'm fine." Secca looked at the notes she had made, then the sheets of paper she had taken from the large envelope Anna had labeled "Armageddon."

"You can't exactly read through those outside."

"No." What troubled Secca, more than when Anna had explained the file, was the understanding that she might have to use the spells—and that the alternative of not using them would mean her defeat and the fall of Liedwahr.

"You may never need these spells, Secca," Anna had said. "I hope you never do. But if you do . . . and if you use them,

Erde will never be the same because everyone will see what sorcery can truly do."

Secca picked up the sheet before her, and slowly read through the spell, as well as the musical notation, which indicated that the spell melody was based on one of the simpler fabrication spells that most players knew.

Remove the air and in emptiness hold fast
till—and all within breathe their last . . .

Anna's gracefully angular writing noted, "This is for use against sorcerers. I doubt any sorcerer can sing without air to breathe, and without air there isn't a spell that can carry."

Secca winced and leafed to the next spell, a long one she didn't remember seeing.

Hydrogen to hydrogen, fuse in pressured desire,
oxygen free to sear just like the sun's fire . . .

The note below was long and cryptic, with words and phrases that Secca didn't understand at all, except for the last words. "If you don't understand this one completely, don't use it. Either it won't work, or it will turn whatever you direct it against into a blast of fire hotter than the center of the sun. Don't sing it unless you're behind three feet of stone and more than three deks away. Even so, it could kill you and everyone around you. This is only to destroy an enemy when you can't possibly escape."

Secca shuddered. Why hadn't she noticed that spell? She turned to the next.

Magma, magma, rise in tubes from the mantle deep
below . . .

The explanation of that was worse than the one before, perhaps because this explanation Secca understood. She'd talked about the creation of the Zauberinfeuer with Anna,

and about the Circle of Fire in Mansuur, and even the glowing mountains of Sturinn.

"With each spell you become more ashen," Alcaren observed. "And with each you sigh more loudly. Surely, those
spells cannot be so tiresome."

"Not tiresome. Terrible. You should read them," Secca
suggested. "Read this one, and Anna's notes." She thrust the
two sheets at her consort.

Alcaren read the age-yellowed sheet, a parchment probably dating from Anna's early years as regent. Finally, he
looked up. He swallowed. "I read the words, but they mean
nothing. That is, except for the last part, and that is indeed
terrible."

Secca nodded.

"None of this she ever used?"

"Nothing as fearsome as that one. Some of the others, I
do not know. I don't know of a time when she did, but she
didn't tell me everything, especially when I was young and
learning sorcery. After her first years as regent, as I told
you, she engaged in more shadow sorcery. Because it was
in the shadows, few would even know that such sorcery had
been practiced."

"The Ladies of the Shadows have more to fear than I
would have thought," Alcaren said slowly.

"If you'd read all of these, you'd understand more."

"Did you not know—about these?"

Secca laughed, ruefully. "Of course I did. I used one of
them to kill the sailors and lancers on the Sturinnese ships
we captured for the Matriarch. That was bad enough, as you
know. I'd hoped not to use more. It's one thing when you
read something, no matter how terrible it *might* be, and another when you look at it and think that you may have to
sing it to save yourself or your forces or your land."

She extended her hand and took back the two sheets from
Alcaren, easing them all into the folder and closing it. "For
a time, I will try my own efforts."

Alcaren looked down at the paper before him. "Mine are child's rhymes against yours."

"You'll do better with practice."

"Perchance."

Secca looked at the blank sheet before her.

Archers . . . archers? What other spell did Secca have that could strike at a distance, that would not be so terrible as those Anna had developed? Secca had done it with the Sturinnese fleet. Could she adapt that spell? Use the wind from a distance before the archers got too close?

She began to write, slowly at first.

Clouds to form and winds to rise
like a caldron in our skies.
Build a storm with winds swirling through . . .

She crossed out the words in the third line, then tried another set. They didn't fit the note values, either.

She paused. This time . . . this time . . . she might avoid the spells Anna had created. But, even if she could develop this spell—and use it—against the Sturinnese, could she again before they had a defense? Or would she have to create ever greater, ever more devastating sorceries? Or use those Anna had already developed?

Even as she tried not to sigh, she found herself moistening her lips.

18

The wind had died away earlier, and the peasant's cottage was warmer than on the previous days, with the afternoon sun falling on the south wall of the dwelling directly enough that the fired mud bricks carried gentle heat into the large room. As the seventh glass of the day passed, in the period between midafternoon and late afternoon, Secca and the others of her informal council watched as Richina sang the scrying spell.

"Show us now and in this day's light
the closest Sturinnese that we might fight . . ."

The image in the glass showed the Sturinnese in a small hamlet, with horses being led into corrals, or tethered on tie-lines, and a set of two four-man patrols, apparently being briefed by an officer. Several drummers were unloading drums wrapped in oiled leather from packhorses and carefully carrying them into one of the small hovel-like cots. Puffs of smoke came from a cooking fire beside one of the larger dwellings.

After everyone had studied the image, Secca nodded to Richina. The younger blonde sorceress sang the release couplet and lowered her lutar.

"If you would show us where they are, Wilten?" Secca gestured to the maps laid out on the table beside the scrying mirror—maps hand-drawn from the views Alcaren, Richina, and she had called up in the scrying glass over the two previous days.

"They have sent out scouts, and they have begun to set up an encampment in this smaller hamlet," Wilten said, touching the map with a stick that had been whittled into a pointer. "It is about ten deks from here."

"How far from the hillside to the south?"

"A fraction over seven deks, I would judge."

Secca glanced to Alcaren, then Richina, and finally, Palian. "Can you have your players ready to ride in less than half a glass? Leaving all but their instruments behind?"

"That we can do."

"And your lancers?" Secca asked the two overcaptains.

"Easily," offered Delcetta.

"That we can do," Wilten said after the briefest of pauses.

"Then, let us make ready." Secca glanced to Palian.

"Have them prepare the third building song, with the flame song in reserve for Richina."

"The third building song, and then the flame song."

"I hope we will not need the second," Secca said, "but with the Sturinnese, it is best to be prepared."

"You do not expect them to give battle, lady?" asked Wilten.

"They may see us drawing up on a hilltop some three or four deks away, but that is a ride of close to a glass. We will either have succeeded or failed long before they can reach us." She smiled. "If we saw the Sturinnese beginning to ride out after we had finished a day's ride, would we wish to ride hard to battle?"

"No, lady," said Delcetta. "But we would be watchful."

"Most watchful," added Wilten.

"I hope they are no different," Secca replied. "Watchfulness will not harm us." She turned to Alcaren. "Would you use the glass to scry what they do as we make ready, and after we reach our position?"

"I would be happy to, my lady." Alcaren inclined his head in acceptance.

"You, Richina," Secca continued, "must stand ready with the flame spell in case we are beset unexpectedly. You may be able to use the players, but you may only have your own voice and lutar."

"Yes, lady." Richina nodded, still holding her lutar, but her eyes going to the corner where the opened lutar case lay.

"Get the lancers and players ready," Secca said.

"Yes, lady."

Palian and Delvor hurried out of the cottage, followed by Delcetta and Wilten, leaving Secca, Alcaren, and Richina standing around the long and battered wooden table.

"You are not pleased with what you must do," Alcaren observed.

"That seems to be my duty in life," Secca replied dryly. "If I do not strike first, then they will. If I do not strike hard enough to destroy them utterly, then we will pay in greater losses later. In turn, in later times, they will try to strike first and with more deadly force."

"Is that not all war, all battle?" asked Alcaren.

"Always it has been, but a sword, an arrow, even a cross-bow . . . they can but strike from a limited distance." She shook her head. "To survive, we will change warfare."

"You fear it will change Liedwahr and us?"

"I know it will change all Erde—and us." Secca forced a smile. "Talking will do us little good now. In a few moments, will you again study the Sturinnese in the glass?"

Alcaren nodded.

Secca walked toward the small bedroom, aware as she stepped through the narrow door that, short as she was, the lintel was less than a span above her head. She donned the green leather riding jacket, and the green felt hat, before stepping back into the main room, where she recased her own lutar.

Richina had already left, and Alcaren had put on his jacket, but not fastened it, as he tuned his lumand. "How long do you want me to wait?"

"Until we're almost all ready to ride," she said. "I'll make sure your mount is waiting."

"I hope they don't intend to ride out against us. I didn't like seeing those patrols."

"Neither do I." Yet, as she left the cottage, Secca wondered. Would she feel better if the Sturinnese mounted an attack? Even if it meant that SouthWomen and Defalkan lancers would die? She frowned as she stepped into the chilly afternoon.

Outside in the cold late afternoon, players were already saddling mounts and strapping their instruments in place. Gorkon rode up, leading Secca's gray and Alcaren's brown gelding. Richina joined Secca as the older sorceress was swinging up into the mare's saddle.

"You do not look pleased, Lady Secca," observed Richina quietly.

"I cannot say that I am, Richina." A tight smile played around Secca's face as she settled herself into the saddle. "If we are successful, there will be few deaths among our forces, but it will encourage the Sea-Priests to try greater sorcery against us from farther away. And then . . . we will have to attempt such before they do . . ." Secca sighed. "And yet, there is no help for it, if we wish to remain free, you and I, especially."

"And a few thousandscore other women," added Palian as she reined up beside Secca. "The players are ready, Lady Secca."

"So are the lancers," added Wilten from behind Palian.

"The SouthWomen," came Delcetta's clear voice.

"Alcaren!" Secca called.

"Not usually late . . . the overcaptain . . ." murmured a voice.

"I asked him to check in the glass once we were mounted," Secca said. "To make sure that the Sturinnese will not surprise us."

It seemed scarcely a few moments before Alcaren hurried out of the cottage, carrying both his lumand and the leather-wrapped scrying glass. As he strapped his lumand and the glass behind his saddle, he told Secca, "There's no sign of their assembling large numbers of archers, but it looks as if they may be sending out another patrol—one almost of a full squad of archers."

"If that patrol sees us, they may well assemble all they have," suggested Richina.

"Not in time," replied Secca. Seeing Alcaren mounted, she called to Wilten and Delcetta, "Overcaptains!"

"Vanguard forward!" Wilten ordered.

The column started forward along the road out of the hamlet, a road that was barely more than a trail, but with clay frozen almost as hard as the stone roads of Defalk or Ranuak. The mounts' breath steamed in the cold clear air that foreshadowed twilight and a colder evening. One-handedly, Secca fastened her jacket around her more tightly.

"Are you cold?" asked Alcaren, leaning toward her.

"I'm fine."

With the slightest of nods, he straightened in the saddle and offered not another word, a silence and an understanding of which Secca was most glad.

They had ridden less than half a glass when the road ahead turned due north along the side of a narrow creek that was a sliver of ice against the low bushes and grass. Wilten and Delcetta had halted the vanguard.

Wilten rode back along the shoulder of the road and reined up before Secca. "Lady Secca, it is best to turn east and follow the long slope of the hill here."

"Is the footing firm in that meadow?" asked Secca.

"The scouts say it is. They also see no sign of any riders."

"Good. Then we will proceed."

Wilten signaled, and Delcetta relayed the order. The vanguard turned off the road and began riding across the meadowlike field, through the browned grass that once might have been hock high on the mounts, but which now was half that, bent over as it was from the wind and winter.

Secca began a series of vocalises, trying to warm up her voice slowly. Shortly, Richina followed her example. Even Alcaren hummed softly. Secca decided she needed to work on some proper vocalises for her consort—she might well need his voice ready in the weeks ahead.

Although the climb up the hill was gentle, it was slower than the road, and the sun hung barely above the Westfels when Secca reined up at the ridge crest that overlooked a series of lower rolling hills to the south and east.

"Chief players," Secca called, "we'll assemble on the flat there." She pointed to an area of grass that was relatively level and sloped but slightly to the southeast. "Quickly, please." She couldn't say why she felt haste was necessary, but trusted the feeling.

After a moment, she turned in the saddle. "Alcaren . . . if you would use the glass once more—"

"Yes, my lady."

"Richina, stand by with your lutar and the flame spell."

"Yes, Lady Secca," replied the taller blonde sorceress.

After Secca had dismounted, along with Alcaren and Richina, Achar took her mount, as well as those of Alcaren and Richina.

Secca walked slowly downhill to the flat where the players were setting up. She glanced to the southeast. That was the direction in which the glass and the maps indicated the hamlet where the Sturinnese had settled in was, roughly three deks away. Was there a faint line of smoke rising above the horizon, above the brown-grassed hills? Secca wasn't sure.

Circled in an arc behind the players were the lancers, the SouthWomen to the north and Secca's own lancers of Loiseau to the south. Immediately to her right, in front of the lancers in green, both first and second players were beginning to tune. Right behind her, she could hear Alcaren singing a scrying spellsong, seeking the Sturinnese yet again, and she waited for his song to die away, and for him to report.

"There is a squad of archers, and they're riding toward us," her consort announced. "You'd best hasten. I'd guess they're but beyond those nearer hills."

"They'll have to dismount, but that won't take long."

"I'll tell Elfens to have his archers ready as well," Alcaren added.

"Good." Secca nodded and turned toward both Palian and Delvor. "Stand ready."

"We stand ready."

Then Secca turned to the two overcaptains, who had remained mounted behind the three who would do sorcery. "Have your lancers ride back north a dek, into the swale there. You can reach us if need be, but this sorcery is untested, and I would not subject the lancers and their mounts to the wild winds that may come."

"Are you certain, Lady Secca?" asked Wilten.

"I'm most certain."

"I would feel better if I left a squad . . ."

"One squad only, then," Secca conceded.

"First squad, green company," called out Wilten. "All others, fall back."

"Fall back to the swale below," echoed Delcetta.

As the lancers repositioned themselves, Secca walked through the cold and dry grass, the thin stalks whispering and breaking against her riding boots and lower trousers, toward Palian and Delvor, and their players.

"We are almost ready, Lady Secca."

"Riders! To the east!" One of the voices was Alcaren's, but a similar call came from a SouthWoman, and another from Achar.

Secca turned more eastward. The white-coated figures were hard to make out in the dimming light, especially against the tan of the grass, but there looked to be only one squad of archers and a handful of players. All had scrambled from their mounts, and some were stringing bows.

"Richina! Use the lutar and flame spell against the archers down there!" Secca turned back to Palian. "Have the players ready to play the moment she finishes. The third building spell."

"Stand ready for the third building spell." Palian's words to the first players were echoed by Delvor's to the second players.

Then, in the sudden stillness, Richina's voice rang out—strong, if not as open a sound as Secca would have liked, and certainly not as open as Anna would have required.

"Turn to fire, turn to flame
all those below of Sturinn's name . . ."

Before the last lines of the spellsong, thin lines of orange fire erupted from the skies, arrowing out of the heavens toward the Sturinnese.

Less than half of those reached the archers and players before a shimmering pale white and gauzy dome appeared in the air above the Sturinnese—a clearly sorcerous creation through which Secca could make out the figures of archers.

Secca glanced toward Palian.

"We stand ready, Lady Secca."

"At your mark." Secca forced herself to relax, to loosen muscles that were tighter than they should have been, and to concentrate on the spellsong ahead—just the spellsong.

"The third building song, at my mark ... Mark!"

Both the first and second players began the building song, with the usual two bars of melody before Secca joined them. She ignored whatever was occurring below, where the hazy white shield had been raised by a Sea-Priest, and concentrated on meshing her words and the players' accompaniment with the visualization of what she intended.

"Clouds to form and winds to rise
like a caldron in darkening skies.
Build a storm with winds of ice and heat
that scythes all Sturinn's men like ripened wheat ..."

Secca slipped a quick breath between the stanzas, still visualizing the storm of all storms, one that would sweep everything before it, ripping and rending all the Sturinnese forces, both those in the lowlands before her, and those deks away in the Dumaran hamlet.

"Clouds to boil and storms to bubble
crush to broken sticks of wind-strewn rubble
all in Sturinn's service or in Sea-Priest white
and let none escape the whirlwind's might ..."

After Secca finished the last words of the spell, she glanced downhill toward the archers. As she watched, the pale white shield vanished, and a dark cloud of arrows arched uphill. Yet, as they did, the skies darkened, and a rushing wind swept from behind Secca, out of the north, with such force that she went to her knees in the winter-tan grass, as did most of the players.

Someone had stood against the wind, for Secca could hear Alcaren and his lumand, singing a spell, one to the tune of the flame song, but with slightly different words.

*"Turn to fire, turn to flame,
in ashes rend all sent 'gainst our name ..."*

"Oh!" The single scream penetrated above the sound of spells, and wind, and a dull heavy roaring, so intense that the very volume of the roar seemed to press Secca farther into the grass. Secca forced her eyes up, just in time to see a lancer transfixed by three yard-long arrows—and to see intermittent blazes of fire—spellfires that turned the incoming arrows to flame and dust, spellfires that blazed as points of light against the almost jet-black clouds that swirled overhead, clouds so dark that they bore a greenish hue.

The roaring of the wind rose so much that Secca could hear nothing else, and the light of dusk darkened so quickly that it appeared as if night had fallen. Gusts of warm, almost summerlike air mixed with air that felt as cold as midwinter ice, flaying Secca with their extremes.

Amid the crashes of thunder, and the howling roar of the wind, Secca felt herself being pummeled, as if she were being poked with a wooden spear. She blinked through eyes that burned enough to blur her vision, to see a rain of hail so thick that she could barely make out the figures of the lancers in the single guard squad that had remained—uselessly—to guard her and the others doing sorcery.

Everywhere, the white globules bounced off everything—her own jacket and head, players and their instruments. In moments, there was a white carpet covering the ground, bending the grass flat. Then, a few more moments later, the hail had passed.

Secca started to climb to her feet, only to find Alcaren's arm lifting her.

"I'm fine, thank you." She softened her words with a quick smile, before her mouth opened involuntarily.

To the southeast, two enormous black funnel-like clouds swirled, visible despite the curtain of hail that trailed them. She watched as the clouds darkened yet more, then seemed to fade behind the curtain of hail. Then, the hail stopped falling, leaving a swath of white, almost like a massive carpet runner over the hills in the direction of the Sturinnese forces.

"Mighty sorcery," Alcaren murmured.

"Your last spell saved many of our lancers and players— and probably both me and Richina," Secca said, turning toward him.

Beyond Alcaren, for the first time, Secca saw the odd coloration on the white hail carpet on the lower hillside, and her eyes darted toward the lower ground from where the Sturinnese players and archers had launched their attack.

"Don't . . ." warned Alcaren.

Secca had to swallow hard as her eyes took in the small swath of devastation. Less than a dek away, where the squad attacking her forces had been, the hailstones were stained various shades of pink, from almost red to a pinkish froth. The sorceress forced herself to keep looking, even as she swallowed to keep her stomach from turning itself inside out. It had been her sorcery . . . her words, her song, that had literally shredded archers and players.

She swallowed again.

Behind her, Secca could hear Richina retching.

"I didn't mean . . . not to be that cruel . . ." Secca said slowly.

"It looks . . . worse," Alcaren said. "It was faster than a blade or an arrow."

That might have been, but Secca couldn't help but shudder.

19

ITZEL, NESEREA

Two men sit alone at the end of the long table nearest the hearth. A single candelabra bearing five candles illuminates their end of the table. The only other light in the dining area comes from the glowing bank of red coals in the hearth.

Belmar finishes a bite of mutton and follows it with a swallow of a dark red wine. he glances at the empty crystal pitcher on the table and lifts the small bell, ringing it twice, before speaking. "The Shadow Sorceress raised the winds to scatter two companies of your best archers, and yet more of your players."

"You could do the same, were you so minded," points out the man who goes by the name of jerGlien. "It is merely a matter of the right melodies supporting the proper words. It is most tiring, and if it fails to destroy the enemy, then the sorcerer is left defenseless."

"She can afford to be defenseless for a short time. She has a sorceress with her. I do not have others."

"Do you wish others to share your powers?" asks jerGlien, looking up as the door to the private dining chamber opens and a slender brunette servingwoman steps inside and bows . . . deeply and silently.

"Another pitcher of the wine, the good red." Belmar turns to jerGlien as the woman bows again and departs.

After a moment, jerGlien continues, "In any case, the sorceress with the shadowsinger is not nearly so strong as she is. Also, she is not your problem. Not now. The Sorceress of Defalk is. You should not be scrying what is happening in Dumar, but what the lady Clayre may be doing in Neserea."

"I have indeed been following the lady Clayre. She hides in that pile of ancient rock on the outskirts of Esaria, as if I could not see where she is. All the time Lord Nysl bows and scrapes, fearing her, yet fearing me more."

"He does her bidding," says jerGlien, his voice mild.

"Because she is a sorceress, and within his hold. Only for those reasons. Once we hold Neserea, he will fall on his knees and grovel. We will let him." Belmar laughs. "If he grovels especially well, we might let him keep his pile of stone."

"Lord Nysl is nothing. You must watch the sorceress."

"That I am. She can do nothing without my knowledge." The Neserean sorcerer takes the smallest of sips of the wine. "You had mentioned her lord, sometime back."

"Ah, yes. I believe I did. The esteemed Lord Robero. He has little love of being indebted to women, and especially women who are sorceresses. He is coming to realize that perhaps he might not be as constrained under other circumstances, and that would be good for both of you."

"Does the shadowsinger know this? If she does, she may well hasten to enter Neserea," Belmar points out. "That being a possibility, I would rather not be surprised if she does."

The door opens, and the slender servingwoman reenters, bowing, and carrying a second crystal pitcher. "Lord."

Belmar watches as the young woman crosses the polished wooden floor. A few droplets of wine spill from the pitcher onto the wood, either from the movements of the server or from the hand which shakes as she sets the pitcher on the table.

"You should not spill good wine." His voice is cold.

"I am sorry, ser. Most sorry, Lord Belmar." The woman's bow is almost a grovel.

"Let it not happen again."

"No, ser. No, lord. I will be most careful."

Belmar does not see the flash in jerGlien's eyes. Nor does the server.

Neither speaks until the door closes once more.

"Even you accept too much sloppiness in women, Lord Belmar," jerGlien observes.

"She is not *my* servingwoman," Belmar points out. "I would not wish to tell those who support me how to discipline their servants. Not yet." He smiles. "You were saying?"

"The shadowsinger cannot cross the Mittfels until the snows melt. That will be weeks from now, at the earliest. By then, you should have disposed of the lady Clayre and the ragtag remnants of the pretender's armsmen and lancers."

"There are still some who refer to her as the Lady High Counselor." A sardonic smile crosses Belmar's face. "You do not care for women in high places."

"No. I do not. No man of Sturinn does. Nor would you, if you but knew the damages wrought by the sorceresses of old. What happened in your petty Spell-Fire Wars is as nothing compared to the Pelaran Devastation."

"I cannot say I have heard of such," replies the younger man.

"Why should you have? Does not the world begin and end in Liedwahr?" The Sturinnese laughs, lightly, before lifting his own goblet. "You can worry about the lessons of days past once you have made your own future certain. What will you do to keep the Lady Clayre from striking at you?"

"Strike first, of course, and in a fashion she will not expect. How could I do otherwise?"

"She will attempt the same, I am certain," points out jerGlien.

"Many attempt; few succeed." Belmar smiles.

So does jerGlien.

20

The gray light that seeped through the warped shutters meant it was sometime around dawn . . . or that the day happened to be cloudy again. Secca doubted it was near dawn as she struggled from under her blanket. She found herself so weak that even the effort to sit up and swing her legs over the side of the narrow double-width bed in the peasant's cottage left every limb trembling. Her eyes burned, and her head throbbed—worse, it seemed, than when she had collapsed into a troubled sleep the night before, and, as she glanced around, daystars flashed intermittently across everything she saw.

Neither Richina nor Alcaren was in the small bedroom, although Secca could hear low voices in the larger common room.

As if he had been listening, Alcaren appeared with a cup of a steaming liquid. "I thought you might need this."

"More of the Matriarch's brew?" Each word felt as though it rasped from her throat and mouth.

Alcaren extended the chipped crockery mug. "I prevailed upon some that I know to provide us with a score of the brew packets. I could not have done so if the Matriarch did not approve, but I thought it best that I not approach her directly."

Secca did not reply, instead taking the mug and sipping slowly.

"Richina and I have checked the glass, but we can find no Sturinnese force headed toward us. None from Dumar, either," Alcaren admitted.

"The weather?" Secca took another small sip of the brew.

"It's chill and windy. There's been some sleet at times this morning, but the clouds are thinning."

Secca nodded.

"Some of the players are as exhausted as you are," Alcaren continued. "I took the liberty of saying that it would be unlikely that we would resume our journey to Envaryl until tomorrow."

"Unlikely?" The way Secca felt, it was most unlikely, and if many of the players were in similar condition, there would be little point in traveling.

"That way . . ." Alcaren looked embarrassed. "Well . . . you could still tell people we were traveling . . . and that I had been mistaken . . ."

Secca laughed—and wished she hadn't as she began to cough.

"Are you all right?" Alcaren stepped up beside her and put an arm around her shoulders to steady her, taking the chipped mug and setting it on the bowed wooden floor.

". . . I'm tired, and we've just started."

"I've just started. You've been at this for almost half a year. You can rest for a while. We're not riding anywhere just yet."

For a time, Secca leaned against his arm and shoulder, but she couldn't help wondering how much her weakness would cost them. If only . . . if only she were stronger. If only she weren't so small.

She straightened. "Let me get the rest of my clothes on. If we're not riding, at least we can see where we'll be going tomorrow."

"There's some bread and cheese waiting for you," Alcaren said, after giving her a last half hug. "You can eat, and then we'll see." He stepped back from the bed and closed the plank door to the common room.

Secca glanced at the single shuttered window, hearing again the moaning of the wind. Spring was supposedly nearing, but the wind sounded like midwinter. With the slightest of headshakes, and another flash of the daystars across what she saw, she threw back the blanket and reached for her boots.

Wind and cold or not, they had to defeat the Sturinnese before more ships and Sea-Priests arrived from the Ostisles.

21

By the next morning, the clouds and wind had passed, and the air was clear, if chill, and by midday Secca and her forces had left the near-deserted hills covered only with winter-tan grass and made their way along a road that had widened enough for Secca, Alcaren, and Richina to ride abreast, although some of the time Alcaren was threading his brown gelding along the road's shoulder in order to ride beside Secca. The higher slopes of some of the hills bore either woodlots, orchards, or the remnants of older forests. The dwellings beside the road had become more numerous, with stubble-turned fields mixed with meadows. Almost all were small cottages—and all were deserted or firmly shuttered as the lancers of Loiseau and the SouthWomen rode by, the hoofs of their mounts thudding dully on the frozen clay of the road.

Ahead of Secca, a half-dek beyond the vanguard of the column, the road curved through a grassy swale between two hills, then appeared to dip. There, at the point where the road began to descend, Wilten and one of Secca's captains—Quebar—had reined up and were talking to a pair of scouts.

"That must be where the road drops into the long river valley," Secca suggested, glancing at Alcaren, riding to her right.

"It should be," he answered.

"Then we're not that far from Envaryl, are we?" asked Richina.

"Not if that's the valley we think it is," replied Secca, reaching up and readjusting the green felt hat.

"We've made good time," Richina observed.

Nodding, Secca reined up short of Wilten and Quebar. The gray mare *whuffed*, as if suggesting that it was well past time for Secca to have stopped. Absently, Secca leaned forward and patted the gray's shoulder, looking at the road that wound down the hill through three switchbacks and then turned almost due north. A thin line of trees marked a watercourse that ran from the horizon where the road seemingly pointed westward toward the foothills and the snow-covered Westfels behind the hills.

"If our maps are right," Secca said, "those trees could mark the course of the Envar River."

"That would mean we're less than thirty deks from Envaryl," Alcaren said, easing his mount to a halt slightly forward of Secca.

"Lady Secca," called Wilten, "there is a town below. The scouts say that there are hoofprints on the road below, the kind that lancer mounts make, but they're headed north, through the town and away from us."

Following Wilten's gesture, Secca studied the valley below and the small town—or large village—that held close to twoscore dwellings. Already, riders and wagons were moving along the road, northward out of the town along the road.

"They aren't staying to see whether we're friendly," observed Delcetta, reining up to join the informal council at the head of the column.

"No armed force is friendly to them," replied Alcaren.

Secca worried about what that meant. Had Dumar become a land where all sides preyed on the people? So much so that they distrusted everyone on sight? She shook her head, wondering how Fehern—and Clehar before him—had ever let matters get to such a state.

After a moment, she forced a pleasant smile. "We'll probably need to send messengers to Fehern before too long. Perhaps tomorrow, after we've had a chance to use the glass tonight and make sure that he still holds Envaryl."

Wilten nodded.

Delcetta glanced from Wilten to Secca, and then to Alcaren. "Ah . . . tomorrow?"

"You think Lady Secca should wait longer?" asked Alcaren, his voice mild.

Secca smothered a smile, for she had seen the twinkle in her consort's eyes.

Delcetta started to speak, then smiled. "Overcaptain Alcaren . . . I would defer to the lady's wisdom. I trust that the reason for leaving messengers until just before we arrive is to make sure there are no surprises?"

"The Sturinnese doubtless know exactly where we are," Secca replied. "If Fehern is less than trustworthy, they will have let him know as well, and there is no reason for us to hazard lancers. If he does not know, why . . ." Secca drew out the pause, "he should be most pleased to see us whenever we arrive."

Secca wasn't sure of the logic of her reasoning, but her senses told her it was too early to send messengers, and so far her feelings had been much more accurate than her logic.

"I am most certain Lord Fehern will profess gladness to see you whenever you arrive, my lady," offered Alcaren.

"But we will send messengers to Lord Fehern?" asked Richina, her eyes going from Alcaren to Secca, then back to the Ranuan sorcerer.

"We will," Secca affirmed. "We don't wish to surprise the acting Lord High Counselor too much, but he should not have too much time to prepare." She smiled more broadly and more falsely. "We would not wish him to spend great effort on welcoming us when the task is to defeat the Sturinnese."

Richina flushed, belatedly understanding the byplay.

"I wish it were otherwise," said Secca, her smile turning

faintly sad. Richina was still young enough that she had to think to consider duplicity and treachery on the part of supposed allies. Secca had been forced to learn that lesson all too early.

"Best we continue," she said quietly, but firmly.

22

Before midmorning, well before, the sun had warmed both air and ground enough that neither the breath of mounts nor lancers steamed, and Secca had loosened her green leather riding jacket. It had been two days since they had left the high hills, and Secca could now see Envaryl before them, on the north side of the narrow river that lay less than a dek ahead.

"There's still no sign of anyone coming out to greet us," observed Richina, riding to Secca's left. "Do you think our messengers got through?"

"I'm most certain that they did," replied Secca. "The glass showed them in comfortable quarters. Fehern was still holding the city. Still, we can't very well just ride into Envaryl. If necessary, we'll stop short of Envaryl on the south side and wait." Her amber eyes flashed. She didn't like the idea of waiting on Fehern, especially not when she was hurrying to his aid.

Alcaren and Delcetta rode back from a point before the vanguard, where they had halted briefly to talk to the scouts and Wilten. As they neared Secca, Alcaren eased his mount around and rode to Secca's right. Delcetta rode behind Alcaren.

"The scouts haven't seen any pickets or patrols," Alcaren said. "There aren't that many tracks on the road, either."

"Less than two deks from the city?" Secca shook her head. "If no one does greet us, we'll stop on this side of the river." There would be no sense in crossing a bridge and then having to fight—if it came to that—with a river at their back.

"That was also what Wilten felt," Alcaren said dryly.

"If you would tell him that we agree with his recommendation . . . ?"

Alcaren laughed.

"Have him bring one company of lancers from Loiseau to the fore, and have Overcaptain Delcetta do the same." Secca felt strange passing the order through Alcaren when Delcetta was riding right behind him, but since that was the way she herself had set up the chain of command, it would have been worse immediately to bypass Alcaren. "Oh . . . Elfens and the archers as well."

Alcaren turned in his saddle, gracefully as always, and said quietly, "If you would, Overcaptain, once we near the bridge?"

"Yes, ser." A faint smile played around Delcetta's lips, one of repressed humor and understanding.

Alcaren eased his mount forward along the shoulder of the road, back past the vanguard and toward Wilten. After that he rode back to talk to Elfens, whose archers rode behind the players.

Less than a glass had passed when Secca reined up on the hint of a rise beside the road, perhaps two hundred yards short of the river and the bridge that crossed it. The Envar River was narrow, less than ten yards across, although the darkness of the water suggested that it was several yards deep. The stone span that crossed the river was narrow and ancient, wide enough for but two mounts side by side. The stones, originally reddish, had faded to pink, and the lower levels, just above the water, bore brown and bleached-out green moss, moss that was doubtless under water in spring and early summer, when the river's water level was higher. The ground around the river and upon each side of the road looked to have been recently cultivated, and the stubble from the previous harvest had been turned under.

There were more than a score of cottages within a dek of where they had halted, but all were set back from the road, and built upon low stilts, suggesting that the river flooded the flatland. As with all the other farm cottages they had passed, the dwellings and outbuildings were shuttered tight.

Secca turned in the saddle, looking for Palian, then called, "Have the players get their instruments ready, so that they can play, quickly if necessary."

"Yes, lady." Palian's smile was knowing, not quite grim. Delvor merely nodded.

"Players dismount!" Palian called. "Dismount and stand ready to play."

"Dismount and tune!" echoed Delvor.

"Gold company to the fore!" ordered Wilten.

"Second company to the fore!" Delcetta's voice cut through the hubbub like a stiletto through rotten meat.

Secca glanced northward across the narrow river. Envaryl presented an odd picture. Dwellings and structures sprouted in groups, seemingly without pattern, except that there were often low hills covered in tan grass and brush between the groupings. A number of the buildings—those whose walls were not plastered—were built of stones of different sizes and colors. On the far side of the river, between the river and the buildings, there was a low hill, or a regular long ridge, covered with the winter-tan grass that grew everywhere in western Dumar and with intermittent brush and trees. A good four yards high, never less than three, nor more than five, the ridge extended east and west of the road, running straight as an iron crossbow quarrel.

From the saddle of the gray mare, after taking her lutar from its case behind her saddle, Secca tuned it. A half smile flitted across her face as she could see Richina starting to follow her example, but she spoke quickly, if evenly, "I'd rather you not show your lutar, Richina."

Richina looked up, startled.

"I'll explain later," Secca said.

"As you wish, lady." The younger sorceress frowned.

Secca knew she'd have more than a little explaining to do. Still holding her own instrument, she studied both the city and the regularity of the ridge. Then she nodded.

"You're nodding," Alcaren said, half-inquiring, as he eased his mount closer to hers.

"Look at that long straight hill," she said. "Closely."

"There's a lot of stone under the bushes and trees. The trees aren't very tall, either."

"That was the city wall," Secca explained. "I'd heard that Anna had turned the city into rubble. I never expected to see it. That's why the city is the way it is. It's not as big as when she destroyed it, and those who live there mined the ruins for the stones."

"She destroyed the entire city?" asked Alcaren.

At Alcaren's question, Richina's head lifted, as if she had heard for the first time about Anna's efforts against Envaryl.

"With one spellsong," Secca replied. "She said she paid for doing that for years, and in ways she'd never expected . . . but she never said what they were." She shifted her weight in the saddle, wondering how long before they received some indication of how to proceed. The scrying mirror had shown that Fehern held the city, and she doubted that could have changed in two glasses, not with the nearest Sturinnese forces still almost fifty deks to the east.

"He'll make you wait," predicted Alcaren, "but not too long."

"Because he doesn't wish to admit he needs us, even though he'll lose everything without us?" Secca had doubts about what she voiced, but what she felt was better left between her and Alcaren for the moment.

"Rulers—or Lord High Counselors—don't like to admit weaknesses."

"No one does." Secca laughed, as much at Alcaren's dry humor as at the implied suggestion that Sorceress Proctectors didn't like to admit to weakness, either.

Secca looked toward the bridge.

A trumpet sounded, and two squads of lancers appeared,

riding out of the city and southward along the road toward the river and bridge—and Secca's forces. All wore tannish leather riding jackets, open enough so that Secca could see the crimson tunics beneath. The Dumaran lancers reined up a good hundred yards short of the bridge on the northern side.

After a moment, a single officer rode forward, slowly, across the bridge.

"Wilten!" Secca called. "If you would greet the Dumaran officer?"

With a nod, the Defalkan overcaptain also rode forward, but only about thirty yards, where he reined up and waited.

Once the Dumaran reached Wilten, he reined up as well, and the two officers conversed for a moment. Then, Wilten and the Dumaran overcaptain rode toward Secca, Richina, and Alcaren. Wilten was careful to rein up a good ten yards short of Secca—and give Alcaren a sharp glance, although Secca's consort had already eased his mount slightly forward and turned the gelding just enough to be able to block any attack on either sorceress.

"Lady Secca." The fresh-faced captain bowed in the saddle. "Lord High Counselor Fehern bids you welcome to Dumar and Envaryl and has sent us to escort you to his headquarters."

"We are most happy to have reached Envaryl, and look forward to meeting with Lord Fehern," replied Secca. "You are?" She raised her eyebrows.

"Captain Kuttyr, lady." The blond officer bowed again.

"Perhaps you would ride with us, Captain Kuttyr, and so enlighten us," Secca suggested. "There is much we should know."

"I would be most pleased," replied the Dumaran captain, his eyes involuntarily drifting to the blonde Richina.

Secca did not replace the lutar in its case as she waited for the players to remount before she rode toward the bridge, following the company of SouthWomen and, then, her own lancers.

"Have there been many attacks recently by the Sturinnese?" asked Secca, after the column had begun to move forward.

"No, lady, not since early winter. Lord Fehern and Arms Commander Halyt have reports that the Sturinnese are gathering their forces and may attack within the next few weeks." Kuttyr offered an almost roguish smile. "I am not certain I should know that, but all the lancers do."

"We will let Lord Fehern tell us what he will," Secca replied with a smile. "How long have you been a lancer?"

"Six years, lady. I just made captain last season." Kuttyr's smile was definitely for Richina.

"You must have distinguished yourself," Richina offered.

Secca kept her smile to herself and listened.

"If surviving and keeping too many lancers from being killed unwisely marks distinction," replied the young captain, "then I distinguished myself." He shook his head ruefully. "The drums, and the waves of white-coats . . . all we could do was attack quickly before they could set up the drums and in places where we knew the land and when they did not expect it. We have slain far more of them than they of us." He laughed, once. "But there are far, far more of them."

"They have many lancers," prompted Richina.

"An endless number, it would seem. And when they use the drums, their archers never miss. It is hard to fight against both sorcery and arms." Kuttyr paused and eased his mount back to let Richina and Secca cross the bridge, then crossed with Alcaren.

"How many companies have you left here in Envaryl?" asked Alcaren.

"Any answer on my part would be a guess," replied Kuttyr with a laugh. "Once we had twenty, but that was when we left Dumaria."

"Only twenty against fifty or more?" said Richina, turning slightly in the saddle. "That speaks for valor."

"You are kind, lady, but valor, alas, does not always bring

success." Kuttyr quickly glanced at Alcaren, as if not wishing to say more about valor. "I note varied livery, Overcaptain, yet yours matches none of them."

Most of the force had crossed the narrow stone bridge, Secca and those riding around her had barely passed the grass-covered rubble of the fallen wall when another squad of lancers appeared, only to turn their mounts to form an honor guard of sorts.

"It does not." Alcaren smiled, spared a more detailed answer by the arrival of the honor guard.

"You do honor us, Captain," Secca said. "Where are we headed?"

"Lord Fehern has taken one of the older villas on the north side of town as his headquarters," replied Kuttyr. "We are headed there."

Secca continued to hold the lutar in readiness as she rode into the city. She was glad that the rebuilding had left wide spaces, where an ambush would have been more difficult than in most cities, but she continued to study everything.

So did Alcaren, she noted, and the two exchanged knowing smiles, as Richina went on talking to Kuttyr.

"How did your forces come to Envaryl?"

"We had little enough choice, lady." Kuttyr smiled ruefully. "The Sturinnese moved up the river from Narial, and then sent one body of lancers to the east to block the pass from Stromwer. They used sorcery, it is said, to fill the lower reaches with rock and snow. Then they swept back westward." He shrugged. "We fought, but we had nowhere to go."

Secca did not comment, but made a mental note to check on the passes from Stromwer with her glass when she had time—and privacy.

"Did the Sturinnese have many archers?"

"More than we did . . ."

For all his words, Kuttyr offered little that Secca had not surmised from the observations she, Richina, and Alcaren had made with their scrying.

Envaryl appeared the same from inside the fallen wall as it had from without. Even from the central avenue that Kuttyr and his squads led Secca's force along, the pattern continued—rubbled sections of land covered with grass interspersed with structures built from bricks and stone mined from the ruins. Once Envaryl had been a substantial city. Now, what amounted to a large town was strewn among the ruins.

Perhaps two-thirds of the way through the town, Kuttyr gestured, even before the leading squad of Dumaran lancers turned. "We will follow the boulevard westward. It is less than a dek from here."

Richina had fallen silent, as if she could think of no more questions.

The villa that stood at the end of the boulevard, flanked by a number of others, was somewhat more than modest, Secca judged, with two wings each of two levels spreading from the entry foyer, and each of those wings close to a hundred yards long. The low wall that enclosed the grounds also contained a number of outbuildings, including a barrackslike structure, and at least one stable of a size able to handle a score of mounts, if not more. The once-white plaster was a pinkish shade from years of red road dust, and the area before the entry circle and the mounting blocks was neither of grass nor gravel, but reddish dirt. The fountain was dry, and looked not to have been used in years.

As Secca reined up opposite the square arch at the top of four wide brick steps that led to an entry foyer, a trumpet sounded, and nearly a score of figures began to march from the villa, first a half-score of lancers in crimson, then several captains and overcaptains, and then a taller and broader officer, and then Fehern. The Lord High Counselor remained standing on the top brick step, along with the tall officer.

Secca eased the gray a bit farther ahead, then turned the mare to face the Lord High Counselor. She did not dismount, and she still held the lutar, if more casually. "Lord

Fehern, we bring you greetings and aid from Lord Robero of Defalk."

Even in the gold-trimmed crimson tunic of the Lord High Counselor of Dumar, Fehern looked more sharp-featured than he had when Secca had seen him in the glass, and his jet-black hair was shot with white, although he could not have been more than a few years older than Secca. Beneath his deep-set and large black eyes were dark pouches.

Fehern offered a wide smile beneath cold eyes, then bowed very slightly. "Lady Secca, we welcome you, Sorceress Protector of the East. Yet here you are in the South. We could have used one such as you several seasons ago." With a vague gesture that seemed to encompass the city-town to the east, he added, "Not that we are less pleased that you have made your way here, for it must have been a most trying journey to reach us from the easternmost part of Defalk."

Secca returned the Lord High Counselor's smile with one doubtless as false as his. She tried to choose her words carefully. "It has been a long journey. We left Loiseau in mid-fall, after harvest, but we hope to be of some assistance in ridding Dumar of the Sturinnese presence."

"My overcaptains have noted women lancers in blue and crimson . . . Surely, they are not of your retinue." Fehern continued to offer a fixed smile.

"When word of your brother's difficulties reached Lord Robero, I was already in Ebra, assisting Lord High Counselor Hadrenn in removing the Sturinnese from his lands. The snows of winter had closed the passes from Defalk to both the south and the east even before we engaged the Sturinnese. By the time we had routed the Sturinnese in Ebra, winter was full upon us. So we made our way to assist you through Ranuak. The SouthWomen's Council was kind enough to offer the assistance of five companies. We made our way here first, to ensure that Envaryl did not fall." Secca offered another broad smile.

"We are most glad that you have." Fehern coughed, clearing his throat. "You must have had a trying journey, and while we hope to hear of that presently, I will not tariff you more until you are rested and refreshed." He paused. "Oh . . . my arms commander, Halyt." Fehern gestured to the burly, almost rotund bear of a man who stood to his right, a figure over two yards in height.

"My pleasure," Secca replied, observing that the man in gray who often appeared in the scrying glass was nowhere visible.

"The pleasure is mine, Lady Sorceress." Halyt offered a deep booming laugh. "To have a sorceress coming to our aid is welcome, and to find she is beautiful is indeed a pleasure."

"Oh . . . this is my consort—Overcaptain Alcaren." Secca nodded to Alcaren. "He represents both the SouthWomen and the Matriarch of Ranuak."

"I am pleased to see you, Overcaptain." Fehern nodded, then said smoothly, "As you can see, Lady Sorceress, we find ourselves in quarters far smaller than in Dumaria. There is an adjoining villa that Arms Commander Halyt's men are making ready for you and your forces. I wish that we could offer more, given that you have traveled half of Liedwahr to come to our assistance . . ."

"After open roads and barns and cottages, a villa would be most welcome." Secca paused. "There are buildings where our lancers can quarter themselves?"

"But of course." Fehern smiled. "Once you are settled and refreshed, I would hope you would join us for the evening meal here, that is, you and your consort and overcaptains . . . and your lovely . . . assistant."

"Alcaren and the overcaptains and Richina and I would be most happy to join you. Also, my chief players."

"They are most welcome, as well. At the ninth glass?"

"We will be here."

"Captain Kuttyr will escort you, and see that you have whatever is in our poor power to supply you." With another nod and a polite smile, Fehern suggested that the first meeting was over.

"We appreciate the hospitality, and we will convey your welcome to Lord Robero." Secca returned Fehern's nod with one equally slight and polite. "And we will enjoy dining with you this evening."

As she and Alcaren followed Kuttyr and his squad down the open lane to the south, toward a structure and set of outbuildings only slightly less extensive than those occupied by Fehern, Secca wondered exactly what the dinner ahead would reveal.

23

ENVARYL, DUMAR

Fehern paces from the massive marble hearth that contains but embers and ashes to the built-in bookcases on the north wall, where he turns and pauses, fixing his eyes on Halyt. "Did you note that overcaptain who is also the sorceress's consort did not wear the same uniform as the SouthWomen? Or the green of the Defalkan lancers?"

"Ah . . . Lord . . . the green is not of Defalk. Those are the sorceress's personal lancers, most loyal to her."

Fehern shakes his head. "Four companies, and they are hers. Five others, and they are SouthWomen. Not a single company from Lord Robero, and yet she comes in his name?"

"Lord Robero has scarce a score of companies to his name, and doubtless many are supporting the other sorceress in Neserea," points out Elyzar.

"Does your glass tell you so, sorcerer?" asks Fehern.

"There are several Defalkan companies with the Sorceress of Defalk. The glass cannot show precisely how many, but

there are more than two and less than a half-score." Elyzar
offers an apologetic shrug.

"So . . . Lord Robero will hazard his lancers in Neserea,
but not in Dumar? And he keeps most of them in Defalk?
A fine lord and supporter he is!"

Halyt coughs, then smiles broadly as Fehern looks to him.

"You have something to say?" demands the Lord High
Counselor.

"This matter about the consort of the sorceress . . . it is a
bit strange, do you not think? Why would a sorceress consort? None have in generations."

"She is a woman, Arms Commander," suggests Elyzar.
"And women . . ."

"To a mere overcaptain?" asks Fehern. "You were the one
who told me that Lady Secca has more lands to her own
name than most lords in Defalk."

"It may be that he is not a mere overcaptain," suggests
Elyzar.

"An emissary of the Matriarch?"

"Ranuak has always needed lands more fertile than those
she possesses," the sorcerer points out. "Since the Spell-Fire
Wars, if not before."

Halyt nods, still smiling jovially. "Since the SouthWomen
are not under the command of the Matriarch . . ."

"She can disavow anything they do," Fehern concludes.

"Did you also notice that she did not introduce the young
woman—Richina?" asks Halyt. "Yet the young woman has
too much of an air of confidence to be a mere lady-in-
waiting or a maid. And never had the sorceresses of Defalk
brought such with them on campaigns."

"It could be that she was tired from the ride and did not
think to introduce her properly," offers the broad-shouldered
sorcerer.

Fehern snorts. "I like this not. I have Sturinnese to the
east, and a sorceress who appears with nearly nine companies, five of them SouthWomen, with an overcaptain from
Ranuak, a mysterious young woman, and two groups of

players. Did you notice that none of them bore wounds? Their gear was dusty, and their weapons used—but not recently."

"She bears no gifts, either," muses Halyt.

"She said that she had left Defalk not knowing she would come to your aid, lord," Elyzar points out. "That was what she said." There is the slightest emphasis on the word "said."

"Yes. That was what she said." Fehern shakes his head. "I do not know which force to fear more—those against me or those who say they support me."

"You must look to your own interests and those of Dumar," reflects Elyzar, "and see which enemy will harm you less or help you more."

"Or see if we can get both enemies to fight while we remain in the background," suggests Halyt with another deep laugh.

Fehern nods. "Both of you listen at table and think upon what you hear. Then, in the morning, we will talk."

24

The second-floor master chambers in the villa offered to Secca were enormous, far larger than those of Lord Robero in Falcor, and three times the size of the master suite at her own hold of Loiseau. In addition to the chambers themselves, there was a long covered balcony more than five yards deep that extended thirty yards along the south side of the north wing of the villa and overlooked a courtyard garden that had seen far better years and care.

Secca stepped from the balcony back into the slightly dusty sitting room, closing the glass-paned doors. Not for the first time, nor the last, she suspected, she wondered at the faded opulence that surrounded her.

"Rather large," said Alcaren dryly, "don't you think?"

"For a town this size that could not afford to rebuild itself completely in a generation . . . yes." Secca shook her head. "The villa Fehern took is even larger. It looks that way from without."

"I am most certain it is." Alcaren stepped toward her.

"You aren't thinking about villas."

"They do have the advantage of privacy." Alcaren grinned.

"Not until after we've bathed."

Alcaren grinned even more widely.

"Separately," Secca said firmly.

Alcaren laughed, generously. "You do make your wishes known."

"And you, yours," she replied, laughing as well, before stepping closer to him and putting her arms around his neck.

It was much, much later when she and Alcaren stood once more in the sitting room, bathed and in cleaner riding clothes, waiting by the rectangular table, a dark-stained expanse of distressed and battered oak with the scrying mirror set roughly in the middle. Secca's lutar rested on one side of the mirror, Alcaren's lumand on the other. Two maps were set before the chair that Secca had decided she would take.

"Do you feel better?" Secca asked with a mischievous smile.

"You *know* the answer to that. The question is whether you do." His smile verged on a leer.

Secca found herself flushing.

"I'll accept that reply," her consort said, grinning widely.

Even as she shook her head, Secca couldn't help but smile.

"Chief Player Palian," announced Achar from the corridor.

"Just have the players, the overcaptains, and Richina

come in when they arrive, Achar. You don't need to announce them all," Secca called.

"Yes, lady."

As she stepped into the room, Palian glanced at Secca, then at Alcaren, and smothered a smile. "Delvor will be along in a moment."

"How are the quarters for the players?" asked Secca, again trying not to flush.

"Somewhat dusty, but far better than anything they expected. There are even provisions in the storerooms, enough for both players and lancers."

Secca wasn't sure she liked what that implied, and a sideways glance at Alcaren, who raised his eyebrows, confirmed that he shared Secca's concerns.

Delcetta stepped inside the room, followed quickly by Wilten, then by Richina, who carried her uncased lutar with her.

The six had barely settled into the spare wooden chairs set around the dark table when the door opened and closed a last time with Delvor's arrival.

"Are the quarters sufficient for the lancers?" Secca asked, looking first to Delcetta and then to Wilten.

"We had to do some rearranging, and some will have makeshift pallets," Wilten said, "but everyone will be warm and dry and fed."

"The Dumarans had already converted the one outbuilding to a barracks," Delcetta added. "It's drafty, but some of my lancers are crafters as well, and they're working on that."

"I have not seen any servants or staff anywhere around," Alcaren said. "Has anyone?"

"None of us," replied Palian.

"Nor us," added Delcetta.

Wilten shook his head.

"No staff . . . but provisions." Secca stood. "We need to see how far we can trust these Dumarans." She lifted the lutar from the table and began to tune it. After pulling on the copper-tipped leather gloves, she immediately offered a spellsong.

> *"Show us now in great details and as you must . . .*
> *weapons set against us by Dumarans we might*
> *trust . . ."*

The glass silvered and then presented an image of only three men—Fehern, Halyt, and the man whom the glass had earlier shown to be a Sea-Priest—but no weapons.

"The weapons are the men themselves," murmured Alcaren.

"Or their words," suggested Secca.

In the mirror image, Fehern snorted visibly at least once before Secca sang the release spell.

She cleared her throat. "Captain Kuttyr said that the Sea-Priests had closed the passes to Defalk through sorcery. Let's see if we can see which one." She lifted the lutar again.

> *"Show me now any pass that to Defalk would go*
> *that through spells the Sea-Priests closed so . . .*
> *if by rock, or dirt, or ice and snow . . ."*

The glass obediently displayed what appeared to be the results of an avalanche, clearly blocking a defile between two low mountains. Secca suspected the pass was the one to Stromwer, but confirming that could wait.

She repeated the spell using "Neserea" in place of "Defalk," but the glass came up silver-blank.

"They haven't closed the trade pass north yet. That's probably because it's narrow and impassable now."

"Or because they don't know about it," suggested Richina.

"That I would not wager on. They know too much about Liedwahr." The redheaded sorceress looked to Alcaren. "Would you see if you can show us the nearest Sturinnese?"

"My songs may not be so well crafted as yours, my lady, but we will try." He rose, then took the lumand, a smaller instrument than the lutars of Secca and Richina. Without the gloves used by Secca, he fingered the strings, checking the tuning, before singing in his strong high baritone voice.

*"Show us now in full and open face
those forces of Sturinn near this place . . ."*

The mirror displayed a scene of white tents in rows, set behind the dwellings of a small hamlet. The view could have been anywhere between Dumaria and Envaryl.

Alcaren quickly sang the release couplet, frowning as he did. "A moment, if you will. We need . . ." His words drifted into silence as he glanced at the maps before Secca. Then he nodded and murmured some phrases to himself.

Wilten looked to Delcetta, who did not return the Defalkan officer's glance, and then to Palian, who watched Alcaren intently.

Finally, Alcaren cleared his throat and sang.

*"Show us where upon a map of this land
these forces of Sturinn now do stand . . ."*

A map appeared, one nearly identical to that Secca and Alcaren had been using on their journey from Stygia to Envaryl. On the mirror-map pulsed a single white star.

Secca squinted, checking the star's location against her own map and recollection, before speaking. "They're about halfway between Dumaria and Envaryl."

"It's almost two weeks since they left Dumaria," mused Delcetta.

Secca nodded to Alcaren to sing the release couplet, then waited for him to finish before speaking. "They're taking their time."

"They wish you to hurry to them," suggested Wilten.

"Because they expect reinforcements from that fleet?" asked Richina.

"That could be," replied Alcaren. "Or they could be setting up some sort of sorcerous trap. Or they want to see what you and Fehern do."

"There are many possibilities," Secca temporized, knowing that none of them were good. She glanced at Richina. "Would you do a map spell the way Alcaren did to see if you can locate the Sturinnese fleet?"

"Yes, lady."

The map called up by Richina's spell was faint, and extremely fuzzy, and only by leaning over almost on top of it could Secca see that it showed the Sturinnese ships northwest of Defuhr Bay—well northwest.

"They should be farther south if they're sailing to Dumar," ventured Alcaren.

Secca nodded, almost to herself, then glanced at the faces around the long dark oak table.

"The Sturinnese here are trying to delay you. The fleet is going to Neserea," Wilten suggested.

"Why . . . ?" began Richina, closing her mouth after the one word.

"They may use sorcery to break the ice on the Bitter Sea," Secca said. "It makes more sense that they support Belmar first. The Sturinnese here will prolong the war, hoping that in the end, they can trap us between two forces. The Sea-Priests plan to take Neserea before the snow in the Mittfels melts enough for us to go north." She glanced at Richina. "You may release the spell."

Richina sang the release couplet, and the mirror blanked. Secca could feel the heat from the frame and the glass.

"But . . . Lady Clayre?" asked Palian.

"The ships heading toward Neserea and the glass both show she is hard-pressed. She is alone, with no other sorceresses, and she has fewer lancers. Belmar's forces continue to grow, and with more support from Sturinn . . ."

Secca shook her head. "We must warn her . . . and Lord Robero—but there is little else we can do."

"We could not reach her if we tried, could we?" asked Palian.

Secca shook her head. "The distance from Envaryl to Esaria is greater than the journey from Mencha to Elahwa, and the roads are far poorer. There are no well-traveled passes, except for the trade pass, and that will be dangerous and late in melting. I would wager that the glass showed us that the longer way through Stromwer has been blocked by the sorcery of the Sea-Priests. Even if we could use sorcery to unblock the pass, to reach it we would have to face the Sturinnese here in Dumar first." She motioned for Alcaren and Richina to reseat themselves at the ancient table with the elaborately carved pedestal legs.

"Everywhere," murmured Palian, "are the Sea-Priests."

"They've been planning this for a very long time," Secca admitted. "The Maitre, whoever he is, has thought out his plans carefully." She offered a ragged smile. "And we still must dine tonight with Lord Fehern and attempt to see which way blows that wind." Her eyes went to the window and the gathering twilight beyond the balcony. "We will be leaving shortly."

"You will need an escort, lady," Wilten replied.

"One squad from Loiseau and one from the SouthWomen, you think?"

Both Delcetta and Wilten nodded their approval.

"And they will stand by Fehern's villa waiting," added the strawberry blonde overcaptain of the SouthWomen. "Captain Peraghn will command our squad."

"If you do not mind, Lady Secca," Wilten said, "I would place the purple company's second squad under Overcaptain Delcetta's captain for the time they are standing by."

Secca managed not to drop her jaw in amazement. "That would be acceptable." She paused. "If it is acceptable to Delcetta and her captains."

"Overcaptain Wilten and I have discussed it already,"

Delcetta offered, inclining her head to Wilten.

"We thought that it would make a certain . . . impression on the Dumarans." Wilten displayed a faintly wry smile.

"I don't think any of us are exceedingly trusting of Lord Fehern and his forces," Secca observed. "I would also ask that none of you mention either Richina's or Alcaren's abilities with sorcery. Richina is my assistant, and Alcaren an overcaptain who is skilled with weapons and as a lancer, and who was once the guard chief for the Matriarch." Secca paused. "Even if Fehern is trustworthy, there is no doubt that some in his headquarters are not."

Both chief players shared a smile before Palian spoke. "The players will be ready to play or ride. They will sup early, and Overcaptain Wilten has agreed to have a messenger ready to ride to inform them if they are needed."

Secca nodded, then stood. "We will meet you below in a few moments." She motioned to Richina. "A word, Richina."

"Yes, Lady."

Once the door closed, Secca faced the younger sorceress. "What we do here could be most dangerous, and I am asking for your discretion, and for you to appear to be but a handmaiden of sorts. It will appear to others that you are barely important. I want you to know that this is not so, and that much of our success may rest on others not knowing the extent of your abilities. I am also asking this of Alcaren. Do you understand why?"

Richina frowned. "You do not wish to appear powerful?"

"I wish Fehern—and possibly the Sturinnese—to think I am the only one with power, and I trust that will give you and Alcaren the ability to act more freely when the time comes, as I fear it will."

"Yes, Lady." A wan smile appeared.

"I am telling you this because whenever others are present, I will treat you as if you were a mere assistant, and I do not want you to think you have fallen from favor because I have consorted with Alcaren." Secca smiled. "I hope I will

not have to require such of you for long, but I wanted you
to understand."

"Thank you." Richina inclined her head.

"Go," Secca said with a laugh. "I'd wager that Captain
Kuttyr will be waiting for a glimpse of you."

"That is all he will get." Richina laughed as well, before
turning and opening the door.

A faint smile played around Alcaren's mouth as he and
Secca waited for Richina to leave the chamber. After the
door closed, he murmured, "That was wise."

"She's still young. If I don't tell her, and tell her directly,
she'll fret. She may, anyway, if this draws out." Secca
smiled at her consort. "You said once that you could play
dinner music. Can you do so with the lumand?"

Alcaren laughed. "That is easy enough. You want an excuse for me to bring the lumand?"

"That, and I don't want Fehern knowing that you are a
sorcerer. I hope you don't mind."

"I've spent most of my life keeping people from knowing
that. I wasn't terribly successful in Ranuak, but let us hope
I can be more so here."

"I do not think they'll be expecting you to be a sorcerer,
and people do not see what they do not expect unless something calls it to their attention," Secca replied. "We had best
go."

Everyone was mounting, or already mounted, by the time
Secca and Alcaren reached the side courtyard between the
villa and the stables.

The ride to the other villa through the deepening gloom
was both short and silent, as Secca wrestled with her concerns and her thoughts about how best to handle Fehern . . .
and her worries that she might be reading the man wrong.

Captain Kuttyr was waiting outside the entry foyer of the
villa serving as Fehern's headquarters. "Greetings. Lord
Fehern awaits you in the dining hall." He bowed deeply as
Secca dismounted and stepped toward him, flanked by Richina and Alcaren, and followed by the two chief players

and the two overcaptains. As Richina passed, his smile widened.

In return, Richina offered the young captain the slightest of nods, along with a warm but pleasant smile.

The Lord High Counselor of Dumar waited, with his arms commander, by the entry to the dining hall. Fehern stepped forward as Secca neared. "Greetings, Sorceress Protector."

"We are most grateful for your hospitality, Lord Fehern." Secca inclined her head.

"Lady Secca." Fehern's eyes studied Secca's green vest, far plainer than the gold-trimmed crimson tunic and trousers he wore. "You travel light, I see."

"Just riding clothes, I fear, Lord Fehern." She smiled. "But then, we are here to fight, not to banquet, although I cannot say how welcome fare such as yours will be after so many days traveling."

Fehern's eyes flicked to Alcaren and the lumand the overcaptain carried.

"My lady requested that I bring the instrument," Alcaren said smoothly. "She thought you might enjoy some afterdinner music in the Ranuan tradition."

"Not sung, I trust?" asked the tall arms commander from behind Fehern's shoulder.

"Harmonies, no," replied Alcaren. "That would be regarded as sorcery in Ranuak." After the slightest pause, he added, "Or anywhere, I suppose."

"We could not bring you gifts, except perhaps for the gift of music," Secca continued. "And Alcaren is accomplished."

"You are most thoughtful, Sorceress Protector." Fehern offered a polite smile, then gestured toward the open double doors.

The dining hall was not overlarge, with a single long table capable of holding twoscore, and set for slightly more than half that. Fehern took the seat at the head, with Secca to his right, and Alcaren to his left, then Halyt beside Secca, and Palian beside Alcaren. Richina was placed above the overcaptains of both Secca's forces and those of Dumar, with several Dumaran captains below the salt.

Fehern gestured for the others to sit, then sat a moment later, leaning toward Secca. "Once the wine is poured, I will offer a welcome and a toast."

"You're most kind and gracious," replied the sorceress.

The wine poured by a servingwoman in brown was a pale amber, and once the server had reached the base of the long table, Fehern stood and lifted his goblet. "For seasons we have struggled against the Sturinnese, but now we will prevail, for we have the assistance of Defalk and one of its greatest sorceresses." He lifted his goblet. "To the Lady Secca and her forces."

"To the Lady Secca and her forces."

Almost immediately a handful of servers appeared with platters of food, all beginning at the head of the table. The meat seemed to be slabs of mutton rolled around a filling of some sort and covered with a white sauce, and the potatoes had been diced, mixed with cheese and spices, and baked again.

Secca sipped her wine sparingly, not difficult under the circumstances, since it was a vintage that had once been lush and was shading toward lush vinegar. Like Dumar, she reflected.

"Did you have any . . . difficulty . . . in reaching Envaryl?" asked the overcaptain farther down the table to Alcaren's left.

"There was a company of Sturinnese," Alcaren replied. "That was three days ago. They tried to ambush us, but Lady Secca discovered them in enough time that we dispatched them." He took a small sip of wine and broke off another chunk of the flat crackerlike dark bread.

"That is too bad," mused Fehern. "The survivors will report your arrival, and the Sea-Priests may attack sooner."

"There were no survivors," Secca said easily, "but that would not matter. The Sturinnese have sorcerers everywhere, and they doubtless know we are here."

"No survivors?" inquired Halyt, raising a single eyebrow.

"None," affirmed Alcaren.

"With all the companies of lancers they have, the Sea-Priests will scarce miss one," added Wilten.

"That is unhappily all too true, Overcaptain," replied Fehern. "Yet it is still an accomplishment to destroy an entire company of Sturinnese without casualties."

Secca laughed ruefully. "Lord Fehern, you give us great credit—more than we deserve. While we have managed this latest engagement without losing lancers, our efforts in reaching you have not been without casualties. We have already lost several companies."

"Several companies?" asked Halyt. "I presume, but I saw no wounded."

"Against the Sturinnese," Alcaren replied, "there are few wounded. There are the dead . . . and the survivors."

Halyt nodded slowly. "That, too, has been our experience. Yet, even against their sorcery and drums . . ."

"We can talk of tactics later," Fehern said smoothly, "when we meet to plan how we will attack the Sturinnese. For now, let us speak of other matters. And shortly, we will hear the overcaptain play."

Secca smiled politely. "He plays excellently, as you will hear."

"I am sure we will, Lady Sorceress." Fehern laughed warmly. "We will need to meet soon, however."

"Tomorrow morning?" suggested Secca. "At my villa at the second glass after dawn? The sooner, the better, do you not think?"

"Ah . . ." Fehern frowned.

"I will have a scrying glass set there so that you may see for yourself." Secca smiled warmly. "And so Halyt can see as well."

"Excellent." Fehern motioned to the servingwoman with the wine, then turned back to Secca. "You must tell me, and Halyt, how you found Ranuak, for none of us has ever traveled there. So much is rumored, yet so little is known."

"I had heard much as well, and I had never visited there, or Elahwa, either," Secca replied. "I was surprised to find Ranuak a poorer land than I had heard. All work, and every morgen of good land is tilled, yet without the fishing and the trade, I think that life in Ranuak would be hard indeed. They abhor sorcery, although the Matriarch was most polite, and we left as soon as we could." Secca laughed lightly. "That I am a sorceress may have added to her willingness to help us leave and come to Dumar."

"The Matriarch helped you?"

"She provided the vessels that carried us to Stygia," Secca admitted.

"And you did not encounter the white-hulled warships?"

"We saw not one," Secca replied.

Halyt looked at Alcaren. "Not one?"

"They had blockaded Encora for a time, but there were none on the seas when we left," Alcaren affirmed.

"But where . . . ?" mused Fehern

"To Neserea, we fear," Secca said. "To support the rebellion there."

The quickest of glances passed between Halyt and Fehern before the Lord High Counselor spoke again. "What of the city of Encora itself. Is it the marvel all say?"

"It has walls on the hills that surround it, and a deep and narrow channel that protects its harbor . . ." As Secca talked, she was all too conscious of how dangerously she wove truth and omission together into a misleading image. Yet there was much she did not wish Fehern to learn—not yet.

25

EAST OF ESARIA, NESEREA

Beyond the faded and heavy wall hangings that fail to keep the winter chill at bay, Clayre stands over the bare wood of the table in the small sitting room of Lord Nysl's keep. Her fingers touch the strings of the lutar, and she begins the spell.

> *"For all who seek me through spell and song*
> *let them see me sitting here as if here long.*
> *Let them see me use the spell and glass*
> *as days and moments come to pass.*
> *Yet a different view will unfold,*
> *for each time one seeks me to behold . . ."*

Clayre smiles as she finishes the spell. After a moment, she lowers the lutar and eases the instrument into the oiled leather case. Then she dons the leather riding jacket, picks up the saddlebags, and walks to the door of the chamber. The ancient oak door creaks on its iron straps as she opens it, and creaks again as she closes it behind her.

At the bottom of the narrow rear staircase, there is a small hall, whose stone walls are unadorned. There, Diltyr waits, beside the door that leads to the rear bailey and the stables. In one hand is a leather case within which is his violino. The other hand is empty. "The players are mounted and ready, Lady Clayre."

A white-haired man in a faded purple tunic trimmed with silver stands beside the chief player. He bows as he speaks. "For all of our sakes, I wish you well, Lady Sorceress."

"I thank you, Lord Nysl, both for your good wishes, and

for your hospitality. I wish you well in the weeks ahead."

"Thank you, lady." Nysl bows again.

"Thank you." Clayre acknowledges the bow with a grace-ful nod. Then she turns as Diltyr opens the bailey door and steps out into the dark gray of an overcast morning before dawn.

Side by side, she and Diltyr walk across the courtyard toward the stables, outside of which players and lancers are already forming up.

"He is relieved that we are departing," says Diltyr in a low voice.

Clayre nods brusquely. "That is to be expected."

"Will not Belmar see us in his glass? Even though we leave before dawn?"

"He will, but what he sees will not be what is." Clayre chuckles.

"With each season, sorcery becomes more devious," murmurs Diltyr.

"And more dangerous. We must make certain that the danger falls upon Belmar, and not upon us."

"That requires lighting a lamp with a short splinter, lady."

"Better than having no light, I think," replies the dark-haired sorceress with a laugh.

26

Once back in the guest villa after a too-long and not-too-enlightening dinner with Fehern, Secca opened the door onto the wide balcony and stepped outside into the night air. Alcaren hurried out after her, his hand on the hilt of his sabre, but the balcony was empty, and the loudest sounds were laughs from the barracks, muted by the brick walls, and the whispering of a wind that was too warm for winter and too chill for spring.

Secca stood at the balcony railing for several moments, looking skyward, but the intermittent clouds obscured any view of either moon. "So many words . . . so little said, and everyone listening for something."

"That is often true," Alcaren said.

"Was it that way in Ranuak?"

"Even less obvious, I fear, my lady. I am not good at such listening, and others would hear what I did not."

"I feel the same way, even here." Secca turned from the railing, and Alcaren followed.

After they had stepped back into the sitting room, Secca slid the door bolt into place, not that it would more than delay a determined intruder. "Did you notice who wasn't there?"

"The disguised Sea-Priest we've seen in the glass with Fehern—unless he was disguised in another fashion. Captain Kuttyr was near the bottom of the table, well away from any of us."

"That's both a precaution and a slight." Secca laughed. "Or a disciplinary action because he said too much to us."

"Or all three."

"What do you think of Fehern?"

"I don't trust him," replied Alcaren, "but he has little enough reason to trust us, either."

Secca yawned. "Dinners such as tonight are more tiring than riding."

"That could be because you rode this morning," he pointed out.

"What do we do when we meet with him tomorrow? Besides develop a battle plan that doesn't put us at his mercy?"

"That could be obvious," mused Secca's consort.

"We have to find a way to make it less so."

"Do we have to do that now?" asked Alcaren, glancing toward the bedchamber.

After a moment, and a shared flush, they both laughed.

27

WEI, NORDWEI

A shtaar is the last one to enter the council chamber, and all eyes focus on the silver-haired Council Leader as she takes her place in the middle of the long dark table. She does not speak immediately. Instead, in the muted light cast by the oil lamps in the sconces on the walls, she looks from one end of the table to the other. The room is silent, except for the breathing of those present, and the occasional rustle of garments.

Her voice is cold and firm when she speaks. "I have heard it said that the future of Liedwahr is being decided as we meet, on the high plains of Dumar somewhere near Envaryl." A tight crooked smile appears, showing teeth shockingly white and even for one so old as Ashtaar. "I would like to say there might be a grain of truth in such a saying, but I doubt that. Our seers have followed the shadowsinger of Defalk. Like the one before her, she is no fool. She did not land at Narial, but picked a small fishing port to the west. She had almost reached Envaryl before the Sturinnese realized her plans and gathered their forces. The sorceress has joined with Lord High Counselor Fehern and is poised to sweep the Sturinnese from Dumar." Ashtaar glances around the Council room. "That is as it appears. Especially in war, early appearances can be deceiving."

"How might they be deceiving, Leader Ashtaar?" asks the balding and young-faced man in gold-trimmed brown. His voice carries both apparent earnestness and an almost-hidden sarcasm. "The Sorceress Protector defeated the Sturinnese in Ebra and destroyed the Sea-Priest fleet off Encora."

The momentary glitter hardens Ashtaar's eyes, but her smile is polite. "High Trader Fuhlar . . . you may recall the Sea-Priest fleet in the Ostisles? It is now northwest of Landende, clearly on its way to Esaria as soon as the ice melts, and perhaps sooner, if the Sea-Priests choose to employ sorcery. But it could turn south at any time. The Liedfuhr of Mansuur has been forced to split his lancers, for even he cannot afford to leave Wharsus undefended, much as he dislikes a greater Sturinnese presence in Liedwahr and much as he would prefer to stand by his sister. By the time the snows melt and allow his lancers in Unduval to cross the Mittpass, they will face a ride of two weeks or more to reach Esaria, and he will be able to send but a third of the force he had earlier assembled."

Ashtaar's gaze rakes across those at the table. She swallows silently to forestall a cough.

"How does this affect the Sorceress Protector in Dumar?" asks a burly man in dark blue.

"The Sturinnese will not fight her unless they can be assured of an easy victory. They will march and retreat, evade and skirmish, and attempt to force her into hasty action because they know that she knows her sister sorceress cannot prevail in Neserea without her aid."

"That will only delay her, from what we have seen," suggests Marshal Zeltaar.

"No." The hard and low negative comes from the hooded Lady of the Shadows. "She will grow impatient, and she will call forth greater sorcery, and the Sea-Priests will be prepared and respond with even greater sorcery—and we will see a disaster greater than the creation of the Zauberinfeuer. It could easily be greater than the Spell-Fire Wars or, the harmonies forbid, the Pelaran Devastation."

"Those are strong words, lady," suggests Fuhlar.

"There is another possibility," Ashtaar says slowly, waiting until all eyes are back on her before continuing. "The shadowsinger may indeed be most effective in her sorceries, and they may be greater than the Sea-Priests anticipate. She has outmatched them so far. According to our seers and calculations, the spells she used to destroy the Sea-Priest fleet should have recoiled and killed any sorceress or sorcerer. They did not."

"They prostrated her," points out Fuhlar.

"It might be most interesting to discover how you found that out, Fuhlar," Ashtaar says slowly, "but that will wait for another time. Would you care to make the conclusion you so carefully interrupted?"

There are smothered smiles around the table.

Fuhlar clears his throat. "You wish us to conclude that the shadowsinger and her compatriots may be powerful enough to destroy the Sturinnese totally in Liedwahr and then unite both Dumar and Neserea under Lord Robero's rule."

"If they succeed against the Sturinnese," Ashtaar says deliberately, "that is highly likely. Lord Robero will not wish a repetition of what has just occurred. Ebra is well on the way to becoming a part of Defalk, and Dumar has shown itself weak and unable to resist invaders. Were you Lord Robero, what would you do?"

"He may do otherwise," suggests a figure in maroon.

"When has he done the unpredictable in the past half-score of years?" The scorn in Ashtaar's voice is almost venomous. "Still . . . there is something else to consider, don't you think, Marshal Zeltaar?"

The black-clad marshal offers a nod. "The Sturinnese have planned all of this very carefully. They may well be playing a far deeper dissonance."

Fuhlar raises his eyebrows in disbelief.

"What if . . ." The marshal pauses. "What if the battles in Dumar leave Fehern and his kin dead, and the sorceresses contend with the Sea-Priests in Neserea . . . and lose?"

Ashtaar nods.

After a silence, the Lady of the Shadows clears her throat. "I will be the one to state the obvious. There would be no one left in Ebra, Dumar, Neserea, or Defalk capable of stopping them."

"Either alternative is intolerable," Fuhlar says. "It will serve us ill to have Liedwahr dominated by either Defalk or Sturinn."

"Can you suggest another?" asks Ashtaar quietly. "If you can, we would all like to hear it."

There are glances exchanged, and frowns around the table, but none speaks.

28

Secca and Alcaren stood in the entry foyer of the villa, a foyer empty of decorations and wall decorations, as indeed was the entire villa, looking through the narrow windows that flanked the closed double doors. Outside, the day was gray, threatening both rain and wind. A squad of the SouthWomen lancers was drawn up as an honor guard for Fehern, with Captain Peraghn mounted in front of them. Secca's overcaptains and chief players were already gathered in the upper-level sitting room.

"Do you think he will come?" asked Alcaren.

"How can he not?" replied Secca. "He needs us more than we need him. Also, it would show fear or distrust for him not to come." She laughed. "He will keep us waiting, and he will have an excuse for that. He will be most apologetic, pleading the press of something."

"I would scarce wager against you on that," replied Alcaren, shrugging his overly broad shoulders. "In truth, I'd scarce wager against you on anything." His gray-blue eyes sparkled as he beheld his consort.

"You say that because you love me."

He laughed. "True as that may be, I'd not have wagered

against you from the day I met you, and that was before I came to love you."

"You speak so fairly—"At the sound of hoofs, Secca opened the doors and positioned herself on the top step of the four that led down to the entry lane, and the sole mounting block there. A clammy mist drifted out of the north, thick enough that the villa to the north was but a blurred shape.

Fehern rode up at the head of a column that comprised a good two companies of lancers. The Lord High Counselor, wearing an oiled gray leather riding jacket over his crimson tunic, reined up by the mounting block and immediately dismounted. Behind him, Halyt and two overcaptains dismounted.

Secca waited as the four walked toward her, then spoke as they started up the steps. "Greetings, Lord High Counselor."

"Greetings, Lady Sorceress. I beg your pardon, but a messenger arrived just as I was leaving." Fehern shrugged. "You understand, I am certain."

"I do indeed. The others are waiting upstairs."

"Others?"

"Just my overcaptains and my chief players." Secca smiled. "The chief players must know so that they can position the players, and so they can inform us if there are situations where the players could not play. One cannot assume that sorcery is equally effective all the time."

"Ah . . . no, but you would know best about such." Fehern smiled indulgently.

Secca kept smiling as she led the way up the stairs, even as she bridled inside at the condescension that welled from the dark-haired lord.

Once they entered the sitting room, with the long conference table, Secca gestured to those waiting. "You recall my overcaptains, Wilten and Delcetta, and my chief players, Palian and Delvor?"

Fehern nodded. "This is Halyt, my arms commander, and Overcaptains Sterkan and Gedhar."

The four chairs were for Fehern and Halyt, and for Secca and Alcaren. Secca offered the chair at one end to Fehern, and took the one at the other end. Alcaren sat to Secca's left, across from Halyt. The other seven people in the room formed a rough oval around the table, standing back several paces.

"The first question," Secca began, "is where might be best to set a battle to halt the Sturinnese. We have looked at the maps, and in the glass, and they show a line of steep hills some deks east of a small town, the closest true town to Envaryl."

"Hasjyl," supplied Halyt. "Some call the hills the east walls of Hasjyl." He laughed heartily. "Most just claim they are a creation of dissonance."

"We should see them." Secca stood and slipped on the copper-tipped gloves, then lifted the lutar, the sole instrument in evidence, and began the spellsong.

> *"Show us now and with details still
> those hills just east of Hasjyl . . ."*

The glass silvered, then displayed the rough and rocky hillside that was but partly covered by winter-tan grass. To the right side of the image was a narrow road, and to the left the Envaryl River.

"You see," pointed out Halyt, "one must cross the river and take a long circular trail for days to avoid the hill route."

"Where would the long way take them, were the Sturinnese to use it?" asked Wilten pleasantly.

"They would have to ford the river west of Hasjyl about four deks, or follow the south side of the river all the way to Envaryl."

"So we would have the advantage if we are rested and upon the heights of Hasjyl before the Sturinnese arrive?" queried Secca.

"So much as any have an advantage against the white priests." Fehern snorted.

"Where do your scouts show the Sturinnese to be?" queried Halyt.

"This morning the reports from scouts and from the glass showed that the main body of the Sturinnese is a two-day ride—a full two-day ride—east of Hasjyl."

"How many might there be?" prompted Halyt.

"Close to sixtyscore," Secca admitted.

"And together we have less than twenty," replied the Dumaran arms commander.

"We also have the use of sorcery," Alcaren suggested.

Halyt frowned, but did not respond.

"What if the Sturinnese do not come to Hasjyl?" asked Fehern.

"Then, we think about how we should attack them," Secca replied. "If they do not come to us, we will indeed have time to consider how to go to them."

"That is true," mused Fehern. "You said that the Sturinnese could make Hasjyl in two days, but when would you think the Sturinnese will actually reach Hasjyl?"

"From where they are . . ." Secca glanced to Alcaren, although she could have answered the question.

"At the pace they are making, four days, perhaps five. They are also sending out squads as scouts. Not all of those are returning to the main body, but none are near Envaryl or Hasjyl as of yet."

"You seem certain of that, Overcaptain," offered Halyt. "How certain?"

Alcaren shrugged. "For now, most certain. As they move west, it will be harder to tell."

"Oh?"

"Past Hasjyl, the high plains and fields look most similar in a glass, and we do not have enough lancers to send scouts in all directions."

"Nor do we," admitted Halyt.

"What sort of plan do you intend, Lady Sorceress?" asked Fehern. "Or do your overcaptains handle the battle plans?"

"Alcaren works with Wilten and Delcetta, and then we talk over what they think and what can be done with sorcery. We use sorcery from higher ground where possible, and against their sorcerers first, then against the first waves of attackers."

"Would they not do the same against you?" countered Fehern.

"They did at Elahwa," Secca admitted.

"How did you handle such?"

"We took a ridge below their position and began lofting arrows into their drummers and sorcerers. That forced them to attack." Secca shrugged. While that had not been exactly what happened, she wasn't about to reveal the full details.

Halyt laughed. "Like stirring up a nest of red ants . . . so mad they don't think, I expect."

"It did work," Secca said.

"If . . . if the Sturinnese continue to advance slowly today, we should leave the morning after tomorrow," suggested Fehern. "Tomorrow, if they ride hard today."

Secca nodded.

"You and your lancers . . . would you prefer the left or the right?"

"The center," Secca replied. "If we are on either wing, I cannot so easily protect the far wing with sorcery."

"Ah . . . but that would split my forces, and to command such . . ." Fehern frowned.

"It does not have to be so," Alcaren offered smoothly. "The Lady Secca takes a position almost in the center, with but one company to one side, and your forces beyond that . . ."

"Yes . . . almost centered . . . like sorcery . . ." Halyt offered another hearty laugh.

Secca smiled once more, hoping she could just keep smiling while the other details were discussed.

29

ENVARYL, DUMAR

In the darkness of the night, there is a tapping, and then a creaking, and then a glow as a man with a hooded lamp slips through the sitting room toward the door to the sleeping chamber. A scraping and another creaking follow as the man with the lamp eases toward the figure in the triple-width bed.

"Lord . . ." The voice is low.

The man bolts awake, and a shimmering short blade appears in his right hand as he lunges toward the man with the lamp, then lowers the blade. "Elyzar . . . I could have killed you." His voice is thick, and he shakes his head, but does not lower the blade farther. "It must be the sixth glass of the night. Why are you here? And how did you get in?"

"I suggested to the guard that the matter was urgent."

In the dimness, Fehern's eyes narrow.

"Lord . . . there is someone to see you."

"At this glass?"

"It is better during this glass than when others might see," offers Elyzar cryptically.

"Oh? And why might that be?"

"You will see, lord."

"Why should I? Why can't he come at a decent glass, whoever he is?" Fehern still does not lower the blade farther.

"To see him could cost you nothing, and it might be advantageous."

"Why?" snaps Fehern.

"He is a Sea-Priest, who wishes to speak with you."

Fehern frowns. "Why would he wish to see me . . . unless . . ." He shakes his head. "All right . . ." The Lord High

Counselor pulls on his trousers, a rumpled tunic, and his boots, then his belt, to which he clips his sabre scabbard, but the weapon remains in his hand. "Where is he?"

"On the balcony, lord."

Fehern crosses the sleeping chamber, then walks to the balcony door, which is bolted. He turns to Elyzar. "How did he get out there?"

"He said he had his ways, and that it would be better if he were outside."

Fehern slides the bolt, then opens the glass-paned door. He steps into the outer darkness and glances around. Chill air seeps around him as he surveys the covered balcony. He stops as he sees a tall cloaked figure standing by the balcony railing. In the distance is a sound like muted thunder, if more rhythmic. Fehern frowns and turns his head, then focuses on the man in the deep gray shadow cloak, who steps forward.

"Lord Fehern."

"Who are you?"

"You know whom I represent. Who else could it be? We have an offer for you."

"Oh? Why should I listen?" Fehern's sleep-roughened voice takes on a sardonic tone.

"Because it is in your interest to listen. There will be a battle. Perhaps there will be many battles. We *will* prevail, but it will be costly. We would rather not lose scores upon scores of lancers."

"Especially with the Liedfuhr of Mansuur considering whether to hurl thousands at you from the north once the snows melt?"

"Let us say that we would prefer a solution that does not squander the lives of valuable armsmen and lancers. Let us say that such battles would be more to our liking and to yours were the Sorceress Protector of the East not present and unable to prolong them."

"Dead, you mean?"

"Let us not concern ourselves with precise terminology.

It matters not *how*, so long as she cannot sing."

Fehern remains silent for several moments. After some silence, he asks, "Why should I trust you?"

"Lord Fehern . . . after these battles you will rule Dumar only under sufferance. It could be our sufferance or Lord Robero's, but it will be sufferance."

"You presume . . . You presume much." Fehern's voice is edged.

"I presume nothing. I could as easily have entered your chamber and killed you while you slept as come to talk to you." A soft laugh issues from the shadowed face.

"That well may be. You did not. That alone proves that you need something from me. It does not provide me with any assurance for what may happen later."

"No. It does not. I would point out that you are a man with few options. Lord Robero and all his sorceresses know that your accession was, shall we say, irregular. To the Maitre, that matters not, so long as a man is the one in charge of Dumar. Have you not noticed the suspicion with which the sorceress and her party regard you?"

"How would you know whether they are suspicious or not?"

"We have our ways." Another soft laugh follows the words. "They do not trust you, and they will never trust you. We do not need to trust you because we can follow whatever you do."

"So I would be the Maitre's puppet? I don't think so."

"You will be as free as any other territorial regent, and that is much to be preferred over being dead."

"You presume that the sorceress will fail."

"Is that presumptuous? Has Sturinn *ever* failed to conquer a land where its ships and lancers have landed?"

"How about Dumar . . . or Ebra?"

"In the past, we did not devote our full forces here. That is not the instance now."

"That may be." Fehern pauses. "Even if you are correct, and there is much doubt about that . . ."

"I do not need an answer now. It will be several days before any battle is joined. Your actions will provide the answer." Another laugh whispers through the cold night air. "Best you think carefully, Lord Fehern."

Fehern stands silently for a moment.

The cloaked figure offers a bow, then steps over the balcony railing and rappels down a rope to the courtyard below. Silence and shadows swallow his form, and Fehern can hear or see nothing.

The Lord High Counselor walks back into the chamber, bolting the outside door. "Elyzar?"

There is no sound.

Slowly, his sabre out, Fehern eases toward the sitting room side table with the lamp. He fumbles with the striker one-handedly, finally lighting the oil lamp, and looking around the sitting room as the orange glow illuminates the chamber. It remains empty. He slips toward the bedchamber door, pulling it open and waiting with the sabre at the ready. He can see no one in the smaller sleeping room.

After several moments, he steps back, picks up the lamp, and walks around the sleeping chamber. No one is there. He steps back into the main chamber, lamp still in one hand, sabre in the other, but finds no sign of anyone.

Finally, the Lord High Counselor of Dumar steps toward the main chamber door, the one to the main corridor. He reaches for the inside bolt. His fingers touch the cold iron. The door is still bolted on the inside—but his chambers are empty, the windows shuttered, and the doors to the balcony bolted. And he had not seen Elyzar leave by the balcony.

30

O ut of the south came a gentle warm breeze under a
sun that hinted that spring might be at last truly on
its way. Even a faint scent of warming earth drifted past
Secca now and again. Her riding jacket but loosely fastened
in the late-morning warmth, Secca rode beside Richina,
with Palian and Delvor directly behind them, and with the
players following the chief players. There was almost a dek
between the last of Secca's force—a company of Delcetta's
SouthWomen—and the Dumaran forces, where Fehern rode
alongside Halyt in the fore of the Dumaran vanguard.

For the moment, Alcaren rode in the van of Secca's
forces, with Wilten, while Delcetta rode behind the last company of Defalkan lancers, from where she could watch the
SouthWomen—and Fehern.

"A better morning than most of late," offered Richina.

"That it is. We should see warmer days in the weeks
ahead," Secca affirmed. "That will be good, since we will
doubtless be riding much."

"That was why you had the lancers take as much provender as we could?"

"One reason."

"Fehern's men do not seem so heavy laden."

"It is his land," said Secca dryly, "and he may have other
views of the days ahead. Not everyone trusts a scrying glass
as we do."

"But Fehern wasn't surprised by the scrying glass," mentioned Richina, riding beside Secca. "And he never even
looked at me."

"Good," replied Secca. "Still, you must be prepared to
use the flame spell, the short one, against anyone who looks

to attack me or Alcaren—or any of the players if I'm not around or occupied."

"You trust him not at all?"

"I trust no one who comes to power in ways that cannot be seen," replied Secca, in a low voice. "A viper does not use its fangs but once."

"Your pardon, Lady Secca . . . but . . . if that be the case . . . ?" Richina's eyebrows lifted quizzically.

"What choice have we? If we do not rid Dumar of the Sturinnese, then we will be fighting all of their forces in both Dumar and in Neserea . . . and, before long, in Ebra once more. For the moment, the Maitre cannot bring more sorcerers and lancers to both Dumar and Neserea. If we can triumph here before summer . . . then we can travel north to aid Clayre."

"Could we not . . . ?" Richina glanced back, in the direction of Fehern and the Dumarans.

"Then we might find ourselves fighting both, as we did in Ebra. For the moment . . . we must only fight the Sturinnese . . . if they will indeed fight."

"You do not think that they will march to Hasjyl?"

"Only far enough to make sure that we must maneuver to keep them from taking Envaryl. They will feint, and march south, or north, so that we must either hasten after them, or hold a position. They may send skirmishers or patrols to extend us, but they will try to avoid a full battle."

"But why? They do not fear you that much, do they?"

"I doubt they fear me at all, but they will be cautious," Secca replied, with a faint smile. "Let us see what the morrow brings."

31

ITZEL, NESEREA

Belmar pours the dark red wine into the two crystal goblets that sit on the small circular table between the two chairs upholstered in green velvet facing the fire in the hearth of the keep's study, then seats himself in the vacant chair. "This is good wine. I thought you might appreciate it, master jerGlien."

"Good wine is always to be appreciated, Lord Belmar." With a smile, jerGlien lifts the goblet, studying it momentarily. "As is good crystal. Is this from Neserea?"

"Of course. There's a holding east of Sperea where they make it and etch it." Belmar frowns. "The name escapes me . . . Lyssin, that's it. The lands were almost part of the holdings Cloftus had. So I suppose they belong to me now . . . or they will." He sips the wine. "Why did you ask?"

"It's good enough to be traded anywhere, and fine crystal brings a truly remarkable return in Pelara and even in some parts of the Ostisles."

"What about in Sturinn?"

"There, too." The Sturinnese takes a small sip of the wine. "This is good, but it might be too delicate to travel far. Like a beautiful woman, it must be restrained and kept close to home."

"Speaking of traveling, we ride out a week from now," Belmar announces, smiling broadly. "All is arranged." He takes a healthy swallow of wine.

"That did not take you long."

"Why should it? Chyalar and Motolla are pleased to know that I will be departing, even if they must wait a week. They will be less than pleased that a squad and some of the play-

ers are remaining, along with you and a junior captain."
Belmar grins boyishly. "I do look like a junior captain, do
I not?"

"By itself, that will not deceive the sorceress."

"Of course not." Belmar takes yet another swallow of
wine from the crystal goblet. "This is indeed good wine."

"I fancy the crystal more." The man in gray gestures for
Belmar to continue. "You were saying?"

"In the morning before we leave, we will sing the spell
that will create the necessary seemings. Whenever anyone
looks for me in a glass, they will find the man who rides
my horse or wears my blue tunic."

"And when you sleep?"

Belmar frowns. "Perhaps I should part with my seal ring."

"That might be better," suggests jerGlien. "It will take
less sorcery as well, because the ring is associated with you
more strongly than are the clothes or the mount. I assume
the lancer who will wear it resembles you?"

"He has dark hair and blue eyes, and he was bearded, but
will be clean-shaven before dawn. I've told him and those
of my personal guard who will accompany him that we will
be rejoining them in a few days, but that we have a dangerous mission that can best be accomplished with but a
handful of lancers." The Lord of Worlan laughs. "All that
is true, so far as it goes."

"What of the Sorceress of Defalk?"

"The glass shows that she remains in Nysl's hold, using
her glass to follow us. Much good it will do her."

"I had thought she might have acted by now," muses the
man in gray.

"Perhaps she has received some word from Lord Robero?"

"It is too soon for such, I would judge. He must be persuaded with great patience and the greatest of care. As you
must be when the Lady Clayre confronts you."

"So I will be, timid as she has been in coming against
us."

"Timid? Or careful?"

"There are times when there is little difference. Fortune favors the bold now."

"So it does. So it does," replies jerGlien with a hearty laugh.

Belmar laughs as well, then takes another sip of the wine, stretching slightly, and enjoying the warmth of the fire.

Unnoticed by the younger man, jerGlien has scarcely drunk any of the dark red vintage.

32

I n the midafternoon light, with the sun falling on her back with welcome warmth, Secca reined up on the low rise looking out over the rough and rocky hills east of Hasjyl.

"Lady?" asked Wilten, also reining up beside her and gesturing toward the lancers waiting on the road to her left.

"Have them remain mounted for a bit. I'll need to check the glass."

The overcaptain nodded.

Secca turned the gray mare and looked toward Palian and Delvor. "Keep them close. I don't think they'll need to play, but we'll have to see."

"We stand ready."

Still mounted, Secca eased the gray around and studied the terrain to the east again. The road wound downhill—and was empty. As far as she could see to the east, there was no one on the dirt track, and not even a sign of dust. A wry smile crossed her face.

"You're scarcely surprised, are you?" asked Alcaren. He and Richina had halted their mounts behind Secca.

"I'd have been surprised if there *had* been any sign of the Sturinnese."

"Where do you think they are?" asked Richina.

"They could be waiting along the river road. They could have headed south to try to go around us. Or they could have split their forces."

Alcaren nodded. "If they split . . . then they think that they could attack successfully with whichever force you do not engage."

"That is if they believe I am the sole sorceress."

"Why would they think otherwise?" asked Richina.

"All it would take would be for one of them to see you in a glass singing and playing."

"They might still think that I was merely accompanying you," Richina pointed out. "No one knows of me, not beyond our lancers and a few armsmen in Ebra."

"And Haddev," suggested Secca. "But your point is well taken. Haddev would say little, and few in Liedwahr wish to speak openly of sorceresses."

"Haddev . . . that seems years ago," mused Richina.

Secca hoped so. She dismounted and unstrapped the lutar and leather-wrapped traveling glass. "Best we see which before Fehern arrives."

"He is about a dek behind Delcetta's rear guard," noted Alcaren, who had also dismounted.

Richina belatedly followed their example, then led the three mounts to Gorkon, for the lancer to hold the reins and watch.

Secca quickly tuned the lutar while Alcaren unwrapped the mirror and set it on a flat section of grass on top of its leather wrappings. Then she sang the spell Alcaren had used earlier.

"Show us where upon a map of this land
these forces of Sturinn now do stand . . ."

The map displayed by the glass showed the Sturinnese in two places. The larger force, from the size of the pulsing star, perhaps as many as fortyscore, looked to be roughly ten deks southeast of where her forces were and upon the south road that circled Hasjyl. Secca noted that a short and narrow road appeared to head due west and intersect the route that had brought the Defalkan and SouthWomen forces to Envaryl.

"That will take them days to reach Envaryl," Alcaren observed.

"If that is indeed what they have in mind."

The smaller group of Sturinnese lancers—if a group larger than the Defalkan and Dumaran lancers together could be called small—had ridden due north, or so it seemed, from their last encampment.

"They are headed for the trade pass," Secca said, immediately singing the release couplet, since she did not want to hold the image any longer than she needed to.

"To use sorcery to block it, you think?" asked Richina.

"I would judge so." Alcaren looked at Secca. "If you use sorcery to clear the pass, it will take longer and weaken you for several days—and that would be after fighting our way to the pass."

"They don't want you to go to Neserea, do they?" Richina glanced back along the road, which followed the ridgeline from Hasjyl. The outbuildings of the town were more than two deks back to the west and barely visible against the hazy horizon. "Here comes Lord Fehern. He's riding a trace faster."

"He would, now that he knows the Sturinnese are nowhere around." Secca's tone was biting.

Richina tilted her head slightly in puzzlement.

"If they were near, we'd have drawn up in battle formation, and the players would be tuning," the older sorceress explained. She finished repacking the mirror and handed it to Alcaren, who fastened it behind Secca's saddle. The gray mare raised her head slightly from nibbling at the dry grass, then lowered it again.

Secca crossed the grass that crackled under her boots, releasing dustlike particles that drifted down in the still air, and took the gray's reins from Gorkon. "Thank you. It looks as though we will not fight today. Nor tomorrow, probably."

Gorkon smiled. "We can wait."

Secca wondered if they could ... and how long. She climbed into the saddle, conscious once again that, unlike the long-legged Richina, she had to climb every time she mounted. Then she turned the gray and eased her mount back toward the road to wait for the approaching Lord High Counselor of Dumar. Alcaren and Richina remounted and followed her, then halted their mounts at the south shoulder of the road behind Secca.

All three watched as Fehern neared, then reined up a good five yards short of Secca, Halyt beside him.

"The Sturinnese do not appear to be anywhere close to here." Fehern looked theatrically to the east.

"Since morning they have changed their path and split their forces," Secca said. "One group is headed north, toward the trade pass to Neserea. The other has taken the road you mentioned, the one that circles Hasjyl to the south."

"And whatever group we pursue, the other will act unopposed?"

"That would seem to be their aim," Secca admitted.

"What will you do, Lady Sorceress? We cannot ride across Dumar chasing them."

Secca knew that all too well. "No. That is what they want." She smiled politely. "I had thought that was possible. Now we know, and we will act accordingly."

"And how might that be?"

"Finding a different way to reach them and destroy them. Do you have another idea?"

Fehern's eyes shifted past Secca's shoulder, looking beyond the sorceress. "Your ... handmaiden ... she is most comely," Fehern murmured.

Secca understood all too well what Fehern meant. "She is indeed. She also comes from one of the more powerful families of the Thirty-three." Secca smiled warmly. "If you would like to consider her as a consort, Lord Fehern, I am sure both Lord Robero and Lady Dinfan would entertain your request."

"Dinfan? That is not a name I recall," replied the dark-haired lord smoothly.

"The demesne of Suhl," Secca added. "Her father is also the brother of Lord Birfels, who holds Abenfel."

"Ah . . . yet she travels with you?"

"Her parents believe she has much to learn." Secca smiled again. "We should repair back to Hasjyl, where the lancers and players can find some quarters. We will leave sentries posted here and overlooking the south road." She paused but briefly. "We will watch the Sturinnese and work out a way to trap them. Then, we will meet early in the morning to discuss it with you." Secca forced yet another smile. "I trust that will meet with your approval?"

"I am not terribly interested in plans, Lady Sorceress. I need results to reclaim my land."

"I need results as well, Lord Fehern. It is difficult to obtain them if one does not plan well. I look forward to your thoughts, and, if you have a better battle plan, to hearing it."

Fehern offered a smile barely more than polite. "Halyt and I will be there, wherever you are."

"We look forward to seeing you."

After a barely perceptible bow, Fehern turned his mount. Secca kept a polite smile on her face.

"He would have liked to have cut you down in the saddle, dearest lady," Alcaren murmured once Fehern was a good hundred yards away on the road back to Hasjyl.

"I know. I'm not charging off and immediately slaying the Sturinnese and handing Dumar back to him, and I'm not turning Richina over to him for his pleasure. So he's angry."

"He is also worried."

"That is more to be concerned over than is his anger," Secca admitted.

The three watched as the Dumaran lancers turned and began to retrace their route back to Hasjyl.

33

HASJYL, DUMAR

The three men sit around a table in a small sitting room, lit but by a single twin-branched candelabra that is far older than any of them. Each has a mug before him, and there is a crockery pitcher on the table near the base of the candelabra.

"I do not like that woman, nor her consort, always lurking behind her. He smiles most pleasantly, and he sings sweetly, and I trust him not at all. And the young one, the one who looks pleasing, why . . ." Fehern shakes his head. "It makes little sense. She was telling the truth about that . . . Richina."

"Even I could tell that," Halyt says with a deep laugh. "The young one looks like a lady, demure, well-bred, and well-spoken."

"Why is she here? On a battle campaign?" asks Fehern, his voice betraying exasperation. "Were it not for the sorceress's consort, I would almost say that the older woman had more than casual affection for the younger."

"A love triangle, you think? Ah . . . what a thought!" Halyt's laugh rumbles forth uncontained. "Both of them are beauties, in different ways."

"No. I am missing something." Fehern shakes his head, then looks at the sorcerer. "What think you, Elyzar? What does your glass show?"

"The sorceress and the Ranuan are indeed consorted, and never have I seen the younger woman with them in such." Elyzar's eyes do not meet Fehern's, not exactly.

"So why is she here?" demands Fehern again.

"Perhaps what the sorceress said was not all that far from

the truth," suggests the man in gray. "Perhaps Lord Robero wishes to bind you more closely to Defalk."

"A consort forced upon me?"

"Not exactly. Who was the Lord High Counselor when the sorceress left Defalk?" questions Elyzar.

"Oh . . ." Fehern nods. "Now . . . now the sorceress is uncertain of what she should do?"

"Or she has received word that she is not to offer the lady to you," muses Halyt. "A shame to miss such a choice morsel because you are not your brother."

"Clehar did suggest that he be given a consort of worth," Fehern says slowly. "The idiot told me that much, as if begging that fop in Falcor would gain him anything." He shakes his head. "So again, I am to be denied? Most consorts required by necessity are pigs. Here is one beautiful and demure, and she is fine for Clehar, but not for Fehern?"

"The sorceress did say you could ask Lord Robero," offers the arms commander. "Perhaps she is not empowered to grant such."

"Aye, you could *ask*," Elyzar repeats.

"What mean you?" snaps Fehern. "Say it outright."

"She does not expect Lord Robero to grant the woman to you. Lord Robero will not go against the sorceress's wishes. He cannot, for the sorceresses are the source of much of his power." Elyzar shrugs. "Is that not clear? Defalk is not Sturinn. In Sturinn, as used to be in Dumar, a male ruled both his keep and his land."

"And I do not?"

Elyzar shrugs again. "It is not my place to say. You know what you know. You know what you must do. I am but a humble self-learned sorcerer barely gifted enough to use a glass or offer a small spellsong here or there."

"Nothing has been the same since that miserable sorceress came from the Mist Worlds." Fehern snorts, his voice rising as he continues. "Everywhere one must look over his shoulder for fear of a woman running to a sorceress, or a sorceress destroying everything a man has striven for and built."

"Not everywhere," replies Halyt with another deep laugh. "I can't see the Sturinnese worrying about women. They chain them and cut out the tongues of sorceresses when they're young."

"Someone should have done that to this one," snaps the Lord High Counselor, "but no, I must bow and scrape if I am to have her assistance. Yes, Lady Sorceress . . . no, Lady Sorceress . . . if you please, Lady Sorceress . . ."

"That is true, if you require the sorceress's assistance," says Elyzar mildly. "Would you rather do without such? What are your alternatives?"

"If I do . . . *if* . . . if I do . . ." He looks at the sorcerer and then at Halyt. "You both may go. I need to consider." His voice drops. "That I do."

Elyzar and Halyt exchange glances before rising, bowing, and then departing, leaving Fehern holding a mug of wine, a vintage well past its prime and ready to turn.

34

The yellow brick dwelling was most modest, with a sitting room on one side and a dining area off the kitchen on the other side of the lower level, and a narrow staircase leading up to two bedchambers on the second level. One reason why Secca had taken over the house was that the merchant who owned it had fled, according to the sole servant remaining. Another was that it was located on the top of a low rise, and there was an inn across the street with a stable and outbuildings. That allowed Secca to have two companies both under roof and nearby while she decided how best to deal with the Sturinnese—and Fehern.

The sky was still the gray of the time just before sunrise and under thin clouds when Secca stepped into space behind the front door—a half foyer between the two rooms on the lower level. Through the narrow window, she could see both lancers—Gorkon and Dymen—stationed at the door as guards—and the squad of SouthWomen mounted and stationed on the street between the inn and the dwelling.

Breakfast had been bread and cheese, with a little cold mutton she had been able to choke down, and she found herself quietly burping from the impact of the heavy food on her system.

"Are you all right?" asked Alcaren, stepping up behind her and sliding his arms around her narrow waist.

"I'll be fine. The mutton was heavy."

"It will stick with you."

"Whether I want it to or not?" Secca laughed, leaning back into Alcaren's arms and enjoying the moment.

Behind her, she heard the sound of Richina's boots coming down the staircase. Almost simultaneously, there was a *thrap* on the weathered oak door.

"The overcaptains and chief players, Lady Secca."

"Once more," Secca murmured before replying, "have them come in."

She turned and touched Alcaren's cheek, then stepped back through the narrow archway toward the sitting room where an assemblage of ill-matched chairs and stools had been circled around a rectangular table. Her lutar was propped in the rear corner against the wall, although she doubted she would be using it for the meeting.

Alcaren picked up a length of shimmering iron that Secca had not seen before.

"What is that?" asked Richina.

"A lance, a short one," Alcaren replied, setting it in the outside corner of the sitting room, the corner farthest from the table, so that the lance rested against the wall. "It's for throwing, but it's not something very useful in battle."

Richina's brow furrowed, but she did not question him as Palian, Delvor, Wilten, and Delcetta stepped into the entryway of the small dwelling.

Secca glanced at Alcaren, and then at the lance, raising her eyebrows in inquiry.

"It may be useful for other matters in the future. I was considering—" He glanced toward those entering. "Later," he said with a smile.

Secca nodded and moved toward the table.

Dymen closed the door after the two chief players and two overcaptains had entered the dwelling.

"Sit down . . . as best you can," offered Secca, gesturing toward the motley assortment of chairs and stools, and then taking a simple straight-backed chair.

Richina took the high stool, and Alcaren a lower one beside Secca.

"What will you propose to Lord Fehern, if we might ask?" inquired the gray-haired Palian.

"That we pursue the group to the south, while he sends a small force northward, in order to keep the Sturinnese guarding the trade pass."

"Do you trust him?" asked Palian. "After what he has done?"

"I have my doubts," Secca replied. At the sound of hoofs, she glanced out through the leftmost of the narrow windows. Fehern had reined up outside the dwelling, along with Halyt. A full company, if not more, of Dumaran lancers was drawn up in formation opposite the inn, across the street from the SouthWomen, and less than twenty yards to the south of the window through which Secca looked.

Secca rose, as did the others.

Fehern stepped into the dwelling, followed by Halyt. Both wore leather riding jackets, unfastened, and a single Dumaran overcaptain followed them. Fehern's sabre rattled against the narrow doorjamb as he made his entrance. The Lord High Counselor of Dumar offered a broad smile. "Good morning to all."

"Indeed it is." Halyt followed his words with a hearty laugh. "And may the day get better as it dawns brighter."

Murmurs of response answered the pleasantry.

Fehern settled into the chair left for him across from Secca, not bothering to remove his jacket. Secca seated herself, as did Halyt and the others. The Dumaran overcaptain stood back a pace, but between the chairs taken by Halyt and Fehern.

"What have you discovered of the whereabouts of the Sturinnese, Lady Sorceress?" inquired Fehern, almost indifferently.

"They remain split into two bodies. The northmost force is half the size of the one to the south of us. The southern force has the greater share of drummers and archers. That would lead one to believe that there are more sorcerers with the southern force as well." Secca smiled politely.

"So we will attack the southern force?"

"I had thought that you would ride toward the northern force," Secca suggested. "They are farther away. If you make a deliberate pace, then it will take several days. Except you will return to Envaryl if it appears they are moving toward you."

"A decoy? We would be a decoy?" Fehern frowned. "Ten companies as a decoy?"

"Only for the first few days. Then we would rejoin forces."

"After you have crushed the larger force, I presume." Fehern's tone verged on sarcasm.

"If it is possible," Secca said. "If we fail, you are no worse off, and perhaps better by the amount of Sturinnese we destroy."

"That is true enough, lord," mused Halyt. "We cannot lose if we proceed."

"Why do you need us to separate?"

"So that the northern force does not ride down upon us from behind," Secca replied. "Also, if you do not have to fight until we rejoin, you will have more lancers."

"You believe we should undertake this effort soon?" asked Halyt, glancing toward the dark-haired Fehern.

"I would suggest tomorrow," Secca replied. "The Sturinnese to the south are on a part of the road where there are no side lanes or ways that lead anywhere, except to local cottages and hamlets, and it will be easier for us to move forward than for them to retreat. If we wait, they can reach a crossroads and avoid us."

"Will that be so on the morrow?"

"Unless they travel far more swiftly than they have. In that instance, we will not have to move that many deks at all."

Fehern fingered his chin, then slowly nodded, looking to Halyt. "Best we do what we must, then."

"I would judge so, lord."

Fehern smiled. "We will leave the larger body in your hands, Lady Sorceress." He paused. "If there is nothing else . . . ?"

"I think not." Secca kept a frown from her lips and face. Fehern's words had disturbed her, for false as they had seemed, they had also seemed true, as though the lord had agreed to commit himself, and that worried Secca. She hadn't expected a sense of commitment from the shifty lord.

"Then . . . we will make ready for the morrow." Fehern stood. "You will send a messenger if the disposition of the Sturinnese alters?"

"That we will," Secca promised.

Fehern took a step toward the door, then paused, turning.

Secca stood waiting, wondering what else Fehern wanted.

"Lady Sorceress . . . a moment," Fehern said. "I would ask your leave to discuss a matter with you." He glanced toward those still standing around the table, then lowered his voice, "About possible consorting . . ."

Secca nodded. "Alcaren, Richina . . . you may remain. Chief players and overcaptains . . . we will discuss matters after I talk with Lord Fehern."

Fehern shifted his weight from boot to boot as Wilten, Delcetta, Palian, and Delvor left, along with the unnamed Dumaran overcaptain who had accompanied Fehern. Look-

ing self-conscious, he fumbled with his sabre belt and then
one of the two belt wallets.

In deference, Alcaren and Richina moved toward the front
of the chamber, affording some space between themselves
and Secca and Fehern.

Halyt followed Alcaren and Secca, offering a low but
hearty laugh.

Secca forced herself to keep smiling after the front door
to the cottage closed, uneasy as she felt. "What did you wish
to discuss?"

"In fact . . . a number of things . . ." Fehern smiled apologetically, reaching inside his riding jacket. "I have something I wished to show you . . . of great interest."

"I see." Rather than moving forward, Secca kept back
from the Dumaran lord, her smile fixed in place.

Fehern's face abruptly contorted, and his gloved hand
swung toward Secca.

She jerked her head aside, but liquid splattered across her
cheeks and forehead, a cool liquid that suddenly began to
burn.

Secca jumped farther back and opened her mouth to offer
a short flame spell, even as she drew her own shorter sabre.

A sabre appeared in Fehern's right hand, and his left fumbled with a belt wallet. He lunged forward.

Secca parried the stroke, beginning the words of the flame
spell.

"Turn to ash and burn with flame . . ."

A mass of fine powder exploded around her face and
mouth, so fine, pervasive, and choking that she could
scarcely breathe, let alone sing. Gasping, she danced back,
her vision blurred. She managed to half parry a second
slashing stroke from Fehern, but took a glancing blow on
her shoulder as she tried to cough her cords clear and avoid
being backed into the corner.

Behind Fehern, she could sense a welter of motion, but

her concentration was on Fehern, and her blurred vision did not reveal more than that.

"Hold still!" snapped Fehern.

Secca moved toward the taller man, blocking another thrust, but feeling the shock and numbness in her sabre hand and arm from the force of his blow.

From the front of the chamber came a spell, sung in Alcaren's voice.

"With this lance, strike him dead,
leave no life in body or in head. . . ."

Secca danced aside as she heard the words, barely managing another parry.

Fehern jerked upright, transfixed by the throwing lance, his mouth opening, then falling slack as he pitched forward toward Secca.

The sorceress stepped aside from the falling body, but kept her sabre ready for a moment. Through a powder-fogged vision, she saw Richina straightening after wiping her sabre clean on the crimson tunic of Halyt, who lay face-down on the dark wooden floor.

"He tried to kill Alcaren. He wasn't even looking at me." Richina smiled bitterly. "I'm sorry, lady, but the sabre was faster, and I was afraid a flame spell would injure you, so close were the two of you."

The sound of weapons and shouts penetrated the chamber.

"Lady Secca! We are attacked!" came the call from outside.

Alcaren started toward the door, his own sabre in hand.

"Outside!" snapped Secca, reaching for her lutar with her free hand.

Richina and Alcaren stood on the lower step, blades ready, as Secca darted out behind them. Below them Achar had joined Gorkon and Dymen, and the three stood shoulder to shoulder to protect the entry to the dwelling.

Mounted lancers in crimson seemed to fill the narrow

street, and the squad of SouthWomen, surrounded on three
sides by Dumarans, was being pushed into a tighter and
tighter circle. Even as Secca brought up the lutar, another
SouthWoman lancer in blue and crimson fell.

"Turn to ash and burn with flame
all those of Dumar against our name,
lash with fire and turn to dust
all those who betrayed our trust . . ."

As she finished the spell, Secca could only hope she had
both words and song right.

She had *something* right, because fire lashes and smoke
appeared from everywhere, and the sky darkened.

Several of the Dumaran lancers looked skyward before
the screams began.

Secca lowered the lutar and shuddered.

Within moments, the stench of burned flesh was over-
whelming, and Secca had to swallow hard to avoid retching.
Dymen was one of those unable to contain his reaction, and
the young lancer was bent almost double at the base of the
steps. Achar appeared pale, but remained alert, his blade out
and poised. Gorkon surveyed the dead and dying Dumarans
with unveiled contempt and anger.

Palian appeared through the smoke and swirling ashes,
with Delvor staggering after her. The gray-haired player
held a bloody sabre. Delvor bore an iron-headed staff, also
bloody.

"The players?" asked Secca.

"They're all right, except for Nuel." Palian lowered the
sabre. "He was standing outside the inn when the Dumarans
rode up. They cut him down. The others were inside."

"You were out here?" Secca laughed at herself, ironically.
"Of course you were. It all happened so fast."

Palian looked at the older sorceress, her eyes narrowing
as she studied Secca's face.

"Fehern tried to kill me, with some burning liquid and a

sabre. He threw flour or talc in my face to keep me from singing a spell."

"He's dead?"

"Quite dead," interjected Alcaren. "So is Halyt. Richina killed him with a sabre."

Wilten rode through the slowly clearly smoke, peering around. When he saw Secca, the relief was obvious on his face, and he guided his mount toward the group.

"They attacked the men where they stood . . ."

"I know. Fehern threw burning water at my face and flour or something at my mouth so that I couldn't sing."

Wilten leaned forward, then winced as he saw Secca's face.

Secca hoped the damage wasn't that bad. "How many did we lose?"

"Perhaps a company's worth for us, and the same for the SouthWomen." Wilten shook his head.

"Where is Delcetta?" asked Secca.

"The overcaptain is pursuing the handful of Dumarans who were beyond your spell. I do not think they will survive her wrath."

Secca hoped not.

"None of the Dumaran lancers within a half-dek of you lived. Some of the local people died also." Wilten's tone was matter-of-fact.

The redheaded sorceress wasn't sure she was even regretful about that. Spells sung in haste often had results beyond their intent, and one sung in a town was bound to have unintended consequences. She also didn't feel that much sympathy for people who allowed plotters like Fehern to triumph. The grim smile faded from her face as she thought of Anna.

Was she coming to be as cynical as her mentor and foster mother? Was that what dealing with power and treachery did?

Secca stiffened, then turned abruptly to Richina. "Get the glass out and see if you can discover if there are any Sturinnese riding toward us. Or if there are any nearby. Now would be the time for them to attack."

Richina scurried back inside the dwelling.

Secca looked up at the still-mounted Wilten. "Best you gather all the lancers and have them stand ready until we know what we might expect."

"Yes, lady." He paused. "Even I did not expect such treachery." Another pause followed. "All will be glad to know you stand prepared." An ironic grin appeared on his face. "Though the last spell would have told them that." With a brusque nod, he turned his mount. "Companies re-form!"

Secca turned and slipped inside the dwelling. Once inside, she sheathed the sabre she had almost forgotten she still held, and then crossed the main chamber to the table.

There Richina stood, lutar in hand, studying the glass. The younger sorceress looked up, then nodded toward the image of the map displayed on the silvered surface. "I have used both spells, and both show that they are on the same roads as this morning, and that there are no Sturinnese lancers near us."

"Then . . . why?" Secca glanced to her consort.

Alcaren looked at Fehern's form, sprawled where he had fallen—transfixed by the shimmering iron of the throwing lance. "We may never know, not for certain. He wanted more, I think, than he was worthy of."

Do not we all? thought Secca, setting the lutar on the table.

"A moment, my lady." Alcaren vanished, only to reappear seemingly within moments, with a bucket of water and some cloths—and a handful of flour.

First, he blotted her face with the flour, gently brushing it away, and then repeating the process. After that, he damp-ened one cloth slightly and blotted the line of the wound. Then he wet a corner of a second cloth and touched her cheek. "Does that burn?"

Secca winced. "Not any more than it did. But touching it hurts."

"I'll be back in a moment." He left the room again, his boots clumping on the stairs.

Secca glanced at Richina. "Could you try a spell to see if anyone from Sturinn is nearby?"

The younger sorceress nodded. She frowned, then began the spell.

*"Show us now and as you may
any of Sturinn near us in any way . . ."*

The sole image was that of a man in gray mounted and accompanied by two Sturinnese lancers and two in the crimson of Dumar.

"That explains much," Richina said.

"We knew he was a Sea-Priest," pointed out Alcaren, who had just come back down the stairs. "What is disturbing is that there were Sturinnese lancers close enough to meet him." He had a length of a dried plant of some sort, which he immersed in the bucket he had brought earlier. He began to knead the plant while keeping it underwater.

"They were here all the time, I'd wager," said Secca. "They were in Dumaran uniforms. Those two probably changed to make sure they don't get attacked by their own forces when they reach the Sturinnese forces."

"You need to hold steady," Alcaren said, taking the damp stringy fibrous mass from the bucket and placing it across her cheek.

"Ooo . . ."

"It's for burns. It is the only thing that might help." He guided her hands. "Just hold it there for a while."

Keeping the plant poultice against her injured cheek with one hand, Secca leaned against Alcaren. Her face still burned, despite the flour he had used to blot away whatever liquid Fehern had thrown. She could feel that her upper left arm was bruised badly and would be sore for days, if not weeks.

"I should have listened to what I felt," she murmured. "Anna told me to trust my feelings. And Palian warned me. I ignored her wisdom. I should have asked more from her. It would have saved much effort and many lives."

"You could not have known," he answered, putting an arm around her uninjured shoulder and gently squeezing. "How could you have known?"

"Known? I couldn't." She straightened, looking her consort in the eyes, and ignoring the concern she saw. "That's why feelings are better."

She wouldn't soon ignore those feelings, and the burning lines on her face would remind her in the days to come, and if she had scars, those would remind her forever.

At least, she had survived this mistake . . . and lesson.

35

Using the late-afternoon light coming through the upper window of the dwelling that remained her temporary headquarters, Secca looked in the mirror, studying her face closely. While most of the red splotches from the morning's encounter with Fehern had begun to fade, the worst remained. A line of red-burned flesh, less than a fingertip wide, ran from the outside corner of her left eye straight down her cheek and under her jaw. The flesh around the acid-water wound was tender, with a lingering burning.

"Dissonance, I was stupid." She shook her head, regretting the motion as the wound on her cheek felt as though it had been whipped with fire. "I did not think he would try to kill me with you and Richina present, not during a meeting. I should have known. I should have thought."

"Wisdom," Alcaren said lightly, "is the product of experience, and experience comes from mistakes."

"It's better if we learn from other's mistakes. It takes much less effort." Secca replied wryly. "I should have asked Palian."

"I will try to remember that," Alcaren said wryly. "We could use less effort."

Giving him a faint smile, Secca turned from the mirror and sat down on the wooden chair beside the bed barely wide enough for the two of them. The chair wobbled as her weight settled in place. "We're in a worse situation than when we started. We have fewer lancers and no allies. We're in the middle of a land without a ruler, and people are likely to be hostile because we killed Fehern. We haven't done anything about the Sturinnese, and I have no doubts that matters are getting worse in Neserea."

"Someone told Fehern how to deal with a sorceress," mused Alcaren. "It was audacious and well planned. It didn't work because you had Richina well trained with a blade and because you didn't let Fehern know everything about her and me."

"At least, I did something right." Secca snorted gently. "Or partly right." She paused. "Did you find out about his pay chests and golds?"

"They were in his quarters. He didn't have that much." Alcaren grinned. "About five hundred golds, plus another smaller chest with some jewels in his own gear. They might be worth a thousand."

"That will help, at least for food."

"Where there's anyone to sell it to us," he said dryly.

"I'm not very good at this," she said slowly. "I have trouble concealing what I feel. I get too angry and act too quickly. I cannot do one thing while feeling something different."

Alcaren waited, listening.

"I could not have turned Richina over to Fehern, no matter what, and I could not have talked sweetly enough to make him think I would." Secca pursed her lips. "Even now, I could not do that."

"You are what you are, my lady, and for that I love you." Alcaren stepped behind the chair and put his overlarge hands on her shoulders.

"You are doubtless the only one."

"Few people like those who do what must be done. Always, that has been." Alcaren laughed, once. "And always it will be."

"I'm not certain I am doing what must be done."

"Lord Robero would not have wanted a traitor as Lord High Counselor of Dumar." Alcaren cocked his head to the side, then stepped sideways to the small window. "I see Delcetta and Wilten riding toward the inn."

"They'll be here shortly, then." Secca stood and headed for the narrow staircase. "I hope she took care of the rest of the Dumaran lancers."

"Given Delcetta, I would not wager on their survival."

Secca smiled briefly, grimly, as she started down the stairs, with Alcaren directly behind her.

As she walked into the lower sitting room, Secca's eyes darted to the rear, where Fehern had died. Both the body and the blood were gone. She had told Alcaren to have the bodies buried quietly. One way or another, with the Sturinnese invaders and the Dumaran succession a mess already, it wouldn't matter, and she had no desire to have what amounted to a state funeral in any form—not after Fehern's treachery.

Richina looked up at the two from where she sat at the conference table. "Lady . . . are you feeling better?"

"My voice is fine, but my face still hurts. It probably will for days." *If not weeks, and it serves you right for being so stupid.*

"Acid-water . . . that . . ." Richina winced.

"What Alcaren did helped."

"Not so much as I would have liked," he said.

"It would have been much worse had you not been there."

Secca smiled at her consort. The smile hurt, too, but not so much. "After the meeting," the older sorceress told Richina, "you will use a spellsong to send the scroll I wrote earlier today to Lord Robero."

Richina nodded.

"He should know of Fehern's treachery. We will see, when this is all settled, but perhaps the younger brother, the one consorted to Aerfor, might be a suitable Lord High Counselor. That is not my decision." Secca cleared her throat. "Before the others arrive, it might be wise to see where the renegade sorcerer is." She looked to her consort. "Would you mind singing the scrying spell?"

"If you had not suggested it, my lady, I would have. You need to recover your strength." Alcaren picked up the lumand and sang.

"Show us now and in clear light
Fehern's sorcerer who took to flight . . ."

The mirror displayed the same man, except he was now clad in white and stood in a tent, talking with three other Sturinnese, all of whom had golden insignia on their tunic collars.

"So it was planned from the beginning," Richina said.

"We knew he was a Sea-Priest," pointed out Alcaren. "What is disturbing is that there were Sturinnese lancers close enough to meet him."

"That is not the only disturbing matter," added Secca.

"You think that Clehar's death was part of it, and that they had groomed Fehern so that he would surrender to them?" asked Richina.

"No." Secca shook her head. "Much as I can be certain of anything. If that were the case, Fehern would not have waited so long."

"The Sea-Priests wanted to use the Dumarans to weaken our forces, because they did not think they could get close enough to you," suggested Alcaren.

"That is closer to what I feel. Yet, if so, they would have already attacked while we were hard-pressed." Secca frowned, then pursed her lips. "There is more to it than that, but what I cannot discern."

"The overcaptains and chief players!" called Gorkon from the door.

"Have them come in." Secca looked at Richina. "If you would sing any spells for scrying?"

"Of course, Lady Secca. You should not be singing now." The younger woman's voice carried more concern than Secca had heard before.

Why? Because Fehern's attempted treachery had shown that even powerful sorceresses could be hurt or killed? Again, Secca wasn't sure her thoughts were on the pitch.

Secca slipped toward the table and the ragtag assemblage of chairs and stools around it.

Traces of road dust still clung to Delcetta's boots, clothes, and hair, although she had clearly washed her face after her pursuit of the fleeing Dumarans. There were also darker splotches on her trousers, most likely blood.

Wilten looked more dusty than Delcetta, and he inclined his head to Secca. "You look better than when I last saw you, Lady Secca."

"I feel somewhat better."

Palian's countenance was drawn, but, after studying Secca's face, the chief player offered a faint smile. Delvor offered a wan smile as well.

Secca returned the smiles, then seated herself at the table, waiting for the others. Finally, once everyone was settled, she turned to the SouthWoman overcaptain. "How fared your pursuit?"

"The rearguard company was the sole one beyond the reach of your spell, Lady Sorceress. We cornered them by the mill. Only two of them escaped. One made the river and dived in, and the other had a fast mount." Delcetta shrugged. "Overcaptain Wilten and I had our lancers inspect all the outlying cots and barns and dwellings. We found one other.

He made it easy. He tried to take Captain Peraghn with a scythe."

Secca nodded slowly. Two lancers surviving from ten companies. What a terrible waste, and yet, under the circumstances, what else could she have done? Could she have come up with another spell? She had put herself in a position where she hadn't had the time. Stupidity, again. "How many lancers are wounded?"

"We have perhaps a half-score, and but one seriously," replied Wilten.

"A quarter-score," said Delcetta. "Saving the squad guarding you, lady, the red beasts did not attack us so quickly as they did your lancers."

"Could you both ride out tomorrow?"

"That we could," Delcetta said.

Wilten nodded slowly.

Secca looked to Palian and Delvor.

"Nuel was the sole player killed. Kylera has a bruised arm and a swollen finger. She laid out a Dumaran with a plank." Palian shook her head, ruefully. "The Dumaran did not rise, even before the flames, but his mount struck the plank and wrenched it from her hands." She looked to Delvor.

"Dossin has a slash on his left arm, but it will heal." Delvor brushed back the unruly lank hair that had flopped down over his forehead ever since Secca had known him.

The redheaded sorceress surveyed those around the table, then said, "We do not know what the Sturinnese may have done since midday. I had thought to have you all here before we decided."

On cue, Richina slipped off the stool and picked up her lutar.

"Show us where upon a map of this land . . ."

The mirror displayed the map that had become all too familiar, with the white stars showing the position of the

Sturinnese forces. The northern force appeared to be settled at the small trading town south of the mouth of the trading pass to Neserea. The larger group of Sturinnese was farther from Hasjyl—and Envaryl—than it had been.

Once everyone had a chance to study the glass, Secca motioned to Richina. The younger sorceress sang the release spell, then set aside the lutar and reseated herself on the stool she had been using.

"They've turned back east—the ones that were heading for Envaryl," observed Wilten.

That didn't surprise Secca at all. She would have been shocked to find the Sturinnese still moving toward her.

"You do not look surprised, Lady Secca," offered Palian.

"The Sturinnese do not wish a battle now. That is clear." Clear it was, but the reasons why an enemy who had always attacked had changed tactics were most unclear. While Secca would have liked to flatter herself that it was because the Sturinnese had come to respect her sorcery, she doubted that was the reason. "It may be that they avoid battle to keep us from going northward to aid the Lady High Counselor."

"Or because they feel that they can triumph in Neserea quickly and then move against you," suggested Wilten.

"All are possible." Secca paused. "We may still ride tomorrow. We will see where the Sea-Priests are in the morning."

Her feelings told her that they would be farther away, but not far enough away for Secca to ignore. They also told her that she needed rest, more than she would probably get for weeks, if not seasons.

She offered yet another polite smile. "We will meet tomorrow at the second glass after dawn. Then we will see what we must do."

36

WEST OF ITZEL, NESEREA

Clayre eases the shutter of the small dwelling ajar and peers out at the fat and fast-falling flakes of snow that have so quickly re-covered the roads and even the field that had shown signs of brown in the days previous. "Already two spans' worth has fallen, and the clouds are darker than earlier in the day."

From behind her, Diltyr shakes his head.

So does the gray-haired lancer captain who paces back and forth before the heap of embers in the small hearth—the remnants of the fire set at midday, after Clayre and her forces had taken refuge from the sudden storm in the nameless hamlet.

"Even the weather is against us," mutters Diltyr.

"At this time of year," Clayre responds, "the weather is against all. The harmonies care not if we need fair weather." She closes and fastens the shutters once more, then steps toward the low embers, where she bends forward to warm her hands.

"If we must wait out the storm, will not Belmar soon discern your sorcery?" asks the captain.

"No. The storm makes it less likely. Were it clear and sunny, he would wonder why his glass shows me in Nysl's keep. Now . . . he will not question." Her lips tighten. "So . . . while we have made little progress toward his forces, we are no worse off. Not for the moment."

"But . . . the storm will fill the roads and passes, and it will be longer yet before any aid can reach us," suggests the chief player.

"There will be little enough of that," Clayre says darkly.

"Lord Robero will not send his last full sorceress to succor us with the Sturinnese holding almost all of Dumar. His last scroll suggests that if we cannot soon defeat the usurper, I should consider returning to Defalk. That . . . that I would rather not, for we might well have to fight again, on our own lands."

The chief player frowns momentarily before speaking quickly. "What of the Liedfuhr? Would his aid assist us?"

"He may well send his lancers—once the snows melt, but the passes to the west are higher and colder. He has too few ships to risk the Bitter Sea. He has no sorcerers to send, and against Belmar even scores of companies of lancers may not suffice."

"You risk much in attempting to destroy Belmar," Diltyr says slowly. "Lord Robero fears such a risk."

"I risk more in not attempting it. He raises more lancers every week, even in winter. Were we to meet in direct battle, our two companies of lancers could not hold back his hordes long enough for me to sing a single spell."

"What will you now?" asks the brown-haired player.

"Take a smaller group to attack his forces once we can ride, and before he thinks we can move. He will expect caution, and he will expect us to move toward Esaria to protect the Lady Counselor."

"How fares she?"

"She still holds Esaria, but not much more. Aerfor and Eryhal have made their way to Nordwei—or so the glass shows."

"How . . . ?"

"They are both quite capable, it appears." Clayre laughs. "They are among the few, it would seem." After a moment, she sighs. "We will wait. That is all we can do. For now."

37

I n the early-afternoon light of a sun that looked warmer than it felt, Secca shifted her weight in the saddle, and the gray mare whuffed as she carried Secca southward on the road from the ford to the west of Hasjyl. The wind was lighter than it had been that morning, and carried the scent of thawing ground and winter-damp vegetation, but Secca still had her green riding jacket fastened snugly. She wore the green felt hat, pulled down over red hair that was always disheveled. Then, and ever since she had been a child, whether her hair had been long or cut short, somehow it had always ended up disarrayed.

According to the glass, the Sea-Priests had taken over a hilltop hamlet some twenty deks to the east and were settling in. Secca had decided to ride eastward to a hamlet eight or nine deks away from the Sturinnese, before attempting an attack on the following day. With Fehern's treachery, she had no longer had to worry about the Sturinnese circling behind her. All she had to do was defeat the Sturinnese. A rueful smile appeared on the redheaded sorceress's face. All?

On the flat and straight stretch of road ahead, Wilten, Delcetta, and Alcaren conferred with the scouts who had just returned. After the brief conference on horseback, Alcaren turned his mount and headed back toward Secca. As he neared, he turned his mount to ride alongside her.

"We are about two deks from that ridge." Secca's consort pointed toward the low rise the road climbed before them. "The hamlet where we plan to overnight is in the swale below that rise."

"We should stop and use the scrying glass to see if there

are any Sturinnese nearby, and what they may be doing. I'd rather not ride into an ambush."

"I'll tell the overcaptains. The lancers and their mounts could use the rest, so long as they don't get chilled."

"It won't take long." Secca smiled and turned to Richina. "Will it, Richina?"

Richina smiled back. "Not at all."

Secca dismounted and unfastened the leather-wrapped glass from behind her saddle. Carrying the mirror with one hand, she walked the mare off the shoulder of the road and to a spot where the grass was thick and had been flattened. Belatedly, Achar rode after her, and took the mare's reins. After loosening the leather thongs, Secca eased the mirror out of the wrapping, then spread the leather on the flattened grass and centered the mirror on the leather.

Richina had followed. She dismounted. Achar took the younger sorceress's mount as well. Richina then unstrapped her lutar and joined Secca.

As Richina tuned her lutar, Wilten and Delcetta eased their mounts to a halt nearby, then dismounted. Handing the reins to a SouthWoman lancer, Delcetta walked toward Richina and Secca. Wilten looked at the lancer, who smiled and took the reins to his mount as well.

The last one to arrive in the circle around the scrying glass was Alcaren.

After looking at Secca's consort, Richina finished a second vocalise, then cleared her throat. She bent over the glass and sang.

*"Show us now and in afternoon light
the Sturinnese we seek to fight . . ."*

The more distant hilltop hamlet appeared much as it had in earlier uses of the scrying glass, except that a patrol of riders—a good half squad—rode northward away from the lake.

"They are sending out scouts," Wilten said.

"Wouldn't you?" asked Alcaren.

"This late in the day?" Delcetta's tone was innocently open, but her eyebrows lifted with the question.

"They're watching us in a glass," Secca said.

"But the camp is quiet," pointed out Wilten.

That worried Secca. Then, whatever the Sturinnese did worried her. She looked at Richina. "Can you do one about the hamlet ahead?"

Richina nodded, then cocked her head. Finally, she sang.

> *"Show us now and as you will*
> *the hamlet ahead below the hill,*
> *and if enemies waiting that there be,*
> *show us clearly so that we may see . . ."*

The glass displayed a view from above of five dwellings. Two men pitched hay from an open cart into a pen containing a handful of cattle. A girl carried two buckets on a yoke, moving from the stream toward one of the houses.

"You wouldn't see that if there were Sea-Priests around," Alcaren observed.

"We will still send scouts first," Wilten declared, looking to Secca.

She nodded. "In dealing with the Sturinnese, when we can, we should be cautious." Despite her words, she had a strong sense that to defeat the Sturinnese she would have to be anything but cautious.

"That we should," affirmed Wilten.

Alcaren caught Secca's eye. They exchanged faint smiles, and Secca knew that her consort felt as she did.

38

I n the grayness before dawn, Secca woke to the faint smell of smoke. She sat up abruptly in the bedroll she had laid on one side of the pallet bed in the cot that was little more than a neatly kept hovel.

Beside her, Alcaren bolted up, shaking his head and looking at her. "What is it?"

"Smoke. It's not like a cookfire." Secca swung her legs over the side of the rickety bed and bent to pull on her boots. Then came the belt and sabre, and then her riding jacket. Absently, she scratched her leg. Despite using her bedroll, she had a few bites from something. She shook her head and headed for the doorway to the one-room dwelling.

Alcaren scrambled to follow her, his jacket half-on as he came through the door behind her and out into the cold morning.

Secca stood in the open space before the cottage, glancing at the lancers who had stood guard before the cottage. "Overcaptain Wilten?"

"He said he'd be back shortly, lady." Gorkon pointed to the southeast. "That be him, I'd think."

Wilten was already riding back into the center of the hamlet, from wherever he had ridden, hurrying past the lancers stationed out as pickets.

Secca sniffed the cold air again, but the odor of smoke remained strong and pungent, and the southeastern horizon was hazy from the smoke.

Richina had joined Secca and Alcaren by the time Wilten reined up his mount.

"The smoke comes from the south, lady," Wilten said. "Overcaptain Delcetta and I have already sent out scouts, but they have not returned."

Secca nodded. She hadn't wanted to try an attack in dawn or darkness, but she feared she knew what the smoke signified. "If you would find Delcetta and join us, we will see what the glass shows."

"She should be here momentarily," replied Wilten.

Secca looked to Richina. "If you would find the chief players . . . ?"

"That I will." Richina hurried toward the cottage to the west.

While the others were gathering, Secca stepped back into the cottage, out of the chill, and, since there had been no table left in the dwelling, laid the scrying glass on the packed-dirt floor of the hovel, then took out her lutar and began to tune it.

Alcaren tuned his lumand as well, and waited.

Richina returned, with both Palian and Delvor, and within moments of their arrival, Wilten and Delcetta stepped inside the single-room dwelling.

Secca did not bother with explanations, but launched into the spellsong.

"Show us now and in this day's clear light
from where the smoke has taken flight . . ."

The mirror displayed the hilltop hamlet that the Sturinnese had held the day before. Half the buildings were already blackened stone or brick and fallen timbers, with mere wisps of smoke trailing upward. A few outbuildings still smoldered.

"They burned it." Wilten's voice was flat. "So we could not reprovision there."

"They would have taken all the supplies, except hay or feed for mounts," Alcaren said. "They burned it to deny us shelter."

Secca sang the release couplet before speaking. "There's more here than shows in the glass." She looked to Wilten.

"I would hear what the scouts have discovered when they return."

Both overcaptains nodded.

Secca looked to Palian and Delvor. "I fear we will have a long and a hard ride in the days ahead. I would that you make certain the players are ready for such."

"We can do that," Palian said. "Might I ask . . . ?"

"The Sea-Priests wish to keep us in Dumar, and to make this a long and arduous campaign. We cannot afford such. I will be looking for a way to shorten that." *If you can.*

After the others filed out of the cottage, except for Richina, Secca turned to Alcaren. "Am I wrong to worry about staying overlong in Dumar?"

"When the Sea-Priests have always attacked swiftly and in force before? I think not." Alcaren glanced toward the door. "I may ride out with one of Delcetta's squads, if you do not mind."

"No. I do not." Secca smiled, if briefly. "We each must trust our feelings."

With a nod, her consort slipped out the door.

As she waited for the scouts to return and report, Secca forced down chunks of the dry crackerlike bread that they had found in Hasjyl, and hard yellow cheese, accompanied by cold water that she had used a songspell to purify the night before. Richina ate with her.

"You were not surprised, Lady Secca," ventured Richina.

"I had hoped for better, but not expected it," replied Secca.

"What will you do?"

"In a moment, we will use the glass to see how Clayre fares. The last time, she was in a hold somewhere in Neserea."

Secca checked the lutar's tuning, but it had held. Then she sang.

"Show us now and in clear light
Lady Clayre for our full sight . . ."

The mirror displayed an image of the dark-haired sorceress holding her lutar and looking into a glass set upon a
bare wooden table in a dark room barely illuminated by a
single twin-branched candelabra.

Secca frowned.

"What is the matter, lady?"

"Something . . ." Secca shook her head. "She is in the
same room as when we looked two days ago." After a moment, the older sorceress sang the release couplet. Then she
repeated the spell.

This time, Clayre appeared in the same room, but sitting
at the table studying the glass. The lutar was nowhere in
sight.

"The lutar . . . it has vanished."

"So has Clayre. She has set a spell that shows these images to any who seek her directly." Secca again released the
spell-image, frowning. "She must be trying something of
great desperation."

"Will that mislead Belmar or whoever seeks her?"

"It may," conceded Secca, "if they do not seek her often
in a glass."

"Is she all right?"

"She has to be alive, for her energies power that spell."
Secca frowned again. "She will not have quite the strength
that she would if she had not used that songspell."

"Should we try to see what she does?" Richina was the
one to frown. "But how . . . ?"

"That will not be difficult." Secca pursed her lips and
thought for a moment.

> "Show us now and as through Diltyr's sight
> Lady Clayre in what is his full light . . ."

Richina offered a low "oh" as the mirror displayed a very
different scene. A small band of players, preceded by one
company of lancers and followed by another rode along a
narrow and winding lane covered with snow. The steam of

the breath of the mounts was clear even through the mirror.

After a moment, Secca sang a second release song and set down the lutar.

"Could not Belmar do as you have?"

"He could indeed—if he suspects all is not as it should be. Clayre's hope is that he will not suspect."

"Should we warn her?" asked Richina.

Secca sighed. "That would be my first inclination. But that will render one of us unable to do much sorcery for a day or longer. Clayre must know that Belmar will not be long deceived. But I cannot risk us losing because we are not strong." She shook her head. "Save it is not that clear. We could avoid a battle with the Sea-Priests easily for a day or two, for that is what they wish. Yet I fear each day we avoid battle brings even greater danger." Secca held up a hand to forestall any questions. "I do not know what that danger may be, only that the Sea-Priests are doing all in their power to keep us in Dumar."

"Could they be giving that appearance to force you into overhasty action?"

Secca laughed, ruefully. "They could, and that makes the dilemma worse." She took out her belt knife and cut off another slice of the hard yellow cheese, breaking off more of the crackerlike bread. The way matters were going, she knew she had to eat more than she wanted—much more.

"Lady Secca?" called Gorkon from outside the hovel. "Overcaptain Wilten."

"Have him come in."

"Lady," began Wilten, almost hesitantly as he closed the rough plank door behind him. He squinted in the dim light, trying to make out Secca more clearly.

"They burned the hamlet, and . . . ?" Secca asked. "What about the people?"

"Most had fled," Wilten said. "Some did not. They are dead."

Secca pursed her lips. "We will see where the Sturinnese are headed, but I would wager that they will retrace their route toward Dumaria, burning each town through which they pass."

"Burning?" asked Richina. "But why? Why not just take the provisions?"

"If we triumph, they wish us great ill in restoring the land, and would lay the blame on Defalk for the devastation because we could not protect them. If they triumph, they will declare that such will always be the fate of those who defy the Maitre of Sturinn."

"But they can retreat as fast as we can advance, can they not?" questioned Wilten.

"Not if they must destroy a town—a larger town," suggested Secca. "If we can circle to the south and move eastward . . ."

"Also, they may wait for the force in the north to join them," suggested Richina.

"That may be. It may not be. That force may wait for us, and then create greater delays in whatever fashion they can."

Wilten nodded slowly and deliberately.

Secca could feel her stomach tightening. Although she could not explain, even to herself, the feelings, she *knew* that she must find a way to defeat the Sturinnese in Dumar quickly. Yet she must do so in a way that would not sacrifice any more of her already slender forces.

39

WEST OF ITZEL, NESEREA

In the dimness of the private study of the keep, Belmar studies the image of the woman in the glass that lies in the center of the dark oak desk. "She has been in the same room for near-on a week."

"Has there not been a snowstorm? And high winds?" asks

jerGlien. "She has but two companies of lancers. She would not risk such against the weather." His tone is close to that of idle speculation.

"She would wish us to think that, I wager."

"Be careful what you wager." The Sturinnese laughs without mirth. "One never knows who might accept your bet."

"She will not gamble." With those words, Belmar clears his throat and sings, without accompaniment.

> *"Paint upon this glass in clearest sight*
> *she who rides Lady Clayre's mount in today's light . . ."*

At the compressed rhyme and stressed note values, jerGlien winces. "You should use the players or learn to play a lute."

"It will work," Belmar says. "See!"

The image in the glass shows the sorceress riding eastward along a snowy road, the sun that has finally broken through days of clouds at her back.

"The devious bitch! I'll set a trap, and not just one for Nysl and his type, but for her. That I will." After a moment, Belmar lets the image fade from the glass, slowly, without singing a release couplet, and turns to jerGlien. "You knew she would do such."

"I knew she could. Any of the sorceresses could do so, were they so minded. I did not know she would. She is usually most direct, and most cautious, as you well have noted." The Sturinnese pauses, then adds, "Women can be most unpredictable. That was noted long ago in Sturinn."

"And that is why you chain them?"

An ironic smile plays across jerGlien's face. "Let us say that it has proven effective over many, many years."

"Well . . . I cannot chain this sorceress. So we must let her believe her stratagem has worked," muses the younger man. "Then she will act, instead of dancing all over the countryside avoiding us." He smiles coldly. "And when she acts, why then, so will we."

"You will follow the decoy lancers more closely so that once she has cast her spells and revealed herself you will crush her?" suggests jerGlien.

"I had thought so. Is aught wrong with that?" Belmar glances down at the blank glass upon the desk.

"Not so long as you use sorcery strong enough to destroy her. She will not give you a second opportunity."

"Nor I her. One must indeed act before she becomes stronger and more devious through experience." Belmar grins at the man in gray. "Is that not the way of Sturinn? To act before another gains strength?"

"That is one way," concedes jerGlien.

"Nothing is simple in Sturinn, is it?"

"Is it anywhere? You should know that appearances can deceive. The shadow sorceress is far stronger than those senior to her, yet all think she is the weakest because she is younger and because she has kept her distance from Falcor." A pleasant smile appears. "As I have told you before, nothing in all Erde is quite what it seems, Lord Belmar."

"Including you? You are here, and then you are not. Whatever you recommend, the Maitre seems to favor."

"The Maitre has not adopted all of the requests you have asked me to convey."

"That is not what I said." Belmar laughs lightly.

"I have conveyed your requests," jerGlien says evenly. "You have done well . . . from what the Maitre has granted."

"As well as any, and yet I cannot say I know you."

"You know me as well as any do," replies jerGlien, "and better than many."

"That is to say, not at all."

The Sturinnese shrugs, as if to end the discussion.

40

T he wind blew harder than on the days before, but it
    came out of the southeast, and was far warmer than in
the recent past. For Secca and her forces, that had meant
more muddy patches of the Dumaran road, and a slower
journey eastward along the side road that roughly paralleled
the river road. Secca had hoped that they could ease closer
to the Sturinnese, enough to flank or circle the Sea-Priests
somehow without overly tiring her own lancers and their
mounts.

She half stood in the stirrups, trying to stretch legs that
felt even shorter after two glasses of riding. As she eased
back down into the saddle, she glanced at Wilten, who rode
beside her for the moment. Alcaren and Delcetta rode close
behind, and Richina and Palian just ahead of Secca and Wilten.

"You are certain that the Sturinnese are moving eastward,
back toward Dumaria?" asked Wilten.

"That is what my glass showed, and Richina's," Secca
replied. "They are retracing their route back along the river
road."

"They are not even attempting to use the hills of Hasjyl,
then, although you left them that opening," Wilten continued.

"They regard such as a trap," suggested Delcetta.

"I think not," Secca replied. "The farther east we go, the
farther we are from the trade pass, and when we vanquish
the Sea-Priests, we will have even more travel to reach
Esaria."

"By then the Sturinnese will have landed their fleet in
Worlan or Esaria," Palian noted, half-turning in the saddle.

"Worlan?" asked Delcetta.

"Those are the lands held by Belmar," replied Secca, "Lord Belmar, who would be the next Prophet of Music. They are west of Esaria, and there is a small port there."

Wilten frowned, but did not speak, keeping his eyes on the narrow road ahead, winding as it did between rich river bottomland, and hills that supported woodlots and orchards with twisted trees that reflected the less fertile higher ground away from the river valley that was less than five deks wide. Still, although the ground was warming, they had seen no signs of the land being tilled or turned in preparation for planting.

Secca tried to recall the details of the map of western Dumar. "Can you send scouts to see if—there's a loop in the river, isn't there, not too far ahead—we could cut across the hills and strike from the higher ground while they follow the river road?"

Delcetta nodded. "Scouts—that we can do."

"They have almost fifty companies of lancers and three of archers," offered Wilten.

"I do not plan to fight that way," Secca said. *Not if you can avoid it.*

"They will not, either," pointed out Alcaren. "So we must surprise them. Would you think of an attack through sorcery at night?"

"We will have to see." Secca shrugged. She wouldn't be at her best if she had to ride most of the day. Neither would the players. Yet she had no doubts that the Sturinnese would not stay close to her for a day to let her rest—not unless she and her forces were so exhausted that any battle promised an easy victory for the Sea-Priests. "I will think of anything that will allow us to fight the Sturinnese when we are rested and have the greatest of advantages."

"You ask much, Lady Secca," offered Wilten.

"Perhaps too much, Wilten," Secca admitted. "Yet we can ill afford to lose many more lancers or any more players." Her eyes went to the winding road ahead. If she could only find a way to sing a spell that would carry farther than the few deks that she had managed in destroying the Sturinnese archers. But her voice had been stretched to its limits to create an effect that had extended three deks. Her voice? She and Richina had destroyed the keep at Dolov by singing harmony together. What if she could manage to add Alcaren? Could the three of them succeed where she could not—in a campaign that now stretched into a future she could neither see nor predict—nor even guess.

41

WEST OF ITZEL, NESEREA

Light powdery snow falls intermittently from the hazy clouds that are somewhere in color between gray and white, and occasionally part to show a blue sky above, then scud together swiftly to dim the day. The road itself appears empty, and the lands beside the road reflect the coming end of winter, with brown spaces in the fields that will be tilled in weeks to come still dotted with snowdrifts. The meadows show the same pattern, save that winter-flattened grass alternates with the snow. Along the road itself, the drifts are fewer, and deeper, usually extending from a fence or stone wall bordering the shoulder of the road.

At one point on the road are three larger and longer drifts in a row, separated by but a few yards of frozen grass. Only four players, Clayre, and a single lancer stand in the space carefully created by hand and sorcery to resemble a snowdrift, the one in the center of the three. Under the white canvas that has been dusted with snow, the six wait for the column of Neserean lancers recruited and trained by Belmar to ride eastward toward Esaria, over the barely melted surface of the still-frozen clay of the road from Itzel to the capital.

"This is most dangerous, Lady Clayre," murmurs Diltyr.

"Indeed." Clayre nods. "But one snowdrift looks like another, and even if he were to see us in his glass, he would not know exactly where we might be."

"He might not come along this road."

"He might not," agrees Clayre. "If they do not, we are no worse off than before."

"True," grudges Diltyr.

"Who will stop this Belmar if we do not? Lord Robero has no more lancers to spare, and the Lady Secca fights her way across the south of Liedwahr. She will not soon reach Neserea, not against the Sturinnese and with the deep snows of the Mittfels blocking all the passes. So it must fall to us."

Diltyr inclines his head in acknowledgment.

They fall silent as the lancer watching the road through the smallest of peepholes in the canvas gestures.

The scouts who ride the road before the column scarcely glance at the snowdrift as they scan the road for signs of hoofs and wagon tracks, and the road farther ahead for riders. The sound of hoofs on the frozen road fades as they pass.

Less than half a glass later comes the main body. Lancers in the ancient green of the Prophet of Music lead the column that follows the road westward. The hoofs of their mounts clop dully on the frozen clay.

Clayre motions the lancer aside and studies the advancing lancers through the peephole in the canvas. Finally, she steps away and nods to the players. "Once the canvas is clear, play on your mark, Diltyr."

"On my mark . . ."

Clayre motions to the lancer. He quickly pulls the canvas away to expose the sorceress and players—and to allow their sound to carry toward the lancers and the figure who wears the colors of Belmar.

Even as the canvas is being cleared, Clayre nods to Diltyr, who brings his hand down, and then begins to play. The other three players join him, and the spellsong accompaniment swells, flowing out into the chill day, each note precise.

Clayre begins the spell on the third measure, lifting her voice into the cold morning air, air solid enough to carry the words and melody more than the half a dek length of the column. She has chosen the players wisely, and though they are few, their notes are firm and forceful, and both spell and accompaniment meld and soar.

> *"Turn to fire, turn to flame*
> *Belmar and all those here in his name,*
> *turn to ashes and scatter as dust*
> *those who follow this prophet's trust..."*

With the spell comes a harmonic chord, reinforcing the words and music, for all its briefness in passing. Then, lightnings flash from the skies, not from the hazy clouds, but from somewhere below them, from where darker clouds begin to form and swirl into being.

From the column of riders come screams and curses, filling the chill morning air. Smoke begins to circle skyward as the lightnings fall like fire lances into the lancers, turning man after man into flaming torches, until the fires and smoke stretch nearly half a dek eastward.

The clouds thicken, and the morning darkens more, until the light resembles dawn or twilight.

As the last sounds of the spellsong die away, Clayre stands, breathing deeply, watching as the last of the lancers in green fall. A grim smile crosses her thin lips, then fades as she beholds the charred figures that once were men. She shakes her head, almost sadly.

"There was no dissonance," offers Diltyr, glancing toward the carnage upon the road.

"No." Claire frowns, and as she does, a deep rolling thunder fills the air, a rhythmic thunder that comes from somewhere behind her, drowning out the more distant rumbling from the roiling clouds overhead, clouds that continue to thicken and darken.

From the direction of the drumming thunder appear more riders—another line of of lancers in green who sweep from the south toward the unprotected players.

Clayre turns and sees the attackers in their cream and green. She bends and snatches the lutar from its case. Without a pause, or a word, she lifts the lutar, her fingers touching the strings precisely. Facing the grim-faced riders who charge across the meadow toward her and who ride through the small snowdrifts, the sorceress faces the riders and begins another spell. Her voice is clear and strong.

"Turn to fire, turn to flame,
all those against our name . . ."

Another line of flame lances drops from the heavens, but this line is far thinner, more like arrows than lances. Thin or not, it is sufficient to turn the entire company that had led the charge across the meadow into charred corpses, so that the colors of the meadow are the dirty white of old snow, the winter tan of last year's grass, and the black of sorcerous death.

Clayre takes a deep and quick breath, then another, listening as she does.

"Lady . . ." begins Diltyr.

Clayre gestures him to silence.

Somewhere beyond the field of death, the rhythmic thunder continues.

She straightens, ignoring the burning in her eyes and chest, and begins another set of chords on the lutar, those that matched the first spell played against the column.

"Turn to fire, turn to flame
Belmar and all those here in his name . . ."

The storm above the sorceress and the small band of players crackles, and more flame lightnings flare to the south . . .

but they do not strike the next wave of lancers, but bend aside near the rear of the attackers, as if they had struck an invisible shield. The lancers ride forward, deliberately.

Clayre staggers as she finishes, then forces herself erect, watching for but a moment, breathing heavily, as the lancers in green gallop toward her and her players.

She swallows, then coughs, and clears her throat.

The rhythmic drumming is louder, more intense, and the sorceress shakes her head, then takes a quick swig from the water bottle at her belt. She squints, as if she has trouble remembering the words to the spell, but her fingers are deft upon the strings of the lutar, and once more, her voice rises, well above the drums, and even above the thunder of the clouds above.

She has but reached the second line of the spellsong when the white-tipped flame lightnings arc from the still-lowering clouds, ripping into her and the players beside her.

The sole lancer's mouth opens, but before he can yell or speak, he too is transfixed with flame. Behind him the white canvas flares into a bonfire, then turns black as the flames consume it.

A single dull harmonic chime sounds, dissonant, unheard except by those few who understand all too well what it means.

42

When Secca and her force stopped for the first break of the day, a good two glasses of travel after leaving their campsite, dawn had barely broken. Orangish light suffused itself across the grasses and low trees of the hills through which wound the narrow trail they had followed in an effort to reach the small unnamed town on the eastern end of the long and narrow bow in the Envar River. The stopping point had been the first wide and halfway-flat spot of ground in several deks, covered mainly with the winter-flattened tan grass of the higher meadows. To the south was a copse of cedar trees, wild and tangled, and twisted by years of neglect.

After chewing through a chunk of the cracker bread that was as hard and tough as ancient dried jerky, Secca took a long swallow of water that was so cold that she shivered, even though the morning was not that chill. She took another bite of the cracker bread, and crumbs sprayed everywhere as her teeth crunched through it.

Beside her, Alcaren smiled.

". . . don't see you eating it . . ." Secca mumbled.

"I am," chimed in Richina from beside the older sorceress.

The three glanced up from where they stood beside their mounts as Wilten and Delcetta rode up.

"We're making good time," Wilten announced. "We could be on the hills overlooking the western end of the town by a bit past midday."

"If the road holds," added Delcetta.

"The glass showed that it will be much the same," offered Alcaren.

A low dull and dissonant chord shook Secca, rattling through her frame so violently that she reached out and grasped Alcaren's shoulder to steady herself. She swallowed, then glanced around.

Alcaren's brows knit. "What was that?"

Richina glanced from Alcaren to Secca. "It was like the battle . . . at Encora."

Secca glanced at the two mounted overcaptains.

"What?" asked Wilten.

"Something . . . happened . . . distant . . . dissonant . . ." Secca forced the words out, even as she turned toward the gray and began to unstrap her lutar.

Alcaren hurried over beside her and untied the leather-wrapped scrying glass.

Both Secca and Alcaren ignored the looks that passed between Wilten and Delcetta as Secca tuned the lutar. Richina laid the leather wrappings on the grass, and Alcaren set the glass on top of those wrappings on the grass. As Secca finished tuning, Palian and Delvor appeared, walking their mounts toward the group.

"Lady . . ." offered Palian.

"We heard," Secca said tightly. "You may watch the glass."

Secca glanced down at the glass, then touched the strings of the lutar.

"Show us now and bring to sight
what caused the dissonance to take flight . . ."

The spell was rough, Secca knew, as she watched the mirror blank into silver and then slowly bring forth an image . . . an image that showed a line of blackened figures within a square of snow. A square of canvas, barely attached to two rough branches, burned brightly.

Secca swallowed as her amber eyes traced out the rough outline of a charred lutar.

"I will sing the release," Alcaren said.

Secca nodded, swallowing again. As Alcaren's voice died away, she looked to her consort. "I must be sure."

"I will—"

"I can, lady," offered Richina.

"No. I must." Secca lifted her lutar and sang.

"Show me now and in the mirror's light
the lady Clayre well within my sight . . ."

The mirror blanked, and then showed almost the same scene, centering on one figure, but . . . even as all gathered around the glass watched, the surface silvered and turned blank.

"Clayre . . . she's gone," Secca confirmed, looking up from the glass. "She's gone."

"So are many of Belmar's armsmen," Alcaren said slowly.

"Would you . . . ?"

Alcaren took the lutar and sang.

"Of Belmar's lancers, show in clear light
all those struck down by sorcery's blight . . ."

The mirror showed a road, in the same snow-studded landscape, along which were strewn the bodies of lancers and mounts, also blackened. The column stretched almost half a dek.

"Not all . . . but many," opined Alcaren. He sang the release couplet, then lowered the lutar.

"What about Belmar?" asked Richina.

Alcaren looked to Secca, who nodded. At Secca's nod, Alcaren handed the lutar to Richina. The younger sorceress ran her fingers over the strings, then cocked her head sideways in thought before singing the viewing spell for Belmar.

The mirror image was clear and sharp, showing Belmar— except that he wore not the garments of a lord, but the uniform of a captain. Beside him rode a man in gray, and behind him at least several players.

For a time, the seven looked at the glass, silently, before Richina sang the release couplet.

"Belmar and his players remain, with nothing between them and Esaria," suggested Palian.

Secca shuddered, silently, numbly, thinking of Clayre, of the dark-haired sorceress who had gone to Neserea with few lancers and less support from the Nesereans. She could still recall first meeting Clayre, when Clayre had been sixteen, and Secca barely nine, and looking up to the tall young woman who had come to Falcor at Anna's behest, to avoid an arranged consorting. Now . . . Clayre was dead, never having known consort or love.

Secca shivered again, then squared her shoulders.

Alcaren put his hand around hers, gently, and squeezed.

"Can you do nothing, my lady?" asked Wilten.

Secca hesitated, then shook her head. "Not beyond what we plan. I dare not. Not until we have dealt with the Sturinnese here in Dumar. We could not reach Esaria within weeks, and if we tried, we would turn Dumar over to those Sturinnese here."

"We could lose both lands, then," suggested Alcaren.

No one mentioned that they could anyway.

Secca took her lutar back from Richina and slipped it into its case, while Alcaren and the younger sorceress rewrapped the all-too-warm scrying mirror and fastened it in place behind the saddle of Secca's gray mare. Then Secca tied the lutar in place. She looked at Wilten. "We had best be riding. I do not intend that the Sturinnese succeed in Dumar." Although she had not intended it, her words fell like ice into the silence—infinitely cold and yet as edged as a freshly sharpened sabre.

Wilten lowered his eyes. "We stand ready, Lady Secca."

Secca forced a smile. "I am not angry with any here, Overcaptains. I am angry, and those with whom I am angry will know it. In time, and in my own way."

Wilten swallowed. Mounted beside him, Delcetta showed a cold and grim smile that bore a hint of satisfaction.

Secca smiled, a hard smile that was becoming too familiar. "Our scouts have said that the ride is less than six deks across the hills. We can make it by midday, and rest for several glasses before the Sturinnese appear."

"If they don't see us coming in their glasses," Wilten said worriedly.

"If they do, how are we worse off? They can hurry, or they can retreat westward. Either way we're in a better position." Secca smiled again. "Besides, I think that their lancers and overcaptains will want to fight. This will give them an excuse."

Alcaren frowned. So did the overcaptains.

Secca looked at her consort. "You said that days ago. That the Sturinnese always liked to attack. How must they feel about retreating from a mere woman with but nine under-strength companies of lancers?"

"They will not want to do that again," suggested Delcetta.

"So they will at least approach more closely to see what we might do," Secca replied. "And if it is close enough, we will strike." Her eyes traveled across each of those around her. "We should be riding once more."

"Yes, Lady Secca." Wilten inclined his head.

After a moment, so did Delcetta. Then the two over-captains turned their mounts eastward and rode back along the trail to where the vanguard had gathered.

Palian mounted, then Delvor, followed by Richina. Alcaren waited until his consort was astride the gray, then mounted last.

Secca's thoughts kept flitting between the Sturinnese ahead, and Clayre and Neserea. How had Belmar destroyed her? Had she relied too much on her deceptive spell? Or was the Neserean even more cunning? And what about the man in gray who resembled all too clearly the man who had advised Fehern? Was he another Sea-Priest? Were they everywhere?

As they rode slowly along the winding trail, following the vanguard, Alcaren turned to his consort. "Whatever you had thought about—for later, after you deal with the Dumarans . . . whatever it be . . . it frightens you."

"You have read Anna's spells and notes. Are you not frightened at what we may unleash?"

Alcaren nodded. "They are fearsome spells. Yet . . . against the fleets and endless forces of Sturinn . . . what else can we do?"

"I think the first Matriarchs asked that same question when they faced the Mynyans," Secca said wryly. "The Mynyans were defeated. Most of the Matriarchs died, and much of the northern and eastern lands of Ranuak remain poisoned to this day. The Ladies of the Shadows may indeed be right about sorcery. And so are you. If I do nothing, the land may survive, but not us and not a way of living I would wish. Yet, if I do something, there is no certainty that our ways of living will survive—or that we can live through the aftermath."

Alcaren laughed, roughly and ruefully. "It is too bad we cannot fight the Sturinnese in the isles of Sturinn, instead of in Liedwahr. Then we would not need to fret about the devastation so greatly."

"It is too bad. The Sturinnese deserve that—or worse." Secca eased the gray forward, frowning as she considered Alcaren's words for a time. Then she returned to thinking about what spellsong to use when the three of them faced the Sturinnese . . . and how she would need to change the underlying melody for each singer to strengthen the harmonic effect.

As she considered what she was about to attempt, she wondered, not for the first time. Was she becoming as ruthless as the Sturinnese? Was there any other way to deal with a land who wanted to put all women in chains—and cut out the tongues of any women who practiced sorcery?

Secca had found no other answers, besides force in some form. It did not comfort her that Anna before her had failed to find an alternative to force backed by sorcery. There might be an answer, but what it might be eluded Secca. The Ladies of the Shadows had no answers, nor had the Matriarch—and they had considered the problem for scores of generations, if not longer. Greater force seemed to be necessary in dealing with a land that had invaded Liedwahr time and time again without provocation.

But still . . . that thought saddened her.

43

Still wearing the uniform and insignia of a junior captain, Belmar rides slowly along the road, eastward toward Esaria. His eyes traverse the charred figures strewn beside the roadside, and the smaller number scattered across the snow-dotted meadow, and he swallows, almost convulsively, whenever there is a lull in the chill northwest wind that numbs his sense of smell.

Behind him, some of the lancers in the six companies that follow are less able to control their visceral reactions.

As Belmar and jerGlien pass the last of the corpses, the Lord of Worlan turns in the saddle, although he does not look directly at the Sturinnese in gray. "I cannot believe she could destroy ten companies of lancers spread out across a dek."

"They are fearsome enemies, Lord Belmar," replies jerGlien. "Had this one been granted even five companies of lancers, you would have had far greater difficulties. Even though she did not know you were on the far rise, or that you had the drums, she sang four spells for your one, and you had great difficulty."

"Such difficulties . . ." Belmar pauses, before his eyes narrow. "You were riding behind them, and you were unscathed. How did such occur?"

With a shrug, jerGlien replies, "You can see the marks of sorcery fire on the vegetation and upon the road. It only carries so far. I was fortunate to have been somewhat farther away."

"You are always fortunate to be just far enough from adverse circumstances."

"It is perchance my one talent." The Sturinnese adds smoothly, "You are most fortunate as well. Were you fighting the Sorceress Protector of the East, who can muster far more lancers, and who has an assistant accompanying her, you might well still be fighting—or even retreating. That is far greater fortune than my small ability to avoid being too close to a distracted sorceress."

"You think so?"

"You need only look to the south." The voice of the man in gray bears a wry tone.

"Oh . . . I do not yet hold my own land, and you would have me look southward?" Belmar shakes his head.

"Once you have Neserea well in hand, the Sorceress Protector of the East must be destroyed. That is, if you and your heirs wish to hold Neserea."

"Not Lord Robero?"

"He is a weakling. Without his sorceresses, you could make *him* your vassal, and he would thank you for letting him hold on to his lands and title. Now, he may be even easier to persuade to accept a change in rule in Neserea."

"He may, but there *are* three other sorceresses."

The man in gray laughs. "Still . . . you do not see. So I must tell you. There was the Sorceress of Defalk, and she was like unto the sorceresses of old. She was indeed powerful, as you have seen, but she would not surrender her power to have heirs of her body. Nor did she wish to work with others, and she would not ask others to work with her, and without asking, none would follow her. Even had she lived, few would have listened as she aged, and all will remember her but for a few score years, and she will have changed nothing."

"Except for those whom she killed," replies Belmar sardonically.

Ignoring the interjection, jerGlien continues, "Then there is the assistant sorceress, and she uses men as men oft use women. Excepting for her gender, she and her use of sorcery are little different from our own sorcerers, save she has no honor, and as a woman prostituting the harmonies, that makes her an abomination and an aberration. In Sturinn, we would make sure she could do little but bear sons. As her own mistress in Defalk, she will have few children, if any, and those she may have will not follow her."

Belmar nods, continuing to listen.

"The third sorceress—the one who assists the Sorceress Protector of the East—she is powerful, but as yet unformed, and unable to stand against us by herself. That leaves the Sorceress Protector of the East. She has the knowledge of the great sorceress, and, if she lives, will take the over-captain from Ranuak as her consort, if she has not already done so, for he is a cousin or some such of the Matriarch. She will have heirs, and already many look to her and follow her. She will turn all Liedwahr in the direction of the Ranuan bitches, and Lord Robero will let her do so, for he cannot stand against her. Indeed, no man in Liedwahr, save you, Lord Belmar, can stand against her."

Belmar fingers his chin with his right hand, the one that does not hold the reins. "This one here, that you say is not so powerful as the younger . . . she even destroyed my seal ring. That had been my grandsire's. Now it is a lump of melted brass."

"You see why I suggested your lancers all see the destruction and death that she wrought?" asks jerGlien mildly.

"That is obvious," Belmar replies. "So that they can observe how evil the sorceresses are, and how little regard they have for a man's life."

"A man's life," says jerGlien with a laugh. "Well put."

"They would turn us all into children."

"As in Ranuak or that so-called Free City. Even in the Ostisles, Sturinn did not behave so terribly."

"That may be, master jerGlien," Belmar replies, "but I would prefer Sturinn far better as ally than as master. I also prefer the Maitre to continue to remain in Sturinn and rule his demesnes and allow me to rule mine."

"The Maitre has never remained just in Sturinn, Lord Belmar. None know where he may appear. That is one of his strengths." A laugh follows. "As for you and Neserea, have we done aught but supply you with golds, arms, and training? Have you seen a single armsman or lancer in Neserea?"

"That I have not, although I would not wager on that." Belmar laughs. "There are no large forces from Sturinn within Neserea. I do know such."

After they have ridden a time, the Sturinnese adds, "You will have some desertions tonight, as well."

"And I should let them go?"

"The lancers who remain will be fiercer in battle, should it come to that."

"It will come to that, will it not, master jerGlien?"

The Sturinnese shrugs, easily. "You will not have to fight any others from Neserea."

"Just the lancers of the Liedfuhr and the other sorceresses of Defalk." Belmar straightens in the saddle, looking westward along the road that leads to Esaria.

"The Liedfuhr . . . one cannot tell. He will not hazard his lancers, much as he is fond of his sister, for a lost cause."

"So . . . if I can slay the Lady Counselor and her mother and her sister and the consort from Dumar, he will not invade Neserea."

"He may not, if you can act before the snows melt in the Mittpass." Another shrug follows jerGlien's words. "Then, he may. It matters not. He has no sorcerers. You have the power to destroy his lancers, and if you do, then none can contest you. Except, of course, the Sorceress Protector of the East."

"You do not care for this Sorceress Protector."

"It matters little what I care. You will do as you will, and so will she. I merely offer you my advice."

"And golds and arms from the Maitre, when he sees fit." Belmar laughs. "He should see fit now, for another sorceress is dead."

"Oh, I have no doubts you will be richly rewarded for

this, Lord Belmar. No doubts at all, and that is how it should be."

"And so will you, for you have helped me, and that has aided Sturinn's cause, else you would not be here."

"You are most perceptive, Lord Belmar. As always."

Belmar looks westward once more, toward Esaria.

44

Under the late-morning sun, Secca had unfastened her jacket, so warm had the day become. She was trying to work on harmonies with Richina and Alcaren as they rode up over the hills, and that was work as well, and contributed to her getting warmer and warmer, although some of the heat was from the sun, enough that she could smell the earth warming. The three rode close together, but the trail was so narrow that Richina and Secca were side by side, with Alcaren trailing close behind.

"Just sing 'la' for every syllable," Secca said, mostly to remind Alcaren, since Secca and Anna had worked such exercises with Richina for several years. "On my mark . . . Mark!"

"La, la, la . . ."

Halfway through what was supposed to have been the first stanza of the third building song, Secca said, "Stop!" She looked to Richina. "You're singing what I do. It won't harm the spell, but it won't be as strong."

"I know you have said it is not so, but it seems so odd," replied the sandy-blonde sorceress, easing herself into a different position in the saddle. "It would seem stronger if we sang the same notes."

Secca shook her head. "We do . . . on the last part of each stanza. That is where we come together. Think of it as . . ." she frowned. "The music has more depth. Anna would have called it color. Depth and color make it stronger."

"But . . . if you spin threads together, they are stronger, and they are all alike," replied Richina.

"The different parts support different things . . . like the braces for a causeway . . . or a bridge," Secca responded.

"If you say so, Lady Secca." Richina's tone remained polite, but dubious.

Secca wanted to yell at the younger sorceress, but swallowed the feeling, and mentally tried to figure out another way of explaining. After a moment, she spoke. "You know, when the second players join in a spell, they do not play the same as the first do?"

"They play chords," Richina admitted.

"If you listen to the chords—closely," Secca went on, "they often have a different sound. Yet, when they play so, the spellsongs we sing are more powerful. What they do with the accompaniment is what we must do with the spellsong."

Richina nodded, too politely for Secca.

"It is like blades, then," offered Alcaren, from where he rode slightly behind the two women. "A sabre must have more than just iron in it. Even a bronze platter is harder than one made of pure copper. Sometimes, something that is all of a kind is weaker than something having different substances."

Secca wouldn't have thought of blades, but the analogy was mostly correct. "That's right. We're forging a stronger kind of spellsong."

This time, Richina's nod seemed to encompass understanding.

"That's why you need to sing the line below mine," Secca repeated. "You are not singing to support me or Alcaren. We are all singing to weld together a powerful spell."

Secca just hoped that they would be able to work out the three-part arrangement. While failure of the spell would not be as deadly as failure in a conventional battle, since they would be trying it from much farther away, her feelings kept telling her that she had far less time than it would seem. Clayre's defeat and death reinforced that sense of urgency, yet even Alcaren did not seem to understand fully her concerns about time.

But then, she told herself, she might not be reading her consort's feelings, since he kept so much hidden, and, to be fair, she had not had a chance to talk to him fully in a place where she felt comfortable explaining how she felt.

"Now . . . can we try it again?" Secca asked.

Alcaren and Richina both nodded.

45

Standing before the bare limbed oak, a tree that had yet to show the buds that would herald spring, Secca glanced from the hilltop to the distant road, shading her eyes against the sun as she studied the ravine a dek or so west and below the hilltop, and the angled lower ridge farther to the southwest. The line of silver that was the Envar River was nearly six deks from the hilltop. In the distance, she could see what looked to be a cloud of dust rising from the river road.

A brief gust of wind swirled around her, a mixture of warm and cold air, but one hinting more at the spring to come than the winter past, with the scent of moisture and a hint of some early-spring flower, although Secca had seen none on the ride through the hills, even in the low bushes on the sunny side of the windbreaking line of firs a dek downhill and to the west.

"They are within two deks of where they must be for us to begin the spellsong." Secca turned to her right, looking to where Palian and Delvor stood before the arrayed players. "A half a glass, I would judge."

"We stand ready," replied the gray-eyed and gray-haired chief of the first players.

Secca turned back to Alcaren and Richina. "Have you the spell words firmly in mind?"

"Yes, lady," replied Richina.

Alcaren nodded. His eyes were dark, and Secca understood why. Richina was preoccupied with the task to come, too young too understand what using the spell meant, and where it well might lead.

"How close must they come?" asked Alcaren in a low voice.

"I do not know," Secca admitted. "When I sang the spell alone, the one against the archers, the effects reached four deks. Anna once sang a spell alone with players that reached more than ten deks. I can but hope that by holding the hillside, and with us singing together, that we can reach the six deks or so from here to where the road passes the closest." She offered a crooked smile. "If we fail, they cannot pursue us directly, not over the ravines and broken ground."

"If we fail badly enough," he said with a laugh, "they will never know we attempted such." The forced smile faded. "You worry more about success."

"I do." She paused. "If this works, we need to think about warding spells, ones that will wake or protect us if sorcery is being tried against us."

"You think we are being watched in a glass?"

"If not already . . . soon. And if we can strike from a distance with spells, we can be struck from a distance."

Richina turned. "They are not so strong as you, lady."

Secca laughed, mirthlessly. "I appreciate your feelings, Richina, but . . . they do not have to be so strong. Anna was attacked in Dumar by a hidden Sea-Priest with a pair of enchanted javelins. There are many more sorcerers among the Sea-Priests than in all the other lands of Liedwahr. What we do, sooner or later they will try."

"Unless you vanquish them all," Richina said.

"And then what?" asked Secca.

Richina's brow wrinkled into a puzzled frown.

"If we destroy all the Sea-Priest sorcerers in Liedwahr, what will the Maitre do? Leave us alone forever? Or just for a few years?" pursued Secca.

"The Sea-Priests left us alone for a score of years." Richina finally replied.

"So we must fight them every score of years? Or should I follow their example, and try to destroy them in their own land? And how am I different from them in that instance?"

"You did not start this war or the last," replied Alcaren bluntly. "You sorceresses have only asked that women be treated as equals. The old lords, the Prophet of Music, and the Sturinnese cannot accept that. You can change the old lords in Defalk . . . and without the meddling of the Sea-Priests, you can change Neserea—but you will never change Sturinn. It is a land that has enslaved and chained its women since before the Pelaran Devastation, and killed or silenced any woman of strength for endless generations."

Secca sighed almost silently. "We don't have to face those questions now. We have to worry about one spell." *Yet . . . will it come to that?* She pushed the thought away and looked to her right, where the players had finished running through a warm-up tune.

"When you are ready, Lady Secca," Palian said quietly.

"It will not be long."

Secca concentrated on the images she intended to use, knowing that her visualization had to be clear and precise, although she had told Alcaren and Richina to concentrate on words and melody, and to leave the imagery to her.

"The main body of the Sturinnese is nearing the bend in the road," called Delcetta from the southern end of the ridge.

"Players, stand ready!" ordered Palian.

Secca glanced from Alcaren to Richina. Both nodded in response.

After looking to the southwest, to confirm as best she could Delcetta's report, Secca cleared her throat, then declared, "At your mark, chief player!"

"At my mark . . . Mark!"

The first bar was only the first players, followed by Delvor's second players. Secca and the other two joined on the third bar, and the spellsong rose from the hillside into the clear sky.

> *"Clouds to form and winds to rise*
> *like a caldron in darkening skies.*
> *Build a storm with winds of ice and heat*
> *that scythes all Sturinn's men like ripened wheat . . ."*

Even before the end of the first stanza, hazy clouds had begun to form, and the light breeze out of the north had strengthened into a solid and stiff wind that pressed against Secca's back and simultaneously carried the spellsong and accompaniment toward the distant Sturinnese force.

A quick breath was all that Secca managed before launching into the second stanza. She concentrated on keeping a clear image of the dark funnel cloud sweeping along the road, sparing none of the Sturinnese force, especially the Sea-Priest sorcerers and drummers.

Beside her, Alcaren's voice held true, strong but supporting, while Richina's provided almost a counterpoint.

> *"Clouds to boil and storms to bubble*
> *crush to broken sticks of wind-strewn rubble*
> *all in Sturinn's service or in Sea-Priest white*
> *and let none escape the whirlwind's might . . ."*

With the last words of the spell, and the deep, not-quite-dull chime of the harmonies that rolled through her, indeed through all nearby who could sense them, Secca looked toward the southwest and the road that held the Sturinnese force. The skies above the river and the road had turned almost black, yet the higher clouds were nearly perfect white—but Secca could see them only for a few moments before the lower and blacker clouds thickened and covered the entire sky, turning the afternoon into twilight.

Her arms felt stiff, and exhaustion had dropped across her like a heavy wet blanket. The exertion of the spell had left her momentarily hot and damp all over, but that lasted only for moments, and she shivered in the rapidly chilling air. Her head ached, and her eyes watered, blurring with the flash of daystars.

The stiff breeze had become a whining, roaring torrent of air, pushing Secca toward the steeper downhill slope before her, with such force that she staggered to hold her balance, before dropping to her knees in the damp and flattened grass. With the gale came snow that whipped around Secca, chill and beadlike. Then, ice pellets began to fall, flaying her back and shoulders.

Abruptly, she felt herself lifted by Alcaren's strong arms.

"We need to get to lower ground," he shouted above the roaring of the wind that had only strengthened. "We are too exposed here."

"Order it!" Secca turned out of Alcaren's grip and, fighting her way into the wind and ice, struggled uphill toward the gray mare that stood stolidly against the sorcery-called storm.

"Down into the trees to the west! Down to the trees!" Alcaren called out.

"To the west . . ." Delcetta's voice rose above the whistle of the wind as well, carrying the same orders.

Wishing she had worn the battered green felt hat, instead of leaving it in her saddlebags, Secca bent farther forward against the wind until she reached her mount. In one moment, when the snow and ice pellets abated for a mere instant, to the south she could see the players lashing instruments to their horses. Secca levered herself up into the saddle with tired legs and arms.

"Here!" called Alcaren, his mount practically beside hers. "This way."

Secca squinted through the whiteness to see Richina on the other side of Alcaren.

"This way," Alcaren repeated, guiding them downhill.

Secca followed, wordlessly, noting that three of her lancers—Gorkon, Rukor, and Achar—had joined them to reform as a guard. The group had gone less than a quarter of a dek, when Alcaren spoke again. "I need to go back and make sure all the players and lancers are getting clear." He pointed downhill. "Beyond the trees you can take shelter. We will rejoin you shortly."

"Be careful!" Secca called out, as her consort turned his mount back uphill. Once again, she wished she were larger and stronger, but for her to follow Alcaren, as she felt, barely able to stay in the saddle, would have served no one well.

"I dare not be otherwise," he replied before vanishing into the flurry of white snow and ice pellets.

Secca kept looking over her shoulder as she and Richina rode northward and downhill. At first, she could see nothing; but Alcaren had been right for the farther downhill she rode, the easier it became to see. Before long, looking back, she could see the players emerging from the worst of the storm, and then a company of SouthWomen, and more lancers. She just hoped that Alcaren would return before long.

"The storm is clearing," Richina suggested to Secca.

Secca gestured for the younger sorceress to turn in the saddle and look back over her shoulder. A sheet of white rose from the ridge behind them, a whiteness that seemed like a wall that climbed from the ridge crest as far skyward as Secca could make out, a wall behind which lay a great darkness.

Richina followed Secca's gesture. "Dissonance . . ." The younger sorceress's voice died away.

"Let us hope it was as effective as it appears," Secca said, turning from the view behind toward the trail road ahead, toward the trees ahead that looked to form a windbreak.

46

I n the glow that the early-morning sun sent through the weathered and stained silk of the small tent, Secca glanced from the closed door panel to Alcaren. The tent was cramped in holding Alcaren, Richina, both overcaptains, both chief players, and Secca, and the air was barely warmer than that outside the tent.

Secca's consort stood over the scrying glass laid on the end of the one cot. In spite of the redheaded sorceress's exhaustion, headache, the daystars that flashed across her eyes, and the intermittently blurring vision, even a day after the massive spellsinging against the Sturinnese, she felt guilty that she had a tent when everyone else had been forced to sleep in lean-tos and other makeshift shelters in and behind the firs that had served as a windbreak.

The overcaptains and chief players had reported some mild cases of frostbite, but nothing worse, and the firs of the windbreak had provided enough wood for cookfires— around which many of the lancers had warmed themselves. There was no fire in the small tent, and the breath of those gathered within steamed in the cold.

"Lady?" asked Alcaren.

Secca nodded at her consort.

He began the scrying song without comment.

"Show us where upon a map of this land . . ."

When Alcaren finished, the mirror displayed but one white star—and that was near the trade pass. Secca looked once more to Alcaren, who lifted his lumand and offered the more conventional spellsong that brought up an image of the Sturinnese force gathered in a small hamlet, with a

patrol about the size of a squad mounting up and preparing
to ride somewhere. There was no sign of snow or of dampness in the clay of the road, and the Sturinnese lancers had
their white riding jackets but loosely fastened.

At Secca's nod, Alcaren sang the release couplet.

"The Sturinnese that were on the road yesterday. They're
gone," murmured Delcetta. "As if they had never been."

Wilten looked up from the blank scrying glass to Secca,
almost reproachfully.

Secca understood the look. "It is hard to believe," she
said quietly, "and some of you may wonder why I did not
use such spells earlier." She offered a bitter smile. "There
is but a single reason." *That you want to tell them.* "First, I
am not experienced in warfare, and there were no such spells
in the books that Lady Anna left to me." *Others far more
terrible than the ones you used, but not the ones you created.* "So I had to learn what I and Alcaren and Richina
could do. There may yet be more that we can do, but we
can only learn by doing."

Palian, who had caught Wilten's expression, added, "Already, what Lady Secca has tried has near-on slain her at
least once, and left her weak and helpless other times. If she
and the others perish in trying too much too soon, we all
will perish soon after, as did those with Lady Clayre. Do
you wish that?"

"Ah . . . no, chief player. No," said Wilten quickly, flinching as much from the fire in Palian's gray eyes as the hard
chill in her voice. "I did not mean such."

"I am most certain you did not," Palian replied warmly.
"You have always been most solicitous of the lady Secca,
and your devotion to her and your duty is well-known. Most
well-known."

Wilten smiled wryly, as if to note that he understood he
was being offered a graceful way out. "As is yours, chief
player."

Alcaren coughed, loudly.

All eyes but those of Secca turned to the broad-shouldered sorcerer.

"Ah . . . a chill. Please excuse me."

Richina smothered a smile.

In the silence, Secca spoke. "Now . . . we need to move northward, against the remaining Sturinnese here in Dumar."

"Lady Clayre?" asked Delvor, almost apologetically.

"I . . . we cannot return her from the dead," Secca answered, her voice heavy. If . . . if she had moved more quickly, could she have reached Neserea in time? She wanted to shake her head. The passes that led north and west had been blocked even before Secca had completed dealing with the Sturinnese in Ebra. "It may be that once we deal with the remaining Sea-Priests it will be warm enough that we can venture through the trade pass and into Neserea. We can but stop this Belmar and make Neserea safe for the Lady Counselor and heir."

"The lancers are almost ready to ride," offered Delcetta.

"And they would be far happier to spend tonight in a warmer and drier place?" asked Secca with an inquiring smile.

"Indeed," replied Delcetta.

"Then we should ride back the way we came, for that is warmer and drier than the route the Sturinnese took." Secca looked to Wilten.

"Our lancers are also ready."

"In a half-glass?" asked Secca.

"No more than a glass," replied Wilten.

Secca nodded, and Alcaren stepped back to open the tent panel. Secca could feel with the light breeze entering the tent that the air remained chill.

Palian waited until the overcaptains and Delvor had left the tent. She inclined her head. "I trust my harsh words to Wilten did not offend you too greatly?"

Secca shook her head and smiled, sadly. "No. They were words that needed to be said, yet not ones that I could say. I thank you."

The chief player smiled, almost wistfully. "You cannot say all that needs to be said. Nor can your consort nor your assistant."

"That may be, but your words were welcome," Secca replied.

"And wise," added Alcaren.

"Wise?" Palian arched her eyebrows. "What we do must be done, but wise? Only if we succeed."

"That is true of all ventures," countered Alcaren. "Success renders the foolish wise, and failure makes the wise foolish."

With a last smile, Palian nodded and slipped out into the cold and clear morning.

"While the lancers strike the tent," Alcaren suggested, "you should ride up to the top of the ridge and see what lies to the south."

"You know. You've seen it, or you wouldn't be suggesting that," Secca replied. "Just tell me."

"My telling you is not the same as your seeing it," he said, smiling.

"I defer to your wisdom." Secca fastened her jacket more tightly and pulled on her riding gloves, then went to saddle the gray mare.

After she had struggled through saddling her mount and refusing aid from Gorkon, knowing she was being foolish, Secca fastened her saddlebags, scrying mirror, and lutar in place.

Then the gray mare carried Secca uphill from the campsite, through snow that would have been nearly knee high had she not been following the track broken by the scouts. Alcaren rode beside her, his breath white against the brilliant blue sky. Richina, wearing both her blue hat and scarf to bundle herself against the cold, followed, as did Palian.

At the crest of the hill, not all that far from where she had sung the storm spell the day before, Secca looked out to the south and east. Despite the warmth of the morning sunlight, everything beyond the hilltop was covered with white, covered deeply enough that not even grass or bushes showed through. Even the valley beyond the road where the Sturinnese had ridden the afternoon before was blanketed in sun-glistening white.

"It is a terrible sight," murmured Palian.

Within herself, Secca had to agree. *But how many more terrible sights will you need to behold before the struggle against the Maitre of Sturinn ends?*

47

WEI, NORDWEI

S etting aside the polished agate oval that she had been stroking with her fingers, Ashtaar covers her mouth with the dark green cloth and muffles the coughs that rack her body. After a time, she straightens and sits erect behind the desk, facing one of the empty straight-backed chair across the table-desk from her, her dark eyes abstracted, as though her thoughts are a continent away.

As the bells that mark the turning of the glass strike, echoing across Wei from the tower to the north of the Council building, there is a single *thrap* on the wooden door.

"You may enter, Escadra." Ashtaar's voice is firm, almost hard.

The dark haired and stocky seer bows twice before stepping toward the desk, and the Council Leader who sits behind its polished and shimmering surface. Escadra sits on the front part of the chair, her eyes slightly downcast, so that she appears to be looking at Ashtaar, but so that she is not meeting the intensity of Ashtaar's scrutiny.

"Go ahead," prompts the silver-haired Council Leader.

"The Shadow Sorceress has found yet another way to use the harmonies for destruction," begins the seer, letting her words drift into silence, and looking to Ashtaar for a reaction.

"Spare me the opinions, Escadra, and tell me what happened."

Escadra flushes, then replies. "She created a cyclone wide enough to destroy more than fortyscore Sturinnese lancers, and their Sea-Priest sorcerers and drummers, from more than ten deks distant, even across a range of hills. So violent was the spell that all the seers here in Wei could feel the harmonies chime."

"Harmonically?" asks Ashtaar.

"Ah . . . yes, your mightiness. It was pure Clearsong, but strong and most violent."

"Did it prostrate the sorceress or her assistant?"

"No, Leader Ashtaar. Or not for long. The recoil from the spell created a snowstorm that dropped a half a yard of snow across the land. Even so, they are riding northwest, back toward the trade pass into Neserea and the remaining Sturinnese forces."

"I see." Ashtaar grips the green cloth in her left hand and takes a sip of the water in the goblet on the side of the desk. She swallows before asking, "What about the Sturinnese? Are they retreating?"

"They appear to be drawing up onto a hilltop near the base of the trade pass."

"A hilltop with a sheer rock cliff behind it, perchance?"

Escadra frowns, tilting her head and closing her eyes, as if trying to call up the image she had seen in the scrying pool. Finally, she opens her eyes. "I believe so, your mightiness."

"And would there be more drums and sorcerers in the remaining Sturinnese force?"

"Yes. It would appear so."

"What does that tell us?" Ashtaar's voice carries a forced patience.

Again, the seer frowns before responding. "That the Sturinnese wish to lure the sorceress into a trap, and that they are more concerned about her traveling into Neserea than in what she may do in Dumar?"

"Is there any other reasonable conclusion?"

"I cannot think of one."

"This time . . . this time . . . you would appear correct. What does that imply for us in Wei?"

There is another pause. "The Lord Belmar has destroyed the Sorceress of Defalk, though she slaughtered more than half his lancers, and the Sturinnese fleet is headed to Esaria. When they reach the last ice of the Bitter Sea, there they will use drum sorcery to break the ice."

"So . . . there are no forces left in Neserea to stop Lord Belmar?"

"The Liedfuhr's lancers are almost through the Mittpass and near the western edge of the Great Western Forest."

"Do they have any sorcerers?"

"No, Leader Ashtaar."

"The younger sister of Annayal is now in Nordwei, is she not? And she is consorted to Eryhal, who is the presumptive heir to Fehern?"

"They are near Morgen, riding along the south branch of the River Nord."

"No one else of import has escaped Belmar, have they?"

Escadra's hand goes to her mouth. "That would give the Sturinnese a reason to . . ."

"It would give them many reasons." Ashtaar clears her throat, and swallows, then takes another sip of water. "Have you discerned who the Sea-Priest sorcerer is who travels upon occasion with Belmar?"

"No, Leader Ashtaar, save that often he is shielded in some fashion or another, and that he must have great power, and that there are others nearby, also shielded. Lord Belmar does not know they are present, from what we can discern." Escadra pauses. "Are you going to send a scroll to Lord Robero . . ." Her words trail away as Ashtaar's eyes seem to flash, and then she stumbles over her next words. "I beg your pardon, your mightiness, I do. I am most sorry . . ."

"I may pardon you, or I may not. That is not for you to
know or decide. Knowing that Lord Robero shies from his
own shadow, and that his failure to send another sorceress
and more lancers with the Sorceress of Defalk, would you
think that such a scroll would prompt him to send greater
aid to Neserea? With a Sturinnese fleet and the Liedfuhr's
lancers both ready to invade?"

Escadra winces.

"You are correct there, at least. Lord Robero will not
learn any of this from us. Do you see why?"

"Yes, your mightiness."

"Good." Ashtaar covers her mouth with the heavy green
cloth and coughs once, before taking another sip from her
goblet. "You may go. Watch both Lord Belmar and the
Shadow Sorceress . . ." Ashtaar gestures, wordlessly, for the
seer to leave the study.

Escadra, her dark eyes lingering on the older woman,
rises and bows.

Once the door closes, Ashtaar collapses into a long fit of
coughing, the paroxysm muffled by the green cloth. Some
considerable time passes before she straightens and takes
another sip from her goblet.

48

Lady Secca . . ."
At the sound of Richina's voice, low and urgent-
sounding, Secca forced open gummy eyes, trying to ignore
the faint throbbing in her head. Her hand touched the canvas, by her cheek, and she frowned. *Canvas? Where . . . ?*

As she looked up from the travel cot and around the
silken tent, a tent whose side panels bore all too many stains
and patches, the scattered fragments of memory swirling inside her head snapped into place. She was on the road back

to Hasjyl, to deal with the last of the Sturinnese forces in Dumar. Slowly, she eased herself upright, looking down toward the closed front tent panel, trying to ignore the daystars that flashed across her vision, if infrequently.

Alcaren had taken to sleeping on a mat laid crosswise at the foot of Secca's cot, claiming that was the best alternative, since he wished to be near his consort, but also wished not to displace Richina. Neither Alcaren nor Richina was anywhere to be seen.

"Lady Secca . . . ?"

"You can come in, Richina," Secca said, her voice cracking, as she turned and sat up sideways on the canvas cot. Even with her feet on the narrow mat, she could feel the chill of the ground below. She fumbled for the water bottle, prying out the cork with stiff fingers and taking a slow swallow.

Richina slipped inside the small tent and stood waiting at the foot of the cot.

Secca looked at the younger woman.

"Lady . . . there is a lord on his way here."

"A lord?"

"He has retainers, and a squad of lancers, and they ride under twin banners—one white and the other a blue banner of harmony."

"He doesn't want trouble, then. No players?"

"None."

Secca took another swallow from the water bottle before speaking. "How far away is he?"

"Lord Alcaren judges that the lord is still two deks to the west. He asked me to wake you."

Secca bent over and pulled on her boots. "Tell him I'm getting ready."

By the time she had eaten some bread and cheese, and made herself vaguely presentable, the dull headache had subsided, as had the daystars—mostly. She fastened the green leather jacket loosely and stepped outside into a day that was not quite so sunny as the one previous. A high thin haze had turned the sky a pale blue, and a gentle and warmer breeze flowed out of the west across the flat of the sheltered meadow that lay slightly below the ridge road.

"Good morning, Lady Secca," offered Rukor, from his post outside the tent. His voice was cheerful.

Secca smiled. "Good morning, Rukor, Dymen. I hope you got some rest."

"That we did, lady," answered Dymen. "We just relieved Achar and Easlon, less than a glass ago."

All three turned as Alcaren rode up, almost as if he had been watching for her. "I hope you don't mind. You were tired, and I thought you should get some more sleep, if you could."

"I was tired," Secca admitted. "Do you know who this lord is?"

"The scouts said that he calls himself Sylonn, and that the area around Hasjyl is his demesne. He told one of them that his uncle was Lord Ehara's cousin."

Ehara? The Lord of Dumar that Anna had defeated and destroyed? Secca frowned.

"He wants something, and he wants you to know that you should treat with him," Alcaren observed.

"He could want almost anything the way matters are now," Secca replied dryly. "Protection from the last of the Sturinnese, my assurance that he will keep his lands, a consort for him or his son, a bridge built . . ." She shook her head, thinking of all the possibilities.

Richina approached from the cookfire. "Lady . . . if I might . . ."

"You may stay," Secca said.

Alcaren turned. "Here he comes."

"If you would stand ready," Secca requested, looking at him.

"I will remain mounted, my lady," her consort said with a laugh, "with my hand near my blade."

Both Dymen and Rukor stepped forward, each standing

a yard to the side and slightly in front of Secca. Richina stepped back toward the tent.

The five watched as Delcetta led two riders away from the column and toward Secca and Alcaren. One was a standard bearer, and the rider who followed the banner wore gray—a gray leather riding jacket, gray trousers and boots, and an odd-looking and short brimmed gray riding hat. The only color in his attire was a scarlet scarf knotted loosely around his neck.

Delcetta reined up a good ten yards from Secca, her eyes still on the two riders who had followed her. "Lady Secca, Lord Sylonn of Dumar has requested a moment of your time."

"Thank you, Overcaptain." Secca nodded to the Dumaran. "Welcome, Lord Sylonn."

Sylonn dismounted, handing the reins of the gray stallion to the standard-bearer, who was also attired all in gray, but without the crimson scarf. Then the Dumaran lord took two steps toward Secca and bowed. "Lady Sorceress. I am Sylonn, Lord of Hesodryll, and most faithful subject of Dumar and of Lord Robero." Sylonn's hair was black and silver, but his square-trimmed beard was entirely silver. His small and deep-set brown eyes went to Alcaren, as if asking for an explanation.

Secca ignored the silent inquiry. "It is good to see a lord and loyal subject of Lord Robero. I must apologize for my appearance and for my not paying my respects to you, but we have been occupied—as you must know—with the Sturinnese."

Sylonn bowed a second time, then straightened. His flat brown eyes did not quite meet Secca's amber ones when he began to speak. "All Dumar is grateful to you for your efforts. We had feared that everything would be lost."

"We have not finished with those of Sturinn," Secca said gently. "There is still another force to the north. There also may be Sturinnese vessels sailing to Narial from the Ostisles."

"Lady Sorceress . . . you have come to Dumar, as did the last great sorceress, and you have destroyed all the Sturinnese that have faced you. All know that you will destroy the remaining Sea-Priests—unless they flee before you can reach them."

"It cannot be a secret that Defalk does not want the Sea-Priests anywhere in Liedwahr," Secca temporized, wondering exactly what Sylonn wanted.

"None would want masters from Sturinn. The Sea-Priests will throw down a lord and a family who have served their people for generations. The Sturinnese give not a thought to what a man has done, only to what increases their power."

Secca didn't see much difference between the lords of most lands and the Sturinnese in that respect, but she merely said, "Sturinn would not be good for Dumar or any land in Liedwahr."

"That is most true. Lord Clehar was a good ruler, and his sons would have been as well," Sylonn continued.

"Would have been?" asked Secca, with a sinking feeling as she realized what was coming.

"You did not know?" Sylonn blinked several times, then shook his head. "Perhaps there would have been no way for you to know." He shook his head once more.

"If I understand you," Secca said, "his sons and daughter . . . ?"

"They were found dead in the palace at Dumaria after Clehar died in battle," Sylonn said. "Many suspected Lord Fehern, but now . . . who can tell?"

"Did not Lord Fehern have sons from his first consort?" Secca recalled Clayre mentioning that one of Clehar's brothers had sons. At the thought of Clayre, even though they had not been that close, Secca felt a rush of regret and sadness.

"He had two. That is true, Lady Sorceress, but they have vanished. None can find them. Likewise, Lord Eryhal was in Neserea with his consort . . ."

"You'd like to know who will be the next Lord High

Counselor?" asked Secca, keeping her voice mild and level.

"Ah . . ." Sylonn glanced away from Secca, toward Al-caren, and then back toward Delcetta, who had also re-mained mounted and close. "Ah . . . my holdings are not far from here, and when I heard you were traveling . . . well . . . I thought it likely that if anyone knew . . . that would be you, Great Sorceress."

Secca managed neither to frown nor to snort at Sylonn's not-so-veiled ambition. "I appreciate your interest, Lord Sy-lonn, but I am not the one who will make that decision. It is Lord Robero's prerogative to name the next Lord High Counselor. I am most certain that he will act as quickly as he can. I will certainly convey your concerns to him as I can . . . and I thank you for being forthright enough to ap-proach me."

"Oh . . . that is all that I can ask." Sylonn bowed quickly. "It is just that matters have been so unsettled."

"Battles and fighting can unsettle the most peaceful of lands," Secca replied. "I will also tell Lord Robero of your concern that matters be settled."

"Thank you, Lady Sorceress. Thank you." Sylonn bowed again, as if uncertain as to what he should do next.

"You may go, Lord Sylonn, and I will convey your con-cerns." Secca felt as though she were endlessly repeating herself, but she knew she could not and should not commit to more.

After yet another bow, the Dumaran lord turned and walked to his horse, mounting quickly, then following Del-cetta and his standard-bearer back toward his personal guard.

Secca watched until she was certain the Dumaran was well out of earshot.

"We haven't even finished with the Sturinnese, and now we'll have to deal with the succession problem here in Du-mar. If we don't . . ." Secca shook her head. "Lords! They won't support their rulers, or support them as little as pos-sible. Now, they're all jostling for position practically before the Lord High Counselor's body has grown cold."

"Such is life among those who seek power," observed Alcaren.

"Do you think they all are like that?" asked Richina.

Secca almost jumped at the voice of the younger sorceress standing behind her. Richina had been so silent that Secca had forgotten she was there. The older sorceress half turned. "Only those lords still alive. Many would not have been even that indirect."

"Witness what is happening in Neserea," Alcaren added. "Lord Hanfor dies, and all wish to be his successor."

"You'll notice that the noble lord Sylonn didn't invite us to share his hospitality," Secca said with a crooked smile.

"Would you want to?" Alcaren laughed.

"No. I'd be looking in the glass and over my shoulder every moment." Still . . . it would have been nice to get a bath and sleep in a good bed—although good beds were rare in most keeps and holdings.

Secca turned to her left to watch as Lord Sylonn's troop made its way back westward along the ridge road. "We'd better check on the Sturinnese."

"Ah . . ." Alcaren flushed.

Secca turned to Richina, who looked down.

"You two already did?"

"Yes, lady," admitted Richina. "They remain in the same hamlet."

Secca laughed.

After a moment, so did the other two. A smile even crossed Rukor's face, although the lancer turned sober-faced as Secca glanced at him.

49

I n the late-afternoon light that slanted through the west
windows, Secca looked around the sitting room in the
merchant's dwelling. Here she was, back in Hasjyl, a week
or so later, with yet another Sturinnese force to confront.
Clayre was dead, along with her lancers, both slain by Belmar's sorcery, and little lay between Belmar and his conquest of Esaria—and Neserea. Not with most of the lords
flocking to him, and those who had not being destroyed by
sorcery and treachery.

Secca snorted. She was mired in Dumar, a land without
a Lord High Counselor, and a land where who knew how
many lords were trying to succeed the nefarious and dead
Fehern—or wanting to know who would so that they could
work their way into positions of power and influence. After
weeks of riding and sorcery and storms, she felt bone-tired.
And she felt guilty about feeling tired, knowing that her
lancers had suffered the weather more, and that Alcaren and
Richina had been through everything she had.

Thinking that water and biscuits might help, she lifted the
water bottle she had put on the oblong table and took a
swallow, following the water with a biscuit that she finished
in three bites, hard as the biscuit had been.

"You should have done that earlier, like I suggested," said
Alcaren from just inside the doorway. "Because you're
smaller, you—"

"I know. I need to eat more often. You told me that."
Secca winced at the sharpness of her words, adding quickly
and more softly, "I'm sorry. You are right. But it is hard
always to be reminded when you're smaller and less strong
than those around you."

Alcaren laughed. "I would never say less strong. Smaller,

yes, and because your stomach is small, it cannot hold as much, and yet because you do more than others, you must eat more often."

"I know," Secca said again, not angrily as before, but tiredly.

Hisss . . . thunk!

A tube of brass appeared on the table, hot enough that Secca could smell the wood under it beginning to heat immediately. She reached for the riding gloves tucked in her belt, but Alcaren was faster, yanking on his gloves and scooping up the tube. He hastened to the end of the long room where he set the tube on the floor. There, he used a wooden dipper to sprinkle water on the tube from the bucket Rukor had brought inside moments before. The water hissed into steam as it struck the heat-tarnished brass.

Alcaren continued to sprinkle the tube with water until the hissing stopped.

Then, almost as quickly as he had seized the tube, Alcaren yanked off his gloves, putting his hands into the bucket of cold water.

"Are you all right?" asked Secca.

"I'm fine. My hands will be a little red, but that will pass."

"Why?" She glanced at the metal tube.

"It was sent by sorcery, and in haste, because it was hot. If you had picked it up, you would have burned your hands. My gloves are heavier, and I could get to the water. If I hadn't the messages inside would be charred and unreadable." Alcaren snorted. "They may be anyway."

After a time he lifted his hands from the bucket, and held one just above the tube, lowering it slowly. "It is cool enough to open." He picked up the message tube and handed it to Secca.

She had to force the end cap off the tube. Although the parchment was brown, the ink on the single scroll was dark enough that she could easily read the words.

Dearest Secca,
As you must know from the wrenching of the harmo-

nies, Clayre perished in attempting to defeat Belmar. She destroyed nearly tenscore of his lancers, but that was not enough, and Belmar lost none of his players.

I have not yet told Lord Robero, for I fear that he will send you orders to return to Defalk. He has already begun to talk about reaching some truce with the Sturinnese if we cannot defeat them. Alyssa has told him that he should decide nothing until he sees how matters turn out with you and Clayre, but he told her that she should not presume, and now he paces and frets that you have shown little success . . .

Secca shook her head and lowered the scroll. Changing his name from Jimbob to Robero hadn't changed the Lord of Defalk's character or his self-centered concern about his own power, rather than his people's needs—or even the needs of the Thirty-three.

"You are angry," remarked Alcaren, who had been reading the words over her shoulder.

"I am more than angry." Secca spaced out the words. "He sent Clayre out without an assistant and with but two companies of lancers."

"Did she not choose to go?"

"She did." Secca took a deep breath. "But he *knew* she would not insist on more. Clayre is . . . she was . . . too proud."

Alcaren nodded slowly.

"You think I'm too proud?"

"There is a difference," he answered carefully, "between pride and foolhardiness. You have trained Richina, and you are training me to help with sorcery. When the need was there, you asked Richina to help. You allow me to assist you. You did not even consider leaving Richina behind, did you?"

"No . . ." Secca admitted slowly. "But when we left Lo-

iseau, I could not have explained why I brought her. I *felt*
it was right."

Alcaren smiled. "That is the difference."

Secca wasn't sure, but she lifted the scroll and resumed
reading.

> . . . He asks me every day whether you have defeated
> the Sea-Priests.. . .

> We have received word from the Council Leader of
> Wei that Aerfor and Eryhal have fled Neserea and
> made their way safely into Nordwei. Lady Aerlya and
> Annayal remain in Esaria, but their forces are dimin-
> ishing. Many are deserting, and others appear to be
> asking that Annayal consort with Belmar or even that
> she request that he become Lord High Counselor—if
> not Prophet of Music.

> The Liedfuhr's lancers are making their way through
> the snows of the Mittpass toward Neserea. He had mar-
> shaled close to five thousand lancers and armsmen, but
> those struggling through the snows number far less than
> that, less than a hundred companies. From what I can
> scry, Belmar is moving to the southwest, and ignoring
> Esaria . . .

"Of course," murmured Secca.

"If he destroys the Liedfuhr's lancers, then he will hold
Neserea—until we can vanquish him," Alcaren said softly.

"You are most hopeful, my love," Secca said softly.

"You can defeat Belmar."

"But can we defeat Belmar and who knows how many
Sturinnese sorcerers?" asked Secca.

"We must."

With a faint and knowing smile, Secca returned to reading
the scroll.

. . . Lord Robero had asked Lythner if he would act as
an envoy to Lord Belmar, should it be necessary. To
his credit, Lythner declined and left Falcor. Lord Robero has summoned Lythner's brother Nerylt from Wendel . . .

Secca winced. Nerylt was a well-meaning bumbler who
would do whatever Robero asked without raising an eyebrow or a question.

. . . but he has yet to arrive. So you can see why I dare
not tell Lord Robero about Clayre. Yet I can keep that
secret only for weeks at best, days at worst. If there is
aught you can do, or that I can do for you, please let
me know. As matters are proceeding, all will be lost in
a season, if not sooner.

Secca looked up from Jolyn's hasty signature. "I do not
know if we can reclaim Dumar in a season."

"Why reclaim it?" asked Alcaren. "It can be reclaimed as
you choose if you can but defeat or drive the Sturinnese out.
Without them and Lord Belmar, any one of your sorceresses, even Richina, young as she is, could return Dumar
and Neserea to Lord Robero's rule."

"That may be true," Secca agreed, "but there is more to
Lord Belmar than meets eye or glass." She eased the scroll
aside.

In the fading afternoon light, sitting in one of the straight-
backed chairs before the table and after taking out several
scraps of the heavy brown paper and a black grease marker,
she began to write.

Alcaren slipped away, only to return with a small wedge
of cheese, some thin strips of jerky, and half a loaf of bread,
all of which he set by her elbow. "As you write, please eat
some of this."

"Thank you." She continued to write, occasionally stopping to eat and nodding appreciatively as Alcaren lit the two

candles in the shaky candelabra he brought to the table. She
ignored the curious look from Richina, who peered into the
long room, then slipped away as her consort murmured
something to the younger sorceress.

Finally, she sat up erect and handed Alcaren a single
sheet. "Can you read that?"

"Yes. Why?"

"I want you to sing that spell."

In the flickering candlelight, Alcaren studied the words
on the brown paper. "You're assuming a great deal here."

"If it isn't so, the glass will come up blank." Secca
smiled. "Can you sing it?"

He frowned. "I might get the glass to show what I want,
not what is."

"It won't do that. The glass can only show what is, not
what was or what might be."

He smiled dryly. "Why do you really want *me* to sing
it?"

"So I can watch the glass." Secca's voice was cold.

"You really hate Belmar, don't you?"

"I do, but I don't think he's the one to hate."

"Sturinn? The Maitre?"

"Who else?" She glanced up once more. "Can you . . . ?"

"Let me try to work out the chords for a few moments."

Secca smiled and took another sheet of the brown paper,
frowning as she looked at the blankness. Finally, slowly, she
began to write the thoughts and words of another spell, trying
not to be distracted by Alcaren's fingers on the strings of his
lumand.

"I'm ready," he finally said.

Secca put aside the paper and marker and looked to the
blank silver of the scrying mirror.

Her consort cleared his throat and began the scrying spell.

*"Show me Belmar now and in the same light
that Sea-Priest who advises him tonight,*

the one who talks of whom to kill or fight
and who would put all Defalk to flight . . ."

Alcaren lowered the lumand and looked into the glass, over Secca's shoulder. The image showed two men sitting across the table from each other in what appeared to be an inn. Neither was speaking.

"Another Sea-Priest," he finally murmured. "You thought as much."

"I did. It could be no other way."

"No other way?" Alcaren raises his eyebrows.

"Belmar. He is a young lord of an impoverished set of lands. The only sorcerer in his family is a distant Prophet of Music. No one has ever heard of him. Lord High Counselor Hanfor dismisses him as unworthy of Annayal. Yet he has the coins to train and pay players, and he has more than five companies of lancers that were trained and ready a year ago? That might have been possible, straining his coffers, but by the middle of last season he had three times that many."

"He had taken the keeps and lands of several in Neserea," Alcaren pointed out.

"That is true, and that is what all were meant to think." Secca paused. "It did not *feel* right, and I should have listened to my feelings earlier."

"All this was planned by the Maitre?"

"All this, and much more, I fear," Secca replied. "Much more, so much more that I cannot guess, only feel." She laughed, harshly. "That sounds mysterious. It is not. The Maitre has a plan to take all of Liedwahr. That is clear. How he intends to do so is what is not clear—except that it has been planned for years, and involves sorcerers and lancers and fleets I fear we have never seen." She paused. "And sorcery as deadly as anything Liedwahr has ever seen."

Alcaren shook his head. "Not so deadly as you might use, and that is why you hesitate and fret."

"Already, you know me too well." Secca pursed her lips

before lowering her voice. "Even knowing what the Maitre plans . . . how could I use such spells? How could I?"

"How could you not, if it meant every woman in Liedwahr in chains, and every sorceress tortured to death or with her tongue ripped out?"

Secca winced.

"You see?" Alcaren said, sadly, gently.

50

The faintest orange of dawn had barely begun to color the eastern sky outside the windows of the dwelling in Hasjyl when Secca looked down at the image Richina had called up in the glass on the oblong table. Alcaren, Palian, Delvor, Delcetta, and Wilten—the others with them—also looked into the scrying glass.

Early as it was in the day, the Sturinnese force was leaving the hamlet to the north, clearly headed toward the trade pass, since the maps showed that the northern road went nowhere else.

Secca nodded for Richina to sing the release couplet, and that the younger sorceress did, easily and with a composure she had not possessed two seasons earlier.

"How many days' travel would it be for us to reach the pass?" Secca asked.

"Three," suggested Wilten. "Two, if we hasten."

Delcetta nodded in agreement.

"I think we need to hasten," Secca suggested. "For the first day, it is almost eastward along the river road, is it not?"

"For a half day, according to the maps," Alcaren replied. "Then the road to the trade pass separates and makes its way north along a stream."

"That stream is the one that comes from the trade pass

and feeds into the Envar River, is it not?" asked Delcetta.

"It is," replied the broad-shouldered sorcerer. "Most passes have rivers or streams, but this is a narrow pass and a small stream as such go."

Secca glanced at Wilten, then Delcetta. "How soon before all can ride?"

"Less than a glass."

"Good." Secca stood, turning to the chief players. "And the players?"

"They will be ready," Palian affirmed.

51

MANSUUS, MANSUUR

In the early-morning grayness caused by two days of steady rain, Kestrin uses a set of calipers to measure a distance on the maps spread across the wide desk in his private study, muttering to himself as he does, "Less than a hundred deks . . . day's sail in favoring winds."

Thrap! Thrap! "Sire!"

"Come in, Bassil," says the Liedfuhr, his voice resigned.

As Bassil enters, the Liedfuhr notes that the maroon uniform is not quite as precisely set as has always been the case with the older lancer officer, and Bassil's hair is slightly disheveled, also unusual. "What has happened now?"

"The Sturinnese have landed a score of companies of armsmen and lancers at Hafen, sire. And at Landungerste." Bassil's voice bears the slightest trace of raggedness, and there are circles beneath his eyes.

"Dissonance! The dissonant sons of sea-sows . . . those . . . unmentionable heaps of dog excrement . . ." Kestrin breaks off the string of expletives, and shakes his head.

"They looted and burned the town and harbor, in both places, did they not?"

Bassil's face reflects surprise. "Yes, sire. But how did—"

"So that I will be forced to keep my lancers close to Hafen and Landungerste—and Wharsus. So that my people will be angry and unhappy that I did not protect them, but sent lancers to a foreign land to protect my sister and niece while leaving my people unprotected. No matter that we have never had more than two companies of lancers in Hafen, and never more than three in Landungerste. No matter that they would have been slaughtered by forces ten times their number." The Liedfuhr shakes his head.

"Will you recall the lancers from the Mittpass to Mansuus, Hafen, or Landungerste?"

"To Hafen and Landungerste? What good would that do? There's little enough left to protect, I imagine. That would be what the blighted Sea-Priests would hope, I wager."

"You wager much on each decision, sire."

Kestrin looks outside at the cold rain of spring, rain that has barely finished melting the accumulated snow and ice of the long winter. "Is that not true of every decision?"

"Ah . . ."

"We just don't always have to pay for the bad wagers so quickly, and sometimes we pay for those of others."

"Others?"

Kestrin ignores the question. "When did this happen, and when did you find out?"

"You had your seers watching the Sturinnese fleet. Part of that fleet had sailed south into the northern part of Defuhr Bay several days ago, and a very small flotilla came even farther south. You were informed."

"That was when I shifted more lancers from Mansuus to Wharsus, in case they attempted to land there." Kestrin stands and walks away from Bassil, toward the windows on the north side of the study, where he stares out into the rain.

Bassil waits.

In time, the Liedfuhr turns. "Send dispatches to all garrisons. Tell them to be especially alert. Send messengers to the forces entering Neserea. Tell them to avoid battle with either the Sea-Priests or Lord Belmar and to make their way to Esaria as quickly as possible." He looks to Bassil. "You have more bad news?"

"Some of each, sire."

"The worst first, then." Kestrin tightens his lips, listening.

"Lord Belmar has defeated and slain the Sorceress of Defalk. Your seers believe that there are already Sea-Priest sorcerers in Neserea."

"Believe?"

"They are encountering wards of some sort against their scrying."

"That makes a sorry sort of sense." The Liedfuhr clasps his hands behind his back, shifting his weight from one foot to the other. "Go on."

"The Sorceress of Defalk slew some ten companies of Belmar's forces, but that still leaves him with almost six companies yet."

"And the support of the dissonant Sea-Pigs."

"Yes, sire."

"The better news?"

"The Sorceress Protector of the East has destroyed close to forty companies of Sturinnese in Dumar, along with their sorcerers and drummers. She is moving northward toward the trade pass and against the last remaining force of Sturinnese in Dumar. Lord Fehern has vanished, and the seers say that he is dead, but know not how."

"He was a traitor to his brother, who was a far better man, and his death is no loss."

"That may be, sire, but that leaves no Lord High Counselor in Dumar."

Kestrin laughs ruefully. "Better a sorceress there than anyone Lord Robero would choose."

Bassil nods slowly.

"We can but hope that the Sorceress Protector will destroy

the last of the Sturinnese opposing her and move northward quickly. Would that we could send her a messenger saying such."

"By the time one reaches her . . ."

"All is likely to be decided," Kestrin finishes the other's sentence. He turns back toward the window and the rain. "Before that, matters will get worse, much worse."

"Sire?"

"I learned a long time ago, watching my father, that when affairs are difficult, and when it seems that they could not be worse, they inevitably become so."

Bassil nods imperceptibly, but does not speak.

Outside the study, the rain continues to fall from clouds of formless gray.

52

Standing in her stirrups for a moment to stretch her legs, Secca glanced forward past the vanguard that wound its way downhill. The clay road descended and curved gently eastward around a hill covered with apple trees showing but the faintest hint of green at the tip of some few leaf buds. Overhead, the sky was clear and cloudless, and a soft warm wind blew at her back. A thin line of smoke rose from the chimney of the dwelling at the end of a muddy lane halfway up the hill, a good dek away. On the lower right side of the road was a field, half-tilled. Secca smiled, suspecting that the tiller had hurriedly taken his mule or horse out of sight when he had seen the column of riders.

According to the maps and the glass, they were but five deks or so from the hamlet that the Sturinnese had briefly garrisoned to defend the trade pass, but the scouts had reported no new tracks on the damp clay of the road and no sign of the Sturinnese. Before they had broken camp that morning, Richina had used the scrying glass, and the image had shown the Sturinnese already partway through the pass, riding beside a stream swollen with runoff.

Secca wondered if her small force would be able to catch the Sturinnese before they joined with Belmar's forces. Yet . . . what else could she try?

As she settled back into the saddle, Secca felt herself shaken—not by something like thunder or the shaking of the earth, but by a harmonic chime, one that indicated major sorcery. But the chime was almost clean, not with the dull undertones of death, or the dissonance of Darksong.

She glanced to Richina, riding slightly ahead and to Secca's right.

Richina had already turned toward Secca, and the younger sorceress's mouth opened as if to frame a question.

Secca nodded. "Sorcery."

Richina closed her mouth.

Alcaren had already turned his mount and was riding back toward them along the shoulder of the road.

"We need to stop and see what has happened," Secca said.

"What do you think?" asked Alcaren as he eased his mount around beside Secca's.

"We need to check the scrying glass. The Sea-Priests have done something."

"The Sea-Priests?" blurted Richina. "But that was Clearsong."

"Who else?" asked Secca. "I cannot see Jolyn essaying such. She could not have reached Neserea from Falcor, and it did not feel like a death chime." She turned in the saddle. "Chief players!"

Alcaren motioned to Gorkon, one of the lancers riding guard behind Secca. "Would you summon Overcaptain Delcetta?"

"Yes, ser."

Even before Gorkon had turned his mount toward the rear guard, Alcaren was urging his brown gelding back forward toward the vanguard where Wilten rode.

Secca began to run through a vocalise to warm up her voice while she kept riding—until Alcaren reached Wilten, and the order echoed back. "Column halt! Stand by!"

From the rear guard came a similar command.

Secca eased the gray mare to the uphill side of the road, looking for a clear space short of the apple trees that was not muddy. She rode another ten yards forward before discovering a square area paved with stones, perhaps four yards on a side, with a narrow lane down to the main road, possibly an ancient loading area. She reined up and dismounted, handing the mare's leads to Easlon, and unfastened the lutar from behind her saddle.

Alcaren was close behind her, followed by Richina. While Alcaren unfastened the scrying mirror, Secca took out her lutar and began to check the tuning on the instrument. She finished the tuning and ran though another vocalise.

She had to cough some mucus from her throat, and then try another vocalise. By the time she felt ready to sing, Alcaren had laid the scrying mirror on its leathers on the weathered stones. Delcetta, Wilten, the chief players, Richina, and Alcaren had formed a semicircle around the glass, flanking Secca on both sides.

Secca took a slow breath, and then sang.

> *"Show us now and in this glass*
> *the change in harmony that's come to pass,*
> *that has chimed throughout this land . . ."*

As Secca watched, the mirror silvered, then shivered to show a solid line of rock between two low mountains. Steam rose from the rock and from behind it. In the foreground, a narrow and winding road ended abruptly at the jumbled mass of rock and soil, and to one side was an empty streambed.

"A wall of rock . . . across the entire trade pass," murmured Palian.

"But why?" said Wilten quietly. "Or have they already crossed into Neserea?"

"I would judge so," replied Secca, "but we should see before we decide what we should do next." She lifted the lutar once more.

"Show us now as if upon a map of this or other land,
where those of Sturinn we've pursued now ride or
*   stand . . ."*

The white star appeared on the far side of the trade pass, clearly well to the north of the sorcerous barricade.

"They used sorcery to melt their way through the pass, and then blocked it behind them," Richina suggested. "They must fear you greatly, lady."

Secca waited for a moment, until all had a chance to study the mirror, before singing the release couplet. Then she considered Richina's thought, frowning before speaking. "No. I think not. There is much more than such involved. They have shown little fear of me, or of Clayre."

"How can we reach Neserea?" asked the younger sorceress. "Will we have to cross Dumar and attempt to return through Stromwer?"

"That pass is also blocked," Secca pointed out.

"There is no way to reach Neserea quickly, not unless you wish to try even greater sorcery and destroy whole mountains," said Alcaren.

"I do not know that we should try that." Secca tilted her head. "That may be what they wish. Even if they do not, we are reacting to what they do."

After a moment, she lifted the lutar.

"Show us now as if upon a map of Neserea's land,
where Belmar's forces now ride or stand . . ."

The map showed most clearly a green star on the road south of the River Salya, a road that swung southwest toward the Mittpass. Secca nodded, then, after singing the release couplet, handed the lutar to Richina. "If you would use the map spell to show where the Liedfuhr's lancers are in Neserea?"

"In Neserea . . . Oh . . . yes, lady." Richina's fingers ran over the lutar's strings. She licked her lips and then cleared her throat. Finally, she sang.

When Richina had finished the third map spell, the mirror showed a maroon star on the road east of the Mittpass, a road that intersected the one on which Belmar's forces rode, if some considerable distance from where the Mansuuran forces appeared to be.

"How far between them?" asked Delcetta from where she stood at Alcaren's shoulder.

"I would judge more than a hundred deks at the moment," replied Alcaren. "Perchance a hundred and fifty."

Secca noted the steam coming from the damp stones and could sense the heat from the scrying mirror. While there was a small spare mirror, there was no sense in breaking the larger mirror. "The release couplet."

"Ah . . . yes, lady."

Looking for a moment at the mirror that reflected familiar faces and the clear sky overhead, if slightly distorted by the heat of sorcery, Secca pursed her lips. "I must think." *Think . . . indeed you must.*

For a long time, she stood, holding a lutar she had forgotten was in her hands, her eyes looking nowhere.

As she stood there, in the spring sunlight, with a warm breeze at her back, she could sense a cold and darkness, not of the day, but of the spirit, descending upon her, and she shivered.

Alcaren eased forward and murmured softly, "Are you all right, my lady?"

"We will talk later," she replied in an even lower murmur, before raising her voice, "I was just thinking of the cold of the Mittfels. But that cold matters not. We will ride for Dumaria. That is all that we can do at this moment." Secca offered a smile she did not feel, then bent and reached for the lutar's case, slowly casing the instrument, and then waiting for Alcaren to wrap the scrying mirror and refasten it behind Secca's saddle.

A puzzled look passed across Richina's face.

The faintest of sad smiles crossed the lips of the gray-haired Palian.

53

Secca stood just outside the plank door of the cottage in the chill evening breeze, looking up to the east at the white disk of Clearsong. In the twilight, hanging over the bare-limbed trees of the woodlot adjoining the hamlet where they sheltered, the moon looked far larger than when it was higher in the sky. In the west, barely visible against the lighter horizon that had not totally faded from the recently set sun, was the red point of Darksong.

Hoping that the rising of Clearsong and the setting of Darksong was a favorable omen, even knowing that it was not, Secca smiled briefly. What would happen depended on what she could do, not upon the moons. *Or what you will do*.

The door of the cottage opened, and Alcaren eased outside into cold and slipped along the wall until he was standing shoulder to shoulder with his consort. For a time, they both looked at the swiftly darkening sky, and neither spoke.

"You have fretted all afternoon, yet you have said nothing," finally offered Alcaren.

"I cannot explain, even to myself," Secca said. "I have read through Lady Anna's terrible spells. I have thought about what needs to be done, and no matter what course I choose, the results look to be equally terrible."

"What about shadow sorcery?" asked Alcaren. "Is there

some smaller, if terrible, sorcery that will foreclose the worst of what you foresee?"

"There is one possibility." Secca shook her head. "For that, I will need a brass or bronze tube perhaps two spans long. If we cannot find brass or bronze, iron may suffice."

"Oh?"

"Do not ask me why. Not now."

Alcaren looked at her, but did not speak.

Finally, Secca murmured. "I must deal with Belmar, I fear. He can use his sorcery to destroy the Liedfuhr's lancers and armsmen."

"Will he?"

"After what he did to Clayre? Is there any question?" Secca's voice was flat in the momentary calm chill that settled around them as the wind subsided.

"And if you use this sorcery, you still fear?"

"I would rather not use it. We will wait . . . to see if Belmar does indeed intend to attack them." She shook her head. "But we will not wait here."

"What do you plan, then? To head back to the trade pass?"

"No. There is a long and narrow road along the western edge of the Great Chasm," Secca said slowly.

"Would it not be wiser to try sorcery to undo what the Sturinnese have done to the trade pass?" asked Alcaren. "Rather than travel days out of our way?"

"Going through the trade pass doesn't feel right," Secca replied.

Alcaren did not reply, letting his eyes rise to rest upon the white orb of Clearsong.

"You think I'm wrong, don't you?" asked Secca.

"You have the power to unblock the pass, if you choose to do so."

"How much water do you think lies trapped behind that wall?" asked Secca.

"It's not that big a stream," reflected Alcaren.

"They had to have used sorcery to melt the snows to go

through the pass," Secca countered. "All that snow couldn't have melted in a week."

"We could avoid that sort of trap."

"But could all those along it or along the Envar River? Or would we have to try even greater sorcery to protect them? Or risk another occurrence of disaster? You saw Envaryl. The people here suffered more than did the Sea-Priests or Lord Ehara when Lady Anna fought here a score of years ago, and Dumar never fully recovered. I should do the same?"

"If you do not do *something* . . . "

"I know," Secca replied tiredly. "I know. But . . . we're missing something." She shivered as the evening wind rose once more and whipped through her loosely fastened riding jacket. *What you're missing you don't know . . . but you fear that it is more terrible than what you can foresee, and yet you can explain neither. Or do you fear both so much that you will not look more deeply?*

She shivered again, and not from the cold and the wind. Her eyes went back to the white orb of the rising moon.

54

W hat *can I do? What should I do? Those awful spells . . . Is it right to use them when so many . . . when such power . . . ?*

Sweating in spite of the chill in the cottage, Secca bolted upright. She glanced to her left. Alcaren was still sleeping, but Secca had to wonder how he could have slept through all her tossing and turning. She had not slept a stitch, but only fretted and turned in her bedroll, with phrases of terrible spells running through her mind, and visions of lands filled with brimstone swamps and figures that had been turned into shimmering black rock.

Slowly, she eased out of the blankets and passed toward the shuttered windows of the cottage, standing before them, wondering whether to open them, whether looking out at Clearsong would help clear her thoughts and cool her feverish body. She shook her head. Opening the shutters would only chill the small cottage and wake the others.

As she stood in the cold, her breath steaming, still uncertain of whether to reach out or climb back into her bedroll beside Alcaren, beside the window a golden haze appeared.

Secca watched as the haze grew into a tall and familiar woman—a girlish-figured, blonde-haired, and commanding presence with penetrating blue eyes both hard as diamond and as warm as a mother's love.

"Anna . . ." breathed the red-haired sorceress as she looked at her mentor and foster mother. "You can't be . . ."

"Don't tell me what I can't be. Or what I can't do." Anna smiled, the warm expression taking the edge off her words. "Don't let anyone tell you, either."

Secca swallowed. "I never realized . . ."

"You don't, not until you have to decide, and your children won't, either," replied the elder sorceress cryptically. "That's the way the world is."

There was so much Secca wanted to say . . . and to ask. But she said nothing, just stood and looked at Anna.

"You have the spellsongs that may allow you to defeat Belmar and the Sea-Priests," Anna went on. "You don't want to use them."

"How could anyone? They're . . . terrible," Secca said.

"So?" asked Anna in the dry tone that Secca recalled all too well. "All effective sorcery is terrible. So are all effective ways to fight any battle. Do you recall all the names I was called? All those who wanted me dead? Do you remember how many people tried to kill me? Or you, because you were a little girl who might inherit power?"

"I don't want to become like them," Secca protested.

"Do you want to die for nothing? Do you want all girl children in Liedwahr chained? Do you want Richina's tongue torn out? Or your brother's daughters turned into broodmares?" Anna's tone turned gentler. "Secca . . . in life we never get the easy choices. Power requires hard choices. Great power requires even harder choices."

"I don't want to unleash another Spell-Fire War. Or another Pelaran Devastation. I don't want people to think of me like that."

"That's not your choice. Someone is going to use great sorceries in the days ahead. You can only choose to see whether Liedwahr becomes the land I hoped for or becomes one like Sturinn."

"Isn't there another way?" Secca asked plaintively. "There must be. There has to be. I shouldn't have to be the one . . ."

Anna offered a sad and almost-pitying look. "Did I have another choice when the chandler raised his bow? Or when Lord Dannel attacked Falcor? Or when Lord Ehara held an entire city hostage? Or when your uncle poisoned your mother and brothers?"

Secca did not answer.

"We all feel better when we can defend ourselves. When we can tell ourselves and everyone else that we did what was necessary and no more. That's easy. What's so much harder is doing what is necessary before others see it and when the actions are harsh and unpopular."

Secca recalled Anna saying those same words once before, years before, and she blinked at that recollection. Then the words had seemed right—and very distant. Now . . . now . . . she was not so certain.

She looked down at the shadowed and rough wooden floor.

When she looked up, Anna was gone. Secca shivered, realizing that her feet were like ice, and she wondered how long she had been standing before the shuttered window.

She shivered again as Alcaren eased out of his bedroll and slipped behind her, wrapping his warm arms around her shuddering figure.

"What were you doing?" he whispered. "You were standing in front of the shutters, murmuring things to yourself.
Was it a bad dream?"

"It helped," Secca whispered back, unwilling at that moment to tell Alcaren what she had experienced and felt. "It
helped."

She glanced back at the window for a moment, before
turning and hugging her consort—hugging him tightly, for
warmth and comfort.

55

MANSUUS, MANSUUR

The Liedfuhr of Mansuur paces back and forth between
the tall windows and the side of the desk in his private
study. His boots are heavy on the polished floor, and he
does not look at Bassil. Finally, he stops and glares.

The older man meets the glare without flinching, but without speaking.

Kestrin clears his throat, and says, "The Sea-Priests have
escaped the Sorceress Protector and sealed the trade pass
with Darksong?"

"Clearsong, sire."

"The method of sorcery matters not. What matters is that
she must tear down mountains to pursue."

"The Sea-Priests may wish her to pursue in another fashion." Bassil pauses. "Or they wish to delay her so that they
may undertake yet another scheme."

Kestrin raises his eyebrows. "You are being obscure, Bassil."

"You seers say that she is riding eastward, away from
Envaryl. These developments mean that your lancers are
greatly at risk, sire."

"Now ... they're *my* lancers, Bassil?" asks Kestrin gently, ironically.

"They always have been, sire."

"Why will she not pursue them?" ponders Kestrin. "Surely, she cannot wish to hand Neserea over to them."

"Lord Robero may not wish her to hazard Dumar—or herself," suggests Bassil. "He has always been reluctant to hazard his lancers or his sorceresses, and with one of them slain by this Lord Belmar, he may not wish the Sorceress Protector of the East to confront both Lord Belmar and the Sturinnese."

"He would not send enough lancers to protect the first, and now, when it is too late to be cautious, he would protect the second?" Kestrin laughs. "Then ... I am no better. I must send armsmen to a burned-out port to reassure my people, and let others sit in Wharsus until at least the Sea-Priest fleet is in the Bitter Sea and about to attack my sister's land—and then it will be too late to aid her."

"That is why the Sturinnese have left a half-score of ships patrolling in Defuhr Bay," Bassil points out.

"I would that I could ride into the fray and impress all with my valor." Kestrin snorts. "Better that than sit here on the hillside and wait for their armies, after they have taken Liedwahr piece by piece. Tell me again why I cannot send another five thousand lancers into Neserea?"

"Because you will lose them all," Bassil says reasonably. "You will likely lose those already there. Lord Belmar is trying to reach them, and, if he does not, the Sturinnese and their sorcerers coming from Dumar likely will."

"It would be so much easier if I could just charge into battle and be done with it." Kestrin sighs.

"Sire ... many a ruler has said such, and some have done so, and a handful have been remembered for their gallant and futile efforts. The others, those who were remembered at all, were written down in the scrolls of history as fools."

"Now I am a fool?"

"Only if you attempt to fight in a way that favors your enemies."

"By not fighting?"

"By letting others fight until you must. So long as you have large numbers of lancers and armsmen, even the Sturinnese must tread with care. If you cast them out into lands where sorcery is rife, then they will fall, not to blades, but to spells."

"Is not sorcery rife everywhere?"

"Not yet, and never has it remained such, for the temptation to use it often means those who employ it must destroy each other—or at the very least all those who oppose them."

"So you think the Sturinnese and the Defalkans will destroy each other? Or that one will destroy the other?"

"Either way, you can make the best peace possible with the winner."

"And let my sister fall to the wolves? Doing nothing?"

"Sire. At this moment, you can do nothing except lose lancers and armsmen. Best you lose as few as you can."

Kestrin winces. "We should have found a way to train sorcerers and players."

"Perhaps you should, but that takes years, and you do not have years."

"Look into it. If we survive this mess, I would not wish to repeat the error." He laughs again. "But in not repeating the present error, doubtless I shall commit another."

"That is the way of ruling, sire." Bassil bows.

Kestrin shakes his head, then looks at the scrolls upon his desk. "See to it, then, and I will content myself with doing what little I can . . . and waiting."

"Yes, sire." Bassil bows before turning.

56

O ver the reddish coals in the kitchen hearth of the cottage hung a heavy iron pot, and in it were the melted remains of candles and candle stubs garnered from throughout the hamlet—barely enough for what Secca needed.

She glanced at the grayish mass of molten wax, swinging the iron arm away from the center of the coals. "We can't let it get too hot, or it will catch fire. I wouldn't want to have to try to find more wax here."

Richina looked from Secca to the small brass tube and matching cap that lay shimmering on the warped and uneven boards of the table. "The tube is beautiful. It's a shame . . ."

"Alcaren did a wonderful job," Secca said, glancing toward her consort.

"It's small, and it's brass," he replied, with a self-deprecating smile. "Very simple Clearsong. Small amounts of metals are easy."

"For you," suggested Richina.

"We're about ready," Secca said. "Please use the dipper to keep stirring the wax, Richina."

The blonde sorceress took the wooden dipper from Secca and gently swirled the molten wax.

Secca moved to the corner of the main room of the cottage, next to the pallet she and Alcaren shared, bent down, and lifted the saddlebags, carrying them across the room and setting them on one end of the table. She unfastened the left saddlebag and began to take out the small jars she had carried all the way from Loiseau, setting them on the table one by one, until she had the one she wanted.

Most carefully, she unstoppered it, then set it back on the table. She lifted the tube with her left hand, and the open jar with her right, and began to pour the gray-green granules into the tube until it was filled to within a fingertip of the smooth brass edge.

Alcaren stepped forward and took the tube from Secca, slipping a cork into the opening, one he had whittled down enough so that it fit flush with the brass edging. Then he eased the brass cap over the top of the tube.

Secca carefully recorked the jar and replaced the jars she had set out back inside her saddlebag. After setting the saddlebags carefully in the corner, she pulled on her riding gloves, took the tube from Alcaren, and nodded to Richina. "I'll be using the wax now."

Richina stepped aside from gently stirring the grayish mixture.

Holding the tube in her gloved right hand, Secca eased it over the pot. She took the wooden dipper to lift molten wax and pour it over the sides and bottom of the tube, slowly coating it. Each time she poured wax, she waited for the hot wax to harden before adding more wax. She was careful to keep the tube over the pot, so that the wax that dripped off fell back into the pot and remelted.

Then, tilting the tube at a slight angle, she began to pour the wax over the capped top of the tube, repeating the dipping, waiting, and cooling process until the entire tube was so thickly coated that no sign of the brass could be seen, and the tube resembled an irregular grayish candle, except without a wick.

Once the last coat had hardened, she set the tube on the table and turned to Richina. "If you would tell Palian that I am ready for the players."

"Yes, Lady Secca." With a nod, the younger sorceress fastened her riding jacket and stepped out of the cottage. Although Richina closed the door behind her, a wave of cold air swept into the small dwelling, and the coals in the hearth flared brighter with the influx of air.

Secca stared at the candlelike tube, then turned toward the closed shutters.

"This bothers you, does it not?" asked Alcaren gently.

"What else can I do? There is no way to reach Belmar before he meets with the Liedfuhr's lancers, and his sorcery is powerful enough to destroy them. I can do nothing to stop the Sturinnese who blocked the trade pass—not in time." She smiled sadly. "I know you think that I might be able to unblock the pass, but that would twist the harmonies, and exhaust the three of us . . . we can only do that so often."

"I would not go against what you feel." Alcaren stepped toward the table, grasping the end closest to the hearth, then lifting it, and swinging it toward the wall. "You'll need more space for the players." He did the same to the other end, then repeated the effort all over again, until the table was flush against the wall and the shuttered window. "That will provide more room for the players."

"Thank you."

At the knock on the door, Gorkon called, "The players, lady."

"Have them enter," Secca replied.

Palian stepped into the cottage, followed by Richina, then the first players. Bretnay, as usual, was the last to enter, carrying her violino case against her chest.

Palian looked to Secca.

"You can take your time to tune," Secca said. "I must warm up as well, and there is no hurry, and this spell must be done right. I will be using the seeking spell."

Palian nodded soberly.

As the players uncased their instruments, Secca stepped to the corner of the room farthest from the players and began a soft vocalise.

Alcaren remained by the table, close enough to grasp the candlelike tube, but saying nothing. Richina stood just inside the door, her eyes going from Secca to Alcaren, and then to the wax-covered tube.

Secca ran through three vocalises before she was satisfied and looked to Palian.

"We stand ready, Lady Secca."

"The seeking spell . . . if you would play it through once?"

"The seeking spell," Palian repeated. "On my mark. . . . Mark."

Secca listened, matching the words in her mind to the notes, mentally checking the values and trying to create the images she wanted.

After the run-through, Palian looked to Secca.

The redheaded sorceress nodded. "The seeking spell, on my mark." She tried not to think too deeply about what the spell she was unleashing would lead to throughout Liedwahr, pausing for a moment before saying, "Mark!"

As the accompaniment rose in the confines of the cottage, Secca launched into the spell.

> *"Take this missile, both north and west,*
> *deliver it in heat to Belmar's breast,*
> *with force to spread its deadly salt,*
> *and bring his life to its sudden halt . . .*
>
> *"Take this missile, in speed and flight . . ."*

As she sang the words, Secca could feel a cold stillness drop across the room, so still that there seemed to be no sound, save that of her voice and the tones of the players. A bone-deep chill infused her, rising from the ground beneath her.

A single, iron-cold harmonic chime shivered through Secca, and she could feel her knees buckling, could see Alcaren moving toward her. But she could not move as she toppled into his arms.

57

NORTH OF NESALIA, NESEREA

The Sea-Priest once known as jerGlien, still in traveler's
gray, looks down upon the body sprawled on the floor
of the study, a figure blackened and charred, except below
the knees, and convulsed in the agony of sudden and excruciating death.

"Who would have thought it?" The Sea-Priest smiles
coldly as he looks up. "Yet . . . if she can do such, then so
can we—"

He breaks off as the study door opens. Through it steps
a tall and lean younger man in the white of a Sturinnese
sorcerer.

"Maitre! I felt the harmonies. As you requested, I immediately used the glass to find the Sorceress Protector. She
had done some great sorcery, but I could not see—" His
eyes drop to the lifeless figure of Belmar on the floor.

"The young sorceress has learned a new trick." The Maitre laughs. "We shall have to learn to master it as well."

"She did that from so far?"

"She did indeed." The older man fixes his eyes on the
younger sorcerer. "Have you sent the scrolls?"

"Yes, Maitre. The fleet is already entering the Bitter Sea
and beginning to fire a channel. The southern waters around
Esaria have already begun to melt, and the fleet will be in
position in close to two weeks—no more than three."

"Unless we hurry and join up with the others, we may
not be back to Esaria by then."

"Will removing the Liedfuhr's lancers and armsmen take
that long?"

The Maitre laughs. "Removing them will not be the most

difficult task. Getting into position to do so will be. Liedfuhr
Kestrin has few illusions. He has ordered them to avoid
Lord Belmar and any sorcerers. Possibly, he has even or-
dered them to avoid us."

"Does he know that we have forces throughout Neserea?"

"It does not appear so. His seers will discover such, but
it will take time for him to get word to them."

"What about the Sorceress Protector of the East?" asks
the younger man. "If she has done this . . ."

The Maitre inclines his head toward the dead Belmar.
"You can see. She is stronger, far stronger, than the Sorceress of Defalk, but strength is not everything. Even if she
tears through mountains, she will be too late."

"If she does not?"

The Maitre smiles. "Where can she go, and what can she
do? Dumar has no ruler and is in chaos. She is unwelcome
in Ranuak, and by the time she returns to Defalk, Neserea
will be ours, and Lord Robero will be more than pleased to
accept our terms. Our agent there has been slowly suggesting that we offer much. Besides, what choice has he? His
power rests on a handful of sorceresses, and he has already
lost one of the more powerful ones. It is most unlikely that
he will hazard the others to save lands that have proven
rebellious and ungrateful."

"But the Sorceress Protector?"

The Maitre shakes his head. "I would not have thought
that she could have struck so hard from so far, but what she
has done, we will do . . . when the time is right."

"Why should we not strike in return? Now?"

The Maitre offers a lopsided smile. "I have no such spell.
Do you? Do you have the accompaniment for the players
and drummers?"

"No, ser."

"That is why you maintain the wards. They were designed
for those closer, but they should work against more distant
sorceries." The Maitre frowns, albeit briefly. "Yet you raise
a good point." He smiles, again coldly. "I give you leave to

craft such a spell and its accompaniment. Then bring it to me, and we will consider its use when the time is right."

"Ah . . . as you wish, Maitre."

"Where is the Sorceress Protector now?"

"In a hamlet along the Envar River. She is prostrate."

"She is doubtless recovering from the sorcery that killed Lord Belmar. Nasty and difficult spell," muses the older sorcerer. "He erupted in flame, and then died of poisoning."

The younger Sea-Priest shudders.

"She is not to be taken lightly. Not as a sorceress. But even great sorcery has its limits, as she is discovering. Our departed ally here"—the Maitre looks down at the dead Belmar—"he never did understand that treachery and good planning can outflank mere sorcery. Even great sorcery." He smiles, half-sadly. "Poor fellow. I could not have set it up better myself." Then he glances back at the other man in white. "You will continue to make sure the wards are held?"

"Yes, Maitre."

"She may not try again soon, for none can repeat such sorcery easily or quickly, but . . . it is far better to be prepared."

"Maitre . . . I must ask again if we should not strike her in the same fashion, before she can discover you are here?"

"We must have the right spell, and it will take time to craft it. I will set jerEstafen on it immediately. For now, until we can strike, I am protected. She cannot attack all of us from that distance, and I would rather save our strength to take Neserea. Also, she can do nothing for the moment." The Maitre gestures for the other to leave him. "I will join you presently."

Once the study door closes, the Maitre walks to the window, where he eases open the shutter and gazes out into the gray day, frowning.

58

On the pallet in the corner of the dwelling's main room, Secca lay in her bedroll, the top blanket rolled back to her waist. Sweat still beaded on her forehead, and her undertunic was soaked with perspiration. She could feel the heat pouring from her, despite the coolness of the air inside the cottage. Outside, the day was gray and windy. A light rain had fallen earlier, Alcaren had said, but not enough to do more than dampen the dust on the roads.

"Here." Alcaren tendered her a chipped mug filled with songspelled and cleaned water. "You need to keep drinking."

"All . . . I . . . do . . . is drink," she murmured.

"It's only been a night and a morning."

"It seems like forever."

"The fever is breaking," he said. "It won't be long."

Secca's fingers still trembled as she drank, and some of the water spilled across her cheek. "Harmonies save me. . . ."

"You'll be fine," Alcaren promised. "The worst is over."

Secca managed to raise her eyebrows in inquiry. "You think so?"

"Belmar is dead," Alcaren said. "Richina used the glass to check. He deserved no better after all those he killed."

"That may be." Secca took a slow breath. Alcaren had been right. She was feeling steadier. Not that much, but clearly she was starting to get her strength back. "How soon will it be before I must do something like it once more? Or before some other sorcerer or sorceress learns what I have done and replicates it?"

"Who else would know?"

"What about the Sea-Priest sorcerer with Belmar?"

Alcaren did not quite meet her eyes, close as he was.

"How soon before I must do more, if we are to survive? And then more, as the Sea-Priests retaliate?"

Alcaren offered a shrug and a rueful expression.

"Or, the harmonies forbid, find some protective spell that takes more strength so that some sorcerer does not do the same to us?"

Both looked up as the door squeaked, and edged open, letting more grayish light into the cottage. With the light came Richina, slipping inside, and closing the door, and shutting off the light. The younger sorceress tiptoed away from the door, awkwardly in her riding boots, and glanced toward the corner.

"She's awake," Alcaren confirmed. "You can come over."

"You frightened us, Lady Secca." Richina pulled over one of the stools and sat down facing the two.

"Again." Secca coughed.

Alcaren offered the mug once more. Secca took another swallow, then handed it back.

Richina glanced toward the warped table, still set against the wall where Alcaren had pushed it the day before, and the scrying glass yet lying upon the uneven wood.

Alcaren lifted the mug, silently urging Secca to drink yet more.

Secca took another sip, noting that Richina shifted her weight on the stool, although she had just seated herself.

The eyes of the younger sorceress drifted to her right, back toward the table again, before she looked straight at Secca. "Your sorcery . . . it was most effective, lady."

"It was effective at prostrating me as well," Secca said dryly, stifling another cough.

"But more effective on Belmar," Alcaren replied quickly.

Secca looked directly at Richina. "Something is fretting you."

"It is nothing. Nothing, lady."

"It is more than nothing. You've looked toward the scrying glass three times since you entered. What is it?"

Richina looked to Alcaren. He nodded.

Stop babying me, Secca wanted to yell, but that would have just made her cough more.

"That Sturinnese fleet . . . it's left Defuhr Bay, and it's sailing northward, Lady Secca," Richina said.

"Northward?" Secca coughed twice before glancing at Alcaren.

"There is more, lady," Richina added apologetically. "The Sturinnese destroyed two port cities in northern Mansuur, and they are using sorcery to melt a channel through the Bitter Sea."

"Toward Esaria, I would wager," Secca croaked.

"That is a wager none of us would take," Alcaren replied.

"I cannot say that I am astounded," Secca finally said. "I had wondered, but it is clear that Belmar was a tool of the Sea-Priests. Perhaps an unwitting tool, but a tool." She took the mug from her consort and took another long swallow.

Richina offered a sound between a cough and a swallow.

"More bad news?" asked Secca dryly.

"I have tried to use the glass to find the Sea-Priest who was with Belmar . . ." Richina's voice trailed off.

"And?"

"The glass shows nothing."

Secca nodded, almost to herself.

"Lady?"

"I must think about that," replied the older sorceress, as she pulled the blanket up to her shoulders, after realizing that she was getting chilled.

"I told you that you were getting better," Alcaren said. "The backlash from sorcery does not last that long."

"If one survives it to begin with," Secca replied, yawning.

"I should go." Richina stood and slid the stool back toward the table.

After Richina slipped out, Secca lay back. "Dissonance, I'm tired. One spell . . . one spell, and it's as bad as . . . well, almost as bad as fighting that Sturinnese fleet."

"I wonder why," mused Alcaren.

"I don't know, but it is." She held back another yawn.

Alcaren stiffened. "It could be the visualization. For the most effective sorcery, you have to visualize the results. Did you visualize what happened to Belmar?"

Secca frowned. "How could I not?" She shivered.

"It could be that creates the effect of Darksong," suggested her consort.

"Because I'm visualizing the effect on something living?" questioned Secca.

"I'm just suggesting. But . . . doesn't the idea fit? I looked over that spell you used against the crews of the Sturinnese ships. If you take the words by themselves, they're pure Clearsong. The effect back on you was more like Darksong."

Secca's mouth opened, then closed.

"When you spellsing, you know that you're affecting something that is living," Alcaren went on. "Did you not tell me that the lady Anna did a great deal of Darksong when she first came to Liedwahr, but that the backlash did not affect her for seasons, if not longer."

Secca nodded. "I never thought about that. She was only affected by what one would call true Darksong, because she was not raised in Liedwahr and had no idea . . ."

"I wonder if that was why Belmar was so effective," mused Alcaren.

"Lady Anna said we were stronger than we thought . . ." Secca let her words trail off. "Strong? I feel like a baby. Or an old woman."

"You'll be fine by tomorrow," Alcaren promised.

"I'm tired. I'm tired of always using force and more force. I'm tired of having to use sorcery to destroy ships and those upon them. I'm tired of shadow sorcery."

"What would you do?" asked Alcaren slowly. "Raise the oceans like the Sea-Priests did? Level entire cities the way Lady Anna did?"

"I'd like to lay a spell on the Sea-Priests. They're the

ones causing all the problems for Liedwahr. I can't. That's Darksong, any way you sing it."

"But they raised two great waves against Encora, and that was Clearsong," he countered. "We just need to find a way to use a great mass of something that isn't living and never lived against them. That would be harmonic justice, wouldn't it?" He laughed.

Secca frowned. "From what Richina said, I have to wonder if the Sea-Priests aren't using spells to protect themselves from spells from us."

"They didn't protect Belmar," he pointed out.

"No, and that is most troubling. Most troubling." She tried to stifle yet another yawn, hoping that Alcaren was right and that she would be stronger by the morrow.

"Everything is that way. Troubling, that is."

"We need to . . ." Secca let her words drift to a halt. She smiled . . . for a moment.

Alcaren studied her for a time. "You have an idea, do you not?"

"I do. But it may not be a good idea." Secca yawned. "I'm too tired to know."

"You can tell me," he suggested.

She yawned again and shook her head. "I need to sleep and think about it. Then, we can talk about it."

"Promise?" he asked.

"I promise," she affirmed, yawning again and trying not to, trying to fix that one idea in her mind. "But . . . have to sleep."

She could feel her eyes closing even with her last words.

59

Secca had awakened with a headache—the kind that came after too much sorcery and too little food—and had quickly washed in chill water, changing into her only other set of riding clothes, and then seated herself at the warped table that Alcaren had returned more to the center of the small cottage. She ate four hard and crumbly biscuits, a small section of a dried apple—all that was left—and two wedges of drying yellow cheese, all helped down with cold water, before she finally looked up at Alcaren and Richina.

"You need to concentrate on the mechanics of the spell, not on the impact," he suggested.

"You told me that last night, and I remember." She took another swallow of water.

"Even when ill, there is little you forget," he said with a smile.

Richina nodded and offered a knowing smile.

"Do you have any maps of the great Western Sea?" asked Secca, between mouthfuls of the last of the dry biscuits.

"Why would I have . . . ?" Alcaren shook his head. "Not here. All those I might lay hands upon are in Encora. I brought the maps I had of Liedwahr." He grinned. "You know, my lady, how fond I am of sea voyages."

Secca laughed. "I scarce can stay afloat in water myself. You know how I fretted about swimming the mounts ashore in Ranuak. I was most glad we did not have to."

"I am glad you did not have to, either." Alcaren lifted his eyebrows, as if he still had a question, but did not wish to ask it.

"Can you sketch a rough map?" asked Secca, ignoring the unspoken question.

"Very rough." He laughed.

256

"If you would . . . please?" Secca opened her eyes wider in a mock-pleading look, and then began to laugh again. "I cannot do that. I cannot counterfeit helplessness or mock-innocence. I would never be a traditional lady."

"I like the way you are."

"Not many have."

"I'm not of the many, as you may have noticed, my lady." Alcaren grinned. "I have better taste."

"You are most rare, my dear." Secca stood and walked to the corner, where she rummaged through the lutar case. She extracted several sheets of brown paper and a sheet of parchment. Returning to the table, she laid the parchment to the side, then looked at Alcaren. "While you sketch out your map, I need to draft a message."

"A message?"

"You'll see." She pointed to the paper. "There's some paper for your map."

"As you command, my lady." Alcaren grinned.

She snorted and picked up the grease marker.

Secca was still writing—and scratching out phrases, and rewriting them—when Alcaren cleared his throat.

"Yes?" she asked, looking up from the papers and the uneven surface of the table.

"I have a map, one most rough, but a map."

Secca set down the grease marker she was using to draft her scroll. The final version would be in ink on parchment. Then she leaned forward as Alcaren set the two sheets before her.

"Here is Mansuur, and Defuhr Bay. Then here are the Ostisles . . ."

"How far from Landende?" asked Secca.

"Close to a thousand deks," Alcaren replied. "And it is another six hundred deks farther west before the border isles of Sturinn—here." He pointed.

"How fast can a ship sail, with the wind?"

"Some can reach twelve deks in an hour, but that is rare

and seldom lasts. Nor can a ship mistress always count on following winds."

"We could help with that," Secca pointed out. She found a corner of the paper she had not used and began to figure. *Even at eight deks, that's but a week to reach the Ostisles* . . . She shook her head, understanding truly for the first time the advantage in travel possessed by those with ships. In a matter of a few glasses a ship could travel more than most riders could in a day.

"You are not . . . not thinking of sailing westward?"

"Where else?"

"We have no ships."

"Not yet." Secca extended two sheets of the brown paper, heavily marked and corrected. "Here is what I had thought of sending to the Matriarch."

"Alya?"

"Read it. It explains itself." Secca tilted her head. "I hope it does."

Secca stood behind Alcaren and reread what she had written as her consort read it for the first time.

Most gracious Matriarch:
I am convinced that, unless Sturinn is dealt with in Sturinn, we will continue to face the threats of invasion and even greater use of sorcery in Liedwahr by the Sturinnese. Those threats will require the need for greater and greater use of sorcery merely for Liedwahr to repulse the Sea-Priests, and for the lands of Liedwahr to keep their freedoms and individual ways of life.

There is a chance, I believe, that we can deal with the problem of Sturinn at its source. For that to take place, we will need several ships to carry us to the isles of Sturinn. While I could request assistance from the Council of Wei, I feel more comfortable requesting those ships from Ranuak . . .

If this is agreeable to you and to the Exchange, I would suggest that we meet the ships in Narial two weeks after the turn of spring . . .

Alcaren looked up. "That's only three weeks from now."

"We can get there in three weeks. Who is likely to stop us?"

"If you use sorcery, and if no one uses it against us," he said, "but would that not exhaust you?"

"There *are* three of us, if one is not too seasick."

"I can do spells, even when turned green."

"Then we shall have a speedy trip—if we can obtain vessels."

"You're not taking everyone? What can they do at sea?"

"I'd rather not," Secca admitted, "but we will need all the players and some lancers for protection. What we do depends on how many ships there are and what we can work out with the mistresses . . . if we get them. I'd thought about having the others wait at Narial for several weeks and then set sail to join us. If we succeed, we could send a message when we depart from Sturinn." *Or what may be left of it.* She paused. "But that way, they would have no protection, and if we did have to land somewhere, we wouldn't either."

"You are most sanguine about this near-impossible venture."

"What else can I be?"

Alcaren nodded slowly, finishing the scroll before looking up at her again. "Do you know whether the Council of Wei would offer you ships?" He smiled as he asked the question, as if he knew the answer.

"If I told them that it would reduce the power of the Sturinnese warships and their control of the Western Sea, I think they would be inclined to offer at least a few. For them, it would cost very little."

"But you are asking the Matriarch."

"Ranuak has far more to lose," Secca pointed out.

"This is a most risky proposition. If you fail . . ."

"I know," Secca admitted. "There is no one but Jolyn to stop the Maitre and his drummers and lancers, and even with Anandra's assistance, she is likely to fail." She sighed. "I do not wish to spend the rest of my life repulsing the Sturinnese—or, like Anna, knowing that they will strike again once I am gone."

"You see that as likely?"

"I see it as inevitable, if the Sturinnese are not destroyed in their own home isles. Nothing besides superior force deters the Sea-Priests. They care not for what any people wishes. They would impose—" Secca shook her head. "In a way, if I am successful, I will be imposing my wishes also." She paused. "But what I wish is for all people to choose what they will in life, not just men, as in Sturinn, or women . . . as in . . . other places."

"You did not say Ranuak," Alcaren said with a laugh. "You thought it, but you did not say it."

"How many years did it take you to become free to do as your talents would let you?" Secca countered.

"Too many, and it would not have happened, save for a beautiful sorceress."

"At the moment, I don't feel beautiful. I'm still tired, and we have close to two weeks riding ahead, and that is without certainty that we will even get assistance from the Matriarch."

"Denyst might volunteer even without encouragement."

"She might want to, but could she afford it?" pressed Secca.

Alcaren shrugged.

"All we can do is ride to Narial and see," Secca said.

"You gamble greatly," he pointed out.

"I do indeed. We could find ourselves in Narial with no ships and a long ride through Stromwer to Falcor—with the need to do mighty sorcery even to reach the borders of Defalk." She offered a crooked smile. "Yet we cannot catch the Sturinnese by chasing them through the Mittfels. If we did, and if once more we destroyed another force, what

would it gain us, save the need to ride northward farther to
fight still another invasion force—and more sorcerers and
drummers?"

"But if you succeeded . . . who else would you have to
fight?"

"The Sturinnese in another handful of years." *When you'd
rather be raising children in a peaceful land.* "They have
not stopped their conquests in a half-score of generations.
Why would they stop now unless something stopped them?
They fight until they wear down their enemies."

Alcaren frowned. "There is something else."

"There is. If we follow them, then we must fight more on
their terms. If I go to Narial, what will they do?" Secca
smiled. "The glass shows no more fleets in Sturinn or the
Ostisles. So they must gather ships from somewhere, or send
ships from that fleet against us—and they would be hard-
pressed to catch us."

"They will have a thousandscore lancers and armsmen
waiting in Sturinn."

"Let them wait."

"What is to stop the Maitre from sending a spell against
you in the fashion you did against Belmar?" asked Alcaren.

"That will happen, once it is clear where we head." Secca
smiled grimly. "So we must develop some spells to set
wards before we ride tomorrow. I will have Richina send
the message later today. That will give her some time to
recover before we ride."

Alcaren shook his head once more.

"Tell Wilten and Delcetta that we ride for Dumaria tomorrow. I'll tell the players."

"We wager much . . ."

"No. We wager far more if we do the expected." *If you
can do all that you plan . . . if . . .* Secca didn't want to think
too deeply about all that she planned beyond what she had
told her consort. Some of it was too wild to put in words.
Far too wild.

60

ENCORA, RANUAK

Outside, a fine mist drizzles down across Encora, so fine and so thick that it is more like fog than rain. In his small study, Aetlen glances from one ledger to the next, shifting them carefully as he makes notes in a fine hand on the sheets of paper to one side. Absently, he scratches his head above his ear, leaving a smudge of ink amid the silver-and-blond hair.

Silently, the Matriarch appears at the doorway to Aetlen's small study. Her face is drawn, but she says nothing until he senses her presence.

He looks up from the ledgers that surround him. "I was trying to balance the ledgers, my dear, and to see who might be shading the accounts."

"I know how tedious that is, and I would not disturb you, save that I wished you to see this." Alya extends the browned scroll to her consort. "It arrived a short while ago. By sorcery, from the Shadow Sorceress."

"By sorcery? Then, it is most urgent." He does not take the scroll.

"I fear it is more urgent than we know, and yet . . ." A tight smile appears on her lips. "I will say no more until you read it."

He sets the quill back in its stand, then looks at his ink-stained fingers. He rubs them on the grayish towel until no more ink appears on the soft fabric. Only then does he take the scroll from Alya.

She watches as he reads, her eyes studying his face intently.

Finally, he looks up. "Will you send her the ships?"

"If I must offer my own body," Alya replies. "If I must sell all that we own. If I must grovel before the Exchange—"

"I understand," her consort says hastily.

"You understand that I am distraught, and that you will say aught to calm me. What the sorceress wrote is disturbing enough, but what she did not write is even more so." The Matriarch clears her throat, then continues. "You know what has occurred. She has used greater and greater sorceries, and so have the Sea-Priests. There is a truly mighty sorcerer in Neserea, perhaps even one as great as the Maitre himself. The Liedfuhr has hazarded too many lancers, and they will perish. Defalk has no defenses left to speak of, except two sorceresses and their assistants. The fleets of Wei are too far south to reach the Sturinnese fleet in the Bitter Sea, even were they inclined to give battle."

Aetlen waits, then speaks when he realizes that she wants words from him. "You fear that she may unleash some great sorceries from the great sorceress?"

"I do indeed. Do you think that Secca is the type to ask for ships on a whim and to sail more than a thousand deks unless she has a plan and a thought of success?"

"She could be mistaken.".

"She could be." Alya smiles wanly. "Consider this. The west of Liedwahr stands within the grasp of the Maitre. But there is a cost. For the first time in generations, most of the ships and lancers of Sturinn are well away from the home isles."

"But . . . how can she defeat them if they are not there?"

Alya looks at him, her eyes unwavering.

His face pales.

"Exactly, my love," she says. "Exactly. Yet . . . do we have any other choice?"

He looks down at the scroll as if it bore the announcement of his daughters' deaths.

"Do we?" she asks again.

He shakes his head slowly.

61

Outside the small dwelling, the wind whispered, not quite wailing, but never subsiding, strong enough at times to send darts of chill air through the shutters and into the cottage. Inside, under the light of the single oil lamp in the hamlet—one Delcetta had brought all the way from Encora—Secca looked once more at the lines on the paper before her.

"From all sorcery near or far, keep us free,
that any spell we can or cannot hear or see,
rebounds full force against whoever sang its cast,
and make sure that this effect will fully last . . ."

Secca rubbed her eyes, stifling a yawn. The idea was good, and the rhymes matched, but there were too many words, and the note values were another question. She looked at the words again and sighed.

"Do you need to do this tonight, and so late, lady?" asked Richina from where she lay in her bedroll on a narrow straw pallet on the far side of the hearth from the larger pallet where Secca's and Alcaren's bedrolls were laid out.

"I should have done it, and cast the spell, before I sent that poisoned tube to kill Belmar. The Sea-Priests have a spell like it, I would guess, from what you have discovered." Secca swallowed another yawn and handed the sheet with the spellsong words to Alcaren, who had seated himself across the table from her. "Would you look at this?"

He took the sheet and began to read. "The lines are long . . ."

"I *know* that. Can you think of any way to shorten them?"

Alcaren finished reading through what she had handed him, then thought, and finally spoke, slowly and distinctly.

*"Keep us free from another's spell
all sorcery turn and repel . . ."*

He broke off and shook his head. "Yours is better."

"It's too long," Secca reiterated.

"How about this," suggested Alcaren,

*"From all sorcery, keep us free,
any spell sent by friend or enemy,
and send it back full force to slay
any with intent . . ."*

"What comes next?"

"I don't know," confessed her consort. "I thought you might have a way to bring it to a close. You are the Sorceress Protector." He grinned, half-apologetically.

"It's your spell, my love," Secca said.

"I am a beginner at this, my lady. Do have mercy upon me and my words."

Both stopped speaking as the wind rose to a whistle and then died to a moaning, before rising to a shrill whistle again.

She looked at Alcaren, his face warm in the golden lamplight. "I want you to sing this one with me in the morning, with all the players. If I finish it." She stopped, then added, "When I finish it, and finish it I will. Tonight."

"As you wish, my lady, although I am not near so accomplished as you."

"Remember how much stronger the spellsong was against the Sturinnese with more voices?" asked Secca.

"Would you like me, also?" Richina inquired from her pallet, her voice sleepy.

"I would like that, but it would not be good for you. Or for the rest of us, either," Secca said firmly.

"I can—"

Secca held up a hand. "You sing well. But this spell is a draining spell, and it takes strength all the time from those who sing it. One of us should not be drained, and because you know more spells than does Alcaren, you must be free to sing those spells should we need them."

"Oh . . ." Richina smiled shyly in the darkness of her corner, but the shyness carried into her voice.

"I am placing a burden on you, as well as on us," Secca said. "Yours is but a different burden." She smiled. "You can do little now. Best you try to sleep."

"I am . . . tired." There was a hint of a yawn in Richina's reply.

Secca looked down at the sheets of brown paper, then turned one, and then another to find a vacant space on one side. It took her three sheets to find one with enough space to write. She picked up the marker and wrote three words, then three more, before scratching out the last, and frowning, then sighing.

Alcaren winced, but said nothing.

Richina rolled on her side in her bedroll.

The wind whistled beyond the walls.

62

Despite the wind of the night before, the air was hushed and still in the orange light of early morning as Secca swung up into the saddle of the gray mare. She glanced back to the western end of the hamlet, where the players were strapping their instruments behind their saddles. Beyond them milled lancers—both the SouthWomen and those from Loiseau.

With a faint smile, she looked eastward out along the river road that would lead to Dumaria, and then to Narial. The one advantage of what the Sturinnese had done in blocking the passes to Neserea was that they couldn't easily turn back and chase Secca or do any more damage in Dumar. Not that they hadn't already done more than enough.

Secca half stretched as she settled into the saddle. The warding spell—if that were what it happened to be—had gone well enough, but Secca supposed she wouldn't know just how effective it might be until or unless the Sea-Priests tried sorcery against her. She glanced around.

Alcaren had already mounted, but had ridden to the western end of the hamlet to talk with Wilten and Delcetta. Richina was mounting, and another rider—gray-haired—was walking her mount toward Secca.

Palian nodded to Dymen as she drew up beside the sorceress. "How long do you think the ward will hold?"

"I don't know," Secca admitted. "A few glasses . . . a few days . . . a few weeks. It could be any." She smiled crookedly. "It might not work at all."

"It will work. I could sense . . . something . . . drawing together."

"Let us hope so."

Palian gestured toward the players. "All are ready, except Bretnay." She turned her mount. "Perchance . . . someday she will learn."

The two women laughed. A vaguely puzzled expression crossed Richina's face as she reined in her mount beside them. Before either Palian or Secca could speak, Alcaren joined the three, his mount moving at a walk, with Wilten and Delcetta following him.

"The lancers are ready," announced Secca's consort.

"Best we be going," Secca said.

"Best I get Bretnay into the saddle," said Palian dryly, turning her mount back toward the players, who all were mounted, save Bretnay, who looked helplessly at a snapped lashing thong while struggling to hold her violino case and the reins to her mount with her other hand.

"There is always one," Secca murmured, more to herself,

before turning to Alcaren. "How do you feel?"

"A little tired," he admitted. "How about you?"

"The same."

"How did you know it would be this way?" he asked.

"Lady Anna told me about spells that have a lasting effect. That was how she created the dam on the Falche, the one that caused the flood of Dumar, but she didn't know what she'd done until she was so tired that it broke in her sleep."

"Column forward!" came Wilten's order.

"Forward!" echoed Delcetta in a slightly higher voice, and one that carried farther.

As she rode past the last small hut, Secca glanced around and back at the dozen or so hovels and cottages seemingly strewn at odd angles beside the road above the narrow Envar River. She hoped the people who had fled their arrival had not suffered too much.

For a time, she rode silently as the sun rose over the low rolling hills to the east, hills that flanked the river on both north and south. She pulled down the brim of the green felt hat, but still found herself squinting against the slowly rising sun.

"I can imagine how sorcery and countersorcery could become ever more involved," Alcaren ventured after a time. "Before one knew it, nothing could be done for all the counterspells to the counterspells."

"And the spells to counter those?" questioned Secca lightly, not really wanting to think, for the moment, about the implications of what she had begun.

"There must be ways around such," offered Richina.

"Indeed?" replied Alcaren.

"You had a thought, Richina?" asked Secca, kindly, turning and smiling at the blonde, trying to draw out the younger sorceress.

"What if the spell were not directed at the sorcerer?" asked Richina.

Alcaren laughed. After a moment, so did Secca, partly

because of Richina's words, and partly because her practical approach again reminded Secca of Richina's mother.

"So simple, yet so profound," Alcaren said. "What did you have in mind?"

"Well," Richina said, almost primly, "what about the great waves of the Sea-Priests? Or if you created a deep pit in the ground under a sorcerer?"

"Or had part of a mountain break off so that it would fall where a sorcerer might be?" suggested Secca.

"Still . . ." Alcaren mused. "Could you not sing a spell against physical harm?"

"I probably could," replied Secca. "How long would we have the strength to hold it?"

Her consort nodded.

Secca frowned. "It might be a good idea to develop such a spell, for use in dire straits."

"It might," Alcaren said. "I would hope we would not need such."

"I wager that the Sea-Priests already know how to do that," Secca replied. "Each season we learn more about what they do know."

"Why did not the Lady Anna—" Alcaren broke off his question. "She was from the Mist Worlds."

"Ah . . . lady, ser . . ." Richina cleared her throat.

"Why don't you explain?" Secca suggested to Alcaren with a grin. "You seem to understand her better than we do."

Alcaren offered a wide and sheepish smile. "I beg your pardon, my lady."

The older sorceress waited.

Alcaren shrugged. "My lady, if you would correct me if I err . . ."

"I'd be delighted, ser." Secca softened the words with a warm smile, "but I may get little chance, since you err so seldom."

Alcaren winced, then cleared his throat. "As you have told me, when the Lady Anna came to Liedwahr, there was but one sorcerer in all of Defalk, and that was Lord Brill. He was most close-mouthed, and he died under the onslaught of the Dark Monks at the Sand Pass. Lady Anna came from the Mist Worlds, where sorcery was less effective, and she had never used sorcery in the fashion that the Evult or the Sea-Priests did. She learned almost all about sorcery, except for the mechanics of singing, in which she was most expert, by reading and by herself. Because she came from elsewhere, she viewed matters differently, and because she was so powerful and so uncontested . . . I would surmise that she never needed spells of defense."

"But there were Sea-Priests then," Richina protested.

Secca shook her head. "Not really. There were but a few sorcerers in Dumar, and most were killed by the river." She cocked her head. "I would also wager that, then, the Sea-Priests had fewer sorcerers and had not thought about such spells, either."

"They have developed such because of you and the others," Alcaren said.

"There is still much we do not know," Secca admitted, "but what has happened has been too well planned not to have been developed over years and years."

"Distance affects spells as well," Alcaren added. "The storm spells . . . your message tubes . . ."

"So a spell of defense should work better against a spell cast from a greater distance," theorized Secca, "because a spell cast from a distance is not so strong?"

"I would guess so." Alcaren shrugged. "But who would know?"

Who would know? There were so many things like that facing them, reflected Secca, and she was stumbling, just trying to outguess a Maitre of Sturinn who had planned his conquest of Liedwahr for years, who had developed an entire company of sorcerers and drummers, and who had already left a quarter of the continent defenseless—except for whatever she and those with her could do.

Secca's eyes drifted over the grasses that flanked the road.

Occasional thin sprigs of green grass had begun to appear at the base of the winter-tan stalks of older grass, and every so often there was the lower white and purple of a spring flower hugging the ground. Spring flowers were a sign of good luck.

She certainly hoped so.

63

WEI, NORDWEI

The faintest of taps echoes from the door to Ashtaar's small audience chamber and private study. Ignoring the sound, Ashtaar coughs once then twice, into the green cloth and takes a sip from the beaker on the corner of the polished ebony of the table-desk, a surface that contains neither scrolls nor papers.

Finally, she replies. "You may enter."

The heavyset and dark-haired seer steps inside and bows, once, and then again, nervously. Her eyes dart around the dimly lit chamber and finally fix on the front of the desk, and not upon the silver-haired woman seated behind it.

"Sit down and calm yourself, Escadra," Ashtaar says tiredly. "I do not torture or kill messengers for the truth of what they bring. I do get angry with those who attempt to hide truth from me or from anyone on the Council."

"Yes, Leader. Yes, Leader." Escadra's eyes still do not light upon Ashtaar, but upon the surface of the desk just before the older woman.

Ashtaar gestures for the seer to begin her report, then sits back in her straight-backed chair ever so slightly, the fingers of one hand lightly caressing the time-and-finger-worn ovoid of dark agate.

"The lord Belmar is dead, slain by sorcery, and the Sea-

Priests have moved all of their forces that remained in Dumar northward into Neserea. They sealed the trade pass and left Dumar before the Shadow Sorceress could reach them." Escadra swallows. "Yet the lancers of Lord Belmar follow the Sturinnese toward the Liedfuhr's forces in the Great Western Forest. They are Nesereans, and they follow a Sturinnese, and willingly so. I am reporting what we have seen. The Shadow Sorceress is riding away from Neserea, southward, and quickly." The chunky seer looks helplessly at Ashtaar. "That is what has happened, Leader Ashtaar, by the harmonies."

"What of the Lady High Counselor and her mother?"

"They remain in Esaria, but only the palace guard remains faithful. Even so, none will yet move against the palace."

"Not yet." Ashtaar lifts the green cloth to her mouth and covers it, then coughs once. She lowers it to her lap, then takes a sip from the beaker. "The Sturinnese fleet?"

"Their sorcerers are melting the ice, but they must clear many deks—"

"How many?"

"We cannot tell. Ice is still water, Leader."

"You can tell whether it seems like a great deal or not a great deal."

"I would guess perhaps fifty deks, but that is a guess."

"Another two weeks at least, then, perhaps three," muses Ashtaar.

"Leader?" Escadra's voice is tentative.

"Yes?"

"I . . . none of us understand why the Shadow Sorceress—"

"Nothing is as it seems, not when sorcery and the Sea-Priests are involved," Ashtaar explains, her words measured. "Most of Belmar's lancers were doubtless Sturinnese or mercenaries hired with Sturinnese gold, but mercenaries posing as Nesereans. He was a fool not to guess such, but all of us can be deceived into seeing what we wish to see. That said, their loyalty is to Sturinn, or its golds. The

Shadow Sorceress is young as sorceresses go, but she is anything but a fool. Belmar is dead, doubtless by Sea-Priest sorcery. It matters not how that happened. He would have died sooner or later, when it served Sturinn's interests. You say the passes are blocked. Even if the Shadow Sorceress could use sorcery to open them, what would it gain her?"

"She could pursue the Sturinnese."

"Could she catch them?"

"Oh . . ."

"The Sturinnese plan that they will hold all of Neserea before she can reach them. They also plan that she will be held from attacking them by the very mountains. She knows both, I wager. There will be ships at Narial, I wager, and she will sail to Esaria, arriving there far more swiftly than if she fought her way through the spring mud of southern Neserea. The Sea-Priests will be slowed, even with their sorcery, by that very mud, and by the need to deal with the Liedfuhr's lancers. Also, how can anyone deliver a message to the Shadow Sorceress while she is at sea?" Ashtaar laughs, a sound more like a cackle. "The real question is whether that spineless idiot in Falcor has enough sense to do nothing."

Escadra's eyes widen, but she says nothing.

"He doesn't do anything well. What he does best is nothing, and that is what he should do now. But we cannot count on that." Ashtaar coughs again into the green cloth, this time repeatedly. It takes several sips from the beaker before she can continue. "After you leave, have a messenger summon Marshal Zeltaar for me, if you would."

"Yes, Leader." Escadra finally meets the dark eyes of the older woman.

"I'm not dead yet, Escadra, and I can still think. Now . . . go fetch the marshal."

"Yes, Leader. Right away, Leader." Escadra rises and backs out of the study.

Ashtaar forces herself to take another sip from the beaker.

64

The closer Secca's forces came to Dumaria, the emptier and more deserted the road seemed to become, with few tracks in the clay, despite the clear and cloudless sky. The hovels, cottages, and dwellings that could be seen from the main road were shuttered and silent, without even the thin plumes of smoke that might have signified someone inside.

Had frightened farmers and their families been huddling inside? Or had they fled when the Sturinnese had swept through, fearing yet to return? Secca wondered.

"Empty, is it not?" asked Alcaren.

Under a hazy sky, the rolling hills had subsided into a flat plain, with untilled fields on either side of the road. A good dek ahead, on the west side of the large plateaulike hill that held Dumaria, were what looked to be two white stone gateposts, tall enough that they were clearly visible, but there was no gate attached to either post, nor walls or earthworks. Behind the gates was a gently rising slope, on top of which were trees and dwellings.

"That must be Dumaria, according to the maps and the scouts," Secca observed.

"The scouts say that the city is half-empty, but there are few signs of destruction or fire, and the Sturinnese have been gone from here for nearly half a season," Alcaren said. "One wonders why."

"There are riders heading toward us." Secca pointed.

As they watched, Wilten and a squad of lancers rode forward to meet the handful of men on horse who approached. After both groups halted and a brief exchange ensued, Wilten turned and rode back toward the vanguard and Secca.

Secca turned in the saddle. "Richina, perhaps you should

bring out your lutar and stand ready with the short flame spell."

"Yes, lady."

"Palian?"

"We stand ready to dismount and play."

Wilten slowed his mount as he neared Secca. "Lady Secca, they are a deputation from the Merchants' Council, welcoming you to Dumaria and beseeching you to treat the city and its inhabitants kindly."

What else would you do? Secca forced a smile. "I will speak to one of them as we ride."

"I will have him escorted with lancers, if you would not mind."

"That would be fine. Richina also has her lutar ready."

"I will tell them that as well." Wilten smiled grimly and turned his mount back toward the deputation.

"Wilten has little love for them," mused Alcaren. "They must have been less than courteous."

"Or excessively so," suggested Secca.

Alcaren laughed.

Before long, three figures rode along the dusty road toward Secca and her entourage—a heavy man flanked by two lancers. Both lancers had their sabres unsheathed. The older man looked from one to the other as he rode, then realized he was nearing Secca and reined up abruptly. He bowed awkwardly and deeply in the saddle.

"Lady Secca, Sorceress Protector of Defalk. Know that we supplicate you," offered the heavyset man in a dark brown leather jacket trimmed in golden braid. "We know that nothing can stand before you, and we offer freely once more our allegiance to you and to Lord Robero. Know that we surrendered unwillingly to the Sea-Priests, and only when we were abandoned by Lord Fehern. We will lead you to the palace. It too stands open to you, as does all Dumaria."

"Thank you," Secca replied. "I trust you will not mind if whatever you say is heard by those around me." She gestured for the merchant to ride so that Alcaren remained between her and the merchant as the column resumed its progress toward Dumaria.

They had traveled less than fifty yards when the man finally spoke once more, his tone of voice uncertain. "Lady Secca, you know that there is no Lord High Counselor in Dumar."

"That is true, but there will be," Secca replied. "I am most certain that there will be. Lord Eryhal and Lady Aerfor have escaped the Sturinnese and are well."

The merchant's eyes widened. "Eryhal—he was said to be much like Lord Clehar, save that he was considered more thoughtful."

"I cannot say what Lord Robero will do," Secca said, "but I would think it likely that he would wish a Lord High Counselor both loyal to Defalk and in favor with the lords and people of Dumar. Also, the Liedfuhr of Mansuur might be better disposed toward Lord Eryhal." She turned in the saddle and leaned forward to fix her eyes on the man. "How would your lords feel about Eryhal?"

"The landed lords . . . there are none left here in Dumaria, and they seldom speak to merchants." The merchant laughed nervously. "I venture that there will be none returned to Dumaria until they see from which quarter the summer wind blows."

After they rode past the white stone gate pillars, the road continued straight for two hundred yards before angling to the right and winding up the slope toward a line of leafless trees. From behind the trees rose a white-marbled palace. As the vanguard turned uphill, Secca could see that the winding way that climbed the hill was also empty, as appeared to be the large and impressive homes that flanked the road.

Across a small parklike space, Secca could see a fountain shaped like a spray of marble flowers standing in the middle of a scallop-shaped pond, but the fountain was not spraying water. Around the pond was a garden, where short green bushes alternated with larger leafless ones. The way into the grounds was barred by a pair of iron gates, as were the lanes into most of the dwellings along the avenue. Not a soul appeared on any of the well-trimmed grounds.

"The wealthy have indeed departed," said Alcaren.

"Along with a few others," Secca replied.

Beside Alcaren, the merchant nodded, quickly and jerkily.

There were no dwellings up the hill, near the top, where the avenue widened and leveled out. A hundred yards farther east was an arched iron gate that straddled the road, but both sides of the gate were swung back. Beyond, past the winter-brown grass of the grounds, lay the marble palace.

As the vanguard and those with Secca rode through what once had to have been the royal park of Lord Ehara, and later his successors, such as Fehern, Secca took in the trimmed topiary displaying a range of game animals, a low boxwood hedge maze, and two marble fountains.

When they neared the palace building, Wilten gestured to the vanguard. "Companies halt!"

In turn, Secca and Alcaren and the others reined up on the smooth-joined paved road less than two hundred yards from the palace.

With the lancers halted, Wilten rode back to Secca. "With your permission, Lady Secca, I would have the lancers search the building and grounds before you enter."

"Please go ahead." Secca smiled. "If our merchant friend is correct, there should be no one here."

Wilten nodded and turned his mount, then reined up and stood in the stirrups. "Purple company. Search the grounds. Green company, the first floor." He turned to Delcetta, who had reined up several yards away.

"Second company, the second floor, third company, the upper floor," ordered the SouthWoman overcaptain.

Secca turned to the merchant in brown and gold. "Once we have determined that no ill lies within the palace, you may go. However . . . we lay upon you the requirement for providing us with adequate supplies. I expect the first wagonload of provisions within a glass of the time you leave. In rough terms, we will need a week's supplies—for now— for . . ." Secca cocked her head and tried to rough out the numbers mentally. "For twenty-five–score lancers and players and their mounts."

The merchant swallowed.

"We have driven the Sturinnese from all of Dumar." Secca smiled. "I do not think provisions for such a small number are an excessive burden. Do you?"

"Ah . . . no, Lady Sorceress."

Secca's voice hardened. "I do not think that any of you wish to anger me—or Lord Robero—over such a minor matter."

"Oh, no, Lady Sorceress. There will be provisions, and they will arrive quickly."

Secca smiled. "Good. It would be much easier on everyone if those who are familiar with provisioning supplied us. If we have to come seeking them . . ."

"You will want for nothing . . ." stammered the merchant.

"Good."

Secca watched silently as lancers began to reappear and to report to Delcetta and Wilten. Before long, Wilten rode up to Secca. "The palace is empty. So are the barracks. The furnishings are mostly here, but anything of greater value has vanished."

"We'll stay here then, with appropriate guards." Secca gestured toward the merchant. "They will be bringing provisions within the glass, and those provisions will be good. If they are not, inform me immediately."

"That I will, Lady Secca," Wilten promised, with a sidelong glance at the merchant.

The man paled, momentarily, then swallowed. "All will be the best we have. The best we have, you understand."

"You may go," Secca said.

"You will inform us . . . Lady Sorceress?"

"For now, you will consider Lord Eryhal as Lord High Counselor, and that he is traveling to return to Dumar. Neither I nor Lord Robero would wish to see any more unrest in Dumar. Matters should proceed as though Lord Eryhal were already here." Secca paused. "Do you understand?"

"Yes, Lady Sorceress."

"Good. You may tell the others, and then you had best start to deliver what we require."

The man bowed from the saddle once more, as awkwardly as the first time.

Secca watched as he eased his mount toward the half-score of other merchants still under guard. The merchant began to speak even before he halted his mount, and soon an animated conversation was occurring, punctuated with looks back at Secca.

"They did not expect that, Lady Secca," said Richina, still holding the uncased lutar at the ready. "Are you still tired?"

"As we have been . . . as we have been," replied Secca dryly.

Slowly, the gaggle of merchants began to ride away from the palace. Several looked back over their shoulders.

"Was that wise, to let them go?" asked Richina.

"I do not know, but they have seen what the Lady Anna did, and, if necessary, one of us can provide a demonstration of sorcery."

"They will supply provisions," Alcaren prophesied. "They will do so, and find a way to make coins as they do."

Secca flicked the reins gently to ease the gray mare into a walk toward the main entrance, where Wilten and a number of lancers were waiting. Once there, she dismounted slowly, trying to hide her tiredness, and methodically untied her lutar and saddlebags.

Alcaren took the scrying mirror, while Easlon took charge of their mounts.

Secca walked through the entry hall, a space nearly twice as broad as that of Loiseau, if with ceilings but a third as high. The walls were bare, but marks and unfaded paint showed where hangings and paintings had been removed.

"Wilten was right. Someone has stripped the palace," Secca said.

"It could have been anyone, from Fehern to the friends of our merchant acquaintance," suggested Alcaren.

"Or all of them," added Richina.

"How many more will ask the same question before we reach Narial, about the next Lord High Counselor, do you think?" Secca turned to Alcaren.

"If the lords do not ask it, they will doubtless think it. Do you think it was wise to suggest Eryhal?"

"They need to think that someone will be taking control, and he is the only one that sounded reasonable." She paused, then frowned. "It is time for us to send a scroll to Jolyn. Or it will be just before we reach Narial. I did not wish to do so earlier."

"What will you tell her?" asked Richina.

"That because the passes are yet blocked, we are arranging passage to Neserea by ship."

"Neserea?" asked her consort. "I thought—"

"I don't think it is necessary to mention details such as a side trip to Sturinn along the way. After all, we do intend to return to Neserea. We will still have to deal with whoever is fighting there. It is most likely to be the forces of Sturinn."

Alcaren shook his head. "Lord Robero will not be pleased."

Behind him, Richina shook hers as well.

"If ... *if* he knows we will head to Neserea," Secca replied, "it may keep him from seeking terms from the Sturinnese or the Liedfuhr."

"Do you think so?" Alcaren frowned.

"I can hope."

You're hoping far too much ... and about far too many things. Secca pushed that thought away as they headed up the wide marble-tiled steps to the second level, following Gorkon and Dymen.

Since the main chambers had been thoroughly plundered, the most habitable chamber was a large guest chamber on the end of the second floor, around a corner and out of the way. Secca smiled as she saw the bathchamber.

Alcaren grinned as he beheld her smile.

Secca flushed. "Later, you lecherous consort."

"Me? How do you know I was thinking anything like that?"

Secca turned even redder.

Alcaren burst into laughter, and, after a moment, so did Secca.

Once the doors were closed, with lancers posted in the corridor outside, Alcaren stepped to the window that overlooked the rear gardens, shaking his head.

Secca stepped up beside him.

Below the window was a boxwood hedge maze, and in the center of the maze was a fountain, with spray playing over the figure of a man. Even in the hazy sunlight, the spray glistened. Beyond the hedge maze was a circular marble pool, its edges outlined in shimmering red tile. The pool overlooked a lawn, evenly cut and deep green, bordered by topiary trees, each sculpted into the semblance of an animal.

Secca could make out several horses, a falcon, a dolphin, and a team of oxen.

"There is nothing like this splendor in Encora," Alcaren said.

"Nor in Falcor," Secca replied, taking out her lutar and tuning it.

"Spellsinging?"

"I would like some warm water for the bath." She arched her eyebrows.

65

The Maitre stands before a large map laid upon a dining table in a long walnut-paneled room. The only illumination is provided by a three-branched candelabra set to one side of the map. He does not look down as he listens to the two men who stand across the table from him.

Neither of the younger Sea-Priests meets his eyes, as the taller one continues to speak.

"Maitre, we have followed the Sorceress Protector, as you requested. She is continuing southward. She has left Dumaria, and is nearing Narial. We have no vessels there or nearby."

"Narial?" For a moment, the Maitre frowns. Then he nods. "She is not to be underestimated, jerEstafen. She knows that we have no vessels in the south, and she also knows that she cannot reach anywhere quickly by land. This is most true in late winter, and in early spring when the mud is everywhere. She will take to the waters. There are no ships from other lands in Narial now. So she must expect a vessel from somewhere." He smiles, and the expression is less than friendly. "Doubtless from the bitch Matriarch."

"We have been able to find none."

"You have not the ability . . ." He shakes his head. "Even had you such, that would be a waste of sorcery."

The younger Sea-Priests wait.

"Have you and jerHalin perfected the spell to cast a sorcerous javelin through the mists at her—the way in which she struck at Lord Belmar?"

"Yes, ser. We have the spell, and the players have practiced it for the past two days. We gave you—"

"I have it."

"That we can do, if we can use a half complement of players and drummers."

The Maitre nods. "Do it quickly, before she erects wards. Take all necessary precautions. She may be a woman, but she has strength you might well envy."

"We will accord her the respect she deserves." JerEstafen bows.

"Indeed, Maitre," adds jerHalin. "Though . . . if we find no wards . . . ?"

"Without wards . . . still she . . ." The Maitre breaks off his words with a smile. "I leave the matter to you two. How you handle it will determine . . . much."

"We will handle the matter, ser."

"I am most certain you will."

The Maitre does not look at the map on the table until he is once more alone.

66

Secca shifted her weight on the stool set before the table, then began to write again, using the grease marker to complete the draft of the scroll. She and Alcaren had taken the largest room in the inn in the town of Stafaal, not that the chamber was especially spacious, measuring as it did all of four yards square. The room held but a narrow double-width bed, a wash table, and the narrow writing table where she sat beside the window. The sole lamp was set in a tarnished bronze bracket-sconce on the wall beside the bed.

Behind her, Alcaren sat on the end of the sagging bed and studied a much-used map of the Western Sea that he had found in the local chandler's shop.

In time, as the sun was nearing the western horizon, Secca finished the last lines of the scroll and stood, leaving the grease ink to dry on the rough brown paper. After stretching, she walked to the second-floor window, where she looked out on the dusty street below. The only figures visible were the lancers posted as patrols and sentries, and most of the windows in the shops and dwellings were dark, as if those inhabitants who had remained did not wish to call any attention to themselves.

Secca could understand that. Stafaal was less than a full day's ride from the port of Narial, near where the Sturinnese had stormed ashore behind their great wave of destruction.

Finally, she turned. "Will you read it?"

"I will. I'm sure it's fine." Alcaren set down the map and stood, also stretching before stepping toward the table beside the unshuttered window. He picked up the two sheets of rough brown paper.

Secca eased herself around behind her consort so that she could look over Alcaren's shoulder as he read the scroll.

Dearest Jolyn,
As you may have seen in the scrying pool, while Lord Belmar has perished, his forces are now commanded by the Sturinnese. Those of Sturinn who were here in Dumar have used mighty sorcery to block all the passes into either Defalk or Neserea. With all the forces of Sturinn now in Neserea, too much is at stake for us to wait for the ice to melt or to exhaust ourselves attacking mountains and solid rock with sorcery. For this reason, we have ridden south and are attempting to engage passage for our forces on vessels that will take us to Neserea . . .

"You write of the mighty sorcery of the Sea-Priests?" asked Alcaren, looking up from the scroll. "This is obviously for her to give to Lord Robero."

"Of course," Secca agreed. "But it will be more convincing as a personal note from me to her. There will be a small scrap of parchment inside which will suggest that if Lord

Robero is uncertain of my meaning or actions that Jolyn should feel free to share the scroll with our dear lord."

Alcaren nodded, and his eyes dropped back to the scroll, before he looked up. "You didn't say who killed Lord Belmar."

"I do not wish Robero to know that." Secca shrugged. "I cannot say why, but it is best that he not know."

"He or Jolyn may guess."

"I doubt it. Has anyone ever used sorcery to kill over that distance? Why would either Jolyn or Robero even consider it?" Secca's voice was cold, almost bleak.

The trace of a frown crossed Alcaren's forehead as he lifted the sheets of brown paper and resumed his perusal of her draft message.

> . . . for now that there are no Sturinnese forces left elsewhere in Liedwahr, we must attack those remaining in Neserea before the Maitre can send another fleet. I am hopeful that in some fashion we will be able to contain the Sturinnese fleet that is somewhere to the north or northwest of Liedwahr . . .

"Somewhere to the northwest?" Alcaren rolled his eyes and laughed. "By now, they must be well into the Bitter Sea, if not almost to Esaria."

"I'm not about to let Robero know that I know that."

"I can see why, but he's shrewd enough to think that you know that."

"Is he?" Secca raised her eyebrows. "Two seasons ago, he was trying to find me a consort so that I'd be happy. He still half thinks of me as naive little Secca."

"Do you think so? Or is that a pose to minimize your influence?"

Secca laughed mirthlessly. "Does it matter? If it's truly a pose, he is trapped with it. How can he suddenly say that the naive little sorceress is devious and deceiving him? Who will believe him?"

"Everyone," replied Alcaren. "They'll believe him because they'll believe anything bad about a woman and a sorceress, even if it contradicts what they thought yesterday. Robero is also cunning enough to blame me. You were just fine until you married the creature of the Matriarch. Now you've been corrupted, and can't be trusted."

Secca sighed. "You're probably right. It doesn't say much for people, but I'd not wager against you." She motioned for him to keep reading.

He lifted the papers once more.

. . . If you would convey to our lord that it is only through this effort that we have any real chance of halting the Sturinnese. Although our efforts are a slim reed, they are better than no reed at all. While we are traveling, we can but hope that the Liedfuhr's forces can defeat or delay the Sturinnese . . .

At the end, Alcaren looked up. A sad smile crossed his lips.

"Have I left anything out?" Secca asked.

"Not for what you intend."

"Would you mind finding Richina?"

Alcaren shook his head and slipped out of the room.

Secca turned back to the window, looking out at the near-deserted street in the twilight. Alcaren was doubtless right in his skepticism about Robero. The Lord of Defalk might have taken a new name when he had come to power, but not much else had changed about the boy with whom she had grown up.

Was she wagering too much on untested sorcery?

She laughed again, a low sound more for herself. Not to try what she planned would doom Defalk and Liedwahr to eternal rule by Sturinn. And it would mean her death, if not worse.

She took a long and deep breath, feeling once more the tiredness, the exhaustion created by the energy drain of the protective spells. Not for the first time since she had cast them, she wondered if they would work, and even if they were necessary.

At the sound of the door opening behind her, she turned as Alcaren ushered Richina into the cramped room.

The younger sorceress bowed. "You wished something of me, lady?"

"We need to send a scroll to Jolyn." Secca looked to Richina. "Can you do such?"

"Is there any reason it would be harder than usual?" Richina frowned.

Secca studied the younger sorceress. "How tired are you?"

"A little," confessed the blonde sorceress, "but I would rather do it tonight, for then I could be rested in the morning for whatever might be needed."

"I hope nothing will be needed, and that there are Ranuan vessels awaiting us."

"The glass shows that a half-score of vessels are somewhere on the Southern Ocean."

"Let us hope that they are heading for Narial." Secca paused. "I have written a draft of the scroll. The one on parchment should be ready in less than a glass." She extended the draft to Richina. "Here is what I've written."

Richina took the sheets and began to read. When she had finished, she looked up, waiting.

Secca moistened her lips. "Is there anything else you think that we should tell Jolyn—or Lord Robero?"

Richina tilted her head to the side, then wrinkled her forehead in thought. "I cannot think of anything that I would add." After a moment, she went on. "Do you wish to send the message before we know that we will actually be sailing?"

Secca shook her head. "No. I would rather wait, but I dare not. If there are any Sturinnese ships to the west, and they choose to sail into the harbor at Narial to bring armsmen or sorcerers against us, you must be rested and able to work sorcery. Likewise, if there are other Sturinnese forces, you must be strong. We dare not send such a message once we are at sea, for it may not arrive—and there is always the possibility of an attack."

"Even if we see none in the glass?"

"What if they have warded ships in the manner as the Sea-Priest in Neserea is warded?"

Richina nodded slowly.

"So, if you would send it tonight? I will call you when it is ready."

"Yes, lady." Richina bowed. "By your leave?"

"You may go."

Once the door closed, Secca and Alcaren exchanged glances.

"It would be better to wait," Alcaren finally ventured.

"It would be," Secca admitted, "if we were not carrying the weight of wards. But we are, and we do not live in a perfect world where all can be done in the manner that is best." She hoped that the manner she chose was just not the worst. After a moment, she added, "We both need sleep, and we will not get it soon until I write the final message on parchment. Could you perhaps find some cheese, or biscuits, or something?"

"That . . . that I can do, my lady." Alcaren smiled.

Secca turned back toward the writing table. The light was dim and getting dimmer, but she could always pull the writing table under the wall lamp, if necessary.

67

A dull ringing chime rolled through the darkness, and Secca bolted upright in the narrow double-width bed— one of the few true beds in which she had slept since leaving Encora so many long weeks before. Sweat poured off her face, and a wall of heat surrounded her and Alcaren, as if they had been placed suddenly within an oven. She found herself gasping for breath against the unbearable heat.

Then, as quickly as the heat had bathed her, with the dying away of the dull, half-harmonic chime it began to diminish. Secca found herself shaking, as if exhausted, as if she had sung a major spell.

"What . . . ?" began Alcaren, also sitting up, then stopping and looking at his consort. "So hot . . ." He flung back the blanket.

"Something with the harmonies." Even as the words left her lips, Secca felt stupid for saying the obvious.

"It had to be," he replied gently, blotting his own sweating forehead with the back of his hand before easing himself out of the bed onto the rough wooden floor that creaked as he moved toward the wall lamp. After picking up the striker from the side of the wash table, he fumbled with it several times before the lamp wick caught.

Secca glanced toward the shuttered window, but outside was still dark, without a hint of an approaching dawn. As dim glow from the oil lamp swelled and illuminated the chamber, Secca studied her consort. While he was not shaking or shivering, he also looked pale, wan.

In the dimness of the inn chamber, the two exchanged glances.

Then both spoke.

"The wards . . ."

"Your wards . . ."

Alcaren smiled and gestured for Secca to continue. He sat down on the edge of the bed facing her.

"I think someone tried some sort of sorcery against us, and not from very close. I could almost feel the distance," she said slowly. "The wards . . ." She smiled, almost wryly, exhausted as she felt. "I guess they worked."

"The Sea-Priests, you think?"

"Who else could it be?" She shook her head. "If there is someone else that powerful whom we don't know about . . .

but why would anyone else attempt it? The Ladies of the Shadows? Do they have that ability?"

"The Matriarch never believed so."

"They limited themselves to assassinations?" Secca took another long swallow from the water bottle.

"And other uses of coins to achieve their ends," he agreed. "They've never used sorcery, and I can't believe they would now." After a time, he added, "Do you think we should use the glass to see who it was?"

Secca frowned. "I'm still tired, but if I can do one spell, it might be a good idea. We'd know who it was. That would tell us what we need to do."

"Then you need to eat. Now." Alcaren rose and walked to the writing table, where he leaned down and lifted the small provisions bag that lay beside the saddlebags. After rummaging through it, he held up a small chunk of bread. "Hard and stale, but it will help." He had to saw into the bread and split it with his belt knife before he could offer a piece to Secca.

The bread was so dry and tough that Secca had to alternate small bites with mouthfuls of water from her water bottle.

"We need to keep more biscuits or something in that," Alcaren mumbled through his own mouthful of bread. "And cheese."

"Where will we find them?"

Alcaren shrugged sheepishly.

"I feel badly about what we're taking from people as it is." Secca held up her hand to keep Alcaren from interrupting. "I know. I can't help them if we don't eat, but it bothers me. I don't have that many golds left, even after taking what we did from Fehern."

"We won't need golds at sea."

Secca nodded, knowing that she would need all that she could gather later, but there was little point in worrying about that now. Still, she worried that she dared not tell anyone, even Alcaren. The risk was too great that someone might hear, through sorcery or simple eavesdropping. *Or are you afraid he won't approve? What are you risking by not telling him?*

"Do you want me to try the scrying spell?" he asked.

"I'll try it. If we need a second, then you will have to do it." Secca eased out of bed and padded across a room that was now cold to get the lutar from its case. She thought for a long time as she tuned the instrument.

In the dim light of the single lamp, Alcaren unpacked the scrying glass from its leathers and set it on the narrow writing table, then stood, waiting as Secca finished tuning the instrument and thinking about the spellsong.

When Secca was ready she turned and stepped up to the table.

"Show us now and so that we can tell those who, against our ward, cast their spell . . ."

As she finished the last words of the spellsong, an invisible hammer seemed to strike her forehead, and she had to force herself to hang on to the lutar. Her eyes watered, and for several moments she could not see anything.

"Are you all right?" Alcaren's voice seemed distant.

Swaying unsteadily, she blinked, once, twice, before the image in the glass slowly filled her vision, if blurrily, and through the daystars that flashed across her field of vision.

Flames licked at what had been a tent. All was charred except for one half-upright side, still partly suspended by the only erect tent pole and two unburned ropes. That sole, and shrinking, section of white canvas diminished as Secca watched the fire flare—and the edge of the tent sink into blackness and orange flames. Around the smoke and fire was a ring of lancers in white riding jackets.

"Let it go," Alcaren said. "They're Sturinnese. Or they were."

Despite the pounding in her head, and the pain and blurring in her eyes, Secca lifted the lutar and managed to sing the release couplet. Just singing the couplet reinforced the pounding in her head, so much that she lurched against the table.

Alcaren took the lutar from her shaking hands, setting it down gently on the floor and against the wall. He straightened and put an arm around his unsteady consort, helping her back to the bed, where she sat down heavily.

"My head . . . it's like being pounded on an anvil." Secca squinted. "It's hard to see." She took the water bottle Alcaren tendered—his, because she had finished hers earlier—and slowly drank. The coolness helped some, and she thought the pounding inside her skull was slightly less intense, but her eyes still hurt, and everything she looked at still blurred and flashed.

"You need to eat more. I'm going to see what I can find." Before Secca could say anything, Alcaren was pulling on his trousers and boots and belting on his sabre. He took Secca's water bottle as well.

Stepping to the door, he slid the bolt.

"Ser?" asked Gorkon, sleepily, as though the lancer had been drowsing at his post outside the door.

"The Lady Secca had to do some unforeseen sorcery, and she needs something to eat."

Secca couldn't hear the rest of what Alcaren said, because he had closed the door. She looked toward the window, but no light slipped through the shutters, and the way she felt she doubted if it was much past midnight. She massaged her forehead with her left hand, then her right, but her head still ached, and she was so exhausted she had to give up the effort.

In the end, she just sat and looked blankly at the door until it opened, and Alcaren stepped back inside and slid the bolt.

He carried a loaf of dark bread, and a small wedge of cheese, and a pouch of some sort, as well as the water bottle. As if reading her thoughts, he answered, "Dried fruit. I persuaded the innkeeper to provide it."

"Persuaded?" Her voice cracked even on the single word.

"I just asked," Alcaren replied, innocently. "Oh, and there's ale in the water bottle. I wasn't sure either of us wanted to try a cleaning spellsong." He handed her the water bottle and then set the cheese on the edge of the wash table, where he hacked off a section, quickly extending it to Secca. "Here."

"I don't . . . my stomach is roiling around."

"Please try it. You can't get better without eating something."

"Can I try some of the bread first?"

The dark bread was surprisingly moist, and tasty. Although Secca took very small mouthfuls, it seemed that she had eaten very little, yet the first chunk was gone, and she was reaching for a second.

"You were hungry." Alcaren managed through his own mouthful of bread. "Could I have a sip of the ale?"

"I thought it was for me." Secca had to force the grin.

"It is, but would you miss a little?"

Secca handed him the bottle.

It seemed as though no time had passed when the two looked up at each other after finishing all the cheese, the entire loaf of bread, and the double handful of dried fruit. Secca licked a last crumb off her fingers.

"How is your head?" asked Alcaren.

"Better. It still hurts, but it's a dull hurt. I can see without it blurring, but there are still daystars, now and again."

"I'm glad you're better." Alcaren frowned. "I worry about the wards."

"About what?"

"Won't there be others who will try? Won't we need to redo them?" Alcaren's question was almost hesitant.

"We should. I'd like to do it now, but I can't. We'd have to wake the players, anyway."

Alcaren frowned. "Can we wait till morning? What if—"

"I can't do it now!" Secca snapped. "I just can't. I

couldn't even see, except in blurs. My head hurt so much I couldn't think. It still hurts. How could I sing anything now?"

"I'm sorry," Alcaren said gently. "I just worry about you."

"I worry, too. I can only hope that they don't have that many strong sorcerers, and that they won't try anything." Secca found tears streaming down her cheeks, and she turned her head toward the wall, hoping that Alcaren wouldn't see in the dim light.

"Are you all right, my lady?"

"My eyes . . . I told you they hurt," Secca choked out.

"You said . . ." He left his words drift into silence as he slipped onto the bed beside her and put an arm around her. "I'm sorry. I just worry. I don't want anything to happen to you."

After a moment, Secca let her head rest against his, but she didn't turn to face him. "I know. I know. We'll see in the morning. That's all I can do. That's all you can do. If you tried any sorcery now, you'd be worse than I am now, and then where would we be?"

Alcaren said nothing, just squeezed her gently.

"We'll be all right," she murmured. In spite of Alcaren's closeness, she shivered.

68

WEST-SOUTHWEST OF NESALIA, NESEREA

At the sound of the drums, and the players, the Maitre nods and steps outside his tent into darkness of the night. He glances upward, into a clear and cold sky where Darksong is at its zenith, a red point of light amid the spray of white stars.

His eyes drop to the large tent to his left, its front panels open to allow the spellsong and accompaniment to fill the night. He listens intently to the two matched voices, the players, and the deep bass of the drums.

As the spellsong ends, a single bright chord echoes through the darkness, unheard except by those who can sense the manipulation of the harmonies.

The Maitre nods, a small smile of satisfaction upon his lips.

Abruptly, the tent where the two Sea-Priests and players had performed flares into a brilliant orange-white light, searing the Maitre's vision into momentary blindness. A dull ringing chord, almost leaden, follows the burst of intense flame.

After blotting the involuntary tears from his eyes, the Maitre takes three steps forward, then stops. Ignoring his blurred vision, he stares at the flaming pyre that had been a tent holding drummers and players. So swiftly has the sorcery struck that there have not even been screams or other sounds.

"The bitch! The murdering bitch!" The words are scarcely more than a whisper, for all their vehemence. "How? She had no wards."

"Maitre?" A tall and young Sea-Priest, his jacket half-fastened, hurries up to the older man. "Are you all right?"

"I am fine, jerClayne." The Maitre's words are cold, almost hissed.

"I am most sorry, ser. I did not mean . . ."

"It is not you," the Maitre replies.

"Fire! Fire!" The cry rings through the camp.

Figures in white appear from everywhere.

"Buckets! A chain from the stream!"

The Maitre nods as the lancers swiftly form up and begin the effort to contain the flames blazing into the night sky.

"Do you know . . . ?" JerClayne breaks off his inquiry, his eyes turning back toward the pillar of flame.

"The Sorceress Protector. She has much to answer for. Much."

"She did that?"

"It could be no other. None. No one could be so deviously evil. So malicious." The Maitre beckons to the younger Sea-Priest. "We need to see what she has done. You need to see this."

"Maitre?"

But the Maitre is striding toward the flaming tent.

After a moment, jerClayne hastens after the older sorcerer.

69

S ecca sat at the battered wooden table in the inn's public room, hoping that the hot spiced cider would quiet her stomach, and wondering how she was going to eat enough to be able to do sorcery to replace the wards before they left Stafaal for Narial—and the Ranuan ships she hoped were there.

The room was empty except for her and Alcaren. Wilten and Delcetta had eaten and left to check on the lancers, as had Delvor and Palian.

Beside Secca on the bench set against the wall sat Alcaren. His eyes flicked from her to the archway through which Richina entered, and then back to Secca.

Richina glanced from Easlon and Dymen, who stood on each side of the archway into the public room, to the couple at the oblong table.

Secca nodded for the younger sorceress to seat herself, not wanting to speak, and wishing that she felt better.

Richina slipped onto the bench on the other side of the table. "I hope I am not . . . but . . . last night . . . there was a disturbance of the harmonies . . ." Her voice trailed away.

Secca took another sip of the cider before speaking. "The wards." She looked to Alcaren. "If you would."

"My lady was most successful in setting up the wards," Alcaren said, with but the faintest dryness in his voice. "The Sea-Priests attempted to cast sorcery from some distance against her. The wards worked. The cost on her was great. She worries that she will have to sing another spell to reset them before the Sea-Priests try once more."

"What happened? How did they work?"

"Their sorcery rebounded upon them and burned them as they would have burned her," Alcaren said. "They did not survive."

"Oh . . ."

"Secca used a glass to see that last night. It was almost too much for her."

"I'm better now," Secca felt compelled to say. "Much better. Later . . . we can redo the wards."

"You look tired, Lady Secca," Richina said. "Must you? Now?"

Secca laughed, harshly, then coughed, shaking her head. She took another sip of the cider before speaking. "I did not sleep well, fearing that before I would wake more sorcery would be sung against us. I do not know that I can rest knowing that unless I sing a ward spell I could die at any moment."

Richina tried to conceal a wince. "Surely there are few who could do such."

"One is sufficient," Secca pointed out. *What have you begun? Will every sorcerer or sorceress have to be warded? Or will you or the Sea-Priests end up trying to destroy anyone else who can use distance sorcery to kill? Just to stay alive?* Secca shook her head once more.

"It may be that sorceresses and sorcerers will have to keep their abilities hidden," Alcaren mused.

"There will be even more shadowsinging," Secca said slowly, "with sorcerers trying to find other sorcerers."

"Could they not work together as have you and I or you and . . . Jolyn?" asked Richina.

"We can work together," Secca agreed, "but would we wish to work for the ends of the Sea-Priests? Or they for our ends?"

"And what of the Ladies of the Shadows? Or the Council of Wei?" added Alcaren. "If they knew that sorcery existed that could destroy sorcerers or sorceresses from so far away that they could not even know they were in danger?"

Richina looked blankly from Alcaren's almost-impassive face to Secca's bleak expression, then back to Alcaren before speaking. "Are there truly that many?"

"I would judge not," Secca replied, "but I would not wager my life, or yours, or Alcaren's, on such. Would you?" She finished the hot cider and set the mug on the time-and-use-distressed wood of the table.

"Do you want more?" Alcaren pointed to her empty mug.

"Please."

Alcaren raised his arm and gestured toward the serving-woman who watched from the doorway back to the kitchen. "Do you want some, Richina?"

The younger sorceress nodded.

Within moments, the rail-thin server stood by the table, her eyes darting between Richina and Secca.

"Two more of the hot ciders," Alcaren said firmly. "What do you have suitable for breakfast?"

"Some of the dark bread. Cheese. Skillet potatoes. Might as have some mutton chops be fried up."

Secca's stomach tightened at the thought of mutton chops.

"We'll have some of the bread, cheese, and potatoes," Alcaren said. "No chops, though."

"Good choice, ser. For the three of you, it'd be five coppers."

Alcaren fumbled out a silver and showed it.

"Yes, ser." With a smile, the servingwoman turned and headed to the kitchen.

"And we don't need more golds?" asked Secca.

"Denyst won't ask for any," Alcaren said.

"If the ships come. If the Matriarch and the Exchange agree. We may get presented with an invoice for services," Secca replied.

"If the ships come to Narial, it will be because the Matriarch has convinced the Exchange to fund them." Alcaren paused before adding, "Or paid for them herself."

"Could she do that?" asked Richina.

"Not very often," admitted Alcaren. "She has some funds, but she is poorer than most rulers, perhaps poorer than Lady Secca."

With two *thumps*, the server deposited another set of mugs on the table, along with two small loaves of dark bread side by side in a grass basket, and a wedge of cheese. "Be a bit for the other." She looked at Alcaren expectantly.

He handed her the silver with a smile, and five coppers appeared on the table. Alcaren left them there.

Once the servingwoman was headed back to the kitchen, Alcaren immediately used his belt knife to slice off a large chunk of the bread, which he tendered to Secca. "Even if you don't do the sorcery now, you need to eat, and you need to eat more than you have been." He handed a second chunk to Richina. "And you as well, lady."

Both women exchanged knowing glances, but Secca took a mouthful of bread. So did Richina.

Alcaren took a smaller slice.

"You eat, too," Secca commanded. "You get to sing the ward spell this time, and I'll support you."

Alcaren grinned sheepishly, then shrugged. "As you command, my lady."

"Best you not forget it." Because she couldn't help smiling at his humorous tone, Secca elbowed her consort in the ribs.

Alcaren laughed, and, after a moment, so did the sorceresses.

70

A perfect semicircle of Sturinnese officers in heavy white riding jackets stands behind the Maitre under a clear but chill blue morning sky. Farther to the west, just barely on the horizon, are the white-covered trees of the Great Western Forest. Closer to the group, upon a square of freshly cut logs, lie two bodies wrapped in white canvas. To the right of the Maitre are a half-score of players. To the left are an equal number of drummers. All stand in precise and symmetrical order, as do the Sturinnese officers.

The Maitre lifts his right hand, and both drummers and players begin. After a bar, his bass-baritone voice follows the accompaniment with the spell.

> *"From the earth, from the land, and to the skies,*
> *go with spirits free, go in greater harmony . . ."*

The rhythm of the drums becomes more insistent with the closing lines of the ceremony.

> *". . . and with celestial fire now take flight*
> *becoming one with harmony's sacred sound and light!"*

The Maitre's last words are followed by a flaring spike of light that flashes skyward, and that light spike is accompanied by a crescendoing drumroll.

For a time, all the Sturinnese stand rigidly in silence before a blackened square of earth that bears no ashes, no remains, where only the wavering of heat lines against the cold day shows that anything has transpired.

The Maitre nods brusquely and turns, walking back toward the largest and most central tent in the encampment. When he reaches it, he steps inside and waits. He does not speak until the half-score of Sea-Priest sorcerers in white— all young-faced and clean-shaven—stand before him and inside.

"Some of you may wonder what occurred last night. You may also wonder why we are heading away from Esaria to engage the Mansuuran invaders." The Maitre's voice is not loud, but it fills the large tent in the stillness of the early morning. "All this is part of a larger plan. It is one that we have labored years to accomplish. Tomorrow, after crossing the bridge at Tryve to the west, we will use sorcery to destroy the bridge, so that the Mansuuran forces must move toward Nesalia. We will take a few companies, along with those we acquired from the unfortunate Lord Belmar, and begin the return to Worlan, where we will be joined by the forces from the great fleet. The forces here will be reinforced by those from Dumar, along with a half-score of sorcerers coming with those forces. Those will be sufficient to destroy the Mansuurans without our aid.

"Once that task is accomplished, it is but seasons before the entire west of Liedwahr is ours." The Maitre smiles. "Now . . . make your preparations to strike camp and ride." Another brief pause follows. "I would like a word with Marshal jerLeng."

A Sea-Priest in a lancer's uniform with eight-pointed gold stars on the collar of his white riding jacket steps forward as the other Sea-Priests offer head bows before turning and filing out of the tent into the still-chill morning.

The Maitre remains silent until the tent is empty except for the two of them. "It is not quite that simple."

"I thought as much, Maitre."

"Almost, but not quite."

"The Sorceress Protector of the East?"

The Maitre nods. "There is no one left, besides me, who could sing a spell against her from this distance."

The other remains silent.

So does the Maitre.

Finally, the lancer officer pauses, clears his throat, and asks, "Why is this one sorceress so important to defeat? And, if she is, why not turn all the sorcerers and drummers here against her?"

"You do not ask why I do not confront her?" The Maitre beckons for jerLeng to come closer before he laughs, without mirth. "I had not thought she was so strong as she has become. Now, the risk is too great. We are close to equal in strength. You know that distance spells only work with one or two voices, and if two, they must be matched—as with jerHalin and jerEstafen. We have no matched voices remaining."

"So . . . can you not focus your sorcery on her, as she did on Belmar?" An almost concealed edge of exasperation colors the lancer officer's voice.

"That was what those two we sent to the harmonies this morning did." The Maitre gestures back toward the site of the ceremony. "Whatever she used is not a ward, but something different, and far more deadly. We have more voices, and in closer combat, as you know, a number of massed voices can overcome the greatest of sorceresses. That was how we destroyed the other sorceress, although Belmar did not realize that his spells were being aided, and that is how we must deal with the Sorceress Protector. She must be destroyed, but that is not certain unless we are closer to her. You must make sure that our forces here, and those coming from Dumar, understand your role. That is to destroy the Liedfuhr's forces and then to rejoin us as you can. If we do not hasten back northward, I fear that she will sail to the Bitter Sea and use sorcery on the fleet from the west."

"They have sorcerers and drummers on board," points out jerLeng.

"But none are experienced, not in sea and sorcery battles,"

the Maitre replies evenly. "If we cannot halt her soon, she will turn all Liedwahr in the direction of the Ranuan bitches, and Lord Robero will let her do so, for he cannot stand against her. Indeed, no man in Liedwahr, save Belmar, could have, and you see how he fared. She is not yet so powerful as she will be if we do not act. Once she is gone, Lord Robero will do as we wish."

"I had thought . . ."

"He may indeed recall her to Defalk, but she is most willful, and we must not count on her obeying her lord. Not until she does. And if she disobeys, and we destroy her, well then, the good Lord Robero is indebted to us."

"But how will you destroy her?"

"I have tested her defenses. They would be difficult to penetrate, even if we could muster all the sorcerers we have here. But they take much energy from her. She cannot do great sorcery and hold those defenses. So we will destroy the bridge and weaken the Liedfuhr's forces as we can before leaving you and most of the lancers to finish them off. You will be reinforced, and you will be able to draw upon those sorcerers, while we will hasten to Worlan to deal with the sorceress when she arrives. With what I know, we will strike the moment she lowers her defenses to attack the fleet. Several of our younger sorcerers will follow her through the glass, and I will lead the rest in striking before she knows what we do."

"What of the other sorceresses in Defalk?"

"The others we can wear down . . . or kill through poison, stealth, or golds." The Maitre shakes his head. "This one . . . if we do not destroy her while we can, she will destroy us and all that Sturinn has built. That must not be, and it will not." The Maitre's eyes blaze.

"We will do our part."

"Good." The Maitre's eyes fix on the marshal. "Good."

71

I n the bright and cloudless midmorning, Secca stood before the small tent at the base of a rise that rose to a low crest a mere fifty yards shoreward of the stone piers of Narial—a rise created and scoured down to bare clay by the sorcerous wave of the Sea-Priests seasons earlier. Dwellings and structures remained standing through the upper reaches of Narial, those on the hillsides, but except for the stone bridge spanning the Falche, virtually no structure around the harbor itself had survived. Near the harbor itself, and just seaward of Secca's tent, were only two crude long buildings, each less than fifty yards in length and but a story high. Built of scavenged bricks and stone, they stood at the base of the one long pier that still had a clear channel to the sea beyond. Both were empty, but from the debris inside, one had served as quarters for some of the Sturinnese, and the other as a warehouse.

Secca had insisted on having her tent erected in the shade beside the more landward of the two, leaving the buildings to the players and lancers. After two days in Narial, although the scrying glass showed no Ranuan ships in the harbor at Encora and a flotilla of ten somewhere at sea, Secca had begun to worry even more about what she could do if the Matriarch had not been able to send ships. The continual tiredness from the drain of the warding spell helped not at all, even if Alcaren had sung it.

Regularly, she continued to scan the harbor and the waters beyond to the south, although she knew that looking would do nothing to make the ships appear or to allay her worries.

"They will be here," Alcaren said, appearing from behind the uneven brick wall of the warehouse. "They would not

have ten ships upon the sea together were they not headed
to aid us."

Secca jumped at his words, but Gorkon did not. Clearly,
the lancer had seen Secca's consort coming, even if Secca
had not. *Are you fretting so much you cannot even see or
hear what is near?* "We cannot wait long, not if we are to
do what we must before it is too late." She paused. "Did
you have any luck in finding better maps?"

Alcaren held up a small rolled scroll, darkened with age.
"I found a section of one, in the papers left to the widow
of a merchant captain. She was pleased to let me have it for
a silver. It shows Stura, as the main isle and the port there
were perhaps a generation or more ago."

"They can't be the same now."

"The buildings may change, but not the land," he pointed
out. "Stura is by far the largest and wealthiest of the isles.
That's from where the Maitre rules. Would you like to see?"
He unrolled the short scroll before she could respond.

In spite of herself, Secca had to admire the cartography,
and the artistry along the borders as she looked at the partial
map.

"These are hard to find," Alcaren said. "The Sea-Priests
have often imprisoned captains or officers who have lost
maps."

"I thought you said you had maps."

He smiled. "There are maps that show the outlines of the
isles, but this one shows more."

Secca squinted against the glare of the morning sun, taking in the minute depictions of towns and mountains, pausing as she came across a jagged line blocking a stream.
"This?" she asked.

"That is a rapids or waterfall. Here . . . that is a volcano,
as in the Circle of Fire in Mansuur. There are a number on
the north end of the isle."

"Like the Zauberinfeuer?"

With a smile, Alcaren nodded. "This symbol means a reef
shallow enough to strand a ship."

"You're pleased with the map?"

"Very much so."

"I must try another scrying," Secca said abruptly.

"Cannot Richina? There are no armsmen near, nor any that could reach us soon," Alcaren said.

Secca knew he was being cautious. There was no sign of any armed force anywhere close, and the surviving Dumarans were happy to provide provisions and leave Secca's force alone. At least so far.

Almost as if she had been prompted by Alcaren, Richina peered from the tent. "Ah ... I could do a scrying, Lady Secca. I am well rested now."

"Why don't you try?" Alcaren suggested quickly.

Secca almost glared at her consort, but looked away quickly. *Why are you so touchy? Wrong time of your season? Or because you're tired? Or are you feeling guilty about keeping things from them?*

Alcaren rerolled the map carefully, then stepped inside the tent, where, after tucking the map into one of his saddlebags, he began to unwrap the scrying mirror.

Richina followed him and began to tune her lutar.

Reluctantly, Secca stepped into the tent to join the other two, waiting until the younger sorceress was ready to begin the spell before moving around to where she could see the glass that Alcaren had placed on the ground between the two cots.

After pulling on the copper-tipped leather gloves, Richina finished tuning, and sang through a single vocalise before clearing her throat and looking at Secca.

Secca nodded, and Richina began the spell.

"Show the ships that sail to meet us here,
as if upon a map with Narial so clear ..."

The image in the scrying glass was fuzzy, distorted, and almost impossible to discern. All three studied the glass.

"They're less than a day's sailing from here. We probably

couldn't even get this image if they weren't close to the coast," offered Alcaren.

"Can you be certain?" asked Secca.

"Not until tomorrow," he replied with a grin.

Secca wanted to shake her head. She knew he was trying to be cheerful, but all she felt was tired and worried. "You can sing the release couplet, Richina."

As the younger sorceress released the image, Secca sat down on her cot and looked at Alcaren, still standing just inside the tent. "Aren't you tired?" Even before the words were out of her mouth, she saw the dark circles under his eyes, and the tightness around his eyes, and she realized that he was at least as exhausted as she was.

"I try not to dwell on it."

A thumping, half-clanging sound filled the tent. Secca turned to see a brass tube rolling across the packed clay between the cots.

Alcaren pulled on his riding gloves and scooped it up, wrenching the top off and extracting the scrolls inside before dropping the tube back on the packed ground. "It was almost glowing." The gloves came off quickly, and he handed the two scrolls to Secca.

The longer scroll was fastened with ribbons and seals, and was, presumably, from Lord Robero. Secca opened it first and began to read.

The Lady Secca, Sorceress Protector of the East, Lady of Mencha and Flossbend, Greetings and best wishes from Falcor, and our deepest appreciation for restoring the lands of Ebra, Elahwa, and Dumar to the oversight of Defalk. You have accomplished what many believed impossible, and for that all in Defalk must be grateful. . . .

Secca didn't like the opening words at all. Fulsome praise from Robero was but honey before the vinegar.

... You are, with the untimely death of Lady Clayre from the sorcery of Lord Belmar, the sole force capable of holding off the Sturinnese forces in Neserea. Defalk's very survival depends on you. For this reason, I must request, order if I must, that you return to Falcor as expeditiously as possible, returning as closely as possible by a route through Stromwer, so that all Defalk can be assured that you will return in safety ...

She managed to keep a faint smile on her face as she continued reading, even as her stomach was clenching at the words before her.

... Any sea voyage, even to Neserea, is fraught with too great a hazard, both to you personally, and to Defalk as a land. You must not embark on such, but return immediately before the situation becomes intolerable. ...

With all that you have done, against near-impossible odds, none will think less of you, and many will think more of you for exercising prudence in defending your land ...

Secca forced herself to keep reading to the end and to the even more flowery conclusion. Then she carefully rerolled the first scroll and read the second and shorter scroll.

Dearest Secca,
I hesitate to send these, yet know I must, if only so that you know how matters be here in Falcor.

A handful of the older lords, led by Ebraak and Fustar, have been catering favor with Robero, suggesting that the only way that he can rule in his own right is with the backing of Sturinn, because only Sturinn can free him of the domination of the sorceresses. You will be happy to learn that Lord Ebraak died of a wasting flux on his way back to Nordfels, although Lord Robero does not yet know this.

Secca shook her head. Lord Cassily would probably be a better lord than his father, but Secca had to worry about Jolyn's motives, for she doubted Ebraak had died accidentally and coincidentally. *Are yours any more pure*? She took a deep breath and continued reading.

Others, such as Dostal and Nerylt, have urged him to talk to envoys of the Maitre, saying that talking can do no harm. Those who have suggested opposing Sturinn, such as Lord Kinor and Lord Birke, Lord Robero will not see. There are murmurs that others have his ear, and I have used what means are at my disposal to seek out who they may be. He has met with men I do not know, but the pool shows little, save that they dress well and that they have oft lodged with Lord Ebraak.

Lord Robero will no longer even heed his own consort. Alyssa has left the liedstadt and taken the children to Morra and her parents. She had not spoken to Lord Robero in the weeks before she left. The old guard captain—Rickel—asked for his stipend and left Falcor, to serve, I believe, under Lady Alseta at Mossbach. Lord Robero growls at everyone, save me and Arms Commander Jirsit. Jirsit has told him, as have I, that seeking any agreement with Sturinn is foolhardy. Robero's only response has been that it is better to seek an agreement while he still has sorceresses left than to be forced to agree to anything when he has none.

I do not know what you will do, but I trust that you will follow your own heart and thoughts. Before Lady Asaro left Falcor, she suggested that the mountain air at Denguic might be refreshing and that she and Lord

Kinor would be most pleased to host me. I might indeed find it so . . . and, of course, I could check the north road to Nordfels, perhaps find some improvements to make there . . . or travel northward, if necessary, perhaps to visit Lysara . . .

Secca slowly lowered the scroll, her face frozen. *Travel northward? Anna had never meant her roads as means of flight. Yet if Jolyn is considering fleeing to Dubaria, or even to Nordwei . . .*

"What is it?" asked Richina.

Secca forced a shrug. "Lord Robero is most concerned and suggests that, if there is any other way to deal with the problems in Neserea, we should attempt such." Secca offered a false and lopsided smile. "If not, we are to proceed with great caution. Very great caution." She snorted. "How does one proceed with great caution against the Sea-Priests?"

Alcaren laughed, sardonically. "By making sure one can destroy them, I would suggest."

"What did the Lady Jolyn say?" asked Richina.

"That she feared Lord Robero was being too cautious." That was certainly true enough. Secca took a deep breath. "I need to think for a moment."

Richina smiled as she replaced the lutar in its case. "I'll be walking along the pier. Easlon or Dymen can come with me."

"Both," suggested Secca.

Alcaren looked up from where he was rewrapping the scrying glass and nodded.

Alcaren and Secca remained in silence for several moments after Richina left.

"That was not what the scroll said, was it?" murmured Alcaren.

Wordlessly, Secca handed the scrolls to him, waiting while he sat down on the cot beside her and read them.

When he had finished, Alcaren bent toward her and whispered in her ear so softly that Secca could barely make out his words. "You are disobeying an order."

Secca put her arms around him and replied in a murmur into his ear, "I'll claim I never received it. If we save his rule, then how can he complain? If we do not . . . then . . . does it matter?"

He pointed toward the scrolls, raising his eyebrows in silent inquiry.

"Sometimes, messages sent by sorcery arrive charred," she murmured. "Sometimes, they do not arrive. Robero need not know which."

Alcaren offered a crooked smile. "The Lady Anna taught you well."

But did you learn it well enough? Or are you over-reaching yourself and ensuring that Sturinn will turn every woman in Liedwahr into a chattel and slave this year— instead of in five?

She shivered.

Alcaren squeezed her in reassurance, but she still felt cold deep inside.

72

Secca sat on the end of her cot in the tent, two sheets of parchment in her hand as she let the ink dry. She glanced down at the parchment, a message that should have been sent days before, had she thought. The stained and worn silk panels fluttered in the light breeze of midday. Outside lay a harbor still empty of ships. At the sound of boots, she looked up.

The tent panel was drawn back, and Alcaren stepped inside. "I wondered where you were."

"I've been trying to remedy what I should have done

sooner. I should have thought of this earlier." Secca rubbed her forehead. "Dissonance, I'm tired." She looked up from the parchment she was rereading.

"Carrying the wards is hard on you," Alcaren replied carefully.

"It makes it harder to think, but . . ." She sighed.

He laughed. "My lady . . . you have defeated the Sturinnese when no others could."

"There is still much I do not know. Everything has happened so quickly, and I've been so tired that I haven't been thinking. We need to send a message with the warding spellsong to Jolyn."

Alcaren's mouth opened, and he shook his head. "That . . . I did not think, either."

"I know," Secca said tiredly. "If they can strike at us, what is to stop them from striking at anyone who is not warded? We should have done it days ago, but the glass shows she is fine, and if we hurry, there will be no harm done."

"You cannot send it," he pointed out.

"Richina can send it. She must." Secca extended the sheets of parchment. "The second one is the spellsong."

Alcaren took the sheet from her and began to read.

Secca stood and moved so that she could see what she had written as he read it.

Dear Jolyn—
We are in Dumar, and awaiting ships from the Matriarch to take us to Neserea . . .

"Clever," Alcaren said. "You would send it as if we had not received the others, and you have even written it so that Richina would not know."

"Richina should read it before she sends it," Secca replied.

He nodded and returned to reading her words.

. . . we hope they will arrive in the next few days.

The Sturinnese forces and their sorcerers are riding northward into Neserea. We have discovered that they now have developed a spellsong that can strike from a distance. It is strong enough to kill unprotected lords or sorceresses. I have attached the warding spell that will protect you from such sorcery and also limit the abilities of the Sea-Priests to see you in a glass. The warding spell lasts until it is attacked, and then it must be resung. Be warned that this spell takes most of your strength just to hold.

The Sturinnese are not yet thinking about you, it would appear, but I have few doubts that they will as time passes, and I would not wish you to be unprotected. I would strongly suggest that you keep Anandra with you, and that one of you sing the ward spell and hold it for a week, and then the other. Whoever holds the ward spells will have little ability besides a few scrying spells.

We will try to let you know once we have arrived in Neserea . . .

Alcaren looked up. "Do you think she will use it?"

"Could I say more?" asked Secca.

"Not that you dare," he reflected. "Nor any words that would do any good." He handed the parchment back to her. "Richina was walking on the end of the pier. I will find her."

"Thank you."

After Alcaren stepped from the tent, Secca pulled the tarnished bronze tube from beneath her cot. *You should have thought about this earlier*. She massaged her forehead once more, trying to reduce the dull aching. *Anna tried to show you, to let you know.* A bitter smile crossed her lips. *Why is it that you don't begin to understand until it's too late . . . or almost so?*

She had no answers for her own questions, only the hope that the warding spellsong would reach Jolyn in time.

73

L ady Secca!" came a voice from outside the tent where Secca had tried to rest and regain more strength—and tried not to worry too much about her failure to warn Jolyn earlier.

She sat up and swung her still-booted feet onto the dust-covered stones that had once been the floor of some structure swept away by the sorcery of the Sea-Priests, or perhaps merely the remnant of an older building revealed by the scouring force of the massive wave. "I'm coming."

Alcaren, who had been napping on the cot normally used by Richina, shook his head sleepily. "What is it?"

"It's a SouthWoman officer, ser," offered Achar from outside the tent.

"Thank you." Secca stepped outside, followed by a sleepy-eyed Alcaren.

Waiting for them in the brisk early afternoon sea breeze was a SouthWoman lancer, an undercaptain Secca did not know. "Lady Secca, ser . . . Overcaptain Delcetta wished you to know that a Ranuan vessel has entered the channel."

Secca looked to Alcaren.

He grinned. "I did say today."

She returned the smile. "Tomorrow, I thought."

"I was wrong." Alcaren's grin was wider.

Secca turned back to the undercaptain. "Please tell the overcaptain that we'll come down to the pier in a moment."

"Yes, lady."

As the undercaptain turned, Secca added, "We'd better have Richina standing by with the lutar, in case this is a trick of some sort."

"Or we could have her scry the ship," Alcaren suggested.

Secca rubbed her forehead. "I'm too tired to think well."

"Do you think we could drop the wards once we're at sea?"

"No." Secca shook her head, ignoring the additional headache the gesture created.

"Are you upset with me, my lady?"

"I'm just upset. You did most of the ward spellsong, but I'm still tired. At times, I *hate* being small."

"You are scarcely small," he replied with a laugh.

"Then why am I always tired?"

"Because you put much energy into everything you do."

"So do you, but you are not . . . never mind."

Alcaren touched her shoulder gently. "Just rest for a moment. I'll get Richina to use the glass. She said she was going to see Palian."

Don't condescend to me. Secca cut off the thought before she spoke it. *What's wrong with you? He's never condescending. He worries, and you aren't helping either one of you.* "Thank you." She managed a smile.

By the time Alcaren returned with the younger sorceress, Secca had drunk half the water in her water bottle, washed up somewhat, and felt slightly less bedraggled.

Richina carried her lutar, uncased, and inclined her head as she stopped before Secca. "Lady . . . Alcaren had said . . . ?"

"If you would sing a spell to determine if the ship in the channel is from Ranuak, that would be most helpful."

While Richina checked the tuning on the lutar, Alcaren retrieved the scrying glass from inside the tent, setting it in the shade of the warehouse wall so that viewing the image called up would be easier.

Then, as Alcaren and Secca watched, the blonde sorceress offered the spellsong.

*"Show us now and in day's clear light,
the closest Ranuan ship to our sight..."*

The glass immediately silvered, then displayed a familiar Ranuan vessel under near full sail, against a backdrop of what seemed to be the island offshore from Narial.

Secca nodded for Richina to let go of the image, and the younger sorceress sang the release couplet.

"It might be a good idea to bring the lutar with you," Secca suggested. "I don't know that I could warm water with a spell right now."

"Nor I," added Alcaren.

While Alcaren replaced the scrying glass in its wraps and replaced it in the tent, Secca looked seaward. At the far end of the channel, she saw a single vessel, sailing northward toward the pier, where a squad of uniformed SouthWomen stood, waiting by the bollards to help tie up the Ranuan ship.

"That's the *Silberwelle*," Alcaren observed after stepping back out of the tent. "Denyst must be worried that we're not here. That's heavy sail for inshore use."

"The SouthWomen on the pier should help show her that we hold Narial," Secca said tersely.

Followed by Achar and Dyvan, Secca, Alcaren, and Richina walked toward the pier where the *Silberwelle* was maneuvering through a tight circle to face offshore before coming to rest at the stone pier. Halfway to where the vessel would tie up, they were joined by Delcetta and Wilten.

"Thank you for sending a messenger," Secca told the SouthWoman overcaptain.

"We thought you should be among the first to know," replied the blonde officer, with a warm smile.

"We told the lancers to make ready to embark," Wilten added. "Though I'd guess it could be today or tomorrow. Or later."

"That depends on how they want to load us aboard," Alcaren said. "We'll see."

The group continued seaward along the pier, walking

slowly, watching the *Silberwelle* easing alongside the stone pier, until they reached a spot between the bollards set far-thest seaward. There they waited, roughly equidistant be-tween the bollards, close to where the midsection of the ship would be when the docking was finished.

The first line was hurled from the bow, striking the lancer waiting at the rearmost bollard with such force that she took two steps backward before recovering and lashing the line around the heavy timber post.

The second line was thrown to a lancer less than five yards from Secca, who immediately ran forward toward the most seaward bollard and lashed the line there.

"Easy in! Easy in!" came the order from the poop deck.

Secca recognized Denyst's distinctive voice, cutting through the afternoon like a jagged blade.

Slowly, the big oceangoing trader eased up to the pier, drawn in by the winches cranked furiously by the *Silber-welle*'s crew. Hempen bumpers festooned the pierward side of the ship, and cushioned the sheathing and timbers as the ship came to rest almost against the bare stone of the pier, stone that had doubtless once been sheathed with softer wood—before the Sea-Priest attack.

"Double up, now!"

Another set of lines went out, so that the ship was doubly held fore and aft.

"Lady Secca, Alcaren! Come aboard!" called the captain.

Secca turned to Richina, and the two overcaptains. "Ri-china, if you wouldn't mind . . . standing by here with the lutar . . . just in case?"

"Not at all, lady."

"Wilten, if you haven't already, would you send someone to tell the chief players that a Ranuan ship is here?"

Wilten smiled. "I dispatched Garyss a while ago."

"Thank you. We need to meet with Captain Denyst. I hope it will not be long."

"We stand ready, lady," replied Wilten.

"As do we," added Delcetta.

Secca walked up the gangway, with Richina and Alcaren just steps behind, almost as soon as it had been extended, noting, once more, how every surface was smoothed and varnished or oiled, and how the brasswork gleamed. They climbed the ladder to the poop deck and found Denyst standing at the railing, watching as her crew checked the lines.

"Wasn't sure we'd find you here. Matriarch was convinced, and so was I, but the other captains . . ." The wiry yet muscular captain shrugged and smiled simultaneously. "So I got to come in to see." She paused, looking at Secca's face, and frowning.

"We had a little trouble with Lord Fehern," Secca said. "He threw burning water at my face and tried to kill me."

"He is dead," Alcaren added.

Denyst nodded slowly. "Knowing what I know of his line, I could not say I am surprised."

"We're glad you're here," Secca said. "Very glad."

"Can't say as I am. Not in some ways, leastwise. Wouldn't be here at all, hadn't seen what you did in Encora." Denyst turned to a taller and more muscular woman. "You've got her now, Elys. I'll be going below with them."

"Aye, Captain."

"You know the way," Denyst said to Secca, gesturing toward the ladder down to the main deck. "Be glad to sit for a bit."

Alcaren scrambled back down the ladder first, then turned, ready to offer Secca a hand, but she didn't need the aid.

"Thank you," she murmured as her feet touched the main deck, before they stepped through the open hatch into the passageway leading back to the captain's quarters.

Secca was struck once more both by how compact everything was on the *Silberwelle*, and yet, comparatively how spacious the captain's quarters were, nearly five yards in width and almost as deep. She wished she could just climb into the recessed double-width bunk, set as it was against the forward bulkhead, and go to sleep. Instead, she eased herself into one of the chairs set around the circular table in the middle of the compartment, a chair secured to the deck itself, as was the table itself and all the other chairs around it.

Denyst was the last to enter, and she carefully closed the doorlike wooden hatch behind her before settling herself in the remaining chair at the table. She looked at Secca for a long moment before speaking. "We brought the ships you captured for us last winter—white hulls and all, but we couldn't bring any inshore until you knew they were ours. I thought they could lead the way once we got close to Stura—if we need a decoy."

"It's a good idea. I wouldn't have considered that," Secca replied.

"What would we be traveling to Sturinn for? Something like what they did here in Narial?" Denyst's eyes were intent as she studied Secca.

"I'd hoped we could do something like that, except to most of the isles, and not just one port." Secca was more than shading the truth, but the less said about specifics the better. *Besides, no one would believe what you plan.*

Denyst nodded slowly. "It took every word and every coin the Matriarch had to get you these ships, Lady Secca."

"I'm not surprised," Secca replied. "I am surprised at the number."

Denyst raised her eyebrows. "You've but seen the *Silberwelle*."

"The glass showed nine others. Were we wrong?" asked Secca with a faint smile.

"Half-score is correct." Denyst shook her head. "Would that we had more. Another score at least."

"So far as we can scry," Alcaren said, "there are no Sturinnese vessels south of the Hoffspitze right now. There may be some small number of ships near Stura, but the last large fleet is in the Bitter Sea."

"That is better news than I'd have hoped."

"Once we deal with Stura," Secca said slowly, "we need

to get as close to Neserea as we can. Esaria, if possible."

"Let us get you to Stura first." Denyst offered a wintry smile. "You still have the same numbers as when you came to Dumar?"

"Almost," Secca said. "Almost."

"And the Sturinnese?"

"More than half their forces destroyed," Alcaren said. "The others fled northward into Neserea and blocked the passes with sorcery."

"Mayhap you *can* do the impossible, lady." Denyst drew out a set of papers and laid them on the stateroom table. "Here be the loading plans . . ."

"You are the expert, Captain," Secca said. "I will need all the players and their instruments on the *Silberwelle* with me. Otherwise, we accept your plans."

"After the battle off Encora, I'd thought as much, about your needing your players," Denyst said musingly. "I'd calculated as much, but we'll be taking but a few of your mounts on the *Silberwelle*. Instead, we'll be carrying more stores." She offered a crooked smile. "For later, should we need them." She cleared her throat and went on. "You two will have my cabin here."

"For such a longer voyage," Secca protested, "we couldn't . . . Besides, the last time you promised you wouldn't give up your cabin . . ."

"Nonsense, lady. My life and that of the Matriarch's are worth more than a few weeks' comfort. You will need rest—that even I can see. I can see the strain of sorcery and battles." Denyst grinned. "You can't always trust a captain to be selfish all the time. Mayhap, I should be saying that you can trust me to be selfish in a way that be wiser."

Alcaren laughed.

Secca looked at her consort.

"You will not win this argument, my lady," he said.

Secca shook her head ruefully, finally admitting, "It has been a long season, and we have not even reached the middle of spring here."

"Even if the worst occurs, you have bought Ranuak time, perhaps years, but already the cost on you has been high." Denyst looked from Secca to Richina, and then to Alcaren. "I can see that it has been high for all of you."

And it will rise even higher. But Secca only nodded and offered a lopsided smile.

74

Under a midday sky that was mostly blue, save for scattered puffy clouds, the *Silberwelle* sliced through the low swells of the Southern Ocean's dark blue water. With the wind in her face, Secca stood at the railing just aft of the bow of the *Silberwelle*, her riding jacket fastened against the chill damp air. Beside her was Alcaren.

"You slept till late morning," he said. "How do you feel?"

"I am still tired, but not so tired as before. What of you?"

He shrugged. "I was so tired my body did not even protest that I was aboard a ship." He laughed.

"You're still tired," she said. "I can see it in your eyes."

"Another few nights of rest, and I will be much better. A good bed helps."

"That was kind of Denyst."

"Both kind and practical. That is the way she is." Alcaren turned and looked steadily at Secca. "Whatever you're—or we're—going to do, my lady, you cannot maintain the wards until just before you try to sing it."

"Without the wards, we may not live to sing," Secca said. "You know that."

Alcaren waited, but Secca did not say more. Finally, he said, "Ships can only sail so fast. If there are no ships within two hundred deks of us, then none can reach us for a day or more."

"Sorcery can strike from any distance. Did we not prove that?"

"You did. But what need is there for Richina to be ready to defend us against other ships?"

"You would have her carry the wards?"

"For a few days."

Secca looked ahead, out across the dark waters to the west.

"We only need a few days to rest up enough for sorcery to defend us," he pointed out. "Then I could spellsing the fire spell against any ship. If that worries you, I will sing the ward spells with Richina. But you must have rest without the drain of the ward spells. Do you not recall the storm spell you used against the Sturinnese fleet?"

Much as she disliked Alcaren's words, Secca knew he was right.

"We have some time," she finally said. *Do you have as much as you need?*

"The more rest you have before you must do great sorcery, the stronger will be your spells. Also, Richina cannot do the water-storm spells, and there may be yet another fleet that will come to test us when we reach the isles of Sturinn." Alcaren smiled wryly. "I cannot believe that those of Sturinn will not have some defenses."

"Nor I," Secca agreed.

"So you will let Richina—or the two of us—carry the ward spells?"

Secca glanced away from Alcaren's piercing gray-blue eyes, instead turning to watch the swells before the *Silberwelle*.

"My lady?" Alcaren asked softly.

"You are right. Yet it worries me. She is still so young." Secca sighed.

"Will the Sturinnese let her live if we fail?"

"No. We both know that." *Why does it have to be this way? Why does it always come back to who can do what to whom?* Secca shook her head.

Alcaren waited, and Secca could feel his eyes on her. At last, she replied, "Tomorrow or the next day. Or perhaps the day after. She will need rest, as well."

Alcaren nodded.

You risk so much. Yet you risk more by doing nothing. Secca tried to push the thoughts from her mind. *You can do nothing at this moment. Nothing.*

Alcaren put his arm around her, silently, so lightly that she almost did not notice it at first, and they remained at the railing, looking westward. Toward Stura.

75

SOUTH OF WORLAN, NESEREA

Two Sea-Priests stand before the Maitre's camp table, erect, their uniforms spotless, waiting, their heads almost touching the overhead fabric of the traveling tent. Outside the tent, the day is gray and chill.

The Maitre shifts his weight on the padded stool and looks up. "Where is she?"

"We do not know, Maitre," offers the shorter man. "As we have told you, when we try to scry her image, we see but our own. By scrying the ships, we can see that she is upon a Ranuan vessel, but it is on the open ocean. Its heading appears to be westward. That would follow if she intends to travel to Neserea by sea."

"The ship is too far from land to say where she is?"

"Yes, Maitre."

"How many vessels?"

"Ten, Maitre." The time the taller Sturinnese sorcerer replies. "Six are vessels she captured from us with sorcery last winter. We think. They have white hulls and our lines."

"So she has embarked her entire force upon Ranuan ves-

sels, and they head westward?" The Maitre frowns. "What
of the fleet of Nordwei?"

"It nears the Ostisles," replies the taller man. "The home
defense fleet is prepared to give chase."

"Is there any sign that they work together?"

"None, Maitre. It is possible, but there are no signs."

"And the Assistant Sorceress of Defalk?"

"She, too, is now warded. We do not know how long her
wards have been there. We had not used the glass to find
her in . . . some time. The wards, they are not like those we
use."

"There is much the bitch sorceresses do that is not as it
should be," the Maitre replies. "You may go. Keep watching, and let me know if you see such and when you can
determine with certainty the destination of the Shadow Sorceress." The dark-haired and sharp-featured Maitre gestures
for the two to leave.

Once they have departed, his eyes fall to the maps spread
across the camp table. "Wards that are not wards, or more
than wards. Ships from all across Liedwahr, and the support
of the Matriarch. Between the Sorceress Protector and that
bitch Ashtaar, we are spread too thin." He shakes his head.
"The shadowsinger . . . that one is too malicious—and too
clever by half. Tearing her tongue out would be too kind.
Far too kind."

The panels of the tent flutter ever so slightly in the light
and chill wind.

76

S pacious as the captain's cabin had seemed, it was
cramped with eight people crowded into it. Cramped . . .
and close. Secca, Alcaren, Richina, and Denyst sat around
the table, with Palian, Delvor, Delcetta, and Wilten standing

behind them. The sole light came through the green-tinted glass of the twin portholes and the prismlike skylenses set in the overhead, leaving the cabin dimly lit, even if far brighter than twilight.

On the circular table were maps—those Alcaren had found and those charts belonging to the *Silberwelle*.

Secca listened closely as Denyst continued to explain.

". . . making near-on twelve deks per glass now, but we've had favoring winds, and they won't hold as they have. Leastwise, can't count on such . . . even if we could, be another three days afore we sighted the Ostisles, a bit less than a week after that before we'd see the fringe isles east of Stura."

"In a few days, even if the winds don't hold, we may be able to help there, as we have before," Secca pointed out.

"I'd rather the winds held," Alcaren said with a laugh. "So that we can save the sorcery for other matters."

"So would I," Denyst responded.

Richina nodded.

Secca looked from the maps to Alcaren and then to Denyst. "All the isles of Sturinn together are not that much larger than Defalk, and the isle of Stura is but half the size of Defalk. Yet they have built many fleets of fivescore vessels and lost hundreds of scores of lancers—with hundreds of scores remaining."

"True enough," the captain agreed.

"Most of the lancer rankers do not come from Sturinn," Alcaren said. "They are from Pelara or the Ostisles. If they survive and are promoted through the ranks to become officers, after a number of years, they can take a stipend and live in great comfort in their homeland. The officers who survive live almost like lords."

"So many do that?" asked Richina. "Enough that thousands upon thousands die willingly year upon year?"

"Stipended lancers and armsmen are free men, anywhere in the Sturinnese lands and isles, no matter from where they came," Alcaren pointed out. "Even crafters and artisans are little better than slaves unless they are from the home isles of Sturinn."

And all women are slaves. Secca kept the thought to herself, instead asking, "Can we avoid the Ostisles and make straight for Stura?"

"We can try," Denyst replied. "If they do not send fleets after us. The Ostisles lie low against the ocean and have many reefs around them. That will work for us. That is less true of the isles of Sturinn." Denyst glanced toward Secca. "Stura is a port city, but Inylt, where they say the palace of the Maitre stands, lies upland and inland."

"We will do what we can," Secca replied, trying to choose her words with great care. "I would rather do all possible by sorcery than try to land lancers in such an inhospitable place." She smiled grimly.

"No offense to you, Lady Secca," observed Wilten, "but we would rather not land there, if other means are possible."

"If . . . *if* the sorcery works as we hope," Secca said slowly, "then we still must return to Liedwahr and Neserea to defeat the forces of the Maitre that remain. No matter what we do to the isles of Sturinn, those forces will never surrender."

"Never have, and never will," added Denyst succinctly.

"Do you know what accompaniment you will use?" inquired Palian.

Secca had been planning to tell the chief player, but merely answered, "You had best keep them well practiced with the first building song. We may need that if the Sturinnese send warships after us. And for the spell against Stura . . . they will need to practice the fifth building spell. I know that they do not use it as much . . ." Secca could not recall when it had been last used, although Anna had insisted on the players knowing and practicing it.

"In a week, they will know it as well as the others," Palian promised. "That they will."

"And the second players as well," Delvor added.

"We still might need the flame spell," Secca said. "And

in another day, we will need to reset the ward spells."

Palian raised her eyebrows.

"Richina will take over the wards," Secca explained.

Both players nodded.

"I had wondered, but did not wish to ask . . ." ventured the gray-haired Palian.

"We are upon the sea, and that makes spellsinging from a distance less effective," Alcaren said. "We will see, but we think that for a few days, Richina will be able to hold the wards if she does little else."

"I can do it," Richina said, her chin stiffening almost imperceptibly.

"You will. You have done everything else needed," Alcaren said warmly.

Secca wished she had been so quick, but she was still tired and not thinking so well as she should be.

Palian and Delvor both smiled briefly.

"Is there aught else that I should know?" asked Secca, taking in each face around and behind the table. After a long moment of silence, she concluded with a smile, "Then we will meet tomorrow."

The overcaptains slipped out of the cabin first, followed by Delvor.

Palian stopped and leaned toward Secca. "They will play them well, and even if the deck throws them from side to side."

Secca smiled warmly at the older woman, murmuring, "I've always been able to count on you, even back when I wasn't the best pupil with the lutar or the violino."

"You have learned, my lady, and for that we are all grateful." With a smile and a nod, Palian turned and eased out through the doorlike hatch.

Denyst nodded brusquely. "Don't know what you plan, but don't go easy on the Sea-Pigs."

"I don't plan to. We have but one chance."

"Good. Need to check topside."

Then the captain was gone, leaving Secca, Alcaren, and Richina.

"You need some more rest, Richina," Secca said. "Are your quarters . . . ?"

"They're small, but the bed is good, and it is good to be with Palian." Richina smiles. "Sometimes, she even tells me stories about when you were young."

Secca winced. "There are such stories, I am sure."

"She said that you sang a spell that lit a fire when you were but nine. Is that so?"

The redheaded sorceress laughed. "It is. I'd memorized part of a spell Lady Anna had used. Lady Anna made me promise not to sing another one until she taught me much more."

"It's good to know you weren't perfect."

"I never was."

"But everyone thinks you are."

Secca just shook her head as Richina stood.

Alcaren closed the hatch door after Richina left, then turned to the table, where he began to reroll the maps that had been spread there.

Secca looked down at the map of Stura for a moment, before Alcaren lifted it and began to roll it.

"You hide much," Alcaren said slowly, after replacing the maps in their cases. He sat back down at the table, waiting for Secca to sit.

Secca remained standing.

"Do you not wish to let them know what you plan?" he asked.

"I have not hidden that we will use terrible spells." Secca shook her head sadly. "It is just that they cannot understand how terrible." She looked across the table at her consort. "Had you not read them, would you know?"

"No," Alcaren admitted. "You fear that some would make the voyage more difficult did they know?"

"I think not, but I would worry that some of the players would not play so well did they know. You recall how Bretnay is, and Rowal would not speak for days after the worst of the storm spells."

Alcaren nodded slowly. "You know which spell, then. Perhaps, you should let me study it, if it must be done. I should know the words and melody as well as you."

Secca eased around the table to the covered bin by the oversize bunk. From there she took a leather folder, opening it and taking out what Anna had called a manila envelope. On the outside was written "Armageddon" in Anna's graceful but angular hand. The sheet Secca wanted was the second one, and she eased it out, then replaced the envelope in the leather folder before handing the single sheet to Alcaren.

He read slowly, swallowing. "You showed me this one before. Why this one?"

"Because of your map," she explained. "The north of the isle is like the Ring of Fire, and the mountains overlook both Inylt and the port city of Stura itself."

Alcaren frowned, as if he did not understand, but did not wish to say so.

"The lady Anna told me, long years ago, that it is easier to use what is than to create all the elements of a spell from nothing. The sea is there, but it cannot reach beyond the towns and cities on the coast, no matter how mighty the spell."

"Whereas this . . ."

"It might reach most of the isle and all the places where those who might seek revenge live and work," Secca finished.

"It is a terrible spell," he murmured.

"It is." Secca sighed. "It is also pure Clearsong."

"But terrible," he repeated.

"Will anything less suffice?" she asked meeting his gray-blue eyes with her amber orbs.

After a moment, he shook his head.

77

B ecause the day is gray, the shutters and hangings in Ashtaar's study and receiving room are drawn back. Outside, dark clouds hang over the city, and occasional fat flakes of spring snow drift past the ancient glass of the window-panes. Inside, the Council Leader sits behind her ebony table desk, the hand in her lap holding a freshly laundered green cloth, the other resting on the polished surface of the table, her fingers less than a span from the polished dark agate oval.

The seer Escadra settles herself into the chair across from Ashtaar.

"What have you to tell me?" asks the older woman.

Escadra clears her throat before she begins. "We still cannot scry the sorceress directly. The glasses show that a half-score of Ranuan ships are bearing and escorting the Sorceress Protector of Defalk westward. They could be traveling toward the Ostisles or the isles of Sturinn, but that is far from certain."

"Not to Neserea?" questions Ashtaar.

"The ships have been sailing due west for days, Leader Ashtaar," Escadra states. "They have been under full sail, and they should have long passed the point where they would turn northward, were they headed to Neserea."

"If they change their course, I am to know at once."

The seer nods.

"What of the Sturinnese in Neserea?"

"The force which left Dumar is nearing the Sturinnese armsmen who have been attacking the Liedfuhr's lancers. Another group, mostly of Sea-Priest sorcerers, is riding northward. They look to be headed somewhere to the west of Esaria. They also are difficult to scry."

"They ride to Worlan, where they will meet the Sturinnese fleet to take Esaria." Ashtaar covers her mouth with the green cloth and coughs, but only once.

"That may be, Leader. The Sturinnese ships have been slowed because the ice in the Bitter Sea is breaking early."

"How far are they from Esaria?"

"We believe within a score of deks, but that was before they were caught in the floes moving."

"Have any been damaged by the ice?"

"Two, so far as we can see. They have used much sorcery, though."

"Good. Best they be tired." Ashtaar gives a hard smile, which vanishes as quickly as it had appeared. "And our fleet?"

"It appears to remain near the Ostisles, as you instructed last fall," replies Escadra. "The Sturinnese have mustered what ships they have remaining in Stura." The seer pauses. "Do you know what the fleet will do?"

"I trust that they will do as instructed, and that is to stay as long as possible without having to fight a sea battle against the Sturinnese. If they do . . . then we may serve the shadowsinger well, and in turn she may serve us even more."

"Do you know, Leader . . . ?" ventures Escadra almost timidly.

"I have no idea what she plans. She may land forces and try to subdue Stura. She may send waves crashing over their cities. She may destroy their ships and fleet. She may do something else. Whatever it may be, it will be less than the Maitre and his white-suited Sea-Pigs deserve."

Escadra's mouth drops open, if but for an instant.

Ashtaar's eyes flare, and her voice snaps. "More coins and more men and women have been lost throughout Erde because the Maitres of Sturinn have decided that women should be chained, if not worse. Our people are poorer, as

are all of those of Liedwahr, because we have had to prepare
to repulse them. Mansuur has lost two port cities to their
raids. Dumar has been prostrated twice in a generation. Ebra
is hardly better. And the rest of Erde is in worse condition.
Most people in Pelara and the Ostisles are slaves in both
name and fact so that a handful of men can live in great
luxury, and a larger number—only of men, mind you—can
live in comfort."

Ashtaar barely gets the cloth over her mouth before she
doubles over in a wave of coughing.

So violent is the attack that Escadra lurches upright and
steps toward the Council Leader. Then she pauses, as if
uncertain as to what she should do.

As Ashtaar's coughing subsides, she straightens and re-
moves the cloth. She takes a sip of the dark liquid in the
beaker on the table, then a second. "Foul stuff. Getting old
is truly awful, seer." A wry smile crosses her lips. "But it's
better than not living that long."

"Ah . . . yes, Leader," stammers Escadra.

"I'm recovered. At least as much as I will be. Think about
what I said."

The seer nods.

"You may go . . . but inform me if anything changes."

"Yes, Leader." Escadra bows and turns.

Ashtaar takes a third sip from the beaker, grimacing after
she swallows the draught.

78

In the breezy afternoon, Secca stood next to the railing at
the forward edge of the *Silberwelle*'s poop deck, looking
down on the first and second players. While the winds had
shifted to a more northerly flow, coming almost directly out
of the south, they were still favorable enough that the small

flotilla continued to maintain a good clip westward. Only a few clouds dotted the sky overhead, and Secca found the warmth of the sun more than welcome.

Mentally, Secca marked each word and note value as the players went through the fifth building song. Beside her, Alcaren did the same, although he still needed to use his own hand-drafted copy of the words, with notes on the sections where he would be singing a different line, what Anna had called supporting harmony, as opposed to "true" harmony. Anna had said it was more like polyphony, but the explanation had never quite made sense to Secca. And now, as in so many things, she couldn't ask. *There is so much you should have asked . . . so much.*

"No!" called Palian. "You are dragging the phrase. A sorceress has but so much breath. If you slow that section, she will not have the power behind the words. Let us try that once more, from the beginning, at my mark . . . Mark!"

Secca tried to concentrate once more on the spell, *the terrible spell.* Except it seemed that with each week, each season, ever more terrible, and ever more powerful spells became more and more necessary.

From the corner of her eye, Secca could see another Ranuan vessel, trailing the *Silberwelle* by less than a dek. The *Schaumenflucht* had been one of the Ranuan ships that had survived the great sea battle off Encora the winter before, a sea battle that foreshadowed the ever-escalating use of sorcery. While Secca had worried about that escalation, she had not foreseen how quickly it would occur.

"Second players . . ." Delvor called.

Alcaren looked up as the accompaniment below halted once more, turning his gaze to Secca and smiling warmly.

Secca returned the smile, and, for that moment, in the open air and the sun, she enjoyed just looking at her consort.

79

WORLAN, NESEREA

In the deep gray of the misty afternoon, the Maitre stands behind the parapets of the ancient structure that had once been the keep of Belmar. He looks beyond the cliffs on which the hold is situated and northward out onto almost black waters of the Bitter Sea, dotted here and again with the white of ice floes. Somewhere to the north, beyond his vision, is the fleet that should port at Worlan on the morrow. After a last glance into the dimness, he turns and descends the narrow stairs two levels before turning off at the landing and stepping into a small room that contains little more than a scrying pool and one tall man in Sturinnese white who is checking the tuning on a stringed instrument more angular than the lutars employed in Defalk, if of similar size.

The man straightens, lowering the instrument. "Maitre."

"What have the pools of the noble Belmar shown you, jerClayne?" asks the Maitre, a humorous tone in his inquiry.

"Ah . . . Maitre . . ." The Sturinnese sorcerer swallows. "The Shadow Sorceress is not headed to Neserea. Nor to Mansuur. The Ranuans carry her westward, and they are nearing the Ostisles."

"You are certain?" The Maitre stares intently at jerClayne.

"We cannot yet scry her directly, but she is aboard one of the Ranuan ships, and she is far nearer to the Ostisles than to Liedwahr. That is all that I can tell with any certainty, Maitre."

"For her, that is more than certain enough." The Maitre tightens his lips for but an instant. "How many vessels?"

"Still just a half-score. The same as before."

"And the ships of Nordwei?"

"They are nearing Osta. They are close enough to land that the glass is more certain. The home defense fleet is within a day's sail."

"Yes. The Assistant Maitre sent a plate this morning stating that. If the northerners will fight, then we will soon hold all the north of Liedwahr."

"You do not think that they will?" inquires jerClayne.

"They are only in the Ostisles to keep our fleet from attacking the Ranuan ships carrying the sorceress. If we form to attack them, they will flee with the wind, and regroup later, closer to Nordwei, and where it will suit them to make a defense, if and when our ships near Wei."

The tall jerClayne nods, waiting.

"I will write a message. Come by my study in a glass to fetch it. Then you will transfer the words to a bronze plate, and have it sent to the Assistant Maitre in Stura. He may not think the shadowsinger a threat, nor understand her goal. He has enough vessels left to intercept their small flotilla. And even should she raise a wave or two against our cities . . . they are well built." The Maitre shakes his head. "While she is in midocean, she can do nothing to save Neserea. Nor is there much she can do against Stura."

"Did she not destroy an entire fleet south of Dumar?"

"Our commanders will not mass their vessels so, but use the tactics of the lancers, to attack in waves until the sorceress and her assistant are too exhausted to cast more spells. They are to harass the Ranuans until they turn from the isles or are defeated, and they will be."

The duty sorcerer nods dutifully.

"Even if she does reach the shores of Stura, what can she do? Our greatest fleets are here, as are our lancers. If she lands, she will be lost, for every man's hand will be against her, and no woman would dare leave her chains." He shrugs. "We may have to rebuild a port or two, and replace some of the defense fleet." A cold smile punctuates his words. "We can suffer great losses, if need be. She can suffer none. She is also malicious, and malice makes a poor guide. For

those reasons, and because we are of Sturinn, we will triumph." He pauses but briefly. "Come and get the message
in a glass."

"Yes, Maitre."

JerClayne's eyes follow the Maitre as the older sorcerer
turns and leaves the scrying room.

The Maitre descends another three levels to the chamber
that had once been Belmar's.

Even as he steps through the door, the waiting serving
girl immediately prostrates herself on the cold stone floor.
She wears but the shortest of armless tunics, and the heavy
chains that restrict her arms so that they cannot rise above
her shoulders clank against the grayish granite. The redness
under the wrist and ankle cuffs has almost faded from her
pale skin. Except for the shivering that she cannot control,
she does not move as the Maitre looks at her.

"You may rise and attend me."

The girl rises, her eyes dull, fixed on the granite floor.

80

So bright was the day outside that not even the captain's
cabin was all that dim, with light flooding through the
portholes and sparkling through the skylenses in the overhead. The lighting did not relieve the closeness of eight
bodies around a table in a small space.

Even though Secca had managed enough sorcery to desalt
a bucket of water to wash off every day or so, there was a
fine layer of salt everywhere, or so it seemed, and with her
all-too-fair skin, Secca felt itchy all over most of the time.
She rubbed her back against the wood of the chair, watching
Alcaren.

Her consort finished tuning the lumand, then glanced

down at the mirror laid upon the circular table in the captain's cabin. Then he began the spell.

"Show us now, and in day's clear light,
ships of Sturinn near enough to fight . . ."

The glass immediately presented three images. In the one to the upper right were five vessels. The lower and smallest grouping was three. In the center was a fleet whose numbers were too great to count easily. All of the ships bore the white hulls of Sturinn.

Secca guessed that the fleet in the center contained a good twoscore vessels, if not more.

"How many ships do they have?" asked Delcetta, almost under her breath. She flushed as she realized that in the closeness of the cabin everyone had heard.

"More than the stars in the sky, some say," replied Denyst with a laugh. "Though I'd not put the numbers so high."

"For generations they have harvested and replanted the forests in their isles so always there will be enough timber for ships," Alcaren said. "Those who cut a tree without the Sea-Priests' permission lose a hand, their heads the second time."

For a moment, there is silence around the table.

"Begging your pardon, Alcaren, sorceresses . . . There any way to tell how close they be?" asked the *Silberwelle*'s captain.

"It will take a different spell," Alcaren admitted. "I need to think a moment."

Secca leaned forward and began to write out a set of lines, ignoring the feeling that all eyes had turned to her. When she finished, she handed the sheet to Alcaren, pointing out the couplet on the bottom, below all the other writing.

He looked over the words she had written, and nodded. Then he sang the same spell, except with a different concluding couplet.

". . . all ships that ours could seek
within a single day of this week . . ."

The mirror showed both the fleet and the three ships, but
not the group of five.

"Thought they might not be so kind as to let us near to
Sturinn." Denyst frowned. "But why they'd be having so
many vessels here off the Ostisles . . ."

"The Ostisles are hundreds of deks from their home
isles," added Palian, voicing Secca's thoughts as well as her
own.

"Could they have two fleets?" asked Richina.

After the quiet following her question, Alcaren softly
sang the release couplet, and the mirror in the center of the
table blanked to silver, and then to reflect the dark timbers
of the overhead.

In the green-tinted light that suffused the cabin, Secca
could see the circles under the eyes of the younger sorceress,
circles that had not yet turned dark. *How much longer can
she hold the wards?* Richina had had to learn and do so
much, and so much younger than Secca had. But then Secca
had grown up in a quieter time. *Quieter? Or had Anna assured that air of peace through shadow sorcery?*

"They could have a score, for all we know," replied Denyst.

"We might as well find out." Alcaren cleared his throat.

"Show us now, and in clear sight,
Sturinn's ships near Stura's noontime light . . ."

This time, the glass showed but two groups of vessels—
four tied up along a white stone pier in a port setting Secca
did not recognize and another three somewhere at sea.

"Most of their ships in the Western Sea are here," mused
Alcaren.

"Could they have known we were headed to Stura?"

asked Palian. "They might not want you to get too close to their home isles."

"Could be," replied Denyst. "Passing strange, though. If we slipped past them and got following winds . . ."

"They'd have trouble catching us?" asked Alcaren.

The captain nodded.

Alcaren sang the release couplet, then looked to Secca.

She realized that everyone was looking to her.

"We won't slip by them. They have sorcerers and seers, and they'll be upon us by morning, if not before." Secca flushed and turned to Denyst. "I know nothing about sailing. That is just my feeling."

"Trust a sorceress's feeling about Sea-Priests over numbers and calculations any day." Denyst paused. "Let me know what you need, same as you did at Encora. We will need some time to signal the others with the flags."

"I will, in a glass or so," Secca promised. She looked to Palian and Delvor. "We'll use the storm spell, the first building spellsong. That's if they attack us in a mass."

"You think that they'll come in small groups to tire you? The way they did with their lancers at Elahwa?" Richina tried to stifle a yawn. "I am sorry."

"You're carrying all the wards. That is work, even with the help of the ocean and distance." After a moment, Secca added, "I would not be surprised. They learn from each encounter, as do we."

That was why Sturinn had taken over so much of Erde, Secca realized, almost belatedly. The Sturinnese changed. Dumar hadn't. Neither had Neserea. And Defalk had changed only because Anna had forced change, and most of those changes Lord Robero wanted to undo. If only Anna could have had children after she had come to Erde, then all might have changed even more, and Secca might never have been faced with what lay ahead.

"You look surprised, lady," offered Palian.

Secca laughed. "I just realized something that I should have seen years ago." She glanced around the table. "There's not much else I can offer at the moment, and I need to go over some spells if the Sturinnese are headed toward us."

"We will practice the first building spell now," Palian said.

After the others had risen and left the cabin, Alcaren motioned to Secca "I need some air. If you would come with me."

Secca glanced at him, realizing that he looked even greener than the others had in the greenish light of the cabin. "I thought you were doing better on this trip."

"Better does not mean I am cured of this affliction." He swallowed and lurched toward the door.

Secca followed at a discreet distance, rejoining him in his favorite spot on the starboard side near the bow. The swells that rose and fell before the *Silberwelle* seemed slightly higher than they had on previous days, and the sea breeze somewhat warmer. Alcaren looked at her briefly, with a faint smile, then turned his face into the wind.

"Are you feeling better? she finally asked.

"Much. The fresh air helps." After a time, he added. "You are right, I fear."

"About what?"

"They will wear you down. That is what they have done to all they have conquered. They send more lancers, more ships, until those they attack have nothing remaining. You cannot let them do that."

Secca snorted. "And what would you have me do?"

"Sing a spell large enough and strong enough to destroy all of their vessels at one time. Let me help. If we do it together . . ."

"We can try," Secca said with a smile.

"Best we tell Denyst, and Palian."

Secca frowned.

"We will have storms, and the weather will be rough. Once the spell is sung, the players need hasten below. The decks should be clear on all our vessels."

"You think so?"

"You are a great sorceress, and when you do great sorcery, best we are all prepared."

"You offer me too much praise," Secca replied. "You are my consort, and I fear love colors your judgment."

"I love you, my lady, but my judgment is also sound." He turned to face her. "You are a great sorceress, and all Erde knows such. Why else would Sturinn send a fleet after you?"

Why else? Because the Sea-Priests don't like even moderately powerful women. "You are kind, my love."

"Truthful," he replied.

Secca wondered. *Can he be? Or does love make one see what one wants?*

81

SOUTHWEST OF ESARIA, NESEREA

In the early-morning light, the Maitre stands on a low rise, overlooking the river to the north, and the city of Esaria beyond the river. To his left, in the waters off Esaria, is the great eastern fleet of Sturinn.

Already, the piers lie in Sturinnese hands, and a wave of armsmen and lancers in white is moving through the city from west to east. Only those inhabitants who resist are being slaughtered. The others will provide supplies and coins and, in time, lancers and armsmen. The Maitre smiles and turns as the shadow of another nears.

"Maitre," offers the tall jerClayne, "all is going as you ordered. Few are resisting." He laughs heartily. "And fewer as others see what happens to those who do resist."

"What of the lady pretender?" asks the Maitre.

"She and her mother have fled eastward, in disguise, it appears. No one has seen them."

"Have you not used your scrying glass, jerClayne?" The Maitre's tone is bland, but his eyes are hard.

"We have tried, Maitre. They wear gray cloaks and are somewhere along the river road to the east. We could use the distance spell to destroy them, but you had requested that we not do so yet. You have also had us reporting on the fighting. There is little of that. And on the shadowsinger. The home defense fleet is encircling her ships and will begin the attacks this morning as you ordered."

"It is morning."

JerClayne shifts his weight. "Ah . . . Maitre, the Ostisles are farther west . . ."

The Maitre laughs, not unkindly. "You are most gentle in reminding me, jerClayne." He turns and studies the city across the river for a moment. "Let us go and see what we find in the palace of the Prophet. Then we will decide what to do with Aerlya and her brat daughter."

82

I n the gray-green dimness of the cabin before dawn, there was a solid rap on the hatch door, followed by a second blow every bit as solid as the first.

Secca bolted upright in the double bunk. "Yes?"

"Captain wanted you to know, sorceress, that there are sails on the horizon and closing."

"I'll be there."

Alcaren was already scrambling for his clothes before Secca finished speaking, and, if but for an instant, she watched his muscular figure, before sliding out of the bunk and onto the cold wooden deck, a deck that felt damp and gritty to her feet. But then, she had gotten used to the almost-invisible salt grit that was everywhere, no matter how often the decks and bulkheads were scrubbed and cleaned. Her skin hadn't adapted, not with itching and red blotches everywhere, but she could tolerate it.

A lighter gray light suffused the sky by the time Secca had pulled on her clothes and splashed some of her limited supply of fresh water across her face. Alcaren followed her up the ladder and then back to the helm platform, where Denyst stood beside the helmswoman.

The wind was cool, not quite cutting, and still mostly from the south. Despite the wind, the air felt heavy, close to oppressive. Secca wondered if she felt that oppression just because she worried about the Sturinnese and the inevitable sorcery to come.

"Didn't want to wake you too early, sorceress," Denyst apologized, "but, any direction the lookouts search, there are sails. Easing in closer over the last glass. Closest is still more than five deks, we'd guess, but with the wind the way it is, that's not much more than half a glass to reach us under full sail, leastwise for those to the west."

"Are they actually sailing toward us?" asked Secca.

"Not yet."

Secca frowned. She didn't want to roust out the players early, not if it could be glasses before the Sturinnese actually decided on an attack, but she didn't want to be caught unprepared, either.

Alcaren leaned forward and said in a low voice, "You need something to eat before you do anything, or you won't be able to sing as well as you need to."

"So do you. We're singing it together."

Denyst waited.

"Can you let me know the moment it's clear that one of them has decided to close on us?" Secca inquired.

"She needs to eat to be at her best," Alcaren said firmly.

Denyst laughed. "Go and eat. We'll find you if the Sea-Pigs make a run."

"Thank you."

"Not be much good to have you not at your best." While the words were gruff, the captain smiled.

"You go back to the cabin and sit down. You'll be standing more than you think today," Alcaren said, as the two stepped away from the helm platform. "I'll see what else I can find besides hardtack and cheese."

"That will be fine." Secca added after a pause, "Unless there's bread."

Alcaren slipped down the ladder to the main deck with an ease that Secca, short-legged as she was, envied, even as she wondered how he could do it, since he wasn't all that much taller than she was. Before she followed, she turned to look astern, but although the eastern sky was lightening, the sun had not peered above the horizon. Alcaren stood waiting below, as if to make sure she did not slip or fall.

"I'll see what the galley has," he promised. "Just sit down and have some water." He grinned. "You don't drink enough before you do sorcery."

"Thank you, dear consort." She let a little trace of irritation show, even though she knew he was trying to be helpful.

He grinned again and offered a sweeping bow.

Secca couldn't help laughing. "Go get the hardtack or biscuits or bread or whatever." Then she headed down the narrow passage back to the cabin.

Once there, Secca took her water bottle from the covered bin, and then seated herself at the captain's round table. She took a slow swallow of water, then another, while she waited. Then she shifted her weight in the wooden chair and glanced toward the door. She turned her eyes to the portholes, and she could see that dawn had come, with sparkles of light on the tops of the long even swells.

She could hear steps through the overhead, steps of sailors, she thought. *Where is he? You should have gone with him.* The *Silberwelle* heeled slightly, and the cabin tilted. Secca grasped the edge of the table, wondering if more gyrations would follow, but the ship settled back into the same kind of long pitching movement through the ocean swells as Secca had come to expect.

"Might as well warm up some more . . ." she murmured to herself and began a vocalise. "Holly-lolly-lolly . . ."

Alcaren stepped into the cabin.

"What took so long?" she asked, even before he had closed the door and set two loaves of bread and a wedge of cheese on the table, along with a handful of dried apple flakes.

"I wasn't but a few moments. It just seems longer when you're worried."

Secca didn't feel convinced. "How did you get all this?"

"I just told the cooks that whether they saw tomorrow depended on how much the sorceress got to eat this morning."

"You said that?"

After seating himself in the chair beside Secca, Alcaren nodded. He broke one of the long narrow loaves in two and handed Secca the longer portion. Then he took out his belt knife and sliced several sections off the cheese wedge.

Between them, they finished off both loaves of bread—and everything else—without speaking.

"You were hungry," Alcaren said, licking the last bits of apple flakes off his fingers.

"And you were not?"

"I never claimed I was not."

"We should go back outside."

"Denyst would send for us," Alcaren pointed out, "but I'd rather be outside in the fresh air."

Secca slipped out from behind the chair. "I'll bring my lutar."

"Why don't you leave it? I can get it in a moment if you need it."

"But . . . oh . . ." Secca nodded. *Best to cast but one mighty spell with players than exhaust ourselves with smaller spell upon smaller spell.* "We'd better go."

"It may be a bit early, but you'll just fret down here." Alcaren gestured for Secca to lead the way.

He followed her back along the passageway and up the ladder to the poop deck.

"Still holding off," Denyst said, even before Secca could ask. "Like as to they're waiting for full sun. Might be that whatever ships are between us and where the sun rises will be the ones leading the way."

"They could get closer before we see them?" asked Secca.

"Some ships, mayhap." Denyst laughed harshly. "My lookouts are better than that." She gestured. "Your other sorceress."

Secca turned to see Richina climbing up the last steps of the ladder. The younger woman made her away aft toward where the three stood just forward and to port of the helm.

Secca studied the younger woman's face, with the dark circles and the haggard expression. "Richina . . ."

"Yes, lady?"

"Find something to eat. Drink as much water as you can, and . . ." Secca paused, then spoke each word clearly, "Go back to sleep."

"But . . . if you need me . . ."

"You're keeping the rest of us safe. If you get too tired to hold those ward spells, we'll all suffer. Please get some food and take care of yourself," Secca concluded warmly.

"Are you . . . ?"

"I am most certain," Secca said firmly. "You are taking care of us as surely as you can."

"Thank you, lady." With a nod, Richina turned, easing her way forward, and then down the ladder.

"Hadn't 'a seen what sorcery does, not sure I'd believe it." Denyst shook her head. "Rather be a ship mistress."

Secca smiled. "If you'll excuse me, I need to warm up."

Denyst nodded.

Secca walked to the port railing and began a vocalise, trying to warm up slowly and evenly. Behind her, she heard Alcaren trying his voice, although his vocalises were still rough. Secca found herself coughing halfway through the first vocalise.

Alcaren appeared with a water bottle, tendering it silently.

She took a swallow, handed it back, and continued with the vocalise. After the second vocalise, Secca slipped back toward the helm platform, beside which Denyst and Alcaren stood.

Denyst pointed off the starboard bow. "Closest ones are there. Just two of them, you see. Still a good three deks from the *Wellereiterin*."

Secca watched. So did Alcaren.

"They're swinging south," Denyst announced after a time, long before Secca could see any change in heading from the Sturinnese vessels.

"They're trying to get you to use sorcery without hazarding many of their ships," Alcaren suggested.

"Can you have the others—our ships—close up a little more?" asked Alcaren.

"Not be a good idea to be closer than half a dek," Denyst pointed out.

"Half a dek would help," Alcaren said. "It will also keep them out of the first lashing of the storms."

"Alcaren did tell you—that there could be storms after the sorcery?" Secca asked.

"He did. We passed that on to the others. Just to rig for heavy weather once the Sturinnese closed. Didn't tell 'em why. The less said the better. Flag signals aren't always secret, even in code."

Secca glanced forward, in the direction of the main deck, still empty of players, then out to the south, where the sails of the Sturinnese vessels seemed fractionally closer. "I think we should get the players tuning."

Alcaren nodded, and started down the ladder.

"I didn't mean you had to—"

"Might as well," he called back. "It's easier on me than standing and watching, and we can't do any sorcery—or I can't—without players."

"Some ways, he hasn't changed much," Denyst said dryly. "Hated to wait for anything as a boy. Hid it well, but those of us who knew him could see that."

"And in other ways?"

"He was always polite, but never has he been so attentive to anyone as he is to you, Lady Sorceress."

Never have you been so attentive . . . except you take him too much for granted at times such as these. Secca looked out to the south. *Perhaps at all too many times.*

"Sorceress?" asked Denyst.

"I was just thinking. He is very special."

"Special he is and may be, but—"

"Sails to stern! Closing!" The warning came from somewhere in the yards above.

Secca glanced up, but she could not tell which lookout had voiced the call.

Denyst glanced aft, quickly, then nodded. "They'll not catch us quickly, but best your players be soon ready."

Secca nodded. Alcaren had already gone to summon them, and there was little enough she could do for the moment—or should.

Alcaren's head had no sooner reappeared as he climbed up the ladder than players began streaming out onto the main deck.

"Palian already had them up. They'd already finished eating," he explained.

Almost immediately, Secca could hear the tuning.

"Quick tune!" ordered Palian. "We need the warm-up song! Places!"

"Second players in places!" Delvor's voice—almost as high as Palian's—rose over the hubbub of the tuning.

Secca glanced aft, but the sails that had appeared to be closing had drifted back.

"Worry more about those forward," Denyst suggested. "They turn into us, and they'll be closing twice as fast."

"They likely to turn so that we'll change course," asked

Alcaren, "and then get caught between them and the ships trailing?"

"Weren't for the fact that they worry about your sorcery, I'd wager they'd already have tried that," replied the captain. "Signs are that they will soon. The ships to the west are trimming sail, just a touch, so little that they hope we won't notice."

Secca turned to her consort. "I'm going to have the players play through the first building song. We should listen and mark it silently."

"That would help me," he said. "I've far less experience than you with such."

Secca walked to the forward part of the poop deck and called down to Palian. "It may not be long now!"

"Quiet!" ordered the chief player.

The warm-up song halted.

"Say that again, Lady Secca, if you will."

"It won't be long. Could you run through the first building song right now?"

"First building song. At my mark!" Palian ordered. "Mark!"

As the players offered the spellsong, there was enough raggedness that Secca was more than glad she had ordered the run-through.

"You must do better," Palian said. "Rowal, you are a half beat behind everyone. Pick it up." Palian glanced to Secca. "Do we have time for another?"

Secca looked to the captain.

"Your call, sorceress. They've not swung their helms yet."

Secca turned. "Go ahead."

Secca noted that Alcaren's eyes almost closed as he followed the accompaniment.

The players finished the second run-through, and, so far as Secca could see, none of the Sturinnese ships was any closer.

For perhaps a quarter of a glass, Secca watched the Sturinnese sails, watched Denyst, and watched Palian.

Abruptly, Denyst turned and gestured. "There's a wedge forming, be coming from the south on the starboard. You want any different course?"

"No," Secca replied. "How long before they're two deks away?"

"Less 'n quarter glass," replied the captain.

"We'll be doing the spells before that," Secca said.

"You tell me when to tell Palian," Alcaren said, stepping to the railing over the main deck. "Stand ready for the first building song!"

"Players standing ready," Palian returned.

Secca had her eyes on the white-hulled ships that seemed to swell up off the starboard bow. "Almost. . . ." She kept watching, absently running through part of a vocalise, looking at the wedge of Sturinnese vessels, perhaps a half-score, and the more distant sails of the ships that held back, hoping that she would cast spell after spell until she could cast no more.

"Now." She didn't raise her voice. Alcaren could do that.

"The first building song!" Alcaren called.

"The first building song on my mark . . . Mark!"

With Palian's direction to the players, Secca pushed the worries out of her mind, the concerns that the Sturinnese fleet was spread too far and across too many deks.

Alcaren stood beside her, just aft of the railing that separated the forward edge of the poop deck from the main deck below.

The Sturinnese ships appeared far closer than the two deks that Denyst had estimated, but, as the accompaniment rose from the first and second players on the main deck, Secca concentrated totally on the spell to come, on the words, on the image of the water and the spouts, spouts that would range for ten deks or more from the *Silberwelle*, and on meshing with the melody that rose from the players below, trusting that Alcaren would support the spellsong in his own way. She made a special effort to visualize the spouts striking the ships, but visualized no more than spouts and ships and winds and rain, just spouts and ships . . . spouts and ships.

From the first words, she and Alcaren and the spellsong were one, and from somewhere behind and underneath all that was Erde came an answering sense of harmony.

> *"Water boil and water bubble*
> *like a caldron of sorcerers' trouble . . .*
> *build a storm with winds swirling through*
> *in spouts that break Sturinn's ships in two . . ."*

With another full breath between the stanzas, Secca continued strongly into the second, knowing that she needed to keep the images, and the intensity, through two full stanzas.

> *"Ocean boil and ocean bubble*
> *crush to broken sticks of floating rubble*
> *ships crewed by those in Sea-Priest white*
> *and let none escape the water's might . . ."*

In the stillness following the last notes, a stillness so absolute that the wind died away and the sails hung limply from the yardarms above, the swells subsided into an unnatural shimmering flatness. The high once-white clouds grayed, and then darkened, and the dark blue expanse of the Western Sea turned almost jet-black under the shimmering surface of the water.

A low and growling rumble, followed by a high-pitched whistling whine, rose, seemingly from everywhere, and the two sounds merged into a rushing and roaring torrent.

In the distance, dark gray funnel spouts appeared, funnel spouts that turned jet-black, funnel spouts that also rushed and roared, as they swelled and moved toward the white-sailed and white-hulled Sturinnese vessels.

Another set of spouts appeared, less than three deks from the *Silberwelle*, one on each side of the wedge of Sturinnese vessels. Around the *Silberwelle*, the ocean remained flat, but the sails of the ships in the Sturinnese wedge pitched forward, and then back. The first spout slid into and over the ship on the right edge of the wedge, and white fragments flew upward, streaking the dark water of the spout but momentarily before the water turned even blacker.

Two more Sturinnese ships vanished into the dark spouts, and the ocean around the *Silberwelle* was no longer calm, as a swell nearly three yards high surged toward the Ranuan vessel. Another higher swell loomed ahead.

The wind continued to rise, tearing at Secca.

"Get below!" Alcaren's voice rose over the roaring of the wind. "Get below!"

"To your quarters! Now!" Palian's higher voice followed Alcaren's.

A gust of wind, more like a wall, swept across the poop deck. Secca locked one arm around the railing, then the other as the combined rush of wind and water buffeted her.

"Keep her steady!" That was Denyst's order.

In what Secca knew had to be a momentary lull, Alcaren helped her down the ladder. They both held tight to the bottom of the ladder as another blast of water and wind lashed them. Then Alcaren thrust Secca inside and closed the hatch door. They staggered along the passageway to the captain's cabin. Secca felt that water gushed from her clothing and her body, and with every step she lurched against one bulkhead or the other.

She had to fumble with the hatch, then was through the open hatchway into the cabin, ramming into the nearest chair. She managed to hold to the chair back and the table and lever herself into one of the chairs. Alcaren staggered, closing the cabin door, and struggled into the chair beside Secca, putting a hand on the table to brace himself.

Secca found herself gripping the wooden arms of the chair so tightly that her hands were aching. As the cabin— and the ship—tilted once again, she had to force herself to relax her grip somewhat. "You . . . were . . . right . . . about . . . storms . . ."

"I . . . wish . . . I had not been," replied Alcaren.

Secca could hear the unhappiness in her consort's voice, could sense the physical discomfort. *He hates being at sea, and yet he has said nothing.* A second thought struck her. *You feel tired, as with heavy roadbuilding, but only with a headache, and without double vision. Was Alcaren right about concentrating on the spell and not on the results of the spell?*

The *Silberwelle* pitched forward, hard forward, and the water rushing by the portholes cut off all light. Then as the bow came up, the light returned, only to vanish again with another dipping pitch into another massive swell.

How long the *Silberwelle* rode through the heavy swells before the pitching began to abate, Secca had no idea, save that it felt like glasses had passed, and that Alcaren appeared as green as the glass in the portholes when he finally pulled himself out of the seat he had taken.

"No worse than a small storm." He swallowed and headed out the passageway.

Secca followed, gingerly. Her head still ached, and most of her muscles hurt, either from sorcery or from her body's dealing with the ship's motions afterward. She was especially careful to hold on to the ladder, and then the poop deck railing, as she trailed Alcaren to the poop deck.

Although the waves had diminished so that *Silberwelle* only occasionally drove through one tall enough for water and spray to cascade over the bow, the entire ship glistened with a thin coat of salt water. The sails had been reefed in so that the Ranuan ship was carrying but a fraction of the sail as before the spellsong.

Denyst eased from the helm platform to the railing at the starboard side, where Secca held to the damp but varnished wood firmly. Alcaren had his face to the wind, and the greenish color of his face had begun to fade. He did not turn to face Denyst as the captain began to speak.

"Never seen spouts like that. Didn't look like many of the Sea-Priest ships survived."

"If we sang the spell right," Secca said, wiping spray from her forehead with her one free hand, "none of them did. What about our ships?"

"Storms and winds scattered us as well, Lady Sorceress. Only seen a few." Denyst gestured to her left. "*Schaumenflucht* managed to stay close, and the *Liedmeer*."

Under the gray clouds, a good dek aft, another Ranuan ship kept station on the *Silberwelle*. Secca thought she saw a third set of sails, on and off as the deck of the *Silberwelle* carried her above and below the crests of the more distant waves.

The captain looked at the sorceress. "Had thought that your glass might tell us more."

"By tomorrow," Secca promised.

"She can only do so much sorcery at once," Alcaren added, without turning his head.

"Is everyone here . . . on the *Silberwelle*?" Secca almost hated to ask.

"The second had to catch one of your players afore he went overboard, but she got him, and everyone else here is fine. Be glad tomorrow, to see how things are on the other ships. Need a calmer sea for the flags." Denyst offered a wry smile. "Best you get some hardtack and some rest."

"In a moment," Secca replied. "The air feels good, even with the spray."

"That it does." A brusque nod, and the captain crossed the deck to the helm platform. "A few points to port."

Secca looked to her consort. "Are you feeling better?"

"Much." He presented a forced grin. "When this is done, can we return to your holdings and leave our feet on solid ground?"

"Solid ground?" Secca laughed. "I would hope so. If the Sturinnese had not left their solid ground, I'd still be there."

"I wouldn't have met you, then."

"One good happening." She smiled, trying not to think

about what came after dealing with Sturinn—if there was an "after."

"There are no other Sturinnese ships here in the Western Sea, and you worry yet."

"There is a fleet in the Bitter Sea, and there are sorcerers in Neserea," Secca pointed out.

"You cannot fret over the battles you cannot yet fight."

"I *should* not," she replied, "but I do."

"As do we all," he replied ironically. "As do we all."

For a long time, as the light in the west dimmed, they stood side by side at the railing, ignoring the infrequent fine spray that drifted over them.

83

By a glass after sunrise the next morning, while not calm, the sea state had returned to one similar to that of a day earlier, before the spellsong, with heavy but regular swells. The sky remained overcast with hazy and indistinct clouds.

Secca stood aft on the windward side of the *Silberwelle*, trying to count the number of Ranuan ships without being too obvious, to see how many were actually close.

Denyst crossed the deck and stood beside her. "You called a storm. Few like that I've ever seen."

"That was the hope."

"We haven't seen any Sea-Pigs."

"The glass shows no Sturinnese ships, except for four in the harbor at Stura, and a few trading vessels scattered throughout the Ostisles and the isles of Sturinn." Secca looked at the wiry and weathered captain.

"And our other vessels?"

"Why don't you come down and look?" Secca said quietly. "I'll show you."

"Fear what I will see in your glass. The *Schaumenflucht*

lost some spars, and so did the *Liedmeer*. The *Ozeanstern* cracked a hatch cover, and took on water, but they got it repaired and pumped out. None of the other captains have seen the *Wellereiterin*. Is that what your glass will tell us?"

Secca nodded slowly. She'd already tried to recall who had been on the *Wellereiterin*, but she hadn't checked with Wilten and Delcetta yet, and hadn't planned to, not until she informed Denyst. As Secca remembered, Quebar's company had been assigned there. Although the young lancer officer had been verbally playful at Loiseau, especially with his cousin Vyren, throughout the battles and travels Quebar had been dutiful, quiet, and effective. He was also one of the few officers from Mencha itself, and all in Loiseau would miss him. "You should see what we see."

"That be not good news."

Secca did not answer, but walked forward to the ladder and climbed down, still careful to keep one hand on something solid as she did, although the height of the waves had continued to decrease, and the *Silberwelle* had settled into an almost-regular motion.

Once below in the captain's quarters, Secca checked the tuning of the lutar, while Alcaren unwrapped the scrying mirror and laid it on the table. Then Secca slipped on the copper-tipped gloves and, without explaining more, sang the spell.

*"Show us clear for all to see
where the Wellereiterin might be . . ."*

The glass blanked, silvered over, and then displayed a stretch of open and empty ocean.

"Afraid of that," murmured Denyst.

"We've tried several different spells," Secca explained. "The glass either comes up blank or shows empty ocean. We thought you should see for yourself. Alcaren and I haven't told anyone else yet."

Denyst nodded slowly, reflectively. "Losing one vessel to

more than twoscore of the Sea-Pigs. No captain can fault that. Still hate to lose a single hand."

"I'm sorry," Secca said, lowering the lutar. "I'd hoped that by using the storm spell early enough . . ."

"The harmonies do not always give us what we wish, no matter how well we plan. Saving grace is that they don't do much better for the Sea-Priests, either." Denyst shook her head. "I'll be missing Sacayla. Good ship mistress she was, and a better friend."

"I'm sorry," Secca said again, knowing she was repeating herself, but with little else to say.

"Did what you had to, sorceress, and more of us'll live through it than without you. Hurts, though. Appreciate your showing me. Better that way."

Secca had hoped so, but she still wasn't sure.

Denyst turned. "Best see about gathering everyone back into formation."

Silently, Secca and Alcaren followed the captain out of the cabin, along the passageway, and then up to the poop deck.

From there, to the west, Secca could see breaks in the clouds, and shafts of sunlight striking the water, turning it from dark blue almost to azure.

"Where are we?" she asked Denyst.

The captain turned. "Best reckoning is that we're a good hundred deks southwest of the southernmost of the Osti-sles," replied Denyst. "We'll be shifting course more to the northwest. With this wind, be four–five days to reach the southern fringes, and another two days to get off Stura. Last two days . . . who knows. Say the wind in the channels is uncertain, shifts a lot."

"Thank you," Secca replied. "If you don't mind, I need to tell Wilten and Delcetta about the *Wellereiterin*."

"Appreciate your letting me know first." The captain turned toward the helm. "Flags! Need to send some course changes."

"She and Sacayla grew up together," Alcaren said quietly,

from where he stood at the railing, just behind Secca's shoulder.

"I did the best I could," Secca said, turning toward him. "No matter what I try, people die."

"Fewer people than if you did not," he replied.

"They are just as dead."

Alcaren nodded, slowly, in agreement, then took her left hand, the one not holding the railing, and squeezed it gently.

84

ESARIA, NESEREA

The Maitre stands in the small study off the far larger pillared chamber that had once served as the audience hall for the Lord High Counselor of Neserea, and, before that, as the throne room for the Prophets of Music. The adjoining study where the Maitre ponders what he must do had been the province of a junior counselor. The Maitre stands beside the desk table with a scroll in his hand.

He studies the scroll, then rereads the one paragraph half-aloud to himself.

> With the aid of the sorcerers from the force that came from Dumar and joined us, we have destroyed more than three thousand of the Liedfuhr's lancers and arms-men. Less than fifyscore remain, and they have scat-tered into the Great Western Forest and the Westfels to crawl back to Mansuur . . .

The signature is that of Marshal jerLeng.

The Maitre smiles, but only for a moment, before rolling the scroll and tucking it into his tunic. Then he turns and leaves the small study, crossing the audience chamber that stands empty except for the armsmen in Sturinnese white and turning down a corridor. In time, he comes to another chamber, one designed and built by the last Prophet of Music specifically for drum sorcery, although a scrying pool had later been added in one corner.

Beside that scrying pool waits jerClayne. The younger Sturinnese moistens his lips as the Maitre strides into the chamber, past another set of armsmen serving as guards, and closes the door behind him.

"Maitre," offers jerClayne, bowing deferentially, but not excessively. His eyes are dark-ringed, and his face is pale.

"Have you found anything more?" The Maitre gestures toward the pool.

"No, ser. There are no signs of the home defense fleet."

"None?" The Maitre's eyebrows rise. "No signs of anything?"

"There was a storm, it appears, a very large storm."

"And how would you know that?"

"Yesterday morning, the seas were almost calm. Today, the waves breaking on the reefs south of the Ostisles—"

"You used the reflecting pool to look at reefs?" A tone of incredulity tinges the Maitre's voice.

"You asked me to discover what happened, Maitre. The pool showed nothing at all or open ocean. I tried a glass, but it was the same. The sorceress still holds wards against us, except they are not the wards we know. I could not view her at all, nor those close around her. I had two others try as well." The younger sorcerer shrugs tiredly. "So I was forced to see if I could find other signs. They all pointed to a large storm. The skies were mostly clear just before the home defense fleet was to attack. I could not follow that, because we were attacking Esaria here. By late yesterday, there was a huge storm breaking up. Storms, as we know, do not appear from nowhere. I can only say what I have seen, and that is that the Shadow Sorceress created a storm mighty enough to sink the entire fleet."

"And her ships were untouched, no doubt?"

"No, Maitre. One of the Ranuan ships is missing, and two others have heavy damage to sails and spars."

"She would lay waste to what has taken generations to build, and she does it thoughtlessly and out of malice!" The Maitre's voice rises. "She has no plan. She has no thought. She travels on a whim! And the bitch Matriarch provides ships." He glares at the younger man for a long moment. "Destruction for destruction, but ours will not be such a waste. Fetch the players."

JerClayne bows and turns, slipping through a side door, and returning almost immediately, followed by a half-score each of players and drummers.

Both sorcerers wait as the players and drummers arrange themselves.

"The sending spell," the Maitre says. "On my sign." He clears his throat, then raises his left hand and drops it.

The accompaniment begins, and the Maitre's baritone is firm and clear, rising above both players and the insistent but muted drumming.

> *"Bring to Aerlya and Annyal the death of fire*
> *the lash of dissonances and certain death's desire . . ."*

By the time he finishes the short spellsong, his face is red, and his forehead soaked in sweat. He takes several deep breaths, then uses a white cloth to blot his face and forehead. After another moment, he turns. "Check the glass, jer-Clayne. Let us see."

"Yes, Maitre." The younger sorcerer turns to the players. "The second seeking song." When he receives a nod from the first player, he signals, then turns and faces the reflecting pool, and sings.

> *"In clear view, show us low and high*
> *where Annyal and Aerlya now lie . . ."*

The scrying pool obediently displays two blackened figures sprawled before a hearth that could have been in any
cottage.

"Good." The Maitre nods. "Good."

Squinting as though he has trouble seeing, jerClayne sings
a release couplet, and the image fades.

The Maitre does not speak, but turns and walks toward
the doorway.

JerClayne bows, then massages his forehead. He sits
down heavily on the tiled edge of the reflecting pool and
closes his eyes.

85

I n the cool damp midmorning air, Secca stood at the poop
deck railing of the *Silberwelle* beside Alcaren, looking
out over the main deck where the players were assembling.
In whatever direction she turned, she could only see water
and more water, except for the other ships and the high hazy
clouds that covered most of the sky, especially to the west.
From the position of the sun, Secca thought the *Silberwelle*
was headed in a slightly more northerly direction than on
the day before, and moving somewhat more slowly, under-
standably so since the wind was not so brisk as it had been.

Richina stood more toward the port side of the ship, to
Secca's left.

Relieved that the younger sorceress did not look quite so
tired as she had previously, Secca slipped toward her.
"You're looking more rested."

Alcaren followed.

"That I should, lady," Richina laughed. "All I have done
is sleep and eat, and sleep and eat, and occasionally practice
a vocalise."

"Can you feel the wards?"

"I can feel them. By evening I am as tired as if I had ridden all day." Richina frowned. "There are times when I can sense chords . . . or discords. They last but a few moments."

"Someone is using a pool or glass to try to see us?" asked Alcaren.

"I would wager so," Secca said, "although we have little experience with this kind of sorcery. Some of the Sea-Priests, I would think."

Both Richina and Alcaren nodded.

"You may feel more as we near Stura. If you feel greatly disturbed, please let us know."

"I will, lady." Richina inclined her head.

All three turned as Palian and Delvor climbed up the ladder and stepped onto the upper deck.

"Good morning," Secca said cheerfully.

"Good morning," replied the chief players, almost in unison.

"You had requested that we practice." Palian smiled as she added, "We would have practiced today even had you not requested it. Players do not play well when they do not play often."

"You must play well this time," Secca replied. She wanted to shake her head at the stupidity of her words. *Has there ever been a time in the past year when you did not need them to play well?*

"The Sturinnese would wish otherwise. We will not grant that wish." The faintest twinkle appeared in the eyes of the gray-haired chief player.

"I'd like you and the players to keep working on the fifth building spell." Secca managed to stop herself from stupidly saying something about the spell being as perfect as possible.

"You are not doing a building spell, not for the Sea-Priests," Palian half said, half asked.

"No. It is a spell of Lady Anna's." Secca added, "Mostly."

Palian nodded slowly. "Will the tempo be the same?"

"It should be, but I need to make sure. That is one reason why I want the run-throughs. We'll need to practice this every day until we reach the isles of Sturinn. I have not used this spell before." She inclined her head to her consort. "So must Alcaren."

"You will both be singing it?"

"The same words, but Alcaren will sing a harmony to mine."

A brief smile flitted across Palian's lips, and Secca recalled Anna telling her that Palian had been present when Anna and Brill had argued over the use of multiple voices singing the same words with different notes. Lord Brill had been adamant against it. He'd also died in that battle, Secca reflected, hoping she would prove to be adaptable as Anna had been.

"We will wait your signal after each run-through before we start the next," Palian said.

"Thank you."

As the two chief players returned to the main deck, where the players were still tuning, Alcaren took out the small sheet of paper with the words and notations of the "terrible" spell. Secca had a copy tucked inside her tunic, but she hoped she would not need it.

Richina looked from Alcaren and his sheet of paper to Secca, inquiringly.

"You may see it later," Secca said. "I don't wish you to be thinking about this spell while you are holding the wards."

"But if you should need me . . ." suggested Richina.

"That is a river we will ford when the time comes. What you do now is more important."

"Yes, lady." Richina did not quite meet Secca's eyes.

"Richina." Secca's voice was firm.

The younger sorceress looked up, almost startled.

"It is a terrible spell. It will do your mind and spirit no good. I wish I did not have to call upon it. I have already asked far more of you than I should. Do not ask even more of yourself." Secca's last words were softer, and warmer.

"I am sorry . . . I did not mean . : ."

"You're curious. So was I when I was your age. So is every good sorceress. But I am still your teacher, and I would rather you not learn what you need not know until you are older—unless it would save your life. Now it would not. Later," Secca promised.

Richina finally smiled.

"We stand ready, Lady Secca!" called Palian.

Secca looked to Alcaren, who nodded.

After a moment, Secca replied, "On your mark, chief player."

"The fifth building song! On my mark . . . Mark!"

On the first run-through, mentally Secca just matched the words of the spell with the notes, trying to make sure that the note values were as Anna had said they were. Unsurprisingly, words and note values matched, but then, Anna had been a greater musician than Liedwahr had seen in generations—if ever.

Secca found her eyes watering, and she had to swallow at the gaping emptiness within her that had reappeared so suddenly and unexpectedly, an emptiness that hurt just as much as the morning Anna had died, if not more.

"Are you all right?" murmured Alcaren.

"I was thinking about Anna," answered Secca in a low voice. She shook her head. "Sometimes . . . sometimes, it still hurts that she's gone, that I can never talk to her. She was so good to me. I can still remember the time, when she was Regent, that she carried me all the way up to my tower room and my bed. Or the times that we played Vorkoffe. She was always so patient. She promised me that she'd always take care of me."

"She did, didn't she?"

Secca nodded and blotted her eyes.

Palian's voice rose from the main deck. "Bretnay! You are holding back the other violinos. Do you want to be cast to the bottom of the Western Sea because the spell accompaniment is not properly played? This is a mighty spell, and if it is not played right, most unfortunate things happen. There once was a violino player who was turned into red dust . . ."

Secca found a wry smile on her face. Palian was embroidering the truth slightly, since the unfortunate player had been turned into dust by Lord Brill for not following instructions, and botching a spellsong accompaniment that had required much additional spellsinging to undo the damage. Still, Bretnay did not have to know the entire story.

Secca closed her eyes for a moment, trying to call up the images she would use. Then she swallowed, realizing something so obvious that she had never thought of it. Anna had taught her the fifth building song with its complicated wording for building . . . but never had Secca ever used that spellsong, because the first three were far easier and covered bridges, roads, walls . . . and most everything else. Most of the spells in the "Armageddon" folder used the fourth, fifth, and sixth building songs.

Secca shook her head, marveling at how many years ahead Anna had thought, giving Secca the tools to use the deadly spells, without burdening her with the knowledge directly.

"Lady Secca?"

The redheaded sorceress opened her eyes and answered Palian. "On your mark."

The accompaniment rose into the morning air and over the waters of the Western Sea. Secca concentrated on words, note values, and the images Anna had suggested in the explanatory words written so many years before, realizing, as she lost the images to the words, that she had as much practicing to do as did the players, or more.

86

MANSUUS, MANSUUR

Kestrin is leaning back in the armchair behind the desk in his private study, reading through a series of requests from the town councils of Landungerste and Hafen. He offers a low and sardonic laugh containing sadness rather than mirth and sets the requests aside, glancing toward the windows and the afternoon clouds beyond that promise rain, though none has yet fallen.

At the *thrap* on the door, he straightens. "Yes?"

"Overcaptain Bassil, sire."

"Have him come in."

Bassil's face is grim as he steps quickly, but firmly, toward the Liedfuhr. He stops and waits a yard short of the desk.

"Just how bad is the news this time, Bassil?"

"As bad as I have ever delivered, sire."

Kestrin gestures for the lancer officer to continue.

"The Sturinnese have used sorcery to slaughter more than three thousand of the lancers and armsmen you dispatched through the Mittpass to Neserea. Perhaps a thousand more are scattered in the Great Western Forest. Many of those will not survive the snows and cold to return."

"When we heard little, I feared as much." Kestrin shrugs sadly. "Yet what could I do? I am not a ruler to stand and do nothing, the way Lord Robero would, had he no sorceresses."

"We knew that risk, sire." Bassil waits.

"You warned me. That I grant, but your face says there is worse to come."

"For you, sire, yes. The seers have discovered that the

Sturinnese have used sorcery to murder your sister Aerlya and your niece Annyal."

"Sorcery?" Kestrin leans forward in the chair, his eyes firmly on the older man.

"Some sort of distance sorcery." Bassil clears his throat gently. "So far, the sole survivors are Aerfor and her consort Eryhal. He also appears to be the only survivor in Lord Clehar's family. They are somewhere in Nordwei."

"Can we do nothing?" Kestrin stands, pursing his lips, then goes on as if he had not asked a question. "No, there is nothing we can do that will not cost us even more dearly. We cannot fight sorcery with lancers, Bassil. We will lose all the lancers we have."

"No, sire. It appears not."

"I must do nothing, cowering in Mansuus, hoping that the Sturinnese will ride eastward rather than westward. Unless you have a better idea?"

"Ah . . . you might inflict great damage by assembling small groups of archers to harass them. They cannot use spells every time an arrow flies into their midst."

"You can start working on that when you leave."

"Yes, sire."

"If we manage to hold Mansuur together, *if* we do, we must have sorcerers, and we must train them from among our own loyal peoples."

Bassil offers a single nod, as if dubious. "Whom would we trust to train them?"

Kestrin laughs, bitterly. "Whom do we distrust least to train them? Who has proved that she can."

"The Shadow Sorceress?"

"I would judge so. If . . . *if* she can defeat the Sturinnese, we will send an envoy with coin and anything else, beseeching her—and I will grovel and mean it—to select and train a sorcerer for us, or more, if she will—out of young Mansuurans we will send to her."

"Will she?" asks Bassil.

"What have we to lose? I would not wish a Sturinnese

presence anywhere in Mansuur, and I could hardly trust
them to teach a sorcerer to act for us against them. We have
seen what has occurred in Dumar and Neserea. The Ranuans
abhor any sorcery beyond scrying, as do those of Nordwei.
Where else can we turn?"

"She might agree—especially if we plead that she does
not wish to happen to Mansuur what happened to Dumar
and Neserea."

"She might. If she can somehow get to Neserea and defeat
the Sturinnese, if she can right matters in Defalk, and shore
up that sagging and self-centered idiot Robero." Kestrin
paces toward the window, then turns on the heels of his
polished boots, and stops. "It would not hurt to see if we
have any sorcerers in Mansuur who have remained hidden.
Cannot my seers use their pools for that?"

"They can but try, sire."

"Then have them try." Kestrin purses his lips. "Small catapults, with flaming oil—can we design some that can be
carried by a single packhorse and set up and fired by one
man?"

Bassil frowns.

"They cannot use a spell for each man. You just told me
that. Not if each is alone and in a different place. Without
sorcerers, we must develop tactics so that sorcery is less
effective. We will meet with the marshals tomorrow morning."

"The Sturinnese have moved from our borders."

"If we do nothing now, what will we do when they return?" asks the Liedfuhr.

Bassil bows his head.

87

I n the warm afternoon, the captain's cabin was crowded with the four around the table and the overcaptains and chief players standing behind Secca, Denyst, Alcaren, and Richina. Secca had edged the maps to one side, right in front of Richina. Green-tinged light from a brilliant day outside poured through the portholes and through the overhead sky-lenses, and the cabin was lighter than usual.

"You have been practicing at great length with the players," Wilten offered. "You have not mentioned what you may require of us."

"Or if there may be any way in which we can assist you," added Delcetta.

"I will be asking much of you both," Secca said, "but not before we reach Neserea. That is my hope, at least." She smiled wryly.

"You do not plan to attack Sturinn as the Sturinnese attacked Dumar and Neserea?" asked Wilten, adding hastily, "If I might ask."

"I hope to deal with the Sturinnese solely through sorcery," Secca said. "I had not planned to land lancers and invade Sturinn. Even if we should be successful in destroying every armsman and lancer in the isles, most hands would still be against us, and there is no way that Lord Robero could ever govern a land more than fifteen hundred deks from Liedwahr. We have no ships and no ports, and far too few lancers and sorceresses for such."

A quick and knowing look passed between the two over-captains.

"Will . . . sorcery . . . suffice?" Wilten's words were almost apologetic.

"I trust so. We would not be traveling this far had I not

thought so." Secca shrugged. "As in many things, there is no way to make sure until the act. We will have to see."

Wilten's face—a face that was so unremarkable—remained impassive, even as he nodded.

"There is one other matter," Delcetta offered after a moment of silence. "Whether it be in Sturinn or Neserea, we could not offer much assistance for a day or more."

"Your mounts?" asked Alcaren.

"Sea travel does not help them. We have lost three already," Wilten said. "That does not include those lost with the *Wellereiterin*."

Secca winced. The effect of a longer voyage on the lancers' mounts was another thing she hadn't thought about. *How many others will there be?* After a moment, she nodded to Alcaren.

He stood and began the scrying spellsong, accompanying himself on his lumand.

"Show us now and in this sun's light
any Sea-Priests near that we might fight . . ."

Before he had finished, the glass in the middle of the table began to display images, and by the time the last note had died away, there were more than a dozen in the silvered glass.

"Look quickly," Secca prompted. She didn't want Alcaren to have to hold the image long, not when she would need all the sorcerous support he could provide in the days ahead.

The images all showed land-based forces, ranging from armsmen in formation to lancers waiting in loose ranks outside a barracks. There were some men in green-and-white uniforms in what looked to be harborside forts, and others drilling on an open green field.

"No ships," offered Denyst. "Strange for the Sea-Priests, isn't it?"

Alcaren glanced to Secca. "That's true. Let me try another

one." He pursed his lips and thought for a moment, before singing a second scrying spellsong:

> *"Show us now and in this sun's light*
> *any ships near that we might fight . . ."*

The mirror remained blank.

"That doesn't mean they don't have some ships, but there aren't any warships or ships with armsmen aboard," Secca explained.

"You have sent a few to the bottom," Denyst acknowledged with a laugh.

"There is still a large fleet in the Bitter Sea," Richina added.

Secca nodded to Alcaren. He sang the release couplet, then slipped the lumand onto the double bunk behind where Palian stood and reseated himself.

Secca eased the map in front of Denyst, pointing. "How long before we can reach this end of Stura?"

"Late tomorrow afternoon, if the wind holds."

"How close can we come to this point, off the mountain here?"

"In these waters, hard to say." The captain tilted her head slightly. "Don't have good charts. Might be able to get within half a dek. If there's a reef, could be as far as three deks."

Secca frowned. "We really need to be about a dek away."

"You need us to be dead in the water?" asked the captain.

"No. It would be better if we were moving, because, if the spell works we'll need to get away quickly. Also . . . we really don't need any other ships close by us. They can't help with the sorcery, and we don't need to worry about them."

"You might create another storm?" Denyst raised her eyebrows.

"It could be worse," Secca admitted. "It might not be, but it could be. No one has ever sung this spell. The accompaniment has been played, but the words have not been sung."

"Could anyone else—" began the captain.

"It's a Mist World spell," Secca said quickly.

Most of the faces around the table, even Richina's, expressed a degree of puzzlement.

"The people of the Mist Worlds know more about worlds—not just our world," Secca replied. "Without that knowledge, the spell would not be possible."

Skepticism replaced puzzlement on Denyst's face.

"You can explain to me," Secca began, "how a ship is built, and why the sails are set so. Could you do that, and could anyone build a ship like the *Silberwelle*, if you did not know how the winds blow and the oceans flow?"

Denyst frowned.

"Do you recall the spell that destroyed the crews of the Sturinnese ships in the battle off Encora?" Secca pressed.

"I recall that it nearly killed you as well."

"Have you ever seen sorcery that kills scores without destroying anything around them? That spell was Lady Anna's, and it worked because she knew something that we did not. This spell is based on something like that."

"You don't want it used again?"

"This is a different spell, and I'd rather not use it at all," Secca admitted, "but I have nothing else that will serve." *Nothing that you have been able to find or write.*

"Your face says that more than your words, Lady Sorceress," Denyst say dryly. "Mighty as this spell must be, would you mind if we were set on a seaward course when you sing it?"

Secca shook her head. "That would be best. The other ships should be at least five deks farther at sea."

"That we will arrange." After a moment, Denyst added, "We'll be in the channel by sunset today or a glass before. Thought we'd stay at the edge of being able to see the isle of Stura itself, leastwise until after midday tomorrow." The captain leaned back in her chair.

Secca looked to Palian. "Can we do another run-through in, say, half a glass?"

"We will be ready." Palian's voice was grave.

Secca suspected it would be far graver if Palian understood the impact of the spell. *Would the players play it well if they knew?* Secca wondered, not for the first time.

88

S ecca found her hands tightening around the port-side railing of the poop deck. She loosened one hand, lifted it, and flexed it, then the other. In the light afternoon air, even under full sail, the *Silberwelle* seemed to be creeping northwestward away from the center of the forty-dek-wide channel between Stura and the smaller isle of Trinn. The sky was deep blue and cloudless, and the rays of the late-afternoon sun were summerlike, so much so that Secca had taken out her green felt hat to protect her face. With the heat of the sun, the air smelled less salty, but Secca still felt itchy, as she had for most of the voyage, despite her use of song-sorcery to come up with the occasional bucket of fresh water for washing.

Except for the nine Ranuan ships, the channel was empty. A brief look in the scrying glass earlier in the morning had shown no ships anywhere in the isles, except for three merchant vessels tied up at the port of Stura, four others at various other piers, and a number of fishing craft almost everywhere. To the west, the dark line that was the shore continued to become more distinct, but Secca could not make out the landmarks that Denyst and the lookouts reported.

Secca flexed her hands again.

Alcaren smiled at Secca's impromptu exercise, but did not speak, his eyes looking aft to the sails of the other ships, now east of the *Silberwelle*, their courses diverging from that of the *Silberwelle* with every moment. For nearly two days, the *Silberwelle* had tracked the coastline of Stura, a land far too large in Secca's mind to be called an isle.

After a time, she eased toward the helm platform, near where Denyst stood.

"How long?" Secca looked to Denyst.

"Another glass and a half, I'd judge. Less if the wind picks up, and more, if it dies off. Looks to stay the same. The channel's so calm it's almost eerie."

"Can you tell how close we can get?"

"Not yet. If it's like this, with no reefs, we can get within a dek and still be in deep water."

"That's important?"

"In deeper water, the Sea-Priests could not raise a wave that would be more than a swell."

Would they raise a wave that could damage their own isle? Secca laughed to herself, realizing how stupid the question was. The Sea-Priests fought to the bitter end when cornered in Liedwahr. Why would that be any different in Sturinn?

"They may not have sorcerers here who can do that, but I agree. I'd rather not chance that." Secca frowned. "But they would have to travel to the shore opposite where we are. They don't know where we're headed, and we're not going to be stopping or anchoring."

"That's much to my liking, sorceress," Denyst said cheerfully. "Much."

"Thank you. I need to tell the players to get ready." Secca nodded and turned away.

"How long?" asked Alcaren, as Secca stepped back toward the railing.

"A glass and a half, if the wind stays as it has. Could you tell Palian . . . ?" Secca laughed. "What am I going to do? Stand here and wait?" She walked forward, turned, and climbed down the ladder to the main deck.

About half the players were in shaded spots on the main

deck, and Secca found Palian and Delvor deep in conversation near the starboard side in a patch of shade created by one of the lower sails. Delvor was nodding in agreement to whatever Palian said.

Both glanced up, almost guiltily, as Secca neared.

"Lady Secca," Palian said.

Delvor bowed, and then straightened and pushed back his forever-flopping lank brown hair. "Lady."

"The captain thinks we will reach our destination for sorcery in about a glass and a half," Secca said. "I thought the players should start to make ready for a last run-through in about a glass. Is that satisfactory?"

"Perhaps a bit before," Palian replied. "I have some—still—who find preparing on a ship challenges their ability. Then, everything challenges the ability of one of them."

Secca smiled sympathetically. She had no doubt that the chief player was referring to the hapless Bretnay.

Palian glanced at Delvor, then looked to Secca. "Delvor and I were talking over some matters. If you and I could repair to the upper deck . . . ?"

"Of course." Secca wondered what the two had been discussing and hoped that it wasn't a problem with the fifth building song or the players. But then, she hoped it wasn't a major problem of any kind. *There are going to be more than enough of those.*

Delvor nodded and stepped away, and the two women crossed the deck, angling aft past the mainmast. Secca gestured for Palian to precede her up the ladder to the poop deck. They moved to the railing a good five yards from where Alcaren stood.

Palian looked at the sorceress. "You never did intend to land on any of the isles of Sturinn, did you, Lady Secca?"

"No." Secca eased the water bottle from her belt and took a swallow, looking toward the dark shore on the western horizon, a shoreline that neared and became more distinct with every fraction of a glass that the *Silberwelle* sailed northwest through the channel and toward the isle of Stura.

"I know not what sorcery you plan," Palian said slowly, "save that it will be terrible, and it will create for you the very problems that it did for Lady Anna."

"Does not all great sorcery create problems?" Secca glanced toward the horizon, then shook her head. "I am sorry, Palian. Those were unkind words, and unkindly said. I am worried. What do you mean?"

"You are much more like her than you would admit, lady."

Palian would know. Of all in Liedwahr, she would know. "Others have said that, and perhaps because I looked up to her, I have become more like her than I would see."

"If your sorcery works, you will destroy Stura. That I know, for you would not risk close to a third of a season upon the open sea for anything less. If you succeed, every man on the face of Erde, saving your consort and the handful that know you, will wish you consigned to eternal dissonance. You will be required to use sorcery more than you ever wish for years to come, and after that, every accident and misfortune in Liedwahr will be laid to your name. Men will whisper your name to sons in hatred for generations."

Alcaren had turned from his all-too-common position at the railing and slid closer to the conversation in his quiet way, so unobtrusively that neither had noticed until he nodded sadly and spoke. "She is right, my lady."

"Because I use sorcery?" asked Secca, fearing she knew the answer, but wanting someone else to say it. "Or because I have not created death and destruction with blades and bows, or tilling salt into croplands? Or slaying the firstborn of my enemies with bloody blades?"

"Men hold great honor in using their strength to defeat other men," Palian said. "Some women also take pride in the strength of their men. With your sorcery, you make their strength of arms as less than the cries of a newborn babe."

Secca laughed, mirthlessly. "Anna said the same, if in different words. Yet it is honorable for a strong-thewed man to slay scores who had the misfortune to be born less endowed with strength and muscles, and dishonorable for me or Alcaren or Richina to slay with song. People take with great willingness the roads and bridges we have built. Or the fords, and the wealth that has flowed from them. A sword builds no bridges and creates few golds. Nor will all the men and their blades or all those slain by blades build what we have built."

"I did not say what people feel is right, my lady," Palian replied gently. "But from this day on, you can trust none you know not well, and perhaps not some of those."

"So I must follow in her footsteps in this as well?" asked Secca.

"Had you any choice, in truth?" replied Palian. "You would do what is right, but what is right accomplishes nothing in our world, save when it is backed with great force."

"A right venal world it is," Alcaren said dryly, "and harmony unsupported is inadequate."

"You two are so cheerful," Secca said, forcing a laugh. "Yet you are right, and I will heed your observations, even as I wish it were otherwise."

"We all wish that, lady," Palian replied, "but wishes have not the weight of blades or spells. Delvor also feels as do I, and we wished you to know that. So I think do Wilten and Delcetta, but they have not spoken to us so directly."

"You're right." Secca inclined her head. "Thank you. Thank you both."

"I need to ready my errant players." Palian offered a wry smile and a parting nod, then headed forward to the ladder and descended to the main deck.

"She is right, my lady," Alcaren said quietly.

"I know she is right," Secca admitted. "I told her that, but I do not have to like what is so."

"You will have to do great sorcery in Neserea as well. The remaining Sturinnese will fight beyond their death. They know that, if you live, Sturinn's way will die out in time. If you die, nothing will change, and in a generation,

two at the latest, another Maitre will return to invade Liedwahr."

"There are other sorceresses," Secca protested. "Jolyn is
strong, and Anandra and Richina could also be most powerful in time."

"There are other sorceresses. There is none like you."

"You say that because you love me." She grinned. "Or
lust after me."

"I do indeed," he replied with a smile, "but my words are
true, and you know they are true."

"You believe them true," Secca admitted.

"Why do you have such trouble in believing them?" he
asked. "Are there others who can raise storms and bridges
or topple holds?"

"There are. Belmar did some of that. So have the Sturinnese. They use their drums to create storms and fog and
raise great waves."

"They are many. You are one."

"As Palian just told me, that is going to be a problem."
If you survive for it to be a problem. She smiled at Alcaren.
"As you become more accomplished, it will be one for you
as well, my love."

He nodded soberly. "Though I will never be able to do
what you do."

"Do not say that yet." Secca took a swallow from the
water bottle and replaced it in her belt holder, cleared her
throat, and began a vocalise.

Alcaren stepped away and cleared his throat, following
Secca's example with a vocalise she had crafted for his
deeper voice.

One good thing about the salt air was that her cords felt
clearer, and it took less time for her to warm up. By the
third vocalise, she was as ready as she would be.

Alcaren still had trouble with warming up, since he'd had
to learn the vocalises from Secca, and they were far from
second nature to him, but he finally turned to her. "I am
ready, my lady."

From the main deck rose the sound of the players beginning to tune. Secca glanced forward, listening for a moment, then looked back toward the large isle once more.

"Lady Sorceress?"

Secca turned to see Denyst standing there.

"Not so much time as I'd thought. There's a reef." Denyst pointed to the left. "The line of breakers there. Looks to be not quite a half-dek offshore. The darker water to this side, that shows that there aren't any shallows, but those breakers directly ahead, that's where the reef turns. Comes out farther on the other side of the bight. Means you'll be closest on this end. I can bring us closer inshore here, but only for about a quarter glass, and then I'll have to run due north, near-on straight out to sea."

"Less than a quarter glass before the second turn after the first?"

"Give or take a bit."

"Then turn in, and we'll sing as soon as we can set up when the ship's steady."

With a nod, Denyst headed back toward the helm. "Two points to port!"

"Two to port. Coming port."

Secca walked to the railing overlooking the main deck, catching Palian's eye. "Time for a warm-up and one run-through. Then we'll do the spell."

"The warm-up tune!" Palian's voice lifted over the rush of the water against the hull of the *Silberwelle* and above the rustling and flapping of the sails above as the *Silberwelle* turned in response to Denyst's command.

Secca could discern, especially as outlined by the low southern sun that was about to set behind the headlands, the volcanic cone that formed the southern end of a half bay, the cone that was the most seaward of the line of volcanoes that ran across Stura from northeast to southwest.

As the sun was dropping behind the higher hills beyond the shoreline, Richina had come up on deck, perhaps to take in the cool of the late afternoon, and to watch the spellsinging, but the younger sorceress remained within a yard of Denyst, and well away from Alcaren and Secca.

Alcaren straightened and cleared his throat. "Are you ready?"

Secca nodded.

"Remember, my lady. Your words, and notes, and thoughts, only on the spell. Only on the spell."

"Only on the spell," Secca repeated. *Only on the spellsong . . .*

"The fifth building song at my mark . . . Mark!" Palian's voice was calm and yet forceful.

Alcaren and Secca moved outward along the railing separating the poop deck from the drop to the main deck until they stood in the corner between the starboard-side railing and the poop deck railing, facing into the early twilight, listening to the players playing through the fifth building song. Secca concentrated one last time on the words and images.

When the players had finished the run-through, and checked tuning and their instruments, Secca considered the spell, wondering, far from the first time, how Anna had learned so much, and why so few in Liedwahr understood just how much her mentor had known about so many things.

She glanced at Denyst, then turned back to look down on Palian and the players. "Stand by for the fifth building song."

"Standing by, at your signal, lady," Palian returned.

Secca took one slow deep breath, then a second, exhaling slowly. She looked toward Alcaren. He nodded.

The redheaded sorceress raised her hand. "At your mark, chief player." She lowered her arm and hand.

For that instant, Secca felt that all Erde paused . . . as if to say that one time was ending, and another beginning.

Then, Palian's voice cut through the slowly fading light. "The fifth building song. At my mark . . . Mark!"

From the first note, the players were strong, the notes clear, the energy focused, and the song lifted toward the shore, toward the isle of Stura, toward the volcanic cones that harbored hidden flame and fire.

Secca and Alcaren joined together, perfectly, with the first note of the third bar.

> *"Magma of the core, fire for Sturinn's woe,*
> *rise and climb from the mantle deep below;*
> *explode in flame, and from the earth in fire flow.*
> *Searing every river, hill and dale, and plain*
> *with gas and ash and lava till none remain*
> *untouched, unstruck, and none escape the fire's*
>   *bane . . ."*

By the end of the first stanza a deep roaring and grumbling filled the air, and the waters between the *Silberwelle* and the white sand of the narrow beach below the steep bluffs shivered. The water calmed, unnaturally, and the spray and whitecaps that had marked where the ocean met the reef vanished. A flat and glassy stillness lay across the water like a blanket, and even the air seemed heavy, leaden.

Secca forced her concentration back onto the notes, the words, and the images of the second stanza.

> *"Lava rise, and lava flare, burst on all below;*
> *cover every town and road in fire's glow,*
> *split the land and force the sea to fire know.*
> *With heat and steam and molten rock bring to bear*
> *all destruction of the earth and sea to Sturinn fair*
> *till none remain, and none will know what is buried*
>   *there . . ."*

With the last note, a single off-key, two-toned note chimed through the air. Not as chord, but one note embodying, it seemed to Secca, all of harmony and all of dissonance.

Her head throbbed, and knives of fire stabbed into her eyes, accompanied by flaring daystars, but her vision was not doubled, as with Darksong-tinged spellsong. Still, seeing was painful enough that tears oozed from her eyes, and her skull ached as if pounded by unseen hammers.

The distant roaring grumble continued to rise. Small ripples flicked across the surface of the unnaturally flat bay, ripples running from the sandy shore toward and past the *Silberwelle*.

For a moment, Secca just stared at the isle, trying to see through the daystars across the dark waters toward the land. Gouts of liquid fire began to spray from the darkness of the shadowed land, from just behind the white line of the sandy beach to the cultivated hillsides and forests above. The fire fountains began to thicken, and the heat—even a dek offshore—began to increase. Within moments, the air was hot, almost like that just above an oven or a fire, so hot that Secca flung up her arm to shield her face.

"Hard starboard! Steady on due north."

"Coming starboard."

Before the ship had even heeled slightly into the turn, a rushing gust of hot air struck Secca, so hard that she staggered. Above her sails cracked in the abrupt gust, and a long ripping sound followed. A huge thundering crash, as though a mountain wall had fallen, reverberated in Secca's ears.

The *Silberwelle* heeled farther, and Secca clutched for the railing to keep her feet. But her eyes remained on Stura. Openmouthed, she watched, frozen at the railing, as cloud of glowing ash surged downhill from the volcanic cone, as trees flattened and burst into flame almost simultaneously with the wind that preceded the avalanche of ash. Then the houses on the lower slopes vanished under the luminous ash.

As the *Silberwelle* turned, crew scrambling through the rigging, and shifting to catch the wind from a different angle, Secca turned away and took a stumbling step toward the ladder that would take her below, out of the heat that she had created. *Didn't know . . . it would be like this . . .*

To the northeast, far into the distance, the sea continued

to flatten and take on an ominous and deadly silvery shimmer.

"Everyone below! Everyone below!" The frantic energy in Denyst's voice was all too clear.

Secca's legs felt like lead, her arms as if she could not lift them, but lift them she did, turning at the top of the ladder. Halfway down the ladder another blast of wind ripped through the *Silberwelle*, slamming Secca against the ladder.

"Bring her round another point! Into the sea! Into the sea!"

The sails flapped in the rising hot winds that gusted round the *Silberwelle*, first blowing from the land, then swirling back southward.

Secca winced as several pinpoints of fire fell from the sky and jabbed at her hands and neck, and she scrambled down the lower part of the ladder, landing with a jolt on the hard planking of the main deck. Her eyes went to the mass of players.

"Into the fo'c's'le!" Delvor's voice was the one that rose above the clamor on the main deck.

Secca took a last glance backward. Above Stura rose an enormous plume of fiery ash, glowing and radiating heat far more intense than any sun Secca had ever felt.

Looking upward, Secca could see Alcaren half-helping, half-dragging Richina to the ladder, and she stopped at the bottom of the ladder to help the younger sorceress, hurrying, and then pushing her into the passageway. Alcaren scrambled after them.

The narrow passageway was far cooler than the deck outside, but Secca did not stop to enjoy the comparative comfort, but staggered into the captain's quarters, half-pushing, half-urging Richina into the nearest chair, and taking the one beside her, grateful once more that the chairs were firmly bolted to the deck.

Secca glanced toward the open wooden bin fastened to the bulkhead, where the cased lutar and wrapped scrying mirror were stowed, glad that the net covering was tied in place.

Alcaren shut the door and scrambled into the chair next to Secca.

"Why . . . ?" stammered Richina.

"Why did she want us below?" asked Alcaren. "Because the spell conjured another great wave. We might be far enough to sea not to be dashed onto the rocks—if it's not too large a wave, or there aren't too many. I hope there aren't."

Secca hoped so as well, recalling both the damages she had seen from such waves and knowing Alcaren's discomfort with sea travel.

The *Silberwelle*'s timbers shivered with a deep bass rumbling, not something of sorcery or harmony, but a sound any could hear, and the ship heeled and then righted herself.

"She's got her headed into the wave," Alcaren said. "Now . . . if we have enough time and enough sea . . ." His eyes flicked toward the forward porthole.

From where she sat, and with the continued stabbing pain in her eyes, Secca could see little, just smudges of darkness and an eerie red glowing. The ship seemed to settle, almost coming to a halt in calm waters.

"Hold on. Hold tight!" said Alcaren, gripping the arms of the chair in which he sat.

In spite of knowing what was coming, and having been through it before, Secca's mouth still opened wide as the deck tilted and the forward bulkhead of the cabin rose more than a yard above the rear one. The bow dropped with a lurch, and a shudder ran through the *Silberwelle*, from stem to stern.

"Didn't break her back," muttered Alcaren. His hand went to his forehead, and he massaged his temples.

The cabin went dark as water surged past the portholes. Then there was a glimmer of grayness, before more water covered the tinted green glass. The *Silberwelle* half corkscrewed, heeled, then righted herself once more.

Secca realized that the air in the cabin had become no-
ticeably warmer and damper, not quite steamy, but hot and
sticky. She swallowed as she realized that the heat was coming from her, especially from her face. She put her fingertips
to her cheek and then her forehead . . . and winced at the
pain.

Alcaren pulled himself out of his chair and, one hand on
the chair, and then on the end of the bunk, made his way
to the porthole, where he watched for a long moment.

"Are we going to be safe?" asked Richina anxiously.
"Can you tell?"

He turned slowly. Even in the dim light, Secca could see
that his face was bright red, as perhaps hers was.

"We've still got headway, and the waves are subsiding
for now," Alcaren finally replied.

Secca feared she understood what he meant. Feared that
their spell had been all too successful. She swallowed, trying
to ignore the pounding in her head and the daystars that
flickered before her.

Alcaren eased himself back into his seat. "We'd only be
in the way topside, at least for a while." Then he tightened
his lips and looked at Secca.

Richina looked from Secca to Alcaren and then back to
Secca, but neither Alcaren nor Secca spoke. Both sat in the
growing darkness, thinking, their faces burning.

89

ESARIA, NESEREA

I n the dimness broken but by a single oil lamp, the Maitre
is standing. He watches the door to the small study where
he waits, off the audience hall, when there is a single rap
on the door.

"You may enter, jerClayne."

"Ser . . ." The younger Sea-Priest bows, then swallows. The blotchiness of his face is obvious, even in the dim light. "Stura is no more, Maitre . . . not as we know it. The isle . . . it is little more than boiling rock."

"I could tell that a glass ago." The Maitre's voice is tight, and yet there is an anger like cold iron underlying his words. "Have you determined what happened?"

"All the great volcanoes, those that have not seen fire in generations . . . all of them . . . it is nothing I have seen, nothing I have read . . . it is not a thing we—"

"Do not tell me what we cannot do!" retorts the Maitre. "What she can do, we can do. We would not destroy a land and its people from spite and malice. What has Defalk done—ever? We have united peoples and brought peace to a quarter of the world. Defalk's lords squabble among themselves. We have brought trade to all. Defalk not a single ship. Yet this . . . this girl . . . she has no thought but to destroy. She does not know what destruction is. But she will learn."

"All of us used the pool, ser," JerClayne stammers. "Stura— the port, it is buried under deks of glowing rock, and the same for Inylt. Even in the night, there is no darkness. Everything is lit with red light . . . and nothing . . . nothing lives . . ." JerClayne's voice breaks.

"What of Trinn?"

"The western half, the lowlands, they . . . were flooded, and many died. Astaal, the northern and eastern half—there the volcanoes spewed forth ash and lava, too."

"And the sorceress?" The Maitre's voice is implacable.

"Her ships sail northward. They did not stop or anchor. They did not even land. They sailed past, and she cast spells." The younger man shakes his head. "How could she?"

"She is a sorceress and an evil woman." The Maitre's lips tighten. "She is spiteful and malicious. Because she cannot face us in open battle, she destroys men from a distance, and slaughters women and children. She has no honor. She has no decency. All Erde will now see her for what she is."

"She also maintains her defense spell. How any—" JerClayne shakes his head. "How could anyone do what she has done? And yet hold a ward?"

"She does not hold the wards. The younger sorceress does. While she knows less than the shadowsinger, she is well trained and strong." The Maitre purses his lips, as if considering whether to say more. "They call us cruel and ruthless, jerClayne. Think of it. We are cruel and ruthless, and we have slain but lancers and armsmen and a sorceress, and perhaps a few handfuls of peasants. They have devastated a land near as large as any of their petty countries. They have not conquered it; they have killed everyone there, as surely as if by a blade or a spear. Yet we are cruel."

JerClayne waits, receptively. Finally, he asks, "How did there come to be so many sorceresses when a generation ago there were none?"

"Because the great evil sorceress from the Mist Worlds was fortunate to arrive in Liedwahr when everyone was at everyone else's throat. First, she was tutored and taught by Lord Brill, who thought to use her as a tool, and instead was used and discarded by her. There were no other sorcerers in Liedwahr—not trained ones. Lord Robero's sire perished at the hands of the Evult, and his grandsire the lord Jecks allowed her to live so that his grandson could become Lord of Defalk."

"She kept that bargain, did she not?"

"He had the title, an added set of lands, and the liedstadt and some trappings. She kept the power, and has passed it on to the shadowsinger and the others. The Ladies of the Shadows, Lord Robero, Lord Mynntar—how could they all have been so blind, you ask?" The Maitre laughs. "Because all were desperate for peace, any kind of peace, and she gave them that. Those who did not wish her kind of peace vanished. By illness, by accident, or by some shadowy means that cast no light on her. That is how it happened, and that is why we are here."

"Can we defeat the shadowsinger, Maitre?"

"We can. She cannot use the spells she used in Stura here in Liedwahr. We must remember that victory comes to those who endure. Victories are not won by destroying lands, but by dominating people. There is no victory in ruling a land where nothing lives. We have already undone much of the damage she and her predecessor created. We hold Neserea, and Dumar is ours, as soon as any lancers return. Ebra will fall to a strong wind. We will move to Defalk, and bring it down, and when she returns, bring her down as well."

"How shall we begin?" asks the younger Sea-Priest.

"I must think. And think I will. For now, have the lancers and all our forces ready to ride by the second glass of the morning tomorrow. And have them bring every wagon that they can find in the city, heavily laden with provisions—the kind that will not spoil."

"Ah . . . where, Maitre?"

"You will see. The shadowsinger will see. The Matriarch will see. The bitch traders of Wei will see what the Sea-Priests of Sturinn are made of. All Liedwahr, and all of Erde will see, and feel what we will do." The Maitre's eyes blaze. "Do not ask of details. Be content to know that Stura will be avenged. Be content to know that none will again cross us without knowing that their days are numbered. In time, when that is clear, the shadowsinger will have to come to us, and when she does she will pay more than she knows can be paid. She will indeed." His words are as cold as frozen iron.

The younger Sea-Priest involuntarily steps back from the restrained anger and chill violence that fills the dimly lighted small room.

90

S ecca lay rigid on the captain's wide bunk, the memory of the internally clashing, agonized single note that embodied chords of both harmony and dissonance still reverberating through her entire body. Her face burned, as if a fire were consuming it again and again, moment by moment. Beyond that, her head throbbed; her body ached; and daystars flashed across her vision.

"Your faces are blistered," Richina said, "as if you had ridden for days under a summer sun." She eased the cloth she had wet once more in fresh water back over Secca's face.

"Or worse," Secca said, her voice muffled by the cloth. Even moving her lips sent faint lines of added pain radiating through her face and skull.

"Worse," mumbled Alcaren from where he sat, leaning back in one of the chairs around the table.

"How do *you* feel?" Secca managed.

"My face is just a little red, but I looked away when all that fire exploded into the sky. I am tired." Richina sighed. "I can feel someone probing the wards again."

"The Sea-Priests in Neserea," said Alcaren. "They have sorcerers."

The cabin door opened, and the captain stepped inside, her eyes going first to Alcaren, then to Secca, and finally to Richina. "How are they?"

"Their faces are blistered from the heat," Richina replied. "In a glass, I will use Alcaren's balm, and, in a day or so, they will be better."

"What about the crew?" Secca asked, sitting up, despite her headache, and the fire in her face, and the pain in her eyes.

"We lost three off the yardarms when the wave hit. Near-on a half-score are burned like you, except more on their arms and necks. Too busy to be looking aft, I'd wager. Some of your players are scorched, too, especially your chief player."

Secca winced. She hadn't even thought of Palian. *So much you haven't thought about . . .*

"She is not so bad as you two," Richina said quickly.

"That's because the poop shielded most of them," replied Denyst.

"How about you?" asked Alcaren.

"Back of my neck. That's it." Denyst half snorted, half coughed. "Thankful we've spare canvas below. Half what we had on was shredded." There was a long silence. "Don't think we'll be worrying about the Maitre and the Sea-Priests ever again."

Secca squinted against the pain in her eyes and face, not that she could see with the damp cloth spread over her cheeks and forehead. "They still have a fleet in the Bitter Sea and more lancers than all of Liedwahr put together."

"You think they'll fight after . . ." There was another pause. "The whole night sky to the south is red—bright enough to steer by or read a chart. The whole place is aflame, and you sang that spell near-on three glasses back."

Secca was silent.

"You said it was a terrible spell," Denyst mused. "Wasn't sure anything could be that awful. Wrong, I guess."

"I made it as strong as I could," Secca said, all too conscious of the stiffness of her mouth and cheeks and lips. "I didn't want them coming back to Liedwahr in another score of years, just waiting, and attacking again."

Denyst sighed. "You'd be right on that. Took 'em two-score years before they took the Ostisles, and threescore before that to take Pelara." There was another sigh.

"You think the cost was too high?" Secca tried to keep the edge out of her voice. *Of course it was too high. It was something like this or watch them take Liedwahr.*

"Lady Sorceress . . . what be done is done, and it's not like they were all servants of harmony. Just . . . so sudden-like."

Secca swallowed, unable to speak.

"Till tomorrow, sorceress."

Secca listened to the door close, still holding herself half-erect, although her arms were beginning to tremble.

"Lady . . . you must rest," Richina said softly, helping Secca lie back down. "You must."

How can you rest? Secca lay in the darkness, her head pounding, knives slashing at her eyes, and her face burning, wondering how she could ever explain. *You can't, except to Alcaren, or Richina, and maybe the Matriarch . . . Robero would never spend the golds to raise thousands of lancers and allow us to train scores of sorcerers and sorceresses, and that wouldn't work because we can't control them the way the Evult did or the Sea-Priests do . . .*

Why was life the way it was? She didn't have scores upon scores of lancers, and scores of sorcerers. She had three people and terrible spells. She could destroy a land, but the three of them were only one force. The Sturinnese were everywhere—in Ebra, in Dumar, in the Ostisles, in Neserea, and the three of them could be but in one. Yet, just as the Ladies of the Shadows faulted the ancient Matriarchs for using sorcery to save their people, she would be condemned—even if she succeeded. *Are there sorceries so terrible that it is better to suffer defeat? Are you wrong to use them? Even when you see no alternatives?*

Under the cloth, the tears oozed from the corners of her eyes, tears that scalded her burned face like steam, and silent sobs racked her.

91

The Maitre stands on the headland to the northeast of the city he and his forces have taken and made theirs— if but for days. Now it stands empty of all those from Sturinn and all those who have served Sturinn, returned for the moment to those inhabitants who dared to remain. As he faces the west-northwest, his eyes study the city below the headland. "You *will* see, all of you. You will see the might of Sturinn."

Then he turns to look over the players and drummers arrayed in a semicircle.

At the sound of boots on gravel he turns back to watch Marshal jerLeng approach, followed by jerClayne.

The lancer marshal bows, slightly, but deferentially, then straightens. "The lancers are drawn up to the east as you requested, Maitre, and we have stripped the city of coin and provisions. We stand ready to travel."

"Good. We will leave shortly. After we complete what must be done here." The Maitre nods to the younger Sea-Priest.

JerClayne also bows, slightly more deeply, before he reports. "The fleet has returned to the open water to the northwest, and the captains will do their best with the sorcerers they have, as the sorceress nears the Bitter Sea. They have your instructions."

"Excellent. Now, we will do our best." The Maitre smiles grimly, and his eyes glitter with determination.

"If I might ask?" inquires jerLeng. "What spell will you use?"

"One that gathers the dust and flame of the heavens and

turns them into fireballs that will fall on Esaria. There is always dust and flame. Why, it might even gather fire and dust from Sturinn. A touch of justice, do you not think?" The Maitre laughs, hauntingly, a sound that rises almost into cackling.

JerLeng barely conceals a wince.

"Maitre . . . might I ask," stammers jerClayne, "what will this destruction do, besides create hatred and enmity?"

"Why, it will deliver a message. It will tell the world that Stura's might still lives, whether the isle of Stura does or not. And that message is necessary," replies the Maitre. "Even though Stura is no more, much of what was Sturinn remains. By bringing down Liedwahr in shambles and destruction, then we give Sturinn the time to rebuild. No matter how mighty this sorceress, she is but one of a kind. She has also shown us what else is possible, and with our players and drummers, we can and will do far more. When we succeed here, then we can return to our isles and the Ostisles and rebuild, knowing that we will have time to do so. If we were to fail to bring down this Shadow Sorceress, then what has made Sturinn great would cease to be for all time. That must never be. Never!" He pauses, then asks, more quietly, "Is that not reason enough?"

Both men stiffen from the fire in the Maitre's eyes, and the iron in his words, as if they wished to step back, but dare not move.

The Maitre turns and steps forward to a position before the players and the drummers. He makes one sharp gesture, and the players begin, followed a bar later by the drums. The Maitre's voice joins them on the third bar.

"Raise waters of the deep to their greatest height . . ."

Before the end of the long stanza, a mournful groaning issues from deep within the earth, and a shudder runs through the land, and then a streaking ripple dances beneath the waters of the Bitter Sea, running northward and vanishing.

For a time, nothing occurs.

The Maitre, now pale-faced, watches the Bitter Sea, as do jerLeng and jerClayne, and the players and lancers assembled behind them.

Shortly, a hummock of water appears on the horizon. Then, with a deep sucking sound, the waters of the harbor below the bluffs of the headland retreat seaward, leaving the few fishing craft stranded on the mud. Two deks seaward rises a wall of dark gray-blue water, which towers over the doomed port and capital as it rushes landward.

The top of the great wave is almost level with the headland before it crashes across the city, flooding all but the highest hills, and flattening structures as though they had been made of fragile sticks and paper, and not of stone and brick.

As the water begins to ooze back seaward, running in streams and torrents and rivulets, carrying debris, planking . . . and bodies, the Maitre turns and makes a second gesture.

A single note issues from a violino, and the players retune.

When they are silent once more, the Maitre raises his hand, and lets it fall, and the accompaniment for the second spell begins.

> "From heaven there beyond let fall the fireballs of
>   might,
> fall in undying flame to turn to ash and dust this city in
>   our sight . . ."

When the spell is complete, the Maitre turns and walks slowly, almost shuffling to the stool set under a canopy, where he reseats himself and listens . . . and watches. His eyes have deep circles under them, circles that had not been there before the spellcasting.

First, there is a distant booming, almost as if an echo of

the drums, and then whistling, hissing, shrieking.

Then the fireballs begin to fall from the sky upon the ruins
of the city and upon those structures that had escaped the
flood—including the buildings that had once comprised the
palace of the Prophet of Music.

"Fire and flood. That is a sufficient beginning." The Maitre slowly rises from the stool and begins to walk toward
his mount, even though the fireballs still bombard what had
once been a city.

92

I n the late afternoon, despite the burning of her face and
continued throbbing in her head, Secca made her way
topside and to the stern of the *Silberwelle*. Alcaren had preceded her, by less than quarter of a glass, but stood near the
bow.

Despite the full canvas, the wind was light, and the ship
barely seemed to move through the dark blue waters of the
Western Sea. For a time, Secca stood at the stern railing,
staring southwest at the wide and dark column of clouds
and smoke and ash that was still visible, for all that the
Silberwelle was more than a hundred deks northeast of
Stura.

Stura had become a funeral pyre, and she had done it.
One spell, sung by two, and Stura would not host life in
generations. Secca had seen the poisoning and the damages
wrought by the conflict of the Mynyans and the Matriarchs,
devastation wrought ages past and still blighting the lands
of Ranuak—and yet she had sung her own terrible spell.

*What else could you have done? What else that you could
do would stop them?* The question circled in her mind, and
still she had no answers.

At the shadow on the deck she glanced up.

Palian slipped to the railing beside the sorceress. Her face was blotchy and red, and had blisters scattered across it, blisters covered with unguent, much in the way Secca had seen her own face that morning in the glass.

"Lady Secca . . ." offered the chief player.

"It was a terrible spell," Secca said quickly. "I know." Her hands clasped together, almost as if they had thoughts of their own. "I knew it was terrible, but I did not realize how terrible it could be."

The gray-haired chief player did not speak, just stood beside Secca.

Secca continued to speak, if in a low voice barely audible to the woman next to her at the railing. "They are defeated, and they return. Their ships are destroyed, and they build more. Their armsmen and lancers are slaughtered, and they raise more and return in greater force. They chain their daughters and consorts, and few beyond Ranuak seem to think it that ill. They tear out the tongues of women who essay sorcery . . ." She shook her head. "My own ruler . . . he would seek peace with such?" Secca swallowed, realizing that she had never mentioned that to Palian, or anyone but Alcaren. She added quickly, "And yet . . . to stop them . . . the only way to stop them . . . and thousands upon thousands died. Many were chained women, or children, helpless babes."

"It *was* terrible, and it is indeed terrible that it needed to be sung," Palian said, her voice firm. "What is more terrible is that few will see that it needed to be sung. They will claim that there must have been another way. Or that you could have threatened the Sea-Priests and forced them from Liedwahr. Some will say that you should have used the spell on some small isle to show its power." The older woman laughed softly, mournfully. "The Lady Anna showed the power of sorcery. As soon as she died, the Sea-Priests attacked. The Lady Clayre died. She did not die because she was a weak sorceress."

Secca turned. "You do not think Belmar was stronger?"

"Belmar had help from the Sea-Priests, it is true," Palian admitted. "The Lady Clayre did not understand that waiting benefits only the Sturinnese and their allies. Your consort said it well. Only you and the Lady Anna have attacked as swiftly as you could, and only you two have prevailed."

"We have not prevailed yet," Secca said.

"You are prevailing, my lady sorceress. You will fail only if you lose the will to prevail. Do not let false sympathy betray you, or all the women of Erde will be lost."

"But thousands upon thousands died . . ."

"Many more of those would have died in the wars that the Sturinnese would wage in the years to come. Many of those gloried in those wars and the spoils of such wars. Those who glory in war have little right to complain about how it is waged. We also have the right to live as we choose, do we not?"

"Yet . . ." mused Secca, "yet Lady Anna changed the way of living in Defalk, and Dumar, and Neserea, and killed many who did not want those changes. And I am no better." *No better at all.*

Palian laughed, ironically. "You could do far worse. Is Defalk a better place for all now? How would it be were the Sea-Priests to rule?"

"Is it always like this . . . having power?" asked Secca, knowing the answer, knowing no one, not even Palian, could absolve her of the guilt and pain.

"No. It is worse to have power and to do nothing. It is worse to have power and use it only to protect one's own lands and golds. It is worse to watch all fall around you, and to know that you might have changed it, but that you did nothing."

Secca winced.

"There are many things worse than what you have done, Lady Secca. I would that I never see them."

After a long and deep slow breath that seemed to burn as much as the light wind did on her skin, Secca turned, and said softly. "Thank you."

"She taught me that," Palian replied, "when I was your age. I have not forgotten."

Secca understood who had taught Palian. Secca also hoped she could hold to what the gray-haired chief player had said, because Palian had shared those thoughts not because the worst was over, but because it was yet to come.

93

WEI, NORDWEI

Ashtaar beckons for the seer to enter the private audience chamber, a chamber kept dim, despite the bright sunlight beyond the shutters and heavy hangings that shroud the window.

Escadra's demeanor is subdued, and she does not meet Ashtaar's dark and piercing eyes, either in approaching the Council Leader or in seating herself across the table-desk from Ashtaar.

"You have something to tell me?" asks Ashtaar.

"Yes, Leader." The seer pauses, then speaks quickly, as if she needs to say all the words at once so that she will not be interrupted. "Stura—there is little left of it. That is, the isle remains, but the northern section, where Inylt and the port of Stura were, it is covered with molten rock and ash, and it appears that few in the southern part escaped the ash and fumes." Escadra swallows.

"How did you discover such?" Ashtaar's voice is mild, as if she were asking about rotation patterns for the seers.

"You knew, Leader?" asks the Escadra.

"There was a great disruption in the harmonies," Ashtaar replies. "I did not know *what* caused it, but I was confident you would discover the cause. What created this disruption?"

"The Shadow Sorceress—we think. It has been most difficult," Escadra says slowly. "When we have tried to scry the Shadow Sorceress, we have seen but images of ourselves. So we have had to scry everything around her. The Ranuan ships are now headed eastward, we think toward Neserea, but they are too far at sea yet to tell."

Ashtaar frowns for a time.

The heavyset Escadra shifts her weight slightly in the straight-backed wooden chair and waits.

Abruptly, Ashtaar laughs. "She is using a ward that mirrors sorcery, or something like it." She shakes her head. "Few are skilled and strong enough to do that. Especially after creating such destruction. Few indeed." After a pause, she asks, "What else can you tell me?"

"The isle of Trinn is greatly damaged by waves, and smoke and ash fall on most all of the inner isles of Sturinn."

"Was there any sorcery to oppose the sorceress? Any ships to attack hers?"

"Only those which attacked near the Ostisles."

"Most strange. Most strange." Ashtaar covers her mouth with the heavy green cloth and coughs, if but once. Then she takes a sip from the beaker. "Dreadful draught. Hope you never have to drink it, Escadra."

"Yes, Leader."

Ashtaar laughs once more, a sound almost like a cackle. "All you young people think that you will be forever strong, that perhaps your hair will turn, but you will be strong enough and your minds will never wander, nor your lungs wheeze. It is not so. You either die young and strong, or live till you are old and weak. All die. The Maitre may well discover that in the weeks ahead."

"The Maitre? Did he not—"

"He could not have so perished. He would have used sorcery to protect Stura. Also, that would explain the most timely death of the Lord Belmar. Yes, it would. The Maitre is with the Sturinnese in Neserea, and he has been for some time."

"How—"

"It is easy to see such in hindsight, but never has a Maitre left Sturinn before. Never has one gone elsewhere and hidden himself. Why would anyone think of that? Until now." Ashtaar clears her throat yet again. "We had best hope that the shadowsinger returns swiftly."

"We?"

"The Maitre is most wroth, I would judge. He had no love of Liedwahr before this. Do you think he does not know what she has done?"

"We are not of Defalk."

"No. That means that he will ravage Neserea and Defalk, and then either Ranuak or Nordwei. That is, if the Shadow Sorceress does not stop him." Ashtaar sighs. "Write me a statement of what you have discovered. Have the scribes make ten copies for the Council meeting."

"Yes, Leader."

Ashtaar waves the seer toward the door.

Even before the seer has closed the door and departed, Ashtaar's head is tilted, and her dark eyes focus elsewhere, as her fingers idly stroke the dark agate oval on her table-desk.

94

Secca awoke with a start. The space in the bunk beside her was empty . . . and cool. Perhaps Alcaren had gotten too hot, or the pitching of the *Silberwelle* had made him uncomfortable enough that he had gone topside for some fresh air. She stretched and closed her eyes.

Even behind closed eyes, she could see once more the clouds of ash and the glowing of molten rock . . . and hear the screams and cries she had caused. *What were you supposed to do? Let them chain every woman in Liedwahr and*

*tear out the tongue of every one who might become a sor-
ceress? Or fight the good fight, but only so far, so that
someone else will have to fight it ten or thirty years from
now?*

Closing her eyes hadn't helped. Neither did staring at the
overhead. She still kept debating and arguing with herself.

Finally, she sat up and threw on the rest of her clothes,
ignoring the pain as her tunic scraped her blistered and still-
sore face. Her head throbbed more when she bent forward
to pull on her boots. Then she made her way out of the
cabin and up toward the bow. There, in the grayness before
dawn, she found Alcaren, on the starboard side, facing into
the occasional spray.

To the east, low in the sky, she could see both moons,
the white disc of Clearsong and the red point of light that
was Darksong, seemingly less than a yard apart in the sky.
She wondered if the near conjunction foreshadowed more
turmoil—or merely reflected what had happened.

"I couldn't sleep," he said.

"After you left, neither could I. I just kept thinking about
Stura."

"You did what had to be done."

"Did I?" she asked. "Could I have done it another way?"

"Yes," Alcaren said. "You could have tried to land, and
risked being killed. If you succeeded in landing, you would
have had to kill almost every man on the isles, probably
even some of the women, and you would have lost lancers
and players. By then, the Sturinnese in Neserea would have
gathered their lancers and their fleets and returned, and then
you would have been trapped, unless you created almost as
great a series of sorceries. And after all that, in another ten
years, or a score of years at most, the Sea-Priests would be
back trying to take Liedwahr with even greater sorcery.
That's what they've been doing for generations."

"I keep telling myself things like that. It doesn't help."

"No . . . it doesn't. It never does. We find it hard to accept that sometimes death and destruction are the only solutions if we want to survive."

"I don't know that this was the only solution," Secca replied.

"In a perfect world, it wasn't," Alcaren admitted. "But we don't have a perfect world. Your Lord Robero is weak and will sell you out to keep his throne. The Matriarch will not take on the Ladies of the Shadows. Lord Fehern would kill his brother to rule as a Sturinnese puppet, and nothing short of their total destruction will keep the Sea-Priests out of Liedwahr. They believe that their way is the only way—"

"And we believe ours is," Secca said.

"That's true." Alcaren paused. "But there is one big difference. You didn't invade Sturinn. You didn't try to conquer three lands that didn't believe as you do."

"Not at first, but . . ." Secca shook her head. The words always ended the same, and Stura was gone.

Alcaren reached out and squeezed her hand.

"What happens next?" Secca asked softly.

"We put our feet on solid ground, and I feel better," Alcaren replied, dryly. "In another week or longer."

Secca laughed softly. "I'm sorry that I've put you through this. I know you never wanted to go to sea again."

"The harmonies have a fine sense of humor," he replied.

"I meant after the battles and the sorcery," she said.

"You keep being a sorceress."

"And what about you?"

"You'll keep teaching me how to be a sorcerer. I hope you will."

Secca looked forward as the *Silberwelle* rode through a swell, spray flying past her, and fine droplets of saltwater mist settling on her. "Life isn't just about doing things."

"No, it's not," he said. "It requires us to do a lot so that we can have time, if we are fortunate, for other things, to enjoy each other, or to watch a sunset without worrying what it means for the battle ahead . . ."

"What other things? It seems so long since I've thought of anything but sorcery and Sea-Priests."

"Do you want children?" he asked softly.

Secca stood frozen. Children . . . she'd once hoped, but she'd seen how so many had grown up. She'd seen a boy named Jimbob go from a bully into a coward named Robero, despite everyone's efforts. She'd seen her own brothers turn cruel, and be poisoned by an even crueler uncle.

"You're afraid . . . aren't you?"

She could not look directly at him. "Do you?"

He smiled sadly. "I don't want them unless you do. You're too strong a person."

"Too strong a person?" Secca laughed. "Every time I do great sorcery, I almost die."

"That is not what I meant, my lady." He paused. "You know where my words lead."

Secca turned her head away. "I don't want to talk about it now. I can't." *How can I even think of children?*

95

Secca had gathered the eight in the captain's cabin in the early morning, hoping that the coolness of the day would help, but even so, the space was getting warm quickly, and her face, still tender, even warmer. As she stood by her seat, lutar in hand, she glanced around the circular table, and at two overcaptains and the two chief players who stood behind the chairs.

"We still have to deal with the Sturinnese in Neserea," Secca began, "and they have a fleet somewhere in the Bitter Sea."

"You don't believe that they'll sail away and let us port at Esaria?" Alcaren's voice carried a hint of mischief. "I cannot imagine why."

A few low chuckles followed his remarks. Palian shook her head, even as she smiled.

"I thought I'd try to show where those ships might be," Secca said, lifting her lutar.

"Show us now where'er the Sea-Priests ships may be
on a map that shows both Liedwahr and the Bitter
*   Sea . . ."*

After Secca's last words, the scrying glass in the middle of the captain's circular table silvered and darkened. The outlines of the map were barely visible against the silvered background of the scrying glass, even in the comparative dimness of the cabin.

Alcaren peered down at the image, finally pointing as he spoke. "They're in the southern part of the Bitter Sea, but not too near Esaria."

Secca sang the release spell and looked at her consort. "We also need to see how Esaria is faring." She sat down.

Alcaren eased himself out of his chair and checked the tuning on his lumand, before clearing his throat and singing.

"Show us now and in clear sight
Esaria in this morning's light . . ."

The second image was far brighter and clearer, but the scrying glass did not display the ordered structures and streets of a city, but of ruins, with thin trails of smoke rising from buildings smoldering on hilltops and pools of water scattered among what had been dwellings and shops and streets in the lower-lying lands. There was no sign of a waterfront or piers, just heaps of wreckage.

"Fire and flood," murmured Richina.

Secca's mouth almost dropped open in shock. *Why should you be shocked? Didn't you know that the Sturinnese would strike back?*

"The Nesereans did not do anything to them," Wilten said slowly.

"It is a message to us," Secca said.

"It's also a way of denying us any supplies in following them," Alcaren added.

"Following them?" blurted Richina.

"To Defalk," replied Alcaren. "That is how they think. They will not surrender. They will lay waste to all that they ride through, and they will try to destroy as much of Neserea and Defalk as they can." He cleared his throat and sang the release couplet.

The mirror blanked.

"How long before we could reach Esaria?" Secca looked at Denyst.

"Be but four days with good winds. The winds aren't the best this time of year. We're having to tack too much. Could be a week, or longer, if they don't change," replied the captain.

Secca nodded slowly before she spoke, addressing her words to the chief players. "We will need the first building song again, and we will use the storm spellsong against ships." She turned her head to face Denyst. "If we come in from the north, and they are the ones closest to the shore, will that make a difference?"

"Aye . . . if the storms you call keep heading south. Otherwise . . ."

"We'll have to go through what we did last time?" Secca said.

"Might not be so bad," replied Denyst. "Storms die out quicker in colder water. Don't see many this time of year that far north."

Secca nodded slowly. "I need to think. Until tomorrow . . . unless anyone has anything I should know about."

There were headshakes around the table, and Secca stood. So did everyone else.

After the others had filed out, Secca and Alcaren reseated themselves and looked at each other across the table.

"I feared, but I was not certain," she began. "They have already left Esaria . . ."

"We travel faster than do they, and the roads will be muddy. We will have a chance to catch them—"

"Who are 'they'?" Secca asked. "What sorcerer would destroy a city for so little—" She laughed bitterly. "I should ask that?"

"I wonder," mused Alcaren. "I wonder."

Secca frowned. "You wonder what?"

Her consort did not answer, but, instead, picked up the lumand and ran his fingers over the strings. After clearing his throat, he sang another scrying spellsong.

> *"Show me now and in day's clear light*
> *those whom for and with the Maitre fight . . ."*

The glass revealed a column of riders in white, riding eastward along a river road. Behind them, barely visible, rose trails of smoke from what Secca thought was a small hamlet.

"They are indeed scorching the earth," she noted, then she shook her head as she realized what else the image showed. "Of course! It makes sense. The Maitre was in Neserea all along. Do you think he was the one with Belmar?"

Alcaren shrugged and smiled. "He was that one, or one in the background."

"I should have seen that sooner." Secca shook her head.

"How would you know?" asked Palian softly. "All the great sorcery till now was done by Belmar? No one in Liedwahr has ever seen the Maitre—"

"I would guess that we could not," suggested Alcaren. "Let me try something else." His voice began another scrying song, this one asking to show the Maitre directly.

The mirror blanked, revealing only the timbers of the overhead.

"You see?" asked Alcaren.

"He's dead," suggested Delvor.

Secca shook her head. "We'd get blank silver with no image at all. As do we, he has wards." After a long pause, she added, "We have wards, and he has wards."

"Why does that bother you so much?" Alcaren asked.

"Because of where it leads," she answered. "We have wards, and so does he. We destroy Stura, and he destroys Esaria. Do you think he is destroying absolutely everything along the rivers?"

"Everything that does not take too much strength," Alcaren said. "He will not weaken himself too much. Also, someone must be holding the wards, and that sorcerer cannot use his strength for destruction."

"There must be a better way than following them." Secca frowned. "There must be . . ."

Alcaren tilted his head. "Let me think. We should also talk to Denyst and perhaps Palian."

"Older and wiser heads?" asked Secca.

"Wisdom and knowledge can save much effort," Alcaren pointed out. "Someone told me that." He grinned.

"And we have made enough mistakes that we could have avoided?" Secca jabbed back.

"No. But I think we could." His eyes twinkled.

"You are most difficult, my love."

"That is *most* necessary when one is consorted to a powerful sorceress."

For a moment, they both smiled.

96

MANSUUS, MANSUUR

The Liedfuhr of Mansuur stands in his undertunic before the desk of his private study. His sky-blue tunic is laid across the back of the desk chair. He holds a lancer's sabre and begins a series of exercises, then proceeds to fence, as if against an imaginary opponent. When he finally pauses, to wipe the sweat from his brow, there is a discreet knock on the study door.

"Yes?"

"Overcaptain Bassil, sire."

"Have him enter." Kestrin replaces the sabre in the scabbard at his belt. Then, he shrugs and takes off the sword belt, laying belt, scabbard, and sword in one of the chairs set at an angle to the desk. He does not redon the tunic, but blots his still-damp forehead once more before turning to address the lancer officer. "Yes, Bassil?"

"You said you wished me to let you know about the reports of great waves crashing over the piers at Wharsus and Landungerste . . . ?"

"Is it good news or bad? We could use a little of the former these days, if you could manage to supply it. That is, if it is at all possible in these troubled times." Kestrin offers a rueful smile, one that vanishes as quickly as it appeared.

"Yes, sire." Bassil bows, showing hair far more silver than it had been even weeks earlier. "It might be considered good news, of a sort."

"Of a sort?" questions Kestrin.

"Stura is no more. That is, it still stands in the middle of the isles, but nothing lives there. It is a seething, smoking expanse of molten rock and noxious gases."

"The volcanoes? You mean the harmonies acted for once?"

"No, sire. The harmonies had great assistance from the shadowsinger. Very great assistance."

"So she has destroyed their home defense fleet, and killed all who live on Stura, and poisoned their home isle so that none can live there?" The Liedfuhr raises his eyebrows. "Exactly how would this be considered good news?"

"Of a sort, sire. I recall that I said, of a sort." Bassil smiles blandly. "Her ships remain mostly intact, although the seers say she has lost one somewhere, and it appears as if she may be sailing to Neserea."

"Revenge will not bring back my sister and my niece, Bassil."

"No, sire. But your other niece lives, and if the sorceress can succeed in defeating the last remnants of the Sturinnese . . . it *may* be possible that she will survive and prosper."

"May? What will stop the shadowsinger after what she has done?"

"The largest of the Sturinnese fleets remains in the Bitter Sea, and it *appears* as though the Maitre himself is with the Sturinnese forces in Neserea."

"Appears?" Kestrin snorts. "Stop making me ask questions and just tell me."

"He and his sorcerers have flooded Esaria and ravaged it with firebolts. They ride eastward and have fired every town and hamlet through which they have passed, and the whole time he has maintained wards which keep a glass from seeing him and where he personally may be. I would judge that he will attack Defalk, or try to, before the Shadow Sorceress can return."

"So that he will turn as much of Liedwahr into burning ruins as he can? I cannot say that all this surprises me that much." Kestrin sighs. "We have sorceresses to our east who wish all women to have the powers of sorcerers and men, and we have Sea-Priests to our west who wish to put all women in chains, and we have the misfortune to be caught between them at a time when great and evil new sorceries are being discovered and used day by day."

"That is true, sire."

"What is worse is that the *best* that can happen is for the sorceresses to triumph."

Bassil nods sympathetically.

"My father had little to fret over, compared to this." Kestrin shakes his head. "What of our plans with the catapults and flaming oil?"

"Marshal Turek has been testing two types. They look

most promising." Bassil raises his eyebrows in inquiry.

"We will still need them, even if the Shadow Sorceress is successful with the last of the Sturinnese. The world will not change back to the way it was. We will need all manner of weapons that a man or small groups of men may use."

"I fear the world is changing faster than I can run, sire."

"That may be true for all of us, Bassil, and even more for the shadowsinger, but we must try." Kestrin shakes his head. "Why? Why could not the Maitre have let dozing dogs lie? Had he left Defalk alone, the sorceresses would have had less power over time."

"You think so? Or merely hope that it would have been so?"

The Liedfuhr laughs, ruefully. "Like all men, I hope for things that might have been. That, I admit. Do not we all so hope?"

97

In the midmorning, Palian, Denyst, Alcaren, Richina, and Secca sat around the table in the captain's quarters of the *Silberwelle*. The air had become decidedly cooler since the day before, for which Secca was grateful, since her face still burned at times. She was also trying to ignore the cramping and the nausea that plagued her—it seemed that she was reminded that she was indeed a woman when it was either dangerous or uncomfortable, if not both. She counted herself fortunate that she was merely uncomfortable.

Denyst stood, bathed in the grayish green light from the overhead skylenses. She looked down on the large chart. "The traders of Wei have always been fearful of being held hostage to but a single port. So they have maintained certain roads and wharfs in other cities. Seldom do they use them. It has cost them dearly to maintain the road from Wei to

Ostwye, but the waters off Ostwye are never frozen, and they value that. Likewise, the port at Sendrye affords not too difficult a trip to Wei, should there be a problem with the River Nord. Lundholn is something else. It was a trading port in the days of the Mynynans, and they say that the stone pier there dates back to the Spell-Fire Wars. Something else, too, about Lundholn. Used to be a trading outlet for the Corians when they held what's now the west of Nordwei. Was their only port, and when the traders forced them out . . . well, that was the beginning of their fall. There's still a good stone road that runs all the way to Morgen, and along the river to Vyel, and then down to Wei. The part that runs east from Morgen goes almost halfway to Nordfels . . ."

"What?" asked Secca, involuntarily.

Palian nodded as Secca spoke.

Secca looked to the older chief player. "Do you know how long the unpaved road is between the old stone road and Nordfels?"

"I do not," Palian replied, "but from what I have heard I would judge it to be fifty deks, no more than sixty. Still, that is a fair distance in the spring on unpaved roads. It might be faster to port at Wei."

"You might consider such, lady," added Wilten.

Secca turned to the captain. "Does your chart show that road?"

Denyst shook her head. "Could make a rough gauge." She took out a pair of calipers from somewhere and spread them, then eased one tip to a point east of Morgen. "If half the distance is on the river road and the road follows the river . . . then the whole distance is ninety deks, and no road runs truly straight. So I'd guess your chief player's thought is close." She frowned. "You still thinking of landing in Lundholn? With unpaved roads in spring?"

"We'll have to look at the old stone road to see what it looks like," Secca temporized. "But ships travel faster than horses, and we can't get provisions from towns flooded and burned out. We can also travel faster on paved roads at this time of year than the Sturinnese can on the muddy roads in eastern Neserea." As she finished speaking, Secca began to look for yet another clear space or yet another corner of her brown paper scraps where she could find a space to craft one more spellsong.

"You certain they'll keep heading east?" asked Denyst.

"About as certain as I am that the sun will keep rising. Vipers don't stop using their fangs." Secca found the grease marker and began to write.

The cabin turned silent, and Secca forced herself to concentrate on the spellsong.

Alcaren beckoned to the captain, then asked Denyst in a low voice, "How long from Esaria to Lundholn?"

"Anywhere from three days to a week or longer, depending on the wind and the seas. Could be longer, if there are too many ice floes."

"Thank you," he murmured in response.

Secca looked at the hasty spell, then stood and reclaimed the lutar from the net-covered bin beside the double-width bunk. After tuning the lutar, she pulled on the supple leather gloves with the copper-tipped fingers, cleared her throat, and offered the short scrying spellsong.

*"Show us in this glass that road of ancient stone
that leads to Morgen from the port of Lundholn,
the section that is the very best and strong . . ."*

The glass showed a narrow stone road flanking a hillside, half covered in snow, half in browned grass and grayish shrubs. The road was clear, and somehow reminded Secca of the road that had taken her the last fifty deks into Encora.

She glanced to Alcaren.

"Mynyan sorcery," he affirmed.

Secca repeated the spellsong, except with wording designed to find the worst section of the road. The image was not that different, except that the paving stones were cracked, and in one place several paving blocks were miss-

ing and the space had been filled in with smaller and far
more roughly cut stones.

A third spellsong followed, one with words about any part
of the road being blocked, but the glass came up blank and
silver. For that, Secca was glad, since she was getting a hint
of dizziness, the kind that preceded daystars across her vision, doubtless because she hadn't eaten that much earlier.
If she ate, at this time in her season, she felt nauseated. If
she didn't, she couldn't do sorcery without being exhausted
and feeling ready to faint.

"We may have to do some more scrying, but the road to
Morgen looks better than any other way to get back to Defalk."

"What about going to Wei? Like Palian, I worry about
the unpaved roads," said Richina. "It's closer to Defalk."

"It is," Secca admitted, "but it's actually east of Falcor,
and that means that we'd have to travel farther to get there.
Also, I'd hoped we could get to the western part of Defalk
so that we could head off the Sturinnese before they do too
much damage."

"Could we obtain permission from the Council of Wei?"
asked Palian.

"Would they be likely to try to stop you?" asked Denyst,
her voice dripping with irony. "You only want to get back
to Defalk to stop the Sturinnese before they try to take over
all of Liedwahr. Last time I checked the chart . . . Nordwei
was part of Liedwahr. Also, the Sea-Priests have never
shown much love of the northern traders."

At the dryness of the captain's tone, chuckles ran around
the table.

Secca smiled. "I'll have to do some more scrying and
thinking, and I'd like you all to think about it as well, at
least until this afternoon. I'll talk to each of you again before
we decide. The unpaved roads bother me, but so do the extra
deks from Wei."

"Best get back topside," said Denyst, nodding at Secca,

then slipping out through the door and along the passageway.

After the others left, Alcaren looked to Secca. "I have been thinking. Most of the roads in Defalk are for trading or going from Falcor to the borders. Yet there is a paved road that goes from Nordfels to Denguic?"

Secca laughed. "Lady Anna called it Lord Kinor's road. He became Lord of Westfort when I was only nine. He kept begging Lady Anna for a road between Denguic and Dubaria so that Lord Nelmor could get to the West Pass. That was because Nelmor was then Lord of the Western Marches. Then, after that was done, he and Nelmor suggested that, if there were a good road to Heinene, the grasslands riders could get—"

"So . . . she built the road just for them?" Alcaren's voice was not quite incredulous.

Secca shook her head. "Anna saw much. She saw that Hanfor was ruling Neserea because he was respected, and because Anna was, but that matters were changing little. At first, Anna had few lancers to station in the west, and later, Lord Robero did not consider Neserea a problem, and he did not station lancers to the west. So Anna started the road, and Jolyn and Clayre finished it. Clayre didn't mind it that much, because her sister Lysara is Lord Tiersen's consort, and she could work on the road and stay with her sister." Secca shrugged. "Most of that was done in the early years, and then Jolyn finished the section to Nordfels later, I think, just to get as far from Falcor as she could, and because she took Lord Ebraak's son Cassily as a lover for a time. But the road meant that the raiders could breed more horses, and that brought more golds, and Lord Ebraak could get more winterwine to Falcor . . . Anyway, the road is there, and it will take us south to the West Pass."

"In time?"

Secca sighed. "I would judge not. But . . . unlike Neserea, Defalk has many holds and keeps, and the Maitre cannot

destroy them all, or even most of those in the west, before
we reach him."

"What if he does not stop and travels straight to Falcor
on your wonderful roads?"

"Then we will catch him there, and there will be far less
destruction."

"You would rather see Falcor fall?"

Secca nodded. "Rather than all those lords and ladies who
have been faithful to Lady Anna and what she meant . . .
yes, I would." A crooked and sad smile crossed her lips.
"Believing so, I would judge that the Maitre would know
such also, and would destroy as much as he can on the way
to Falcor—or even to provoke us into undue haste to meet
him. Also, Jolyn is possibly in the west, and he would wish
to draw her into a conflict so that he could destroy her."
Secca paused. "We should send her a message once we
know our way and offer advice."

"Will she take it?"

Secca shrugged, her smile turning wistful. "At times she
has, but she will do as she will please."

This time Alcaren was the one to nod—slowly.

98

It was just past noon, and the two sorceresses and the
sorcerer sat around the captain's circular table. Frowning,
and trying to ignore her all-too-frequent cramping, as well
as the increasing pitching of the *Silberwelle*, Secca looked
up from the rough figures she had scrawled on the corners
of the paper.

"We have little choice," she finally said. "Lundholn it
must be."

"Lady . . ." ventured Richina, almost delicately, "how will
you know if we dare to land at Lundholn?"

"We ask," Secca replied with a laugh. "Very politely, and we send the request in a message tube."

"That will convey both courtesy and power, all in one," Alcaren pointed out. After a moment, he fingered his chin. "To whom can you send it?"

"They have a Council," Secca replied. "Let us see if the glass will recognize such." She stood and stretched, then reclaimed the lutar. After checking the tuning, she pulled on the playing gloves, and launched into the scrying spellsong.

"Show us so clear and bright in this glass
the leader of the Council of Wei in all that may
*   pass . . ."*

The glass immediately showed a silver-haired woman seated before an ebony table desk, one hand resting on a polished oval dark agate, the other clutching a cloth. Even through the glass, the Council Leader seemed to shimmer with an inner force.

Secca studied the woman for a moment, then sang the release spell. "After I send the scroll, Alcaren can use the glass to make sure she is the one who receives it." After setting aside the lutar, Secca glanced at Richina, taking in her still-drawn face and the dark circles that persisted under the eyes of the younger sorceress. "You need to get something more to eat and then to rest."

"I'm feeling better," Richina protested.

"You need to feel much better," Secca replied.

"I feel so useless. You and Alcaren do everything."

Secca shook her head. "We do everything only because you keep us safe from sorcery sent against us from a distance. How many times have you sensed someone probing at you and the wards?"

"Every day . . . sometimes more often," admitted the younger woman.

"Could we do anything were you not holding the wards?" Secca fixed her amber eyes on Richina.

A wan smile crossed the blonde's lips. "I would wager not. But still . . ."

"Enough," said Secca firmly. "Find something to eat and then get some sleep. Go!" She motioned for Richina to depart.

Richina smiled mischievously as she eased out of the chair.

"What?" asked Secca.

"It's just . . ." Richina stopped.

Secca raised her eyebrows.

"You could have been Lady Anna the way you said all that." Richina bowed. "Sometimes, you are so like her, Lady Secca."

For a moment, Secca could say nothing. Finally, she replied, "You credit me too much, Richina. Now, off with you."

"Yes, lady." Richina smiled warmly, and then turned and slipped out of the cabin.

Secca shook her head as she began to rummage through the stack of materials.

"You do not think you resemble her?" asked Alcaren.

"Me? Hardly. She was tall; I'm small. She was blonde and beautiful; I'm plain and petite. She was strong and forceful; I still do not know what I do half the time—" She stopped as Alcaren held up his hand.

"You are most beautiful, and others have said so besides me. You are indeed strong and forceful, and size has nothing to do with that. And I imagine that the Lady Anna often felt that she did not know what she was doing or where it would lead when she was faced with rebellions and invasions. You saw her from the view of a child looking at her mother. How could she not have been wonderful?" He laughed warmly. "You are all the things you say you are not, and in time, Richina . . . or . . . others . . . they will look at you in the way you looked at Lady Anna."

Secca shook her head once more. "I need to find some parchment or vellum." She leafed through the papers on the table another time, then looked into the covered bin.

"You have no more parchment left?" asked Alcaren.

The redheaded sorceress shook her head. "We are short on much."

"Find one of those scrolls sent to you that you can do without. We will have to make a palimpsest. I can do that while you put down your thoughts."

Secca turned to one of the saddlebags, opening it, and checking the scrolls one by one, then stopping and handing one to Alcaren.

He looked at it and then smiled. "Perhaps it is best that these words of Jolyn be erased."

"I thought so." Secca reseated herself at the table.

Alcaren began to sharpen his belt knife.

"You don't mind doing that?" Secca asked as she leaned forward, looking for a section of paper on which to draft her thoughts.

"It's simple work," he replied. "Much easier than scrying or composing a scroll to the Council Leader. It also keeps me from recalling that I am upon a ship."

"You're doing better, I think."

"No. We have been fortunate that the weather has not been too bad, except at times."

"The times when I created storms."

Alcaren shrugged. "Better to feel uneasy than to have been sunk by the Sea-Priests."

Secca laughed gently. "I'd better get to writing this. I want a few days of rest after sending it."

Alcaren nodded, then bent forward, using the new-sharpened edge of the knife to scrape away the dark ink, letter by letter, line by line, until the parchment appeared to have been used not at all. He studied the apparently clean surface, then took the knife and went back over several sections.

By then, Secca was straightening. "Would you read this?"

"I'd be happy to." He wiped the knife blade before

sheathing it, then took the rough brown paper sheets from his consort.

As Alcaren read, Secca stood behind him and reread the lines.

> . . . the Maitre of Sturinn is laying waste to Neserea . . . heading toward Defalk and will most likely turn north to Nordwei . . . if he is not halted . . . Stura has been destroyed and will not pose a threat for generations to come—if the Sturinnese forces in Liedwahr are destroyed . . .

> Therefore, we are requesting your permission to land at Lundholn and disembark our forces to travel south along the road to Morgen and from there to Nordfels . . . quickest route to reach Defalk, and speed is most necessary . . .

> We have some limited golds with which to purchase supplies and quarters, as necessary, and will pledge not to forage off your people . . . If you and your Council agree, we would suggest that you raise a pale blue banner on a pole at the end of the pier in Lundholn, where it can be seen easily by glass or from a vessel . . .

When he finished, Alcaren looked up. "It is good. Perhaps . . . you might consider a few words about how Wei and Defalk have been such good neighbors in recent years, and how you look forward to that continuing once the Sturinnese are vanquished."

"Implying that if they don't let us use their roads, they'll have far worse neighbors?"

"I had thought that," he admitted. "So should they."

"So they should," Secca agreed. "Is there aught else?"

He shook his head. "Not so far as scrolls might go . . ."

His eyes flicked past her toward the double bunk.

"We will see, dearest consort, *after* the scroll is written and dispatched." Despite the sternness of her words, she could not help flushing, and hoped that the lingering redness of her face covered it, even as she tried to hide a smile.

99

WEI, NORDWEI

Ashtaar looks neither surprised nor even puzzled when the bronze tube appears upon her table-desk, although she has to fumble with the green cloth and another she takes from the single drawer in the table in order to pry off the cap of the tube of blistering metal.

She ignores the burns on the wood and the slight reddening on one aged hand as she reads the brief scroll. After she finishes reading, she begins once more until she comes to a line, which she murmurs aloud, if but to herself, "we are requesting your permission to land at Lundholn . . ." After a single barklike laugh, she says, "At least, she is requesting."

After rerolling the scroll, she takes the small bell from the drawer and rings it—twice. She does not have to wait long before the door opens, and Escadra appears.

"You rang, Leader Ashtaar?"

"I am calling an immediate meeting of the Council. At the sixth glass."

"Leader . . . this is six-day. Many will not be—"

"Then they will not be there. This cannot wait."

Escadra bobs her head up and down.

"You may tell those who are in Wei that I am not losing my mind or my temper, but that it concerns the threat of invasion of Nordwei by the Maitre. If they wish no part of the decision, why then, I will act in the Council's name."

The chunky seer's eyes widen.

Ashtaar stands. "Since it takes me longer than once it did to walk to the other end of the building, I will begin now." She smiles politely, but her dark eyes are cold.

Escadra bows quickly. "Yes, Leader. I will find all those that I can and send messengers for the others."

"Only if they are in Wei."

The seer nods once more and scurries out.

Ashtaar, for all her words about age, leaves her small audience chamber and study briskly. She walks quickly along the dark-paneled corridor until she comes to the steps. Her sole concession to age is her use of the handrail as she descends.

She is the first counselor to reach the Council chamber, but Escadra has sent word to someone, because the oil lamps in the bronze wall sconces are all lit. With a nod, Ashtaar takes the center place at the long dark table and sits down to wait.

The Lady of the Shadows is the next to arrive in the Council chamber, and she bows to Ashtaar. "Did I not tell you that the Sorceress Protector of Defalk would cause great difficulty?"

"You did, but I believe she is going to cause great difficulty for the Maitre, as I will explain when all are here who choose to come."

"It should be most interesting, especially on how you plan to keep us out of the problem after our fleet has acted as a decoy for the sorceress."

Ashtaar but nods as a second member of the Council appears—Marshal Zeltaar, wearing a black informal uniform. The marshal seats herself to the left of Ashtaar without speaking.

Next is High Trader Fuhlar, who swirls off a hooded golden cloak to reveal his customary apparel—brown trousers with gold piping, and a rich brown tunic also trimmed with gold. He hangs the cloak on one of the ancient wooden pegs set beside the door for such a purpose, and surveys the table, then takes a position directly across from the marshal.

Three others ease in, but only the third—a hard-faced blonde woman wearing dark green and silver—turns and speaks. "I trust this will be well worth our time, Ashtaar."

"Oh, it will, Adgan. Even you, I think, will find it so." Ashtaar surveys the chamber. "There are enough for us to proceed."

"This is most irregular," offers the brown-clad Fuhlar. "On a six-day, late on a six-day, no less."

Ashtaar holds up a heat-tarnished bronze tube. "So is this. Do any of you recognize what this might be?"

Fuhlar shakes his head. The hint of a smile plays across Marshal Zeltaar's mouth, but she does not speak.

The Lady of the Shadows is the one to break the silence. "I would gather it is a message tube, one that a sorceress could employ to send a message a great distance. That you have it means that the Shadow Sorceress has sent it to you, and that greater mischief is brewing."

"A message from the Shadow Sorceress?" questions Adgan. "A mere message—"

"As the lady has suggested," Ashtaar states firmly, interrupting Adgan, "this message arrived by sorcery. We have known that the Sea-Priests will sometimes send messages engraved on brass by sorcery. I had not known that the sorceresses of Defalk also had found a way to do the same—"

"How can they without the paper—"

"They use parchment, which resists heat far better than paper, and they send it in this bronze tube lined with a gray substance that keeps the tube from getting hot enough to char the parchment. That is not the reason for the meeting. The message request is. The sorceress is requesting passage through Nordwei to return to Defalk. She is requesting the use of the stone road from Lundholn to Morgen, and thence to Nordfels. The Sea-Priests are using sorcery to destroy all of Neserea. Every span of land along the Saris River has been burned to ashes. The Sea-Priests are beginning to do the same as they follow the road along the River Saria toward Elioch."

"Why does she want—"

"Insane . . ."

"Cannot let her . . ."

"Quiet!" snaps Ashtaar. "She knows of the old paved road from Lundholn to Morgen. She would take the pass to Nordfels, and then the metaled road created by the great sorceress down to Denguic. As I told you two days ago, the Shadow Sorceress has destroyed all the cities and half the land on the isle of Stura. This is a grave insult to any man of Sturinn"—Ashtaar laughs, a hard and ironic sound—"and the Sturinnese have gone mad. There is a great sorcerer, perhaps the Maitre himself, in Neserea. The sorceress would use our roads to get to hers to head off and attack the Sturinnese. She pledged to pay for provisions and not to forage off our people."

"Even if we do agree to this . . ." asks Fuhlar, "how would we let her know we accept?

"She requests that we fly a plain blue banner on a tall staff at the end of the pier in Lundholn."

"How—?"

"She will see it in her glass," Ashtaar says tartly. "We need to decide. Do we give the sorceress the means to stop this insanity on her lands before it gets farther out of hand, or do we refuse her passage and have both Defalk and Sturinn at our throats?"

"I do not believe—" begins Fuhlar.

"You're an ass, Fuhlar, if you think it stands any other way," snaps Ashtaar.

"While I would not use such terms," adds the lady in black, "I do believe that the Council Leader has stated this situation accurately."

"You who oppose all sorcery would allow a sorceress to cross Nordwei?" asks Adgan.

"That is why," replies the Lady of the Shadows. "These two will fight a terrible sorcerous battle. Nothing we can do will stop that. Therefore, the sooner this battle is fought, and the farther from Nordwei, the less we will suffer."

"You have said little, marshal," said Fuhlar, almost winningly.

"What else is there to say?" asks the officer in her black uniform. "We could not stop the sorceress if we wished, and we would lose all the lancers we could send against her. She has pledged not to harm our people and to pay for what she takes. She is desperate to reach Defalk before it is totally destroyed. Would *you* stand in her way?"

"Ah . . . no." Fuhlar frowns, then adds, "but could we not refuse to grant her permission, but not actually oppose her. That way, if the Sturinnese do prevail . . ."

"We could claim we were invaded?" suggests Marshal Zeltaar.

"While that sounds most reasonable," Ashtaar replies, "it is stupid and foolish. The Sturinnese hate us already, not because of our allies, but because we are ocean traders and rivals. Should they defeat the sorceress, they will destroy us whether we support her or not. We gain nothing by refusing permission, and should the sorceress win, we well may lose far more."

Fuhlar had begun to open his mouth, but he does not finish whatever he might have said and closes it abruptly.

"Exactly," the marshal concludes. "We might also be best served by sending messengers to Lundholn and Morgen to tell all those there, and to suggest that the merchants and chandlers offer a fair price. They should not give away goods, but at this time, it is not a good idea to charge in excess."

"But . . ." protests Fuhlar, "we should not even profit from our generosity?"

"You will profit, Fuhlar," Ashtaar says smoothly. "We will not have to fight on our lands, even if the worst occurs, until much later. If the sorceress wins, we will control all the trade in the Western Sea, and that should be more than enough profit for any of your trading cronies."

Fuhlar looks down at the table.

"There is one more matter—the heirs of Dumar and Neserea. Marshal Zeltaar had agreed to provide them transport, but we now have a quicker alternative that will send them farther from the Maitre, as well as upon the ocean while the conflict proceeds."

"Why . . . ?"

"Again, it cannot hurt," Ashtaar says, "especially if the Shadow Sorceress does not know, and there should be no reason for her to learn."

"You could turn them over to her," suggests Fuhlar.

"I dislike having all coins in a single strongbox, and so should you."

The trader nods reluctantly.

"I gather we are agreed," Ashtaar says. "I will have messengers sent to Lundholn and Morgen."

Not a single figure seated around the table objects.

100

S ecca had her green leather riding jacket fastened as she stood near the bow of the *Silberwelle*, beside Alcaren. The swells had increased once more, and the water of the Northern Ocean was a dark blue that seemed almost black, even in the midday sunlight. The spray from the bow was fine and chill, almost like mist, and she had to blot it off her face frequently—and gently. To the south, she could make out a fine dark line on the horizon—the northeastern coast of Mansuur, east of the Circle of Fire.

"I know we travel faster than if we rode," she said to her consort, "yet I feel we do nothing. Before long we will have to deal with the Sturinnese fleet, and that will take time . . ." Her words faded into the chill breeze.

"Need we deal with them?" asked Alcaren. "If they remain to the south, close to Esaria, then we could sail directly to Lundholn."

Secca's brows wrinkled in thought. "That would leave them behind us, and once we disembarked, there would be little protection for the ships."

"If they were far enough south—"

"Then we could disembark and Denyst could leave," Secca finished his sentence. "The Sturinnese would not dare to chase her ships and leave the Maitre unsupported." *Yet who truly knows what they would do?*

"That might be."

"And it might not." Secca shook her head. "When we go below, we will use the glass and see where the ships are—if we can." She shivered, and reached up to refasten her riding jacket against the chill. "It's colder now."

"It is, and the water will get even colder now that we are close to the Bitter Sea," Alcaren said, his eyes still looking eastward at the empty sea before them. "Does the cold air help your face?"

"It feels better in the chill air. I don't know as it helps much. I'll still have scars, I fear," Secca replied.

"You may not. Even the lines where Fehern threw the acid-water are beginning to fade."

The sorceress shook her head. "I still cannot say I understand his acts."

"You understand, my lady." Alcaren's tone is wry.

"Oh . . . I *know* why he did what he did—just as I know why the Sturinnese act as they do. But I cannot say that I understand within my heart why they take such pleasure in forcing others to do as they wish, or in wanting to make sure women have little power and less say in how matters are run. Some of it makes little sense. Lord Robero would have nothing, were it not for the sorceresses. He would be dead and have been lying in an unmarked grave for nearly thirty years. Yet, he listens to those who counsel him against sorceresses?"

"We all believe what we wish to believe," Alcaren said.

"I know, and that also is frightening. How much do I delude myself into believing what I do is good, because that is what I wish to believe?"

"At least you ask such questions." Alcaren laughs. "The Sea-Priests follow their beliefs without questioning, and without looking at the world beyond."

"Is that our weakness?" mused Secca. "Those who try to do what is right . . . are we always at a disadvantage because of our doubts, while those who never question their beliefs can justify anything to further what they believe?"

"That is possible," Alcaren replied. "But is it not better to question than to accept blindly?"

"I wonder. Because I question, and must suppress my own doubts in order to act, then do I act more harshly to overcome both my own doubts and my adversaries?"

"You ask hard questions, my lady. But in the end, you must act."

"I know." Secca sighed. "In the end, refusing to decide is every bit as much a decision and an action as acting."

"Sometimes, refusing to act," he pointed out, "creates more death and hardship than acting, however harsh those actions may seem. Would not many more have died and suffered had you not acted to save Elahwa? Would not many more have suffered and died had you not destroyed the Sturinnese in Dumar?"

Secca nodded slowly. "Yet . . ."

Alcaren laughed again. "Yet never can we prove the dangers and deaths that might have been. Never can we prove how awful might have been the alternative, not without allowing it to occur."

"And that we cannot do," Secca said slowly, reflecting. Anna had been right there, too, as in so many things. To make decisions for others meant having to take the responsibility—and the blame—even when matters would have been far, far worse without the action.

"No. We cannot."

Secca looked eastward, wondering how long it would be before they neared the Sturinnese ships—and what else might be required of her and Alcaren.

101

Even after the *Silberwelle* entered the Bitter Sea, the swells remained heavy, but regular and long. The water stayed dark, and the sky turned to a hazy overcast, leaving the poop deck where Alcaren and Secca stood damp and chill. Keeping one hand on the taffrail, Secca glanced aft. A dek or so behind the *Silberwelle* followed the *Schaumen-flucht*, and then farther aft was the *Liedmeer*.

Denyst checked the heading and studied the helmswoman briefly before turning back to the couple. "This heading, the way the wind is swinging, we could make better time if we didn't have to turn south to deal with the Sturinnese. That course would bring us right into the teeth of the wind before long."

"Let us see if they will come to us," Secca suggested.

Alcaren nodded slowly.

"You think they will?" asked Denyst.

"I've been thinking about it. We've looked in the glass, and their ships are close to Esaria," Secca said. "I don't know, but we could save several days if we did not have to go all the way to Esaria, could we not?"

"That we could . . . but I would not wish to be caught unloading at Lundholn," Denyst said dryly. "The wind there makes leaving the harbor long and tricky. Or so it is said."

"I don't think that will happen," Secca said. "If the Maitre is trying to destroy Neserea and then Defalk, and we look

to be sailing past Esaria, what would you do if you were
the fleet commander? Let us sail blithely by?"

Denyst laughed.

"What if they do?" questioned Alcaren.

"Then . . . we'll have to come back later and destroy the
fleet. Right now, it has done as much damage as it can to
much of Liedwahr. That is not true of the Maitre."

"For that reason, you think that they will sail north to
attack us?" asked Denyst.

"The Sea-Priests are angry," Secca pointed out. "If we
seem to be avoiding them, they would have to believe that
we either fear them or wish to avoid them. If they think we
fear them, then they may be bolder to attack. If they think
we wish to avoid them to make haste to Defalk, will the
Maitre let those ships sail a useless picket and do nothing?"

"When you tell it that way," Denyst said, "it seems likely
that they will come to us."

"I'd wager golds on it."

"I don't think I'd wager against that." Denyst laughed.

"We'll have to keep a close watch on their ships in the
glass," Alcaren added, swaying on his feet as the *Silberwelle*
pitched forward, then up and into a heavier swell. Some of
the spray from the bow drifted far enough aft to mist down
across the three by the helm platform.

"We can do that," Secca said.

"They'd be trying a stern chase, as well, and that will
give you more time to use your sorcery when it suits you
and not them." Denyst inclined her head. "You set on this?"

Secca nodded.

"Then, if you'd excuse me, I'd like to check the charts
for a bit. We could angle more northeast and pick up more
speed . . . as I recall." With a nod, the mistress of the *Silberwelle* slipped away.

Secca grasped the taffrail firmly as the ship nosed down
between swells, more steeply than before, waiting for another misting of spray.

"This war has changed," Alcaren mused.

"Oh?"

"When it began, you and all of Liedwahr needed to react to the Maitre. Now, you are forcing him to react to you."

"Only in this one matter," Secca pointed out.

"More than just this. By burning towns and hamlets in Esaria, he is acting as much in rage as in calculation."

"Perhaps . . ." Secca conceded. "Perhaps." *What if he is not? What if he is the one forcing us to react? Yet . . . ?* There was so much yet that she did not know, could not know, and they were racing toward Lundholn, without having seen, yet, any signal that the traders of Wei would allow them to land uncontested. *You hope you don't have to make that choice, either.*

Secca gripped the taffrail even more firmly, and not just because of the motion of the ship.

102

ALONG THE RIVER SARIA, NESEREA

A warmish wind wafts over the two Sea-Priests who stand at the hillcrest, looking down at the hamlet below.

In the late afternoon, a cordon of mounted lancers surrounds the score of cottages and hovels. All have their swords unsheathed. A squad of lancers approaches each dwelling. The process is quick—and efficient. Any man or male child is dragged out and cut down, his body left on the bloodstained dirt. The women's hands are bound, and each is tied into a long coffle that has already begun the march up the hill to the Sturinnese camp.

"They will serve us, one way or another," the Maitre observes.

As the last of the women is tied into the coffle, Sturinnese squad leaders apply torches to the hovels, the cottages, and the barns and outbuildings.

The Maitre nods and turns, walking back across the hill-crest to his tent. The wind that ruffles the panels of the Maitre's tent, as he enters it, also brings with it the odor of burning wood . . . and the sweet-acrid smell of other materials burning as well. The Maitre seats himself on a camp stool, ignoring the sounds and smells from the hamlet to the west, as he considers the maps spread on the camp table.

A time later, jerClayne enters the tent and clears his throat.

After a moment, the Maitre looks up from the maps. "Yes?"

"Fleet Marshal jerStolk has sent a plate requesting your instructions," offers jerClayne. Mud spatters dot his boots and white riding trousers.

"He had instructions," snaps the Maitre. "What problem has he with them? Must I spell out everything to everyone?"

"The ships carrying the Shadow Sorceress are on a course to bypass Esaria, and appear to be heading to Wei," replies the younger Sea-Priest, his voice carefully neutral. "He will have to sail north to engage them." After a moment, he adds, "We have used the glass, and that seems to be so. The Ranuan vessels are on a northeasterly heading."

"Why would she bypass Esaria?" the Maitre muses. "Has she given up on retaking Neserea . . . ?"

"Perhaps she knows that we will leave her no supplies or provisions," suggests jeClayne.

"She could take another route, even if it were slower . . ." The Maitre stops. "The bitch . . . the devious bitch. Speed! I should have thought of that. Ships are faster. The Council of Wei is in league with her. That's why their fleet was in the Ostisles. So she can sail to Wei and take the river roads, and then the metaled roads of Defalk . . ."

The hollow-cheeked jerClayne sways slightly on his feet, then stifles a yawn, waiting. Finally, he speaks. "Ser . . . instructions?"

"Send a plate back telling him to attack, but using the group tactics. He must at least delay her. He should know that. And tell him to destroy her ships!"

"Yes, ser." The tall and ever-thinner Sea-Priest coughs, then asks. "And what will we do, then?"

"Keep as we are. Time is still on our side. While we must reduce Neserea to rubble, we will still be in Defalk in two weeks. Even if she avoids the fleet, she cannot be out of Wei by then. She will gain some time, but little enough." He shakes his head. "Make it clear to jerStolk that she must not escape him."

"Yes, ser."

"Why must I spell out everything in letters large enough for the least intelligent of schoolboys and acolytes?"

JerClayne says nothing.

"Well . . . go and have the plate made and sent—quickly."

The younger Sea-Priest bows and departs.

The Maitre looks down at the maps, his expression between a glare and a frown.

103

Bright as the early-afternoon sun shone in the blue southern sky, little of its warmth reached Secca where she stood beside the helm platform, between Alcaren and Denyst. The heavier swells of the days previous had subsided into long and low masses of water that rose and fell far less than a yard. The wind had dropped to little more than a light breeze, just enough to keep the sails of the *Silberwelle* taut.

"Might not be that long." Alcaren gestured toward the south. "But the lookouts haven't spotted sails yet."

"They will be there," replied Secca. "The glass showed sails filled with wind."

"Sorcery," added Denyst. "Wind's so light we're barely more than making headway."

"They can't use sorcery for everything," Secca said. *You hope they can't.*

"They'll do anything to stop you, sorceress," suggested the ship mistress.

"I know." Secca cleared her throat. "We need to warm up." She glanced forward.

The players had begun to assemble below on the main deck, and a few discordant bowings and off-tune horn notes drifted aft.

Secca coughed, and began slowly. "Holly-lolly-lolly . . ."

Alcaren slipped away to the port side, where, more quietly, he began to warm up, his vocalises clearly better than in weeks previous.

The sorceress was midway through a second vocalise when the cry came from the yards above. "Sail ho! Starboard quarter."

Secca finished the second vocalise and then a third before she turned and strained to see the vessels that the lookouts had reported and that Alcaren had earlier discovered in the scrying glass, but either her eyes were not sharp enough, or the Sturinnese ships were at the edge of vision and she was too short—or both.

"Sail to the south and to the west, still closing, Lady Sorceress. You were right." The captain of the *Silberwelle* gave an off-center smile. "How many ships do they have?"

"The glass showed close to threescore, but there were no more than five in any one group and each group was deks from any other group."

"And each group has at least one sorcerer, I would wager," Alcaren added.

"Are they all to the south?" asked the captain. "The lookouts only see sail there."

"To the south and west."

The sounds of the players tuning rose from the main deck, drifting aft to Secca and Alcaren, only to die away abruptly.

"First warm-up, at my mark," ordered Palian. "Mark!"

As the warm-up song filled the air, Secca walked forward across the poop deck, until she stood just aft of the railing overlooking the main deck. From there, she watched, her eyes finding Bretnay, and then Elset, the woodwind player. Both looked to be in good form.

Alcaren stepped up beside her, offering an inquiring gesture toward the south. "How much longer before we must spellsing?"

"I do not know. They're closing but slowly, and that bothers me. What if they have some sorcery that strikes from even more distance than does our storm spell?"

"They could," he said, "but I cannot imagine what that might be."

"That does not mean they do not have such."

Alcaren nodded slowly.

The two glanced to the starboard side of the poop deck where Richina stood, a faint smile on her face, a face somehow older than before. Secca wondered just what it was that made the younger sorceress look older, but her thought was interrupted by a distant, whistling roaring that slowly grew until it rose over the sound of the players' warm-up tune, its intensity seeming to vibrate the very deck of the *Silberwelle*.

Alcaren stiffened.

Secca glanced to the south, but saw nothing, then turned aft, to the west, but saw nothing except for the sails of the other Ranuan ships. A *hissing* roar shook Secca as *something* passed overhead, coming not from the south, but out of the northeast. A gout of water geysered into the air less than a dek to the south of the *Silberwelle*, and even as the spout subsided a froth of steamy fog formed above the dark blue waters of the Bitter Sea.

Secca watched for a moment, openmouthed, but the fog began to shred and dissipate within moments. "Huge fireballs . . . What . . . what kind of sorcery . . . is that?"

Another whistling roar began to rise out of the north.

"We need to sing. Now!" She turned and took three steps toward the railing overlooking the main deck where, below her, the players had finished the warm-up—or perhaps Palian had halted it.

Alcaren followed and drew up beside her at the railing.

As if Palian had not a care in all Erde, the chief player called up to Secca, "Your players stand ready."

"The first building song—on your mark!" Secca ordered.

"The first building song, on my mark. Mark!"

Alcaren coughed, as if trying to clear his throat, caught unaware, but somehow his baritone was there, matching and joining Secca, with the beginning of the words of the spell-song.

"Water boil and water bubble
like a caldron of sorcerers' trouble . . . "

In the moments when Secca was singing the last words of the first stanza, the second fireball roared overhead, so close to the *Silberwelle* that Secca could feel the heat, and with such a rush of wind that she found herself swaying on her feet. Somehow, she managed to keep the words, images, and rhythm all together as she and Alcaren began the second stanza. So did the players.

A dull *boom* shivered the *Silberwelle*. Even with that, the players did not falter, and the two singers continued with the spellsong. Secca concentrated especially on waterspouts spread widely enough to destroy the scattered Sturinnese vessels as she came to the last phrases.

". . . crewed by those in Sea-Priest white
and let none escape the water's might!"

The by-now-too-familiar sounds of wind and water and forming storms began to rise, even over the hissing of another gout of steam rising out of the dark waters of the Bitter Sea aft of the *Silberwelle*. Three patches of mist obscured the view so that she could not see clearly the other Ranuan vessels.

In the distance between Secca and the groups of sails that were the Sturinnese, dark spouts began to form, first as hazy patches of air, then as darker wedges, and finally as black funnels rising out of the dark waters of the Bitter Sea. The funneled waterspouts seemed darker ... more menacing than those Secca had raised in the isles of Sturinn.

Secca gripped the railing, exhausted, just hanging on, as the skies continued to darken, and the wind to rise, whipping her short red hair around her face. Her head and body ached, and daystars flashed before eyes that had trouble focusing.

Alcaren stood beside her, breathing deeply, also with both hands on the railing.

"Lady Sorceress!"

At the words from the Ranuan ship mistress, Secca turned.

"Those fireballs." Denyst was shouting to lift her voice above the rushing and roaring of the winds. "Struck two of ours. One was the *Liedmeer*. Can't tell about the other. Will there be any more?"

Rather than fight the wind and strain her voice, Secca offered an exaggerated shrug. *You hope there won't be, but who knows?*

"Sorceress!" The ship mistress suddenly jabbed a hand in the direction of Secca's right. "There!"

Secca turned to see Richina sprawled on the deck, the younger woman's body sliding toward the railing. Alcaren moved first, darting around Secca and reaching the fallen sorceress just before Secca did.

Needle-like droplets of rain began to sting Secca's exposed neck and face, and the skies continued to darken. The roaring of the wind took on a howling overtone.

"Get her below! Best get everyone below!" Denyst called. "Another blow coming. Won't be so bad as the last, but won't be easy."

"Clear the decks!" came a call from somewhere. "Clear the decks!"

"Storm rigging! Storm rigging!"

"Players below!" ordered Palian, a rasping edge to her voice.

Alcaren lifted Richina, almost as if she were a child, although the younger woman was as tall as he was. "Go! Wait at the bottom of the ladder in case I need help."

Secca hesitated.

"Now!"

With a quick look backward, the redheaded sorceress turned and made for the ladder, squinting to make her way through the increasingly heavy rain and the daystars that flashed in front of her eyes. By the time she was on the main deck, Alcaren was at the top, Richina over his shoulder. He started down.

His boots came down hard on the planks of the main deck, and Secca reached out to steady him as he turned toward the hatch door that led aft. Secca held the door, and Alcaren carried the limp form into the passageway and then into the first small cabin.

Palian appeared in the passageway behind Secca. "If you would let me see her, lady?"

"Of course." Secca stepped back, flattening herself against the bulkhead.

The chief player and healer slipped into the small cabin behind Alcaren, who had laid Richina on the lower bunk. He slipped back as the chief player entered. The space, Secca judged, was barely larger than one of the wardrobes in Lord Robero's suite in Falcor, and she stood in the doorway because there was no space for her to enter.

"What happened?" asked Palian.

"After the fireballs flew by," Alcaren said, "while we were singing the spellsong, she collapsed." He glanced up at Secca.

Secca opened her mouth. For a moment, no words came as she realized what must have happened. Finally, she spoke. "Those . . . fireballs . . . they were sorcery . . ."

"The wards?" asked Alcaren.

"They kept them from hitting the *Silberwelle*," Secca said.

"But not the other ships?"

Secca had no answer, but had to reach out and brace herself against the bulkhead as the *Silberwelle* listed to port, then pitched forward.

"She's breathing, Lady Secca," Palian said, "but she is very weak."

"Chief player," Alcaren said. "Can the players perform the ward spell?"

Palian looked up, and Secca turned.

"We need the wards, it is clear," her consort said quietly. "Lady Richina has done all she can for now. I must hold them."

The redheaded sorceress finally nodded.

"In a few moments . . ." began Palian.

The *Silberwelle* pitched forward, this time abruptly enough that Alcaren had to brace himself against the bulkhead to avoid slamming into Secca.

"After the storm subsides," Secca suggested. "We would lose players and more on the deck now." She doubted that anyone would be doing much sorcery for the next few glasses. *You hope so.* Repressing a sigh, she looked back toward Palian and the unconscious Richina.

"She will recover," predicted the chief player.

Secca hoped so. All around her, others were paying the price for sorcery. Another two ships had perished, if not more, with crews and lancers from both Loiseau and Encora. Richina had fallen on the deck of the *Silberwelle*. The Maitre was burning his way across Neserea toward Defalk.

And for all of that, Secca had yet to set foot on land in Liedwahr.

104

I n the gray light of an overcast morning that oozed, green-tinged, into the tiny cabin, Secca sat on the edge of the lower bunk and handed Richina yet another sliver of bread, then offered her a cup of water. The younger sorceress sipped quietly for a moment and, after letting Secca take the cup back, slowly chewed another morsel of bread.

"I feel so weak . . ." Richina murmured.

"Keep eating, and it will pass." Secca did not look directly at the deep and dark circles under the younger woman's eyes, nor at the reddish welt along her jawline that was already beginning to purple.

"Not in time, I fear."

"In time for what?" asked Secca with a laugh. "It will be another two days at least before we port in Lundholn. Just eat and rest for now."

"Do we have a signal? From the Council Leader?"

"Not yet . . . but it could take almost a week to get a message to Lundholn by messenger."

"Am I so tired . . . just from the wards?"

Secca shook her head. "The Sturinnese sent those firebolts against us. They were guided by sorcery . . ."

"The wards moved them?"

"We think so. You collapsed after the second one just missed the *Silberwelle*. Alcaren and I think the effort to protect us caused that. We may never know with certainty." Secca offered a rueful smile. "I would not wish to see such again."

"We are unprotected?" Richina lurched upright, as if alarmed.

"No. Everything is fine." Secca leaned forward, easing Richina back against the thin single blanket folded into a pillow. "You need not worry. Alcaren took over the wards this morning."

"I am so sorry I failed you, Lady Secca. I am so sorry . . . I tried, but I was so tired—"

"Nonsense," replied Secca tartly. "You allowed us to destroy the Sturinnese fleet. The very last Sea-Priest fleet. If you had not held the wards, we could not have done that." She extended the cup of water. "You need to drink some more."

Richina took another swallow of water. "You'll have to do everything now . . . if Alcaren . . ." She yawned. "So . . . tired."

Secca shook her head. "You'll have time to recover. Now . . . you need to rest."

Once she had Richina—already half-asleep—settled back into the narrow bunk, Secca eased out of the tiny cabin and made her way up to the poop deck, where she found Denyst and Alcaren beside the helm platform.

A faint chill drizzle fell from the formless gray clouds overhead, and while the wind was stronger than before the battle, it was still comparatively light. Without full forward speed and the heavier swells, the *Silberwelle* seemed, at least to Secca, to be pitching more, and she grabbed the taffrail for support.

"How is she?" asked Alcaren.

"I got her to eat more, and she's sleeping." Secca shook her head. "She looks so tired and frail. Weeks ago, she was a strong, almost strapping, young woman."

"Sorcery," commented Denyst. "What it does to others is terrible, but it takes a terrible toll on you sorceresses. And sorcerers," she added as her eyes fell on Alcaren.

There was a moment of silence.

"One of those fireballs struck the *Liedmeer*," Denyst said. "And another took the *Morgenstern*. She was one of the ships you captured for us. Not a trace of either. Did your glass show aught?"

Alcaren shook his head. "There was no sign of either, nor of any Sturinnese ship."

"Didn't think it could be done, Lady Sorceress," Denyst said. "Oceans swept clean of the Sea-Pigs. Had it been any others, would have felt poorly at their fate. Terrible it was, and no more than they deserved."

"It's far from over," Secca said slowly. "Unless we can defeat the Maitre, it will just go on and on."

"We cannot just defeat him, my love," Alcaren replied. "Defeat the Sturinnese never accept. We must destroy him, or he will destroy us."

Secca's lips tightened, even as she nodded. *He's already destroyed so many. Why is it that everything you do hurts those around you and those who follow you? Why must you destroy all the Sturinnese just in order to survive? Why?*

She didn't have an answer. Not really, although she knew that what Alcaren had said was true, and that everything that had happened in the past year was proof of that.

Proof or not . . . an enormous blanket of sadness wrapped itself around her as she looked aft, back west. Back across the dark waters that held too many shattered ships and broken bodies.

105

NORTHWEST OF ELIOCH, NESEREA

The white-clad lancers are unfastening the side panels of the Maitre's tent. The remaining panels flap in the stiff breeze, but the Maitre remains seated on the folding stool behind the camp table, even as his tent is being disassembled around him, studying the scrying glass and the image of empty dark blue waters it holds.

On the other side of the table, still standing and holding

the angular lute, is jerClayne, his forehead damp. His eyes are dark-rimmed and bloodshot.

The Maitre looks up from the scrying glass, his eyes cold. "Two ships . . . that is all? Two ships? JerStolk lost an entire fleet of two and a half–score vessels to destroy two ships?"

The younger Sea-Priest remains mute.

"I have spent a lifetime building Sturinn. I have spent a score of years creating ships and fleets. The moment I am not there, there is failure! One small woman. One! And she has turned them all into mewling children! A fleet commander, and he has five times the number of ships, and all are armed. He has a half-score of sorcerers, and he can destroy but two ships! Two unarmed ships crewed by women!"

"Yes, ser," murmurs jerClayne.

"Were he not already dead . . ." The Maitre shakes his head. "Incompetent idiot! And now the Ranuans have more ships than do we. Never . . . seven ships, and they have more than do the Sea-Priests of Sturinn. How did this happen?"

"Her storm sorcery . . . their wards . . ."

"They are still warded, are they not?" asks the Maitre.

"Ah . . . yes, ser," replies jerClayne. "That is, we cannot use the glass to view the sorceresses or the consort of the shadowsinger. Or the Assistant Sorceress of Defalk."

"Two sorceresses—one of them barely more than a girl—and a Ranuan tool of that weakling Matriarch . . ." The older Sea-Priest stops, as if at a loss for words. "A half-score of our sorcerers—gone."

"They were on different vessels, as you ordered," jerClayne points out.

"Did they even *try* sorcery against them after the firebolts?"

"How could we tell, Maitre?"

The Maitre's eyes harden, as does his voice. "*We* must do better. Much better. We *will* do better."

The younger Sea-Priest does not speak.

"You say nothing, but your eyes ask me how." A tight

smile appears on the Maitre's face. "It is simple. We make her hasten. We ride directly to Defalk . . . and there we begin to ravage the country. We turn keeps into piles of stone. We do not kill the peasants, but we kill the lords and the merchants. We move to where we have an advantage, and then we wait while she comes to us."

"What about the other sorceress, ser? The one protecting Lord Robero?"

"She has fled from Falcor, did you not say?"

"That we know. She is in one of the western keeps." Tilting his head slightly, jerClayne frowns. "Dubaria. She also is warded."

"Then . . . we will bring it down around her. When we get there. We will take Denguic first, and then Fussen so that we need not worry about troublesome lords following us . . . and so that those in Dubaria will know what we can do."

"What of Lord Robero and Falcor?"

"Once we have crushed his sorceresses, what can he do? Many of the old lords will prefer a rule under our sufferance to one under that of the sorceresses . . . and those who do not will either submit or perish. They will indeed." His voice rises into a laugh.

"Submit or perish," repeats jerClayne, a hollow smile on his gaunt face, even as his eyes glitter almost as much as those of the Maitre.

106

S ecca stood beside Denyst near the helm platform as the *Silberwelle* edged toward the single long pier that jutted out almost half a dek from the semicircular stone shingle beach. Alcaren stood by the starboard railing, trying to ignore the ship's motion. The wind had picked up over the past days, and Denyst had shifted the sails into harbor rig well out from the port. With the wind had come clouds, still high and gray and scudding southward swiftly, and higher waves.

Secca herself felt better than she had in weeks, but when she glanced at Alcaren, she could see the tiredness in his eyes, and she still worried about Richina.

"No lancers, no armsmen?" asked the ship mistress again, as if to make certain, even though Secca's glass had shown the blue banner flying, to confirm the Council's agreement with a landing by Secca's force.

"The glass shows none," Secca confirmed. "None except two officers and a single squad of lancers." She gestured toward Elfens, the chief archer, and his squad.

As if he had seen her gesture, the long-faced archer turned and inclined his head. "We stand ready, Lady Secca."

"We shouldn't need you, Elfens, but we'd rather be prepared."

"As would we, lady."

"Looks as though he'd just as soon nock that arrow and send it whistling through someone as spit," noted Denyst, before turning her head and calling an order to the woman at the helm. "Another point to starboard!"

"Coming starboard."

Secca just watched the pier while the ship mistress began to issue commands, and sails were reefed in, and crew members scampered through the rigging as the vessel eased toward the long stone pier. She could tell Lundholn was an old town, a gray ancient whose stone walls and streets had had all color bleached from them by endless generations of brutal winters and winds off the Bitter Sea. Even the few shutters that she could see on the warehouses behind the pier were gray and weathered, as were the heavy timbers that sheathed the stone pier.

The blue pennant at the end of the pier was held almost horizonal by the stiff wind out of the northwest, and almost directly below it stood a man and a woman, each wearing a black-and-silver uniform, with silver bars on the collars of their uniform jackets. Their eyes remained on the *Silber-welle* as Denyst called out commands, and the mooring lines were thrown to a pair of men in faded brown jackets and trousers. Neither officer on the pier moved as the *Silberwelle* was winched into position at the second berth from the sea-ward end of the pier.

Secca stepped toward the railing to watch, and to get a better view of the two officers who waited. "What do you think?" she asked Alcaren.

"They're waiting for us."

"Double up . . . make her snug!" ordered Denyst.

The hull creaked as the harbor waves lifted the ship and pushed her against the pier and the hempen bumpers. Still, there was no one on the long pier, save the two hands who had taken the mooring lines and made them fast to the bol-lards and the two officers in silver and black.

Delcetta appeared on the poop deck and halted before Secca. "If you would not mind, Lady Sorceress, I would first meet with those on the pier."

"Let her," murmured Alcaren.

Secca nodded. "Tell them I would be happy to talk with them."

"That I will." Delcetta bowed and turned.

From the forward section of the poop deck, Elfens glanced toward Secca.

"If you would stand ready for a bit yet," Secca called to the chief archer, "until we have a company disembarked and on the pier."

"We will stand ready so long as you need us," returned the long-faced archer. An incongruous smile appeared, then vanished.

Secca watched as the blonde overcaptain of the SouthWomen walked down the gangway, followed by two lancers, and neared the two Norweians. The conversation was brief, and then all five turned and walked back up the gangway. Delcetta and the two Norweian officers climbed the ladder to the poop deck and walked toward Secca.

Both officers halted a good two yards from Secca and bowed deeply.

The woman spoke first. "Lady Sorceress. I am Captain Salchaar. This is Undercaptain Eztaar. We have been sent to serve as your guides and escorts to Morgen and to the border with Defalk. The Council is more than happy to grant you passage and any supplies you may need. If you do not have the golds at hand, we will take draughts that you can repay once your campaign against the Sea-Priests is complete. The Council felt that if we led you, there would be no misunderstandings, and all would understand that you are a welcome guest in Nordwei."

"We thank the Council, and we thank both of you for your service and duty," replied Secca. "We may have to wait a day or so for our mounts to recover some strength."

"We had thought so, and we have arranged quarters throughout Lundholn." Salchaar added quickly, "Always by company and in secure locales."

"You and your players and officers and a company can have the larger inn—the Snow Gull," added the undercaptain. "We have two smaller inns as well and an older barracks—it is clean and snug, if spare. We had guessed at ten companies."

"We will need to see to the unloading," Secca said. "We still have six other ships to see to. We have but seven companies and a company's worth of players and archers."

The Norweian captain frowned slightly.

"We lost two ships and all aboard in the battle with the Sea-Priests," Secca explained.

"We did not know . . . we left Wei before . . ."

"There are no Sturinnese vessels left in the Bitter Sea," Alcaren added, "or in any other ocean around Liedwahr."

"Yet you need to travel . . . ?"

"The Maitre has scores of companies of lancers riding through Neserea to Defalk. This morning they were but two days' ride from Elioch. They are destroying every town and hamlet they ride through," Secca explained. "So we must unload and prepare."

"We will wait until you are ready, Lady Sorceress," replied Captain Salchaar. "Then we will show you what we can offer."

"You and the Council are most kind," Secca replied, "and we appreciate that friendship and kindness. And we will remember it."

"We have few lancers, Lady Sorceress, and we appreciate your efforts against the Sturinnese." Captain Salchaar offered a slight head bow. "We would not delay your off-loading, and we will await you at the foot of the pier."

"Thank you." Secca returned the bow.

As the two Norweian officers climbed down the ladder to the main deck, the cool wind gusting around them, Secca turned and walked over to Denyst. She bowed to the ship mistress. "I cannot give you thanks enough for all that you have done, and for your grace and warmth in surrendering your own quarters to us for such a long time."

The wiry captain smiled. "Lady Secca, was my pleasure, and my duty. If the Sea-Pigs win, we'd never sail again."

"We haven't won yet."

"That may be, but the seas will be free for years to come, and I'd not be wagering against you in your campaign against the Maitre."

Secca wondered if the Ranuan ship mistress didn't have more confidence than she did. "I trust in the harmonies that you will win those wagers."

"I will. You have a way with the harmonies, Lady Secca. That you do." Denyst glanced toward the main deck, where several crew members had opened the hatch and were rigging a crane and hoist.

Secca's eyes followed the captain's. "You have much to do. We'll leave you to that, and gather our people and gear." She tried not to think about the several days before the mounts would be ready to ride—or the more than eight days necessary even to reach Nordfels.

"We should be able to unload all you need within a glass. I've signaled the *Schaumenflucht* to tie up behind us. We can mostly unload by twos. Wouldn't want to use the in-shore positions on the pier with our draft."

Secca smiled. "In all matters such as those, we defer to you." She bowed again before she turned and headed forward to the ladder.

Alcaren had already gone below to the captain's cabin, and when Secca rejoined him, he had already stacked all the gear that they had packed earlier and placed it on the table. He looked up from the lumand case he had just set down. "I thought I'd get all this ready."

"Thank you. Denyst says she will have us off-loaded in a glass or so."

"If she says so, then she will." Alcaren paused. "I just talked to Richina. She is ready." He tilted his head slightly, as if he were not quite certain of the next words. "She's still so frail."

"She shouldn't have to do any sorcery for close to two weeks, if not longer," Secca said. "That should help."

Alcaren nodded.

"We'll have to alternate singing and holding the ward spells," Secca said. "We can't have you looking like that, either, not when I'll need you to sing with me against the Maitre. Perhaps I can hold the wards for a few days on the journey."

"Let us see," Alcaren replied.

Secca laughed. "I think that's as close to a disagreement as you'll offer."

Alcaren's first reply was a sheepish smile. "I should be able to hold them until Richina is better, and she and I can alternate. You have to be rested."

"Let us see," answered Secca, using Alcaren's own words in return.

He shook his head, ruefully, then stepped forward and embraced her.

Secca returned the embrace and clung tightly to him for a time, just hanging on to the moment, knowing all too well that, under the best of circumstances, death and devastation lay along the road before them.

107

In the late afternoon, Secca stood under the overhanging eaves of the Snow Gull's side porch, looking down from the rise on the now-empty harbor of Lundholn. In the shadows cast by the headlands to the west and north, the water near the shore looked almost a shimmering black. The wind had subsided to a light breeze, so that only gentle wavelets lapped on the shingled beach and against the stone buttresses of the long pier. Less than a glass before, the last Ranuan ship had reprovisioned from the stores that had been mustered by the Council of Wei, and all were, Secca hoped, on an uneventful return voyage to Encora.

She had noted a pair of passengers being escorted to the *Ozeanstern*, the last ship to leave the harbor of Lundholn, just before the big trader cast off, and absently wondered who would take passage to Ranuak in such unsettled times. *Then, they really aren't that unsettled on the oceans, now . . . but who would know that?* She shook her head. She had more than enough with which to concern herself without worrying about two passengers.

She glanced sideways at Alcaren. "It's been two days, and Delcetta tells me that the mounts still are not ready, even to be walked more than a few deks." Her lips tightened. "The glass shows that the Maitre is nearing Defalk, and all we can do is wait. There are not even a double handful of mounts to purchase here."

Alcaren cleared his throat. "I did purchase some ponies. I thought that if they could carry provisions . . ."

Secca laughed, ruefully. "That will help."

"But not enough." He paused. "Do you know where Jolyn is?"

"She is in a hold, Dubaria, and she seems safe for now, although we cannot scry her directly." Secca frowned. "You think we should warn her?"

"She probably knows that the Maitre approaches. And she may try something. He is not thinking about her, but he will be if she does."

"Send her a warning to strike from afar, and only at the lancers and animals well away from the Maitre and his Sea-Priests." Secca nodded. "We should—I should do that now, before other sorcery is called for. I should have thought of that sooner, but with the mounts and the maps and the draughts for supplies, and the study of the . . . those spells . . ." She pushed back a lock of unruly red hair that was getting far too long. "We should have her warn the lords around there to abandon their keeps. The Maitre will pull them down around them."

"You think so?" Alcaren laughed at himself. "Of course he will. If he has done that in Neserea, why would he not do worse in Defalk?"

Secca took a last look at the shadowed harbor. "I should have done this earlier." *Why does it always seem that way? Because you are still not that experienced in planning battles and travels and sorcery and all that goes with it?* She wasn't, Secca reflected, but the problem was simple. There wasn't anyone else who was, except Alcaren and Palian. Alcaren still didn't know enough about Defalk to see what she was missing or had overlooked, and Palian had her hands full managing the players and keeping Delvor in line. "We'd better check the scrying glass first, then I'll write a message."

The two walked along the narrow corridor to the large room in the southeast corner of the sprawling stone-walled inn that sat on the bluff overlooking the town proper. Secca nodded to Mureyn as she and Alcaren passed the lancer acting as guard, and closed the door behind them.

Alcaren unwrapped the scrying mirror from its leathers while Secca moved the pitcher and basin off the small wash table. Then he set the mirror in place. Secca tuned the lutar quickly, then sang the seeking spell, asking to see the dwelling in which Jolyn was staying.

When the image of a redstone-walled keep appeared, they both studied the glass.

"Dubaria—that's Tiersen's keep. Good. I'm glad she's still there. She should be, but she could have ridden somewhere else." At Alcaren's puzzled look, she added, "Tiersen's consort is Lysara. She saved my life and almost lost hers doing it. I would want them warned above all others. Then Kinor."

She sang the release spell and recased the lutar. Then she went to the narrow wardrobe and opened it. A smile crossed her lips as she took out a fresh sheet of paper, one of the twoscore sheets she had managed to find in the chandler's the day after they had landed—along with a half-score of fresh parchment sheets. For a time, at least, she wouldn't have to be writing notes and spell drafts on the sides and corners of papers that already had every span covered with writing.

"I'm going to draft the letter to Jolyn. I'd like to read it to you when I'm finished. You can tell me if there's something I should add." She paused, then swallowed, as she lifted out the leather folder and the manila envelope within—Anna's "Armageddon" file—and handed it to Alcaren. "While I'm writing, if you would read these, and see which ones might be useful against the Maitre."

His eyes widened as he took the aged parchment and recognized what she was handing him. "Me? How would I . . . ?"

"You'll know, my love."

A wry smile crossed his face. "You would share these with me?"

"Who else?" asked Secca. "You will be the one singing with me against the Maitre."

"Me? Why not Richina?" Alcaren rewrapped the scrying mirror and set it in the corner beside the narrow wardrobe.

"Because the spellsongs are stronger—at least, Anna said so—with a man's voice and a woman's voice. And because I do not wish Richina to be singing such until she is older." Secca pulled a stool over to the wash table and seated herself.

Alcaren took the folder and sat down on the foot of the bed that was barely of double width, narrower even than the bunk in Denyst's cabin aboard the *Silberwelle*.

Even from the first words of the first sheet, Secca could see he was frowning. She forced her thoughts back to the message she should have written earlier. She had sent the warding spell in time, and Jolyn was still fine. *You should have done it earlier.* Secca winced, but she kept searching for words.

After almost a glass, as the sun was dropping behind the conifer-covered hills to the west of the Snow Gull, Secca finally scratched out the last words she disliked and replaced them with another phrase—her third attempt. Then she cleared her throat.

Alcaren looked up.

"Will you listen?" she asked.

He nodded.

"Dear Jolyn—

"We are in Wei, and will be traveling to Defalk from the north as soon as our mounts recover from sea travel. That will be within two days, I hope. We will take the road from Nordfels and hope to reach you before the Maitre of Sturinn can accomplish too much devastation in Defalk.

"The Maitre is nearing Defalk, with at least a handful of strong sorcerers and a spell that can kill unprotected lords or sorceresses from a great distance. We can tell that you have used the warding spell that will protect you from such sorcery and also limit his abilities to see you in a glass. Because the warding spell takes most of your strength just to hold, if you attempt any sorcery against the Maitre, you must direct it at his lancers, those that are distant from the Maitre.

"He has been pulling down liedburgs and keeps around lords in Neserea and will do so in Defalk. Warn Tiersen and Kinor and others, as you can, that the best way to survive is to abandon keeps and fortifications, and to attack scouts and other smaller forces where there are no sorcerers.

"We will be there as soon as we can. Remind them that we can help them rebuild structures, but that we cannot bring them back to life. . . ."

Alcaren laughed softly as she read those words.
"What do you think?" Secca asked.
"Are there any other spells you should send?" he asked.
"I would not send the terrible ones. Her players are half the number of ours and do not know the fourth, fifth, and sixth building spells."
"That is not the only reason why you will not send them," he said quietly.
"She cannot use them," Secca protested.
"That well may be true," Alcaren agreed, his gray-blue eyes meeting her amber ones.
"I fear to have many see or hear them," she admitted.
"Do you think to keep them hidden?"
"If I can . . . if I can."

"It will be even harder if we succeed," Alcaren replied.

Secca understood all that he meant, for if they succeeded, sorcerers around Erde would search for the means they had used. If they failed, no one would look further.

They shared sad and knowing smiles.

108

NORTHWEST OF ELIOCH, NESEREA

The column of men in white stretches more than two deks westward, back toward yet another hamlet whose demise is marked by trails of smoke winding skyward, but lost soon against the high gray overcast. The lancers ride in precise formation, as always.

A lancer undercaptain in Sturinnese white rides up to the Maitre, slowing his mount, then bowing in the saddle. "Maitre . . ."

"What is it?" The Maitre reins up, as do all those who follow.

"The riders we reported—they were Defalkans, bearing a scroll from Lord Robero. They wished to deliver it personally." The undercaptain flashes a hard smile.

"I see you persuaded them otherwise."

"Yes, Maitre." The undercaptain extends the scroll, not to the Maitre, but to jerClayne, who rides to the left of the leader of Sturinn.

The younger Sea-Priest breaks the seal and checks the document without reading it before handing it to the Maitre. In turn, the Maitre takes a quick look at the seal on the bottom, then impatiently reads through the document.

Beside him, jerClayne waits, a puzzled frown upon his face.

The Maitre laughs—harshly—and lowers the scroll.

"Ser?"

"That weakling suggests that we meet to discuss an agreement of mutual advantage. I can guess what that will be."

The younger Sea-Priest waits.

"He realizes he is about to lose control of his land. He does not know that he lost it to the Great Sorceress years ago. So he would like us to remove the sorceresses and let him rule his tabletop demesne."

"He wrote that?"

"Of course not. He is less than brilliant, but not that stupid. His words mean the same thing." The Maitre flicks the reins to urge his mount forward, ignoring the undercaptain, who has turned his mount to ride behind them. "He is right to be worried. No matter what happens, if the fighting continues, he will lose. So he will do anything to stop it. Anything that will allow him to keep his title and lands." The Maitre laughs again.

"What will you do?"

"What any prudent man would do. Promise him that we will talk, but I will neglect to say when or where."

Another look of puzzlement crosses jerClayne's face.

"Yes, we will talk . . . when the time is right." The Maitre continues to ride, his eyes studying the road ahead, as the column moves eastward along the river, toward the road that will take them south to Elioch.

109

Secca walked beside the gray mare, the reins held loosely in her right hand, her boots hitting heavily on the gray paving stones of the ancient Corian road to Morgen. Her feet, legs, and back were sore, and her face raw from the damp winds off the endless low hills of western Wei.

A good hundred yards ahead rode the Norweian officers
and their squad of lancers. Their mounts didn't need extra
care, Secca reflected. Something bothered her, and she had
not been able to grasp what it was . . . what might be wrong
that she wasn't seeing. She looked to the hillside to her
right, but the brown grasses and the leafless bushes, and the
scattered low junipers could have been anywhere. Anywhere. Then, she nodded and turned to Alcaren, who walked
beside her, leading his chestnut gelding.

"You have that look, my lady," he said with a smile.

"I realized what has been fretting at me." She gestured to
the hillside. "What is wrong with the hillside?"

He frowned. "Little that I can see."

She nodded. "Did you not tell me that Nordwei had also
suffered in the Spell-Fire Wars?"

Alcaren smiled. "There was not so much sorcery used
here in the west—except that many of the forests burned
and have never regrown. The places that look like Ranuak
are to the south and east of Wei itself, mostly along the
River Ost. That was closer to the Mynyan holdings."

"No one ever mentions that in schooling in Defalk," she
said slowly.

Her observations were cut short as the toe of her boot
caught the slightly upraised edge of a paving stone, and she
stumbled forward, barely catching her balance. "Dissonance!" *You were the one who suggested walking the
mounts* . . . And she was. She'd just forgotten how slow and
painful walking was, even on the antique metaled road. And
how cold in a land where spring came late, and winter lin-
gered.

"Are you all right?" asked Alcaren.

"I am." She shook her head, aware once more how her
feet hurt. "How far?"

"About a dek since you last asked," he said with a smile.

"I didn't look pleased when you didn't feel well on the
Silberwelle," she replied, forcing a smile. "Walking is hard
on sorceresses with small feet and short legs."

"I am sorry, my lady. I was not taking pleasure in your discomfort."

"Then . . . why the smile?"

"It was more of a wistful smile," Alcaren said slowly. "I was thinking about music. I don't suppose I'll ever look at it or listen to it the same way." He paused. "Yes . . . you know that music is the basis of sorcery, but in Ranuak, instrumental music was acceptable—without words and only on a single instrument. Now . . . it's more of a tool."

Secca tilted her head, recalling Anna's words.

"You look thoughtful," her consort observed.

"I was thinking about Anna. She said something like that. She missed music by what she called the great masters."

"Who were they?"

Secca shrugged. "She used many names. They were all from the Mist Worlds. I remember Mozart and Schumann and Poulenc. She talked about them more than the others. Sometimes, she'd say something about the tragedy of music in Liedwahr was that it was nothing more than a tool and never would be more than that because complexity introduced the possibility of greater error and because no working tool needed greater errors."

"Hmmmm. I can see that. But . . . how could it be otherwise? Even dinner music is a tool of sorts, something to put people at ease."

"Only in Ranuak," Secca replied. "It didn't put Fehern at ease."

"Nothing would have put him at ease."

"Any use of music puts off most people," Secca suggested.

"Like dancing?"

Secca shook her head. "There is a reason for that. Spell music that affects the body is Darksong. People dance to music, and the old books talk about dance music with drums being especially harmful."

"So, because dancing *looked* like Darksong, the old rulers banned it?" Alcaren snorted.

"I didn't say it made sense." Secca shrugged. She found her steps slowing as she climbed the last few yards of the gentle hillside curve in the road, until she reached the crest, where her eyes took in the mist of the valley that opened below. "There is supposed to be a town here, at the far end, with an inn. That's what Salchaar said."

"Good. We could use the rest—if we can get there before dark."

Secca hoped so, even as she tried not to think about where the Maitre and his sorcerers and lancers might be and what they might be doing.

110

Although the sun had just dropped behind the hills to the west, the sky above remained a bright and clear blue that had not yet begun to fade into twilight. Only the lightest breeze—coming out of the south with a trace of dampness and the hint of warming ground—drifted past the riders.

Secca shifted her weight in the saddle of the gray mare, her eyes dropping to the road momentarily. The ancient gray paving stones had begun to show more cracks as the road, descending gradually from the bluffs on the eastern side of the River Nord, neared Morgen. At least, Secca hoped they were nearing Morgen. Her legs and back were stiff, but not so sore as they had been for the first days out of Lundholn, when she had not ridden for weeks.

Riding beside Secca, Richina took a deep breath.

Secca glanced at the younger sorceress, pleased to see that Richina no longer looked absolutely gaunt. Nor did the younger woman have the deep black circles under her eyes. Secca frowned. While Alcaren merely looked tired, Secca had to wonder how long it would be before he started showing the strain.

She glanced ahead, where a good five yards before her Alcaren rode with Captain Salchaar. The Norweian captain gestured to an oblong stone set beside the road—a dekstone around which the brush had recently been cut back.

Secca leaned forward in the saddle as the mare carried her toward the grayish dekstone. It read: Morgen—2 d. Two deks to the edge of the town she could handle. She urged the mare forward to close the gap between her and Alcaren and Salchaar. Just beyond them, the road angled to the right with a steeper descent toward the town, which lay in the valley below.

"The town is on the point between the two rivers," Salchaar was saying, as Secca eased her mount almost beside Alcaren's gelding. The Norweian captain turned in the saddle, half-toward Secca. "Morgen has five inns, even more than Lundholn. We told the keepers that you would doubtless be needing both quarters and provender."

Secca nodded. "That we will." She'd already put her signature and seal to draughts for close to two hundred golds, and they weren't even out of Nordwei.

"The River's Edge is the largest and the best, although," Salchaar added with a twist to her lips, "I must admit that it has seen better days. Annalese has refurbished many of the rooms since she took it over and since trade with Defalk has continued to improve. It is much better than making a bivouac. It also has a bunkhouse that we have used as a barracks. I thought that would serve for you, your players, and some of your lancers. How long do you think . . . ?"

"One night," Secca said. "We will not rise at dawn, and we will allow more time for rest, but we have already lost too many days." She just hoped a slightly slower, but continued, pace would get them to Nordfels and then to the south before the Maitre had ravaged too much of Defalk.

"We had thought as much." Salchaar glanced to Alcaren, then back at Secca. "The road to Nordfels will be more difficult."

"We fear that, but that is still the swiftest way to Defalk, is it not?"

"That it is," replied Salchaar with a laugh. After a moment, she added, "We should be at the River's Edge before full twilight." She shifted her weight in the saddle to face full forward.

Alcaren had slowed his mount until he dropped back to ride beside Secca. He gestured toward the town. "From here, the buildings look like the older dwellings in Encora."

"They couldn't have been built with sorcery, the way the walls of Encora were," Secca pointed out. "The Corians banned sorcery from the beginning."

"That's true," mused Alcaren.

"And they turned women into chattels," Secca added mischievously.

Alcaren offered a puzzled expression.

"They also lost." Secca grinned.

Behind her, Secca could hear a smothered giggle from Richina.

"My lady," Alcaren said, presenting a long face, an exaggerated expression of penance, "I would never have the ability to do either, and I would hope to have the wisdom not to try."

Secca laughed, and, after a moment, so did he.

"I think they had to use stone," Alcaren said after a time of silence, "because the Spell-Fire Wars destroyed so many of the trees. Here, they cut it by hand and with chisels."

While Morgen was not a city, neither was it a small town, Secca reflected, and cutting the amount of stone she saw in the dwellings beyond the river could not have been accomplished in any short period.

At the base of the long grade to the valley, the road curved more to the right and headed due south between flat fields toward a group of dwellings and small shops clustered on the north side of the river.

"Those aren't stone," Richina said from where she rode behind them.

"They were built later, I'd wager," replied Alcaren.

Secca wasn't about to take the wager, and instead surveyed the browned grass and the yet unturned soil of the fields flanking the road, then the dwellings on the outskirts of the town ahead.

The wooden plank siding of the first dwelling she rode by was stained a grayish blue, as if to emulate some form of stone, and the shutters were painted a yellow that had long since faded. The space between the dwelling and the road was damp clay, filled with dead weeds, except for two gravel paths—one to the front porch steps and the other to an outbuilding that looked to be a stable. From the sagging porch, a boy in an overlarge stained sheepskin jacket watched the riders, his eyes dark and solemn.

The next dwelling—on the left side of the road—had clearly been abandoned for years, with the roof caved in from winters of heavy snow, Secca guessed, and gaping windows with missing shutters. While the other dwellings, and a pair of shops of some sort without signs, were in better repair, none had been stained or painted recently.

Beyond the dwellings was a cleared space, perhaps of one hundred yards, leading to the River Nord. Its greenish waters were less than thirty yards wide. The riverbed itself was three times that and spanned by a flat, gray stone structure, supported by thick buttresses. The railings were not stone, but timber, and although weathered, appeared strong enough to restrain the largest of trading wagons.

The gray's hoofs clicked on the stones of the bridge's roadbed. Near the center, Secca looked east to the point of land beyond which a plume of more brownish water joined the greener waters of the Nord.

"The Nord is much larger," she said.

"Much, lady," replied Undercaptain Eztaar, turning slightly from where he rode in front of her. "The waters were near flood when we passed this way before. From the melted runoff of the Nordbergs."

"Thank you." Secca looked around as the mare carried

her off the bridge and into what had to be a stone-paved square almost a hundred yards on a side, a square empty of people or horses.

"The market square," Eztaar volunteered, letting his mount drop back beside them. "In summer and in harvest it is filled. Now . . ." he shrugged.

Beyond the square, the gray stone buildings began—all at least two stories high and barely set back from the narrow stone streets that reminded Secca vaguely of Falcor, save that Morgen smelled older, even if she saw little refuse in the growing twilight. The acrid odor of wood burning in stoves and hearths was noticeable in the narrow streets, but that was the only sign of the inhabitants—that and a mottled gray cat that watched from the top of a covered rain barrel set in an alley.

A half-dek beyond the market square, the dwellings and shops were replaced by an open expanse that was parklike, with the first real trees Secca had seen since leaving Elahwa two seasons earlier.

"The River's Edge is below the green, and to the west," Eztaar volunteered.

Secca peered in the direction of his gesture, but they rode at least another two hundred yards before she could make out the gray building. The River's Edge was a two-story structure almost fifty yards long, one of the larger inns Secca had seen, with rust-streaked gray stone walls and a split-slate roof that showed traces of ancient moss everywhere. The shutters had once been painted red, but the paint had faded into a duller shade that almost matched the rust lines in the stone walls.

As the column rode along the narrow stone-paved lane toward the inn, Secca could see that the old inn was not exactly on the river, but on a low rise on the south side of where the smaller and browner Fehl River joined the Nord. A paved circle with time-softened mounting blocks formed an unloading area before the entry to the inn. Behind the mounting blocks was a small front entry porch, no more than five yards by three, supported by two of the rust and gray stone columns.

Salchaar eased her mount to one side, to let Alcaren and the sorceresses ride to the mounting blocks. "We'll see that all is well here, and then escort Overcaptain Delcetta and her lancers to the Stone Oven and the Copper Skillet."

"Thank you," offered Secca.

"Captain Salchaar!" A rail-thin woman with a round face bustled out from under the eaves of the porch to stand in front of the mounting block closest to the inn.

"Annalese," replied Salchaar, "I said we'd be returning."

"Expected you yesterday or the day before, not that it makes the difference this time of year." The edge on Annalese's voice suggested that it did indeed make a difference. Her bright gray eyes, almost the color of the thatch of gray hair, remained fixed on the Norweian officer.

"Annalese, this is the Sorceress Protector of Defalk, Lady Secca, and her consort, Lord Alcaren of Ranuak. And Lady Richina."

Secca noted that Alcaren raised his eyes at the title, but said nothing.

"A pleasure to have you and your lancers here. Specially at this time of season." A wry smile crossed the round face. "You ready to come in?"

Secca glanced back at the lancers acting as guards.

"We'll take care of the mounts, lady," Easlon said quickly.

"Chief players . . ." Secca called.

Another woman appeared, a younger version of Annalese.

"My daughter Rekka. She'll settle your players and your officers," the innkeeper said.

"This is Chief Player Palian, Chief Player Delvor, and Overcaptain Wilten." Secca gestured, then looked at Palian and then Wilten. "Rekka here is charged with helping you."

The younger innkeeper bowed.

As Rekka began to explain the quarters arrangements to Palian and Wilten, Secca dismounted, hiding a wince as her weight came to rest on her sore feet. She quickly turned and handed the gray's reins to Easlon, then unfastened the saddlebags and lutar. Alcaren had already dismounted. His saddlebags were slung over his shoulder, and he carried the leather-wrapped scrying mirror, following Secca up the stone steps to the porch of the inn. Behind them came Richina.

Inside was a long and narrow foyer, the walls paneled in plain but oiled oak that shimmered in the light of the four oil lamps set in bronze wall sconces.

Annalese walked toward the archway on the left, stepping through it and into a long, white-plastered corridor.

"We only have one grand room, and the Council said it was for you, lady," Annalese said as she led the way along the yard-wide corridor, past frequent oak doors, all with bronze locks. "Also, we set aside the private dining room for you and your personal party and commanders. The private dining room is the one with the golden hangings in the archway. Not hard to find, seeing as it's the only one."

"That's most kind."

"Most practical. You're paying, and you're the one who's going to stop the Sea-Pigs. Much as I like silvers, I like being free to run my own life even more." Annalese snorted. "Should have all been strangled in their cradles." Abruptly, she stopped at one door, producing a key. "This one is for you, Lady Richina, not quite so grand, but the best we have."

"Thank you." Richina offered a head bow.

"If you would join us in a moment," Secca murmured to Richina as the younger woman started to enter her chamber.

The blonde sorceress nodded.

Annalese continued the last fifteen yards to the end door of the corridor, and produced a second heavy bronze key. "Here we go."

Secca let Alcaren enter first with the innkeeper, then followed. She smiled. The chambers were actually large, with a small conference table before the hearth in which already burned several logs, a writing table against one wall, two large wardrobes, and a triple-width bed and clean white linens.

"This is wonderful." Secca didn't have to hide her pleasure and relief.

"Even has a bathing chamber . . . boys will be bringing up kettles soon as you wish," added the innkeeper, handing the bronze key to Secca.

"They can bring them now," Secca said with a smile. "And thank you."

"Be thanking you, Lady Sorceress. Oh, and there are kettles for the other sorceress, too." Annalese bowed and slipped out through the still-open door, past Dymen and Gorkon, who had stationed themselves at the doorway.

Secca barely had a chance to lay out the saddlebags and set down the lutar when Richina reappeared.

"Yes, Lady Secca?"

"Before the bathwater arrives," Secca said, "I want to see where the Maitre's forces are."

"Before you eat?" asked Alcaren.

Richina offered an inquiring look as well, but said nothing.

"I can do one scrying spell," Secca replied.

"Just one," Alcaren said.

While Secca uncased the lutar, Alcaren set the scrying mirror on the foot of the bed and began to unwrap it from its leathers. The he lifted the mirror and set it in the middle of the square conference table.

Secca finished tuning the lutar and stepped to the table, beginning the spellsong without preamble.

"Show us now and in clear light . . ."

The image in the scrying glass was that of a small hamlet set to the east of rolling hills still covered with brown grass. After a long look, Secca sang the release couplet, then turned to Alcaren. "They look to be in the grasslands just north of Elioch."

"Can you tell how far north?"

"It could be one or two days. No more." Secca tightened her lips. The Sturinnese were within four days of the West Pass, and five of Denguic. *Less if they hasten.*

"Should we send a message to Jolyn?" asked Richina.

"No," Alcaren said firmly. "She received the last scroll. She knows what she must do. You must recover, Lady Richina, and my Lady Secca needs no additional strain upon her now."

There was a *thrap* on the oak door.

"The boys with kettles," announced Dymen.

"Have them come in, one at a time," Alcaren said before Secca could respond. His hand rested on the hilt of his sabre. He watched as the three boys in brown robes paraded into the chambers one at a time and poured the steaming water into a tub that already had several spans of cooler clean water in it.

When both servers and Richina had departed, Secca slid the bolt across the outer door. "Do you mind if I bathe first?"

"Not if I can watch." He grinned.

"You . . ." she shook her head and walked toward the bathchamber.

For all his words, Alcaren did not follow her.

After Secca had bathed, she stood in one corner of the bathchamber, with a too-small towel wrapped around her. Finally, she pulled out the rolled green gown from her saddlebags, the one she hadn't worn since Encora, if not before, and looked at the wrinkled fabric.

Alcaren leered from the tub, where he was now bathing. "You're wearing that?"

"We are going to do some other sorcery, my dear." She flushed, realizing what she implied. "It's called washing out riding clothes. If I wear this tonight . . ."

"You won't be wearing it that long," he suggested.

Secca flushed even more and had to turn away for a moment before she continued, "I can wash both sets of riding clothes and spread them before the hearth."

"That is a good idea."

"You could wear that formal uniform."

From the tub, he shrugged. "It's packed with the gear we didn't bring in. I'll have to do with washing one set of uniforms."

Secca decided against providing more temptation and slipped out into the larger main chamber to dress.

By the time Secca and Alcaren had dressed and used a spell to wash their soiled gear, and then gathered Richina, more than a glass had passed, and faint daystars intermittently crossed Secca's vision. She said nothing to Alcaren, not after she'd insisted that the laundry spell would not hurt her.

Both chief players and Wilten were waiting in the private dining area, but Secca was relieved to see that each had ale and that the remnants of a loaf of bread lay in a basket on the large round table.

"The lancers?" asked Secca.

"They are already being fed in the public room," Wilten replied. "They can serve scores at once."

"I'm sorry." Secca took one of the empty wooden chairs. "We took a moment to use the glass to see where the Maitre might be. His forces are still in Neserea, but they appear close to Elioch."

Palian shook her head. "We can but do our best, lady."

"If Lord Robero had sent more lancers with Lady Clayre," added Delvor, "we might not be so pressed."

Except that Lord Robero isn't the one who will suffer. That was a thought Secca wasn't about to say aloud.

She looked up as a servingwoman, red-faced and smiling, appeared. "We have but two meals tonight, noble lady. The first is a small half chicken served with cream sauce and sautéed harvest mushrooms. We also have a quinced goose stuffed with nutbread and flamed with Vyelan brandy."

Alcaren lifted his eyebrows, then smiled, as did most of the others around the table.

"The chicken," Secca said, "with an ale." Much as she liked the change from hard bread, cheese, and other travel fare, she wasn't sure she wanted to see the draught she'd have to sign and seal for the River's Edge. Then again, whatever the cost, it was cheaper than trying to follow the Maitre through burned-out lands or forcing a march through Nordwei.

She might as well enjoy the chicken, since quince was less than her favorite fruit, and even the best goose had a chance of being greasy.

111

U nder a warm spring sun and a clear afternoon sky, Secca glanced down at her boots and trousers, splattered with mud, and probably worse, then at Alcaren, riding in front of her. He was even muddier than Secca, or perhaps it showed more on his light blue uniform.

Her entire force was riding single file across a soggy hillside bordering what had been a road, moving at the pace of a three-legged ox, if not slower. For the first day out of Morgen, the road had been damp clay, and fairly well packed, if at times slippery, but their luck with roads had ended roughly five deks behind them, where the road had narrowed and followed a stream on a gentle incline. The stream had recently overflowed its banks and flooded the road. Because the road had been used by wagons and horses for generations, they had gradually worn out a track that was below the terrain on either side, and that track had become a series of small ponds and muddy canals.

Looking at the long ridgeline that stretched south farther than she could see, Secca doubted they would cover ten deks in the entire day. *At this pace, two or three days more than you'd calculated just to get to Nordfels.*

A dollop of mud splatted against Secca's thigh, followed by small droplets of dark water thrown by Alcaren's chestnut. Secca sighed.

Salchaar had told Secca that the roads were bad because spring had come late and hard, and everything had melted in days, rather than weeks.

Alcaren turned in the saddle and called back to Secca, "We're going to have to climb higher on the hillside to circle around a bog in that dale ahead."

"How much higher?" asked Secca.

"Several hundred yards," he called back.

By the time they got around the bog, the detour would add another half-dek or more, and then there would probably be another one, if not more, when they reached the next valley.

Secca took a deep breath. *There's nothing you can do.* Sorcery wouldn't help, or rather any that might would only clear or dry a few deks and leave her worthless for days, scarcely the best of ideas with the Maitre and his forces riding toward Defalk.

112

Secca frowned as she reined up on the rise behind the two Norweian officers. The tiny town lying at the foot of the slippery clay road that wound down the hillside appeared to be more hamlet than town. Late-afternoon shadows from those peaks of the Nordbergs that lay to the west enfolded the clump of buildings.

"The scouts say that it is called Talseite." Undercaptain Eztaar turned in the saddle and addressed Secca. "Myself, I have never heard of it. They say that the border with Defalk is but a day's ride to the south."

"Now? Or in the summer?" asked Secca dryly.

Eztaar shrugged, half-apologetically. "Summer, I would guess."

The sorceress nodded. In the three days since leaving Morgen, they had covered perhaps forty deks—little more than a day's ride on the roads of Defalk—and almost half of that had been on the first day. She tried not to think about how far the Maitre's forces might have gone on the far better roads in Neserea and how much faster they could move once they entered Defalk.

"It is windier to the south," suggested Captain Salchaar. "That may dry the ground faster."

"Or melt everything faster," replied Alcaren.

As the column resumed its slow ride down the slippery and muddy road, Secca would have wagered on Alcaren's judgment. So far, the unpaved roads had been slow—and they had been lucky not to have had to ride through rain. Yet.

Talseite had one inn, marked by a large iron kettle hung from a gallowslike frame beside the road, a good two hundred yards to the north of any of the other buildings in the hamlet. With its recently whitewashed plank walls, and graveled half courtyard between the main building and the stables, the Iron Kettle looked to be the house of a prosperous farmer converted to an inn to make a profit off the trade that had resumed during and after Anna's Regency.

After discussing the arrangements for the players and lancers with the chief players and overcaptains, Secca dismounted and brushed off as much of the dried mud as she could before unstrapping her gear. She used the bootscraper and climbed the two wide plank steps up to the narrow covered porch that sheltered the entrance. Behind her came the others, led by Alcaren.

Once inside the inn, she glanced through the square archway into the public room, a space with worn split-plank

floors stained by age and grease, with rickety pine tables as
dark as ancient oak. The entire public room was barely large
enough for a score of diners. Then she turned to Wilten,
Delcetta, and Palian. Delvor was still on the front steps.
"We'll eat in a glass, after the lancers and mounts are settled
as best they can be."

"Ah . . . ummm."

At the sound of the apologetic bass voice, Secca turned.

"The scouts have explained all, Lady Sorceress." The
once-muscular innkeeper bowed twice, mostly with his
head, since a large midsection precluded any deeper a gesture of respect. "You have the best room, that you do." He
bowed again. "And the other lady the one adjoining. Yes,
indeed."

"Thank you." Secca inclined her head slightly.

"If you would show us?" Alcaren stepped forward, smiling pleasantly.

"Oh, yes. Yes, ser." The balding innkeeper turned and
waddled through a narrow rectangular archway that he
barely seemed to clear. "This way. This way, if you please."

Alcaren followed, with Gorkon behind him, then Secca
and Richina.

The corridor was short, and held but five doors, the last
two for the sorceresses.

The "best" room had a double-width bed, a ledge attached
to the wall beside it, on which was a small oil lamp. There
was one narrow window, a wash table, and a rough pine-
sided wardrobe without a door.

"Anything you want, we would please. Yes, we would."
Bowing effusively, the innkeeper backed away.

Secca suspected that, again, there would be draughts or
golds required that were not quite excessive, but close to it.

As Alcaren and Secca closed the door and surveyed the
small chamber, Secca could see that Alcaren's eyes looked
more dark-rimmed. Should she take the wards for at least a
day?

He caught her glance and shook his head. "Richina will

be well enough to carry them by the time we reach Nordfels."

"You are most stubborn, my love."

"Most practical, I fear," he replied.

"While the others are settling in," Secca said, "let me see
where the Sea-Priests are."

While Alcaren removed the bronze pitcher and basin and
laid the mirror on the small wash table, Secca tuned the lutar
and quickly sang the scrying spellsong.

> *"Show us now and in clear light*
> *where those with the Maitre spend this night . . ."*

The glass displayed a town square. On one side was a
two-story wooden building, its slab-planked sides covered
with a recent whitewash. The shutters were swung back and
revealed narrow casements with glass windows. Several
lancers in the white of Sturinn were posted as guards on the
front porch. Even through the glass, Secca could see the
sharpness of the white uniforms and the hard edge of discipline.

"That looks to be Elioch," Secca observed. "That's not
any town in Defalk, and the only town of any size in eastern
Neserea is Elioch."

"You could try a map spell."

She shook her head. "For now, that is good enough."

"At least they're not in Defalk yet."

"Not for another two or three days." Secca frowned.
"They should be traveling faster than they are."

"It's hard to travel fast," Alcaren replied, "if you have to
destroy everything along the roads you ride. That's true even
using sorcery, I'd wager."

Wincing at the images created by Alcaren's words, and
knowing that by the next evening Elioch would be ashes,
Secca sang the release couplet. She didn't need to see more,
and she certainly didn't want to call up scenes of the sorcerous carnage the Sturinnese had doubtless created, not

when there was nothing she could do but fret. "Tomorrow, we'll need to send a messenger to Lord Cassily, telling him we are coming."

"How will he take such?" asked Alcaren.

"That . . . I do not know. He was pleasant enough to Jolyn when she was his lover, and he now is lord because of her shadow sorcery, though he may not know such." Secca shrugged. "She said that he would make a good lord of the old style."

Alcaren nodded slowly.

Are there any good lords of the old style? Secca wondered.

113

A fine misting rain drifted around Secca, foglike enough that she had trouble seeing any riders except those within a few yards. Although it was close to midday, there was no sign of the sun or its warmth, and the air felt like that of a chill early-spring morning, or perhaps even a warmish winter morn. Even the green felt hat helped little because the fine rain drifted sideways as much as fell.

Alcaren had been right about the warmth creating just more mud, Secca reflected, as the Norweian officers led her forces along the road, if it could have been called such, leading to Nordfels. She doubted that she had been able to go a hundred yards all morning without having to ride through or around a puddle of muddy water. Some seemed as large as small ponds. Mud coated everything—the legs and belly of the gray mare, Secca's stirrups and boots, and her trousers practically halfway up her thighs.

She edged forward in the saddle, then reined in the mare as she saw that the scouts and the two Norweian officers had come to a halt at the low rise ahead. She eased up beside Alcaren and the two officers, then brought her mount to a halt.

"Sorceress Protector, the border lies here." Captain Salchaar bowed slightly in the saddle, a graceful gesture from a tall and lean woman, then gestured toward a weathered square stone post set on the right-hand shoulder of the muddy track, barely visible in the foggy rain.

Secca squinted, but could make out no inscriptions on the yard-and-a-half-high marker, and she turned her eyes back to the Norweian. "We appreciate your guidance and all that you have done, and all that the Council has provided."

"Nordwei is most appreciative of all that you have done, and we wish you triumph in the battles to come."

"That would be best for both Defalk and Nordwei," Secca replied. "We will do all we can."

"That is all the harmonies ask, all any can expect." Salchaar bowed again.

Secca returned the bow. "A good and safe return to Wei for you."

"Thank you, Lady Sorceress." Captain Salchaar turned her mount, as did Undercaptain Eztaar, and the two headed back northward, joined by the squad of Norweian lancers that had been in the rear. Shortly, the Norweians vanished into the mist.

The sorceress turned the gray mare, looking south from the gentle road crest, but there was little to see, except a few yards of muddy road, descending slowly, before the misting rain and fog obscured what lay beyond. Secca could guess what was there—more deks of muddy road and soggy ground, winter-browned grasses, and bare-limbed bushes.

Beyond that . . . Nordfels and the paved road that would lead to the Maitre and battles she wished not to contemplate and could not afford not to.

With a deep breath, she gestured to Alcaren, then Wilten. "We need to ride on."

114

West Pass, Denguic

Three men stand around the camp table on which rests a scrying glass. The Maitre faces the closed door flaps of the tent, while Marshal jerLeng and jerClayne face the Maitre. The faint scent of roasting mutton drifts into the tent from outside, where, in the growing twilight, cookfires have died from blazes into deep banks of coals.

"Your scouts were attacked?" asks the Maitre. "Why do you tell me that? You were told that the Defalkans had abandoned the keep at Westfort. Lord Kinor has always maintained five companies of his own lancers. He is Lord of the Western Marches, and he was placed as such under the recommendation of the evil one. Is it so surprising that they attacked? What were you thinking?"

"No one else has, not in two hundred deks of travel," points out jerLeng. "Nor have they abandoned a keep."

"That only shows that they fear us and that they know what sorcery can do." The Maitre smiles coldly. "That will not save them long. We will still destroy the keep."

"With no one in it?"

"Do you want them to be able to return to it once we move toward Falcor?"

"We could use it," suggests jerLeng. "After you destroy this Lord Kinor and his lancers."

"We cannot use spellsong to destroy every lord in western Defalk," the Maitre explains, his words deliberate, yet cold. "They have split up their lancers into squads, and all move separately. Kinor has his sons and even his dissonant daughter commanding each group. To use sorcery would require more than ten spells for just the lancers, possibly twice that to find and identify them enough for effective sorcery. It is more efficient to destroy the keep and town with a single spell. In weeks, there will be little for any to eat, and we will not have to worry about attacks."

The younger Sea-Priest does not move, but his eyes flit from the marshal to the Maitre as each speaks. He clears his throat.

"Yes?" The Maitre's tone suggests that jerClayne had best have something of value to offer.

"Ser . . . they have also removed all the food from the towns and keeps, and even the peasants are fleeing."

The Maitre offers a tight smile. "At Denguic and West-fort? Or all through the west?"

"Fussen has done little. Nor Aroch. We have a scroll from Lord Dostal, suggesting that he might be willing to supply us . . . in return for certain conditions."

"Tell him we'll spare his precious keep on our march to Falcor," the Maitre says. "Use those exact words—spare his keep on our march to Falcor."

"Yes, ser."

A knowing smile plays across the lips of Marshal jerLeng. "What of the Sorceress Protector and the Assistant Sorceress of Defalk?" His eyes travel to jerClayne.

"The Assistant Sorceress of Defalk remains in Dubaria, from what we can tell," jerClayne replies.

"From what you can tell?" The Sturinnese marshal frowns.

JerClayne sways on his feet, then steadies himself. "Both sorceresses use those strange wards. They cannot be seen directly in a glass, but that limits what sorcery they can use against us."

The Maitre looks at jerLeng, then jerClayne. After a long moment of cold silence, he speaks. "Tomorrow, we will raze Denguic and Westfort, then travel south to Fussen."

"What of Dubaria and the keeps to the north?"

"After Fussen, we will see. We may go to Dubaria—or take Lord Dostal's kind offer." The Maitre tilts his head, his

eyes on jerClayne. "Oh . . . and draft a scroll for me to send
to Lord Robero, suggesting that, if he wishes to save his
precious title, he had best have his lords supply us."

"Yes, ser."

"Once a few keeps come down in fire and rubble, he may
be more . . . accommodating . . ." The Maitre smiles once
more.

115

The rain of the previous days had vanished, and only
scattered and puffy white clouds scudded across the
midafternoon sky. The wind was stiff, blowing Secca's hair
back from her ears, but warm, as she rode up the causeway
to the keep at Nordfels, following the squad of SouthWomen
led by Delcetta.

Alcaren studied the ancient stone walls, rising a good fifteen yards above the berms they overlooked. "I'm glad you
used the glass. Then again, the walls of Dolov were more
impressive."

"I'd just as soon not create any more destruction in Defalk," Secca replied.

Whatever else she might have said was halted by a trumpet fanfare as the first riders neared the massive oak gates
swung wide in welcome. A second look revealed to Secca
that the gates had been chained open, and the chains were
both ancient and rusted in place.

Inside, the courtyard was barely large enough for the
squad of SouthWomen, Secca, Richina, Alcaren, Secca's
guards, and the players. A tall, dark-haired man attired in
deep blue and black, and wearing a black mourning band
on his left sleeve stood on a mounting block by the narrow
entrance to the keep building. Beside him was the trumpeter,
who played a second fanfare as Secca reined up.

"Welcome! Nordfels welcomes the Sorceress Protector of Defalk!" For all his size Lord Cassily had a strong but high tenor voice. Following his words, a broad smile showing large and uneven white teeth appeared on his squarish face.

Secca eased the gray mare forward. "Lord Cassily."

The tall dark-haired lord bowed as Secca reined up. "Lady and Sorceress Protector, we are most pleased to see you."

"We are glad to see you, Lord Cassily," Secca replied, "though we will not be staying long."

"I had thought not." Cassily's smile faded into a somber, almost stern expression. "Not when I considered your message." He paused. "We had received a scroll from Lord Robero . . . He had not heard of the death of my sire until a few weeks ago. Yet you knew . . ."

"I cannot say that I have heard much from Lord Robero," Secca replied. "We have been far beyond Defalk since last fall." She offered a smile she hoped was not too false. "I had used the glass, and it showed you. Since your father was not a young man . . ."

"You have not been in Defalk since harvest? Lord Robero did not mention such." Cassily smiled more warmly. "But I am chattering here when I should be allowing you to settle yourself in to refresh yourself before we eat." He cleared his throat. "My keep is small . . . and I do not have proper barracks, but we have the drying rooms we use for the apples, and I have had them swept, and the kitchen has prepared a hearty meal for all your companies. We did bring in some women from the town to help . . ."

Secca did not quite relax, but the burly lord's demeanor was at least accepting, if holding a heartiness that seemed slightly forced. "We are most grateful, and we will tariff you as little as possible, Lord Cassily. I know from Lady Jolyn that you are an honorable and honest lord. She has spoken most highly of you."

"She is a most . . . remarkable lady."

Secca laughed gently, and disarmingly, she hoped. "That she is." She half turned in the saddle and gestured. "This is

my consort, Lord Alcaren of Ranuak; Lady Richina, my
assistant sorceress; Palian, my chief of players . . ." When
she had finished introducing the chief players and the overcaptains, she added, "Without Overcaptain Delcetta and the
support of Ranuak, we would not now be here."

"Then we thank them as well." Cassily beckoned, and
from the handful of figures on the steps behind him, a slender and gray-bearded man slipped forward. "Anseln is my
saalmeister, and he will take all care to see that you and
your party are settled in as much comfort as we can offer.
We look to see you at table and to hear all that has come
to pass since you left Defalk."

Secca inclined her head. "We appreciate your hospitality
and look forward to sharing what we know and what lies
ahead for you and Defalk."

For the briefest moment, the hint of a frown crossed the
lord's face.

Secca wasn't about to tell Cassily everything, but what
she would tell him would be more than enough to leave him
quite sobered.

116

MANSUUS, MANSUUR

B right sunlight—from the first clear day in over a
week—poured through the Liedfuhr's study windows.
Kestrin stands in front of the desk, away from the light that
warmed the heavy fabric of his winter tunic too much for
comfort, listening to Bassil. As he stands listening, he
shifted his weight from one foot to the other.

"We have threescore of the catapults ready, and more than
tenscore of the oil vessels with fuses." Bassil inclines his
head.

"And sorcerers . . . or even sorceresses?" asks the Lied-fuhr.

The graying lancer overcaptain shakes his head. "The seers have found none in Mansuur, and the glasses do not lie."

"Have them look for children who have the talent."

"They have. There are scores of those."

"But no one to teach them." Kestrin sighs.

"Nor do we have more than a handful of players."

"Can it be that hard? It looks and sounds so simple."

"Does a perfect circle look difficult, sire? Yet how many can draw one? Does blade work look difficult when shown by an expert lancer? Does—"

"Enough! You have made your point, Bassil. You always do." Kestrin frowns, half-turning from the older man. "There is another problem. The shadowsinger was in Morgen, and she did not even know that Aerfor was there?"

"Aerfor is no longer there, sire," Bassil says. "The Norweians must have smuggled her aboard one of the Ranuan ships just before they left Lundholn."

"What? And you did not tell me?"

"I did not know until this morning, when the seers discovered she was on a ship. They had great difficulties . . ."

"Why?"

"Upon the ocean—"

"No. Why would they put her . . ." Kestrin's fist slams the desk. "Of course! They did not want her and Eryhal to remain in Nordwei, and also the farther they are from the Maitre the more difficult sorcery would be, especially on the ocean when the Sturinnese have no ships." A smile of relief crosses his face, but then fades. "Make sure that they follow her to make sure she is safe."

Bassil nods. "The Council of Wei thinks the sorceress will triumph."

Kestrin shakes his head. "That I doubt. They do not know, any more than do we. What that cunning old Ashtaar does understand is that by saving Aerfor, she can gain my gratitude and possibly that of the shadowsinger. She can also preserve the claims of both Eryhal and Aerfor, and perhaps keep Defalk from taking over Neserea and Dumar outright if the sorceresses can defeat the Maitre. That would be why she did not tell the sorceress." He pauses. "It galls me yet that I must hope that they do."

"From gall, one can recover," Bassil says mildly.

Kestrin laughs. "Always the practical one, Bassil."

"We try, sire. Even in times such as these."

117

The banquet hall was traditional Corian, a long room with a polished gray stone floor and ancient oak-paneled walls, with bronze lamps set in wall sconces. The table itself was a good ten yards in length, although places were set only on the half closest to the hearth. Lord Cassily sat at the head, in a thronelike chair upholstered in dark blue velvet. Secca sat to Lord Cassily's right, and to his left was Cassily's consort Andra, the very much younger woman he had taken as a consort almost a year before, after Jolyn had broken off her dalliance with Cassily. Beside Andra was Alcaren, with Richina beside him.

When the servers had filled the rose-tinted crystal goblets with a dark red wine, Cassily rose and lifted his own. "To the Sorceress Protector and all her company and friends."

"To the Sorceress Protector . . ."

Secca smiled politely, reminded how little she enjoyed the formal dinners and ceremonies, but gratified that Cassily seemed honestly glad to see her, especially after the sobering sights she had beheld in the scrying glass before she and Alcaren had descended to the hall for dinner.

"Thank you," she murmured as the lord reseated himself. "It is good to be here, and back in Defalk."

"It is good that you are here." The burly lord shifted his weight in the large chair, then paused as one of the serving boys eased before him a platter of sliced beef, covered with a brown sauce and toasted nuts of some sort.

Secca started to lift her goblet, but then stopped as Cassily served her three large slices of the beef before serving his consort, and then himself. With a knowing smile, he looked at Secca as he handed the platter to Alcaren. "I trust that you will be needing that, and perhaps more?"

Secca returned the smile, catching herself before referring to Jolyn. "Sorcery leaves one famished, and we have traveled far." She did lift the goblet and take the slightest sip of the wine, while Alcaren served Richina, then himself.

"You had said you had news . . ." offered Cassily.

"Not much of it is good," Secca admitted. "We sent a message scroll to the Lady Jolyn, and Lord Kinor and Lord Tiersen have cleared their keeps. The scrying glass shows that Kinor has attacked some Sturinnese patrols, but that has not slowed them. The Maitre has used sorcery to level the keep of Westfort. Not one stone remains upon another."

Andra's mouth opened, just fractionally before she closed it.

"That is why you warned them to leave their holds?" asked Cassily.

"That is also why I do not wish to take any of your armsmen and lancers, now, save for perhaps a few as scouts and to send back messages." Secca took a sip of the wine, then went on. "Sorcery is limited and cannot be used endlessly. If lancers and lords and ladies are scattered and spread throughout the lands, while the Sturinnese can destroy buildings and keeps and some lancers . . ."

"So . . . should they march north, we should do the same?" Cassily's mouth tightened. "Abandon all that we have?"

"The glass shows that both Kinor and Tiersen live, as do most of their followers and lancers. None of those who holed themselves within their keeps in Neserea survived their destruction under the sorcery of the Maitre."

Cassily nodded, slowly and reluctantly, more that he had heard Secca than he necessarily agreed. "Do you know which way they ride?"

"They are camped in Denguic. I would wager that they will level it as well once they move on, but I cannot tell in which direction they will ride until they do. If I know in the morning, I will tell you."

"We will send scouts southward. They could ride with you for a time."

"And return with news to you, although, I would guess," Secca said, "that you will not see the Maitre's forces this far north." *Not unless we fail.*

"Unless Defalk falls, you mean?" Cassily's smile was knowing and off-center.

"I am most hopeful that will not happen, but you are fortunate that he attacked from the west."

"Perhaps that makes up for the years when the Suhlmorrans attacked so often from the south." The burly lord laughed, ruefully. "My sire's forebears would not have called it fortunate, but we will take what fortune we can." He took a swallow of the wine. "And offer all that you can use in the fashion you see most fit."

A foreboding silence fell across the table.

"You're Lord Mietchel's daughter?" Secca asked Andra, who was but two years older than Richina, from what Secca recalled. It was an awkward question, because she very well knew the answer, and Andra doubtless knew that Secca knew, but Secca wanted Andra to give her an opening.

The younger woman smiled gently, but warmly. "His very youngest, as he has so often told all who would listen. He also says that I am more like his sister than him. Or than Alyssa."

"That would seem to be quite a compliment," Secca replied. From what she recalled of Andra's aunt, the Lady Wendella, that meant that Andra was probably a bit headstrong behind the pleasant front. But then, Andra's older sister was Lord Robero's consort, and while Alyssa presented a demure and charming front, she definitely had a mind of her own, enough that she had left her consort behind to visit her parents.

"We both have been known to express our views when it would have been better that we had not," Andra admitted.

Lord Cassily laughed. "You still do, my lady, and doubtless always will."

Secca nodded. Since Cassily hadn't been able to hold on to Jolyn, he'd tried to find a forthright woman like her, or so it seemed.

"My aunt has said that syrup catches more wishes than vinegar, but . . ." Andra shrugged helplessly. "Much as I try, too often I speak before considering, unlike Alyssa. My lord is most tolerant of this weakness, and for that I am grateful." Andra smiled at Cassily.

The love and affection in the smile, and in the smile with which Cassily responded, warmed Secca. From what she was seeing, she suspected that Cassily had learned much from Jolyn, yet was far better off consorted to the younger Andra.

"How is your sister?" Secca asked innocently.

Andra's eyes flicked to Cassily, who nodded. After the nod, Andra replied, "She found that it would be best if she took the children and repaired to Morra. She felt that the children would be safer there. My father still maintains five companies of lancers."

Secca held in a shiver at the matter-of-fact tone. Five companies meant nothing against the Sturinnese, but everything against Robero. "I have always liked and respected your sister," Secca answered.

"She respects you greatly, Lady Secca. She even sent me a scroll several weeks ago saying that and conveying her respects and her support for your bravery in defense of Liedwahr."

"She is most kind, indeed. We can only do what we think is best."

"You have shown that, Lady Secca," Cassily interjected, with the faintest emphasis on the pronoun. "Not all have." He gestured toward the server.

As another platter was held before her, Secca took a large helping of the lace-fried potatoes covered in butter-cream, then cut a morsel of the beef. As she began to eat, realizing that matters in Defalk were far worse than even Jolyn had conveyed, she also realized that she was sampling the best food she had eaten in seasons, if not in years, and that the food was also a statement of sorts, as well. So hungry she was that she had finished most of the lace-fried potatoes and all of the meat before looking up, almost embarrassed.

"I am so sorry . . ." she began.

"It is not a fault to be famished, or to enjoy a meal, Lady Sorceress," replied Cassily, half-laughing.

"This is excellent," Secca said simply.

"More than excellent," added Alcaren.

"We had hoped you would find it so," Andra replied. "The potatoes are fixed the way my aunt always has. The beef is an old favorite of my lord's."

There was a momentary silence.

"As you may have heard, Lady Secca," Cassily began slowly, "my father and I, for all that I loved him, did not see Defalk or Nordfels with the same eyes. My older brother believed as did my father, but after the accident in Heinene, my father was left to choose between me and my sister Asaro. Since Asaro had long since consorted to Lord Kinor, my sire had few choices, and we talked but seldom."

"I had heard something along those lines," Secca replied cautiously, even though she had not heard about the death of Cassily's older brother. Knowing what she had known about the late Lord Ebraak, she had few doubts about the nature of the "accident."

"We wish you to know that you are always welcome here," Cassily continued, "and that we will support you as we can."

"I cannot tell you how much that means."

"I will say more," Cassily went on, almost hurriedly. "While we can do nothing in this respect, my lady and I would say that Defalk would be far better off..." He paused. "Let us just say that we admire the heritage of the first years of the Lady Anna's efforts in Defalk." Cassily offered a smile, one somehow both defiant and yet supportive. "In some ways, it was a great tragedy that she and Lord Jecks..." The lord left his sentence unfinished.

Secca managed not to swallow or choke on the wine she had just sipped. "I also admired Lady Anna." She offered her own smile. "I may not be the best judge, though, for she was not only my mentor, but my mother from the time I was nine years. She wanted to do what was best for Defalk, as do I."

"That is most clear, Lady Secca," Andra said. "Anything we can do to aid you in defeating the Maitre, that we will support. And anything you may need after such, that too will we support."

Cassily nodded. "My lady speaks as I feel and will act."

"Thank you." Secca paused. "For now, we *could* use some provender for travel and a few extra mounts, could you spare such."

"You shall have them," Cassily declared.

Richina's eyes had widened at the turn in the conversation, but the younger sorceress had taken refuge behind the rose-tinted goblet.

"You are most kind," Alcaren said smoothly. "This is my first encounter with any of the Thirty-three, and I must confess that you have overwhelmed me with your kindnesses to my lady and your understanding."

"It is said that you are a lord of Ranuak," Andra offered.

Alcaren laughed. "That is a title of courtesy. Most properly, I was an overcaptain of lancers in the service of the Matriarch. Neither she nor I wished it known that I was also her cousin, if for very differing reasons." His voice turned wry. "So I was sent as part of the relief force to lift the siege of Elahwa, and there my lady Secca arrived in time

486 L. E. MODESITT, JR.

to save us all from annihilation. In an attempt to repay that which could never be repaid, we supported her in the efforts which expelled the Sea-Priests from Ebra, and later from Ranuak and Dumar—"

"Along the way," Secca interrupted firmly, "he saved my life and nearly lost his own in the effort. That was when we learned that we belonged together. I prevailed upon the Matriarch to consort us."

"Is that why you have three companies of SouthWomen?" asked Cassily.

Secca gestured down the table to Delcetta. "Overcaptain Delcetta might better explain that."

Delcetta smiled, half-proudly, half-sadly. "The South-Women's Council offered its services and lancers to the Sorceress Protector even before she consorted with Lord Alcaren. Five companies we brought. We lost two and Lady Secca one in the sea battles against the Sturinnese, but all my lancers and I will follow her and Alcaren until there are no Sea-Priests left in Liedwahr."

"Thank you." Cassily nodded slowly. "I have heard that even Lord Selber sent lancers to serve under you in Ebra, and that Lord Hadrenn of Ebra put all his forces under your command."

"That is so," Secca acknowledged.

"I do not recall any lords doing so for any lord or lady since Lady Anna," observed Cassily.

"There has not been the need," Secca pointed out.

"Nor do I see any lords or ladies placing their forces under any but you during this time of need," Cassily continued.

"I believe Lord Tiersen and Lord Kinor are working with Lady Jolyn," Secca said.

"They are wise to do so, and while they will work with Lady Jolyn, I would wager that only to you would they cede command."

"I cannot say, Lord Cassily," Secca replied, "but your support is most appreciated. How much I cannot tell you."

Cassily laughed, softly, but warmly. "Enough of this. You know where we stand. Now let us talk of what we do not know. Perhaps Lord Alcaren can tell us of Ranuak and what it was like to grow up there."

Alcaren smiled broadly. "Are you most certain you wish to hear the ramblings of a man whose only success has been in consorting?"

A loud snort came from somewhere down the table, from Delcetta, Secca thought.

"There are some who think otherwise," Cassily said. "Come, let us hear . . ."

Secca's consort cleared his throat. "In Ranuak, as you have heard, the women are the traders, and my mother was and is most successful at such, and my younger sister promises to be so as well. Alas . . . there are certain virtues a trader must have, such as a love of the sea, and the ability to remain hale and healthy on sea voyages through all manner of weather . . ."

Secca smiled, knowing where Alcaren's tale was headed. She tried not to yawn, but could not help but think of the triple-width bed in the opulent guest quarters above, and the sleep she would dearly like to have after the trek through the Nordbergs—even if the section they had traversed had been little more than hills compared to the peaks to the east and west. Yet for all her tiredness, she felt almost chill as she considered Lord Cassily's declarations. Had Robero so alienated the Thirty-three? Or had Jolyn so altered Cassily's perceptions about Defalk?

Would Secca ever really know? Did it matter against the certainty that the Maitre was creating an ever-increasing swath of destruction across Neserea and into Defalk? Yet, neither she nor her lancers could have traveled faster than they had.

A faint and sad smile crossed her lips as she took another tiny sip of the red wine. Bed and sleep would have to wait, and she hoped she could remain alert.

118

F or dek after dek, Secca and her forces had ridden south along the great gray stone road across the seemingly endless valley, where faint green shoots had begun to appear at the base of the winter-browned prairie grass. The ground was so level that the only depressions were the small ponds created years before when sorcery had removed the rock beneath the soil to provide the paving stones and gravel for the road itself. The wind remained warm and light, although Secca could see clouds building up over the Mittfels to the west.

After the struggle to cross the Nordbergs, Secca felt almost as though they were flying southward. Yet so wide were the glasslands that they seemed to make little progress. Still, for Secca, it was a relief that they could ride abreast, with Alcaren to her left and Richina to her right, and that they had escaped the muddy roads of the north.

"They say that there are snakes in the grass," Richina said. "Large ones."

"It is too early in the year for the snakes, and for that I am glad." Secca hid a smile as she continued. "The old Rider of Heinene told Lady Anna that some were five yards long and could swallow a gazelle."

Alcaren raised his eyebrows, before adding, "That is nothing compared to the serpents of the Southern Ocean. Traders say that they have been known to swallow longboats whole. Only the largest serpents, that is."

Richina frowned slightly as she turned in the saddle toward him.

"Others say that they must snap the boats in two with their tails before they can swallow them." Alcaren grinned. "What are grass snakes compared to those?"

"Gazelles move far more swiftly than longboats," Secca countered, stifling a laugh. "I would rather face a sea serpent than a grass snake."

"Especially here," riposted Alcaren.

Then, both Secca and Alcaren burst into laughter.

After a moment, so did Richina, flushing as she did so.

After the laughter died away, Richina, still flushed, peered southward. "How much farther, do you think?"

"We should see the hilltop where the Rider has his Kuyurt before long," Secca promised Richina.

Secca was curious about what she would find at the Kuyurt, a hilltop domicile, not really a keep, of Lord Vyasal, the Rider of Heinene. Vyasal's father had been an early and strong supporter of Anna, and Vyasal had continued his vocal support after his sire's death. Especially after having seen the smoldering ruins of Denguic in the glass that morning, Secca could only hope that the Maitre would move slowly and that Vyasal would support her as well as had Cassily, at least in terms of supplies. She would need all the support she could muster in the aftermath of the Maitre's destruction of towns and keeps.

119

FUSSEN, DEFALK

The wind blows out of the north, across the granite-studded ridgeline and toward the town of Fussen in the shallow valley below. To the southwest, above the town, looms the keep. Not a single wisp of smoke rises from the silent town, for all that it is chilly, even in the sunlight. Not a body or a mount is visible in the town. Nor is there any sign of life from the keep. The faint high haze that weakens the sun lends an additional sense of chill to the morning.

The players and drummers have formed in an almost-perfect arc on the ridge, facing the town below. Behind them are twenty-five companies of lancers, mounted and ready to attack or defend, should either be necessary. Another sixty-five companies are stationed along the stone-paved highway from Denguic. Standing before the players and drummers are a half-score of Sea-Priest sorcerers, headed by the Maitre, and Marshal jerLeng. Their white uniforms are spotless and shimmer under the cold morning sun.

"They have abandoned the town and keep, Maitre," jerClayne reports.

"Are there men with arms nearby?" questions the Maitre. "Those of Defalk or Fussen itself?"

"The glass shows small groups of armed men. Some are lancers, and some wear livery of a lord. They have avoided our sweeps. They are not near the town, but many would be within several deks, we would judge."

"Good. They will not escape the way the last ones did." The Maitre's voice is cold. "We may not get all of them, but enough will suffer."

JerClayne looks to Marshal jerLeng, but jerLeng neither acknowledges the glance nor speaks.

The Maitre steps forward and gestures to the players and drummers. "The firebolt song! On my signal."

"We stand ready, Maitre," comes back the response.

The Maitre raises his left hand, then drops it. The drumming rises from a rhythmic backdrop into a pulsing roar, then softens to fall beneath the Maitre's baritone as he begins the spellsong.

"Blast with fire, blast with flame,
all men in Fussen not of Sturinn's name,
sear with whips of sound, and fire's lash,
turning all against us into ash . . . "

Lines of flame sear through the high overcast, narrow needles of color seemingly jabbing at the ground randomly.

As the lines of fire subside, the Maitre sits down heavily on the camp stool that awaits him.

He watches, his head moving from side to side, until no more flame needles flash down from above the overcast. Only then does he turn and look to jerClayne and the two younger Sea-Priests. "That will leave their women for suitable use. You will handle the spells to turn the keep and town into rubble."

"Yes, Maitre." JerClayne bows, then steps forward. "The hammer song."

"The hammer song. We stand ready," replies the head player, the only one with gold rings on the sleeves of his white tunic.

Squaring his shoulders, jerClayne lifts his left hand, then drops it. He waits, then joins the players and drums with his voice and words.

"Smash all brick and break all stone,
so no building, wall, or hall shall stand alone.
Then with flame and fire's heat . . ."

As the words and accompaniment fade, the ground, and even the hard granite underlying the ridge shivers underfoot to the rhythm of blows, as if delivered by an unseen hammer that flattens everything in the town, and all structures of the keep to the west against the anvil of the very earth. Dust rises dozens of yards into the sky, creating veils that shroud the land and the rubble beneath those shrouds.

Within moments of the last words of the spellsong lifting into the air, jerClayne pitches forward, his fall barely stopped by the taller of the young sorcerers.

"Make sure he gets food and rest," the Maitre says. "We have much more to do. Much more." He turns and walks toward his tent.

To the southwest reddish dust swirls around the crushed and crumbled stone that had been the keep of Fussen. In the valley below the keep, where the town had been, tongues of fire roar into the sky, creating a wall of flame and smoke that obscures even the outlines of the shattered hilltop keep.

To the south and the east, lines of thin black smoke rise everywhere, out of woodlots and from behind hills high and low.

120

The hilltop Kuyurt of the Rider of Heinene was not a keep, but a series of stone-walled and white-plastered rooms built in an oval and joined by an enclosed corridor set on the inside of the rooms. Separate from the Kuyurt were the guest stables, slightly downhill and to the west. At the south end of the oval was a walled garden. At the north end were a great room and the banquet hall where Vyasal had feted them the night before and where Secca and Alcaren sat at one end of the long table, eating a breakfast of fried flatbread, soft white cheese, and honey-spiced baked apple slices.

Vyasal had eaten earlier, but sat at the table with Secca, Alcaren, Richina, and the two chief players. His dark brown eyes, intent and deep above his trimmed black beard, fixed upon Secca. "You still do not wish me and my riders to come with you?"

Secca took another sip of the warm cider, thinking, before answering. "We face sorcery. For now, I would not wish any riders because the Maitre might destroy them before they could ride against his lancers. Against such sorcery, we cannot protect a large force. If we prevail in sorcery, then . . . then we will need riders." She paused. "If you could spare a few riders, and one or two that we could send back to summon you when the time comes . . . ?"

Vyasal nodded. "That . . . that we can do, and my daughter Valya, she will ride with you." The Rider of Heinene laughed. "Always, she has said that she would do as the men do. Now, I can send her with a true battle sorceress."

Secca nodded, hoping she had not shown her concern inadvertently, for she had met Valya the evening before, and the girl—while tall, muscular, and wiry like her father— was a good three years shy of her score.

"She is the eldest, and since I have but daughters, best she learn from a woman who commands."

While the words were a statement, Secca understood the appeal as well. She smiled. "I will see that she is with me or Richina at all times."

Vyasal inclined his head ever so slightly. "Valya has made ready, in hopes that she would accompany you."

"She will." Secca forced herself to take another deep swallow of the warm cider as she finished a second section of the hot flatbread, onto which she had piled apple slices.

"How long before the lancers are ready, do you think?" She glanced at Alcaren, who looked somewhat more rested than the night before, although there were still dark circles under his gray-blue eyes.

"A glass or so."

"Before you go," insisted Vyasal, "you must see our horses." His dark eyes sparkled. "I must insist."

"I am not a rider," Secca protested, even as she wondered if she could see the horses quickly enough so that they would not be delayed. It was still a good two days' ride to Dubaria, and a day and a half beyond that to the ruins of Westfort and Denguic. Her lips tightened at the thought of the destruction the Sturinnese had already created and the concern about what else might be devastated before she could reach the Sturinnese. She tried not to think about her fears that what she knew might not be enough—or that she might have to use even more terrible spells than those she had already employed.

Vyasal laughed. "Once, perhaps, that was true. I saw you ride into the Kuyurt. You are a rider. So you must see our horses."

Secca rose. "Best we do so now, then, for I fear to delay much will offer the Maitre more opportunities for destruction."

Vyasal stood as well, saying in a low voice, "Would that others had such concerns." He added more loudly, "I will meet you by the guest stables."

"We will be there as soon as we get our gear." Secca turned to Palian. "You will have a bit more time to gather the players."

"I fear some will need it." Palian's voice was dry. "We will be ready when you return."

Delvor merely nodded.

Secca, Alcaren, and Richina walked from the banquet hall.

As they made their way along the stone-walled inside corridor, Richina spoke. "Lady Secca, might I accompany you to see the horses?"

"Of course. So long as you are packed and ready to ride from there."

"I am already packed."

Alcaren said nothing until he had closed the door to the guest chamber, a room nearly as large as the one they had occupied in Nordfels, but whose white-plastered walls and arched ceiling were draped with dun silks, giving it the impression of an enormous tent. "Those words referred to Lord Robero."

"They did indeed, unhappily." Secca set the lutar on the foot of the low bed, which was a circular affair in the middle of the room with no headboard or footboard, but with dun silk quilts and more than a half-score of pillows. "If what Jolyn wrote us earlier is correct, Defalk is splintering once more, into the factions of the old traditions and the new ways."

"I have but seen those favoring the new ways." Alcaren shouldered his saddlebags.

"Most of those in the west favored Anna," Secca pointed out, "save Ustal, and Falar is the warder of his heir." She slipped on her riding jacket and tucked the green felt hat into her belt.

Alcaren shrugged helplessly.

Secca shook her head, realizing, belatedly, that Alcaren would not have known. He was so good at understanding that at times she forgot he was unfamiliar with much of the history of Defalk. "The demesne of Fussen. Falar was the younger son, and Ustal the older. Ustal nearly destroyed the demesne with his insistence on following the old traditions, but he died when a crossbow wire frayed and slashed out his throat. Falar is also the consort of Lady Herene of Pamr, but he has been acting as warder for the heir. I think young Uslyn reached his score while we were at sea. There was talk of that just before we left Defalk in the fall. In any case, the other western lords supported Lady Anna. Many of those in the center of Defalk, or in the south, did not, and still some of those favor the older traditions."

"The ones who never had to shed their blood against invaders," Alcaren observed dryly, "or who never had to worry about such."

"Just so." Secca lifted the saddlebags and lutar.

Alcaren opened the door, and they walked out past Dymen and Easlon, who fell in behind them. Richina was waiting by the guest stables and had already saddled her mount. Gorkon had saddled the gray and held the mare while Secca strapped on the saddlebags, then the scrying mirror and lutar.

Vyasal rode up on one of the huge raider beasts, a stallion with a coat of so deep and lustrous a blackish brown that it shimmered in the early-morning light almost like polished black stone. Riding beside him was Valya. Like Secca, and unlike the other women Secca had seen in the Kuyurt, her black hair was cut short. She wore the black leather shoulder harness of a rider, with the twin short blades across her back. A small circular shield rested in front of her right knee.

"Good morning, Valya," Secca said. "I see you are prepared for the worst."

"Or the best, Lady Sorceress." Valya inclined her head. "Thank you."

The Rider of Heinene studied the gray mare intently, then looked to Secca. "Are you ready, Lady Sorceress?"

Secca tightened the straps holding the lutar and mounted.

"The horses I want you to view are downhill and just to the west," Vyasal said, easing his mount to Secca's left.

Alcaren rode to the right, while Richina and Valya followed the three down the gentle slope. Easlon and Gorkon brought up the rear.

The ride was indeed short, less than a dek, Secca judged, when Vyasal reined up beside a stone wall little more than a yard high that formed a circle with a circumference of roughly a dek. There was a gate of sorts formed by two poles crossing an opening perhaps two yards wide in the stones. The area inside the wall was heavily grassed, and a narrow creek ran through it, with openings in the wall to accommodate the thin line of cold rushing water. There were five large horses—raider beasts—standing less than fifty yards from the wall.

"They could jump this if they wished. It pleases them to stay," Vyasal said with a laugh. "I could whistle, and they would come, but I will not." He turned in the saddle and faced Secca, the smile fading. "You must have a beast that matches your spirit."

"How will you know that one of them does?" Secca asked, amused in spite of herself at the Rider's assurance, amused and wondering whether to be offended.

"Your mother?—the great sorceress? She was fortunate to find her first beast because she had no Rider to aid her. I am the Rider. I can tell you will find a mount. You must walk up to them by yourself . . . you will find the one that suits you."

Alcaren's eyes widened.

Secca slowly nodded, understanding more than Vyasal would ever say. She dismounted and handed the gray's reins to Gorkon, who took them solemnly. Then she walked to the gate and ducked between the two poles. There were some advantages to being small.

Secca wondered what she was doing—walking up to the largest horses in all Erde, beasts trained to kill enemies and any threat to their riders—if they accepted a rider. She smiled, ruefully. Perhaps she was so small that she would be seen as no threat, even if none liked her.

Her eyes ran over the five horses, all of whom had lifted their heads from where they had been grazing. The one farthest to Secca's left was a mare, her coat a shade that Secca could only have described as firegold. Beside her was another mare, with a darker coat, more the shade of the mount that Vyasal rode. On the right side was a palomino stallion, almost like Farinelli, the first beast that Anna had ridden. The stallion snorted once, and turned, neither moving closer, nor farther away, but just watching Secca. The other two horses, both mares, with more silvery tinges in their palomino coats, also looked at Secca, almost indifferently.

Secca took another few steps, looking at the two mares to her left. The firegold mare raised her head slightly, then lowered it, and her eyes seemed to meet Secca's. The sorceress took another step toward her. The mare with the darker coat eased back, away from both Secca and the firegold.

Before she quite realized it, Secca stood by—or beneath, she felt—the firegold mare. Slowly, very slowly, she extended an open hand. The mare lowered her head just enough to sniff Secca's hand. After a moment, Secca's fingers gently touched the mare's shoulder. The mare continued to look at Secca, almost impatiently, Secca felt.

Now what do I do? Secca glanced toward Vyasal.

"You walk toward us. She will follow. It must be her choice as well," the Rider called.

Feeling foolish, Secca turned and walked slowly back toward the gate. She could feel the firegold's breath on her neck, following her step for step. She stopped at the pole gate and turned.

The firegold mare snorted, gently, her muzzle just spans from Secca's face.

"She is ready for you to saddle her," Vyasal said.

"I . . . never have I seen mounts do that," Richina murmured, if loudly enough for Secca to hear.

"Then never have you seen a well-trained raider beast," replied Vyasal. "They know who will be their rider."

Alcaren dismounted and began to unfasten the gear strapped behind Secca's saddle.

"You will need a Rider bridle." The Rider of Heinene grinned as he lifted one in his left hand. "I thought to bring one."

Secca shook her head. "You *knew*."

"You are a sorceress, Lady Secca. I am the Rider."

Secca leaned across the gate and took the bridle, then studied it. The bridle had no bit, and appeared to be a modified hackamore. Somehow, that didn't surprise Secca. A Rider-trained raider beast would obey because it valued its rider, not through pain or force. When Secca turned, bridle in hand, the mare had actually lowered her head to be bridled. With a smile, Secca slipped the bridle over the mare's head and ears, and fastened it in place.

"Here." Alcaren handed the saddle blanket across the gate to his consort.

Secca was still dazed. Here she was, saddling a beast whose shoulders she could barely reach, even stretching, and what was amazing was that the firegold mare was letting her, even seeming to encourage her. Secca wondered about the length of the girths from her own saddle, but they were long enough—if with little to spare.

Once she had finished, Secca mounted, and this time she definitely had to jump-mount, just to get her foot in the stirrup. The mare did not move, except once Secca was in the saddle, to toss her head slightly, as if to indicate that she would be glad to be moving on.

Vyasal had dismounted and removed the two poles to let

Secca ride out of the stone corral. He remounted and did not replace them.

Secca looked down at the faithful gray mare, then turned to Vyasal, inquiringly.

"You worry about the little gray? Do not." Vyasal smiled. "She has carried you far. She should be honored, and we will feed her and pamper her so long as she lives. We do not mistreat or discard even the oldest and the smallest."

At that moment, a low, evil-sounding note—a dissonant harmonic—shivered through Secca. Secca glanced toward Alcaren, who had paled. Richina shivered.

So cold . . . so deadly. Secca swallowed.

"You are troubled," Vyasal said. "Do not be. We will take your little mare and we will give her the best of care and pasture, but she is tired . . ."

Secca shook her head. "I'm sorry. It is not that. Somewhere, someone has done some terrible sorcery, and I fear it is the Maitre."

Vyasal nodded, if sadly. "You are like your mother in that as well—sensing what most could not and would not."

"We need to see." Secca feared what the glass would show.

Alcaren had already dismounted, once more, and laid the scrying glass in its leathers upon a flat area of ground, amid the tan winter-browned grass stalks of the previous season and the green shoots that were beginning to herald the spring.

She dismounted and offered the firegold's reins to Vyasal. "If you would . . ."

The Rider just smiled as Secca took the lutar from behind the saddle, where she had just refastened it. Secca checked the tuning, and then thought for several moments. Finally, she sang.

> *"Show us now what sorcery has shivered through the land . . ."*

The mirror in the heat-darkened frame silvered, then centered on a panoramic view.

Secca looked down into the glass. Smoke swirled from the town where some structure smoldered and others still burned. The keep on the hillside was little more than scattered stones, licked by the intermittent flames of those items that flared in fire from the heat.

Vyasal licked his lips nervously. "I had heard . . . but to see an image from so far away . . ."

"It looks like Esaria," Richina said.

"It felt worse," Secca mused.

"What about the people?" asked Alcaren.

Secca looked at him, inquiringly.

"That kind of chord . . . it wasn't pure Clearsong," he said.

Vyasal's eyes flicked from the mirror to Secca, and then to Alcaren.

Secca tried another spellsong.

> *"Show us now from Fussen, Uslyn, Falar and their*
> *   best,*
> *and of those who fought or fled the fate of the rest . . ."*

The silver of the mirror twisted, and for the briefest of moments filled with hundreds of separate images, all blackened corpses. Then, with a splintering *crackkk!*, silvered glass sprayed across the grass.

Secca looked blankly at the shattered and scattered glass, the fragments glinting in the early-morning sunlight. Scores of scores had died . . . scores of scores . . . Falar, Lady Herene's consort, who always had a ready smile, and Uslyn, who had barely become lord of his demesne. Lady Herene and her family had always supported Anna, and now Secca, and once again it seemed as though they had been punished for that support.

Vyasal looked from the shards of glass and then to Secca.

"You must do what you must." A concerned smile appeared. "The mare, she will help."

"Might you have a mirror such as this one was?" asked Alcaren. "We have a smaller one, but going into battle against the Maitre . . ."

"A mirror—that is little to supply. There is a sturdy one in the corridor off my chamber." Vyasal laughed. "I will send for it." He turned in the saddle and looked at his dark-haired daughter.

"The one with the plain dark wood border?" asked the young woman.

"That is the one."

As Valya turned her mount and urged the silver-gold stallion into a trot up the hill, Secca glanced at the firegold mare, who had not moved. "Songfire. You're Songfire." She had never named a mount before, but the mare was not just a mare. That she knew.

Then, she recased the lutar and strapped it behind the saddle. Pointing to the steaming wood frame that had once held a mirror used for scrying, she asked, "Would you mind if we left that . . . ?"

Vyasal laughed. "Ha! Unlike so many, you ask, and for that courtesy alone I would bring every rider in the grass-lands behind you, Lady Secca. We will take care of it once you are on your way."

"Thank you." Secca remounted Songfire, leaning forward in the saddle and patting the mare's shoulder and getting a slight *whuff* in return.

As she settled herself in the saddle, Secca was suddenly conscious that she seemed to tower over Alcaren and Ri-china, or so it seemed, although her head was probably only a few spans higher than theirs. But after years of being the smallest on smaller mounts, the change seemed enormous.

"You see," Vyasal proclaimed, "now you have an advan-tage none can match. You are small, and your Songfire can carry you more swiftly and for longer than any. Even I could not catch you if you had the slightest of starts." The Rider grinned, clearly pleased with himself as the group rode back uphill.

Secca was more than conscious of Richina's eyes on her back as they neared the stone walls of the Kuyurt. There, by the guest stables, the lancers and players were already formed up. Across a space of fifty yards from them was a line of men and woman in the battle garb of the Riders, with the twin blades in shoulder harnesses.

Secca glanced toward Vyasal.

"Only an honor guard," The Rider replied. "We could not send you off without showing our support for you." The emphasis on the pronoun was slight, but it was clear.

Secca felt a chill at Vyasal's words, but turned as Palian rode toward them.

The chief player reined up, and declared, "The players stand ready, Lady Secca." A knowing smile crossed her face. "Your mount . . . she is beautiful."

"A Sorceress Protector who must defend her land against the Sea-Priests must have a mount that declares who she is," Vyasal said.

Valya reappeared on her mount, carrying an oblong object, wrapped in a brown blanket of some sort, and rode toward Secca and her father. Alcaren intercepted her and took the replacement mirror, further wrapping it in the leathers, before he eased his gelding beside the raider mare Secca rode. There he leaned over and fastened the new scrying mirror behind Secca's saddle.

"Lancers ready!" called out Wilten.

"SouthWomen ready!" came from Delcetta.

Secca nodded and eased Songfire toward the front of what would be a column. Vyasal rode beside her on the left, with Alcaren on the right, and Valya and Secca riding directly behind them. Secca had barely to touch the reins to signal the firegold mare to stop.

Vyasal eased his mount closer beside Secca, and leaned toward her. "I trust you with my daughter and my heir. I would trust you with my life. All those in Defalk who think beyond their petty appetites would trust you, for you will not fail us, Sorceress-Protector." He straightened, and proclaimed loudly, "Go in victory!"

The riders mounted as an honor guard repeated the cry. "Go in victory."

Secca swallowed, thought for a moment, then replied, "With your support and your faith, we will bring victory and peace to Defalk once more." *You hope you can.* Even with the doubts inside her, she smiled as she touched the reins, and Songfire carried her toward the road that led southward—toward Dubaria and Fussen and the Maitre. And toward all those who had already died . . . and those who would.

121

EAST OF FUSSEN, DEFALK

The Maitre, jerClayne, and Marshal jerLeng sit on stools around the camp table under the silk canopy of the Maitre's tent. A single oil lamp offers dim but adequate illumination, casting shadows across the faces of all three.

"The Shadow Sorceress is traveling south. She has passed the grasslands and enters the hills to the south of Heinene. She has added no lancers from either Nordfels or from the raider chief." JerClayne pauses. "Not in any numbers that we can see."

"That would show that even the western lords are less than fond of a woman with power," points out the Maitre. "Or that they do not trust her not to lose their lancers in battle."

"I would that your scrying could show more," says the marshal.

"Her wards keep us from seeing her directly, or those

close to her," replies the younger Sea-Priest, "just as ours keep her from seeing the Maitre or us when we are close to him."

"Doubtless she heads for Dubaria," the Maitre observes. "She can have Dubaria."

The younger Sea-Priest and the marshal wait.

"We have an invitation of sorts, do we not? From Lord Dostal of Aroch?" A hard smile curls across the lips of the Maitre.

"You would leave Dubaria?" asks jerLeng.

"Only for now. Only for now. If we ride directly to Aroch, we are closer to Falcor, and she must come to us to save the liedstadt. So we will go there and let her come to us. Then we will see."

"See what?" questions jerLeng.

"Aroch controls the access to Falcor. It is time to draw Lord Robero into this. Holding Aroch will let us do so. From there we will send emissaries to Falcor. We will threaten to destroy Falcor unless Lord Robero orders the Shadow Sorceress to allow us to return to Neserea unmolested."

"Why would he do such when Stura is in ruins and we have no fleet?"

The Maitre smiles crookedly. "Does he know such? Neither sorceress is near him, and your scrying has shown that he paces and frets. There are no message tubes upon his desk. We do have sorcery and close to one hundred companies of lancers. He can muster less than a score, if that."

"So he thinks that he is likely to lose all unless he treats with us . . ."

"We can hope that he sees matters in that light. From what we have seen, it is most likely."

"Still . . . will she not come after us?"

"If she obeys one order, she will obey another. If she obeys neither, then we will level Aroch and move on Falcor. Either way, she will get no support from Lord Robero, and he will get none from her. We will destroy them each in turn." The Maitre leans forward. "You, jerLeng, will take thirty companies and leave early in the morning to take advantage of the good Lord Dostal's invitation. I will send a younger sorcerer with you, should it be necessary to destroy a section of the wall or the gates."

The marshal nods. "And . . . what of Lord Dostal?"

"Once you have the hold well in hand . . . the usual. Leave the women, restrained suitably, of course. We will need serfs and servants in the years to come."

122

Gray clouds filled most of the afternoon sky, with occasional patches of blue. The wind came and went, as did quick pattering rain, never enough to more than dampen the dust on the road stones before the rain stopped and the sun shone, if briefly, before another series of gusts and more showers scudded over the low and rolling hills that were mostly forest. While some of the scattered cottages had small fields ready to be tilled, most of the open ground was pasture, and here and there were some flocks of sheep.

Secca had the green felt hat tucked in her belt but preferred not to wear it. She bent forward slightly in the saddle and patted Songfire on the shoulder, still marveling that she was riding a raider beast and enjoying it.

Abruptly, she straightened as she saw riders coming from the south along the great western road. She squinted to make them out, then relaxed as she saw the green uniforms mixed with several of blue and crimson. Some of the lancers Wilten and Delcetta had sent out as scouts were returning.

"They must have something to report," Alcaren suggested.

"I hope it's good." Secca shifted her weight in the saddle. As she continued to ride southward along the western road, she watched as Wilten finished talking to the scout.

Then the overcaptain turned his mount and headed around the vanguard and back toward Secca and Alcaren. Wilten eased his mount around and rode beside Secca. "The scouts have returned with a messenger from Lord Tiersen. His forces are scattered through the lands ahead, but he will meet you at a small hamlet several deks farther to the south." The overcaptain frowned, wrinkling his forehead. "The hamlet is called Sedak. It has a sawmill, and is in the woods a dek to the east of the road."

"Where it is more difficult to scry," Secca noted.

"I would judge so, lady."

"Have they had any trouble with the Sturinnese?"

"They attacked a scouting party," Wilten reported. "None of the Sea-Priest lancers survived, but Lord Tiersen lost some of his lancers."

"Not too many, I hope."

"The messenger did not say."

"Send back a messenger to tell Lord Tiersen we will be there shortly."

Wilten nodded, if dubiously.

"The glass showed no Sturinnese near here this morning. They cannot have reached here yet, and we have more than enough lancers and sorceresses to deal with anything else," Secca pointed out.

"You will let us send out an advance squad?"

"Of course. You have my leave. Remember . . ." Secca shook her head. Wilten wouldn't know what she was thinking. "Tiersen and his consort saved my life when I was a child. She almost died in doing it. I owe them greatly."

Some of the stiffness left the overcaptain's face.

"Tiersen is a good lord, and he will help us in any way he can," Secca added. "Your squad should be careful, but I would doubt that the dangers lie with him."

Wilten bowed. "I will accompany them."

"Thank you." Secca wasn't about to countermand that decision by Wilten, not when doing so would have implied that all she had just said was false or misleading—and it wasn't. "Tell Lord Tiersen I look forward to seeing him as soon as we arrive."

"That I will, Lady Secca."

As Wilten rode back toward the vanguard, Alcaren laughed softly. "He still trusts not those he does not know."

"Better that than trusting blindly," Secca replied.

As they rode the next dek of the road, Secca did notice that she saw no flocks in the meadows and no smoke from chimneys. She glanced back over her shoulder. Had it been that way for a time, and she hadn't noticed, or was there a change as they neared Dubaria?

While the road was smooth and level, it did wind around the hills, and when they rode around another gentle curve, they came to a crossroads of sorts. There two lancers had reined up, one a SouthWoman and the other in the green of Loïseau. The lane led eastward into a heavy forest.

Delcetta, who had taken over command of the vanguard in Wilten's absence, rode back to Secca. "They say that the hamlet is a dek to the east."

"We might as well follow the lane, then," Secca replied.

"I would send the vanguard at least a half-dek ahead," counseled the SouthWoman overcaptain.

"As you see fit, overcaptain. I will also uncase my lutar."

"I trust we will need neither," Delcetta replied, "yet I would be prepared."

Secca waited until the vanguard was almost out of sight on the lane that rose slowly along an ancient ridge, then urged Songfire forward. While the mare's ear's lifted slightly for a moment, she seemed relaxed.

The lane had been cut through ancient oaks, whose trunks were a good fifteen yards back from each shoulder of the clay track. The heavy trunks and the towering crowns overshadowed the entire lane, and in the gloom the air was colder and far damper.

"It would be hard to find someone hidden here with a glass," Alcaren pointed out.

"I'm certain Tiersen—or Lysara—thought about that," Secca replied.

After less than a dek, the lane curved to the south and began to descend. Abruptly, the ancient trees ended, revealing a clumping of buildings set against a hillside, where an older building overlooked a millpond and millrace. Below the mill was a long lumber barn, and Secca could smell damp sawdust.

Wilten's advance squad was drawn up before another group of riders, headed by a tall and muscular blond figure.

"Secca!" The call came from the muscular blond man.

"Tiersen!" Secca replied, grinning in spite of herself as she rode toward the dwellings of the hamlet behind the SouthWomen. The lancers eased aside as Secca neared Tiersen and his lancers.

Favoring Secca with a broad smile, Tiersen noted, "I see you've taken to riding raider beasts." Even after more than a score of years, the Lord of Dubaria retained the same lankiness he had possessed as a youth.

"Songfire was a gift from Lord Vyasal." On the mount behind the Lord of Dubaria, Secca recognized another figure, although the red hair was now streaked with gray. "Lysara!"

"You haven't changed at all," Lysara offered.

"Not in some ways," Secca replied. "I'm still small." She paused. "I didn't tell you, not directly." She gestured to Alcaren. "This is Alcaren. We were consorted by the Matriarch in Encora at the turn of spring."

"By the Matriarch," said Tiersen with a laugh. "I am impressed." He smiled openly at Alcaren. "Welcome to the lands of Dubaria, such as they are. If Secca chose you, you must have many talents. She is very choosy; she even turned down the Lord of Defalk."

Alcaren glanced toward Secca.

Secca flushed, in spite of herself.

"She did," Lysara insisted, with a mischievous grin. "She even once told him he was a worthless bully."

"I doubt that I can compare to the lord of a land," Alcaren said.

"He doesn't compare to you, my love," Secca replied. "Not in any way."

Tiersen cleared his throat.

The others looked to him.

"I saved the largest dwelling in the hamlet for you and your immediate party," Tiersen offered.

"Thank you." Secca felt confused by all the crosscurrents. "Oh . . . you recall Palian, and Delvor. They head my players. And Richina, and this is Valya, the oldest daughter of Vyasal."

"It has been years since we have seen Palian and Delvor," Lysara said, "but it is good they are here."

Palian returned the pleasantry with a nod.

"We have seen both Richina and Valya, if a few years back, when they were neither so old, nor so beautiful and capable," Tiersen said.

"It is a good thing you added the word 'capable.' " Lysara laughed.

"I am slow, but over the years I have learned," Tiersen replied. "Now . . . can we escort you to your dwelling, such as it is, and dismount? We have been riding since before dawn."

Both Lysara and Secca laughed. Secca turned in the saddle toward Wilten and Delcetta. "Can you work out some arrangements for all the lancers?"

"They say the lumber barn is mostly empty," Wilten called back. "We will manage."

Delcetta nodded.

Secca hoped so, but there was at least some shelter.

Less than half a glass passed before a group of ten was crowded around a too-small table in the common room of the dwelling that Tiersen had commandeered for Secca. Besides Secca and Alcaren, Tiersen and Lysara, and the two younger women, Palian and Delvor had joined them, and last, Wilten and Delcetta. Richina and Valya stood, while

the others sat on the battered wooden benches, except for
Secca, who perched on a stool.

"We have been trying to protect the road to Falcor by
ambushing their scouts and foraging parties, but we pulled
back when they sent thirty companies east," Tiersen said.
"Jolyn sent a messenger—she's with Kinor now—saying
that they had a sorcerer with them and to be careful."

"Thirty companies? Where are they headed?"

"To Aroch, it would appear. Dostal was in favor of at
least talking to the Sturinnese." Tiersen frowned. "Klestayr
was cruel, but even he wasn't that stupid. His son . . ."

"Is a fool. He's always been one," Lysara said. "I warned
Ruetha, but she wanted to leave Falcor no matter what."

Secca looked at the mirror on the table. "We should see
where the Maitre and the other Sturinnese lancers are." After
leaving the table and returning with the lutar, she quickly
tuned it, then sang the seeking map spell.

The dark-bordered mirror displayed a map of western Defalk, showing the Sturinnese in two places, the larger body
being on the main road perhaps fifty deks west of Aroch,
and the smaller body perhaps twenty deks from Lord Dostal's keep.

The second spell, focused on the easternmost Sturinnese,
showed a column of lancers in white riding along the stone
road to Falcor.

"More than twenty companies," suggested Alcaren.
"Could be thirty."

Secca pointed. "That's a drum cart. Just one, though."

"They're sending a sorcerer, then?" asked Lysara. "Poor
stupid Dostal."

Tiersen glanced to Secca.

"There's nothing we can do," she said. "It's a good two-
day ride from here, maybe three."

"Two and a half," Tiersen replied. "If it doesn't rain. The
stone roads go the longer way and are a hard four and an
easy five."

"We'll still have to go to Aroch," Secca said. "Let them take it. We'll bring it down around them."

"If it doesn't rain," said Delcetta. "If it does, they could be gone."

Secca frowned. "Perhaps. They may want us to come to them."

"So that they can fight where they want?" asked Lysara.

"What is the land like there?" Alcaren looked at Tiersen.

"The keep overlooks the town from the north, and the land slopes down. To attack the keep from the main road, you have to ride uphill."

"And from the north?"

"There are hills that overlook the keep, perhaps as close as a dek, but there is a gorge between them. There are bridges to the east and west, but they are several deks away." Tiersen frowned. "I do not recall exactly."

Secca nodded. "It might work."

"What?" Tiersen looked at Secca.

"What I'm thinking about." Secca looked to Palian. "Can the players practice later this evening? I may need a spell-song we haven't used recently."

"That we can. Today's ride has not been hard."

"As can we," Delvor added.

"Perhaps you should run through the fifth and sixth building spells now—or once they are settled?" asked Secca.

Palian rose. "By your leave?"

Secca nodded, and both chief players left. Then she turned to the overcaptains. "I don't know about their lancers, but you may have to be prepared to hold those bridges. I will know more later tonight, or in the morning. We will be riding tomorrow."

After Wilten and Delcetta left, Secca looked into the lined faces of her friends, recalling how youthful Lysara had appeared so many years before, when the now-graying Lady of Dubaria had taken up a blade, almost losing her life to save Secca's. "You yet look most serious."

"The Sturinnese are but half the problem," Tiersen said slowly.

"Robero?"

"He's still the same Jimbob you called a bully," Lysara said.

Richina's eyes widened, as did Valya's, but neither spoke nor moved.

"He would rather rule badly by himself than well with aid," Tiersen added. "Even Alyssa has left him, though she merely pleaded her need for the healthful air of the mountains of the south."

"We heard something of the sort from Lady Andra," Secca replied.

"Cassily was most fortunate there," Lysara said.

"Do you think Anna foresaw this?" asked Tiersen. "That we would be working together?"

Both Secca and Lysara looked at him.

"That was the whole point of Anna's fostering so many with ability, my dear," Lysara said. "If you recall. Think about where they all are now."

Tiersen shook his head, mock-ruefully.

"Was abandoning Dubaria hard?" Secca asked Lysara.

"Not that hard. Not after Jolyn showed us in the glass what the Maitre did to Esaria. The hard part was sending Lystar and Terlen to Abenfel. Birke insisted that, no matter what happened, they'd be safer there. Lystar didn't want to go. A year past his score and he wants to fight the Sturinnese on his own."

"I suppose he points out that you fought?" Secca grinned.

Lysara grinned back. "I told Lystar that he could fight once he could find a sorceress to protect him from sorcery and not until. I fear he might."

"One of Birke's daughters?" Secca asked.

"Birke says that Bireya is much like Clayre, except she has red hair. She is almost fifteen, and he was thinking of sending her to study with you."

"Fylena must approve, then."

"Bireya's a younger daughter," Lysara said, "and both Laron and Stefan are strong and healthy. Laron is looking to consort with one of Cataryzna's daughters." Lysara grinned. "Her name is Annya."

Secca swallowed as a sudden emptiness filled her, that sadness she could never exactly predict when she felt so deeply the loss of Anna.

"It still hurts, doesn't it?" Lysara asked softly.

"At times. Sometimes, I miss her so much. I wonder if she really knew."

"I'm sure she did. You always wanted to please her so much." Lysara shook her head. "Seeing you on that raider beast . . ."

"Songfire," Secca supplied automatically.

". . . you looked so much like her, yet you're not. But you had that air, that presence."

"I'll never be like her. No one will," Secca demurred.

"You are her daughter. Not by blood, but in every way that counts, Secca. Even Tiersen saw it." At the cough from outside the dwelling, Lysara broke off whatever else she might have said.

"Lady Secca," Gorkon called, "there will be food in a glass. Overcaptain Delcetta wanted you to know that."

"Thank you," Secca replied.

Lysara rose, glancing at Tiersen.

"You and your consort could use a few moments' rest," said the Lord of Dubaria, "and we need to see to our lancers and the supplies we brought." He grinned. "You will eat better, even if we are on the run, so to speak."

Secca returned the smile, warmed by both the presence and words of two old friends.

123

In the dimness of the common room, a single oil lamp oozed light over the sheets of parchment and paper before Secca on the table. Alcaren sat across from her, watching as she pored over them.

Secca nodded and lifted a single sheet, which she set beside two others.

"Which one was that?" Alcaren gestured to the parchment in Secca's hands.

"It is a release spell for the wards."

He frowned.

"If, as the messengers say, Jolyn joins us tomorrow, I will have her sing it, and then have Richina and Anandra take the wards for the next days to allow you and Jolyn to rest. That way, we will have one set of wards guarding us all."

"Will you have Jolyn sing against the Sturinnese?"

"In some fashion, but she must have some rest. I would have her join us, if I can. There is a greater complement to our three voices with hers, rather than Richina's."

"And you do not wish Richina to sing one of the terrible spells?" Alcaren murmured, inclining his head toward the smaller room where the two young women had retired, ostensibly to sleep, but more probably to share stories.

"I would prefer not. I would rather have her, Valya, and Anandra well back from the players."

"The spells are that deadly?"

Without speaking, Secca passed two sheets across the battered wooden table to Alcaren.

He took them, looked at them, but did not immediately begin to read the words. Instead, his eyes went back to Secca.

"Those two are the only ones that look to have the power

to break through the wards of the Maitre," she explained. "Read them. Anna also wrote notes explaining each. Those are the words below the spell itself. Tell me which spellsong you prefer. You will have to sing them with us if they are to succeed."

"Did she say that?"

Secca shook her head.

"But you know so?"

"I *feel* such, and Anna warned me never to go against my feelings. When I have, I have regretted doing so. We cannot afford regrets now." Secca's voice was cold, almost flat.

Alcaren lifted the sheet holding the first spell, his lips moving as he whispered the words almost soundlessly.

Secca could hear the first few lines.

"Fuse all of heaven's sun above this land,
and focus through a lens held by harmonic hand . . ."

Then, Alcaren stopped whispering, and his eyes widened slightly as he took in the last words of the spellsong. His eyes dropped from the spell to the explanation below that ran half a page on one side, and the full page on the back side.

When he finished, he looked up. "How can things be split into parts so small that they are no longer what they were, but just . . . whatever they are?"

"I could not explain in the way Anna did," Secca replied. "I think of it so. A spellsong, the way it is sung, is one thing. Yet it is composed of smaller things that are not the song. There is a note on a lutar, and there are many lutars. That note in turn comes from smaller things—the vibration of the string, and the echo from within the instrument. Why is the same not true of a stone or a tree? Perhaps everything is really a vibration of the harmonies, and that is why sorcery works."

Alcaren shook his head. "I do not know."

"You saw what happened to the Sturinnese crews, did you

not?" asked Secca, almost tartly. "When I used that first spell?"

"It near killed you," Alcaren countered.

"It worked, and it was based on what Anna knew. She warned me. She wrote that it was dangerous to the singer; I chose to use it." Secca pointed to the sheets he had been reading. "Her words say that this one and the other one are pure Clearsong."

"Pure Clearsong, but so dangerous that you should be three deks away, and hide behind stone or in an earthen trench the moment you finish the spell?"

"I would not use it first. I would try the one that destroyed Dolov before it."

"But you would use it?" pressed Alcaren.

"Dear one, what choice have I? If the spell works, and I live, all is well. If I die, and the Maitre dies, Defalk survives, and women will not be chained or enslaved. Only if the Sturinnese survive will we have failed, and that I cannot allow to come to pass." Secca's amber eyes blazed. "I cannot."

Alcaren glanced down at the sheets of parchment without speaking.

As Secca watched, he continued to read.

After a time, he looked up. "The first one, the one that is like unto the sun. The images are easier, and the second one . . ." He shuddered. "That is even more terrible than the first." After a moment, he added, "Would that you have to use neither."

"I would not use either, were it my choice." Secca smiled sadly. "I do not know as we are given such choices. Too often, no matter what simpering savants say, there is no real choice. Not if life is to have meaning."

Alcaren nodded, and slowly passed back the sheets, while the single oil lamp cast wavering shadows across both their faces.

124

ENCORA, RANUAK

Alya settles herself upon the blue cushion that is the sole soft aspect of the blue crystalline chair of the Matriarch, then nods to the guard in the pale blue uniform who stands beside the door. "She may enter."

A woman in black enters, although the hood of her cloak is thrown back, revealing her lined face. The guard steps outside the receiving chamber and closes the door behind him. Because the day is cloudy, and no direct sunlight falls through the tall windows, the air in the hall seems chill.

"Greetings, Santhya," offers the Matriarch.

The gray-haired and round-faced woman bows, with a gesture only slightly more than perfunctory. "Matriarch."

"You requested to see me. Again. I trust that you are well, and your daughter." Alya's eyes remain upon the former Assistant Exchange Mistress.

"We have no complaints about our care while in the towers. The SouthWomen were more solicitous than one could have ever imagined." Santhya squares her shoulders. "We are far more worried about what is about to happen in Defalk."

"As are we all."

"Do you not see? Now?" asks the woman in black. "Stura is no more. Half of Trinn is destroyed, and more than a third of Astaal. Esaria is half-molten, half-flooded, and every town and hamlet along the Saris River and the River Saria has been destroyed beyond rebuilding. Already Elioch, Denguic, Fussen, and their keeps have been ravaged. The Sea-Priests have called down the fires of the sun on the land,

and the Shadow Sorceress has called up the deep fires of the earth. Between them, they will turn all Liedwahr into ashes."

"Only Stura has been destroyed beyond rebuilding," the Matriarch answers evenly, "and it will take a generation to replace the warships the sorceress has destroyed. *That* can scarcely be a concern for you or for the Exchange."

"Ships must have goods to trade, and one cannot trade goods between lands that are poisoned and devastated, where the ground is so seared plants will not grow and where the forests have been turned to ash so there is no timber for building or for firewood. The Maitre and the Shadow Sorceress have yet to meet. When they do, all Lied-wahr will suffer."

"Only if the Maitre prevails." Alya's voice remains level. "If the Lady Secca prevails, then you will thank the har-monies, and well you should."

"If she does not?"

"You will get your wishes—or part of them. For no woman in Liedwahr will ever be a sorceress again, and there will be little sorcery, save by the Sea-Priests."

"With Sturinn ravaged?"

"People create their lands; lands do not create people. If the Maitre prevails, Lord Robero will surrender, and the Sea-Priests will control not only the Western Sea, but Nes-erea, Defalk, and Dumar. Within ten years, Nordwei will fall, and Mansuur will fall when the Liedfuhr attacks, for he will, if he sees the power of Sturinn growing in Lied-wahr."

"You see no choice? We must be enslaved or suffer the second set of Spell-Fire Wars? You cannot believe that," Santhya insists.

"Did the first Matriarchs have a choice? A true choice?" replies Alya. Her eyes are cold as they rest upon the Lady of the Shadows. "Tell me that they did. If you can. Hon-estly."

Santhya does not raise her eyes.

125

The clouds of the days previous had given way to a clear day, but a cooler one, with a brisk wind out of the northeast. Secca wore her riding jacket, but had left it unfastened as Songfire carried the sorceress along the narrow clay track that wound—generally—southeast through the rolling hills and toward Aroch. Although it was barely midmorning, Secca stood in the stirrups and stretched. Beneath her, Songfire *whuffed*, but did not break gait.

Because Secca had asked the players to run through the sixth building spell twice before they left the hamlet of Sedak, they had not gotten as early a start as either Secca or Alcaren would have liked, and that would delay their meeting with Kinor, Jolyn, and Anandra. But there were only so many glasses in the day, Secca reflected, and sleep was one need that could not be neglected or cut short, not if the best spellsinging were needed, and it would be before long.

She glanced to Valya, riding to her left. "When did you get your mount?"

"Stormwind? He is but five, and I raised him. I had thought to see if he would take the Lady Anna as his rider, but—" Valya laughed. "He had other ideas."

"Did you know Anna?" asked Secca.

"I saw her once, when I was but six," Valya reminisced. "She was riding a mare like your . . . Songfire, and she was far taller than I had thought. She looked so young that I first thought she had yet to be consorted, until I saw her eyes." The Rider heir shook her head. "I never forgot those eyes. They were deeper than blue." She looked at Secca. "Your eyes are like that, too. They are amber, but they are more amber than amber, and there is fire in them."

From behind Secca, where he rode with Richina, Alcaren

laughed softly. Secca thought she also heard Lysara laugh, although the lady of Dubaria rode with Tiersen behind Richina and Alcaren.

"My father thought so when you rode up to the Kuyurt," Valya added, "but after you dined with them, he and my mother said you were the Great Sorceress' daughter, because no one else's eyes looked that way, and they have both met the other sorceresses."

Secca wasn't sure how she could respond. Finally, she said, "The Lady Anna was the one who raised me and cared for me after I left my own hold. I was eight, and she taught me all she could."

"Even the blade?"

Secca laughed. "Anna could only use a knife, and she insisted that I *would* know more."

"You are like a Rider woman," Valya mused. "We are all taught the same, boys and girls. My father says that all mounts must be ridden well, whether by men or women. No one has threatened us in ages, because we all ride and all use the shortswords."

"Until now," Secca said. "The Sturinnese would chain all women."

"No. We will not be chained. We will fight. We may die, but we will not be chained." The absolute certainty in the young woman's voice was chillingly matter-of-fact.

"I wish that more felt that way," Secca replied instantly. Once the words were out, she wondered. *If everyone feels that way about their way of life . . . is that not how we got into this war of devastation?* Except, as Alcaren had said, neither Secca nor the Riders of Heinene had tried to force their way of life on others, or at least not until others had attacked them first.

126

Secca glanced to the west, where, in midafternoon, scattered thunderclouds had begun to form. Even now, in late afternoon, she could see none of the mist below the clouds that would have indicated rain. Rain was the last thing she needed, not with the Maitre's lancers using the stone-paved main road eastward and her forces using the back roads because, from where she 'was, the good roads ran in the wrong directions. *Is that symbolic of something?* Secca shook her head. *Thinking in that way lies madness.*

Delcetta rode back from the vanguard. As she neared Secca, the SouthWoman overcaptain smiled. "Lady, the scouts report that the sorceress Jolyn and the lord Kinor are waiting at the crossroads ahead. They await you rather than double-track the road."

"Do we know how far it may be to a place where we can find shelter—of sorts?"

"Lord Kinor's messenger says that a glass to the east on the crossroad is a hamlet that has some barns and outbuildings. He also said to tell you that while it belongs to Lord Dostal, Lord Dostal is now unable to protest."

Secca winced. She feared she knew exactly what Kinor meant.

Delcetta turned her mount alongside Secca. "You are close to Lord Kinor and Lord Tiersen, are you not?"

"We spent several years together in Falcor when we were younger. They are almost a half-score of years older than I am, though. Why?"

"Lord Tiersen watches you as though you were a younger sister, and so does his consort. I would wager that Lord Kinor will do the same."

Secca smiled, somewhat in rue. "That may be."

"The Great Sorceress chose better than she knew," suggested Delcetta.

"I don't think she ever *knew*," Secca replied. "She understood and felt how matters should be without having to think or know. At times, I wish I could trust what I felt as well as she did."

"You trust yourself more than you know," Delcetta replied, before heading back toward the vanguard and the head of the column.

The damp clay road ran, for once, straight through a set of fields still showing the stubble of the fall before, untilled and unplanted. On the far side of the field, there was a hedgerow that doubtless marked the crossroad that led eastward.

Just to the north of the hedgerow was a line of mounted figures. As the vanguard, followed by Secca and those around her, drew closer, Secca could make out individuals. Kinor's once-flaming red hair, like Lysara's, was no longer red, except his was a thick thatch of brilliant white, almost as striking as red might have been.

Kinor caught sight of the column and turned his mount northward, riding ahead of his lancers and everyone else. He rode on the shoulder of the road, half in the fields, until he saw Secca. Then he grinned, rode forward, and eased his mount around, joining her. "You're still small and redhaired, but you're riding a raider beast."

"A gift of Vyasal." Secca gestured behind her. "Valya is riding with us. You might recall Richina."

Kinor bowed in the saddle. "You have grown into a full sorceress, Richina, and we are most glad to see you. You, Valya, have changed little in a season, except for the battle gear." He glanced at Alcaren.

"This is my consort, Alcaren. Alcaren, this is Kinor. He used to tease me, many long years ago."

"I am happy to meet you." Alcaren inclined his head. "Anyone she recalls fondly as teasing her must indeed be special."

In answer to Kinor's unspoken question, Secca continued, "Alcaren was one of the overcaptains sent by the Matriarch to aid Elahwa. He is also a sorcerer, and he saved my life, and almost lost his. The scars on his cheeks are a memory of that. Oh . . . he is also a cousin of the Matriarch."

Kinor shook his head, then smiled at Alcaren. "She would find the only lord in Liedwahr who is both a warrior and a sorcerer. She always did have high standards."

Alcaren laughed softly. "She insists that I am more than I am."

Kinor laughed in return, far more heartily. "Secca *never* made anyone into more than they are. Ask Lord Robero if you have the chance."

Secca blushed, but was gratified to see that Alcaren was flushed as well.

Another rider eased up almost behind Kinor—Lysara. "Kinor?"

The white-haired lord of the Western Marches turned in the saddle. "Yes? Oh . . . Lysara, I didn't see you."

"I'm not surprised. I'm not as striking as Secca. I just wondered. Where is Asaro?"

"I insisted she take the children to Mossbach."

"Good."

"Kinor!" called Tiersen. "If you have a moment, I need a few words."

Kinor inclined his head to Secca. "If you would not mind?"

"Go," Secca replied with a smile. "We'll all be together for some days yet."

As Kinor slowed his mount to fall back beside Tiersen, Lysara rode up to Secca. She leaned forward, and murmured, "Asaro is not well, and even Jolyn could do nothing. Since Kinor cannot fight that, he will fight the Sturinnese. Be most careful in what you ask of him."

"Thank you," Secca murmured, still looking for Jolyn and Anandra.

Lysara let her mount fall back beside that of her consort.

They had almost reached the crossroads before Jolyn and Anandra rode forward to meet Secca. This time, as mounts and riders mingled, in exasperation, Secca suspected, Wilten raised a hand. "Column halt!"

Delcetta echoed the command, as did Palian.

In the mix of mounts and riders, Jolyn reined up opposite Secca, with the thin and gray-eyed Anandra slightly back of her.

"I am glad to see you." Jolyn's brown eyes swept across the column stretched behind Secca. "Those aren't all yours?"

"They all serve her," Alcaren offered.

Almost as if she had not seen the officer in the Ranuan uniform, Jolyn stared at Alcaren, taking in the pale blue of Ranuak.

Secca shook her head ruefully. "Jolyn, this is Alcaren. We were consorted by the Matriarch at the turn of spring."

Jolyn's mouth opened. "And you never told anyone?"

"I didn't want Robero to know at first and then . . . well . . . somehow, I never got around to it," Secca confessed.

"What does he have that all the others didn't?"

Secca smiled at Jolyn's all-too-customary bluntness.

"He's a sorcerer, and he almost died saving my life because he loves me," Secca replied just as bluntly.

"A Ranuan sorcerer?" Jolyn laughed. "How . . . ?"

"He was an overcaptain sent to relieve Elahwa, and he is a cousin of the Matriarch. She was pleased that she could consort us and send him off somewhere that people didn't mind male sorcerers."

Jolyn's eyes ran over the younger sorceress, then turned to Alcaren. "She looks happier than in years. You must be treating her well. Just don't let her order you around too much."

"Like you do?" countered Secca.

"I treat men well. At least for a time," Jolyn conceded with a smile.

As Secca studied the older and taller blonde sorceress more closely, she could see that Jolyn's face was pale, ashen, and her eyes red and sunken in black circles. "As soon as we can find a suitable place to stop this afternoon, you need to sing the release spell for the wards," she blurted.

"I look that bad?" Jolyn's deep contralto voice carried an ironic twist and humor at odds with her exhausted appearance.

"Worse," Secca replied. "Richina and Anandra can carry the wards together for the next few days. We need you to get some food and rest."

"I could not rest easily," Jolyn replied. "Kinor insisted that while he could not stop full companies of lancers, he needed to kill all stragglers and scouts. So I had to accompany him, as did Anandra."

"But she was not carrying the wards."

Jolyn offered a quizzical look.

"We've been singing some of the spellsongs together. It makes for a stronger spell."

"Dissonance," murmured the older blonde sorceress. "I could sense you were doing something different. Is it safe?"

"Anna thought so. She tried to get Brill to do it years ago. Don't you remember her talking about that?"

Jolyn raised her eyebrows. "No. I don't think she ever did."

"Oh . . ."

"We have much to talk about, but it should wait for later," suggested Jolyn.

Secca nodded. "We'd better sort out this mess and get riding so that we're not caught in the middle of nowhere in the dark."

"That might be wise."

Secca stood in Songfire's stirrups, conscious that now, when she did so, she could actually see above others. "Wilten! Delcetta! Form up to head east on the crossroad!"

"Form up! Vanguard! To the east road! To the left!"

Secca settled into the saddle.

"You've changed in other ways, too," offered Jolyn. "We do need to talk."

"We do," agreed Secca.

Alcaren watched, saying nothing.

127

WEST OF AROCH, DEFALK

The Maitre looks up from behind the camp table at the officer who faces him. To his left and slightly behind him stands jerClayne.

"She is moving eastward along the back roads, toward Aroch," offers the grizzled Sturinnese overcaptain. "Her forces are larger than before, and they are moving swiftly."

"We will reach Aroch first, and we now hold it, do we not?"

"Aye, Maitre. We hold Aroch, but as for your forces holding it against an attack... Marshal jerLeng did have to breach the walls in two places, and it may be a day more afore they're repaired, even with sorcery."

"So... we must delay her. We have the better roads, and we can flank her and attack from the south," declared the Maitre. "That should slow her, and we can slay some of those lancers with her."

"Begging your pardon, Maitre, but how might you suggest that we do so against her sorcery?"

"You will do so. I will send one of the Sea-Priests and some players. Take... jerWyal... have him create a fire in her path... or a flood... or both. Or whatever he can do. A rainstorm to turn the back roads into mud. Then, while she deals with such, attack the outliers."

"Yes, ser."

"Fall back, and do it again, or something like it, each time. Don't charge her directly. Kill those away from her protections, and that will slow her advance enough to give us time to prepare at Aroch."

The overcaptain bows. "Yes, Maitre."

After he departs, the Maitre looks to jerClayne. "Does she still hold the wards?"

"Someone does, and the other sorceress has joined her."

"Good. We will not have to chase them both, and we will finish this whole matter within a week, if not sooner."

They both nod in agreement.

128

Twilight had turned into early evening by the time the players had recased their instruments, after the last sounds of the warding spell died away. Secca stood in the damp clay of the lanelike road that ran between the small cottages of the unnamed town. A light wind ruffled through her hair, a wind with a chill that signified that spring had yet to come fully.

Secca looked at Richina, then at Anandra. "Remember. Eat well and rest as much as you can. Your strength allows us to do what we must."

Both younger sorceresses bowed slightly. "Yes, Lady Secca."

Secca looked to Alcaren, then Jolyn. "Is there anything else I should tell them?"

"Not to talk all night," suggested Jolyn. "There are three of them now, with Valya."

A guilty look passed from Richina to Anandra. Behind them stood the Rider heir, and a smile crossed her lips.

"You can talk for a while," Secca said. "I need a few words with Jolyn."

Alcaren nodded. "I should talk to Wilten and Delcetta about our order of march tomorrow, and as we near Aroch." With a smile, he bowed slightly and turned away.

The hamlet was larger than Sedak, in that there were almost twoscore dwellings, but none of them were much more than one- or two-room cottages, rudely built of dried mud bricks. Secca and Jolyn walked toward one of the larger ones, the one that would hold the sorceresses, Alcaren, and Valya. The two-room cottage had not even a table, but just a plank wedged between a course of bricks and supported by two bricks protruding from the rough mud brick wall.

Secca pulled one of the two stools to a corner of the plank. Jolyn took the other. Before sitting down, Secca found a striker and lit the stub of a candle set in a crudely carved wooden holder, then slid the holder to a more level spot on the plank, not quite against the grease-splattered mud brick wall.

"You have much to say, from your eyes and carriage," Secca offered gently, easing herself onto the stool, far less comfortable than her saddle. Although Jolyn was less than a head taller than Secca, she was far more muscular, and Secca had always thought of her as taller than she was.

"You know I enjoy using a blade or both blade and board, don't you?" Jolyn asked quietly.

Secca laughed gently. "You've always enjoyed it, and there are more than a few men who wished you did not." She frowned. "Now it bothers you?"

"No," answered the older sorceress. "I'd rather use a blade. I can't say I like using sorcery to destroy people. Even Sea-Priests."

"After what they've done?"

"I don't like what they've done, and I'd cheerfully lop off their maleness myself and then slit their throats. It's doing it with sorcery that bothers me. It's like they're bricks in a wall, or stones in a road." Jolyn shook her head. "Death is too final, too important, for people to be cut down as if they were grain before a scythe."

"The Sea-Priests started this war by using the ocean as a scythe against Narial," Secca pointed out. "And in all battles, they have used or tried to use sorcery to allow their blades to control the field. That isn't much different from using sorcery directly. In a way," Secca reflected, "it's even more dishonest. They use sorcery to weaken or disable their opponents, and then overwhelm them with lancers and blades."

"You would see it that way. So did Lady Anna."

Secca thought. *What can you say against feelings?*

"You don't agree with what I feel. I can tell that," Jolyn said.

"I can see why you feel the way you do," Secca replied, her words slow and careful. "Sorcery is terrible, and I have used the most terrible spells. If we are to defeat the Maitre, there will be others. As Alcaren keeps telling me, we are not the ones who keep invading others' lands. We are not the ones who insist that women—or men—be chained as slaves. Or that women who essay sorcery have their tongues cut out. We should be able to live as we choose, so long as we do not harm others, or harm them as little as possible. And we should not lose that freedom simply because we do not have scores upon scores of half-captive lancers with sharp blades."

Jolyn sighed. "I know. You're right. I tell myself that time after time. And I do what spells I must. But it does not *feel* right to kill so with sorcery."

Secca's laugh was hard and brittle. "You believe I *enjoy* such spells?"

"No. They will tear at you until you bleed inside." Jolyn paused. "But you will do what you must, and you will use whatever spell may be needed. In that, you are no different from Lady Anna. You know, she thought herself a small woman?"

"I know. She always felt she was small. She said that was because she was small in the Mist Worlds." Secca raised her eyebrows. "Because we believe ourselves small, you think we have less aversion to using terrible spells?"

"I had wondered."

Secca pursed her lips, thinking. Finally, she spoke. "I may have less aversion to such spells, but I cannot say that it is because I am small. I have slain men with sorcery and with a blade. Those slain one way are as dead as those slain another. And I cannot see much difference between a ruler who slays scores upon scores with thousands of lancers and one who slays the same number with sorcery."

"But at least in combat, a better lancer has a chance."

"Does he?" asked Secca. "I have seen many slain from behind where their skill mattered little. I wonder if you value the illusion of such chance more than its worth merits."

This time Jolyn was the one to pause before speaking. "That could be, but is not most of what we value in life at least part illusion? You will strip that illusion from us, Secca, and while you may weep bitterly, you will not hesitate." Jolyn held up her hand. "I will sing whatever you wish, and I will sing it as well as I can. For, as you have said, there is no choice now. Perhaps there never was. But I will regret, as long as I live, that sorcery must be used such, and it will feel wrong that long, if not longer."

"I'm sorry," Secca said.

Jolyn offered a crooked smile. "Do not be. Liedwahr needed Lady Anna, and it needs you even more. You will do what you must, however much it pains you, and your spirit will bleed for the rest of your life, and all will walk in fear of you and the long shadow you cast, even as they revel in the freedom you have given them."

"You make it sound as though it will be nothing to defeat the Maitre," Secca protested.

"No. I did not mean that. You are overmatched. He still has a half-score of sorcerers and twoscore players and drummers, and close to a hundred companies of lancers. All will fight beyond death, if they can. Against all that, if you can but survive, you will prevail, for there is nothing you will not do to be free to choose your life. Because you believe all women should have such choice, you will survive. You are like fire, Secca, and one does not wager against fire, no matter what the odds." Jolyn laughed, softly, sadly. "And your Alcaren worships that fire."

Secca was silent.

"Show me your terrible spells," Jolyn said. "It is too late for aught else."

With a slow deep breath, Secca stood. "They *are* terrible."

"How could they be otherwise?"

129

Secca shifted her weight in the saddle, then looked to the right, across a wide and empty meadow that had but scattered shoots of green peering through the winter-browned grass. The light wind and high hazy clouds had left the midafternoon pleasant enough for riding, but she remained uneasy. Once more, she reseated herself in the saddle. This time, Songfire *whuffed*.

"I know," Secca replied to her mount, her voice low. "I'm fretting too much." That morning, the scrying glass had shown a large column of Sturinnese lancers headed eastward on the main road, clearly moving to reinforce Aroch. The Maitre's main force, twice that size, was farther west, if far closer to Aroch than was Secca.

Worried as she was, Secca had ordered Wilten and Delcetta to send out more scouts than usual, and farther. She didn't want to spend too much energy or time scrying every glass, but she had checked the scrying mirror at noon. From what she and Alcaren could determine, the nearer group of Sturinnese had been more than ten deks away, and heading eastward on the main road, already farther eastward than Secca, if parallel to Secca's track on the back roads.

She stiffened as a rider in red livery raced toward the

vanguard, reining up before Wilten and Delcetta. Scarcely
moments passed before Wilten had urged his mount back to
Secca, who reined up. Behind her, the column slowed, then
stopped.

Beginning even before he fully reined up, Wilten offered
words that were clipped, precise, but spoken very quickly.
"There is a fire three deks ahead. The woods are burning,
so fiercely that the road is blocked. The scouts have seen
tracks of riders, but have not seen the riders."

Secca sniffed the air. She should have noted it earlier.
The scouts were right. Something was burning somewhere.

Kinor eased his mount closer to Secca and called to her,
over both Wilten and Jolyn. "The ground and the trees are
too wet. A fire is not natural at this time of year."

Secca looked at Wilten, then stood in the stirrups. "Chief
player! We will stop here. Prepare the players. The first
building spellsong, for the storms."

"We will prepare," Palian called back. "First players assemble!"

"Second players assemble!"

"First SouthWomen to the fore!"

"Green company! . . ."

Alcaren had eased his mount up beside Songfire and
leaned over to unstrap the scrying mirror. Songfire *whuffed*
and edged sideways.

"Easy, lady," Secca said, patting the mare's neck. "Easy."
She guided Songfire to the side of the road, looking for a
half-clear space that wasn't muddy, settling on a patch of
flattened brown grass, beside which she dismounted. She
looked up to find Valya offering to take Songfire's reins,
and let the Rider heir have the leathers.

By then, Alcaren had the mirror on the grass.

Secca quick-tuned, and then tried the seeking spell.

"Show us now, as we desire,
the one who set this land afire . . ."

Instead of showing a blank silver mirror, as Secca had half expected, the image of a young-faced Sea-Priest appeared, riding beside a gray-and-black-bearded overcaptain in Sturinnese white. A column of riders in white followed, and not a particularly long column. That bothered Secca.

"He has no wards," Richina murmured from the side, still mounted, beside Jolyn.

"They mean to exhaust you, and they will sacrifice even a young sorcerer to do that," Alcaren said. "I can do the storm spell this time, if we can get within two or three deks, I think."

"But—"

"This I can do," Alcaren said. "The Lady Jolyn must get more rest, and you must not be worn-out when you face the Maitre."

"Let us see what riders they have," Secca said. "And where." She lifted the lutar again.

"Show us now and in clear light
Sea-Priest lancers close enough to fight . . ."

The mirror displayed five separate images, but all were large bodies of mounted lancers. The first column was crossing a bridge. A second was riding through a stubble-filled field. Secca looked at the second one, seeing wisps of smoke. She gestured to Wilten, who remained mounted, and back from Valya. "There's one group coming from the east, from near the fire."

Alcaren turned to Palian. "Can you set up the players on that rise there." The spot to which he pointed was barely a yard higher than the rest of the field and meadowland through which the road they had followed had run.

"Here?"

"I fear that by the time the players set up and tune, one group of Sturinnese will be upon us," Alcaren replied.

"Companies! Form up by squads!" Wilten and Delcetta were not waiting. That was clear, and Secca had the feeling that, once more, everything was on the edge of reeling out of control.

Alcaren was singing a vocalise and walking toward where the players were quick-tuning.

"Bretnay! Now!" Palian snapped at the laggard violinist.

"Yes, chief player."

As the sounds of tuning died away, and the players began their warm-up tune, Secca looked to the east, where two companies of lancers had formed into an attack line, even though no Sturinnese were visible. To the south, halfway across the field, a company of SouthWomen had taken station.

A distant and dull rumbling began to rise, and Secca could feel the air tremble, or so it seemed. Secca turned, looking at Richina, then to the north. With the rumbling came a too-familiar hissing scream as a blaze of fire whooshed out of the north and plunged toward the ground perhaps a dek to the south. A dull *boom* followed. Then the ground shook, and a column of smoke, mostly whitish, rose against the hazy sky.

Both Richina and Anandra had paled. Secca looked at the two.

"It was like someone was pushing at us," Richina said.

"Just hold on," Secca urged them, looking toward the players.

"We stand ready, Lord Alcaren," Palian called.

"On your mark," Alcaren called back.

"At my mark," ordered Palian, "the third building song. Mark!"

Standing on the low rise, the grass now somewhat muddy from the players' boots, both the first and second players began the spellsong. Secca almost joined in at the third bar, but shut her mouth as Alcaren's baritone filled the air.

> *"Clouds to form and winds to rise*
> *like a caldron in darkening skies . . ."*

Secca found herself breathing faster, nervous for Alcaren, and yet visualizing the storm of all storms, and hoping that her consort was as well as he began the second stanza.

"Clouds to boil and storms to bubble . . ."

After Alcaren completed the last words of the spell, Secca looked to the east, where the pall of smoke was definitely thicker, as her nose insisted.

The skies darkened, particularly to the west, and the rushing of the wind rose swiftly into the roaring torrent that Secca disliked more each time she heard it. So strong was the wind that Secca found herself holding on to Songfire's stirrup strap. Valya yelled something, but, against the wind, Secca could hear nothing, even though the Rider heir was less than a handful of yards from her. Gusts of bitter-chill air blasted through the warmer springlike air, pulling and pushing at the sorceress. Amid the crashes of thunder, and the darkened skies, fine ice needles pelted Secca, flying across the open fields and meadows almost sideways.

The ice pellets vanished, and the air turned strangely still, and the sky was almost dark green as, to the west, two enormous black funnel clouds swirled, with the dark misty moisture of rain surrounding and trailing them. Faint yells and cries rose in the distance.

Then rain, not ice, swept back over Secca and the others, and she held herself against the comforting bulk of Songfire. The rain lashed at her with cold needles, so hard and thick that she could see nothing. The howling roar filled her ears, seemingly coming from both east and west.

After some fraction of a glass—Secca wasn't sure how long—the hard rain subsided into a lighter rain, and then stopped, leaving a foggy mist rising from the ground.

Secca looked around Songfire to the east, where she watched for several moments, perhaps longer, as the last funnel cloud slowly vanished. Then she turned.

Alcaren was sitting on the grass. His face was ashen, al-

most corpselike, and he was slowly eating some bread and
sipping from a water bottle that Valya was holding while
he ate the bread.

"He swooned," the Rider woman explained.

Alcaren looked up at Secca sheepishly. "I did finish the
spell."

Secca wanted to protest that he shouldn't have done the
spellsong, but, looking at him, she knew he'd been right.
And so was she—they were being stretched to their limits.

Behind Alcaren were Richina and Anandra. The two
youngest sorceresses also were eating, but did not look so
pale as Alcaren.

Farther to the south were the players, frantically using
cloths to dry instruments and strings. Secca hoped that there
had not been too much damage, but usually the players had
more time to prepare and had a better idea of what to expect
after the spellsong.

"Secca?" The contralto voice was that of Jolyn.

The redheaded sorceress half turned.

"That firebolt. Is that what they used on Denguic?" Jolyn
stood by her mount, reins in hand, water from the sudden
rain and ice storm oozing from her hair across her forehead.

"And Esaria, and Elioch, and Fussen," Secca replied, absently blotting away the water she belatedly realized was
dripping from her own hair.

Jolyn nodded slowly. "Then we must do what we must,
and I will sing with both heart and voice."

That was as much of an apology—or a reconsideration—
as Secca would get from Jolyn, and it was enough. "Thank
you."

Jolyn glanced sadly across the fields, then looked up at
the sound of a rider against the silence.

Secca looked to the west and watched as Wilten rode
toward her. The overcaptain swallowed once, then again.
Like Alcaren, he was pale.

Secca wanted to ask him what the problem was, but she
had a good idea, from the yells she had heard just before

the funnel cloud had swept across the long field to the west of her force. Instead, she waited.

"The Sturinnese . . . mayhap five companies, they were charging the green company and overcaptain Delcetta's second . . . when the storm struck them . . ."

"How many did we lose?" asked Secca quietly.

"A score and a half, lady, and there are five who will survive but will not soon fight."

Secca nodded slowly. "I am sorry." *It's your fault. You should have checked the glass more often.* But everything was a trade-off. If she checked too often and became exhausted, she wouldn't have the strength left to use the sorcery she needed. Alcaren was physically stronger than she was, but the strain of carrying the wards for nearly two weeks had worn on him as well.

"There are none of Sturinn surviving. Not near here." Wilten swallowed convulsively. "I would not have any ride west. The grass is pink, and . . ."

Secca waited again.

"We will have to ride north for a time, Lady Secca. The winds snapped the trees across the road, as if they were kindling. The rain did douse the fire, and so there are steam and smoke, but few flames. If we ride north for a dek or two, we can head eastward once more, or so the scouts say."

"We need to travel eastward some. Perhaps we can find shelter before dark."

"That would be good, Lady Secca."

"Thank you, Wilten."

Secca watched as the overcaptain turned his mount toward the intact companies still stationed on to the east. Then she looked toward Alcaren, and the others. "We need to ride and find shelter. There will be more attacks." Of that, she had no doubts.

130

S ecca looked at the damp logs half-burning, half-
steaming in the open hearth of the cottage. The intermittent flames cast shifting shadows on the plastered walls
of the main room, walls that had not been whitewashed in
years. The plank floors were gritty with years of sand
ground into the wood.

Outside a drizzle, not quite a rain, drifted across the
dwellings of the small town of Frowlet. It had been almost
dark when Secca's force had ridden into the quiet lanes.
Someone had clearly warned everyone, because the town
was empty, but there were coals in the hearths, unshuttered
windows, and fresh tracks in the damp clay of the road.
Secca felt guilty for driving out the local people, but if she
did not succeed in defeating the Maitre, she had no doubts
that the folk around Aroch would suffer far more.

Secca cleared her throat and looked around the crowded
room. From a small group of five or six people two seasons
earlier, her unofficial council had grown to more than a half-
score, with all the sorceresses, overcaptains, lords, and chief
players—plus Lysara and Valya. With thirteen people in the
common room, it was far too close and cramped for Secca's
taste, yet she did not feel right in asking any of them to
leave. Everyone stood, most with their backs to the hearth,
facing Secca, because the square table in the corner could
have held but five or six, and because only a single bench
and two stools had been left in the cottage.

"According to the scrying glass and to the scouts sent out
by Lord Kinor, Lord Tiersen, and by Wilten and Delcetta,"
Secca began, "the Maitre's main force could reach Aroch by
midday tomorrow. The Sturinnese have repaired the breaches
in the walls and have scouts and picket lines around the town

and keep. They have close to twenty companies at Aroch. There are only a few scouts to the north, but the two bridges across the gorge are already heavily guarded."

"Do you think they will attack us tomorrow?" asked Tiersen. "Or are they still too far from Aroch?"

"Tomorrow would seem most unlikely," Alcaren replied. "They do have fifteen or twenty companies at Aroch, but only a few sorcerers and but one drum cart. They would have to ride twenty deks or more and they would only outnumber us by less than two to one. Their drum carts would slow them as well if they took their sorcerers. The Maitre's force has close to fifty companies and several sorcerers, but they would have to reach Aroch, then immediately ride north for almost twenty deks, again with the drum carts."

"We will have to use the scrying glass more often as we near Aroch," Secca added. "We can expect more attacks like the one yesterday once all the Maitre's forces are settled in Aroch."

"Why will they gather all together?" asked Tiersen.

"For the same reason that we are," Secca replied. "To protect against sorcery from a distance. If we are together, one or two sorceresses can handle the wards, and the rest of us can use sorcery against them. If we split up, then most of the sorceresses will have to spend their efforts protecting against sorcery."

Both Wilten and Delcetta nodded knowingly.

"That means that they sent out that young sorcerer to die," Jolyn said. "They had to know he could not have defeated us."

"His attack cost us near-on a company and a half," Delcetta pointed out.

"They want to exhaust us," Secca said. "They almost did at the battle for Elahwa. It was close. Richina and I could hardly stand. Their last charge came from all sides. I didn't see the lancers from the rear. If they had had another ten companies, they would have taken us. Once they are ready, they will send as many attacks as they can mount, and as close together as possible."

"Should we just back away, and let them hold Aroch?" asked Jolyn.

Secca frowned. "I think not. I could not tell you why, but that feels most wrong."

"It would certainly strengthen those in Defalk who urge that we treat with the Sea-Priests," said Kinor. "It would also leave Dumar and Neserea open to mischief, either from Mansuur or even from Nordwei."

"Not immediately," Secca pointed out. "They will wait some weeks, but if we do not show Defalk as strong and able, all will scramble to treat with the Maitre—or to take any lands they think they might hold."

"Defalk is *not* strong and able," pointed out Lysara, from the corner by the hearth. "Its sorceresses are. Defalk cannot afford to have you seen as unable or unwilling to deal with the Maitre, not if we wish to avoid unending battles in the years to come."

Secca feared that Lysara was all too close to the truth. Even if they did prevail, unless they could utterly destroy the Sturinnese, they would be fighting skirmishes and visiting every lord in Dumar, Neserea, and Defalk for years and years to come just to keep order. It was certain Lord Robero could not. "That may be, but we need to work on the spells as well." Secca looked to Palian. "Did the players have a chance to practice the sixth building song?"

"We practiced for almost a glass tonight. We will practice in the morning before we ride."

"And the first building song?"

"They know that one well, and we ran through it but once."

"We will try that first when the time comes," Secca said. "If they can shield against it, then we will use the sixth building spell."

"You have not used that spell before, Lady Secca?" asked Palian, the faintest trace of a smile betraying that she already knew the answer and wanted Secca to elaborate.

"No. It is more terrible than any you have seen or heard."
Secca paused, then looked at Wilten, Delcetta, and then at
Tiersen and Kinor. "We will need spades and mattocks.
These spells will have to be sung where the spellsingers and
players can immediately take shelter behind berms and walls
of earth."

"From deks away?" asked Wilten.

"Yes. From deks away."

Wilten looked down. Delcetta did not. Tiersen shifted his
weight from foot to foot. Kinor nodded slowly.

"We will use the glass in the morning before we ride out,
and let you all know what we have seen." Secca forced a
smile. "Until then."

She watched as the others began to file out, then gestured
to Jolyn. "Once they leave, we will need to practice, using
blank syllables."

"Ah . . . in a few moments?"

"Are you well?"

Jolyn smiled uncomfortably. "I hope to be. It is not the
best time of my season."

Secca nodded. "A little later? A half-glass from now?"

"That would be better."

The older blonde sorceress slipped out of the cottage, and
Secca turned to the two younger sorceresses and Valya.
"You may remain here, if you wish, so long as you are
quiet."

"Thank you . . . if it truly would not bother you, lady?"
asked Valya.

"If you are quiet," Secca replied with a smile, "you may
enjoy the fire."

Richina and Anandra grinned, and Richina began to drag
the bench in front of the hearth.

Secca walked over to Alcaren, who had commandeered
one of the stools and sat facing a fire that had mostly
stopped hissing, his lumand held loosely in one hand, a single sheet of paper in the other.

"How are you feeling?" she asked.

"Tired," he admitted. "But better than yesterday." He smiled at her. "You know that sorcery is also like exercise?"

"Exercise?" Secca frowned.

"When we first did the wards, and the Sea-Priests sent sorcery against us, neither of us could do much more than hold those wards. Now . . ."

Secca nodded slowly. What Alcaren said was true. Yet that opened another box of dangers. Did that mean that she had to offer ever-stronger spells to maintain some sort of superiority over the Sturinnese—or whoever might try to follow the Sea-Priests? That there would be someone, should they succeed, of that she had no doubts.

"I have been studying the spellsong," Alcaren continued, "and I have played out the melody and sounded out the note values. It is not difficult . . . not too difficult." He paused. "I worry that after tomorrow we will face attack upon attack."

"So do I. Yet . . . if we wait, they will only strengthen their hold on Aroch. With the exception of the Maitre, I do not believe their sorcerers are as strong as we are, but there are more of them, and in time . . ."

"They will either prevail or keep us spending every moment containing them. So we must be prepared to do what we must."

Secca worried that doing just that would leave everyone exhausted before they could establish themselves on the hills to the north of Aroch . . . before they could sing a spell that would change Liedwahr forever—either because they would fail, or because they would succeed.

131

The mist and rain of the previous days had vanished, and the late-morning sky was clear. The day was also cold, as if a touch of winter had blown in with the northerly winds that had swept out the clouds. The column was now riding nearly directly south, toward Aroch, or more properly toward a hamlet about two deks to the north of the gorge that protected the rear of the keep.

As a splatter of something struck Songfire's shoulder, Secca glanced down at her legs. Although the road was only slightly muddy, the vanguard had churned the road somewhat, and Secca would have hated being at the end of the column. Still, she had far less of the stuff splattered across her legs. She smiled—another advantage of riding a raider beast. Then, perhaps Richina and Valya, who were riding directly behind her, might be receiving a greater amount of mud thrown from Songfire's hoofs.

Secca looked up to see Wilten riding toward her, along the shoulder of the road. With him was a lancer in the bluish green tunic of Defalk. Secca frowned, then nodded.

"A messenger?" asked Alcaren from where he rode to her left.

"It has to be, and I'd guess we won't like what it says," Secca replied. "Not if it's coming from Lord Robero."

"Lady Secca," began Wilten even before he reined up short of where Secca had halted Songfire, "the undercaptain bears a message scroll from Lord Robero, and he insists that he must deliver it to you personally, and take a response from you back to Lord Robero."

"Lady Secca." The undercaptain bowed in the saddle, then extended a scroll circled in blue ribbon.

Wilten intercepted the scroll, then eased his mount closer to Secca before passing the scroll to her.

Secca took the scroll.

Wilten looked to Secca, as did the messenger.

"I will read Lord Robero's message, and then I will decide whether there needs to be a return message."

"Your pardon, Lady Secca. Lord Robero asked for a response."

"I'm most certain that he did, Undercaptain," Secca replied politely. "At the very least, I will need to read his message and consider it." She paused. "You may go." Secca looked to Wilten. "Perhaps the undercaptain could ride with you or overcaptain Delcetta in the vanguard for the moment."

Wilten smiled in return. "That might be best." He nodded to the square-bearded but young undercaptain. "Shall we ride up to the vanguard, Undercaptain?"

"Yes, ser." Both words were filled with fatalistic resignation.

"Undercaptain," Secca said, "Lord Robero may punish messengers who do not tell him what he wishes to hear. I do not. You may go," she repeated.

Once the two had turned their mounts back southward, Secca broke the seal on the scroll and untwisted the long blue ribbons. With a slow deep breath, she began to read.

Sorceress Protector Secca—
You were ordered to secure Dolov, and then aid Elahwa. You aided Elahwa, and then destroyed Dolov. You were ordered to aid the Lord High Counselor of Dumar, and help him defeat the invaders. You killed him, and failed to destroy all the invaders, allowing them to invade Neserea and devastate it. You were ordered to return to Defalk, in order to protect the land, and you did not do so, but took a ship to Neserea, arriving too late to save Esaria, or indeed, any of the towns in the northern part of the country, and also al-

lowing an invasion of Neserea by the Liedfuhr of Mansuur because Defalk had not honored its commitment
to protect Neserea and the Lady High Counselor.

For all these reasons, and others which we need not
enumerate herein, we have been required to treat with
the Maitre of Sturinn and reach an accommodation in
order to prevent further devastation and depredation of
Defalk . . .

Secca took another long and deep breath, forcing herself
to read the remainder of the lines written on the parchment.

As Lord of Defalk, I must insist that you honor the
agreement reached between Defalk and Sturinn and do
not attack the Sturinnese forces as they return to Neserea. Further, once they are withdrawn, I must insist
that you return to your ancestral lands, and turn over
the demesne of Mencha to a suitable successor to be
named appropriately . . .

Secca snorted, then turned in the saddle and thrust the
scroll at Alcaren. "When you finish it, Jolyn should read it
as well. But no others."

Alcaren read silently, his face expressionless until he finished the scroll. "He has lost his mind."

"He never had much of one," suggested Jolyn, as she
eased her mount forward to take the scroll from Alcaren.

"No. He has lost his scorceresses." Secca smiled wanly.
"Do you not see? Jolyn left Falcor before we reached the
Ostisles. We have sent Robero no messages." Secca turned
to Jolyn. "Have you?"

"Why would I have done that? He would not listen to
aught I said."

"He believes that all Sturinn will descend upon him."

"Send him a message and tell him otherwise," suggested

Richina, who had also eased her mount forward to hear what was occurring.

"Let Jolyn read the scroll," Secca temporized. All too conscious of those pressing their mounts nearer to hear what was happening, she stood in the stirrups. "We have received a message from Lord Robero. He does not seem to be aware of what has happened, and we will be considering how to answer his scroll in a way that benefits the people of Defalk."

No one moved away.

"That is all!" Secca said loudly, not quite snapping. "We still must deal with the Maitre and the Sturinnese. Let us ride on." After gesturing to Wilton, she settled back into the saddle, then eased Songfire forward.

Slowly, the column began to move.

Jolyn rode forward and passed the scroll back to Secca, who tucked it inside her green leather riding jacket.

"You will not obey," Jolyn said.

Secca steeled herself inside. "I think not. Nor will we respond. Any response that is good for Defalk will merely enrage Lord Robero. We will do what we must against the Maitre. Then we will decide how best to reply to Lord Robero. The undercaptain can remain with us for the time."

"We will do as you feel we must," Jolyn said. "It cannot be otherwise."

"No, it cannot," Alcaren said firmly. "Not now." His gray-blue eyes fixed on Jolyn.

The older sorceress looked down after a moment.

Secca wondered if the moment had been foredestined years ago, when a tiny redheaded girl had told an heir that he was a bully and defended Anna by saying that Anna was only nasty when people made her be. *Will you end up repeating that pattern, as well?*

Secca looked bleakly southward as Songfire carried her toward Aroch . . . and a future she had never imagined, could never have imagined.

132

AROCH, DEFALK

The Maitre stands on the northwest corner of the north tower, under an overcast that threatens rain at any time. Beside him, on his right, is Marshal jerLeng, and on his left is jerClayne. The Maitre surveys the hills beyond the gorge that lies nearly a dek to the north of the walls of the keep.

After a time, he points. "She will take the high ground there, and they will arrive there later this afternoon. I want to make them fight for it." He turns to jerLeng. "Send fifteen companies over each bridge, and have them attack as soon as she nears. You should understand which tactics work."

Marshal jerLeng looks straight at the Maitre. "You wish me to send another thirty companies to their deaths?"

"In a good cause, yes," the Maitre replies.

The marshal does not respond.

"Do you recall what happened at Elahwa?" The Maitre glances from jerLeng to jerClayne.

"We lost," points out jerLeng. "Only five companies survived."

"Had jerClayne and I been there, we would not have lost. At the end, neither sorceress could sing a spell. They had to use blades to save themselves. One more charge . . . *one more charge* would have finished them."

"That is easy to say now. We had but five companies remaining after all their sorcery, and they had three times that," the marshal points out wearily.

"That is not the point," the Maitre counters, his voice sharp. "They have but two sorceresses now."

"I count three and an assistant, and possibly the Ranuan."

"The Ranuan cannot have learned that much in a season,

and it takes one sorceress and the assistant to hold their wards, just as it takes two Sea-Priests. That means they have but two sorceresses. We will transfer the wards to the three junior Sea-Priests as soon as we leave this tower. This afternoon, you will attack them, using companies in groups large enough to overwhelm their camp unless they use sorcery. I will send two apprentice Sea-Priests with you. They are strong enough to deflect any sorcery but the most powerful."

"That will gain us some time, but little more."

"Even with the lancers she has gained from Lords Kinor and Tiersen, she has but eleven companies, and half are understrength. Lord Robero has told her not to attack, and she will not gain lancers from him—"

"Do you believe his message?"

"He is neither that deceptive nor that willing to risk lying to us. He truly believes that we will triumph." The Maitre smiles. "That should say much to your lancers, marshal. As for the sorceress, she lost near-on two companies from Captain jerDrall's attack, and that attack greatly weakened the sorceresses. I can tell that from the scope of the wards."

"We are to keep attacking until they can use sorcery no more?"

The Maitre nods. "By attacking this afternoon, we will make sure that they get no rest, and we can hold Aroch under a shield. Tomorrow, we will destroy them with fireballs and fire whips as we did those in Fussen."

The marshal waits, as if expecting more.

"There is one other way you might break through," the Maitre adds. "She is using sorcery that cannot strike within her own troops without destroying them. Her lancers have become used to this. That was how jerDrall destroyed nearly two companies. If you have a company with strong mounts that can sprint forward before she begins her dissonant sorcery, they might well reach her."

"We will offer that to the captains." JerLeng pauses, then asks, "What if thirty companies are not enough—"

"You have sixty remaining at present," the Maitre replies coldly. "What are they for but to assure victory?"

"Yes, Maitre."

"Do you want that . . . those abominations . . . to survive? Do you want the home isles to fall to the bitch traders of the north—or the Matriarch?"

"No, Maitre."

"We are all that remains of the power of Sturinn, and we are all that can reclaim it. To do that, we must destroy the sorceress. Do you understand that?"

"Yes, Maitre."

"Then do your duty." The Maitre turns and makes his way toward the steep stone steps that lead downward into the keep.

133

Secca had hoped that the skies would remain clear, but by the end of the two days it had taken them to ride around the fire and storm damage created by Alcaren's sorcery, the winds had shifted once more. Low clouds had slid across the sky from the south, and the air was chill and damp, although it had not rained, not yet.

Ahead of the vanguard, partly visible to the left of the hill around which the road curved eastward and then south, and above the low and bare limbs of an apple orchard, were the back sides of the hills that overlooked Aroch. After finishing a vocalise so that she would be ready whenever the Sturinnese appeared, Secca stood momentarily in the saddle, then reseated herself, reflecting that a year before she'd had no idea that she would have ridden across half the continent of Liedwahr, fighting a war that would have seemed inconceivable.

She had checked the scrying mirror a little over a glass

earlier. Then, the images in the glass had shown companies of Sturinnese lancers massed around the bridges, half on each side roughly, but without any columns or scouts riding farther northward. Wilten and Delcetta had sent out even more scouts to warn them of any possible attacks, and Secca had been watching the road carefully.

Almost with that thought, a rider in the crimson and blue of the SouthWomen appeared from behind the trees where the road curved and galloped northward toward the column, her speed indicating that all was not well.

Secca took a swallow from her water bottle and began a second vocalise, slowly, trying not to force anything. Riding beside her, Alcaren cleared his throat and also continued his warm-up.

Delcetta listened to the messenger but for a moment, and then the two SouthWomen rode along the shoulder of the narrow road toward Secca.

Before they reached her, Secca reined up Songfire, though the gesture took but the slightest pressure, and stood in the stirrups, signaling for the column to halt. "Chief player!"

"First players!" echoed Palian.

"Second players!" followed Delvor.

Delcetta and the messenger reined up, and the South-Woman overcaptain said, "Report to Lady Secca."

"Lady Secca, there are two forces of Sea-Priests. There are at least fifteen companies in each force. One is riding from the southeast and the other from the southwest. They are about three deks away."

"Over each of the bridges from Aroch," Secca said, not quite asking.

"Yes, lady."

"We can ride up the hill to the west, lady," offered Delcetta. "That will give us some advantage. The south side of the crest is mostly clear."

Secca glanced to her right, noting that the hillcrest rose less than twenty yards above the road. On the left, the meadows and the unleafed orchard actually sloped downward from the road, if gently.

"That's the best we can do," she finally acknowledged. "Order it." Her eyes went to Palian and Delvor, who had eased their mounts closer by circling beyond the shoulder of the road. "We'll be setting up on the top of the hill, on the south side. We'll have less than a half glass, if the scouts are correct."

"We will quick-tune and be ready," Palian promised.

Following the column, Secca turned Songfire to her right and urged the raider mare up the hill. Alcaren and Jolyn rode on each side of her, and the two younger sorceresses and Valya followed.

Alcaren eased his gelding almost shoulder to shoulder with Songfire. "I will do it. You must lead in the terrible spells tomorrow."

"You cannot. You have not recovered from holding the wards so long. There are more than thirty companies coming."

"Then, at least let us do it together," he replied. "If I can spare you some of the effort, it will make what you do on the morrow more effective."

"I can help," Jolyn offered.

Secca turned in the saddle and took in the older sorceress's still-tired visage and the dark circles around her eyes before responding. "If we need a second spell, you can support me. Alcaren will support me for the first."

Jolyn nodded.

When Secca reached the southern side of the crest of the hill, already most of the lancers were forming in an arc by companies. Kinor's companies were on the left flank—to the east—while Tiersen's were on the right—beside a company of SouthWomen. Secca turned Songfire and glanced out to the south. Were there white tunics in the woods to the south beyond the large and yet-leafless orchard? She could see none, but felt that they were there and nearing quickly.

Since there was little else she could do except ready herself to sing, Secca dismounted. She looked around, half-expecting Valya to take Songfire's reins, but the Rider heir had stationed herself to the right of Richina and Anandra, effectively acting as another guard for the younger sorceresses. With a smile, Secca handed Songfire's reins to Easlon and stepped forward into the center of the arc formed by the first players. Alcaren also handed the reins to his gelding to Easlon and followed Secca.

"Quick-tune! Now, Bretnay!" snapped Palian.

The true tone issued forth from the violino of Kylara—the lead violinist after Palian herself. Secca found herself standing on one foot and then the other as the players tuned. Her eyes flicked to check the slope below and beyond the bare-limbed trees of the orchard, as well as to the road to the left of the orchard.

"Warm-up tune. One time through, at my mark. Mark!" announced Palian.

As the players reached the midpoint of the warm-up tune, Secca saw a rider in white burst out of the forest and began riding uphill through the wider lanes between the trees of the orchard. Others followed.

"Sturinnese below!" called Wilten.

As Secca turned to the chief player to signal that they needed to begin the spellsong, the sorceress heard a low rumbling, like thunder. She swallowed as she recognized the sound of the Sturinnese drummers. So close were they from where she had last scried them that they must have quick-trotted all the way from the bridges—or even galloped some of the way.

She wanted to shake her head, but instead just signaled to Palian.

"The players stand ready, Lady Secca," Palian announced.

"On your mark," Secca replied, raising her hand, and then lowering it.

"At my mark," ordered Palian, "the third building song. Mark!"

Secca followed the beat, strong and even, and joined in at the first note of the third bar, gratified that Alcaren's baritone came in exactly with her, and not trailing.

"Clouds to form and winds to rise
like a caldron in darkening skies . . ."

Although she concentrated on the melody and the spellsong, Secca could not help but sense the waves of horsemen in white who had appeared at the base of the hill and had already begun to race up through the apple trees to close the last dek between them and Secca's forces. She could also sense the heaviness and the interference of the drums, and had to force herself to keep up the tempo as she and Alcaren began the second stanza.

"Clouds to boil and storms to bubble . . ."

Before they could complete the second stanza, the rumbling roar of yet another fireball grew, and then a rush of hot air whipped around the hillcrest as the firebolt whipped overhead, clearing the lancers by less than twenty yards, and plunging into the meadow beside the road less than a half a dek to the southeast.

Despite the hot wind that pushed and pulled at them, Secca concentrated on the storm spell and on the images of the storm funnels sweeping across the front and sides of the hills, as close as she dared bring the storms.

Her forehead was pouring sweat by the time the last note faded, and once the discipline of the spellsong dropped away, she found herself breathing hard, with her head throbbing and daystars flashing before her eyes, but not with great intensity or frequency. The drumming rose in intensity, and another rumbling and rushing roar was building somewhere behind them.

Secca could only hope that Richina and Anandra could hold the wards yet again.

"Third company! To the fore!" At the command, a score of lancers in SouthWomen crimson rode out in front of the players.

At a muffled sound from beside her, Secca half-turned in time to see Alcaren sway, and then start to pitch forward as his knees buckled. She jumped toward him, but only managed to grab his tunic. That was enough to swing his limp figure enough so that he landed in the damp winter-tan grass gently on his side, rather than pitching forward and landing far harder on his face.

The skies darkened, turning the sickly dark grayish green that Secca hated, and the winds rose. Then, for a moment, there was an instant of silence, and the firebolt plowed into the hillside less than fifty yards in front of Kinor's forces on the left flank. Fragments of trees flew like spears and quarrels.

Secca shivered as four or five men and mounts in the forwardmost line went down. She hoped Kinor had been farther back.

The roaring of a funnel cloud sweeping through the orchard below followed the explosion of the firebolt. The yells of men and the screams of mounts rose with the wind and the darkness that swept before Secca, pulling and tugging at her.

She went to her knees with the force of the wind, barely avoiding her unconscious consort. She rolled Alcaren on his back, then staggered erect and ran toward Easlon and Songfire. She took the mare's reins and scrambled up into the saddle, ignoring the daystars as well as she could.

The roaring of the winds was stronger than before, even as the funnel clouds swept away from the hillcrest, but the spell should have been that strong with the support of two voices.

A glance downhill showed Secca that at least a score or two of the Sturinnese had escaped the funnel and had been met by the SouthWomen and part of the gold company of Loiseau. There were also gaps in the defenders' line, gaps that had been there before the attackers had reached them, Secca feared.

"To the sorceress! The sorceress!" With the yell from massed voices, a wedge of white-clad lancers burst out of the low brush and trees to the west, spurring their mounts toward the slight gap between the SouthWomen and Tiersen's lancers, clearly sprinting their mounts toward Secca and players.

"To the right, charge!"

"Left, charge!"

At the command, Delcetta's companies wheeled and met the charge, as did Tiersen's lancers, but the angle and the ferocity of the charge allowed three of the Sturinnese lancers to break through the gap, leaving two or three bodies in their wake. Secca turned Songfire and unsheathed her sabre.

From Secca's right, Valya charged the Sea-Priests. Behind her were Richina and four of the lancers acting as Secca's guards.

The first lancer went down under Valya's shortswords, and a second doubled over his mount's neck with a thrown blade through his chest.

When the melee cleared, moments later, the last Sturinnese lancer was dead. From what Secca could see, neither Valya nor Richina appeared injured. Nor did Gorkon or the other guards appear wounded.

Secca turned Songfire, her sabre still at the ready, but all she could see were her own players and lancers—and a wall of black rain that was advancing up the hill in waves.

"Case your instruments! Case your instruments!" Both Delvor and Palian were shouting the command.

Amid the still-roaring and -rushing winds that had faded somewhat as they swept southward, Secca turned Songfire back toward Alcaren. Jolyn had helped him into a sitting position. He was drinking from a water bottle, if pale as winter ice. Beside him, on the ground, was Anandra, equally pale and drawn.

At least a score of lancers and mounts in blue and crimson

and in green lay across the area just below the hillcrest, and
those Secca could see all too well, even through the intermittent daystar flashes. Mixed with the Defalkan and Ranuan dead were the bodies of more than a score of Sturinnese
lancers.

Secca turned away, slightly. Her head ached, and her eyes
burned, as much from frustration and anger as from exhaustion.

Delcetta walked her mount toward Secca. Secca turned in
the saddle and waited.

"You have destroyed yet another army, Lady Sorceress."

"This time we lost more," Secca said.

"A company's worth of SouthWomen and almost as many
of yours. Close to half a company each from your lords, I
would judge."

Secca nodded slowly. *And we still have not reached Aroch . . . or the Maitre.*

134

AROCH, DEFALK

The Maitre is seated behind a wide desk of cherry that
appears warm in the light from the lamps and the
hearth. His eyes, unlike the wood of the desk, glitter like
the ice of Pelara lit by the heatless sun of midwinter. His
words are even colder as he beholds the two lancer officers
in white who stand before the desk.

"You are telling me that you fear your lancers will not
obey? Lancers of Sturinn?"

"I do not fear that they will not obey. I am telling you
that they will not make another fruitless suicide attack," replies Marshal jerLeng. "That is exactly what I am telling
you."

Standing behind the Maitre's shoulder, jerClayne shakes his head, as if to warn the marshal against his words.

"We have lost more than fifty companies in less than a week, thirty of them this very afternoon. Every lancer and every officer out there knows that. They also know that no lancer has survived in going against the Sorceress Protector." JerLeng smiles grimly. "My officers are not stupid, Maitre. You can do no worse to them than can the sorceress, and perhaps not so much as she has done. They will not attack again until you attack with sorcery."

"And if I replace you?"

"Then you will have to replace me, as well," offers the overcaptain who stands slightly behind jerLeng. "No officer will give such an order. If he did, no lancer would obey it."

"*No* lancer?"

"No, ser," replies the overcaptain.

"We have almost won, and you would back away?" snaps the Maitre.

"We have destroyed two weak lands, and we have lost our homeland," counters jerLeng. "We have lost over four hundred companies of lancers in less than a year, and the enemy has lost twenty—if that. It may be that others cannot stand against our sorcery, but it is also clear that our lancers cannot stand against the sorcery of the Sorceress Protector. You have said you are her superior. It is time for you to make good on that claim."

"I am the Maitre. I decide when—"

"No." JerLeng's voice is chill, colder than the Maitre's eyes and words, cold enough to freeze the chamber into silence. "You may well have the power to destroy me and every lancer in Aroch. If you do, then you will still have to face the sorceress. And if you should defeat her . . . then . . . without lancers, how can you rule? And what will you have to rule? Or for whom?"

"I see." The Maitre stands, slowly. "You make matters difficult. Then, I want your promise that, after we destroy

558 L. E. MODESITT, JR.

the sorceress tomorrow, that you and your lancers will not question my orders."

"If you destroy the sorceress, we will follow you as we always have." The marshal does not bow as he finishes his sentence. He turns and walks from the chamber without another word, followed by the overcaptain.

"Fools!" The Maitre shakes his head, then looks at jerClayne. "It would have been so much easier with one more attack. So much easier. She lost three companies, and the two junior sorcerers almost broke their wards."

"You cannot make them attack," jerClayne points out.

"I cannot. Now. But they will pay for their insubordination. That they will." A hard smile crosses his face. "For now, we must plan how we will break the sorceresses."

He points to the map laid across the desk. "Here. You will direct the junior Sea-Priests to begin with an attack with firebolts—as many as they can muster against the sorceresses. Darksong will not be above the horizon until dawn. A glass later, you will begin . . ."

.As the Maitre details his strategy, jerClayne nods, listening intently.

135

I n the late evening, sitting on her bedroll, with Alcaren beside her, Secca looked into the embers in the hearth of the tiny cot. In one corner, Richina, Anandra, and Valya slept. In the corner closest to the hearth, so did Jolyn.

"You are worried about more than the battle to come," offered Alcaren in a low voice. "Are you not?"

"If I do not worry about the battle, I will not be worrying about anything else," Secca temporized, her voice barely above a whisper. "The glass shows that the Maitre still has something like forty companies of lancers. I have perhaps three in name and less than two in fact. I have lost more than half the lancers I brought from Loiseau. The SouthWomen have lost more than half their numbers. Kinor and Tiersen have lost close to half their lancers. Fewer than ten companies against more than forty?"

"The Sturinnese have lost hundreds of ships and hundreds of companies of lancers," Alcaren pointed out.

"They have them to lose. We do not."

"Kinor has the trenches and berms ready. The players have run through the sixth building song until they know it well. Richina knows the first building song, and even carrying the wards, she can do one spellsong . . ."

"That is asking much of her," Secca said. *Yet Alcaren and Jolyn can do but one as well.* In everything she tried to do, they were stretched, asking too much of everyone.

"You will not let me do the first one," Alcaren pointed out.

"You almost did not finish the storm spell," Secca replied, "and I need you and Jolyn for the sixth building spellsong."

Alcaren nodded. "You know what is best. But you must believe in yourself, my lady, and your preparations. The glass shows that no lancers have left the keep of Aroch, and there are scouts watching the bridges. There is little more that you can do this evening except to get sleep so that you will be rested for the morrow."

"That I know. Yet . . ." Secca shook her head. "I am a sorceress. I am barely a lady in experience, and must rely on others to handle even my own demesnes. I am not an arms commander." She offered a low and bitter laugh. "What good arms commander would lose half his lancers?"

"Secca, my love . . ." Alcaren drew out the words. "You have won every battle you have fought. You have destroyed more than thirty times the number of lancers that you have lost. You have conquered three lands and destroyed the power of a fourth. You have lords and ladies who would die for you—and lancers and players who have followed you across half of Liedwahr. If those are not what make a successful arms commander, please tell me what does."

"One who does not have to fight her way across an entire continent. One who does not have to call on sorcery to rend lancers and players limb from limb." Secca sighed. "I hate fighting. Yet . . . I can see no end to it."

"If you triumph tomorrow, there will be no more fighting in Liedwahr," Alcaren promised.

"How can you say that?"

"Was there any after Lady Anna triumphed?" he countered.

"But when she died . . ." Secca pointed out.

"She prepared you. If you defeat the Maitre tomorrow, it will prove that you are a worthy successor. And if you prepare a successor, there is less chance of war for her."

"You offer many 'ifs' there, my love," Secca replied.

"Life is filled with them," he admitted with a smile. "Yet, you cannot refuse what will be. Lady Anna turned her rule to a weak successor, and all Liedwahr has paid."

Anna had no choice. She could have no heirs. Secca did not say those words, instead replying, "But I'm not strong like her."

Alcaren shook his head slowly. "I am strong, or so I thought, but I swoon, after a single one of your spells. Do you think the Rider of Heinene would entrust his daughter to a weakling? Do you think that the Council of Wei would offer passage to such? Or the Matriarch and her ship mistresses would follow one with no strength? You had the courage to defy an heir when you were but nine. All remember it. You had the courage to defy the greatest sorcerers and fleets ever assembled, and all you need do tomorrow is act as you always have." He slipped his arm around her shoulder. "I will be there, but you do not need me."

"I want you beside me," Secca admitted.

Alcaren smiled at her, warmly. "For that I am most glad, and grateful." He squeezed her gently. "You must sleep."

Then he yawned. "So must I, for I am not so strong in this craft of sorcery as are you."

"I've had more practice," Secca murmured.

"Enough," he replied, leaning back and stretching out, stifling yet another yawn. "I must sleep, and so must you."

Secca lay back beside him.

136

I n the grayness of the cloudy early morning, the four sorceresses and Alcaren stood on the mud-smeared grass of the southeastern side of the hill facing Aroch, just below the crest. With them were the two overcaptains and Tiersen and Kinor. Lysara stood back from the group, but her posture indicated that she had no intention of leaving. The air was chill and damp, and the winter-killed grasses held dew that looked almost like ice where it clung to the few blades of grass that had not been trampled into the hillside by the boots of the lancers who had dug the trenches the evening before. The two berms of raw earth rose almost a yard above the grass. Yet to Secca, they appeared fragile, almost useless against what she knew was to come. She looked toward Aroch once more, where the outlines of the keep were half-shrouded in ground mist, although it was less than half a glass past dawn.

To her left the players had gathered and begun to tune their instruments. The deep chords of the grand lutars of the second players sounded almost menacing to Secca. *Is that because you know what your spells may do?*

Secca let her fingers run over the lutar, checking the tuning once more, while Alcaren laid the scrying glass on the leathers over the hillside grass. Then, after strumming the lutar a last time, she sang an unforced spellsong, the one seeking the players of the Maitre.

The glass silvered over, turning blank, and showing nothing, nothing at all.

Secca sang the release couplet nearly immediately. She replaced the lutar in its leather case. Alcaren took both the mirror, which he had rewrapped in its leathers, and Secca's lutar and carried them to Easlon, who strapped them behind his mount.

"They are preparing," Richina observed. "They must be, for they wish not that we have even a glance at the keep or their players."

"But there are no lancers beyond the keep walls. Not a one," observed Wilten, "except for the squads guarding the bridges."

"The scouts report that no lancers have crossed the bridges. None has even neared them," added Delcetta.

Alcaren frowned. "That I do not like. Do they plan such sorcery—"

"As we do?" asked Secca ironically, raising her voice slightly to carry over the discordant sounds of the players beginning to tune their instruments. She winced at a particularly off-key squawking that came from one of the falk-horns. Still, she turned and gestured toward the chief player.

"Finish tuning, now!" called Palian, an edge to her voice, the first true edge that Secca had heard ever from the seasoned chief player. "Make ready for the warm-up tune!"

"Ready for the warm-up tune," echoed Delvor.

The players launched into the warm-up, and Secca turned to the four commanders of lancers, and Lysara, who remained standing several paces back of the others. Before Secca could speak, a long and dull-sounding series of thunder-rolls—or giant drumbeats—echoed through the air from the north. Then came the ever-increasing rumbling shrieking roar as the firebolt seemed to accelerate out of the clouds.

Secca barely had time to moisten her lips before four enormous balls of fire flashed above them and arced down to the south, splashing across the bare-limbed brush-and-hardwood forest on the lower hill below. The hillside shook, and columns of flame arose in a half-score places, with trails of smoke and steam rising almost immediately.

The players' warm-up finished raggedly.

"Finish what you play. You do that when they're singing, and you'll end up fried by one of those fireballs!" snapped Palian.

After glancing to Alcaren, Secca looked to Richina and Anandra. Some of the color had already drained from Anandra's face, and Richina had taken a step back as if an invisible hand had pushed her.

Secca gestured toward the four commanders of lancers. "Best you make sure all the lancers are behind the crest of the hill." Secca looked first to the overcaptains, then to Kinor, Tiersen, and, finally, Lysara, who stood several paces back. "No one should be able to see Aroch. No one!" she repeated.

"What of you?" asked Lysara softly, although her voice carried.

"Richina and I will try the spell that brought down Dolov." Secca looked to the overcaptains. "Now see to your lancers." Without waiting for a response, she turned back toward Palian.

"If it does not work?" asks Alcaren, his voice quiet, but tense.

"Then we will sing the terrible spell," Secca replied. "We will have no other choice." *Not that you or anyone else has been able to find. Not that will stop the Sturinnese.* She stepped toward the chief player. "The first building song."

Palian inclined her head, then addressed the players. "You will play once, twice at most. No matter what happens, or falls from the sky, do not hesitate. Concentrate solely on the spellsong." She glanced quickly toward Secca. "We stand ready, Lady Secca."

Another series of distant thunder-rolls echoed from the northern sky. Secca could feel the shuddering of both air and the harmonies. Richina and Anandra still stood firm.

Secca raised her voice. "As soon as this fireball passes, we will sing." *You hope it will pass, but they will not play without the possibility of error in the midst of a falling firebolt.*

The redheaded sorceress forced herself to listen, to watch, and to wait, as the hissing, shrieking, and roaring rumble rose into an ear-numbing storm of sound, then swept past. There were three firebolts, but they were no closer than the first attack, and slightly to the east of the first, when they sprayed across the lower hill and beyond, plowing up ground, and shattering trees.

Even before the ground shook and more columns of flame erupted into the sky, Secca motioned to Palian, and then to Richina. The younger blonde sorceress smiled confidently and stepped up beside Secca.

Secca knew they were taking a chance with Richina, but she knew that Alcaren could sing but one spell, and the same was true for Jolyn, and Secca would need both for the terrible spell.

She gestured to Palian.

"Now!" ordered the chief player. "The first building spell . . . at my mark! Mark!"

The sounds of both first and second players rose into the gray morning, climbing over the smoke of the numerous small fires started by the firebolts, and out over the valley below and the gorge beyond. Secca's and Richina's voices melded with the melody from the first players, supported as it was by the chorded harmony of the second players.

"Break the brick and rend the stone
leave not a single course alone
break to rubble and to dust
all the walls in which they trust . . ."

From the first words that Secca and Richina sang, the low overcast thickened and began to descend, forming into black and roiling clouds. With the growing darkness came more

dull rumblings, angrier and closer than those of the Sturinnese firebolts.

The triplet of chimes that Secca remembered from Dolov
cascaded across the hills, past the gorge and the bridges
guarding it. Secca could feel, even as she finished the last
words of the spellsong, that the song had surrounded the
rise on which sat the keep of Aroch.

Then came the lightnings, yellowish bolts flashing toward
the keep, bright against the darkening sky. Secca opened her
mouth soundlessly, as the lightnings flared harmlessly
against a circular dull white dome that arched over the keep,
appearing only to absorb or deflect the lightnings.

From deep within the depths of the earth issued a deep
rumbling groan. The hillside below the sorceresses and the
players rippled, and waves of soil and earth, less than a span
high at the base of the hill, began to head southward toward
the keep. Trees toppled, falling in all directions, but mainly
to the north. Secca spread her feet to keep her balance, but
her eyes remained on Aroch, even as her head rang with the
reverberations of an unseen chime.

A rampart of earth surged toward the gorge, and parts of
that chasm's ancient granite edges tumbled inward over each
other, down into the depths carved by the unseen stream.
But the gorge did not stop the moving of the earth, nor the
felling of trees beyond the gorge. The rippling of soil and
stone rumbled toward the gray walls of the keep—and
halted, impossibly, just short of the stones, leaving an
earthen rampart almost as high as the chisel-cut stones.

Beside Secca, Richina sank onto the brown grass. Anandra already lay flat on the grass, her eyes closed.

Secca whirled, almost unaware of the slight throbbing in
her head, calling to Palian. "We must sing the sixth building
song spell. Now! The very moment that the players finish,
they must run behind the berm and lie flat on the ground in
the pit. Any who look up may be struck blind."

Palian swallowed.

"Now," Secca insisted. "We must sing the sixth building

song before they can bring their firebolts upon us. We have no wards remaining, and if we do not strike now, they well may strike first."

Palian turned to the players. "Ready the sixth building spellsong."

Secca bent and touched the dazed Richina on the shoulder, then shook her. "Richina! Behind the hill! Now!"

Richina staggered to her feet and took a half-score of steps, unsteadily. From where she had remained mounted with the lancers serving as Secca's guards, Valya rode forward and half-lifted, half-dragged the near-limp blonde sorceress up before her, before turning her raider stallion northward and toward the top of the hill and beyond.

Dymen and Achar had ridden forward with Valya. Achar vaulted from his mount and lifted the unconscious Anandra up to Dymen, then remounted. The two lancers turned their mounts to follow the Rider heir.

"Lancers! The rest of you. Both of you, follow Valya and Dymen! Now!"

Gorkon looked at Secca.

"Go!" she snapped. "I'll need you later. You'll be hurt if you remain, and then you can't help us."

Slowly the last two lancers turned their mounts, following Valya.

Secca turned back to check the players, sensing Alcaren to her left. As Jolyn stepped up to Secca's right, the red-headed sorceress motioned to Palian.

"The sixth building spell. At my mark . . . Mark!"

Secca focused her entire being on the spellsong, on the words, on the images, on the meaning behind those words and images, letting herself become one with the song, thinking only of the sorcery itself. Even so, she could feel the energy, from both Alcaren and Jolyn, as the three voices fused into one near–harmonically perfect spellsong, one great and terrible working of voice, accompaniment, and knowledge better left unused—if it but could have been.

*"Fuse all of heaven's sun above this land,
and focus through a lens held by harmonic hand,
pour through it the beam of white-blue light,
with power to shatter all matter with its might . . ."*

As Secca launched into the second stanza, the clouds above Aroch began to glow with a white light. Even the darkest of the sorcery-created storm clouds from the first spell began to shred into foggy fragments, then white mists. A circle of dazzlingly clear sky appeared directly above and around the keep of Aroch.

*"Split harmonic whole into its smallest parts
with greater power than the sun or dissonance's
     arts . . ."*

Then, a beam of white light lanced downward from high in the heavens, growing wider and so intense that Secca had to close her eyes with the last few words of the spellsong. Even her closed eyelids provided little relief as she whirled away from the light that seemed to burn right through her entire body. *Never . . . never thought it would be like this . . .*

With the light came a single chime, a single harmonic chime that shivered through Secca, through the dazzle-cleared skies, through the solid stones of the world, through . . . everything, as powerful and ear-numbing as the light was blinding—beyond blinding.

137

AROCH, DEFALK

From the northwest tower of the keep, where he sits upon a stool, the Maitre glances eastward toward where the sun would be, were there not clouds, then looks to jerClayne. "Darksong is high enough, though it would be better without the clouds. Far better." He laughs and adds. "Not that the marshal or the sorceresses have given us the choice. Already, they gather behind their puny earthen ramparts on their hilltop."

Behind the Maitre and jerClayne are three younger Sea-Priest sorcerers, the last of the twoscore that had left Stura nearly a year before. Behind them are the players, and a double set of drums. Although the space on the top of the tower is large for a keep, there is scarcely a fraction of a yard in which to move, except for that area before the players and around the sorcerers.

"It might be well," offers the Maitre, with an imperious gesture toward jerClayne, "that you begin—before the sorceress calls upon her players and spells."

After stepping forward into position before the players and the drummers, jerClayne speaks clearly, "The firebolt spellsong, on my signal." He raises his arm, then drops it in one abrupt movement. The players start the spell melody, followed a bar later by the drums, which begin as a low rolling and rise into a muted thunder.

JerClayne's voice joins them on the next bar, supported by the voices of the three younger Sea-Priests.

*"From heaven there beyond let fall the fireballs of
    might,*

*fall in undying flame to turn to ash the enemy in our
      sight . . ."*

When the drumming and playing die away, and the spell
is complete, jerClayne steps toward the parapet and leans
against the stone, resting. One of the younger Sea-Priests
has crumpled and lies on the stones of the tower. The other
two drag him gently to a place beside the parapet wall.

To the far north, beyond the overcast clouds, there is a
dull series of thunderlike rolls, followed by a low rumbling
that grows with every instant. The clouds to the immediate
north of Aroch and beyond the gorge and the hills glow.
Then comes a whistling, hissing shriek.

From the low gray clouds four lines of fire burst, spraying
away from the tallest hilltop and scattering across the hillside to the south of that hilltop, a hillside covered with
bare-limbed trees. The walls of the keep vibrate, ever so
slightly. Lines of smoke rise from the hillside nearly immediately, followed in places by tongues of flame, and then
by lines of smoke rising into the morning.

"Again!" snaps the Maitre.

JerClayne straightens and steps back before the players.
He gestures, and the players and drums repeat the spellsong
accompaniment. The voices of the two remaining young sorcerers support him, but this time, when he finishes, his steps
toward the parapet are close to a lurching stagger, and he
breathes deeply as he leans against the stone rampart.

Both of the other Sea-Priests have fallen, and there is no
one to move them. One of the players looks at the two fallen
sorcerers, and then at the Maitre, before licking his lips and
remaining in his position with the other players.

The firebolts once more spew from the northern skies and
blast through the gray clouds that hang over the keep and
the lands to the north, but once again they spray away from
the hilltop where the Defalkan sorceresses have set up their
berms.

"Retune!" snaps the Maitre, rising from his stool. "Once more and their wards will fall."

After a long pure note from a violino, the players begin to retune.

Before they can complete the task, the faintest shiver shakes the tower of the keep, and jerClayne raises his head. His red-rimmed eyes survey the ground to the north. Then he squints and looks more closely.

"Maitre! She is moving the entire earth against us. See how the ground ripples." JerClayne's words run into each other. He pauses, then lifts his hands to clasp and massage his forehead.

The Maitre's eyes take in the moving earth but for a moment, before he calls out to the players. "The short safety spell! Now!" His hand drops with his words.

The players play, and the drummers drum, and the Maitre's bass-baritone dominates both as he sings the spellsong he has called forth.

> *"Shield us now in safety and for this glass*
> *till all sorcery against us will fail and pass . . ."*

Still holding to the parapet, jerClayne watches as the wave of earth rumbles, groaning, toward the walls of the keep. For a moment, the entire keep shivers, even as a shimmering white glow begins to enfold the tower, and indeed the entire keep. Then, the shivering halts.

"That . . . will . . . stop her . . ." pants the Maitre. "That . . . will stop . . . any sorcery. Now . . . the firebolts against her. Both of us will sing. In a moment." He walks slowly to the stool and laboriously bends to take a long swallow from the bottle beside the stool. Then he lifts the bottle and crosses the few yards between the stool and the parapet, where he hands the bottle to the younger sorcerer.

"Thank you," says jerClayne, before taking a deep swallow and setting the bottle on the battlement.

The Maitre massages his forehead, then turns and addresses the players. His eyes appear as sunken red orbs in a sagging face, but his voice holds rage under iron control. "The full firebolt spell with the double drumming."

With a nod, the head player acknowledges the order. "On your signal, Maitre."

The Maitre clears his throat, once, then again, before glancing sideways at jerClayne.

The younger sorcerer nods.

The Maitre drops his arm, and both sorcerers join in the spellsong after the opening bars.

> *"From heaven there beyond let fall the fireballs of might—"*

Abruptly, their words are stilled, not by their will, but by a single clear harmonic chime that lances through the tower almost like an unseen and invisible knife. So cuttingly powerful are the vibrations of its passage that both men are unable to utter a word for a long moment.

Tiny flakes shiver from the battlements around them, falling like a stone rain around the feet of the Sea-Priests and the players. The strings of the players' violinos vibrate, creating a strange and eerie accompaniment, and the drums groan, as if in protest, or in resistance to that sole harmonic note.

JerClayne looks askance at the Maitre.

"Damp your strings! Again! From the beginning!" snaps the Maitre.

Even as he speaks, a circle of ever-brighter light enfolds the tower, rising from the intensity of noonday sun in the Dunes of Doom to a glare that cannot be measured, a knife-like light that cuts through clouds, through stone and white robes.

Flames burst from the varnished and seasoned woods of the violinos used moments before by the players. The skins of the drums snap under the instant and violent heat, and tongues of fire leap from within those same drums.

Steam erupts from the water bottle on the battlement stones beside jerClayne. Yet as that steam flares forth, the heat that has created it sucks all moisture from the Maitre's body, and from the bodies of all those on the tower, and their faces shrivel.

"Abominations—"

The Maitre's words are seared from existence by the beam of heat and light so intense that everything—from the Sea-Priests and their players and their instruments to the very stone around them—is vaporized into a mist of fire that rises straight up, creating a white pillar of living flame that explodes skyward through clouds and rain, searing both from existence.

The very stones of the tower become a glowing mist, a fiery death mist that envelops the entire keep. So swift is that envelopment that not one lancer within the walls has time for more than a single syllable, not before the entire keep and all around it explode into primeval flame.

At the base of that pillar of light, where the keep of Aroch had stood, a lake of liquid molten rock forms, a lake of liquid fire containing the heat of the sun, a lake that, as crystal droplets fall from the fire pillar, is covered with molten silver glass.

138

Secca staggered under the double impact of both the harmonic chime and the column of brilliant and burning light. Under the force of both, she found her feet carrying her backwards, where she stumbled into the trench, then dropped flat onto the uneven surface. The clay there was cold and damp despite the searing intensity of the light above her. Her head throbbed, and her eyes burned, and daystars flashed across eyes that also burned long after she had closed them tight against the unrelenting glare.

She had been lying in the trench but instants before she found herself shielded by Alcaren's body. His figure blocked the worst of the unyielding light, but she had to squirm sideways to move to where his weight did not squeeze her chest against the clay so that she could breathe more easily. A crackling flared somewhere in the sky, blazing through even her closed eyelids, and a wave of heat cascaded over the part of her shoulder unshielded by her consort.

She could sense that at least one other besides Alcaren was in the trench, but when she tried to open her eyes just the slightest to see who, the glare was so intense that it sent needles through her eyes, and she had to close them. She could only hope that Jolyn was with them, and that the players had all managed to scramble into the pit behind them.

Was this necessary? Did you need such a terrible spell-song? Even as she asked herself the question, she suspected the answer was that she had no choice—but that, if she survived the terror she had created, the question would come back to haunt her for the rest of her days. *If you even survive to be haunted.*

Anna had written cautions, but cautions and warnings were nothing compared to the terrifying reality of the blinding light, and the shivering harmonic chord that had run through her. *Nothing at all.* Secca had thought the destruction of Stura was terrible, but the blinding intensity of the pillar of light was also terrible—and it had happened in Defalk.

The warmth of Alcaren beside her helped some, but Secca felt buffeted by light and heat from above and damp and cold from below, and by the unseen crackling sound that half hissed through the skies far above. The glare waxed and waned, even through her closed eyelids, although the waning was merely uncomfortable, while the waxing was excruciating painful.

How long she lay there, Secca had no idea, only that

when the glare finally faded, and she opened her eyes, she could barely see. Everything was silvered, silver against silver, all shades of silver . . . and colors were barely visible. Against that silvered background, daystars flashed, each one like a bright needle playing counterpoint to the throbbing headache that made Secca simply want to curl up in the trench, cold and damp as the soil was.

Finally, she eased herself into a sitting position and watched through squinting and slit eyes as Alcaren struggled to do the same.

She swallowed. "Can you see?" she finally whispered to her consort.

Alcaren blinked, his eyes not quite focused on her as he turned in the narrow trench. "It's . . . all silver."

Jolyn levered herself up in the trench. "Never saw anything so bright. Did you bring the sun down?"

Secca looked at Jolyn. "Can you see?"

"Mostly. Everything has a shiny silver cast," replied the older sorceress. Her eyes seemed to widen as she looked at Secca.

"What is it?" asked the redhead.

"Your eyes. Somehow . . . they're amber, like always, but their centers are dark silver, almost like quicksilver." Jolyn turned and leaned to look past Secca at Alcaren. "So are yours."

Secca glanced at the sky, no longer glaring bright white, but totally clear. "All the clouds—they're gone."

"They're mostly water," reflected Alcaren. "The light must have burned them all away."

"We need to get out of here and over the hilltop," Secca said. She just hoped she was strong enough to walk or run the hundred yards or so. She cleared her throat. "Don't look back."

She could not have said why, but she felt that. "Don't look at Aroch. Not now."

Alcaren boosted her up the back wall of the trench, then helped Jolyn out before levering himself up.

"Players!" Secca called. "To the other side of the hill. Don't look back! Don't look back." She hoped everyone would obey. Her legs felt unsteady, and she was glad that Alcaren took her arm as they walked toward the low rise that marked the hilltop.

"To the rear," called Palian. "Keep your instruments, but don't look back. You could burn your eyes. Don't look back."

Secca wasn't sure about that, but it was a good idea to give a reason, and she hadn't been able to think of one. By the time they reached the crest and started down, Secca could feel heat radiating from behind her, and smell the smoke of woods and grasses burning.

She nearly stumbled, but Alcaren caught her.

"Aren't you feeling weak?" she murmured.

"I've felt better," he admitted. "We just have a little farther to go. Just another fifty yards, I'd wager. Just a little farther."

The tone of his voice told Secca that he wasn't in much better shape than she was, but his arm felt sturdy supporting her.

"A few more yards," Secca called out, hoping her voice would carry back to Palian and the players who followed.

"Lady Secca says we have but a few more yards," Palian repeated. "Take care with your instruments."

Secca hoped that they would not need those instruments anytime soon. She certainly wouldn't be spellsinging for a time.

As they began to walk down from the back side of the hillcrest, through the scrub oak and scattered junipers, Delcetta was the first to ride toward them. There were others behind her, but Secca could not make them out with her silvered vision.

"Are you . . . can you . . . ?" Delcetta didn't seem to want to complete the question.

Secca wondered if she looked that bad.

"The Lady Secca will need some assistance," Alcaren said.

Secca felt as though his voice were deks away, and it faded and then roared in her ears, and the daystars before her vision rushed toward her and then receded. She forced herself to put one foot in front of the other . . . one foot in front of the other.

"The ground rumbled," Delcetta declared, "and then it was brighter than if there were a score of suns in the sky. Those suns blazed away the clouds as if they did not exist. Now"—she gestured southward—"smokes rises as if all Aroch were aflame."

Secca turned and looked back over the hillcrest, feeling that would be safe enough, since she could not see Aroch itself. Even through her silvered vision, she could make out the immense pillar of swirling smoke that rose into a clear sky—an otherwise totally clear sky.

Abruptly . . . suddenly, Secca could feel her legs begin to shake.

She started to sit down, helped by Alcaren, but a wave of silvered blackness swept up over her.

139

Secca woke with darkness all around her. Her eyes opened slowly, and daystars flashed before her, silver-tinged flashes that made it nearly impossible for her to see anything. She was almost afraid to move, but she let her eyes travel to her right, where she could make out the embers in a hearth, red embers also tinged with silver. She seemed to be lying on her bedroll in the same small cot where she had struggled to get sleep the night before. Had it been the night before? Just the night before?

She tried to roll over because her shoulder was both burning and stiff. With that motion, her entire face turned into flame. "Ohhhh."

"Here, lady. You must drink," said Richina, easing a water bottle to Secca's lips. "The water will help."

Secca drank, but the water seemed so cold that she shivered as it eased down her throat, and the drops that spilled on her face were like ice.

"You must have more," Richina insisted, easing the bottle back to Secca's mouth.

Secca took the water, until she was shivering all over and could drink no more. Then she asked, "The wards. What of the wards?"

"Lady Secca," Richina offered softly, "there is no one left who can cast sorcery from a distance—save you. Do you not remember?"

"Alcaren?" Secca's voice was raspy, hoarse.

"He sleeps now, almost beside you. He is better than you," murmured the younger blonde sorceress, "though his face is also flushed and painful. That is true of everyone who sang or played the last spellsong, but yours is the most flushed. The Lady Jolyn suffered less than you two."

"What . . . of the players?"

"Palian and Delvor are much like Lord Alcaren, but I would say they will recover, as will most of the players."

"Most?"

"Bretnay and Rowal . . . they did not seek shelter as you ordered. The light . . ." Richina's voice broke off, as if she did not wish to explain.

Secca did not wish to force her. That the two had died, she regretted, as with all the deaths of those who had helped and followed her. In a sense, how the two died did not matter, save that she would have willed it otherwise, and she hoped it had not been painful or lengthy. Yet, with the Sea-Priests bent on taking Liedwahr, could the war have been fought without deaths? Secca doubted that, but had there needed to be so many?

It could have been, had you studied more when Anna lived. Or had you considered better spells. But, by the time she faced the Maitre, Secca had had no other choices. The

whole point of shadowsinging was to avoid having to use
great and terrible sorcery, and Secca had not fully understood. She had thought that terrible spellsongs and shadow
sorcery were simply different tools, and that shadow sorcery
could at times preclude terrible spellsongs. She had not understood how closely the two were linked, as if they were
two sides of the same coin. If one side were not used, the
other had to be. Sometimes there might not have been a
choice, but Secca feared she had erred all too many times
in not seeing the opportunities. *And you will always wonder
. . . as did Anna.*

Secca yawned in spite of herself, and the yawning sent
fresh waves of fire across her face, and a deeper throbbing
through her skull.

"You must sleep, Lady Secca."

". . . don't . . . want to . . ." She had so much she needed
to consider, and so much she wanted to tell Richina, for fear
that she could not, that she would sleep and not wake.

"Tell us tomorrow, lady. You can tell us then."

Secca's eyes closed.

140

Under a clear and cloudless sky, Secca rode eastward
through the morning on the paved main road that
would lead her to Falcor—and Lord Robero. She wore the
green felt hat pulled low across her forehead, not because
the spring weather was cold, but to shade her too-sensitive
eyes, eyes that, after four days, still showed her the world
tinged with silver, if not quite so heavily silvered as right
after the terrible sorcery.

She turned once more in the saddle, looking back toward
the spot where Aroch and the town had been—now a fused
expanse of silver glass, glass that from a distance appeared

to be a circular silver lake. Kinor and Tiersen had promised to set up warning stones on the roads that led to the ruins of town and keep—when they had time after returning to their demesnes. Secca had promised Kinor that she or Richina would return to help rebuild Westfort with sorcery.

Following Anna's instructions, Secca had not been closer than five deks to the ruins since she and her forces had escaped the heat and devastation. Even from that distance and after four days, she could feel the heat.

While she felt no sympathy for the Maitre and the Sturinnese, who perished within Aroch, the cost to Liedwahr had been dear, dearer than any could have foretold—except the Ladies of the Shadow. So many Secca knew had died, and one of the last had been the unfortunate Ruetha, who had accepted a consorting with a weak lord out of fear of being poor and abandoned, as her mother had been before Anna had rescued her. *Is that a lesson of sorts?* Secca shook her head. No one should be punished for weakness. *But the strong and the thoughtless so often do punish the weak . . .*

With a sigh, Secca turned back in the saddle to face the road ahead.

"You cannot change what has been," Alcaren offered from where he rode beside her. "Nor should you regret what you did." He laughed softly, warmly, and yet ruefully. "Yet you will, for all the days of your life. That I know."

"How can I not regret all those who died?" Secca gestured to the vanguard riding before them and then swung her arm to encompass those who followed. "Stura is destroyed. The north of Neserea is devastated. Nearly two-thirds of the SouthWomen died to follow us. I have less than half the lancers who rode out from Loiseau little more than two seasons ago . . ."

"Let us say, my love," Alcaren offered calmly, "that you had been able and ready to use shadow sorcery on the Maitre the day you discovered he was in Neserea—"

"That would have been too late."

"So . . . you are faulting yourself for not knowing all that happened in the world? When no others did?" Alcaren's silvered eyes twinkled. "You would fault yourself for what you could not have known?"

Secca shook her head, knowing that, in the use of words, she could not overcome Alcaren's logic, and while what he said made sense, it also made no difference, because too many people had died. She could not have accepted women in chains, and the Maitre could not accept them free of chains. Secca could justify her actions because she had not been the one to attack and force her way on others, but could there have been another way?

At the time it all had begun, after Anna's death, it had probably been too late. Secca's lips tightened. But now . . . now she had to make certain that another such conflict did not arise—not in her life, and perhaps beyond.

"Lord Robero is still in Falcor," Alcaren said, his voice neutral.

"He was this morning."

"You do not intend to send him any messages except the one you dispatched two days ago?"

"No. He knows that the Sturinnese and the Maitre have been destroyed. That is enough until we meet."

"Will he meet with you?"

Secca shrugged. "How can he not?"

"He fears you."

As well he should . . . as well he should. Secca smiled.

"Yet even he does not know how strong a sorceress you have become," Alcaren added. "Nor do you."

"Because I have done terrible spellsongs? Does that make me stronger? Or just more cruel?" asked Secca.

"You know you are stronger in what spells you can sing. So am I, and so is Richina. That is good for Defalk and Liedwahr."

But is it good for me . . . for us? "Perhaps."

"What will Lord Robero do, do you think?" asked Alcaren, clearly understanding that Secca was uncomfortable in talking about her strength as a sorceress. "I know him but through your eyes."

"He will blame me for his misfortunes, and for the deaths and destruction. Perhaps he will say he had no choice. He should not have threatened to take Loiseau from me."

"It means more to you than Flossbend?"

"In a way. I earned Loiseau, and it was given with love." Even thinking of Loiseau, of Anna, Secca could feel the emptiness, wondering again if that would always be with her.

"Perhaps he will reward you."

"It's too late for that. Defalk deserves better." *Are you the one to provide it? But who else is there?* Secca took a long and slow breath, then leaned forward and patted Songfire on the shoulder.

Behind them, Jolyn rode, talking with Palian, and the two younger sorceresses told Valya about Falcor. Secca looked eastward, silver-tinged eyes slit against the brightness of the day, and against the decisions she had made and would have to carry out.

141

ENCORA, RANUAK

In the shadows of the balcony, the Matriarch looks southward at the sun setting behind the low hills overlooking the harbor. Beside her stands Aetlen, one arm loosely around her waist.

"I feel happy for her and sorry for her," Alya muses.

"Lady Secca?" asks Aetlen.

"She will not see it yet, but she has no choice. She wrestles with a decision that is not a choice."

"She feels it within her heart, but would wish to deny it,"

suggests Aetlen. "As did you, once, as I recall. Within, you two are much alike."

"I suspect so. Except she has been forced to learn in blood and pain that good principles and feelings are far from enough to ensure peace and prosperity—or free actions for people."

"You feel sorry for her."

"Don't you?" asks the Matriarch. "Every joy she will know will be tinged with bitterness and loss. Every action taken will be chosen knowing the pain of those who will suffer."

After a time, Aetlen asks, "What of the Ladies of the Shadows?"

Alya shrugs. "I imagine that they will claim that either luck or the discipline of the Great Sorceress or the greed of the Sea-Priests, or some such, were all that prevented Liedwahr from being turned to molten rock by sorcery, and that what happened to Stura is a lesson about sorcery misused. Saying so, they will continue to oppose it here."

"You do not seem terribly upset." Aetlen grins.

"No. We can now send young men with a talent for sorcery, or even headstrong young women, to foster with Lady Secca and Lord Alcaren. She could scarce refuse such."

"Not now."

"She will be far more careful than any suspect," predicted the Matriarch.

"She will be far more ruthless in using the shadows," added Aetlen sadly. "Truly, she will have to be the shadowsinger for all Liedwahr, but she will not see that yet. All she sees is that Lord Robero must be replaced, and she questions whether it is right that she should."

"There is no one else."

They both nod, then watch as the sun slips behind the hills, and the harbor waters turn from silver into dull gray.

142

S ecca shifted her weight in Songfire's saddle, then leaned
forward to see better the oblong stone by the shoulder
of the road. The dekstone read: Falcor: 5 d.

Secca looked to Alcaren. "Not that much farther."

"There has been no word from Lord Robero."

"The glass showed him riding somewhere," Secca pointed
out.

"He does not wish to meet with you. That is most clear."
Alcaren laughed. "Nor would I, were I in his boots."

Secca nodded, then looked back over her shoulder. For
the first time in the two days since they had ridden away
from the glass lake that was Aroch, she could see clouds to
the west, just a few white puffs, and in the light wind of
midafternoon, she doubted that, even if the clouds darkened
and promised rain, they would reach her force before they
entered Falcor.

"Look!" Alcaren gestured.

Delcetta and Wilten rode back along the side of the stone-
paved highway, then turned their mounts and flanked Secca
and Alcaren.

"A company of lancers rides toward us, lady," announced
Wilten. "They wear the blue-green of Defalk."

"After all that has happened," Delcetta added, "we would
prefer to be ready."

"That might be best," Secca replied. "I doubt there will
be trouble, but I will have the lutar ready as well." She
suspected she would be good for about one spell, but that
was one more than some of the players could take.

"I will bring up a full company to the vanguard." Delcetta
smiled. "They should see the blue and crimson."

"I think they should," Secca agreed, returning the smile.

In less than a half-glass, after they had ridden over a gentle rise in the road, Secca could see the company of Defalkan lancers. They had stopped and were drawn up in formation, less than a dek ahead on the gray paving stones of the road.

"Column halt!" The order came from both Delcetta and Wilten, near simultaneously. "Ready arms!"

Secca let her fingers touch the strings of the lutar, checking its tuning once more, before watching as a single officer in the blue-green of Defalk rode forward, his hands open, and extended to show that they were empty. He was accompanied by a single lancer bearing a white banner. He stopped his mount as he neared Wilten and Delcetta. The three talked for a moment, then all three followed the banner bearer along the shoulder of the road toward Secca.

As they neared, Secca recognized the gray-bearded Defalkan officer. "That's Jirsit."

"And?" asked Alcaren dryly.

"Oh . . . he's Lord Robero's arms commander. I've known him since I was a child. Anna always found him honest and solid."

"Let us see how honest and solid," suggested Alcaren.

After reining up a good ten yards from Secca, Jirsit bowed. "Lady Secca, the lancers of Defalk welcome you to Falcor, and we stand ready and willing to do your bidding as Sorceress Protector."

"We have come to see Lord Robero," Secca replied evenly.

"He is not in Falcor, Lady Secca. When he received word of your victory and your message that you were returning to discuss the future of Defalk with him, he ordered us to oppose you. This morning, we formed up and rode out, and then sent a message to Lord Robero that since you had defeated the Sturinnese, we were bound to you as the Sorceress Protector." Jirsit laughed ironically. "In less than a glass, he had gathered his personal guard and left Falcor. He was riding toward Elheld."

Secca nodded slowly. "We will enter Falcor, but we will only spend a day or so allowing the lancers and players some rest. Then we must go to Elheld."

"We know, Lady Secca. We ask to be placed under your command and to accompany you there." Jirsit's eyes held the hint of a smile. "We will abide by *your* decisions. Every officer and every lancer has so agreed."

Will it be this simple? Secca doubted that, since nothing in the past year had turned out as it first seemed—except her foreboding feeling about the Sturinnese.

143

MANSUUS, MANSUUR

The two men stand on the balcony outside the Liedfuhr's private study, looking out over the city and at the River Toksul in the quiet of twilight.

The younger and taller Liedfuhr glances sideways at Bassil. "So I must plead to the Sorceress Protector now?"

"I think not, sire. She will entertain a simple request, courteously sent, and accompanied with several thousand golds as a token of your esteem and gratitude for ridding Liedwahr of the scourge of the Sea-Priests. You could even suggest that because she used her own resources on behalf of Liedwahr you are sending the golds to her personally as the merest token of recompense."

Kestrin laughs. "Such words reek worse than steer manure."

"She knows that, and you know that, but she will accept them, and she will entertain your request."

"The woman could destroy all we have in a season, and you think she will entertain such a request?"

"Yes, sire. It is simple. First, she will have to become

Lady of Defalk. She may protest, and rail, for she is clearly
not one to enjoy dealing with scheming lords and ladies, but
there is no one else. She is young enough to bear heirs, and
against that too, she may rail, but she is a woman who will
do what needs to be done. Only sorcery will rebuild Neserea
and western Defalk, and the only sorcerers and sorceresses
are of Defalk. Neserea will become part of Defalk. That
means that Dumar will not."

"Not now," snorts Kestrin.

"There is already word in Dumar that the Sorceress Protector had suggested your niece and her consort as the Lord
and Lady High Counselors of Dumar. The Sorceress Protector will have her hands filled to overflowing in consoli-
dating her power in Defalk and in rebuilding Neserea. You
merely congratulate her on her wise decision in naming your
niece and young Eryhal and promise another installment of
golds in a year, once Mansuur has recovered from its own
losses."

"She might accede there, at that," muses the Liedfuhr.

"Later, when she feels more secure, you request that she
train a sorceress for the defense of Mansuur. She can say
yes or no, but I would wager that she will accede if you are
gracious enough."

"Perhaps. Perhaps." The Liedfuhr's lips twist into an
ironic smile.

"Given what might have happened, we have lost little,"
suggests the older man.

"Is that not the usual refrain, Bassil? That matters could
have been so much worse?"

"Always, sire. Always."

Kestrin laughs once more.

144

Secca rode the last dek toward Elheld, northward from the town of Elhi, which lay several deks to the south of the hold, a town that had been little more than a hamlet until the time of Robero's great-grandsire. Her lutar was already tuned and held ready while she guided Songfire left-handed. As she neared the ancestral hold of Lord Robero, Secca glanced at the ancient gates to Elheld—open, as they had always been—but deserted. Even at midday, under a warm spring sun and a cloudless sky, the reddish granite stones held a silver shade. But then, everything that Secca saw still held silver tinges, and always would, she suspected. The gates were not to a keep or liedburg proper, but set on each side of the lane and in the low walls that surrounded Elheld at a distance of well over a dek. Elheld was a sprawling stone mansion, not a true keep, and never had been high-walled in the fashion of Loiseau or Falcor.

The vanguard preceding Secca and Alcaren contained a company of lancers from Loiseau and one of SouthWomen. Jolyn and Anandra had remained in Falcor, and Jirsit had been persuaded to leave half of the surviving companies— five companies—of the Lancers of Defalk in Falcor under his assistant, Elber. Jirsit himself had insisted on accompanying Secca. So the column that stretched out behind her ran almost a dek back toward the town of Elhi and the Fal River.

Past the open gates, the lane leading up to the main dwelling was empty—except for a single lancer officer, mounted on a roan stallion. The officer wore the bright blue tunic of Lord Robero's personal guard.

The column halted while Delcetta and Jirsit rode forward to talk to the officer, then all three rode back toward Secca.

Alcaren left his sabre unsheathed, his eyes on the approaching officer. Secca continued to hold the lutar ready.

The tall lancer officer reined up well back from Secca, and bowed in the saddle. "Lady Secca, I am Overcaptain Bryn, commanding Lord Robero's personal lancers."

"Yes, Overcaptain?" Secca's voice was impersonal.

"Might I speak with you, Lady Secca?" asked Bryn.

"You may speak here, Overcaptain Bryn, where my consort and all may hear. About this, I would have no secrets."

"So it has always been said about you, lady." Bryn inclined his head. "Very well. Our problem is most simple. We are pledged to Lord Robero. Lord Robero has not carried out his duties and has exceeded his authority in trying to take your demesne from you. He has, if I may be perfectly blunt, also exceeded his intelligence. Nonetheless, we are pledged to him. You have the power to destroy us all, possibly without losing a single lancer. We neither wish to break our pledge, nor to die needlessly."

"I can see your problem." Secca nodded slowly. "Yet, here is mine. Lord Robero ordered me to allow the Sturinnese to depart after they had destroyed all of northern Neserea and too many keeps and towns in Defalk. He feared losing his power and position more than he feared his people losing their lives and their freedoms." She paused. "I cannot release you from your pledge. Only Lord Robero can do that. Nor can I fail to do my duty to Defalk and its people. All I can offer you is that whatever happens between Lord Robero and me will occur between us—as woman to man, man to woman." Her smile was cold. "Surely, Lord Robero does not need his lancers to protect him against one small woman." Her silver-pupiled amber eyes fixed on the overcaptain.

As if for the first time, Bryn saw her eyes. He swallowed.

"Yes . . . or no, Overcaptain? Does your pledge mean attacking one small woman who has done right by Defalk in order to defend a man who has done wrong? Does it mean losing all your lancers to defend a man who has already broken his pledge to his people?"

Bryn looked away. "If we do not attack . . . what will you do?"

"Leave you free to tender your pledge to Lady Alyssa, to protect her and her children. They may hold Elheld here, but no more than Elheld."

Bryn slowly nodded. "We will not interfere. Should you prevail, as you will, we will protect the Lady Alyssa. Our men are drawn up in formation to the west of the hold house."

"Overcaptain Delcetta and her first company will accompany you to ensure that naught occurs, if you do not mind, while I meet with Lord Robero."

Jirsit cleared his throat. "Lady Secca . . . we would also accompany the SouthWomen. All five companies."

"I would appreciate that, Arms Commander." Secca turned in the saddle. "Richina! Palian?"

The younger blonde sorceress rode forward. "Yes, Lady Secca?"

Palian followed.

"You and the players will follow Arms Commander Jirsit and set up by the hold house. There are several companies of Lord Robero's personal guards drawn up there in formation. If Overcaptain Bryn and his men make one move to leave or attack, you will use the flame spell and destroy them all."

"Yes, Lady Secca." Richina looked coldly, imperiously, at the older overcaptain.

"Your players stand ready, Lady Secca," added Palian, her voice colder than Secca's or Richina's.

Secca could see a hint of silver in Richina's eyes as well. *Will that mark all of us who were at Aroch and survived? Forever?*

Bryn looked away from Richina and Palian.

"Unlike some, Overcaptain, I keep my word," Secca said. "So does Richina, and she is almost as powerful as I am."

She looked to Alcaren and Wilten. "We need to meet with
Lord Robero."

"Lady . . . you must not step into the dwelling," Wilten
said. "Not until we have secured it."

Secca did not argue. "Go ahead. Except . . . tell everyone
that if even one of your lancers is harmed, I will use sorcery
against every man in Elheld. Everyone."

"That I will be pleased to announce. We will disarm them
all."

Secca eased Songfire to the side of the lane. As most of
the column of lancers and players rode northward and up
the long gentle slope, Secca and Alcaren watched.

"Do you think any will try to trouble you?" asked Alcaren.

"I would think not," Secca replied, "but I trust no one
here who is not pledged to me." *And it is sad that it must
be that way.*

Less than half a glass passed before Captain Peraghn of
the SouthWomen rode back down the lane and reported.
"Elheld is yours, lady."

"Was there any trouble?"

Peraghn shook her head. "Some faces were sad. I think
all expected this."

That, too, was sad, Secca reflected as she urged Songfire
up the lane. Anna had hoped and worked for a stable lineage
to rule Defalk, but Robero had proved, in the end, unequal
to the task. *You would have to be the one to tell him.*

As she neared the hold itself, Secca studied the ranked
guards in blue to the west—and the Defalkan lancers arrayed between them and the entrance to the mansion itself,
and then the players set up just beyond the entrance and the
mounting blocks. She doubted that ever had Elheld seen so
many lancers at once, and never so many from such different
sources.

Wilten stood by the archway that led inside, waiting.

"I will meet him in the open hall outside his study," Secca
said as she reined up, "where all can see." *Where he cannot*

hide some treachery. She dismounted, and then recased the lutar and restrapped it to Songfire. If she needed sorcery against Robero himself, her voice would be enough.

After patting Songfire once on the shoulder, Secca turned, climbed the two low steps, and walked through the archway and then the foyer. Alcaren's sabre was out, as were those of the four lancers who flanked her. Their boots echoed hollowly on the polished floors of the ancient building.

Near the end of the corridor stood Robero, his paunch more noticeable than when Secca had last seen him two seasons earlier, his thinning mahogany hair longer and disarrayed. Secca's lancers lined the corridor, their blades out.

"All hail the usurper, the new Lady of Defalk." Robero offered a deep and mocking bow. His face bore a reddish mark across one cheek, but his scabbard still held a blade. "You have always wanted to pull me down, Secca, and now you have done it. Are you happy? How much else of Liedwahr will you destroy to prove you're more of a man than any man?"

Secca just looked at him, shaking her head. "You were always a bully, Jimbob," she said, using his childhood name to emphasize her point. "Nothing Anna did could change that. And the more she did, the angrier you became. In the end, you would have enslaved every woman in Liedwahr and turned the land over to the Maitre rather than admit your weaknesses."

"Will you burn me down with fire, Secca?" asked Robero. "The way Anna destroyed Behlem? Or will you poison me the way you handled Kylar and so many others you never bothered to tell me about?"

"I think not," Alcaren said, lifting his sabre. "All know you cannot stand up to a woman. Perhaps you can try to stand up to a man."

"Ah . . . the loyal consort. Such devotion."

Secca held up her hand, gesturing for Alcaren to stand back. "When you were fourteen, I said that you were a self-centered bully. Anna did her best, and when she gave you back your lands, you even changed your name. Neither was enough."

"Words, dear little Secca. Words. You would replace me. How could you, when the great Anna couldn't? Everyone will fear you, but none will love you."

"You may well be right." Secca smiled coldly, then sang.

> *"Robero strong, Robero wrong,*
> *turn to flame with this song,*
> *singing turn, music burn,*
> *die the death you've richly earned."*

Robero's mouth opened as she began to sing. "You can't . . ." He fumbled for the decorative sabre at his belt, then lunged forward.

Alcaren stepped in front of Secca, slashing once with his own blade.

Robero's blade clattered on the polished stone of the corridor.

There were no screams as the whips and lances of fire ripped into the lord called Robero, who had once been a bullying boy named Jimbob.

Tears streamed down Secca's cheeks.

Alcaren looked on, his face impassive.

Secca forced herself to stand and watch, watch until a charred figure lay on the polished stone.

145

Ashtaar muffles the coughs that have become more insistent—and more bloody—with another green cloth. When they finally subside for a moment, she takes first a sip from the beaker on the polished table-desk, and then a swallow.

Marshal Zeltaar looks across the table at the silver-haired Council Leader. "How long can you keep up the façade, Ashtaar?"

"Long enough. Long enough." Ashtaar takes another swallow from the beaker. "Long enough for the shadowsinger to become Lady of Defalk in name as well as fact." Her lips curled into a smile, almost a grimace. "All of Liedwahr knew it before she did."

"A sorceress as ruler? I cannot say that I like such."

"You'll like it very well, Zeltaar," predicts Ashtaar. "It will be very useful for you as Council Leader."

Zeltaar's eyes narrow. "Is that your idea of a joke?"

"Not at all. Escadra is the best of the seers, and she is far too young and trusting. Fuhlar is a fool, as we both know. The lady . . . need I say more? And as for Adgan, she is so cynical that she believes nothing, and that is worse than being too trusting." As she takes yet another sip from the beaker, Ashtaar waves off any objection the marshal may have. After finishing that swallow of the bitter draught, she continues. "Your hardest task will be to convince the Council to back a resumption of trading with the Ostisles, and to combine that with establishing a naval base there totally under our control. You will need a second base there, probably at the western harbor of Alphara, say . . . three years after the first. I'd suggest trying to find our trading concerns solid partners out of Defalk, or Dumar, but even someone out of Wharsus will do in a pinch ..." The Council Leader covers her mouth with the green cloth and doubles over in another fit of coughing.

The marshal waits.

Ashtaar recovers and takes another swallow from the beaker.

Then Zeltaar asks, "I assume you plan for Nordwei to take over the Ostisles?"

"What else?" Ashtaar smiles, an expression as much of pain as pleasure. "Defalk has neither ports nor ships. The Matriarchy cannot expand. There is an absence of trading power with the destruction of Stura, but it will not last. We fill it, or the Sturinnese will as they recover. If you make that clear to both the Liedfuhr and the shadowsinger, they might even support you. They certainly will not oppose you. No one wishes a resurgence of Sturinnese fleets and power."

"And the shadowsinger?"

"Let her do as she will. She will have to take over Neserea. There is no help for that, and that will take most of her life and effort. She hates fighting, and that is what makes her such a terrible enemy."

The marshal frowns.

"Do you not see? She does not believe there is honor in any form of fighting. So ... whatever works most effectively is what she will use. Do you think the Neserean lords will rise against her—after they have seen what sorcery can do? They are not terribly bright, but they are bright enough to see that they suffered the sorcery of the loser, and that the Sturinnese lost every last lancer and sorcerer. The Liedfuhr will beg for assistance. It may not look like begging, but he is no fool. The Ladies of the Shadows do not wish the shadowsinger back in Ranuak, nor do Lord Hadrenn and his sons wish to contest her. So, Defalk will hold the midsection of Liedwahr, from Ebra to Worlan, and Dumar will do as Lady Secca wishes, and will do so gladly. And we, we will prosper, with our southern flank protected by the greatest power in Erde. Can you think of a better position in which to be? Or would you rather be the shadowsinger, who must watch every shadow for envy and ingratitude, even as she builds and rebuilds, and who must wonder if she will ever outgrow the shade of her mentor, even after she casts a shadow over all of Erde?"

The marshal smiles wryly. "Being Council Leader sounds much better."

They both smile.

146

Secca paced across the floor of the chamber she had always used in Falcor. Somehow, she never wanted to live in the large chambers Robero had created by remodeling the liedburg. If she had to be in Falcor, then those Anna had used would suffice. Her eyes flicked to the open shutters, whose dark wood was silvered in her sight, as was everything. *Silver, not gold.* Even the perfect white rose that lay upon one corner of the writing table was silvered. Secca slowed her pacing and smiled, thinking about the moment when Alcaren had presented the rose to her, a moment that she would treasure always, both for the love it showed and the innocence it had represented.

Her eyes lifted from the rose to Alcaren.

"You *must* be Lady of Defalk," her consort insisted. "You have known that for weeks, if not longer. Why do you hesitate now?"

"I just wanted to stop the killing and the destruction. I didn't want women to lose all that Anna gave us." Secca paused. "And I killed more people than she ever did."

"Did you have any choice, if you did not want Liedwahr under the hands of the Maitre?"

"I did not see any," Secca admitted.

"No one else did, either. Not the Matriarch or the Council of Wei or even the Ladies of the Shadows." Alcaren paused, and then continued, his words measured. "My lady . . . that is why you must be Lady of Defalk, and why Defalk must include Neserea, Ebra, and Dumar. Only then will there be no killings by the scores."

"By expanding Defalk threefold?"

"You already hold it," he said. "They all will bow to whoever you appoint as Lord High Counselor in Dumar. Neserea's lords should become part of the Thirty-three, and you should call all the lords, including Hadrenn and his sons, the Fifty or some such."

"What will the Thirty-three say?"

"They will say little. You stopped the Sea-Priests, and only three holds in Defalk were destroyed. Two of those belonged to loyal lords. You can at least help rebuild those two with sorcery. Leave Aroch as an example. The cost to you and the SouthWomen was great, but the SouthWomen will recall with pride for generations their role in repulsing the Sturinnese and in supporting the Lady Sorceress. All will know the price you paid to save them, and that is as it should be."

Secca glanced toward the open window, catching a hint of the summer to come, with the spring flowers from the garden Alyssa had planted. Secca shook her head. Alyssa, like Anna, had done her best with Robero, and it had not been enough. *Will your best fail to be enough? Will you always be looking over your shoulder? Wondering what devastation and disaster may lie ahead?*

"I don't like being the person one has to be to rule effectively." That was it, pure and simple.

"So long as you remember that, all will be well. Was that not Lord Robero's greatest failing?" asked Alcaren. "That he liked power more than ruling?"

"One of them," Secca acknowledged.

"People follow you," Alcaren said.

"Now."

"They know that you went into danger for them."

"They will forget."

Alcaren laughed. "Have you an objection to everything?"

"No . . . yes." Secca turned toward the window. Finally, she turned back. "As . . . as Lady of Defalk . . . the reason why Anna could not be Lady . . ." Secca flushed and looked down, her eyes straying to the hearth before which she had once played Vorkoffe, never dreaming how she would one day return to the chamber.

Alcaren waited, a supportive smile on his face.

"As Lady . . ." She stopped, then began again. "Lady Anna was but regent because she could not have children, and a ruler . . ." She found herself flushing even more brightly.

Alcaren took her hand, then reached up with his other hand and turned her face to him, looking at her with gray-blue eyes that saw into her, but did not judge or condescend. "Would that be so terrible, my love? So very awful to have a child?"

Secca eased her arms around him, brushed his cheek with her lips, and then held tightly to him for long moments . . . and for the future.

In time, she took a half step back and looked again into his eyes—silver-centered amber meeting silver-centered gray-blue. She tilted her head back ever so slightly, and then their lips met.

Outside the unshuttered window, the spring song of a red-bird rose liltingly, and with promise.